PENGUIN ⟨P⟩ CLASSICS

# THE HISTORY OF HENRY ESMOND

WILLIAM MAKEPEACE THACKERAY was born in 1811. He was educated at Charterhouse and Trinity College, Cambridge, and studied art and law at The Middle Temple. He then turned to journalism. In London, Thackeray wrote for many periodicals, principally for *Fraser's Magazine* for which he wrote a social satire *The Yellow Plush Correspondence*. This appeared in book form in 1841. *Vanity Fair*, Thackeray's masterpiece, was published in monthly parts, 1847–8. His other novels include *The Luck of Barry Lyndon* (1844), later revised as *The Memoirs of Barry Lyndon, Esq.* (1856), and *The History of Pendennis* (1848–50). He also published many volumes of *Miscellanies* of both prose and verse. *The Four Georges: Sketches of Manners, Morals, Court and Country Life* first appeared in the *Cornhill Magazine* in 1860. His 1851 lectures, *The English Humourists of the Eighteenth Century*, were published in 1853. Thackeray died suddenly in 1863, having suffered from heart trouble for some time.

JOHN SUTHERLAND, who has edited Anthony Trollope's *The Eustace Diamonds* and *Phineas Finn* for Penguins, was Reader in English at University College, London, until 1984 and is now a Professor of English at the California Institute of Technology in Pasadena. His other publications include *Fiction and the Fiction Industry* and *Best Sellers: Popular Fiction of the 1970s*.

MICHAEL GREENFIELD received his M.A. degree from the University of Sussex in 1966, and is now an Assistant Lecturer in English at the University of Singapore.

*William Thackeray*

# THE HISTORY OF
# HENRY ESMOND

*Edited by John Sutherland and
Michael Greenfield,
with an Introduction and Notes
by John Sutherland*

*Penguin Books*

Penguin Books Ltd, 27 Wrights Lane, London w8 5tz (Publishing and Editorial)
*and* Harmondsworth, Middlesex, England (Distribution and Warehouse)
Viking Penguin Inc., 40 West 23rd Street, New York, New York 10010, USA
Penguin Books Australia Ltd, Ringwood, Victoria, Australia
Penguin Books Canada Ltd, 2801 John Street, Markham, Ontario, Canada l3r 1b4
Penguin Books (NZ) Ltd, 182–190 Wairau Road, Auckland 10, New Zealand

First published 1852
Published in the Penguin English Library 1970
Reprinted 1980, 1982
Reprinted in Penguin Classics 1985, 1987

Introduction and notes copyright © John Sutherland, 1970
All rights reserved

Made and printed in Great Britain by
Richard Clay Ltd, Bungay, Suffolk
Set in Monotype Ehrhardt

# CONTENTS

# INTRODUCTION

IN its own day *Henry Esmond* commanded superlatives. With the air of a man stating the incontrovertible Trollope asserts, in *An Autobiography*, that Thackeray is the foremost novelist, and elsewhere that *Henry Esmond* is his best novel, the master's masterpiece. The more modest assertion that *Henry Esmond* was the best *historical* novel ever written was a nineteenth-century commonplace so widespread that it sometimes seems like a ritual genuflexion. It was not, of course, the first of its kind, and those who praised it so extravagantly tended to see it as a literary consummation, 'The crown and flower of the historical novel' as Saintsbury called it. Curiosity can trace the ancestry of Thackeray's novel back to the moment in 1813 when Walter Scott, then a well-known poet, turned up a long-lost manuscript while rummaging in a desk for fishing tackle. It was a sample of historical fiction, an attempt to spice antiquarian erudition with Gothic romance. The publishers had not thought well of it and Scott had turned to other things, but now he felt like diversifying his talent into prose narrative, so the work was refurbished and concluded with the usual prodigious speed. The result was *Waverley* and a revolution which tilted the whole field of literary endeavour towards the novel. The esteem of the historical novel has never stood higher than it did in that second decade of the nineteenth century; then it must have seemed the most exciting development in fiction since Richardson started Pamela corresponding with her parents. A century later, after a brief Stevensonian flowering, it had sunk below the level of respectable critical view into the limbo of 'Romance' to join there its *déclassé* genre-cousins, 'the cowboy', 'the love-story', 'the thriller'. In order to appreciate *Henry Esmond* the modern reader has to recover a certain open-mindedness about the historical romance, to suspend, as it were, a verdict which literary history has brought, and accept with Trollope that 'great historical novel' is not a paradox.

Writing within the memory of Scott's greatness almost all the nineteenth-century novelists we respect tried their hand at the historical form. Often they went harder at the task than at their work-a-day fiction, as if to achieve something special. One thinks of the legendary labours of Victorian fiction; George Eliot beginning *Romola*, as she said, a young woman and emerging from her research 'an old woman', the barrow load of books at Dickens's front door waiting to be digested into *The Tale of Two Cities*, the acres of historical fact which Charles Reade scissors-and-pasted into *The Cloister and The Hearth*. *Henry Esmond* has a place in the list. Since Thackeray's acknowledged flaw was idleness, a tendency to pull the same strings on the same old puppets, his pride in *Henry Esmond* was correspondingly the greater for the unusual pains which had gone into it. It had cost him he said 'as much trouble as Macaulay's *History*'. In later life he called it his 'careful novel'. An unaccustomed preparatory effort was writing it entire before publication; it is the only one of his full-length novels produced of a piece in the traditional three volumes at a guinea and a half, and not in monthly or magazine numbers, and is thus of all his works the one that most positively severs a degrading connexion with hand-to-mouth journalism. More importantly it was revised before and not during its issue, allowing Thackeray to reserve the virtuosity which elsewhere goes into extemporizing and the 'life and death struggle' with the unwritten instalment. Consequently *Henry Esmond* has structure in an architectural sense, not simply 'Roundabout' extension. The groundwork had been laid by his Lectures on the eighteenth-century English Humourists the year before. These were primarily money-spinners (the easiest money, Thackeray said, he had ever earned), but they equipped him uniquely well for his novel. They were also the link between *Esmond* and a life's ambition to write a History of Queen Anne's reign.

The novel was written part among his family, part in the British Museum and part 'on club notepaper' at the *Athenaeum* to which he had been elected in 1851. The tripartition matches the accents heard in the narration, those of a gentleman, a scholar and a defender of English domestic values. Eyre Crowe, his secretary, has left us a picture of the great man at work, for

whom every facility was made available: a private part of the
Museum, and a partitioned section of the club library where he
would dictate 'not *sotto voce*'. It is not merely fanciful to claim
that we can hear the voice in *Henry Esmond* more clearly than
elsewhere, and the man who steps down to talk with us in this
novel is not *Vanity Fair*'s 'brother of the story telling trade' but
Esmond, Colonel of the Queen's Service and reluctant Marquis,
the most patrician narrator Thackeray, who always ventrilo-
quized his novels, attempted outside burlesque. Tactically
dignity is vital to the novel's immunization against satires on
vulgar historical fiction which Thackeray himself had been foremost in devising. None the less from the Author of *The Book of
Snobs* it was, perhaps, risky and he had had doubts about
Esmond being a 'prig', but it worked; 'Never could I have
believed,' wrote Landor when the book was published, 'that
Thackeray, great as his abilities are, could have written so noble
a story as Esmond!' 'Grand' is Saintsbury's epithet. The work
was, in short, a claim on literary fame; Thackeray had arrived
and this was his 'card'; he would, he hoped, 'stand or fall by
*Esmond*'.

*Henry Esmond* was written between autumn 1851 and summer
1852. Then Thackeray was personally at the height of his powers
and publicly at the top of the tree fighting it out with Dickens.
Publishers solicited him. George Smith waited with 'a thousand
pounds in his pocket' for the new novel (in fact, Thackeray
received £1,200 for the first 2,500-copy edition from the
successful Smith, Elder and Co.). With *Vanity Fair* he had
established a moral authority, based to some extent on a mis-
anthropy which worried him, for which the less satiric Boz
might well have exchanged his greater sales. Charlotte Brontë,
in an embarrassingly psalmodic preface to *Jane Eyre*, had hailed
him as the 'social regenerator' of the age, 'whose words are not
framed to tickle delicate ears: who to my thinking comes before
the great ones of society, much as the son of Imlah came before the
throned kings of Judah and Israel'. The bad time to come, when
Thackeray could be unthinkingly dismissed as a penny-a-liner
made good, was still a decade off – in 1862, for example, without
apparently intending insolence *The Westminster* could talk of his

'fame' being 'a large balance at the bankers'. But in 1852 Thackeray had great unrealized capacities, and *Henry Esmond* is a measure of the novelist he might have been.

The veneration for the historical novel, of which *Henry Esmond* is so supreme an example, can easiest be accounted for in two words – 'Scott' and 'Carlyle'. Scott had achieved a remarkable double, he had inaugurated a tradition of popular fiction and yet had retained for himself the status of a gentleman. To achieve large sales with dignity remained the dual prize in fiction throughout most of the century, and it was the combination of wide readership with high respectability that gave the nineteenth-century novelists the sense that their profession was, as Thackeray put it, 'as serious as the Parson's own'. Carlyle, on the other hand, historicized the thought of his age. History he urged, evangelically, was society's 'letter of instruction. . . . Only he who understands what has been, can know what should be and will be' (*On History Again*, 1833). Fascinated by crisis, Carlyle offered the vision of history's tides culminating in revolution, of societies 'shooting Niagara', and the salvationary image of the Hero stemming and turning the courses of history into destiny. Like the novel, history was a best-seller; the first two volumes of Macaulay's *History of England* sold thirteen thousand in the first four months, vying with its contemporaries *Dombey and Son* and *Vanity Fair*. Indeed, when he wanted to make capital for his daughters rather than income Thackeray himself turned to history with his public lectures on the Humourists and the Georges.

Although the twin popularities of history and the novel, and a great example created the vogue for it, the course of the post-Scott historical novel is littered with ruins and cheapened by poor imitations. The context of *Henry Esmond*, which Thackeray is conscious of throughout, is debased literature. Most successful of the run of imitators were those who emulated Scott at a self-consciously inferior level – the 'teeming father of romance', G. P. R. James who turned the craft into an industry with his hundred or more historical romances, or Harrison Ainsworth who sensationalized the form with an admixture of violence and glamorous crime. Those like Bulwer Lytton, George Eliot or

Charles Kingsley who tried to do something great in the historical novel had farther to fall, and fell. To himself Scott observed with Aguecheek's complacency that they might do it with better grace, but he did it more naturally. Had he lived to see *Henry Esmond* he would have discovered a novel as 'natural' as his own, partly because like Scott, Thackeray was steeped in the past, but primarily because Thackeray had arrived at his own sophisticated and heterodox aesthetic of historical fiction.

A principal difficulty was in finding the right blend of romance and historical erudition, uniting, as it were, Mrs Radcliffe and the Rev. Jonas Dryasdust. It is a specific instance of fiction's larger struggle to integrate what Wilde called inartistic 'truth' and artistic 'lying', but more acute since 'historical fiction', pedantically considered, means 'factual fiction'. The problem was one which Thackeray had isolated well before he came to write *Henry Esmond*. Thackeray is, incidentally, a great critic, and certainly one of the best where the historical novel is concerned. This stature is not always recognized because his finest criticism is embodied in burlesque and parodic strata in his novels, where we find the critical intelligence working within rather than outside the stuff of fiction. The theoretic Preface to *Henry Esmond* is to be found in the series of burlesque novelettes by 'Eminent Hands' which *Punch* published in 1847. Since Thackeray here works out the practice of the historical novel by comic exaggeration of vulgarity and naïvety, the effect is more of an 'etiquette' than an aesthetic. But this corresponds with what we find to be the tone of the later novel, a 'well-mannered' avoidance of the *faux pas* which others have committed. One such is the tendency to become tied up in circumstantial historical detail, rendering the work either like a prose museum or a melodrama of fustian, pasteboard and costume spuriousness. In this extract from *Barbazure* (ostensibly a spoof on G. P. R. James) the prose is as overloaded with outlandish nouns as the horse is with accoutrements:

The warrior who bestrode the noble beast was in sooth worthy of the steed which bore him. Both were caparisoned in the fullest trappings of feudal war. The arblast, the mangonel, the demiculverin, and the cuissart of the period, glittered upon the neck and chest of his war-steed; while the rider, with chamfron and catapult, with ban and ariere-ban, morion and tumbrel, battleaxe and rifflard, and other appurtenances of ancient chivalry, rode stately on his steel-clad charger, himself a tower of steel.

The opposite fault is the over-indulgence of romance – in Scott's definition of it – fiction 'the interest of which turns upon marvellous and uncommon incidents'. There is obviously a special strain when 'historical' characters are introduced. This little verbal cartoon is from *George de Barnwell*, Thackeray's more spiteful squib on Bulwer:

And the boy – for he who addressed the most brilliant company of wits in Europe was little more – emptied the contents of the brandy-flask into a silver flagon, and quaffed it gaily to the health of the company assembled. 'Twas the third he had taken during the sitting. Presently, and with a graceful salute to the Society he quitted the coffee-house, and was seen cantering on a magnificent Arab past the National Gallery.

'Who is yon spark in blue and silver? He beats Joe Addison himself, in drinking, and pious Joe is the greatest toper in the three kingdoms,' Dick Steele said, good-naturedly.

'His paper in the Spectator beats thy best, Dick, thou sluggard,' the right Honourable Mr Addison exclaimed. 'He is the author of that famous No. 996, for which you have been giving me all the credit.'

'The rascal foiled me at capping verses,' Dean Swift said, 'and won a twopenny piece of me, plague take him!'

'He has suggested an emendation to my "Homer" which proves him a delicate scholar,' Mr Pope exclaimed.

'He knows more of the French King than any man I have met with; and we must have an eye on him,' said Lord Bolingbroke, then Secretary of State for foreign affairs, and beckoning a suspicious looking person who was drinking at a side table, whispered to him something.

Meanwhile who was he?

The answer is Bulwer Lytton, in his wildest dreams. Thackeray is aiming the charges of vulgarity, vanity and historical ignorance at Bulwer's *Devereux*, a novel which resembles *Henry Esmond* in everything except ability. Thackeray's version of the coffee-house scene, with virtually the same dramatis personae, is to be found in the third volume of *Henry Esmond*. The difference is that Esmond, as much Thackeray as Devereux is Bulwer ('a handsome likeness of an ugly son of yours' he called the hero in a letter to his mother), is modestly restrained from even speaking, let alone dazzling, 'the most brilliant company' in Europe. He is 'a dull fellow' at their table and says of the wits that he 'never [had] a great intimacy with any of them except with honest Dick Steele and Mr Addison'. 'Mr' Addison reveals that there is some distance even in this intimacy. As for Pope, the 'puny lad . . . appearing seldom in public places', he does not enter the novel at all except as a brilliantly precocious reputation. As always in Thackeray, good sense is the great preservative. Esmond, the fictional character, is kept on the edge of historical events, like Blenheim, for example, just as historical characters are kept on the fringe of the novel's crises. The exception is, of course, the restoration conspiracy in the last third of the novel, by which time Thackeray has earned the right to relax his rules somewhat. Too loose a rein on romance results in the historical work being either juvenile fantasy ('jellies' which the artistically middle-aged Thackeray tolerated with a little avuncular mockery) or insufficiently earnest about morality, which he would not tolerate, and which roused him to great corrective outbursts such as *Catherine*. His special aversion had been the Newgate school of historical romance, which glorified the criminal as hero; heroes made Thackeray satiric, but crime lightly handled in literature made him splenetic; the only good to be got from the contemplation of it he insisted 'is abhorrence'.

The historical novel should be distinguished from the novel which is merely set in the past, like *Middlemarch*, *Vanity Fair* or *Tess of the D'Urbervilles*. It is significant that the prototype *Waverley* is subtitled ''Tis sixty years since', and insists on standing a life-span away from the reader. This 'then' rather than 'now' tone produces technical disruptions. Alienation by at least one generation tends to violate tacit contracts and relationships between what, for the sake of the reading illusion, are usually considered time–space cohabitants, the reader, the narrator and the fictional personage. The connecting medium, language, feels the strain most. The historical novel's idiom, especially, in dialogue, becomes notoriously false, fabricating 'tushery' or 'gadzookery' in its attempt to find the equivalence between the modern and the past modes of language. The failures can be dramatic. When, for example, in Lytton's *Harold* the King describes Hilda as 'sibbe to Githa, wife of Godwin', a crevasse opens which the most suspended disbelief cannot cross. There is, consequently, a critical death sentence on the historical novel which states that it can survive only in the absence of that same good sense which the great fictional moralists have set out to cultivate. And, the argument goes, this can be traced back to the verbal stilts on which the historical novel must walk. 'To reject the rhythms of the contemporary idiom by returning to the language of the past is to sacrifice everything. That is why historical novels cannot be taken seriously by the critic, however seriously they may be taken by their authors' (Q. D. Leavis: *Fiction and the Reading Public*).

Thackeray's solution in *Henry Esmond* is a daring one. The novel is written throughout in pastiche – though 'creative parody' might be a more flattering term. Linguistically, though less flamboyantly, the work is uniform with the famous *Spectator* paper in the third volume, and what cannot be done unobtrusively is made virtuosic. The thoroughness of the imposture is remarkable; the pseudo-authenticity of the elaborate editorial frame in the preface and the footnotes is immediately apparent, but the first edition of *Henry Esmond* almost deserves a facsimile reproduction, not to be read (it is not very legible to modern eyes) but to be looked at. It was set up in the obsolete type of Queen Anne's Age, with carefully old-fashioned spelling. The consistency of the anachronism amounted to benevolent forgery, and it caused Thackeray chagrin when he first saw *Henry Esmond* normalized and his counterfeit undone.

The literary models Thackeray chose for Colonel Esmond's memoirs were not the intimate journals of the age, Swift or Evelyn, for example, nor the great correspondents, but the public voice of the *Tatler* and *Spectator*, with here and there an infusion from the eighteenth-century stage. The result is less falsetto than might have been expected. Thackeray's style, like his personality, had a natural affinity with the earlier period, Isaac Bickerstaff and Mr Spectator are ancestors of Michelangelo Titmarsh and Mr Roundabout. The assumed environment of the earlier period, it can be argued, actually accommodates Thackeray's characteristic classical quotation, sententious worldliness, satire and sentimentality more comfortably than the nineteenth century. But whatever loss of naturalness there is in the slight change of pitch is more than compensated for by the discipline which the formal third-person narrative imposes on the essayistic flights of Thackeray's normal 'confidential talk'.

*Henry Esmond*'s success can be largely attributed to Thackeray's taking the historical novel as something to be solved in his own idiosyncratic way and not as something to be cut from Scott's pattern. This is nowhere more apparent than in the sense of history which gives it shape. Scott was essentially a political historian who perceived through the clash of party the larger opposition of ideology and so laid hold on a dialectical interpretation of the past. Although *Henry Esmond* is politically opinionated, hovering between Whig sense and Tory sentimentality, Thackeray's approach is basically that of the debunking, apolitical biographer: 'The dignity of history,' he wrote in an early review, 'sadly diminishes as we grow better acquainted with the materials that compose it.' Defamation is, essentially, the Thackerayan method, the reduction of all aspiration to the same basic human comedy. The prelude to *Henry Esmond* demonstrates it in terms of juxtaposed public and private images – the false Louis sitting in state for his portrait, the real Louis: 'A little wrinkled old man, pock-marked, and with a great periwig and red heels to make him look tall – a hero for a book if you like, or for a brass statue or a painted ceiling, a god in Roman shape, but what more than a man for Madame Maintenon, or the barber who shaved him, or Monsieur Fagon, his surgeon?' Louis is 'merely enacting through life the part of Hero', and court-ridden history itself acts, decently muffled by its mask and cothurnus. Through the theatrical metaphor Thackeray is making the same point as in the preface *Before the curtain* in *Vanity Fair* – that the backstage view is always the right one. It is the make-up man, not the audience, who sees things as they really are. Anne is 'a hot, red-faced woman', not

the regal statue left to posterity outside St Paul's, and the exiled
Stuarts not martyrs but drunken lechers. The pose is that of the
anti-historian, just as elsewhere Thackeray appears the anti-
romancer and anti-novelist. History is lies, just as the novel is
largely lies. The process of *Henry Esmond*, and the progress of
its hero, is a stripping-away of illusions, painful in Esmond's
case, since they are ideals, until the final denouement at Castlewood when the king and mistress he has served are exposed as
sham. In *The Four Georges* Thackeray's 'familiar rather than
Heroic' muse spurns ceremonial obligations with a characteristic excuse: 'We are not the historical muse, but her ladyship's valet de chambre for whom no man is a hero.' The *mot*,
which is alluded to more than once in *Henry Esmond*, evokes
Carlyle's continual descant on the theme in *Past and Present* and
*On Heroes*: 'While we ourselves continue valets, how can any
hero come to govern us? We are governed very infallibly by the
"sham-hero".' Thackeray's social–historical critique, like
Carlyle's, can be summed up in a pungent anti-social vocabulary
– 'sham, flunkeydom, humbug, cant, vanity' – and Thackeray's
personal addition – 'snob'. Both moralists believe in the virtue
of stripping of the meretricious 'clothes' with which falsity hides
itself, fashion, pretension, rank. This is expressed particularly in
*Sartor Resartus*'s 'the philosophy of Clothes' and everywhere in
Thackeray – 'sweep out the tailor-made ones' is Carlyle's cry.
Compare his iconoclasm from *On Heroes* with Thackeray's: 'No
man can be a Grand-Monarque to his valet-de-chambre. Strip
your Louis Quatorze of his king-gear, and there *is* left nothing
but a poor forked radish with a head fantastically carved; –
admirable to no valet' (*Heroes and Hero Worship*, the Hero as
Man of Letters). Thackeray, then, in the same spirit of literary
sansculottism sets out to show history without its high heels and
periwigs. Where he differs from Carlyle, and it is a wide diver-
gence, for it calls into question what he stands for rather than
against, is over hero-worship. *Henry Esmond* is as much a novel
without a hero as *Vanity Fair*, and here the polemic turns
against Carlyle. The sham heroes in the novel are Marlborough
and The Pretender. Esmond's divesting eye discovers them a
bloodthirsty miser and a lecherous trifler, but to the mean,

REX.     LUDOVICUS.     LUDOVICUS REX.

AN HISTORICAL STUDY.

sham heroism destroyed by his artistic 'Valetism' he does not oppose the true hero. The positive which we find in the novel is a different genus – the gentleman. Thackeray's version of Tennyson's 'grand old name of gentleman/defamed by every charlatan' is complex, and is perhaps best understood by simply contemplating Esmond. Undoubtedly one of the strands in it is Carlyle's regenerate aristocracy, who are to replace the old aristocrats and their empty titles. 'Aristocracy has become Phantom Aristocracy, no longer able to *do* its work.' Thackeray plays with the idea whimsically in the early pages of *Henry Esmond* with the joke on the 'Warden of the Butteries and Groom of the King's Posset'. These 'unworkers', as Carlyle labelled them, should be replaced by the 'virtual aristocracy'. In a sense this title suits Esmond well enough – 'I think you are like a king,' says the rarely perceptive Frank. But Esmond is not a 'great man', a Carlylean Hero. He is a gentleman, ethically noble, he can refuse his title with an unironic '*noblesse oblige*', because it would be ungentlemanly to hurt the family who sheltered him, but it is not the '*noblesse*' of the whoring, duelling, gambling Castlewoods. He is not a leader in society but an ideal Everyman, if he reforms society it will be because there are enough like him to make the mass substantially better from inside. He is in a sense Steele's 'Christian Hero', made on good principles not great actions. There are almost as few true gentlemen in Thackeray's world as there are Carlylean heroes, but the difference is that the aristocrat is born, the gentleman can be made. It is a democratic ideal with overtones of universal suffrage that Carlyle could never have tolerated. And it enables Thackeray in his fiction to make his great appeal to 'us' rather than to 'them'.

Judged simply as novel, irrespective of sub-categories, *Henry Esmond* deserves its nineteenth-century reputation rather than the comparative twentieth-century neglect. But it has suffered a double devaluation with the slump in the historical novel and the slower but unreversed depreciation of Thackeray's stock. Nor is it a novel which lends itself to easy classification. A typical response is the first recorded verdict – that of Charlotte Brontë –

who when shown part of the novel in manuscript pronounced it 'admirable and odious', mixed feelings which have followed the work ever since. Basically *Henry Esmond* is a psychological drama crossed with a romantic plot in a historical setting; the historical scenery and the romantic adventure may be scored as outright successes – but the love story provokes a more vexed reaction. George Eliot's casual comment in a letter puts the problem bluntly: 'the most uncomfortable book you can imagine . . . the hero is in love with the daughter all through the book and marries the mother in the end.' Either George Eliot had not been reading carefully or she was being deliberately flippant in ignoring all the hints which Thackeray lays, such as Rachel's jealousy of the blacksmith's daughter when Harry brings the smallpox to Castlewood, and Harry's jealousy of Tom Tusher in Chapter Four of the second book. The drift is unmistakable in the third volume when Esmond asks his younger mistress:

'How long was it that Jacob served an apprenticeship for Rachel?' 'For Mamma?' says Beatrix. 'Is it Mamma your honour wants, and that I should have the honour of calling you Papa?'

None the less when it comes, the denouement is a shock if it is not a surprise, the implied 'incest' and 'adultery' still scrape a taboo and a commandment, if not as sharply as they did a hundred years ago.

Certainly *Henry Esmond* seems charged with strange emotions and tensions. Although publicly he vaunted the novel, privately it seems to have depressed Thackeray; he talks of its 'cutthroat melancholy', 'it is clever,' he says echoing Charlotte Brontë, 'but it is also stupid and a mistake'. Writing to Mrs Gore he says, 'You will remark Bon Dieu . . . in what a state of mind this man must have been when he wrote these thousand dismal pages!' There are a number of keys which have been suggested for the novel. An obvious temptation is to work from Thackeray's known fixation on his mother, but the best of the biographical explanations is that by the official biographer, G. N. Ray. Professor Ray accounts for the novel in terms of a crisis in Thackeray's sentimental friendship with his friend's wife, Jane Brookfield. This accounts for the embittered mood of the novel, and wish-fulfilment for the 'happy ending'. The danger of theses like this is that they explain the novel *too* completely, so that we throw it away like a solved crossword clue. One is tempted to say that in this respect the novels are of more use to the biographer than the biography is to the reader. As an alternative to the Harry-Thackeray, *cri-de-cœur* theories we may list schematically, perhaps, a number of other significances of the hero which enrich rather than impoverish the novel by offering explanations of the conflict whose logic does not have to go outside the novel as we have it. For convenience these are titled Harry as eighteenth-, nineteenth- and twentieth-century man.

## (a) *Harry as eighteenth-century man*

Like Macaulay, Thackeray saw 1688 as a date as significant to English history as 1789 was to French. Both revolutions had rebalanced society towards a certain class. In England it was the middle class whose emergent ideology, in *Henry Esmond*, is expressed in the 'manly' politics of Addison and the 'manly' morality of Steele. Implanted in the novel is the great value judgement that society is getting better and moving away from the bad old days of the Restoration Court, which we see receding in Harry's childhood. But the Revolution posed a terrible dilemma, for it involved English society in an act of collective disloyalty. Harry, whose motto 'Servetur ad imum . . .' is absolute loyalty, acts out in his painful progress from Tory to Whig the conflict and exculpation of his guilt. This is why his great anti-type in the novel is the 'Judas' Marlborough whose disloyalty sprang not from moral but selfish motives.

The two women in Harry's life reflect his divided world. One, the witty beauty Beatrix, belongs in type to the Restoration stage; the other, the good woman Rachel, to the pages of the *Spectator*, whose improving tea-table sermons were designed to encourage 'female virtues of a domestic turn'. It is significant that Beatrix should be criticized in the mock *Spectator* – it is also significant that Esmond, in spite of the catalogue of faults, cannot give her up. Beatrix, who wants to be the mistress of a king, like 'Jezebel' Castlewood, rejects the Darby and Joan decency which Harry offers her. She is a dangerous resurgence of the past which Harry can reject intellectually but not emotionally. When, as a sign of his servitude, Harry kneels to kiss her toe the memory goes back twenty years to when he knelt as a little Papist to the 'Goddess' Rachel. It is a grave lapse. By plotting to restore the Jacobite king Esmond will undo the Revolution. It is England's destiny as well as his own which is at stake, and he knows, though he cannot help, the unwisdom of his action – it is as Monsieur Simon, the 'Simple Cymon' of the *Spectator* paper, that he goes across to arrange the conspiracy. Fortunately the Pretender lets the crown slip from his hand and fortuitously England is preserved. The last of the 'Faithful Fool's' loyalty for wrong causes is purged away in disgust, and with it his bondage to Beatrix. 'His love of ten years was over, it fell down dead on the spot.'

Harry has been poised between the siren of the past and the madonna of the future. That he eventually chooses the future, marries a woman just like his mother (too like for some), and goes to work in the aptly named Virginia for the reward of domestic bliss makes him seem, as critics have pointed out, a Victorian. But it is quite feasible to see in *Henry Esmond* the nineteenth-century mind tracing the genealogy of its civilization in the eighteenth century.

## (b) *Harry as nineteenth-century man*

'An intelligent man of the nineteenth century,' wrote Dostoyevsky, 'is bound to be a spineless creature.' 'Bound' because although he is free to choose his belief, he can never find certainty in it. The role fits Esmond, Marquis and bastard, Protestant and Catholic, Jacobite and Hanoverian, Tory and Whig, scholar and soldier, son and lover. Occasionally the outcome is nihilism and the premature desire to try a 'new life in a new world', but for most of the novel he is in search of a final meaning. The many references to Esmond as the 'knight of the Rueful Countenance' are appropriate, he is Quixotic. His many-turned coat belongs with Tennyson's 'damned vacillating state', his chronic *angst* with Arnold's 'darkling plain', and the rather desperate domesticity in which he finally finds consolation is a typically Victorian way out.

### (c) *Harry as twentieth-century man*

In terms of its motifs *Henry Esmond* has adultery, incest and, arguably, Oedipean murder. Admittedly as these filter through the elegant narrative demeanour they are less alarming than they sound. A typical hint at the novel's psychic underworld is the recurrent identification of the hero and heroine with passionate criminals like Medea and Othello. Not all the 'abnormality' is as allusive as this, however. Harry marries a woman who has said, with good reason, 'I am your mother, you are my son.' Nor is it an arbitrary conclusion. Rachel's adultery, so to call the illicit love which flourishes before her husband's death, is established early in the novel by the instability of her attitude to her young 'knight'. In one of Beatrix's later speeches it is corroborated: 'she has had a great sorrow in her life and a great secret and repented of it'. Beatrix does not know what this 'secret' which requires 'repentance' is, but the reader does, and many nineteenth-century readers would rather not have known it.

The murder requires a larger imaginative leap. Thackeray changed the name of the villain, Charles Mohun, who was historical, to Harry Mohun. It could not have been accidental, since Thackeray had followed his duelling career with some pains through Howell's *State Trials*. One small justification for the change is the *coup de théâtre* when it is reported to Rachel that 'Harry' has been killed in the overturned chariot and she faints, thinking that Esmond is meant. More suggestive, since Mohun wants to make Rachel his mistress in the practical sense of seducing her, and kills Harry's two rivals in love, the fourth Viscount and the Duke of Hamilton, is that he is conceived of as a kind of *alter ego*, acting out the other Harry's unexpressible desires. 'The most normal people,' as Birkin says in *Women in Love*, 'have the worst subterranean selves.'

This may seem far-fetched. But there is uncovered in the novel, demonstrably, a layer of motive astonishing in fiction of this period. Rachel especially, with her jealousy of her daughter, persecution of her husband and love of her 'son', seems to be a contradiction as well as an affirmation of the novel's ostensible idealism. The modernity of the psychological analysis comes from the many suggestions, in Rachel's hysteria and Esmond's mystical spirituality, for example, that social attitudes are a mask, not an expression, of real motives. Thackeray does not, of course, think of it as sub-conscious but as 'sub-moral', and therefore infinitely more dangerous to a world built on duty and principle. The result is what T. S. Eliot describes in *Hamlet*, an emotion 'in excess of the facts as they appear'. The following passage, in which Rachel has just discovered Harry's sacrifice for her family, illustrates the discrepancy well:

'Dearest saint,' says he – 'purest soul, that has had so much to suffer, that has blest the poor lonely orphan with such a treasure of love! 'Tis for me to kneel, not for you; 'tis for me to be thankful that I can make you happy. Hath my life any other aim? Blessed be God that I can serve you. What pleasure, think you, could all the world give me compared to that?'

'Don't raise me' she said, in a wild way, to Esmond, who would have lifted her. 'Let me kneel – let me kneel, and, – and – worship you.'

This welter of erotic–religious fervour, if it were not psychologically 'right', would be atrociously bad writing. In this respect the literary company we should choose for *Henry Esmond* is not *Ivanhoe* and *Westward Ho!* but *Oedipus Rex*, *Hamlet* and *Sons and Lovers*, Thackeray's novel being no more a simple historical romance than Shakespeare's tragedy is a simple revenge play.

Harry as heroic scapegoat for the 'justified disloyalty' of the revolution, Harry as victim of nineteenth-century intellectual *anomie*, Harry as a man half-controlling, half-controlled by his unconscious self; these are the lights by which we can examine the hero's puzzling moods and strange intensities. But not even in sum with the more fashionable theory that *Henry Esmond* is Thackeray's personal catharsis do they make up an explanation of the novel, though they attest its many-sidedness and complex refusal to yield to solve-all formulas.

Taine thought *Henry Esmond* the only novel Thackeray ever wrote (the rest were satires); Pater called it 'a perfect fiction'. More judiciously his fellow Victorian Brownell qualified the compliment – '*Esmond* is not the greatest of the novels, it is the most perfect.' In a performance which has so much of the *tour de force* about it, it is perhaps natural that admiration for the technical excellencies should be exacted almost as a critical due. Any one of the following features could provide the text for an extended eulogy – the depth of plotting and density of connected detail beneath the brilliant glaze of the style; the integration of fictional and historical characters; the cleverly terraced narrative strategy in which Esmond Senior (in about 1740) philosophizes mellowly on the passionate activities of his youth, forty years before, with the occasional distancing interjections of his daughter (about 1780); the shapeliness of the three individual volumes, each with its cadence to the lowest point of a phase of the hero's career; the pictorial and scenic 'solidity' of the novel (no novel needs illustrations less). Above all, the ironic structure of the novel, which hinges on the hero's ignorance and which, uncharacteristically, Thackeray does not sabotage by narrative omniscience, so that the action is sprung on a last-page denouement which is as unexpected as, in retrospect, it is seen to have been inevitable. But in the last analysis *Henry Esmond* is much more than the perfect shell of an extinct literary species. If it had been no more than the 'best historical novel' there would have been none of the unease about its 'uncomfortable', 'painful' and 'unsavory' quality which echoes the nineteenth-century praise. The cleverness of the work is a surface which to some extent obscures, but through which we can see into a novel which is more complex and deeply felt, if less funny, than any other Thackeray wrote.

# A NOTE ON THACKERAY AS HISTORIAN

THE historical backing to *Henry Esmond* is remarkably thorough. A lifetime's affectionate saturation in the period has been sharpened by the effort of the lectures on the English humorists. Consequently, Thackeray's sources are, at any one point, manifold. To support a fictional scene he might, for example, use Boyer's *History of the Reign of Queen Anne* for the general sweep of events, Swift's private writing for the inside gossip and the *Spectator* for stylistic and period colouring. There are numberless other tributaries feeding into the narrative from Thackeray's private reading, and the overall effect is that multiplicity which Mr Roundabout admired in Macaulay – 'he reads twenty books to write a sentence.'

The similarity with Macaulay is suggestive in other ways. The careers of the two men trace a curious parallel, both Trinity men, both journalists until 1848, when huge literary successes put them among the great men of the age. Macaulay's friendship after they met in 1849 and the first two volumes of the *History of England* probably helped form the Whig historical thesis which we find in *Henry Esmond*. This it is which vindicates the Revolution by casting James and his progeny as the villains and William as the hero, the verdict at which the hero painfully arrives. The same thesis singles out Marlborough, the man who went over to William too soon, as party scapegoat, and Thackeray joins Swift and Macaulay as Marlborough's greatest slanderers. The opinion of Winston Churchill, the official biographer of Marlborough, that Macaulay is a liar and *Henry Esmond*, in this respect, 'malicious' should perhaps be appended to any edition.

It is interesting to note that, as he worked on the novel, Thackeray likened himself to Macaulay: 'It costs as much trouble as Macaulay's History almost, and he has the vast advantage of remembering everything he has read, whilst everything but impressions – I mean facts, dates, and so forth – slip out of my head.' As he worked at the British Museum on his 'family papers' (he was very distantly related to General Webb, Marlborough's great antagonist), Thackeray may consciously have tried something Macaulayan, and seen in it a way out of the novel-writing trade into the dignity of literature. But one of the most interesting features of the novel is the way in which Thackeray the moralist overcomes Thackeray the historian. Finally, he is as much against 'filthy' Swift as against Marlborough, because Swift is, as the Lecture on him points out, against marriage and children. Here the political alliances go wrong. And *Henry Esmond*, which shapes as a *roman à thèse*, becomes something much more complex, for which the reader may be grateful.

*J.S.*

# A NOTE ON THE TEXT

*Esmond* was first published in 1852, 'in periwig and embroidery, in beautiful type and handsome proportions', as Thackeray's daughter said. The three volumes, printed in an eighteenth-century type-face, and sprinkled with archaisms, masqueraded as the memoirs of Colonel Esmond, published in 1778. The last text to be supervised by the author, that of the one-volume 1858 edition, modernized the type and most of the usage, corrected some errors, and also deleted a piece of personal satire which had served its purpose.

The 1858 text is the basis of this edition. Errors persisting in that text, and some newly introduced by it, have been corrected. The satire is relegated to the notes. I have retained, however, the first edition's archaic spellings where they are distinctive, for they seem right in a 'history' on which Thackeray lavished his 'care and antiquarianism'. Few readers will puzzle long before making out that a turbant is a turban, and that yatches are yachts.

The Queen Anne type-face had to be discarded. The idea of a Penguin in periwig and embroidery is pleasant but, alas, not practical.

*M.C.G.*

# A NOTE ON THE MANUSCRIPT

THE manuscript of *Henry Esmond* was given to Trinity College, Cambridge, by Leslie Stephen in 1887. The gesture was a graceful one, since Thackeray in fact and Esmond in fiction had attended that college (neither with any great success). The most remarkable feature of the manuscript is that it seems to bear out the claim by the novelist's daughter that this was the only draft of the work that Thackeray made. So with nothing more than his notebooks and a very clear prevision Thackeray contrived to write a novel which most critics have agreed in finding supremely intricate and carefully wrought.

The manuscript presents a rather quilted appearance to the eye. It is written on letter-paper (at least three club crests are to be found), Thackeray had two handwritings and two amanuenses (used largely for the more historical passages), and it was his habit to write or dictate a little often, rather than to prolong any period of composition. As a result of this desultory procedure, and the fact that he did not conceive of the narrative in chapter units, the reader will find *Esmond* abrupt in its transitions, though perfectly unified in mood. He seems to have the main outline of the novel firm in his mind from the beginning, though there are a few wrong turnings. The old Viscountess Isabella, for example, was originally to have been much more villainous, killing Mrs Tusher (who, the reader will notice, mysteriously disappears after the fifth chapter) by making her play picquet in wet shoes. Holt was to have been less fallible and comic than he finally turns out to be. But on the whole there are remarkably few major corrections. The only places in which Thackeray really loses control are those where dates, places and names are concerned. In these matters the novelist seems to have been wildly erratic and forgetful. Harry Esmond of Trinity is on occasion George Esmond of Christchurch, Oxford. Rachel for a large part of the novel was prenamed, less felicitously, Dolly. Beatrix was first Beatrice and Mohun variously Roydon and Poyns. Originally Castlewood was to have been in Norfolk not

Hampshire, with Chatteris for Hexton, and Thackeray did not entirely clear up this muddle in the version he passed for press (see p. 439 et al.). Small errors of this kind abound, and many have slipped through to the final text. Attentive readers will not find it difficult to catch Thackeray out, though it is doubtful whether such small-mindedness increases one's pleasure in the novel. About three-quarters of the way through the novel Thackery hit on the idea of having the memoirs edited by Rachel Esmond Warrington, with interjections by others of the Esmond family. Hence the elaborate frame which the novel has. And this frame, of course, is *The Virginians* in embryo. There was one long footnote which Thackeray intended to add to the end of the second book, a quotation, *in extenso*, from Macpherson's *Original Papers*. This collection of documents was one of the source books for *Esmond*, and the extract concerned was one which confirmed Thackeray's black portrait of Marlborough. In his description of Wynendael the reader will notice that Thackeray goes so far as to say that the Commander in Chief deliberately let Webb fall into a trap which should destroy him. Thackeray must have felt this was going too far, hence the balancing footnotes which we have and the major one which, for presumably technical reasons, he could not fit in.

In general, the manuscript bears out what might have been expected from one's first reading of the novel, that Thackeray wrote it quickly, confidently and buoyed up throughout by a sure flow of inspiration.

*J.S.*

# BIBLIOGRAPHICAL NOTE

THE best introduction to *Henry Esmond* is probably still Thackeray's own essays on the eighteenth-century English humourists. Those interested in matching the novel with its historical background will find a congenial account in the consecutive narrative histories of Macaulay, *The History of England* (which in fact covers the reigns of James II and William III) and Trevelyan's *England under Queen Anne* (1932). The best single study of *Henry Esmond* is G. N. Ray's *The Buried Life* (1952), though possibly its brilliant biographical insights tend to reduce the novel to a *roman à clef*. Professor Ray has also compiled the four-volume edition of the *Letters* (1946) and has written the official two-volume biography *Thackeray: The Uses of Adversity: 1811–1846* (1955) and *Thackeray: The Age of Wisdom: 1847–1863* (1958). These are indispensable for the student and, in view of Thackeray's genius as a letter writer and his practice of sublimating his life in fiction, of more than average interest to the general reader. Geoffrey Tillotson's *Thackeray the Novelist* (1954) is, as its title implies, a purely literary appreciation. Those who want to taste the flavour of criticism which felt no need to apologize for the author might try Saintsbury's *A Consideration of Thackeray* (1931) or the even earlier *Thackeray* (1879) by the friend and disciple Trollope.

# FAMILY TREE OF THE ESMONDS

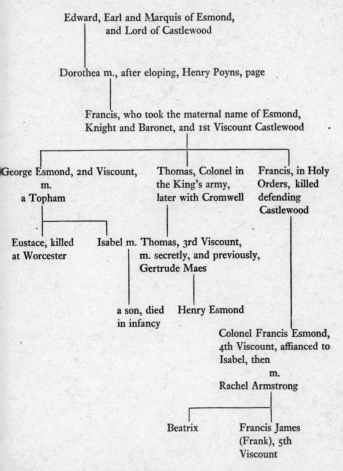

Edward, Earl and Marquis of Esmond,
and Lord of Castlewood

Dorothea m., after eloping, Henry Poyns, page

Francis, who took the maternal name of Esmond,
Knight and Baronet, and 1st Viscount Castlewood

George Esmond, 2nd Viscount,
m.
a Topham

Thomas, Colonel in
the King's army,
later with Cromwell

Francis, in Holy
Orders, killed
defending
Castlewood

Eustace, killed
at Worcester

Isabel m. Thomas, 3rd Viscount,
m. secretly, and previously,
Gertrude Maes

a son, died
in infancy

Henry Esmond

Colonel Francis Esmond,
4th Viscount, affianced to
Isabel, then
m.
Rachel Armstrong

Beatrix

Francis James
(Frank), 5th
Viscount

Henry and Rachel Esmond's grandchildren, Harry and George Warrington,
are the heroes of *The Virginians*, and George Warrington is the grandfather
of his namesake in *Pendennis*.

*Facsimile of the title page
of the first edition of Henry Esmond*

# THE HISTORY

OF

# HENRY ESMOND, Esq.

A COLONEL IN THE SERVICE OF HER MAJESTY
Q. ANNE.

## WRITTEN BY HIMSELF.

Servetur ad imum
Qualis ab incepto procefferit, et fibi conftet.

**IN THREE VOLUMES.**

VOLUME THE FIRST.

*LONDON:*

PRINTED FOR SMITH, ELDER, & COMPANY,
OVER AGAINST ST. PETER'S CHURCH IN CORNHILL.

1852.

# PREFACE

## THE ESMONDS OF VIRGINIA

THE estate of Castlewood, in Virginia, which was given to our ancestors by King Charles the First, as some return for the sacrifices made in his Majesty's cause by the Esmond family, lies in Westmoreland County, between the rivers Potomac and Rappahannoc, and was once as great as an English Principality, though in the early times its revenues were but small. Indeed, for near eighty years after our forefathers possessed them, our plantations were in the hands of factors, who enriched themselves one after another, though a few scores of hogsheads of tobacco were all the produce that, for long after the Restoration, our family received from their Virginian estates.

My dear and honoured father, Colonel Henry Esmond, whose history, written by himself, is contained in the accompanying volume, came to Virginia in the year 1718, built his house of Castlewood, and here permanently settled. After a long stormy life in England, he passed the remainder of his many years in peace and honour in this country; how beloved and respected by all his fellow-citizens, how inexpressibly dear to his family, I need not say. His whole life was a benefit to all who were connected with him. He gave the best example, the best advice, the most bounteous hospitality to his friends; the tenderest care to his dependants; and bestowed on those of his immediate family such a blessing of fatherly love and protection, as can never be thought of, by us at least, without veneration and thankfulness; and my son's children, whether established here in our Republic, or at home in the always beloved mother country, from which our late quarrel hath separated us, may surely be proud to be descended from one who in all ways was so truly noble.

My dear mother[1] died in 1736, soon after our return from England, whither my parents took me for my education; and where I made the acquaintance of Mr Warrington, whom my children never saw. When it pleased Heaven, in the bloom of his youth, and after but a few months of a most happy union, to remove him from me, I owed my recovery from the grief which that calamity caused me, mainly to my dearest father's tenderness, and then to the blessing vouchsafed to me in the birth of my two beloved boys. I know the fatal differences which separated them in politics never disunited their hearts; and as I can love them both, whether wearing the King's colours or the Republic's, I am sure that they love me, and one another, and him above all, my father and theirs, the dearest friend of their childhood, the noble gentleman who bred them from their infancy in the practice and knowledge of Truth, and Love, and Honour.

My children will never forget the appearance and figure of their revered grandfather; and I wish I possessed the art of drawing (which my papa had in perfection), so that I could leave to our descendants a portrait of one who was so good and so respected. My father was of a dark complexion, with a very great forehead and dark hazel eyes, overhung by eyebrows which remained black long after his hair was white. His nose was aquiline, his smile extraordinary sweet. How well I remember it, and how little any description I can write can recall his image! He was of rather low stature, not being above five feet seven inches in height; he used to laugh at my sons, whom he called his crutches, and say they were grown too tall for him to lean upon. But small as he was he had a perfect grace and majesty of deportment, such as I have never seen in this country, except perhaps in our friend Mr Washington; and commanded respect wherever he appeared.

In all bodily exercises he excelled, and showed an extraordinary quickness and agility. Of fencing he was especially fond, and made my two boys proficient in that art; so much so, that when the French came to this country with Monsieur Rochambeau,[2] not one of his officers was superior to my Henry, and he was not the equal of my poor George, who had taken the King's side in our lamentable but glorious war of independence.[3]

Neither my father nor my mother ever wore powder in their hair; both their heads were as white as silver, as I can remember them. My dear mother possessed to the last an extraordinary brightness and freshness of complexion; nor would people believe that she did not wear rouge. At sixty years of age she still looked young, and was quite agile. It was not until after that dreadful siege of our house by the Indians, which left me a widow ere I was a mother, that my dear mother's health broke. She never recovered from her terror and anxiety of those days, which ended so fatally for me, then a bride scarce six months married, and died in my father's arms ere my own year of widowhood was over.

From that day, until the last of his dear and honoured life, it was my delight and consolation to remain with him as his comforter and companion; and from those little notes which my mother hath made here and there in the volume in which my father describes his adventures in Europe, I can well understand the extreme devotion with which she regarded him – a devotion so passionate and exclusive as to prevent her, I think, from loving any other person except with an inferior regard; her whole thoughts being centred on this one object of affection and worship. I know that, before her, my dear father did not show the love which he had for his daughter; and in her last and most sacred moments, this dear and tender parent owned to me her repentance that she had not loved me enough: her jealousy even that my father should give his affection to any but herself; and in the most fond and beautiful words of affection and admonition, she bade me never to leave him, and to supply the place which she was quitting. With a clear conscience, and a heart inexpressibly thankful, I think I can say that I fulfilled those dying commands, and that until his last hour my dearest father never had to complain that his daughter's love and fidelity failed him.

And it is since I knew him entirely, for during my mother's life he never quite opened himself to me – since I knew the value and splendour of that affection which he bestowed upon me, that I have come to understand and pardon what, I own, used to anger me in my mother's lifetime, her jealousy respecting her husband's love. 'Twas a gift so precious that no wonder she who had it was for keeping it all, and could part with none of it, even to her daughter.

Though I never heard my father use a rough word, 'twas extraordinary with how much awe his people regarded him; and the servants on our plantation, both those assigned from England and the purchased negroes, obeyed him with an eagerness such as the most severe taskmasters round about us could never get from their people. He was never familiar, though perfectly simple and natural; he was the same with the meanest man as with the greatest, and as courteous to a black slave-girl as to the governor's wife. No one ever thought of taking a liberty with him (except once a tipsy gentleman from York, and I am bound to own that my papa never forgave him): he set the humblest people at once on their ease with him, and brought down the most arrogant by a grave satiric way, which made persons exceedingly afraid of him. His courtesy was not put on like a Sunday suit, and laid by when the company went away; it was always the same; as he was always dressed the same whether for a dinner by ourselves or for a great entertainment. They say he liked to be the first in his company; but what company was there in which he would not be first? When I went to Europe for my education, and we passed a winter at London with my half-brother, my Lord Castlewood and his second lady, I saw at her Majesty's Court some of the most famous gentlemen of those days; and I thought to myself, none of these are better than my papa; and the famous Lord Bolingbroke,[4] who came to us from Dawley, said as much, and that the men of that time were not like those of his youth:— 'Were your father, Madam,' he said, 'to go into the woods, the Indians would elect him Sachem';[5] and his lordship was pleased to call me Pocahontas.

I did not see our other relative, Bishop Tusher's lady,[6] of whom so much is said in my papa's memoirs – although my mamma went to visit her in the country. I have no pride (as I showed by complying with my mother's request, and marrying a gentleman who was but the younger son of a Suffolk Baronet), yet I own to *a decent respect* for my name, and wonder how one, who ever bore it, should change it for that of Mrs *Thomas Tusher*. I pass over as odious and unworthy of credit those reports (which I heard in Europe, and was then too young to understand), how this person, having *left her family* and fled to Paris, out of jealousy of the Pretender betrayed his secrets to my Lord Stair, King George's Ambassador, and nearly caused the Prince's

death there; how she came to England and married this Mr
Tusher, and became a great favourite of King George the
Second, by whom Mr Tusher was made a Dean, and then a
Bishop. I did not see the lady, who chose to remain *at her palace*
all the time we were in London; but after visiting her, my poor
mamma said she had lost all her good looks, and warned me not
to set too much store by any such gifts which nature had
bestowed upon me. She grew exceedingly stout; and I remember
my brother's wife, Lady Castlewood, saying 'No wonder she
became a favourite, for the King likes them old and ugly, as his
father did before him.' On which papa said – 'All women were
alike; that there was never one so beautiful as that one; and that
we could forgive her everything but her beauty.' And hereupon
my mamma looked vexed, and my Lord Castlewood began to
laugh; and I, of course, being a young creature, could not understand what was the subject of their conversation.

After the circumstances narrated in the third book of these
Memoirs, my father and mother both went abroad, being advised
by their friends to leave the country in consequence of the transactions which are recounted at the close of the volume of the
Memoirs. But my brother, hearing how the *future Bishop's lady*
had quitted Castlewood and joined the Pretender at Paris, pursued him, and would have killed him, Prince as he was, had not
the Prince managed to make his escape. On this expedition to
Scotland directly after, Castlewood was so enraged against him
that he asked leave to serve as a volunteer, and join the Duke of
Argyle's army in Scotland, which the Pretender never had the
courage to face; and thenceforth my lord was quite reconciled to
the present reigning family, from whom he hath even received
promotion.

Mrs Tusher was by this time as angry against the Pretender as
any of her relations could be, and used to boast, as I have heard,
that she not only brought back my lord to the Church of
England, but procured the English peerage for him, which the
*junior branch* of our family at present enjoys. She was a great
friend of Sir Robert Walpole, and would not rest until her
husband slept at Lambeth, my papa used laughing to say. However, the Bishop died of apoplexy suddenly, and his wife erected

a great monument over him; and the pair sleep under that stone, with a canopy of marble clouds and angels above them – the first Mrs Tusher lying sixty miles off at Castlewood.

But my papa's genius and education are both greater than any a woman can be expected to have, and his adventures in Europe far more exciting than his life in this country, which was passed in the tranquil offices of love and duty; and I shall say no more by way of introduction to his Memoirs, nor keep my children from the perusal of a story which is much more interesting than that of their affectionate old mother,

RACHEL ESMOND WARRINGTON

Castlewood, Virginia,
*November* 3, 1778

# CONTENTS

## BOOK I

### THE EARLY YOUTH OF HENRY ESMOND, UP TO THE TIME OF HIS LEAVING TRINITY COLLEGE, IN CAMBRIDGE

## BOOK II

### CONTAINS MR. ESMOND'S MILITARY LIFE, AND OTHER MATTERS APPERTAINING TO THE ESMOND FAMILY

## BOOK III

### CONTAINING THE END OF MR ESMOND'S ADVENTURES IN ENGLAND

# THE HISTORY OF
# HENRY ESMOND

## BOOK I

### THE EARLY YOUTH OF HENRY ESMOND,
### UP TO THE TIME OF HIS LEAVING TRINITY
### COLLEGE, IN CAMBRIDGE

THE actors in the old tragedies, as we read, piped their iambics
to a tune, speaking from under a mask, and wearing stilts and
a great head-dress. 'Twas thought the dignity of the Tragic
Muse[1] required these appurtenances, and that she was not to
move except to a measure and cadence. So Queen Medea[2] slew
her children to a slow music: and King Agamemnon perished
in a dying fall (to use Mr Dryden's words):[3] the Chorus standing
by in a set attitude, and rhythmically and decorously bewailing
the fates of those great crowned persons. The Muse of History
hath encumbered herself with ceremony as well as her Sister
of the Theatre. She too wears the mask and the cothurnus,[4] and
speaks to measure. She too, in our age, busies herself with the
affairs only of kings; waiting on them obsequiously and stately,
as if she were but a mistress of Court ceremonies, and had
nothing to do with the registering of the affairs of the common
people. I have seen in his very old age and decrepitude the old
French King Lewis the Fourteenth, the type and model of
king-hood – who never moved but to measure, who lived and
died according to the laws of his Court-marshal, persisting in
enacting through life the part of Hero; and, divested of poetry,
this was but a little wrinkled old man, pock-marked, and with a
great periwig and red heels to make him look tall – a hero for a
book if you like, or for a brass statue or a painted ceiling, a god
in a Roman shape, but what more than a man for Madame
Maintenon, or the barber who shaved him, or Monsieur Fagon,
his surgeon? I wonder shall History ever pull off her periwig
and cease to be court-ridden? Shall we see something of France

and England besides Versailles and Windsor? I saw Queen
Anne at the latter place tearing down the Park slopes, after her
stag-hounds, and driving her one-horse chaise – a hot, red-faced
woman,[5] not in the least resembling that statue of her which
turns its stone back upon Saint Paul's, and faces the coaches
struggling up Ludgate Hill. She was neither better bred nor
wiser than you and me, though we knelt to hand her a letter or
a washhand-basin. Why shall History go on kneeling to the end
of time? I am for having her rise up off her knees, and take a
natural posture: not to be for ever performing cringes and
congees like a Court-chamberlain, and shuffling backwards
out of doors in the presence of the sovereign. In a word, I
would have History familiar rather than heroic: and think that
Mr Hogarth and Mr Fielding will give our children a much
better idea of the manners of the present age in England, than
the Court Gazette and the newspapers which we get thence.

There was a German officer of Webb's, with whom we used
to joke, and of whom a story (whereof I myself was the author)
was got to be believed in the army, that he was eldest son of the
hereditary Grand Bootjack of the Empire, and heir to that
honour of which his ancestors had been very proud, having been
kicked for twenty generations by one imperial foot, as they drew
the boot from the other. I have heard that the old Lord Castlewood, of part of whose family this present volume is a chronicle,
though he came of quite as good blood as the Stuarts whom he
served (and who as regards mere lineage are no better than a
dozen English and Scottish houses I could name), was prouder
of his post about the Court than of his ancestral honours, and
valued his dignity (as Lord of the Butteries and Groom of the
King's Posset) so highly, that he cheerfully ruined himself for
the thankless and thriftless race who bestowed it. He pawned
his plate for King Charles the First, mortgaged his property for
the same cause, and lost the greater part of it by fines and
sequestration: stood a siege of his castle by Ireton, where his
brother Thomas capitulated (afterward making terms with the
Commonwealth, for which the elder brother never forgave him),
and where his second brother Francis, who had embraced the
ecclesiastical profession, was slain on Castlewood tower, being

engaged there both as preacher and artilleryman. This resolute old loyalist, who was with the King whilst his house was thus being battered down, escaped abroad with his only son, then a boy, to return and take a part in Worcester fight. On that fatal field Eustace Esmond was killed, and Castlewood fled from it once more into exile, and henceforward, and after the Restoration, never was away from the Court of the monarch (for whose return we offer thanks in the Prayer-Book)[6] who sold his country[7] and who took bribes of the French king.

What spectacle is more august than that of a great king in exile? Who is more worthy of respect than a brave man in misfortune? Mr Addison has painted such a figure in his noble piece of Cato.[8] But suppose fugitive Cato fuddling himself at a tavern with a wench on each knee, a dozen faithful and tipsy companions of defeat, and a landlord calling out for his bill; and the dignity of misfortune is straightway lost. The Historical Muse turns away shamefaced from the vulgar scene, and closes the door – on which the exile's unpaid drink is scored up – upon him and his pots and his pipes, and the tavern-chorus which he and his friends are singing. Such a man as Charles should have had an Ostade or Mieris[9] to paint him. Your Knellers and Le Bruns[10] only deal in clumsy and impossible allegories: and it hath always seemed to me blasphemy to claim Olympus[11] for such a wine-drabbled divinity as that.

About the King's follower the Viscount Castlewood – orphan of his son, ruined by his fidelity, bearing many wounds and marks of bravery, old and in exile, his kinsmen I suppose should be silent; nor if this patriarch fell down in his cups, call fie upon him, and fetch passers-by to laugh at his red face and white hairs. What! does a stream rush out of a mountain free and pure, to roll through fair pastures, to feed and throw out bright tributaries, and to end in a village gutter? Lives that have noble commencements have often no better endings; it is not without a kind of awe and reverence that an observer should speculate upon such careers as he traces the course of them. I have seen too much of success in life to take off my hat and huzza to it as it passes in its gilt coach: and would do my little part with my neighbours on foot, that they should not gape with too much

wonder, nor applaud too loudly. Is it the Lord Mayor going in
state to mince-pies and the Mansion-House? Is it poor Jack of
Newgate's procession, with the sheriff and javelin-men, conducting him on his last journey to Tyburn? I look into my
heart and think that I am as good as my Lord Mayor, and
know I am as bad as Tyburn Jack.[12] Give me a chain and red
gown and a pudding before me, and I could play the part of
Alderman very well, and sentence Jack after dinner. Starve me,
keep me from books and honest people, educate me to love
dice, gin, and pleasure, and put me on Hounslow Heath,[13] with
a purse before me and I will take it. 'And I shall be deservedly
hanged,' say you, wishing to put an end to this prosing. I don't
say no. I can't but accept the world as I find it, including a
rope's end, as long as it is in fashion.

## Chapter 1

### AN ACCOUNT OF THE FAMILY OF ESMOND
### OF CASTLEWOOD HALL[1]

WHEN Francis, fourth Viscount Castlewood, came to his title,
and presently after to take possession of his house of Castlewood,
county Hants, in the year 1691, almost the only tenant of the
place besides the domestics was a lad of twelve years of age, of
whom no one seemed to take any note until my Lady Viscountess
lighted upon him, going over the house, with the housekeeper on
the day of her arrival. The boy was in the room known as the
book-room, or yellow gallery, where the portraits of the family
used to hang, that fine piece among others of Sir Antonio Van
Dyck of George, second Viscount, and that by Mr Dobson of
my lord the third Viscount, just deceased, which it seems his
lady and widow did not think fit to carry away, when she sent
for and carried off to her house at Chelsey, near to London, the
picture of herself by Sir Peter Lely,[2] in which her ladyship was
represented as a huntress of Diana's court.

The new and fair lady of Castlewood found the sad lonely

little occupant of this gallery busy over his great book, which he laid down when he was aware that a stranger was at hand. And, knowing who that person must be, the lad stood up and bowed before her, performing a shy obeisance to the mistress of his house.

She stretched out her hand – indeed when was it that that hand would not stretch out to do an act of kindness, or to protect grief and ill-fortune? 'And this is our kinsman,' she said; 'and what is your name, kinsman?'

'My name is Henry Esmond,' said the lad, looking up at her in a sort of delight and wonder, for she had come upon him as a *Dea certè*,[3] and appeared the most charming object he had ever looked on. Her golden hair was shining in the gold of the sun; her complexion was of a dazzling bloom; her lips smiling, and her eyes beaming with a kindness which made Harry Esmond's heart to beat with surprise.

'His name is Henry Esmond, sure enough, my lady,' says Mrs Worksop the housekeeper (an old tyrant whom Henry Esmond plagued more than he hated), and the old gentlewoman looked significantly towards the late lord's picture, as it now is in the family, noble and severe-looking, with his hand on his sword, and his order on his cloak, which he had from the Emperor during the war on the Danube against the Turk.

Seeing the great and undeniable likeness between this portrait and the lad, the new Viscountess, who had still hold of the boy's hand as she looked at the picture, blushed and dropped the hand quickly, and walked down the gallery, followed by Mrs Worksop.

When the lady came back, Harry Esmond stood exactly in the same spot, and with his hand as it had fallen when he dropped it on his black coat.

Her heart melted I suppose (indeed she hath since owned as much) at the notion that she should do anything unkind to any mortal, great or small; for, when she returned, she had sent away the housekeeper upon an errand by the door at the farther end of the gallery; and, coming back to the lad, with a look of infinite pity and tenderness in her eyes, she took his hand again, placing her other fair hand on his head, and saying some words to him, which were so kind and said in a voice so sweet, that the boy, who had never looked upon so much beauty before, felt as if the touch of a superior being or angel smote him down to the ground, and kissed the fair protecting hand as he knelt on one knee. To the very last hour of his life, Esmond remembered the lady as she then spoke and looked, the rings on her fair hands, the very scent of her robe, the beam of her eyes lighting up with surprise and kindness, her lips blooming in a smile, the sun making a golden halo round her hair.

As the boy was yet in this attitude of humility, enters behind him a portly gentleman, with a little girl of four years old in his hand. The gentleman burst into a great laugh at the lady and her adorer, with his little queer figure, his sallow face, and long black hair. The lady blushed, and seemed to deprecate his ridicule by a look of appeal to her husband, for it was my Lord Viscount who now arrived, and whom the lad knew, having once before seen him in the late lord's lifetime.

'So this is the little priest!' says my lord, looking down at the lad; 'welcome, kinsman.'

'He is saying his prayers to mamma,' says the little girl, who came up to her papa's knee; and my lord burst out into another great laugh at this, and kinsman Henry looked very silly. He invented a half-dozen of speeches in reply, but 'twas months afterwards, when he thought of this adventure: as it was, he had never a word in answer.

'*Le pauvre enfant, il n'a que nous,*' says the lady, looking to her lord; and the boy, who understood her, though doubtless she thought otherwise, thanked her with all his heart for her kind speech.

'And he shan't want for friends here,' says my lord, in a kind voice, 'shall he, little Trix?'

The little girl, whose name was Beatrix, and whom her papa called by this diminutive, looked at Henry Esmond solemnly, with a pair of large eyes, and then a smile shone over her face, which was as beautiful as that of a cherub, and she came up and put out a little hand to him. A keen and delightful pang of gratitude, happiness, affection, filled the orphan child's heart, as he received from the protectors, whom Heaven had sent to him, these touching words, and tokens of friendliness and kindness. But an hour since he had felt quite alone in the world: when he heard the great peal of bells from Castlewood church ringing that morning to welcome the arrival of the new lord and lady, it had rung only terror and anxiety to him, for he knew not how the new owner would deal with him; and those to whom he formerly looked for protection were forgotten or dead. Pride and doubt too had kept him within doors: when the Vicar and the people of the village, and the servants of the house, had gone out to welcome my Lord Castlewood – for Henry Esmond was no servant, though a dependant; no relative, though he bore the name and inherited the blood of the house; and in the midst of the noise and acclamations attending the arrival of the new lord (for whom you may be sure a feast was got ready, and guns were fired, and tenants and domestics huzzaed when his carriage approached and rolled into the court-yard of the hall), no one ever took any notice of young Henry Esmond, who sate un-observed and alone in the book-room, until the afternoon of that day, when his new friends found him.

When my lord and lady were going away thence, the little girl, still holding her kinsman by the hand, bade him to come too. 'Thou wilt always forsake an old friend for a new one, Trix,' says her father to her good-naturedly; and went into the gallery, giving an arm to his lady. They passed thence through the music-gallery, long since dismantled, and Queen Elizabeth's rooms, in the clock-tower, and out into the terrace, where was a fine prospect of sunset, and the great darkling woods with a cloud of rooks returning; and the plain and river with Castle-wood village beyond, and purple hills beautiful to look at – and the little heir of Castlewood, a child of two years old, was already here on the terrace in his nurse's arms, from whom he ran across the grass instantly he perceived his mother, and came to her.

'If thou canst not be happy here,' says my lord, looking round at the scene, 'thou art hard to please, Rachel.'

'I am happy where you are,' she said, 'but we were happiest of all at Walcote Forest.' Then my lord began to describe what was before them to his wife, and what indeed little Harry knew better than he – viz., the history of the house: how by yonder gate the page ran away with the heiress of Castlewood, by which the estate came into the present family, how the Roundheads attacked the clock-tower, which my lord's father was slain in defending. 'I was but two years old then' says he, 'but take forty-six from ninety, and how old shall I be, kinsman Harry?'

'Thirty,' says his wife, with a laugh.

'A great deal too old for you, Rachel,' answers my lord, looking fondly down at her. Indeed she seemed to be a girl; and was at that time scarce twenty years old.

'You know Frank I will do anything to please you,' says she, · 'and I promise you I will grow older every day.'

'You mustn't call papa, Frank; you must call papa my lord, now,' says Miss Beatrix, with a toss of her little head; at which the mother smiled, and the good-natured father laughed, and the little, trotting boy laughed, not knowing why – but because he was happy no doubt – as everyone seemed to be there. How those trivial incidents and words, the landscape and sunshine, and the group of people smiling and talking, remain fixed on the memory!

As the sun was setting, the little heir was sent in the arms of his nurse to bed, whither he went howling; but little Trix was promised to sit to supper that night – 'and you will come too, kinsman, won't you?' she said.

Harry Esmond blushed: 'I – I have supper with Mrs Work-sop,' says he.

'D——n it,' says my lord, 'thou shalt sup with us, Harry, tonight! Shan't refuse a lady, shall he, Trix?' – and they all wondered at Harry's performance as a trencher-man, in which character the poor boy acquitted himself very remarkably; for the truth is he had no dinner, nobody thinking of him in the bustle which the house was in, during the preparations ante-cedent to the new lord's arrival.

'No dinner! poor dear child!' says my lady, heaping up his plate with meat and my lord filling a bumper for him, bade him call a health; on which Master Harry, crying 'The King,' tossed off the wine. My lord was ready to drink that, and most other toasts: indeed only too ready. He would not hear of Doctor

Tusher (the Vicar of Castlewood, who came to supper) going
away when the sweetmeats were brought:[4] he had not had a
chaplain long enough, he said, to be tired of him: so his reverence
kept my lord company for some hours over a pipe and a punch-
bowl; and went away home with rather a reeling gait, and
declaring a dozen times, that his lordship's affability surpassed
every kindness he had ever had from his lordship's gracious
family.

As for young Esmond, when he got to his little chamber, it
was with a heart full of surprise and gratitude towards the new
friends whom this happy day had brought him. He was up and
watching long before the house was astir, longing to see that
fair lady and her children – that kind protector and patron; and
only fearful lest their welcome of the past night should in any
way be withdrawn or altered. But presently little Beatrix came
out into the garden, and her mother followed, who greeted
Harry as kindly as before. He told her at greater length the
histories of the house (which he had been taught in the old
lord's time), and to which she listened with great interest; and
then he told her, with respect to the night before, that he
understood French, and thanked her for her protection.

'Do you?' says she, with a blush; 'then, sir, you shall teach
me and Beatrix.' And she asked him many more questions
regarding himself, which had best be told more fully and
explicitly, than in those brief replies which the lad made to his
mistress's questions.


## Chapter 2

### RELATES HOW FRANCIS, FOURTH
### VISCOUNT, ARRIVES AT CASTLEWOOD


'TIS known that the name of Esmond and the estate of Castlewood, com.[1] Hants, came into possession of the present family
through Dorothea, daughter and heiress of Edward, Earl and
Marquis of Esmond, and Lord of Castlewood, which lady

married, 23 Eliz.,[2] Henry Poyns, gent.; the said Henry being
then a page in the household of her father. Francis,[3] son and
heir of the above Henry and Dorothea, who took the maternal
name which the family hath borne subsequently, was made
Knight and Baronet by King James the First; and, being of a
military disposition, remained long in Germany with the
Elector-Palatine, in whose service Sir Francis incurred both
expense and danger, lending large sums of money to that
unfortunate Prince; and receiving many wounds in the battles
against the Imperialists, in which Sir Francis engaged.

On his return home Sir Francis was rewarded for his services
and many sacrifices, by his late Majesty James the First, who
graciously conferred upon this tried servant the post of Warden
of the Butteries, and Groom of the King's Posset, which high
and confidential office he filled in that king's, and his unhappy
successor's, reign.

His age, and many wounds and infirmities, obliged Sir
Francis to perform much of his duty by deputy; and his son,
Sir George Esmond, knight and banneret,[4] first as his father's
lieutenant, and afterwards as inheritor of his father's title and
dignity, performed this office during almost the whole of the
reign of King Charles the First, and his two sons who succeeded
him.

Sir George Esmond married rather beneath the rank that
a person of his name and honour might aspire to, the daughter
of Thos. Topham, of the city of London, alderman and goldsmith, who, taking the parliamentary side in the troubles then
commencing, disappointed Sir George of the property which
he expected at the demise of his father-in-law, who devised his
money to his second daughter, Barbara, a spinster.

Sir George Esmond, on his part, was conspicuous for his
attachment and loyalty to the royal cause and person, and the
King being at Oxford in 1642, Sir George, with the consent
of his father, then very aged and infirm, and residing at his
house of Castlewood, melted the whole of the family plate for
his Majesty's service.

For this, and other sacrifices and merits, his Majesty, by
patent under the Privy Seal, dated Oxford, Jan., 1643, was

pleased to advance Sir Francis Esmond to the dignity of
Viscount Castlewood, of Shandon, in Ireland: and the Viscount's
estate being much impoverished by loans to the King, which in
those troublesome times his Majesty could not repay, a grant
of land in the plantations of Virginia was given to the Lord
Viscount; part of which land is in possession of descendants of
his family to the present day.

The first Viscount Castlewood died full of years, and within
a few months after he had been advanced to his honours. He
was succeeded by his eldest son, the before-named George; and
left issue besides, Thomas, a colonel in the King's army, that
afterwards joined the Usurper's Government; and Francis, in
holy orders, who was slain whilst defending the House of Castlewood against the Parliament, anno 1647.

George Lord Castlewood (the second Viscount) of King
Charles the First's time, had no male issue save his one son
Eustace Esmond, who was killed, with half of the Castlewood
men beside him, at Worcester fight. The lands about Castlewood
were sold and apportioned to the Commonwealth men; Castlewood being concerned in almost all of the plots against the
Protector, after the death of the King, and up to King Charles
the Second's restoration. My lord followed that King's Court
about in its exile, having ruined himself in its service. He had
but one daughter, who was of no great comfort to her father;
for misfortune had not taught those exiles sobriety of life; and
it is said that the Duke of York and his brother the King both
quarrelled about Isabel Esmond. She was maid of honour to
the Queen Henrietta Maria; she early joined the Roman
Church; her father, a weak man, following her not long after at
Breda.[5]

On the death of Eustace Esmond at Worcester, Thomas
Esmond, nephew to my Lord Castlewood, and then a stripling,
became heir to the title. His father had taken the Parliament side
in the quarrels, and so had been estranged from the chief of his
house; and my Lord Castlewood was at first so much enraged
to think that his title (albeit little more than an empty one now)
should pass to a rascally Roundhead, that he would have
married again, and indeed proposed to do so to a vintner's

daughter at Bruges, to whom his lordship owed a score for lodging when the King was there, but for fear of the laughter of the Court, and the anger of his daughter, of whom he stood in awe; for she was in temper as imperious and violent as my lord, who was much enfeebled by wounds and drinking, was weak.

Lord Castlewood would have had a match between his daughter Isabel and her cousin, the son of that Francis Esmond who was killed at Castlewood siege. And the lady, it was said, took a fancy to the young man, who was her junior by several years (which circumstance she did not consider to be a fault in him); but having paid his court, and being admitted to the intimacy of the house, he suddenly flung up his suit, when it seemed to be pretty prosperous, without giving a pretext for his behaviour. His friends rallied him at what they laughingly chose to call his infidelity. Jack Churchill,[6] Frank Esmond's lieutenant in the Royal regiment of foot guards, getting the company which Esmond vacated, when he left the Court and went to Tangier in a rage at discovering that his promotion depended on the complaisance of his elderly affianced bride. He and Churchill, who had been *condiscipuli* at St Paul's School, had words about this matter; and Frank Esmond said to him with an oath, 'Jack, your sister may be so-and-so, but by Jove my wife shan't!' and swords were drawn, and blood drawn too, until friends separated them on this quarrel. Few men were so jealous about the point of honour in those days; and gentlemen of good birth and lineage thought a royal blot was an ornament to their family coat. Frank Esmond retired in the sulks, first to Tangier, whence he returned after two years' service, settling on a small property he had of his mother, near to Winchester, and became a country gentleman, and kept a pack of beagles, and never came to Court again in King Charles's time. But his uncle Castlewood was never reconciled to him; nor, for some time afterwards, his cousin whom he had refused.

By places, pensions, bounties from France, and gifts from the King, whilst his daughter was in favour, Lord Castlewood, who had spent in the Royal service his youth and fortune, did not retrieve the latter quite, and never cared to visit Castlewood, or repair it, since the death of his son, but managed to keep a good house, and figure at Court, and to save a considerable sum of ready money.

And now, his heir and nephew, Thomas Esmond, began to bid for his uncle's favour. Thomas had served with the Emperor, and with the Dutch, when King Charles was compelled to lend troops to the States, and against them, when his Majesty made an alliance with the French King. In these campaigns Thomas Esmond was more remarked for duelling, brawling, vice, and play, than for any conspicuous gallantry in the field, and came back to England, like many another English gentleman who has travelled, with a character by no means improved by his foreign experience. He had dissipated his small paternal inheritance of a younger brother's portion, and, as truth must be told, was no better than a hanger-on of ordinaries, and a brawler about Alsatia and the Friars,[7] when he bethought him of a means of mending his fortune.

His cousin was now of more than middle age, and had nobody's word but her own for the beauty which she said she once possessed. She was lean, and yellow, and long in the tooth; all the red and white in all the toy-shops[8] in London could not make a beauty of her – Mr Killigrew called her the Sybil,[9] the death's-head put up at the King's feast as a *memento mori*, &c. – in fine, a woman who might be easy of conquest, but whom only a very bold man would think of conquering. This bold man was Thomas Esmond. He had a fancy to my Lord Castle-wood's savings, the amount of which rumour had very much exaggerated. Madame Isabel was said to have Royal jewels of great value; whereas poor Tom Esmond's last coat but one was in pawn.

My lord had at this time a fine house in Lincoln's-Inn-Fields, nigh to the Duke's Theatre and the Portugal ambassador's chapel. Tom Esmond, who had frequented the one as long as he had money to spend among the actresses, now came to the church as assiduously. He looked so lean and shabby, that he passed without difficulty for a repentant sinner; and so, becoming converted, you may be sure took his uncle's priest for a director.

This charitable father reconciled him with the old lord his uncle, who a short time before would not speak to him, as Tom passed under my lord's coach window, his lordship going in state to his place at Court, while his nephew slunk by with his battered hat and feather, and the point of his rapier sticking out of the scabbard – to his twopenny ordinary[10] in Bell Yard.

Thomas Esmond, after this reconciliation with his uncle, very soon began to grow sleek, and to show signs of the benefits of good living and clean linen. He fasted rigorously twice a week to be sure; but he made amends on the other days: and, to show how great his appetite was, Mr Wycherley said, he ended by swallowing that fly-blown rank old morsel his cousin. There were endless jokes and lampoons about this marriage at Court: but Tom rode thither in his uncle's coach now, called him father, and having won could afford to laugh. This marriage took place very shortly before King Charles died: whom the Viscount of Castlewood speedily followed.

The issue of this marriage was one son, whom the parents watched with an intense eagerness and care; but who, in spite of nurses and physicians, had only a brief existence. His tainted blood did not run very long in his poor feeble little body. Symptoms of evil broke out early on him; and, part from flattery, part superstition, nothing would satisfy my lord and lady, especially the latter, but having the poor little cripple touched by his Majesty[11] at his church. They were ready to cry out miracle at first (the doctors and quacksalvers being constantly in attendance on the child, and experimenting on his poor little body with every conceivable nostrum) – but though there seemed from some reason a notable amelioration in the infant's health after his Majesty touched him, in a few weeks afterward the poor thing died – causing the lampooners of the Court to say, that the King in expelling evil out of the infant of Tom Esmond and Isabella his wife, expelled the life out of it, which was nothing but corruption.

The mother's natural pang at losing this poor little child must have been increased when she thought of her rival Frank Esmond's wife, who was a favourite of the whole Court, where my poor Lady Castlewood was neglected, and who had one child, a daughter, flourishing and beautiful, and was about to become a mother once more.

The Court, as I have heard, only laughed the more because the poor lady, who had pretty well passed the age when ladies are accustomed to have children, nevertheless determined not to give hope up, and even when she came to live at Castlewood, was constantly sending over to Hexton for the doctor, and announcing to her friends the arrival of an heir. This absurdity of hers was one amongst many others which the wags used to play upon. Indeed, to the last days of her life, my Lady Viscountess had the comfort of fancying herself beautiful, and persisted in blooming up to the very midst of winter, painting roses on her cheeks long after their natural season, and attiring herself like summer though her head was covered with snow.

Gentlemen who were about the Court of King Charles and King James, have told the present writer a number of stories about this queer old lady, with which it's not necessary that posterity should be entertained. She is said to have had great powers of invective; and, if she fought with all her rivals in King James's favour, 'tis certain she must have had a vast number of quarrels on her hands. She was a woman of an intrepid spirit, and it appears pursued and rather fatigued his Majesty with her rights and her wrongs. Some say that the cause of her leaving Court was jealousy of Frank Esmond's wife: others, that she was forced to retreat after a great battle which took place at Whitehall, between her ladyship and Lady Dorchester, Tom Killigrew's daughter, whom the King delighted to honour, and in which that ill-favoured Esther got the better of our elderly Vashti.[12] But her ladyship for her part always averred that it was her husband's quarrel, and not her own, which occasioned the banishment of the two into the country; and the cruel ingratitude of the Sovereign in giving away, out of the family, that place of Warden of the Butteries, and Groom of the King's Posset, which the two last Lords Castlewood had held so honourably, and which was now conferred upon a fellow of yesterday, and a hanger-on of that odious Dorchester creature, my Lord Bergamot;* 'I never,' said my lady, 'could have come to see his Majesty's posset carried by any other hand than an Esmond. I should have dashed the salver out of Lord Bergamot's hand, had I met him.' And those who knew her ladyship are aware that she was a person quite capable of performing this feat, had she not wisely kept out of the way.

Holding the purse-strings in her own control, to which, indeed, she liked to bring most persons who came near her, Lady Castlewood could command her husband's obedience, and so broke up her establishment at London; she had removed from Lincoln's-Inn-Fields to Chelsey, to a pretty new house she bought there; and brought her establishment, her maids, lap-dogs, and gentlewomen, her priest, and his lordship, her husband, to Castlewood Hall, that she had never seen since she quitted it as a child with her father during the troubles of King Charles the First's reign. The walls were still open in the old house as they had been left by the shot of the Commonwealthmen. A part of the mansion was restored and furnished up with the plate, hangings, and furniture, brought from the house in London. My lady meant to have a triumphal entry into Castlewood village, and expected the people to cheer as she drove over the Green in her great coach, my lord beside her, her gentlewomen, lap-dogs, and cockatoos on the opposite seat, six horses to her carriage, and servants armed and mounted, following it and preceding it. But 'twas in the height of the No-Popery cry; the folks in the village and the neighbouring town were scared by the sight of her ladyship's painted face and eyelids, as she bobbed her head out of the coach window, meaning no doubt to be very gracious; and one old woman said, 'Lady Isabel! lord-a-mercy, it's Lady Jezebel!' a name by which the enemies of the right honourable Viscountess were afterwards in

---

*Lionel Tipton, created Baron Bergamot, ann. 1686, Gentleman Usher of the Back Stairs, and afterwards appointed Warden of the Butteries and Groom of the King's Posset (on the decease of George, second Viscount Castlewood), accompanied his Majesty to St Germain's where he died without issue. No Groom of the Posset was appointed by the Prince of Orange, nor hath there been such an officer in any succeeding reign.

the habit of designating her. The country was then in a great No-Popery fervour; her ladyship's known conversion, and her husband's, the priest in her train, and the service performed at the chapel of Castlewood, (though the chapel had been built for that worship before any other was heard of in the country, and though the service was performed in the most quiet manner), got her no favour at first in the county or village. By far the greater part of the estate of Castlewood had been confiscated, and been parcelled out to Commonwealthmen. One or two of these old Cromwellian soldiers were still alive in the village, and looked grimly at first upon my Lady Viscountess, when she came to dwell there.

She appeared at the Hexton Assembly, bringing her lord after her, scaring the country folks with the splendour of her diamonds, which she always wore in public. They said she wore them in private, too, and slept with them round her neck; though the writer can pledge his word that this was a calumny. 'If she were to take them off,' my Lady Sark said, 'Tom Esmond, her husband, would run away with them and pawn them.' 'Twas another calumny. My Lady Sark was also an exile from Court, and there had been war between the two ladies before.

The village people began to be reconciled presently to their lady, who was generous and kind, though fantastic[13] and haughty, in her ways; and whose praises Doctor Tusher, the Vicar, sounded loudly amongst his flock. As for my lord, he gave no great trouble, being considered scarce more than an appendage to my lady, who as daughter of the old lords of Castlewood, and possessor of vast wealth, as the country folks said (though indeed nine-tenths of it existed but in rumour), was looked upon as the real queen of the Castle and mistress of all it contained.

## Chapter 3

## WHITHER IN THE TIME OF THOMAS, THIRD
## VISCOUNT, I HAD PRECEDED HIM AS
## PAGE TO ISABELLA

COMING up to London again some short time after this retreat, the Lord Castlewood despatched a retainer of his to a little cottage in the village of Ealing, near to London, where for some time had dwelt an old French refugee, by name Mr Pastoureau, one of those whom the persecution of the Huguenots by the French king had brought over to this country. With this old man lived a little lad, who went by the name of Henry Thomas. He remembered to have lived in another place a short time before, near to London, too, amongst looms and spinning-wheels, and a great deal of psalm-singing and church-going, and a whole colony of Frenchmen.[1]

There he had a dear, dear friend, who died and whom he called Aunt. She used to visit him in his dreams sometimes; and her face, though it was homely, was a thousand times dearer to him than that of Mrs Pastoureau, Bon Papa Pastoureau's new wife, who came to live with him after aunt went away. And there, at Spittlefields, as it used to be called, lived Uncle George, who was a weaver too, but used to tell Harry that he was a little gentleman, and that his father was a captain, and his mother an angel.

When he said so, Bon Papa used to look up from the loom, where he was embroidering beautiful silk flowers, and say, 'Angel! she belongs to the Babylonish scarlet woman.' Bon Papa was always talking of the scarlet woman. He had a little room where he always used to preach and sing hymns out of his great old nose. Little Harry did not like the preaching; he liked better the fine stories which aunt used to tell him. Bon Papa's wife never told him pretty stories; she quarrelled with Uncle George, and he went away.

After this Harry's Bon Papa, and his wife and two children of her own that she brought with her, came to live at Ealing.

The new wife gave her children the best of everything, and Harry many a whipping, he knew not why. Besides blows, he got ill names from her, which need not be set down here, for the sake of old Mr Pastoureau, who was still kind sometimes. The unhappiness of those days is long forgiven, though they cast a shade of melancholy over the child's youth, which will accompany him, no doubt, to the end of his days: as those tender twigs are bent the trees grow afterward; and he, at least, who has suffered as a child, and is not quite perverted in that early school of unhappiness, learns to be gentle and long-suffering with little children.

Harry was very glad when a gentleman dressed in black, on horseback, with a mounted servant behind him, came to fetch him away from Ealing. The noverca, or unjust stepmother, who had neglected him for her own two children, gave him supper enough the night before he went away, and plenty in the morning. She did not beat him once, and told the children to keep their hands off him. One was a girl, and Harry never could bear to strike a girl; and the other was a boy, whom he could easily have beat, but he always cried out, when Mrs Pastoureau came sailing to the rescue with arms like a flail. She only washed Harry's face the day he went away; nor ever so much as once boxed his ears. She whimpered rather when the gentleman in black came for the boy; and old Mr Pastoureau, as he gave the child his blessing, scowled over his shoulder at the strange gentleman, and grumbled out something about Babylon and the scarlet lady. He was grown quite old, like a child almost. Mrs Pastoureau used to wipe his nose as she did to the children. She was a great, big, handsome young woman; but, though she pretended to cry, Harry thought 'twas only a sham, and sprung quite delighted upon the horse upon which the lacquey helped him.

He was a Frenchman; his name was Blaise. The child could talk to him in his own language perfectly well: he knew it better than English indeed: having lived hitherto chiefly among French people: and being called the little Frenchman by other boys on Ealing Green. He soon learnt to speak English perfectly, and to forget some of his French: children forget easily. Some earlier and fainter recollections the child had, of a different country; and a town with tall white houses; and a ship. But these were quite indistinct in the boy's mind, as indeed the memory of Ealing soon became, at least of much that he suffered there.

The lacquey before whom he rode was very lively and voluble, and informed the boy that the gentleman riding before him was my lord's Chaplain, Father Holt – that he was now to be called Master Harry Esmond – that my Lord Viscount Castlewood was his *parrain* – that he was to live at the great house of Castlewood, in the province of ——shire, where he would see Madame the Viscountess, who was a grand lady. And so, seated on a cloth before Blaise's saddle, Harry Esmond was brought to London, and to a fine square called Covent Garden, near to which his patron lodged.

Mr Holt the priest took the child by the hand, and brought him to this nobleman, a grand languid nobleman in a great cap and flowered morning-gown, sucking oranges. He patted Harry on the head and gave him an orange.

'*C'est bien ça,*' he said to the priest after eyeing the child, and the gentleman in black shrugged his shoulders. 'Let Blaise take him out for a holiday,' and out for a holiday the boy and the valet went. Harry went jumping along; he was glad enough to go.

He will remember to his life's end the delights of those days. He was taken to see a play by Monsieur Blaise, in a house a thousand times greater and finer than the booth at Ealing Fair – and on the next happy day they took water on the river, and Harry saw London Bridge, with the houses and booksellers' shops thereon, looking like a street, and the Tower of London, with the armour, and the great lions and bears in the moats[2] – all under company of Monsieur Blaise.

Presently, of an early morning, all the party set forth for the country, namely, my Lord Viscount and the other gentleman; Monsieur Blaise, and Harry on a pillion behind them, and two or three men with pistols leading the baggage-horses. And all along the road the Frenchman told little Harry stories of brigands, which made the child's hair stand on end, and terrified him; so that at the great gloomy inn on the road where they lay, he besought to be allowed to sleep in a room with one of the servants, and was compassionated by Mr Holt, the gentleman who travelled with my lord, and who gave the child a little bed in his chamber.

His artless talk and answers very likely inclined this gentleman in the boy's favour, for next day Mr Holt said Harry should ride behind him, and not with the French lacquey; and all along the journey put a thousand questions to the child – as to his foster-brother and relations at Ealing; what his old grandfather had taught him; what languages he knew; whether he could read and write, and sing, and so forth. And Mr Holt found that Harry could read and write, and possessed the two languages of French and English very well; and when he asked Harry about singing, the lad broke out with a hymn to the tune of Doctor Martin Luther, which set Mr Holt a-laughing; and even caused his *grand parrain* in the laced hat and periwig to laugh too when Holt told him what the child was singing. For it appeared that Dr Martin Luther's hymns were not sung in the churches Mr Holt preached at.

'You must never sing that song any more, do you hear, little mannikin?' says my Lord Viscount, holding up a finger.

'But we will try and teach you a better, Harry,' Mr Holt said; and the child answered, for he was a docile child, and of an affectionate nature, 'That he loved pretty songs, and would try and learn anything the gentleman would tell him.' That day he so pleased the gentlemen by his talk, that they had him to dine with them at the inn, and encouraged him in his prattle; and Monsieur Blaise, with whom he rode and dined the day before, waited upon him now.

' 'Tis well, 'tis well!' said Blaise, that night (in his own language) when they lay again at an inn. 'We are a little lord here; we are a little lord now: we shall see what we are when we come to Castlewood where my lady is.'

'When shall we come to Castlewood, Monsieur Blaise?' says Harry.

'*Parbleu!* my lord does not press himself,' Blaise says, with a grin; and, indeed, it seemed as if his lordship was not in a great hurry, for he spent three days on that journey, which Harry Esmond hath often since ridden in a dozen hours. For the last two of the days, Harry rode with the priest, who was so kind to him, that the child had grown to be quite fond and familiar with him by the journey's end, and had scarce a thought in his little heart which by that time he had not confided to his new friend.

At length on the third day, at evening, they came to a village standing on a green with elms round it, very pretty to look at; and the people there all took off their hats, and made curtsies to my Lord Viscount, who bowed to them all languidly; and there was one portly person that wore a cassock and a broad-leafed hat, who bowed lower than anyone – and with this one both my lord and Mr Holt had a few words. 'This, Harry, is Castlewood church,' says Mr Holt, 'and this is the pillar thereof, learned Doctor Tusher. Take off your hat, sirrah, and salute Doctor Tusher!'

'Come up to supper, Doctor,' says my lord; at which the Doctor made another low bow, and the party moved on towards a grand house that was before them, with many grey towers and vanes on them, and windows flaming in the sunshine; and a great army of rooks, wheeling over their heads, made for the woods behind the house, as Harry saw; and Mr Holt told him that they lived at Castlewood too.

They came to the house, and passed under an arch into a court-yard, with a fountain in the centre, where many men came and held my lord's stirrup as he descended, and paid great respect to Mr Holt likewise. And the child thought that the servants looked at him curiously, and smiled to one another – and he recalled what Blaise had said to him when they were in London, and Harry had spoken about his god-papa, when the Frenchman said, '*Parbleu*, one sees well that my lord is your godfather;' words whereof the poor lad did not know the meaning then, though he apprehended the truth in a very short time afterwards, and learned it and thought of it with no small feeling of shame.

Taking Harry by the hand as soon as they were both descended from their horses, Mr Holt led him across the court, and under

a low door to rooms on a level with the ground; one of which
Father Holt said was to be the boy's chamber, the other on the
other side of the passage being the Father's own; and as soon
as the little man's face was washed, and the Father's own dress
arranged, Harry's guide took him once more to the door by
which my lord had entered the hall, and up a stair, and through
an ante-room to my lady's drawing-room – an apartment than
which Harry thought he had never seen anything more grand –
no, not in the Tower of London which he had just visited.
Indeed the chamber was richly ornamented in the manner of
Queen Elizabeth's time, with great stained windows at either
end, and hangings of tapestry, which the sun shining through
the coloured glass painted of a thousand hues; and here in state,
by the fire, sate a lady to whom the priest took up Harry, who
was indeed amazed by her appearance.

My Lady Viscountess's face was daubed with white and red
up to the eyes, to which the paint gave an unearthly glare: she
had a tower of lace[3] on her head, under which was a bush of
black curls – borrowed curls – so that no wonder little Harry
Esmond was scared when he was first presented to her – the
kind priest acting as master of the ceremonies at that solemn
introduction – and he stared at her with eyes almost as great as
her own, as he had stared at the player-woman who acted the
wicked tragedy-queen, when the players came down to Ealing
Fair. She sate in a great chair by the fire-corner; in her lap was
a spaniel-dog that barked furiously; on a little table by her was
her ladyship's snuff-box and her sugar-plum box. She wore a
dress of black velvet, and a petticoat of flame-coloured brocade.
She had as many rings on her fingers as the old woman of
Banbury Cross; and pretty small feet which she was fond of
showing with great gold clocks[4] to her stockings, and white
pantofles[5] with red heels; and an odour of musk was shook out
of her garments whenever she moved or quitted the room,
leaning on her tortoiseshell stick, little Fury barking at her heels.

Mrs Tusher, the parson's wife, was with my lady. She had
been waiting-woman to her ladyship in the late lord's time, and,
having her soul in that business, took naturally to it when the
Viscountess of Castlewood returned to inhabit her father's house.

'I present to your ladyship your kinsman and little page of honour, Master Henry Esmond,' Mr Holt said, bowing lowly, with a sort of comical humility. 'Make a pretty bow to my lady, Monsieur; and then another little bow, not so low, to Madame Tusher – the fair priestess of Castlewood.'

'Where I have lived and hope to die, sir,' says Madame Tusher, giving a hard glance at the brat, and then at my lady.

Upon her the boy's whole attention was for a time directed. He could not keep his great eyes off from her. Since the Empress of Ealing he had seen nothing so awful.

'Does my appearance please you, little page?' asked the lady.

'He would be very hard to please if it didn't,' cried Madame Tusher.

'Have done, you silly Maria,' said Lady Castlewood.

'Where I'm attached, I'm attached, Madame – and I'd die rather than not say so.'

'*Je meurs où je m'attache*,' Mr Holt said with a polite grin. 'The ivy says so in the picture, and clings to the oak like a fond parasite as it is.'

'Parricide, sir!' cries Mrs Tusher.

'Hush, Tusher – you are always bickering with Father Holt,' cried my lady. 'Come and kiss my hand, child,' and the oak held out a *branch* to little Harry Esmond, who took and dutifully kissed the lean old hand, upon the gnarled knuckles of which there glittered a hundred rings.

'To kiss that hand would make many a pretty fellow happy!' cried Mrs Tusher: on which my lady crying out, 'Go, you foolish Tusher,' and tapping her with her great fan, Tusher ran forward to seize her hand and kiss it. Fury arose and barked furiously at Tusher; and Father Holt looked on at this queer scene, with arch grave glances.

The awe exhibited by the little boy perhaps pleased the lady to whom this artless flattery was bestowed; for having gone down on his knee (as Father Holt had directed him, and the mode then was) and performed his obeisance, she said, 'Page Esmond, my groom of the chamber will inform you what your duties are, when you wait upon my lord and me; and good Father Holt will instruct you as becomes a gentleman of our name. You will pay him obedience in everything, and I pray you may grow to be as learned and as good as your tutor.'

The lady seemed to have the greatest reverence for Mr Holt, and to be more afraid of him than of anything else in the world. If she was ever so angry, a word or look from Father Holt made her calm: indeed he had a vast power of subjecting those who came near him; and, among the rest, his new pupil gave himself up with an entire confidence and attachment to the good Father, and became his willing slave almost from the first moment he saw him.

He put his small hand into the Father's as he walked away from his first presentation to his mistress, and asked many questions in his artless childish way. 'Who is that other woman?' he asked. 'She is fat and round; she is more pretty than my Lady Castlewood.'

'She is Madam Tusher, the parson's wife of Castlewood. She has a son of your age, but bigger than you.'

'Why does she like so to kiss my lady's hand? It is not good to kiss.'

'Tastes are different, little man. Madam Tusher is attached to my lady, having been her waiting-woman, before she was married, in the old lord's time. She married Doctor Tusher the Chaplain. The English household divines often marry the waiting-women.'[6]

'You will not marry the Frenchwoman, will you? I saw her laughing with Blaise in the buttery.'

'I belong to a church that is older and better than the English church,' Mr Holt said (making a sign whereof Esmond did not then understand the meaning, across his breast and forehead); 'in our church the clergy do not marry. You will understand these things better soon.'

'Was not Saint Peter the head of your church? – Doctor Rabbits of Ealing told us so.'

The Father said, 'Yes he was.'

'But Saint Peter was married, for we heard only last Sunday that his wife's mother lay sick of a fever.' On which the Father again laughed, and said he would understand this too better soon, and talked of other things, and took away Harry Esmond, and showed him the great old house which he had come to inhabit.

It stood on a rising green hill, with woods behind it, in which were rooks' nests, where the birds at morning and returning home at evening made a great cawing. At the foot of the hill was a river with a steep ancient bridge crossing it; and beyond that a large pleasant green flat, where the village of Castlewood stood and stands, with the church in the midst, the parsonage hard by it, the inn with the blacksmith's forge beside it, and the sign of the Three Castles on the elm. The London road stretched away towards the rising sun, and to the west were swelling hills and peaks, behind which many a time Harry Esmond saw the same sun setting, that he now looks on thousands of miles away across the great ocean—in a new Castlewood[7] by another stream, that bears, like the new country of wandering Æneas, the fond names of the land of his youth.

The Hall of Castlewood was built with two courts, whereof one only, the fountain court, was now inhabited, the other having been battered down in the Cromwellian wars. In the fountain court, still in good repair, was the great hall, near to the kitchen and butteries. A dozen of living-rooms looking to the north, and communicating with the little chapel that faced eastwards and the buildings stretching from that to the main gate, and with the hall (which looked to the west) into the court now dismantled. This court had been the most magnificent of the two, until the Protector's cannon tore down one side of it before the place was taken and stormed. The besiegers entered at the terrace under the clock-tower, slaying every man of the garrison, and at their head my lord's brother, Francis Esmond.

The Restoration did not bring enough money to the Lord Castlewood to restore this ruined part of his house; where were the morning parlours, above them the long music-gallery, and before which stretched the garden-terrace, where however, the flowers grew again, which the boots of the Roundheads had trodden in their assault, and which was restored without much cost, and only a little care, by both ladies who succeeded the second viscount in the government of this mansion. Round the terrace-garden was a low wall with a wicket leading to the wooded height beyond, that is called Cromwell's battery to this day.

Young Harry Esmond learned the domestic part of his duty, which was easy enough, from the groom of her ladyship's chamber: serving the Countess, as the custom commonly was in his boyhood, as page, waiting at her chair, bringing her scented water and the silver basin after dinner – sitting on her carriage step on state occasions, or on public days introducing her company to her. This was chiefly of the Catholic gentry, of whom there were a pretty many in the country and neighbouring city; and who rode not seldom to Castlewood to partake of the hospitalities there. In the second year of their residence the company seemed especially to increase. My lord and my lady were seldom without visitors, in whose society it was curious to contrast the difference of behaviour between Father Holt, the director of the family, and Doctor Tusher, the rector of the parish – Mr Holt moving amongst the very highest as quite their equal, and as commanding them all; while poor Doctor Tusher, whose position was indeed a difficult one, having been chaplain once to the Hall, and still to the Protestant servants there, seemed more like an usher than an equal, and always rose to go away after the first course.

Also there came in these times to Father Holt many private visitors,[8] whom after a little, Henry Esmond had little difficulty in recognizing as ecclesiastics of the Father's persuasion; whatever their dresses (and they adopted all) might be. These were closeted with the Father constantly, and often came and rode away without paying their devoirs to my lord and lady – to the lady and lord rather – his lordship being little more than a cypher in the house, and entirely under his domineering partner. A little fowling, a little hunting, a great deal of sleep, and a long time at cards and table, carried through one day after another with his lordship. When meetings took place in this second year, which often would happen with closed doors, the page found my lord's sheet of paper scribbled over with dogs and horses, and 'twas said he had much ado to keep himself awake at these councils: the Countess ruling over them, and he acting as little more than her secretary.

Father Holt began speedily to be so much occupied with these meetings as rather to neglect the education of the little lad who so gladly put himself under the kind priest's orders. At first they read much and regularly, both in Latin and French; the Father not neglecting in anything to impress his faith upon his pupil, but not forcing him violently, and treating him with a delicacy and kindness which surprised and attached the child, always more easily won by these methods than by any severe exercise of authority. And his delight in our walks was to tell Harry of the glories of his order, of its martyrs and heroes, of its brethren converting the heathen by myriads, traversing the desert, facing the stake, ruling the courts and councils, or braving the tortures of kings; so that Harry Esmond thought that to belong to the Jesuits was the greatest prize of life and bravest end of ambition; the greatest career here, and in heaven the surest reward; and began to long for the day, not only when he should enter into the one church and receive his first communion, but when he might join that wonderful brotherhood, which was present throughout all the world, and which numbered the wisest, the bravest, the highest born, the most eloquent of men among its members. Father Holt bade him keep his views secret, and to hide them as a great treasure which would escape him if it was revealed; and proud of this confidence and secret vested in him, the lad became fondly attached to the master who initiated him into a mystery so wonderful and awful. And when little Tom Tusher, his neighbour, came from school for his holiday, and said how he, too, was to be bred up for an English priest, and would get what he called an exhibition from his school, and then a college scholarship and fellowship, and then a good living – it tasked young Harry Esmond's powers of reticence not to say to his young companion, 'Church! priesthood! fat living! My dear Tommy, do you call yours a church and a priesthood? What is a fat living compared to converting a hundred thousand heathens by a single sermon? What is a scholarship at Trinity by the side of a crown of martyrdom, with angels awaiting you as your head is taken off? Could your master at school sail over the Thames on his gown? Have you statues in your church that can bleed, speak, walk, and cry? My good Tommy, in dear Father Holt's church these things take place every day. You know Saint Philip of the Willows appeared to Lord Castlewood and caused him to turn to the one true church. No saints ever come to you.' And Harry Esmond, because of his promise to Father Holt, hiding away these treasures of faith from T. Tusher, delivered himself of them nevertheless simply to Father Holt, who stroked his head, smiled at him with his inscrutable look, and told him that he did well to meditate on these great things, and not to talk of them except under direction.

## Chapter 4

### I AM PLACED UNDER A POPISH PRIEST AND BRED TO THAT RELIGION – VISCOUNTESS CASTLEWOOD

HAD time enough been given, and his childish inclinations been properly nurtured, Harry Esmond had been a Jesuit priest ere he was a dozen years older, and might have finished his days a martyr in China or a victim on Tower Hill: for, in the few months they spent together at Castlewood, Mr Holt obtained an entire mastery over the boy's intellect and affections; and had brought him to think, as indeed Father Holt thought with all his heart too, that no life was so noble, no death so desirable, as that which many brethren of his famous order were ready to undergo. By love, by a brightness of wit and good-humour that charmed all, by an authority which he knew how to assume, by a mystery and silence about him which increased the child's reverence for him, he won Harry's absolute fealty, and would have kept it, doubtless, if schemes greater and more important than a poor little boy's admission into orders had not called him away.

After being at home for a few months in tranquillity (if theirs might be called tranquillity, which was, in truth, a constant bickering), my lord and lady left the country for London, taking their director with them: and his little pupil scarce ever shed more bitter tears in his life than he did for nights after the first parting with his dear friend, as he lay in the lonely chamber next to that which the Father used to occupy. He and a few domestics were left as the only tenants of the great house: and, though Harry sedulously did all the tasks which the Father set him, he had many hours unoccupied, and read in the library, and bewildered his little brains with the great books he found there.

After a while the little lad grew accustomed to the loneliness of the place; and in after days remembered this part of his life as a period not unhappy. When the family was at London the whole of the establishment travelled thither with the exception of the porter, who was, moreover, brewer, gardener, and woodman, and his wife and children. These had their lodging in the gate-house hard by, with a door into the court; and a window looking out on the green was the Chaplain's room; and next to this a small chamber where Father Holt had his books, and Harry Esmond his sleeping closet. The side of the house facing the east had escaped the guns of the Cromwellians, whose battery was on the height facing the western court; so that this eastern end bore few marks of demolition, save in the chapel, where the painted windows surviving Edward the Sixth had been broke by the Commonwealthmen. In Father Holt's time little Harry Esmond acted as his familiar, and faithful little servitor; beating his clothes, folding his vestments, fetching his water from the well long before daylight, ready to run anywhere for the service of his beloved priest. When the Father was away he locked his private chamber; but the room where the books were was left to little Harry, who, but for the society of this gentleman, was little less solitary when Lord Castlewood was at home.

The French wit[1] saith that a hero is none to his *valet-de-chambre*, and it required less quick eyes than my lady's little page was naturally endowed with, to see that she had many qualities by no means heroic, however much Mrs Tusher might flatter and coax her. When Father Holt was not by, who exercised an entire authority over the pair, my lord and my lady quarrelled and abused each other so as to make the servants laugh, and to frighten the little page on duty. The poor boy trembled before his mistress, who called him by a hundred ugly names, who made nothing of boxing his ears – and tilting the silver basin in his face which it was his business to present to her after dinner. She hath repaired, by subsequent kindness to him, these severities, which it must be owned made his childhood very unhappy. She was but unhappy herself at this time, poor soul, and I suppose made her dependants lead her own sad life. I think my lord was as much afraid of her as her page was, and the only person of the household who mastered her was Mr Holt. Harry was only too glad when the Father dined at table, and to slink away and prattle with him afterwards, or read with him, or walk with him. Luckily my Lady Viscountess did not rise till nooon. Heaven help the poor waiting-woman who had charge of her toilet! I have often seen the poor wretch come out with red eyes from the closet, where those long and mysterious rites of her ladyship's dress were performed, and the backgammon-box locked up with a rap on Mrs Tusher's fingers when she played ill or the game was going the wrong way.

Blessed be the king who introduced cards, and the kind inventors of piquet and cribbage, for they employed six hours at least of her ladyship's day, during which her family was pretty easy. Without this occupation my lady frequently declared she should die. Her dependants one after another relieved guard – 'twas rather a dangerous post to play with her ladyship – and took the cards turn about. Mr Holt would sit with her at piquet during hours together, at which time she behaved herself properly; and, as for Doctor Tusher, I believe he would have left a parishioner's dying bed, if summoned to play a rubber with his patroness at Castlewood. Sometimes, when they were pretty comfortable together, my lord took a hand. Besides these my lady had her faithful poor Tusher, and one, two, three gentlewomen whom Harry Esmond could recollect in his time. They could not bear that genteel service very long; one after another tried and failed at it. These and the housekeeper, and little Harry Esmond, had a table of their

own. Poor ladies! their life was far harder than the page's. He
was sound asleep tucked up in his little bed, whilst they were
sitting by her ladyship reading her to sleep, with the News
Letter² or the Grand Cyrus.³ My lady used to have boxes of
new plays from London, and Harry was forbidden, under the
pain of a whipping, to look into them. I am afraid he deserved
the penalty pretty often, and got it sometimes. Father Holt
applied it twice or thrice, when he caught the young scapegrace
with a delightful wicked comedy of Mr Shadwell's or Mr
Wycherley's under his pillow.

These, when he took any, were my lord's favourite reading.
But he was averse to much study, and, as his little page fancied,
to much occupation of any sort.

It always seemed to young Harry Esmond that my lord
treated him with more kindness when his lady was not present,
and Lord Castlewood would take the lad sometimes on his
little journeys a-hunting or a-birding; he loved to play at cards
and tric-trac⁴ with him, which games the boy learned to pleasure
his lord: and was growing to like him better daily, showing a
special pleasure if Father Holt gave a good report of him,
patting him on the head, and promising that he would provide
for the boy. However, in my lady's presence, my lord showed
no such marks of kindness, and affected to treat the lad roughly,
and rebuked him sharply for little faults – for which he in a
manner asked pardon of young Esmond when they were
private, saying if he did not speak roughly, she would, and his
tongue was not such a bad one as his lady's – a point whereof
the boy, young as he was, was very well assured.

Great public events were happening all this while, of which
the simple young page took little count. But one day, riding
into the neighbouring town on the step of my lady's coach, his
lordship and she and Father Holt being inside, a great mob of
people came hooting and jeering round the coach, bawling out
'The Bishops for ever!'⁵ 'Down with the Pope!' 'No Popery!
no Popery! Jezebel, Jezebel!' so that my lord began to laugh,
my lady's eyes to roll with anger, for she was as bold as a
lioness, and feared nobody; whilst Mr Holt, as Esmond saw
from his place on the step, sank back with rather an alarmed

face, crying out to her ladyship, 'For God's sake, madam, do not speak or look out of window, sit still.' But she did not obey this prudent injunction of the Father; she thrust her head out of the coach window, and screamed out to the coachman, 'Flog your way through them, the brutes, James, and use your whip!'

The mob answered with a roaring jeer of laughter, and fresh cries of 'Jezebel! Jezebel!' My lord only laughed the more: he was a languid gentleman: nothing seemed to excite him commonly, though I have seen him cheer and halloo the hounds very briskly, and his face (which was generally very yellow and calm) grow quite red and cheerful during a burst over the Downs after a hare, and laugh, and swear, and huzza at a cockfight, of which sport he was very fond. And now, when the mob began to hoot his lady, he laughed with something of a mischievous look, as though he expected sport, and thought that she and they were a match.

James the coachman was more afraid of his mistress than the mob, probably, for he whipped on his horses as he was bidden, and the post-boy that rode with the first pair (my lady always went with her coach and six), gave a cut of his thong over the shoulders of one fellow who put his hand out towards the leading horse's rein.

It was a market-day, and the country-people were all assembled with their baskets of poultry, eggs, and such things; the postilion had no sooner lashed the man who would have taken hold of his horse, but a great cabbage came whirling like a bombshell into the carriage, at which my lord laughed more, for it knocked my lady's fan out of her hand, and plumped into Father Holt's stomach. Then came a shower of carrots and potatoes.

'For Heaven's sake be still!' says Mr Holt; 'we are not ten paces from the Bell archway, where they can shut the gates on us, and keep out this canaille.'

The little page was outside the coach on the step, and a fellow in the crowd aimed a potato at him, and hit him in the eye, at which the poor little wretch set up a shout; the man laughed, a great big saddler's apprentice of the town. 'Ah! you d—— little yelling Popish bastard,' he said, and stooped to

pick up another; the crowd had gathered quite between the
horses and in the inn door by this time, and the coach was
brought to a dead stand-still. My lord jumped as briskly as a
boy out of the door on his side of the coach, squeezing little
Harry behind it; had hold of the potato-thrower's collar in an
instant, and the next moment the brute's heels were in the air,
and he fell on the stones with a thump.

'You hulking coward!' says he; 'you pack of screaming
blackguards! how dare you attack children, and insult women?
Fling another shot at that carriage, you sneaking pigskin cobbler,
and by the Lord I'll send my rapier through you!'

Some of the mob cried, 'Huzza, my lord!' for they knew
him, and the saddler's man was a known bruiser, near twice as
big as my Lord Viscount.

'Make way, there,' says he (he spoke in a high shrill voice,
but with a great air of authority). 'Make way, and let her
ladyship's carriage pass.' The men that were between the
coach and the gate of the Bell actually did make way, and the
horses went in, my lord walking after them with his hat on his
head.

As he was going in at the gate, through which the coach had
just rolled, another cry begins, of 'No Popery – no Papists!'
My lord turns round and faces them once more.

'God save the King!' says he at the highest pitch of his
voice. 'Who dares abuse the King's religion? You, you d——d
psalm-singing cobbler, as sure as I'm a magistrate of this
county I'll commit you!' The fellow shrunk back, and my lord
retreated with all the honours of the day. But when the little
flurry caused by the scene was over, and the flush passed off
his face, he relapsed into his usual languor, trifled with his little
dog, and yawned when my lady spoke to him.

This mob was one of many thousands that were going about
the country at that time, huzzaing for the acquittal of the seven
bishops who had been tried just then, and about whom little
Harry Esmond at that time knew scarce anything. It was
assizes at Hexton, and there was a great meeting of the gentry
at the Bell; and my lord's people had their new liveries on, and
Harry a little suit of blue and silver, which he wore upon

occasions of state; and the gentlefolks came round and talked to my lord: and a judge in a red gown, who seemed a very great personage, especially complimented him and my lady, who was mighty grand. Harry remembers her train borne up by her gentlewoman. There was an assembly and ball at the great room at the Bell, and other young gentlemen of the county families looked on as he did. One of them jeered him for his black eye, which was swelled by the potato, and another called him a bastard, on which he and Harry fell to fisticuffs. My lord's cousin, Colonel Esmond of Walcote, was there, and separated the two lads, a great tall gentleman with a handsome, good-natured face. The boy did not know how nearly in after life he should be allied to Colonel Esmond, and how much kindness he should have to owe him.

There was little love between the two families. My lady used not to spare Colonel Esmond in talking of him, for reasons which have been hinted already: but about which, at his tender age, Henry Esmond could be expected to know nothing.

Very soon afterwards my lord and lady went to London with Mr Holt, leaving, however, the page behind them. The little man had the great house of Castlewood to himself; or between him and the housekeeper, Mrs Worksop, an old lady who was a kinswoman of the family in some distant way, and a Protestant, but a stanch Tory and king's-man, as all the Esmonds were. He used to go to school to Doctor Tusher when he was at home, though the Doctor was much occupied too. There was a great stir and commotion everywhere, even in the little quiet village of Castlewood, whither a party of people came from the town, who would have broken Castlewood Chapel windows, but the village people turned out, and even old Sieveright, the republican blacksmith, along with them: for my lady, though she was a Papist, and had many odd ways, was kind to the tenantry, and there was always a plenty of beef, and blankets, and medicine for the poor at Castlewood Hall.

A kingdom was changing hands whilst my lord and lady were away. King James was flying, the Dutchmen were coming; awful stories about them and the Prince of Orange used old Mrs Worksop to tell to the idle little page.

He liked the solitude of the great house very well; he had all the play-books to read, and no Father Holt to whip him, and a hundred childish pursuits and pastimes, without doors and within, which made this time very pleasant.

## Chapter 5

### MY SUPERIORS ARE ENGAGED IN PLOTS
### FOR THE RESTORATION OF KING JAMES II

NOT having been able to sleep, for thinking of some lines for eels which he had placed the night before, the lad was lying in his little bed, waiting for the hour when the gate would be open, and he and his comrade, Job Lockwood, the porter's son,[1] might go to the pond and see what fortune had brought them. At daybreak Job was to awaken him, but his own eagerness for the sport had served as a reveillez long since – so long, that it seemed to him as if the day never would come.

It might have been four o'clock when he heard the door of the opposite chamber, the Chaplain's room, open, and the voice of a man coughing in the passage. Harry jumped up, thinking for certain it was a robber, or hoping perhaps for a ghost, and, flinging open his own door, saw before him the Chaplain's door open, and a light inside, and a figure standing in the doorway, in the midst of a great smoke which issued from the room.

'Who's there?' cried out the boy, who was of a good spirit.

'Silentium!' whispered the other; ' 'tis I, my boy!' and, holding his hand out, Harry had no difficulty in recognizing his master and friend, Father Holt. A curtain was over the window of the Chaplain's room that looked to the court, and Harry saw that the smoke came from a great flame of papers which were burning in a brazier when he entered the Chaplain's room. After giving a hasty greeting and blessing to the lad, who was charmed to see his tutor, the Father continued the burning of his papers, drawing them from a cupboard over the mantel-piece wall, which Harry had never seen before.

Father Holt laughed, seeing the lad's attention fixed at once on this hole. 'That is right, Harry,' he said; 'faithful little famuli[2] see all and say nothing. You are faithful, I know.'

'I know I would go to the stake for you,' said Harry.

'I don't want your head,' said the Father, patting it kindly; 'all you have to do is to hold your tongue. Let us burn these papers, and say nothing to anybody. Should you like to read them?'

Harry Esmond blushed, and held down his head; he *had* looked as the fact was, and without thinking, at the paper before him; and though he had seen it, could not understand a word of it, the letters being quite clear enough, but quite without meaning. They burned the papers, beating down the ashes in a brazier, so that scarce any traces of them remained.

Harry had been accustomed to see Father Holt in more dresses than one; it not being safe, or worth the danger, for Popish ecclesiastics to wear their proper dress; and he was, in consequence, in no wise astonished that the priest should now appear before him in a riding dress with large buff leather boots, and a feather to his hat, plain, but such as gentlemen wore.

'You know the secret of the cupboard,' said he, laughing, 'and must be prepared for other mysteries'; and he opened – but not a secret cupboard this time – only a wardrobe, which he usually kept locked, and from which he now took out two or three dresses and perruques of different colours, and a couple of swords of a pretty make (Father Holt was an expert practitioner with the small sword, and every day, whilst he was at home, he and his pupil practised this exercise, in which the lad became a very great proficient), a military coat and cloak, and a farmer's smock, and placed them in the large hole over the mantelpiece from which the papers had been taken.

'If they miss the cupboard,' he said, 'they will not find these; if they find them, they'll tell no tales, except that Father Holt wore more suits of clothes than one. All Jesuits do. You know what deceivers we are, Harry.'

Harry was alarmed at the notion that his friend was about to leave him; but 'No,' the priest said; 'I may very likely come back with my lord in a few days. We are to be tolerated,[3] we are not to be persecuted. But they may take a fancy to pay a visit at Castlewood ere our return; and, as gentlemen of my cloth are suspected, they might choose to examine my papers, which concern nobody – at least, not them.' And to this day, whether the papers in cypher related to politics, or to the affairs of that mysterious society whereof Father Holt was a member, his pupil, Harry Esmond, remains in entire ignorance.

The rest of his goods, his small wardrobe, &c., Holt left untouched on his shelves and in his cupboard, taking down – with a laugh, however – and flinging into the brazier, where he only half burned them, some theological treatises, which he had been writing against the English divines. 'And now,' said he, 'Henry, my son, you may testify, with a safe conscience, that you saw me burning Latin sermons the last time I was here before I went away to London; and it will be daybreak directly, and I must be away before Lockwood is stirring.'

'Will not Lockwood let you out, sir?' Esmond asked. Holt laughed; he was never more gay or good-humoured than when in the midst of action or danger.

'Lockwood knows nothing of my being here, mind you,' he said; 'nor would you, you little wretch, had you slept better. You must forget that I have been here; and now farewell. Close the door, and go to your own room, and don't come out till – stay, why should you not know one secret more? I know you will never betray me.'

In the Chaplain's room were two windows; the one looking into the court facing westwards to the fountain; the other, a small casement strongly barred, and looking on to the green in front of the Hall. This window was too high to reach from the ground; but, mounting on a buffet[4] which stood beneath it, Father Holt showed me how, by pressing on the base of the window, the whole framework of lead, glass, and iron staunchions, descended into a cavity worked below, from which it could be drawn and restored to its usual place from without; a broken pane being purposely open to admit the hand which was to work upon the spring of the machine.

'When I am gone,' Father Holt said, 'you may push away the buffet, so that no one may fancy that an exit has been made that way; lock the door; place the key – where shall we put the key? – under Chrysostom[5] on the bookshelf; and if any ask for it, say I keep it there, and told you where to find it, if you had need to go to my room. The descent is easy down the wall into the ditch; and so, once more farewell, until I see thee again, my dear son.' And with this the intrepid Father mounted the buffet with great agility and briskness, stepped across the window, lifting up the bars and framework again from the other side, and only leaving room for Harry Esmond to stand on tiptoe and kiss his hand before the casement closed, the bars fixing as firm as ever seemingly in the stone arch overhead. When Father Holt next arrived at Castlewood, it was by the public gate on horseback; and he never so much as alluded to the existence of the private issue to Harry, except when he had need of a private messenger from within, for which end, no doubt, he had instructed his young pupil in the means of quitting the Hall.

Esmond, young as he was, would have died sooner than betray his friend and master, as Mr Holt well knew; for he had tried the boy more than once, putting temptations in his way, to see whether he would yield to them and confess afterwards, or whether he would resist them, as he did sometimes, or whether he would lie, which he never did. Holt instructing the boy on this point, however, that if to keep silence is not to lie, as it certainly is not, yet silence is, after all, equivalent to a negation – and therefore a downright No, in the interest of justice or your friend, and in reply to a question that may be prejudicial to either, is not criminal, but, on the contrary, praiseworthy; and as lawful a way as the other of eluding a wrongful demand. For instance (says he), suppose a good citizen, who had seen his Majesty take refuge there, had been asked, 'Is King Charles up that oak-tree?' His duty would have been not to say, Yes – so that the Cromwellians should seize the King and murder him like his father – but No; his Majesty being private in the tree, and therefore not to be seen there by loyal eyes: all which instruction, in religion and morals, as well as in the rudiments of the tongues and sciences, the boy took eagerly and with gratitude from his tutor. When, then, Holt was gone, and told Harry not to see him, it was as if he had never been. And he had this answer pat when he came to be questioned a few days after.

The Prince of Orange was then at Salisbury, as young Esmond learned from seeing Doctor Tusher in his best cassock (though the roads were muddy, and he never was known to wear his silk, only his stuff one, a-horseback), with a great orange cockade in his broad-leafed hat, and Nahum, his clerk, ornamented with a like decoration. The Doctor was walking up and down, in front of his parsonage, when little Esmond saw him, and heard him say he was going to pay his duty to his Highness the Prince, as he mounted his pad and rode away with Nahum behind. The village people had orange cockades too, and his friend the blacksmith's laughing daughter pinned one into Harry's old hat, which he tore out indignantly when they bid him to cry, 'God save the Prince of Orange and the Protestant religion!' but the people only laughed, for they liked the boy in the village, where his solitary condition moved the general pity, and where he found friendly welcomes and faces in many houses. Father Holt had many friends there too, for he not only would fight the blacksmith at theology, never losing his temper, but laughing the whole time in his pleasant way, but he cured him of an ague with quinquina,[6] and was always ready with a kind word for any man that asked it, so that they said in the village 'twas a pity the two were Papists.

The Director and the Vicar of Castlewood agreed very well; indeed, the former was a perfectly bred gentleman, and it was the latter's business to agree with everybody. Doctor Tusher and the lady's maid, his spouse, had a boy who was about the age of little Esmond; and there was such a friendship between the lads, as propinquity and tolerable kindness and good-humour on either side would be pretty sure to occasion. Tom Tusher was sent off early however to a school in London, whither his father took him and a volume of sermons in the first year of the reign of King James; and Tom returned but once, a year afterwards, to Castlewood for many years of his scholastic and collegiate life. Thus there was less danger to Tom of a perversion of his faith by the Director, who scarce ever saw him, than there was to Harry, who constantly was in the Vicar's company; but as long as Harry's religion was his Majesty's, and my lord's, and my lady's, the Doctor said gravely, it should not be for him to disturb or disquiet him: it was far from him to say that his Majesty's church was not a branch of the Catholic church; upon which Father Holt used, according to his custom, to laugh and say, that the Holy Church throughout all the world, and the noble army of martyrs, were very much obliged to the Doctor.

It was while Doctor Tusher was away at Salisbury that there came a troop of dragoons with orange scarfs, and quartered in Castlewood, and some of them came up to the Hall, where they took possession, robbing nothing however beyond the hen-house and the beer-cellar; and only insisting upon going through the house and looking for papers. The first room they asked to look at was Father Holt's room, of which Harry Esmond brought the key, and they opened the drawers and the cupboards, and tossed over the papers and clothes – but found nothing except his books and clothes, and the vestments in a box by themselves, with which the dragoons made merry, to Harry Esmond's horror. And to the questions which the gentlemen put to Harry, he replied, that Father Holt was a very kind man to him, and a very learned man, and Harry supposed would tell him none of his secrets if he had any. He was about eleven years old at this time, and looked as innocent as boys of his age.

The family were away more than six months, and when they returned they were in the deepest state of dejection, for King James had been banished, the Prince of Orange was on the throne, and the direst persecutions of those of the Catholic faith were apprehended by my lady, who said she did not believe that there was a word of truth in the promises of toleration that Dutch monster made, or in a single word the perjured wretch said. My lord and lady were in a manner prisoners in their own house; so her ladyship gave the little page to know, who was by this time growing of an age to understand what was passing about him, and something of the characters of the people he lived with.

'We are prisoners,' says she; 'in everything but chains, we are prisoners. Let them come, let them consign me to dungeons, or strike off my head from this poor little throat' (and she clasped it in her long fingers). 'The blood of the Esmonds will always flow freely for their kings. We are not like the Churchills – the Judases,[7] who kiss their master and betray him. We know how to suffer, how even to forgive in the royal cause' (no doubt it was to that fatal business of losing the place of Groom of the Posset to which her ladyship alluded, as she did half-a-dozen times in the day). 'Let the tyrant of Orange bring his rack and his odious Dutch tortures – the beast! the wretch! I spit upon him and defy him. Cheerfully will I lay this head upon the block; cheerfully will I accompany my lord to the scaffold: we will cry "God save King James!" with our dying breath, and smile in the face of the executioner.' And she told her page a hundred times at least of the particulars of the last interview which she had with his Majesty.

'I flung myself before my Liege's feet,' she said, 'at Salisbury. I devoted myself – my husband – my house, to his cause. Perhaps he remembered old times, when Isabella Esmond was young and fair; perhaps he recalled the day when 'twas not *I* that knelt – at least he spoke to me with a voice that reminded *me* of days gone by. "Egad!" said his Majesty, "you should go to the Prince of Orange, if you want anything." "No, Sire," I replied, "I would not kneel to a Usurper; the Esmond that would have served your Majesty will never be groom to a traitor's posset." The royal exile smiled, even in the midst of his misfortune; he deigned to raise me with words of consolation. The Viscount, my husband, himself, could not be angry at the august salute with which he honoured me!'

The public misfortune had the effect of making my lord and his lady better friends than they ever had been since their courtship. My Lord Viscount had shown both loyalty and spirit, when these were rare qualities in the dispirited party about the King; and the praise he got elevated him not a little in his wife's good opinion, and perhaps in his own. He wakened up from the listless and supine life which he had been leading; was always riding to and fro in consultation with this friend or that of the King's; the page of course knowing little of his doings, but remarking only his greater cheerfulness and altered demeanour.

Father Holt came to the Hall constantly, but officiated no longer openly as Chaplain; he was always fetching and carrying: strangers, military and ecclesiastic (Harry knew the latter though they came in all sorts of disguises), were continually arriving and departing. My lord made long absences and sudden reappearances, using sometimes the means of exit which Father Holt had employed, though how often the little window in the Chaplain's room let in or let out my lord and his friends, Harry could not tell. He stoutly kept his promise to the Father of not prying, and if at midnight from his little room he heard noises of persons stirring in the next chamber, he turned round to the wall and hid his curiosity under his pillow until it fell asleep. Of course he could not help remarking that the priest's journeys were constant, and understanding by a hundred signs that some active though secret business employed him: what this was may pretty well be guessed by what soon happened to my lord.

No garrison or watch was put into Castlewood when my lord came back, but a guard was in the village; and one or other of them was always on the green keeping a look-out on our great gate, and those who went out and in. Lockwood said that at night especially every person who came in or went out was watched by the outlying sentries. 'Twas lucky that we had a gate which their worships knew nothing about. My lord and Father Holt must have made constant journeys at night: once or twice little Harry acted as their messenger and discreet little aide-de-camp. He remembers he was bidden to go into the village with his fishing-rod, enter certain houses, ask for a drink of water, and tell the good man, 'There would be a horse-market at Newbury next Thursday,' and so carry the same message on to the next house on his list.

He did not know what the message meant at the time, nor what was happening: which may as well, however, for clearness' sake, be explained here. The Prince of Orange being gone to Ireland, where the King was ready to meet him with a great army, it was determined that a great rising of his Majesty's party should take place in this country; and my lord was to head the force in our county. Of late he had taken a greater lead in affairs than before, having the indefatigable Mr Holt at his elbow, and my Lady Viscountess strongly urging him on; and my Lord Sark being in the Tower a prisoner, and Sir Wilmot Crawley, of Queen's Crawley,[8] having gone over to the Prince of Orange's side – my lord became the most considerable person in our part of the county for the affairs of the King.

It was arranged that the regiment of Scots Greys and Dragoons, then quartered at Newbury, should declare for the King on a certain day, when likewise the gentry affected to his Majesty's cause were to come in with their tenants and adherents to Newbury, march upon the Dutch troops at Reading under Ginckel; and, these overthrown, and their indomitable little master away in Ireland, 'twas thought that our side might move on London itself, and a confident victory was predicted for the King.

As these great matters were in agitation, my lord lost his listless manner and seemed to gain health; my lady did not scold him, Mr Holt came to and fro, busy always; and little Harry longed to have been a few inches taller, that he might draw a sword in this good cause.

One day, it must have been about the month of July, 1690, my lord, in a great horseman's coat, under which Harry could see the shining of a steel breastplate he had on, called little Harry to him, put the hair off the child's forehead, and kissed him, and bade God bless him in such an affectionate way as he never had used before. Father Holt blessed him too, and then they took leave of my Lady Viscountess, who came from her apartment with a pocket-handkerchief to her eyes, and her gentlewoman and Mrs Tusher supporting her.

'You are going to – to ride,' says she. 'Oh, that I might come too! – but in my situation I am forbidden horse exercise.'

'We kiss my Lady Marchioness's hand,' says Mr. Holt.

'My lord, God speed you!' she said, stepping up and embracing my lord in a grand manner. 'Mr Holt, I ask your blessing': and she knelt down for that, whilst Mrs Tusher tossed her head up.

Mr Holt gave the same benediction to the little page, who went down and held my lord's stirrups for him to mount; there were two servants waiting there too – and they rode out of Castlewood gate.

As they crossed the bridge Harry could see an officer in scarlet ride up touching his hat, and address my lord.

The party stopped, and came to some parley or discussion, which presently ended, my lord putting his horse into a canter after taking off his hat and making a bow to the officer who rode alongside him step for step: the trooper accompanying him, falling back, and riding with my lord's two men. They cantered over the green, and behind the elms (my lord waving his hand, Harry thought), and so they disappeared.

That evening we had a great panic, the cow-boy coming at milking-time riding one of our horses, which he had found grazing at the outer park wall.

All night my Lady Viscountess was in a very quiet and subdued mood. She scarce found fault with anybody; she played at cards for six hours; little page Esmond went to sleep. He prayed for my lord and the good cause before closing his eyes.

It was quite in the grey of the morning when the porter's bell rang, and old Lockwood waking up, let in one of my lord's servants, who had gone with him in the morning, and who returned with a melancholy story.

The officer who rode up to my lord had, it appeared, said to him, that it was his duty to inform his lordship that he was not under arrest, but under surveillance, and to request him not to ride abroad that day.

My lord replied that riding was good for his health, that if the Captain chose to accompany him he was welcome, and it was then that he made a bow, and they cantered away together.

When he came on to Wansey Down, my lord all of a sudden pulled up, and the party came to a halt at the cross-way.

'Sir,' says he to the officer, 'we are four to two; will you be so kind as to take that road, and leave me to go mine?'

. 'Your road is mine, my lord,' says the officer.

'Then,' says my lord, but he had no time to say more, for

the officer, drawing a pistol, snapped it at his lordship; as at the same moment Father Holt, drawing a pistol, shot the officer through the head.

It was done, and the man dead in an instant of time. The orderly, gazing at the officer, looked scared for a moment, and galloped away for his life.

'Fire! fire!' cried out Father Holt, sending another shot after the trooper, but the two servants were too much surprised to use their pieces, and my lord calling to them to hold their hands, the fellow got away.

'Mr Holt, *qui pensait à tout*,' says Blaise, 'gets off his horse, examines the pockets of the dead officer for papers, gives his money to us two, and says, "The wine is drawn, M. le Marquis," – why did he say Marquis to M. le Vicomte? – "we must drink it." '

'The poor gentleman's horse was a better one than that I rode,' Blaise continues; 'Mr Holt bids me get on him, and so I gave a cut to Whitefoot, and she trotted home. We rode on towards Newbury,[9] we heard firing towards midday: at two o'clock a horseman comes up to us as we were giving our cattle water at an inn – and says, all is done. The Ecossois declared an hour too soon – General Ginckel was down upon them. The whole thing was at an end.

' "And we've shot an officer on duty, and let his orderly escape," says my lord.

' "Blaise," says Mr Holt, writing two lines on his tablebook, one for my lady, and one for you, Master Harry; "you must go back to Castlewood, and deliver these," and behold me.'

And he gave Harry the two papers. He read that to himself, which only said, 'Burn the papers in the cupboard, burn this. You know nothing about anything.' Harry read this, ran upstairs to his mistress's apartment, where her gentlewoman slept near to the door, made her bring a light and wake my lady, into whose hands he gave the paper. She was a wonderful object to look at in her night attire, nor had Harry ever seen the like.

As soon as she had the paper in her hand, Harry stepped back to the Chaplain's room, opened the secret cupboard over the fireplace, burned all the papers in it, and, as he had seen the priest do before, took down one of his reverence's manuscript sermons, and half burnt that in the brazier. By the time the papers were quite destroyed it was daylight. Harry ran back to his mistress again. Her gentlewoman ushered him again into her ladyship's chamber; she told him (from behind her nuptial curtains) to bid the coach be got ready, and that she would ride away anon.

But the mysteries of her ladyship's toilet were as awfully long on this day as on any other, and, long after the coach was ready, my lady was still attiring herself. And just as the Viscountess stepped forth from her room, ready for departure, young Job Lockwood comes running up from the village with news that a lawyer, three officers, and twenty or four-and-twenty soldiers, were marching thence upon the house. Job had but two minutes the start of them, and, ere he had well told his story, the troop rode into our courtyard.

## Chapter 6

### THE ISSUE OF THE PLOTS – THE DEATH OF THOMAS, THIRD VISCOUNT OF CASTLE-WOOD; AND THE IMPRISONMENT OF HIS VISCOUNTESS

AT first my lady was for dying like Mary, Queen of Scots (to whom she fancied she bore a resemblance in beauty), and, stroking her scraggy neck, said, 'They will find Isabel of Castlewood is equal to her fate.' Her gentlewoman, Victoire, persuaded her that her prudent course was, as she could not fly, to receive the troops as though she suspected nothing, and that her chamber was the best place wherein to await them. So her black Japan casket which Harry was to carry to the coach was taken back to her ladyship's chamber, whither the maid and mistress retired. Victoire came out presently, bidding the page to say her ladyship was ill, confined to her bed with the rheumatism.

By this time the soldiers had reached Castlewood. Harry Esmond saw them from the window of the tapestry parlour; a couple of sentinels were posted at the gate – a half-dozen more walked towards the stable; and some others, preceded by their commander, and a man in black, a lawyer probably, were conducted by one of the servants to the stair leading up to the part of the house which my lord and lady inhabited.

So the Captain, a handsome kind man, and the lawyer, came through the ante-room to the tapestry parlour, and where now was nobody but young Harry Esmond, the page.

'Tell your mistress, little man,' says the Captain, kindly, 'that we must speak to her.'

'My mistress is ill a-bed,' said the page.

'What complaint has she?' asked the Captain.

The boy said, 'The rheumatism!'

'Rheumatism! that's a sad complaint,' continues the good-natured captain; 'and the coach is in the yard to fetch the Doctor, I suppose?'

'I don't know,' says the boy.

'And how long has her ladyship been ill?'

'I don't know,' says the boy.

'When did my lord go away?'

'Yesterday night.'

'With Father Holt?'

'With Mr Holt.'

'And which way did they travel?' asks the lawyer.

'They travelled without me,' says the page.

'We must see Lady Castlewood.'

'I have orders that nobody goes into her ladyship – she is sick,' says the page; but at this moment Victoire came out. 'Hush!' says she; and, as if not knowing that anyone was near, 'What's this noise?' says she. 'Is this gentleman the Doctor?'

'Stuff! we must see Lady Castlewood,' says the lawyer, pushing by.

The curtains of her ladyship's room were down, and the chamber dark, and she was in bed with a nightcap on her head, and propped up by her pillows, looking none the less ghastly because of the red which was still on her cheeks, and which she could not afford to forego.

'Is that the Doctor?' she said.

'There is no use with this deception, Madam,' Captain Westbury said (for so he was named). 'My duty is to arrest the person of Thomas, Viscount Castlewood, a nonjuring peer – of Robert Tusher, Vicar of Castlewood – and Henry Holt, known under various other names and designations, a Jesuit priest, who officiated as Chaplain here in the late King's time, and is now at the head of the conspiracy which was about to break out in this country against the authority of their Majesties King William and Queen Mary – and my orders are to search the house for such papers or traces of the conspiracy as may be found here. Your ladyship will please to give me your keys, and it will be as well for yourself that you should help us, in every way, in our search.'

'You see, sir, that I have the rheumatism, and cannot move,' said the lady, looking uncommonly ghastly as she sat up in her bed, where however she had had her cheeks painted, and a new cap put on, so that she might at least look her best when the officers came.

'I shall take leave to place a sentinel in the chamber, so that your ladyship, in case you should wish to rise, may have an arm to lean on,' Captain Westbury said. 'Your woman will show me where I am to look'; and Madame Victoire, chattering in her half French and half English jargon, opened while the Captain examined one drawer after another; but, as Harry Esmond thought, rather carelessly, with a smile on his face, as if he was only conducting the examination for form's sake.

Before one of the cupboards Victoire flung herself down, stretching out her arms, and with a piercing shriek, cried, '*Non, jamais, Monsieur l'officier! Jamais!* I will rather die than let you see this wardrobe.'

But Captain Westbury would open it, still with a smile on his face, which, when the box was opened, turned into a fair burst of laughter. It contained – not papers regarding the conspiracy – but my lady's wigs, washes, and rouge-pots, and Victoire said men were monsters, as the Captain went on with his perquisition.

He tapped the back to see whether or no it was hollow, and as he thrust his hands into the cupboard, my lady from her bed called out with a voice that did not sound like that of a very sick woman, 'Is it your commission to insult ladies as well as to arrest gentlemen, Captain?'

'These articles are only dangerous when worn by your ladyship,' the Captain said with a low bow, and a mock grin of politeness. 'I have found nothing which concerns the government as yet – only the weapons with which beauty is authorized to kill,' says he, pointing to a wig with his sword-tip. 'We must now proceed to search the rest of the house.'

'You are not going to leave that wretch in the room with me,' cried my lady, pointing to the soldier.

'What can I do, madam? Somebody you must have to smooth your pillow and bring your medicine – permit me——'

'Sir!' screamed out my lady——

'Madam, if you are too ill to leave the bed,' the Captain then said, rather sternly, 'I must have in four of my men to lift you off in the sheet: I must examine this bed, in a word; papers may be hidden in a bed as elsewhere; we know that very well and——'

Here it was her ladyship's turn to shriek, for the Captain, with his fist shaking the pillows and bolsters, at last came to 'burn', as they say in the play of forfeits, and wrenching away one of the pillows, said, 'Look, did not I tell you so? Here is a pillow stuffed with paper.'

'Some villain has betrayed us,' cried out my lady, sitting up in the bed, showing herself full dressed under her night-rail.[1]

'And now your ladyship can move, I am sure; permit me to give you my hand to rise. You will have to travel for some distance, as far as Hexton Castle to-night. Will you have your coach? Your woman shall attend you if you like – and the Japan-box?'

'Sir! you don't strike a *man* when he is down,' said my lady, with some dignity: 'can you not spare a woman?'

'Your ladyship must please to rise and let me search the bed,' said the Captain, 'there is no more time to lose in bandying talk.'

And, without more ado, the gaunt old woman got up. Harry Esmond recollected to the end of his life that figure, with the brocade dress and the white night-rail, and the gold-clocked red stockings, and white red-heeled shoes sitting up in the bed, and stepping down from it. The trunks were ready packed for departure in her ante-room, and the horses ready harnessed in the stable: about all which the Captain seemed to know, by information got from some quarter or other; and, whence, Esmond could make a pretty shrewd guess in aftertimes, when Doctor Tusher complained that King William's government had basely treated him for services done in that cause.

And here he may relate, though he was then too young to know all that was happening, what the papers contained, of which Captain Westbury had made a seizure, and which papers had been transferred from the Japan-box to the bed when the officers arrived.

There was a list of gentlemen of the county in Father Holt's handwriting — Mr Freeman's (King James's) friends – a similar paper being found among those of Sir John Fenwick and Mr Coplestone, who suffered death for this conspiracy.[2]

There was a patent conferring the title of Marquis of Esmond on my Lord Castlewood, and the heirs-male of his body; his appointment as Lord Lieutenant of the County, and Major-General.*

There were various letters from the nobility and gentry, some ardent and some doubtful, in the King's service; and (very luckily for him) two letters concerning Colonel Francis Esmond; one from Father Holt, which said, 'I have been to see this Colonel at his house at Walcote near to Wells, where he resides since the King's departure, and pressed him very eagerly in Mr Freeman's cause, showing him the great advantage

---

*To have this rank of Marquis restored in the family had always been my Lady Viscountess's ambition; and her old maiden aunt, Barbara Topham, the goldsmith's daughter, dying about this time, and leaving all her property to Lady Castlewood, I have heard that her ladyship sent almost the whole of the money to King James, a proceeding which so irritated my Lord Castlewood that he actually went to the parish church, and was only appeased by the Marquis's title which his exiled Majesty sent to him in return for the £15,000 his faithful subject lent him.

he would have by trading with that merchant, offering him large premiums there as agreed between us. But he says no: he considers Mr Freeman the head of the firm, will never trade against him or embark with any other trading company, but considers his duty was done when Mr Freeman left England. This Colonel seems to care more for his wife and his beagles than for affairs. He asked me much about young H. E., "that bastard," as he called him: doubting my lord's intentions respecting him. I reassured him on this head, stating what I knew of the lad, and our intentions respecting him, but with regard to Freeman he was inflexible.'

And another letter was from Colonel Esmond to his kinsman, to say that one Captain Holton had been with him offering him large bribes to join, *you know who*, and saying that the head of the house of Castlewood was deeply engaged in that quarter. But for his part he had broke his sword when the K. left the country, and would never again fight in that quarrel. The P. of O. was a man, at least, of a noble courage, and his duty and, as he thought, every Englishman's, was to keep the country quiet, and the French out of it: and, in fine, that he would have nothing to do with the scheme.

Of the existence of these two letters and the contents of the pillow, Colonel Frank Esmond, who became Viscount Castlewood, told Henry Esmond afterwards, when the letters were shown to his lordship, who congratulated himself, as he had good reason, that he had not joined in the scheme which proved so fatal to many concerned in it[3]. But, naturally, the lad knew little about these circumstances when they happened under his eyes: only being aware that his patron and his mistress were in some trouble, which had caused the flight of the one, and the apprehension of the other by the officers of King William.

The seizure of the papers effected, the gentlemen did not pursue their further search through Castlewood House very rigorously. They examined Mr Holt's room, being led thither by his pupil, who showed, as the Father had bidden him, the place where the key of his chamber lay, opened the door for the gentlemen, and conducted them into the room.

When the gentlemen came to the half-burned papers in the

brazier, they examined them eagerly enough, and their young guide was a little amused at their perplexity.

'What are these?' says one.

'They're written in a foreign language,' says the lawyer. 'What are you laughing at, little whelp?' adds he, turning round as he saw the boy smile.

'Mr Holt said they were sermons,' Harry said, 'and bade me to burn them'; which indeed was true of those papers.

'Sermons indeed – it's treason, I would lay a wager,' cries the lawyer.

'Egad! it's Greek to me,' says Captain Westbury. 'Can you read it, little boy?'

'Yes, sir, a little,' Harry said.

'Then read, and read in English, sir, on your peril,' said the lawyer. And Harry began to translate:–

'Hath not one of your own writers said, "The children of Adam are now labouring as much as he himself ever did, about the tree of the knowledge of good and evil, shaking the boughs thereof, and seeking the fruit, being for the most part unmindful of the tree of life." Oh, blind generation! 'tis this tree of knowledge to which the serpent has led you' – and here the boy was obliged to stop, the rest of the page being charred by the fire: and asked of the lawyer – 'Shall I go on, sir?'

The lawyer said – 'This boy is deeper than he seems: who knows that he is not laughing at us?'

'Let's have in Dick the Scholar,'[4] cried Captain Westbury, laughing: and he called to a trooper out of the window – 'Ho, Dick, come in here and construe.'

A thick-set soldier, with a square good-humoured face, came in at the summons, saluting his officer.

'Tell us what is this, Dick,' says the lawyer.

'My name is Steele, sir,' says the soldier. 'I may be Dick for my friends, but I don't name gentlemen of your cloth amongst them.'

'Well then, Steele.'

'Mr Steele, sir, if you please. When you address a gentleman of his Majesty's Horse Guards, be pleased not to be so familiar.'

'I didn't know, sir,' said the lawyer.

'How should you? I take it you are not accustomed to meet with gentlemen,' says the trooper.

'Hold thy prate, and read that bit of paper,' says Westbury.

' 'Tis Latin,' says Dick, glancing at it, and again saluting his officer, 'and from a sermon of Mr Cudworth's,'[5] and he translated the words pretty much as Henry Esmond had rendered them.

'What a young scholar you are,' says the Captain to the boy.

'Depend on't, he knows more than he tells,' says the lawyer. 'I think we will pack him off in the coach with old Jezebel.'

'For construing a bit of Latin?' said the Captain, very good-naturedly.

'I would as lief go there as anywhere,' Harry Esmond said, simply, 'for there is nobody to care for me.'

There must have been something touching in the child's voice, or in this description of his solitude – for the Captain looked at him very good-naturedly, and the trooper called Steele put his hand kindly on the lad's head, and said some words in the Latin tongue.

'What does he say?' says the lawyer.

'Faith, ask Dick himself,' cried Captain Westbury.

'I said I was not ignorant of misfortune myself, and had learned to succour the miserable, and that's not *your* trade, Mr Sheepskin,' said the trooper.

'You had better leave Dick the Scholar alone, Mr Corbet,' the Captain said. And Harry Esmond, always touched by a kind face and kind word, felt very grateful to this good-natured champion.

The horses were by this time harnessed to the coach; and the Countess and Victoire came down and were put into the vehicle. This woman, who quarrelled with Harry Esmond all day, was melted at parting with him, and called him 'dear angel', and 'poor infant', and a hundred other names.

The Viscountess, giving him her lean hand to kiss, bade him always be faithful to the house of Esmond. 'If evil should happen to my lord,' says she, 'his *successor* I trust will be found, and give you protection. Situated as I am, they will not dare wreak their vengeance on me *now*.' And she kissed a medal she wore with great fervour, and Henry Esmond knew not in the least what her meaning was; but hath since learned that, old as she was, she was for ever expecting, by the good offices of saints and relics, to have an heir to the title of Esmond.

Harry Esmond was too young to have been introduced into the secrets of politics in which his patrons were implicated; for they put but few questions to the boy (who was little of stature, and looked much younger than his age), and such questions as they put he answered cautiously enough, and professing even more ignorance than he had, for which his examiners willingly enough gave him credit. He did not say a word about the window or the cupboard over the fireplace; and these secrets quite escaped the eyes of the searchers.

So then my lady was consigned to her coach, and sent off to Hexton, with her woman and the man of law to bear her company, a couple of troopers riding on either side of the coach. And Harry was left behind at the Hall, belonging as it were to nobody, and quite alone in the world. The Captain and a guard of men remained in possession there; and the soldiers, who were very good-natured and kind, ate my lord's mutton and drank his wine, and made themselves comfortable, as they well might do, in such pleasant quarters.

The captains had their dinner served in my lord's tapestry parlour, and poor little Harry thought his duty was to wait upon Captain Westbury's chair, as his custom had been to serve his lord when he sat there.

After the departure of the Countess, Dick the Scholar took Harry Esmond under his special protection, and would examine him in his humanities, and talk to him both of French and Latin, in which tongues the lad found, and his new friend was willing enough to acknowledge, that he was even more proficient than Scholar Dick. Hearing that he had learned them from a Jesuit, in the praise of whom and whose goodness Harry was never tired of speaking, Dick, rather to the boy's surprise, who began to have an early shrewdness, like many children bred up alone, showed a great deal of theological science, and knowledge of the points at issue between the two churches; so that he and Harry would have hours of controversy together, in which the

boy was certainly worsted by the arguments of this singular
trooper. 'I am no common soldier,' Dick would say, and indeed
it was easy to see by his learning, breeding, and many accomplishments, that he was not. 'I am of one of the most ancient
families in the empire; I have had my education at a famous
school,[6] and a famous university; I learned my first rudiments
of Latin near to Smithfield, in London, where the martyrs were
roasted.'

'You hanged as many of ours,' interposed Harry; 'and, for
the matter of persecution, Father Holt told me that a young
gentleman of Edinburgh,[7] eighteen years of age, student at the
college there, was hanged for heresy only last year, though he
recanted, and solemnly asked pardon for his errors.'

'Faith! there has been too much persecution on both sides:
but 'twas you taught us.'

'Nay, 'twas the Pagans began it,' cried the lad, and began to
instance a number of saints of the Church, from the protomartyr
downwards – 'this one's fire went out under him: that one's oil
cooled in the cauldron: at a third holy head the executioner
chopped three times and it would not come off. Show us
martyrs in *your* church for whom such miracles have been done.'

'Nay,' says the trooper gravely, 'the miracles of the first
three centuries belong to my church as well as yours, Master
Papist,' and then added, with something of a smile upon his
countenance, and a queer look at Harry – 'And yet, my little
catechiser, I have sometimes thought about those miracles, that
there was not much good in them, since the victim's head
always finished by coming off at the third or fourth chop, and
the cauldron, if it did not boil one day, boiled the next. Howbeit,
in our times, the Church has lost that questionable advantage of
respites. There never was a shower to put out Ridley's fire,[8]
nor an angel to turn the edge of Campion's axe. The rack tore
the limbs of Southwell the Jesuit and Sympson the Protestant
alike. For faith, everywhere multitudes die willingly enough. I
have read in Monsieur Rycaut's[9] History of the Turks, of
thousands of Mahomet's followers rushing upon death in battle
as upon certain Paradise; and in the great Mogul's dominions
people fling themselves by hundreds under the cars of the idols

annually, and the widows burn themselves on their husbands' bodies, as 'tis well known. 'Tis not the dying for a faith that's so hard, Master Harry – every man of every nation has done that – 'tis the living up to it that is difficult, as I know to my cost,' he added with a sigh. 'And, ah!' he added, 'my poor lad, I am not strong enough to convince thee by my life – though to die for my religion would give me the greatest of joys – but I had a dear friend in Magdalen College in Oxford; I wish Joe Addison were here to convince thee, as he quickly could – for I think he's a match for the whole College of Jesuits; and what's more, in his life too. In that very sermon of Doctor Cudworth's which your priest was quoting from, and which suffered martyrdom in the brazier,' Dick added with a smile, 'I had a thought of wearing the black coat (but was ashamed of my life you see, and took to this sorry red one) – I have often thought of Joe Addison – Doctor Cudworth says, "A good conscience is the best looking-glass of heaven" – and there's a serenity in my friend's face which always reflects it – I wish you could see him, Harry.'

'Did he do you a great deal of good?' asked the lad, simply.

'He might have done,' said the other – 'at least he taught me to see and approve better things. 'Tis my own fault, *deteriora sequi.*'[10]

'You seem very good,' the boy said.

'I'm not what I seem, alas!' answered the trooper – and indeed, as it turned out, poor Dick told the truth – for that very night, at supper in the hall, where the gentlemen of the troop took their repasts, and passed most part of their days dicing and smoking of tobacco, and singing and cursing, over the Castlewood ale – Harry Esmond found Dick the Scholar in a woeful state of drunkenness. He hiccupped out a sermon; and his laughing companions bade him sing a hymn, on which Dick, swearing he would run the scoundrel through the body who insulted his religion, made for his sword, which was hanging on the wall, and fell down flat on the floor under it, saying to Harry, who ran forward to help him, 'Ah, little Papist, I wish Joseph Addison was here!'

**Though the troopers of the King's Life Guards were all**

gentlemen, yet the rest of the gentlemen seemed ignorant and vulgar boors to Harry Esmond, with the exception of this good-natured Corporal Steele the Scholar, and Captain Westbury and Lieutenant Trant, who were always kind to the lad. They remained for some weeks or months encamped in Castlewood, and Harry learned from them, from time to time, how the lady at Hexton Castle was treated, and the particulars of her confinement there. 'Tis known that King William was disposed to deal very leniently with the gentry who remained faithful to the old King's cause; and no prince usurping a crown, as his enemies said he did (righteously taking it as I think now), ever caused less blood to be shed. As for women-conspirators, he kept spies on the least dangerous, and locked up the others. Lady Castlewood had the best rooms in Hexton Castle, and the gaoler's garden to walk in; and though she repeatedly desired to be led out to execution, like Mary, Queen of Scots, there never was any thought of taking her painted old head off, or any desire to do aught but keep her person in security.

And it appeared she found that some were friends in her misfortune, whom she had, in her prosperity, considered as her worst enemies. Colonel Francis Esmond, my lord's cousin and her ladyship's, who had married the Dean of Winchester's daughter, and, since King James's departure out of England, had lived not very far away from Hexton town, hearing of his kinswoman's strait, and being friends with Colonel Brice, commanding for King William in Hexton, and with the church dignitaries there, came to visit her ladyship in prison, offering to his uncle's daughter any friendly services which lay in his power. And he brought his lady and little daughter to see the prisoner, to the latter of whom, a child of great beauty, and many winning ways, the old Viscountess took not a little liking, although between her ladyship and the child's mother there was little more love than formerly. There are some injuries which women never forgive one another; and Madam Francis Esmond, in marrying her cousin, had done one of those irretrievable wrongs to Lady Castlewood. But as she was now humiliated, and in misfortune, Madam Francis could allow a truce to her enmity, and could be kind for a while, at least, to her husband's discarded mistress. So the little Beatrix, her daughter, was permitted often to go and visit the imprisoned Viscountess, who, in so far as the child and its father were concerned, got to abate in her anger towards that branch of the Castlewood family. And the letters of Colonel Esmond coming to light, as has been said, and his conduct being known to the King's council, the Colonel was put in a better position with the existing government than he had ever before been; any suspicions regarding his loyalty were entirely done away; and so he was enabled to be of more service to his kinswoman than he could otherwise have been.

And now there befell an event by which this lady recovered her liberty, and the house of Castlewood got a new owner, and fatherless little Harry Esmond a new and most kind protector and friend. Whatever that secret was which Harry was to hear from my lord, the boy never heard it; for that night when Father Holt arrived, and carried my lord away with him, was the last on which Harry ever saw his patron. What happened to my lord may be briefly told here. Having found the horses at the place where they were lying, my lord and Father Holt rode together to Chatteris, where they had temporary refuge with one of the Father's penitents in that city; but the pursuit being hot for them, and the reward for the apprehension of one or the other considerable, it was deemed advisable that they should separate; and the priest betook himself to other places of retreat known to him, whilst my lord passed over from Bristol into Ireland, in which kingdom King James had a court and an army. My lord was but a small addition to this; bringing, indeed, only his sword and the few pieces in his pocket; but the King received him with some kindness and distinction in spite of his poor plight, confirmed him in his new title of Marquis, gave him a regiment, and promised him further promotion. But titles or promotion were not to benefit him now. My lord was wounded at the fatal battle of the Boyne, [11] flying from which field (long after his master had set him an example), he lay for a while concealed in the marshy country near to the town of Trim, and more from catarrh and fever caught in the bogs than from the steel of the enemy in the battle, sank and died. May the earth lie light upon Thomas of Castlewood! He who writes this must speak in charity, though this lord did him and his two grievous wrongs: for one of these he would have made amends, perhaps, had life been spared him; but the other lay beyond his power to repair, though 'tis to be hoped that a greater Power than a priest has absolved him of it. He got the comfort of this absolution, too, such as it was: a priest of Trim writing a letter to my lady to inform her of this calamity.

But in those days letters were slow of travelling, and our priest's took two months or more on its journey from Ireland to England: where, when it did arrive, it did not find my lady at her own house; she was at the King's house of Hexton Castle when the letter came to Castlewood, but it was opened for all that by the officer in command there.

Harry Esmond well remembered the receipt of this letter, which Lockwood brought in as Captain Westbury and Lieutenant Trant were on the green playing at bowls, young Esmond looking on at the sport, or reading his book in the arbour.

'Here's news for Frank Esmond,' says Captain Westbury; 'Harry, did you ever see Colonel Esmond?' And Captain Westbury looked very hard at the boy as he spoke.

Harry said he had seen him but once when he was at Hexton, at the ball there.

'And did he say anything?'

'He said what I don't care to repeat,'[12] Harry answered. For he was now twelve years of age: he knew what his birth was and the disgrace of it; and he felt no love towards the man who had most likely stained his mother's honour and his own.

'Did you love my Lord Castlewood?'

'I wait until I know my mother, sir, to say,' the boy answered, his eyes filling with tears.

'Something has happened to Lord Castlewood,' Captain Westbury said in a very grave tone – 'something which must happen to us all. He is dead of a wound received at the Boyne, fighting for King James.'

'I am glad my lord fought for the right cause,' the boy said.

'It was better to meet death on the field like a man, than face it on Tower-Hill, as some of them may,' continued Mr Westbury. 'I hope he has made some testament, or provided for thee somehow. This letter says, he recommends *unicum filium suum dilectissimum*[13] to his lady. I hope he has left you more than that.'

Harry did not know, he said. He was in the hands of Heaven and Fate; but more lonely now, as it seemed to him, than he had been all the rest of his life; and that night, as he lay in his little room which he still occupied, the boy thought with many a pang of shame and grief of his strange and solitary condition: – how he had a father and no father: a nameless mother that had been brought to ruin, perhaps, by that very father whom Harry could only acknowledge in secret and with a blush, and whom he could neither love nor revere. And he sickened to think how Father Holt, a stranger, and two or three soldiers, his acquaintances of the last six weeks, were the only friends he had in the great wide world, where he was now quite alone. The soul of the boy was full of love, and he longed as he lay in the darkness there for some one upon whom he could bestow it. He remembers, and must to his dying day, the thoughts and tears of that long night, the hours tolling through it. Who was he and what? Why here rather than elsewhere? I have a mind, he thought, to go to that priest at Trim, and find out what my father said to him on his death-bed confession. Is there any child in the whole world so unprotected as I am? Shall I get up and quit this place, and run to Ireland? With these thoughts and tears the lad passed that night away until he wept himself to sleep.

The next day, the gentlemen of the guard who had heard what had befallen him were more than usually kind to the child, especially his friend Scholar Dick, who told him about his own father's death, which had happened when Dick was a child at Dublin, not quite five years of age. 'That was the first sensation of grief,' Dick said, 'I ever knew. I remember I went into the room where his body lay, and my mother sate weeping beside it. I had my battledore in my hand, and fell a-beating the coffin, and calling Papa; on which my mother caught me in her arms, and told me in a flood of tears Papa could not hear me, and would play with me no more, for they were going to put him under ground, whence he could never

come to us again.[14] And this,' said Dick kindly, 'has made me
pity all children ever since; and caused me to love thee, my
poor fatherless, motherless lad. And, if ever thou wantest a
friend, thou shalt have one in Richard Steele.'

Harry Esmond thanked him, and was grateful. But what
could Corporal Steele do for him? – take him to ride a spare
horse, and be servant to the troop? Though there might be a
bar in Harry Esmond's shield, it was a noble one. The counsel
of the two friends was, that little Harry should stay where he
was, and abide his fortune: so Esmond stayed on at Castlewood,
awaiting with no small anxiety the fate, whatever it was, which
was over him.

## Chapter 7

### I AM LEFT AT CASTLEWOOD AN ORPHAN,
### AND FIND MOST KIND PROTECTORS
### THERE

DURING the stay of the soldiers in Castlewood, honest Dick the
Scholar was the constant companion of the lonely little orphan
lad Harry Esmond: and they read together, and they played
bowls together, and when the other troopers or their officers,
who were free-spoken over their cups, (as was the way of that
day, when neither men nor women were over-nice), talked un-
becomingly of their amours and gallantries before the child,
Dick, who very likely was setting the whole company laughing,
would stop their jokes with a *maxima debetur pueris reverentia*,[1]
and once offered to lug out against another trooper called Hulking Tom, who wanted to ask Harry Esmond a ribald question.

Also, Dick seeing that the child had, as he said, a sensibility
above his years, and a great and praiseworthy discretion, confided
to Harry his love for a vintner's daughter, near to the Tollyard,
Westminster, whom Dick addressed as Saccharissa [2] in many
verses of his composition, and without whom he said it would be
impossible that he could continue to live. He vowed this a

thousand times in a day, though Harry smiled to see the love-lorn swain had his health and appetite as well as the most heart-whole trooper in the regiment: and he swore Harry to secresy too, which vow the lad religiously kept, until he found that officers and privates were all taken into Dick's confidence, and had the benefit of his verses. And it must be owned likewise that, while Dick was sighing after Saccharissa in London, he had consolations in the country; for there came a wench out of Castlewood village who had washed his linen, and who cried sadly when she heard he was gone; and without paying her bill too, which Harry Esmond took upon himself to discharge by giving the girl a silver pocket-piece,[3] which Scholar Dick had presented to him, when, with many embraces and prayers for his prosperity, Dick parted from him, the garrison of Castlewood being ordered away. Dick the Scholar said he would never forget his young friend, nor indeed did he; and Harry was sorry when the kind soldiers vacated Castlewood, looking forward with no small anxiety (for care and solitude had made him thoughtful beyond his years) to his fate when the new lord and lady of the house came to live there. He had lived to be past twelve years old now; and had never had a friend, save this wild trooper perhaps, and Father Holt; and had a fond and affectionate heart, tender to weakness, that would fain attach itself to somebody, and did not seem at rest until it had found a friend who would take charge of it.

The instinct which led Henry Esmond to admire and love the gracious person, the fair apparition of whose beauty and kindness had so moved him when he first beheld her, became soon a devoted affection and passion of gratitude, which entirely filled his young heart, that as yet, except in the case of dear Father Holt, had had very little kindness for which to be thankful. *O Dea certè*, thought he, remembering the lines out of the Æneis which Mr Holt had taught him. There seemed, as the boy thought, in every look or gesture of this fair creature, an angelical softness and bright pity – in motion or repose she seemed gracious alike; the tone of her voice, though she uttered words ever so trivial, gave him a pleasure that amounted almost to anguish. It cannot be called love, that a lad of twelve years of age, little more than a menial, felt for an exalted lady, his mistress: but it was worship. To catch her glance, to divine her errand and run on it before she had spoken it; to watch, to follow, adore her, became the business of his life. Meanwhile, as is the way often, his idol had idols of her own, and never thought of or suspected the admiration of her little pigmy adorer.

My lady had on her side her three idols; first and foremost, Jove and supreme ruler, was her lord, Harry's patron, the good Viscount of Castlewood. All wishes of his were laws with her. If he had a headache, she was ill. If he frowned, she trembled. If he joked, she smiled and was charmed. If he went a-hunting, she was always at the window to see him ride away, her little son crowing on her arm, or on the watch till his return. She made dishes for his dinner; spiced his wine for him; made the toast for his tankard at breakfast; hushed the house when he slept in his chair, and watched for a look when he woke. If my lord was not a little proud of his beauty, my lady adored it. She clung to his arm as he paced the terrace, her two fair little hands clasped round his great one; her eyes were never tired of looking in his face and wondering at its perfection. Her little son was his son, and had his father's look and curly brown hair. Her daughter Beatrix was his daughter, and had his eyes – were there ever such beautiful eyes in the world? All the house was arranged so as to bring him ease and give him pleasure. She liked the small gentry round about to come and pay him court, never caring for admiration for herself; those who wanted to be well with the lady must admire him. Not regarding her dress, she would wear a gown to rags because he had once liked it; and, if he brought her a brooch or a ribbon, would prefer it to all the most costly articles of her wardrobe.

My lord went to London every year for six weeks, and the family being too poor to appear at Court with any figure, he went alone. It was not until he was out of sight that her face showed any sorrow; and what a joy when he came back! What preparation before his return! The fond creature had his arm-chair at the chimney-side – delighting to put the children in it, and look at them here. Nobody took his place at the table; but his silver tankard stood there as when my lord was present.

A pretty sight it was to see, during my lord's absence, or on those many mornings when sleep or headache kept him abed, this fair young lady of Castlewood, her little daughter at her knee, and her domestics gathered round her, reading the Morning Prayer of the English Church. Esmond long remembered how she looked and spoke, kneeling reverently before the sacred book, the sun shining upon her golden hair until it made a halo round about her. A dozen of the servants of the house kneeled in a line opposite their mistress; for a while Harry Esmond kept apart from these mysteries, but Doctor Tusher showing him that the prayers read were those of the Church of all ages, and the boy's own inclination prompting him to be always as near as he might to his mistress, and to think all things she did right, from listening to the prayers in the antechamber, he came presently to kneel down with the rest of the household in the parlour; and before a couple of years my lady had made a thorough convert. Indeed, the boy loved his catechiser so much that he would have subscribed to anything she bade him, and was never tired of listening to her fond discourse and simple comments upon the book, which she read to him in a voice of which it was difficult to resist the sweet persuasion and tender appealing kindness. This friendly controversy, and the intimacy which it occasioned, bound the lad more fondly than ever to his mistress. The happiest period of all his life was this; and the young mother, with her daughter and son, and the orphan lad whom she protected, read and worked and played, and were children together. If the lady looked forward – as what fond woman does not? – towards the future, she had no plans from which Harry Esmond was left out; and a thousand and a thousand times in his passionate and impetuous way he vowed that no power should separate him from his mistress, and only asked for some chance to happen by which he might show his fidelity to her. Now, at the close of his life, as he sits and recalls in tranquillity the happy and busy scenes of it, he can think, not ungratefully, that he has been faithful to that early vow. Such a life is so simple that years may be chronicled in a few lines. But few men's life-voyages are destined to be all prosperous; and this calm of which we are speaking was soon to come to an end.

As Esmond grew, and observed for himself, he found of necessity much to read and think of outside that fond circle of kinsfolk who had admitted him to join hand with them. He read more books than they cared to study with him; was alone in the midst of them many a time, and passed nights over labours, futile perhaps, but in which they could not join him. His dear mistress divined his thoughts with her usual jealous watchfulness of affection: began to forebode a time when he would escape from his home-nest; and, at his eager protestations to the contrary, would only sigh and shake her head. Before those fatal decrees in life are executed, there are always secret previsions and warning omens. When everything yet seems calm, we are aware that the storm is coming. Ere the happy days were over, two at least of that home-party felt that they were drawing to a close; and were uneasy, and on the look-out for the cloud which was to obscure their calm.

'Twas easy for Harry to see, however much his lady persisted in obedience and admiration for her husband, that my lord tired of his quiet life, and grew weary, and then testy, at those gentle bonds with which his wife would have held him. As they say the Grand Lama of Thibet is very much fatigued by his character of divinity, and yawns on his altar as his bonzes kneel and worship him, many a home-god grows heartily sick of the reverence with which his family-devotees pursue him, and sighs for freedom and for his old life, and to be off the pedestal on which his dependants would have him sit for ever, whilst they adore him, and ply him with flowers, and hymns, and incense, and flattery; – so, after a few years of his marriage, my honest Lord Castlewood began to tire; all the high-flown raptures and devotional cere-monies with which his wife, his chief priestess, treated him, first sent him to sleep, and then drove him out of doors; for the truth must be told, that my lord was a jolly gentleman, with very little of the august or divine in his nature, though his fond wife per-sisted in revering it – and, besides, he had to pay a penalty for this love, which persons of his disposition seldom like to defray: and, in a word, if he had a loving wife, had a very jealous and exacting one. Then he wearied of this jealousy: then he broke away from it; then came, no doubt, complaints and recriminations; then, perhaps, promises of amendment not fulfilled; then upbraidings not the more pleasant because they were silent, and only sad looks and tearful eyes conveyed them. Then, perhaps, the pair reached that other stage which is not uncommon in married life, when the woman perceives that the god of the honeymoon is a god no more; only a mortal like the rest of us – and so she looks into her heart, and lo! *vacuæ sedes et inania arcana*.[4] And now, supposing our lady to have a fine genius and a brilliant wit of her own, and the magic spell and infatuation removed from her which had led her to worship as a god a very ordinary mortal – and what follows? They live together, and they dine together, and they say 'my dear' and 'my love' as heretofore; but the man is himself, and the woman herself: that dream of love is over, as everything else is over in life; as flowers and fury, and griefs and pleasures, are over.

Very likely the Lady Castlewood had ceased to adore her husband herself long before she got off her knees, or would allow her household to discontinue worshipping him. To do him justice, my lord never exacted this subservience: he laughed and joked, and drank his bottle, and swore when he was angry, much too familiarly for any one pretending to sublimity; and did his best to destroy the ceremonial with which his wife chose to surround him. And it required no great conceit on young Esmond's part to see that his own brains were better than his patron's, who, indeed, never assumed any airs of superiority over the lad, or over any dependant of his, save when he was displeased, in which case he would express his mind, in oaths, very freely; and who, on the contrary, perhaps, spoiled 'Parson Harry', as he called young Esmond, by constantly praising his parts, and admiring his boyish stock of learning.

It may seem ungracious in one who has received a hundred favours from his patron to speak in any but a reverential manner of his elders; but the present writer has had descendants of his own, whom he has brought up with as little as possible of the servility at present exacted by parents from children (under which mask of duty there often lurks indifference, contempt, or rebellion): and as he would have his grandsons believe or represent him to be not an inch taller than Nature has made him: so, with regard to his past acquaintances, he would speak without anger, but with truth, as far as he knows it, neither extenuating nor setting down aught in malice.

So long, then, as the world moved according to Lord Castle-wood's wishes, he was good-humoured enough; of a temper naturally sprightly and easy, liking to joke, especially with his inferiors, and charmed to receive the tribute of their laughter. All exercises of the body he could perform to perfection – shooting at a mark and flying,[5] breaking horses, riding at the ring,[6] pitching the quoit, playing at all games with great skill. And not only did he do these things well, but he thought he did them to perfection; hence he was often tricked about horses, which he pretended to know better than any jockey; was made to play at ball and billiards[7] by sharpers who took his money; and came back from London woefully poorer each time than he went, as the state of his affairs testified, when the sudden accident came by which his career was brought to an end.

He was fond of the parade of dress, and passed as many hours daily at his toilet as an elderly coquette. A tenth part of his day was spent in the brushing of his teeth and the oiling of his hair, which was curling and brown, and which he did not like to conceal under a periwig, such as almost everybody of that time wore (we have the liberty of our hair back now, but powder and pomatum along with it. When, I wonder, will these monstrous poll-taxes of our age be withdrawn, and men allowed to carry their colours, black, red, or grey, as nature made them?) And, as he liked her to be well dressed, his lady spared no pains in that matter to please him; indeed, she would dress her head or cut it off if he had bidden her.

It was a wonder to young Esmond, serving as page to my lord and lady, to hear, day after day, to such company as came, the same boisterous stories told by my lord, at which his lady never failed to smile or hold down her head, and Doctor Tusher to burst out laughing at the proper point, or cry, 'Fye, my lord, remember my cloth,' but with such a faint show of resistance, that it only provoked my lord further. Lord Castlewood's stories rose by degrees, and became stronger after the ale at dinner and the bottle afterwards; my lady always taking flight after the very first glass to Church and King, and leaving the gentlemen to drink the rest of the toasts by themselves.

And, as Harry Esmond was her page, he also was called from duty at this time. 'My lord has lived in the army and with soldiers,' she would say to the lad, 'amongst whom great licence is allowed. You have had a different nurture, and I trust these things will change as you grow older; not that any fault attaches to my lord, who is one of the best and most religious men in this kingdom.' And very likely she believed so. 'Tis strange what a man may do, and a woman yet think him an angel.

And as Esmond has taken truth for his motto, it must be owned, even with regard to that other angel, his mistress, that she had a fault of character, which flawed her perfections. With the other sex perfectly tolerant and kindly, of her own she was invariably jealous, and a proof that she had this vice is, that though she would acknowledge a thousand faults that she had not, to this which she had she could never be got to own. But if there came a woman with even a semblance of beauty to Castlewood, she was so sure to find out some wrong in her, that my lord, laughing in his jolly way, would often joke with her concerning her foible. Comely servant-maids might come for hire, but none were taken at Castlewood. The housekeeper was old; my lady's own waiting-woman squinted, and was marked with the small-pox; the housemaids and scullion were ordinary country wenches, to whom Lady Castlewood was kind, as her nature made her to everybody almost; but as soon as ever she had to do with a pretty woman, she was cold, retiring, and haughty. The country ladies found this fault in her; and though the men all admired her, their wives and daughters complained of her coldness and airs, and said that Castlewood was pleasanter in Lady Jezebel's time (as the dowager was called) than at present. Some few were of my mistress's side. Old Lady Blenkinsop Jointure, who had been at Court in King James the First's time, always took her side; and so did old Mistress Crookshank, Bishop Crookshank's daughter, of Hexton, who, with some more of their like, pronounced my lady an angel; but the pretty women were not of this mind; and the opinion of the country was, that my lord was tied to his wife's apron-strings, and that she ruled over him.

The second fight which Harry Esmond had, was at fourteen years of age, with Bryan Hawkshaw, Sir John Hawkshaw's son, of Bramblebrook, who advancing this opinion, that my lady was jealous, and henpecked my lord, put Harry into such a fury, that Harry fell on him, and with such rage, that the other boy, who was two years older, and by far bigger than he, had by far the worst of the assault, until it was interrupted by Doctor Tusher walking out of the dinner room.

Bryan Hawkshaw got up, bleeding at the nose, having, indeed, been surprised, as many a stronger man might have been, by the fury of the assault upon him.

'You little bastard beggar!' he said, 'I'll murder you for this!' And indeed he was big enough.

'Bastard or not,' said the other, grinding his teeth, 'I have a couple of swords, and if you like to meet me, as a man, on the terrace tonight ——'

And here the Doctor coming up, the colloquy of the young champions ended. Very likely, big as he was, Hawkshaw did not care to continue a fight with such a ferocious opponent as this had been.

## Chapter 8

### AFTER GOOD FORTUNE COMES EVIL

SINCE my Lady Mary Wortly Montagu brought home the custom of inoculation[1] from Turkey (a perilous practice many deem it, and only a useless rushing into the jaws of danger), I think the severity of the small-pox, that dreadful scourge of the world, has somewhat been abated in our part of it; and remember in my time hundreds of the young and beautiful who have been carried to the grave, or have only risen from their pillows frightfully scarred and disfigured by this malady. Many a sweet face hath left its roses on the bed, on which this dreadful and withering blight has laid them. In my early days this pestilence would enter a village and destroy half its inhabitants: at its approach it may well be imagined not only the beautiful but the strongest were alarmed, and those fled who could. One day in the year 1694 (I have good reason to remember it), Doctor Tusher ran into Castlewood House, with a face of consternation, saying that the malady had made its appearance at the blacksmith's house in the village, and that one of the maids there was down in the small-pox.

The blacksmith, beside his forge and irons for horses, had an alehouse for men, which his wife kept, and his company sate on benches before the inn door, looking at the smithy while they drank their beer. Now, there was a pretty girl at this inn, the landlord's men called Nancy Sievewright, a bouncing fresh-looking lass, whose face was as red as the hollyhocks over the pales of the garden behind the inn. At this time Harry Esmond was a lad of sixteen, and somehow in his walks and rambles it often happened that he fell in with Nancy Sievewright's bonny face; if he did not want something done at the blacksmith's he would go and drink ale at the Three Castles, or find some pretext for seeing this poor Nancy. Poor thing, Harry meant or imagined no harm; and she, no doubt, as little, but the truth is they were always meeting – in the lanes, or by the brook, or at the garden-palings, or about Castlewood: it was, 'Lord, Mr Henry!' and 'How do you do, Nancy?' many and many a time in the week. 'Tis surprising the magnetic attraction which draws people together from ever so far. I blush as I think of poor Nancy now, in a red boddice and buxom purple cheeks and a canvass petti-coat; and that I devised schemes, and set traps, and made speeches in my heart, which I seldom had courage to say when in presence of that humble enchantress, who knew nothing beyond milking a cow, and opened her black eyes with wonder when I made one of my fine speeches out of Waller or Ovid. Poor Nancy! from the mist of far-off years thine honest country face beams out; and I remember thy kind voice as if I had heard it yesterday.

When Doctor Tusher brought the news that the small-pox was at the Three Castles, whither a tramper, it was said, had brought the malady, Henry Esmond's first thought was of alarm for poor Nancy, and then of shame and disquiet for the Castle-wood family, lest he might have brought this infection; for the truth is that Mr Harry had been sitting in a back room for an hour that day, where Nancy Sievewright was with a little brother who complained of headache, and was lying stupefied and crying, either in a chair by the corner of the fire, or in Nancy's lap, or on mine.

Little Lady Beatrix screamed out at Doctor Tusher's news; and my lord cried out 'God bless me!' He was a brave man, and not afraid of death in any shape but this. He was very proud of his pink complexion and fair hair – but the idea of death by small-pox scared him beyond all other ends. 'We will take the children and ride away tomorrow to Walcote': this was my lord's small house, inherited from his mother, near to Winchester.

'That is the best refuge in case the disease spreads,' said Doctor Tusher. ''Tis awful to think of it beginning at the ale-house. Half the people of the village have visited that to-day, or the blacksmith's, which is the same thing. My clerk Simons lodges with them – I can never go into my reading-desk and have that fellow so near me. I *won't* have that man near me.'

'If a parishioner dying in the small-pox sent for you, would you not go?' asked my lady, looking up from her frame of work, with her calm blue eyes.

'By the Lord, *I* wouldn't,' said my lord.

'We are not in a Popish country: and a sick man doth not absolutely need absolution and confession,' said the Doctor. ''Tis true they are a comfort and a help to him when attainable, and to be administered with hope of good. But in a case where the life of a parish-priest in the midst of his flock is highly valuable to them, he is not called upon to risk it (and therewith the lives, future prospects, and temporal, even spiritual welfare of his own family) for the sake of a single person, who is not very likely in a condition even to understand the religious message whereof the priest is the bringer – being uneducated, and likewise stupefied or delirious by disease. If your ladyship or his lordship, my excellent good friend and patron, were to take it ——'

'God forbid!' cried my lord.

'Amen,' continued Doctor Tusher. 'Amen to that prayer, my very good lord! for your sake I would lay my life down' – and, to judge from the alarmed look of the Doctor's purple face, you would have thought that that sacrifice was about to be called for instantly.

To love children, and be gentle with them, was an instinct, rather than a merit, in Henry Esmond, so much so, that he thought almost with a sort of shame of his liking for them, and of the softness into which it betrayed him; and on this day the poor fellow had not only had his young friend, the milkmaid's brother, on his knee, but had been drawing pictures, and telling stories to the little Frank Castlewood, who had occupied the same place for an hour after dinner, and was never tired of Henry's tales, and his pictures of soldiers and horses. As luck would have it, Beatrix had not on that evening taken her usual place, which generally she was glad enough to have, upon her tutor's lap. For Beatrix, from the earliest time, was jealous of every caress which was given to her little brother Frank. She would fling away even from the maternal arms, if she saw Frank had been there before her; insomuch that Lady Esmond was obliged not to show her love for her son in the presence of the little girl, and embrace one or the other alone. She would turn pale and red with rage if she caught signs of intelligence or affection between Frank Esmond and his mother; would sit apart, and not speak for a whole night, if she thought the boy had a better fruit or a larger cake than hers; would fling away a ribbon if he had one; and from the earliest age, sitting up in her little chair by the great fireplace opposite to the corner where Lady Castlewood commonly sate at her embroidery, would utter infantine sarcasms about the favour shown to her brother. These, if spoken in the presence of Lord Castlewood, tickled and amused his humour; he would pretend to love Frank best, and dandle and kiss him, and roar with laughter at Beatrix's jealousy. But the truth is, my lord did not often witness these scenes, nor very much trouble the quiet fireside at which his lady passed many long evenings. My lord was hunting all day when the season admitted; he frequented all the cock-fights and fairs in the country, and would ride twenty miles to see a main[2] fought, or two clowns break their heads at a cudgelling match; and he liked better to sit in his parlour drinking ale and punch with Jack and Tom, than in his wife's drawing-room: whither, if he came, he brought only too often blood-shot eyes, a hiccuping voice, and a reeling gait. The management of the house and the property, the care of the few tenants and the village poor, and the accounts of the estate, were in the hands of his lady and her young secretary, Harry Esmond. My lord took charge of the stables, the kennel, and the cellar – and he filled this and emptied it too.

So it chanced that upon this very day, when poor Harry Esmond had had the blacksmith's son, and the peer's son, alike upon his knee, little Beatrix, who would come to her tutor willingly enough with her book and her writing, had refused him, seeing the place occupied by her brother, and, luckily for her, had sate at the further end of the room, away from him, playing with a spaniel dog which she had (and for which, by fits and starts, she would take a great affection), and talking at Harry Esmond over her shoulder, as she pretended to caress the dog, saying, that Fido would love her, and she would love Fido, and nothing but Fido, all her life.

When, then, the news was brought that the little boy at the Three Castles was ill with the small-pox, poor Harry Esmond felt a shock of alarm, not so much for himself as for his mistress's son, whom he might have brought into peril. Beatrix who had pouted sufficiently (and who whenever a stranger appeared began, from infancy almost, to play off little graces to catch his attention), her brother being now gone to bed, was for taking her place upon Esmond's knee: for, though the Doctor was very obsequious to her, she did not like him, because he had thick boots and dirty hands (the pert young miss said) and because she hated learning the catechism.

But as she advanced towards Esmond from the corner where she had been sulking, he started back and placed the great chair on which he was sitting between him and her – saying in the French language to Lady Castlewood, with whom the young lad had read much, and whom he had perfected in this tongue – 'Madam, the child must not approach me; I must tell you that I was at the blacksmith's to-day, and had his little boy upon my lap.'

'Where you took my son afterwards,' Lady Castlewood said, very angry, and turning red. 'I thank you, sir, for giving him such company. Beatrix,' she said in English, 'I forbid you to touch Mr Esmond. Come away, child – come to your room. Come to your room – I wish your reverence good-night – and you, sir, had you not better go back to your friends at the alehouse?' Her eyes, ordinarily so kind, darted flashes of anger as she spoke; and she tossed up her head (which hung down commonly) with the mien of a princess.

'Hey-day!' says my lord, who was standing by the fire-place – indeed he was in the position to which he generally came by that hour of the evening – 'Hey-day! Rachel, what are you in a passion about? Ladies ought never to be in a passion. Ought they, Doctor Tusher? though it does good to see Rachel in a passion – Damme, Lady Castlewood, you look dev'lish handsome in a passion.'

'It is, my lord, because Mr Henry Esmond, having nothing to do with his time here, and not having a taste for our company, has been to the alehouse, where he has *some friends*.'

My lord burst out with a laugh and an oath – 'You young slyboots, you've been at Nancy Sievewright. D—— the young hypocrite, who'd have thought it in him? I say, Tusher, he's been after——'

'Enough, my lord,' said my lady, 'don't insult me with this talk.'

'Upon my word,' said poor Harry, ready to cry with shame and mortification, 'the honour of that young person is perfectly unstained for me.'

'O, of course, of course,' says my lord, more and more laughing and tipsy. 'Upon his *honour*, Doctor – Nancy Sieve——'

'Take Mistress Beatrix to bed,' my lady cried at this moment to Mrs Tucker her woman, who came in with her ladyship's tea. 'Put her into my room – no, into yours,' she added quickly. 'Go, my child: go, I say: not a word!' And Beatrix, quite surprised at so sudden a tone of authority from one who was seldom accustomed to raise her voice, went out of the room with a scared countenance and waited even to burst out a-crying, until she got to the door with Mrs Tucker.

For once her mother took little heed of her sobbing, and continued to speak eagerly – 'My lord,' she said, 'this young man – your dependant – told me just now in French – he was ashamed to speak in his own language – that he had been at the alehouse all day, where he has had that little wretch who is now ill of the small-pox on his knee. And he comes home reeking from that place – yes, reeking from it – and takes my boy into his lap without shame, and sits down by me, yes, by *me*. He may have killed Frank for what I know – killed our child. Why was he brought in to disgrace our house? Why is he here? Let him go – let him go, I say, to-night, and pollute the place no more.'

She had never once uttered a syllable of unkindness to Harry Esmond; and her cruel words smote the poor boy, so that he stood for some moments bewildered with grief and rage at the injustice of such a stab from such a hand. He turned quite white from red, which he had been.

'I cannot help my birth, madam,' he said, 'nor my other misfortune. And as for your boy, if – if my coming nigh to him pollutes him now, it was not so always. Good-night, my lord. Heaven bless you and yours for your goodness to me. I have tired her ladyship's kindness out, and I will go'; and, sinking down on his knee, Harry Esmond took the rough hand of his benefactor and kissed it.

'He wants to go to the alehouse – let him go,' cried my lady.

'I'm d——d if he shall,' said my lord. 'I didn't think you could be so d——d ungrateful, Rachel.'

Her reply was to burst into a flood of tears, and to quit the room with a rapid glance at Harry Esmond, as my lord, not heeding them, and still in great good-humour, raised up his young client from his kneeling posture (for a thousand kindnesses had caused the lad to revere my lord as a father), and put his broad hand on Harry Esmond's shoulder.

'She was always so,' my lord said; 'the very notion of a woman drives her mad. I took to liquor on that very account, by Jove, for no other reason than that; for she can't be jealous of a beer-barrel or a bottle of rum, can she, Doctor? D—— it, look at the maids – just look at the maids in the house' (my lord pronounced all the words together – just-look-at-the-maze-in-the-house: jever-see-such-maze?) 'You wouldn't take a wife out of Castlewood now, would you, Doctor?' and my lord burst out laughing.

The Doctor, who had been looking at my Lord Castlewood from under his eyelids, said, 'But joking apart, and, my lord, as a divine, I cannot treat the subject in a jocular light, nor, as a pastor of this congregation, look with anything but sorrow at the idea of so very young a sheep going astray.'

'Sir,' said young Esmond, bursting out indignantly, 'she told me that you yourself were a horrid old man, and had offered to kiss her in the dairy.'

'For shame, Henry,' cried Doctor Tusher, turning as red as a turkey-cock, while my lord continued to roar with laughter. 'If you listen to the falsehoods of an abandoned girl—'

'She is as honest as any woman in England, and as pure for me,' cried out Henry, 'and as kind, and as good. For shame on you to malign her!'

'Far be it from me to do so,' cried the Doctor. 'Heaven grant I may be mistaken in the girl, and in you, sir, who have a truly *precocious* genius; but that is not the point at issue at present. It appears that the small-pox broke out in the little boy at the Three Castles; that it was on him when you visited the alehouse, for your *own* reasons; and that you sate with the child for some time and immediately afterwards with my young lord.' The Doctor raised his voice as he spoke, and looked towards my lady, who had now come back, looking very pale, with a handkerchief in her hand.

'This is all very true, sir,' said Lady Esmond, looking at the young man.

''Tis to be feared that he may have brought the infection with him.'

'From the alehouse – yes,' said my lady.

'D—— it, I forgot when I collared you, boy,' cried my lord, stepping back. 'Keep off, Harry, my boy; there's no good in running into the wolf's jaws, you know.'

My lady looked at him with some surprise, and instantly advancing to Henry Esmond, took his hand. 'I beg your pardon,

Henry,' she said; 'I spoke very unkindly. I have no right to inter-
fere with you – with your—'

My lord broke out into an oath. 'Can't you leave the boy
alone, my lady?' She looked a little red, and faintly pressed
the lad's hand as she dropped it.

'There is no use, my lord,' she said; 'Frank was on his knee as
he was making pictures, and was running constantly from Henry
to me. The evil is done, if any.'

'Not with me, damme,' cried my lord. 'I've been smoking' –
and he lighted his pipe again with a coal – 'and it keeps off
infection; and as the disease is in the village – plague take it – I
would have you leave it. We'll go to-morrow to Walcote, my lady.'

'I have no fear,' said my lady; 'I may have had it as an infant,
it broke out in our house then; and when four of my sisters had
it at home, two years before our marriage, I escaped it, and two
of my dear sisters died.'

'I won't run the risk,' said my lord; 'I'm as bold as any man,
but I'll not bear that.'

'Take Beatrix with you and go,' said my lady. 'For us the
mischief is done; and Tucker can wait upon us, who has had the
disease.'

'You take care to choose 'em ugly enough,' said my lord, at
which her ladyship hung down her head and looked foolish: and
my lord, calling away Tusher, bade him come to the oak parlour
and have a pipe. The Doctor made a low bow to her ladyship (of
which salaams he was profuse), and walked off on his creaking
square-toes after his patron.

When the lady and the young man were alone, there was a
silence of some moments, during which he stood at the fire,
looking rather vacantly at the dying embers, whilst her ladyship
busied herself with her tambour-frame[3] and needles.

'I am sorry,' she said, after a pause, in a hard, dry voice – 'I
*repeat* I am sorry that I showed myself so ungrateful for the
safety of my son. It was not at all my wish that you should leave
us, I am sure, unless you found pleasure elsewhere. But you
must perceive, Mr Esmond, that at your age, and with your
tastes, it is impossible that you can continue to stay upon the
intimate footing in which you have been in this family. You have

wished to go to the University, and I think 'tis quite as well that you should be sent thither. I did not press this matter, thinking you a child, as you are, indeed, in years – quite a child; and I should never have thought of treating you otherwise until – until these *circumstances* came to light. And I shall beg my lord to despatch you as quick as possible: and will go on with Frank's learning as well as I can, (I owe my father thanks for a little grounding, and you, I'm sure, for much that you have taught me), – and – and I wish you a good-night, Mr. Esmond.'

And with this she dropped a stately curtsey, and, taking her candle, went away through the tapestry door, which led to her apartments. Esmond stood by the fireplace, blankly staring after her. Indeed, he scarce seemed to see until she was gone; and then her image was impressed upon him, and remained forever fixed upon his memory. He saw her retreating, the taper lighting up her marble face, her scarlet lip quivering, and her shining golden hair. He went to his own room, and to bed, where he tried to read, as his custom was; but he never knew what he was reading until afterwards he remembered the appearance of the letters of the book (it was in Montaigne's Essays), and the events of the day passed before him – that is, of the last hour of the day; for as for the morning, and the poor milkmaid yonder, he never so much as once thought. And he could not get to sleep until daylight, and woke with a violent headache, and quite unrefreshed.

He had brought the contagion with him from the Three Castles sure enough, and was presently laid up with the smallpox, which spared the Hall no more than it did the cottage.

## Chapter 9

### I HAVE THE SMALL-POX, AND PREPARE TO LEAVE CASTLEWOOD

WHEN Harry Esmond passed through the crisis of that malady, and returned to health again, he found that little Frank Esmond had also suffered and rallied after the disease, and the lady his

mother was down with it, with a couple more of the household.
'It was a Providence, for which we all ought to be thankful,'
Doctor Tusher said, 'that my lady and her son were spared,
while Death carried off the poor domestics of the house'; and
rebuked Harry for asking, in his simple way for which we ought
to be thankful – that the servants were killed, or the gentlefolks
were saved? Nor could young Esmond agree in the Doctor's
vehement protestations to my lady, when he visited her during
her convalescence, that the malady had not in the least impaired
her charms, and had not been churl enough to injure the fair
features of the Viscountess of Castlewood, whereas in spite of
these fine speeches, Harry thought that her ladyship's beauty
was very much injured by the small-pox. When the marks of the
disease cleared away, they did not, it is true, leave furrows or
scars on her face (except one, perhaps, on her forehead over her
left eyebrow); but the delicacy of her rosy colour and complexion
were gone: her eyes had lost their brilliancy, her hair fell, and
her face looked older. It was as if a coarse hand had rubbed off
the delicate tints of that sweet picture, and brought it, as one has
seen unskilful painting-cleaners do, to the dead colour. Also, it
must be owned, that for a year or two after the malady, her ladyship's nose was swollen and redder.

There would be no need to mention these trivialities, but that
they actually influenced many lives, as trifles will in the world,
where a gnat often plays a greater part than an elephant, and a
mole-hill, as we know in King William's case, can upset an
empire.[1] When Tusher in his courtly way (at which Harry
Esmond always chafed and spoke scornfully) vowed and protested that my lady's face was none the worse – the lad broke
out and said, 'It *is* worse: and my mistress is not near so handsome as she was'; on which poor Lady Esmond gave a rueful
smile, and a look into a little Venice glass she had, which showed
her I suppose that what the stupid boy said was only too true,
for she turned away from the glass and her eyes filled with tears.

The sight of these in Esmond's heart always created a sort of
rage of pity, and seeing them on the face of the lady whom he
loved best, the young blunderer sank down on his knees, and
besought her to pardon him, saying that he was a fool and an

idiot, that he was a brute to make such a speech, he who had caused her malady, and Doctor Tusher told him that a bear he was indeed, and a bear he would remain, at which speech poor young Esmond was so dumb-stricken that he did not even growl.

'He is *my* bear, and I will not have him baited, Doctor,' my lady said, patting her hand kindly on the boy's head, as he was still kneeling at her feet. 'How your hair has come off! And mine, too,' she added with another sigh.

'It is not for myself that I cared,' my lady said to Harry, when the Parson had taken his leave; 'but *am* I very much changed? Alas! I fear 'tis too true.'

'Madam, you have the dearest, and kindest, and sweetest face in the world, I think,' the lad said; and indeed he thought and thinks so.

'Will my lord think so when he comes back?' the lady asked with a sigh, and another look at her Venice glass. 'Suppose he should think as you do, sir, that I am hideous – yes, you said hideous – he will cease to care for me. 'Tis all men care for in women, our little beauty. Why did he select me from among my sisters? 'Twas only for that. We reign but for a day or two: and be sure that Vashti knew Esther was coming.'

'Madam,' said Mr Esmond, 'Ahasuerus was the Grand Turk, and to change was the manner of his country, and according to his law.'

'You are all Grand Turks for that matter,' said my lady, 'or would be if you could. Come Frank, come my child. You are well, praised be Heaven. *Your* locks are not thinned by this dreadful small-pox: nor your poor face scarred – is it, my angel?'

Frank began to shout and whimper at the idea of such a misfortune. From the very earliest time the young lord had been taught to admire his beauty by his mother: and esteemed it as highly as any reigning toast valued hers.

One day, as he himself was recovering from his fever and illness, a pang of something like shame shot across young Esmond's breast, as he remembered that he had never once, during his illness, given a thought to the poor girl at the smithy, whose red cheeks but a month ago he had been so eager to see. Poor Nancy! her cheeks had shared the fate of roses, and were

withered now. She had taken the illness on the same day with
Esmond – she and her brother were both dead of the small-pox,
and buried under the Castlewood yew-trees. There was no
bright face looking now from the garden, or to cheer the old
smith at his lonely fireside. Esmond would have liked to have
kissed her in her shroud, (like the lass in Mr Prior's pretty
poem)[2]: but she rested many foot below the ground, when
Esmond after his malady first trod on it.

Doctor Tusher brought the news of this calamity, about which
Harry Esmond longed to ask, but did not like. He said almost
the whole village had been stricken with the pestilence; seventeen persons were dead of it, among them mentioning the names
of poor Nancy and her little brother. He did not fail to say how
thankful we survivors ought to be. It being this man's business
to flatter and make sermons, it must be owned he was most
industrious in it, and was doing the one or the other all day.

And so Nancy was gone; and Harry Esmond blushed that he
had not a single tear for her, and fell to composing an elegy in
Latin verses over the rustic little beauty. He bade the Dryads
mourn and the river-nymphs deplore her. As her father followed
the calling of Vulcan, he said that surely she was like a daughter
of Venus, though Sievewright's wife was an ugly shrew, as he
remembered to have heard afterwards. He made a long face, but,
in truth, felt scarcely more sorrowful than a mute at a funeral.
These first passions of men and women are mostly abortive; and
are dead almost before they are born. Esmond could repeat, to
his last day, some of the doggrel lines in which his muse be-
wailed his pretty lass; not without shame to remember how bad
the verses were, and how good he thought them; how false the
grief, and yet how he was rather proud of it. 'Tis an error, surely,
to talk of the simplicity of youth. I think no persons are more
hypocritical, and have a more affected behaviour to one another,
than the young. They deceive themselves and each other with
artifices that do not impose upon men of the world; and so we
get to understand truth better, and grow simpler as we grow older.

When my lady heard of the fate which had befallen poor
Nancy, she said nothing so long as Tusher was by, but when he
was gone, she took Harry Esmond's hand and said—

'Harry, I beg your pardon for those cruel words I used on the night you were taken ill. I am shocked at the fate of the poor creature, and am sure that nothing had happened of that with which, in my anger, I charged you. And the very first day we go out, you must take me to the blacksmith, and we must see if there is anything I can do to console the poor old man. Poor man! to lose both his children! What should I do without mine!'

And this was, indeed, the very first walk which my lady took, leaning on Esmond's arm, after her illness. But her visit brought no consolation to the old father; and he showed no softness, or desire to speak. 'The Lord gave and took away,' he said; and he knew what His servant's duty was. He wanted for nothing – less now than ever before, as there were fewer mouths to feed. He wished her ladyship and Master Esmond good-morning – he had grown tall in his illness, and was but very little marked; and with this, and a surly bow, he went in from the smithy to the house, leaving my lady, somewhat silenced and shamefaced, at the door. He had a handsome stone put up for his two children, which may be seen in Castlewood churchyard to this very day; and before a year was out his own name was upon the stone. In the presence of Death, that sovereign ruler, a woman's coquetry is scared; and her jealousy will hardly pass the boundaries of that grim kingdom. 'Tis entirely of the earth, that passion, and expires in the cold blue air, beyond our sphere.

At length, when the danger was quite over, it was announced that my lord and his daughter would return. Esmond well remembered the day. The lady, his mistress, was in a flurry of fear: before my lord came, she went into her room, and returned from it with reddened cheeks. Her fate was about to be decided. Her beauty was gone – was her reign, too, over? A minute would say. My lord came riding over the bridge – he could be seen from the great window, clad in scarlet, and mounted on his grey hackney – his little daughter ambled by him in a bright riding-dress of blue, on a shining chestnut horse. My lady leaned against the great mantelpiece, looking on, with one hand on her heart – she seemed only the more pale for those red marks on either cheek. She put her handkerchief to her eyes, and withdrew it, laughing hysterically – the cloth was quite red with the rouge

when she took it away. She ran to her room again, and came back
with pale cheeks and red eyes – her son in her hand – just as my
lord entered, accompanied by young Esmond, who had gone out
to meet his protector, and to hold his stirrup as he descended
from horseback.

'What, Harry, boy!' my lord said, good-naturedly, 'you
look as gaunt as a greyhound. The small-pox hasn't improved
your beauty, and your side of the house hadn't ever too much of
it – ho, ho!'

And he laughed, and sprang to the ground with no small
agility, looking handsome and red, with a jolly face and
brown hair, like a beef-eater; Esmond kneeling again, as soon as
his patron had descended, performed his homage, and then went
to greet the little Beatrix, and help her from her horse.

'Fie! how yellow you look,' she said; 'and there are one, two,
red holes in your face'; which, indeed, was very true; Harry
Esmond's harsh countenance bearing, as long as it continued to
be a human face, the marks of the disease.

My lord laughed again, in high good-humour.

'D—— it!' said he, with one of his usual oaths, 'the little slut
sees everything. She saw the Dowager's paint t'other day, and
asked her why she wore that red stuff – didn't you, Trix? and
the Tower; and St. James's; and the play; and the Prince
George, and the Princess Anne – didn't you, Trix?'

'They are both very fat, and smelt of brandy,'[3] the child said.
Papa roared with laughing.

'Brandy!' he said. 'And how do you know, Miss Pert?'

'Because your lordship smells of it after supper, when I embrace you before I go to bed,' said the young lady, who, indeed,
was as pert as her father said, and looked as beautiful a little
gipsy as eyes ever gazed on.

'And now for my lady,' said my lord, going up the stairs, and
passing under the tapestry curtain that hung before the drawing-
room door. Esmond remembered that noble figure handsomely
arrayed in scarlet. Within the last few months he himself had
grown from a boy to be a man, and with his figure, his thoughts
had shot up, and grown manly.

My lady's countenance, of which Harry Esmond was accustomed to watch the changes, and with a solicitous affection to note and interpret the signs of gladness or care, wore a sad and depressed look for many weeks after her lord's return: during which it seemed as if, by caresses and entreaties, she strove to win him back from some ill-humour he had, and which he did not choose to throw off. In her eagerness to please him she practised a hundred of those arts which had formerly charmed him, but which seemed now to have lost their potency. Her songs did not amuse him; and she hushed them and the children when in his presence. My lord sat silent at his dinner, drinking greatly, his lady opposite to him, looking furtively at his face, though also speechless. Her silence annoyed him as much as her speech; and he would peevishly, and with an oath, ask her why she held her tongue and looked so glum, or he would roughly check her when speaking, and bid her not talk nonsense. It seemed as if, since his return, nothing she could do or say could please him.

When a master and mistress are at strife in a house, the subordinates in the family take the one side or the other. Harry Esmond stood in so great fear of my lord, that he would run a league barefoot to do a message for him; but his attachment for Lady Esmond was such a passion of grateful regard, that to spare her a grief, or to do her a service, he would have given his life daily: and it was by the very depth and intensity of this regard that he began to divine how unhappy his adored lady's life was, and that a secret care (for she never spoke of her anxieties) was weighing upon her.

Can anyone, who has passed through the world and watched the nature of men and women there, doubt what had befallen her? I have seen, to be sure, some people carry down with them into old age the actual bloom of their youthful love, and I know that Mr Thomas Parr[4] lived to be a hundred and sixty years old. But, for all that, threescore and ten is the age of men, and few get beyond it; and 'tis certain that a man who marries for mere *beaux yeux*, as my lord did, considers his part of the contract at end when the woman ceases to fulfil hers, and his love does not survive her beauty. I know 'tis often otherwise, I say; and can think (as most men in their own experience may) of many a house, where, lighted in early years, the sainted lamp of love hath never been extinguished; but so there is Mr Parr, and so there is the great giant at the fair that is eight feet high – exceptions to men – and that poor lamp whereof I speak, that lights at first the nuptial chamber, is extinguished by a hundred winds and draughts down the chimney, or sputters out for want of feeding. And then – and then it is Chloe, in the dark, stark awake, and Strephon snoring unheeding; or *vice versâ*, 'tis poor Strephon that has married a heartless jilt, and awoke out of that absurd vision of conjugal felicity, which was to last for ever, and is over like any other dream. One and other has made his bed, and so must lie in it, until that final day when life ends, and they sleep separate.

About this time young Esmond, who had a knack of stringing verses, turned some of Ovid's epistles[5] into rhymes, and brought them to his lady for her delectation. Those which treated of forsaken women touched her immensely, Harry remarked; and when Œnone called after Paris, and Medea bade Jason come back again, the lady of Castlewood sighed, and said she thought that part of the verses was the most pleasing. Indeed, she would have chopped up the Dean,[6] her old father, in order to bring her husband back again. But her beautiful Jason was gone, as beautiful Jasons will go, and the poor enchantress had never a spell to keep him.

My lord was only sulky as long as his wife's anxious face or behaviour seemed to upbraid him. When she had got to master these, and to show an outwardly cheerful countenance and behaviour, her husband's good-humour returned partially, and he swore and stormed no longer at dinner, but laughed sometimes, and yawned unrestrainedly; absenting himself often from home, inviting more company thither, passing the greater part of his days in the hunting-field, or over the bottle as before; but, with this difference, that the poor wife could no longer see now, as she had done formerly, the light of love kindled in his eyes. He was with her, but that flame was out; and that once welcome beacon no more shone there.

What were this lady's feelings when forced to admit the truth whereof her foreboding glass had given her only too true warning, that with her beauty her reign had ended, and the days of her love were over? What does a seaman do in a storm if mast and rudder are carried away? He ships a jurymast and steers as he best can with an oar. What happens if your roof falls in a tempest? After the first stun of the calamity the sufferer starts up, gropes around to see that the children are safe, and puts them under a shed out of the rain. If the palace burns down, you take shelter in the barn. What man's life is not overtaken by one or more of these tornadoes that send us out of the course, and fling us on rocks to shelter as best we may?

When Lady Castlewood found that her great ship had gone down, she began as best she might, after she had rallied from the effects of the loss, to put out small ventures of happiness; and hope for little gains and returns, as a merchant on 'Change,[7] *indocilis pauperiem pati*,[8] having lost his thousands, embarks a few guineas upon the next ship. She laid out her all upon her children, indulging them beyond all measure, as was inevitable with one of her kindness of disposition; giving all her thoughts to their welfare – learning, that she might teach them, and improving her own many natural gifts and feminine accomplishments, that she might impart them to her young ones. To be doing good for some one else, is the life of most good women. They are exuberant of kindness, as it were, and must impart it to some one. She made herself a good scholar of French, Italian, and Latin, having been grounded in these by her father in her youth: hiding these gifts from her husband out of fear, perhaps, that they should offend him, for my lord was no bookman – pish'd and psha'd at the notion of learned ladies, and would have been angry that his wife could construe out of a Latin book of which he could scarce understand two words. Young Esmond was usher, or house tutor, under her or over her, as it might happen. During my lord's many absences, these school-days would go on uninterruptedly: the mother and daughter learning with surprising quickness; the latter by fits and starts only, and as suited her wayward humour. As for the little lord, it must be owned that he took after his father in the matter of learning – liked marbles and play, and the great horse, and the little one which his father brought him, and on which he took him out a-hunting – a great deal better than Corderius and Lily,[9] marshalled the village boys, and had a little court of them, already flogging them, and domineering over them with a fine imperious spirit, that made his father laugh when he beheld it, and his mother fondly warn him. The cook had a son, the wood-man had two, the big lad at the porter's lodge took his cuffs and his orders. Doctor Tusher said he was a young nobleman of gallant spirit; and Harry Esmond, who was his tutor, and eight years his little lordship's senior, had hard work sometimes to keep his own temper, and hold his authority over his rebellious little chief and kinsman.

In a couple of years after that calamity had befallen which had robbed Lady Castlewood of a little – a very little – of her beauty, and her careless husband's heart (if the truth must be told, my lady had found not only that her reign was over, but that her successor was appointed, a Princess of a noble house in Drury Lane somewhere, who was installed and visited by my lord at the town eight miles off – *pudet hæc opprobria dicere nobis*),[10] a great change had taken place in her mind, which, by struggles only known to herself, at least never mentioned to any one, and unsuspected by the person who caused the pain she endured – had been schooled into such a condition as she could not very likely have imagined possible a score of months since, before her misfortunes had begun.

She had oldened in that time as people do who suffer silently great mental pain; and learned much that she had never sus-pected before. She was taught by that bitter teacher Misfortune. A child, the mother of other children, but two years back her lord was a God to her; his words her law; his smile her sunshine; his lazy commonplaces listened to eagerly, as if they were words of wisdom – all his wishes and freaks obeyed with a servile devotion. She had been my lord's chief slave and blind wor-shipper. Some women bear farther than this, and submit not only to neglect but to unfaithfulness too – but here this lady's allegiance had failed her. Her spirit rebelled and disowned any more obedience. First she had to bear in secret the passion of losing the adored object; then to get a farther initiation, and to find this worshipped being was but a clumsy idol: then to admit the silent truth, that it was she was superior, and not the monarch her master: that she had thoughts which his brains could never master, and was the better of the two; quite separate from my lord although tied to him, and bound as almost all people (save a very happy few) to work all her life alone. My lord sat in his chair, laughing his laugh, cracking his joke, his face flushing with wine – my lady in her place over against him – he never suspecting that his superior was there, in the calm resigned lady, cold of manner, with downcast eyes. When he was merry in his cups, he would make jokes about her coldness, and, 'D—— it, now my lady is gone, we will have t'other bottle,' he would say. He was frank enough in telling his thoughts, such as they were. There was little mystery about my lord's words or actions. His fair Rosamond did not live in a labyrinth, like the lady of Mr Addison's opera,[11] but paraded with painted cheeks and a tipsy retinue in the country town. Had she a mind to be revenged, Lady Castlewood could have found the way to her rival's house easily enough; and, if she had come with bowl and dagger, would have been routed off the ground by the enemy with a volley of Billingsgate,[12] which the fair person always kept by her.

Meanwhile, it has been said, that for Harry Esmond his bene-factress's sweet face had lost none of its charms. It had always the kindest of looks and smiles for him – smiles, not so gay and artless perhaps as those which Lady Castlewood had formerly worn, when, a child herself, playing with her children, her husband's pleasure and authority were all she thought of; but out of her griefs and cares, as will happen I think when these trials fall upon a kindly heart, and are not too unbearable, grew up a number of thoughts and excellences which had never come into existence, had not her sorrow and misfortunes engendered them. Sure, occasion is the father of most that is good in us: As you have seen the awkward fingers and clumsy tools of a prisoner cut and fashion the most delicate little pieces of carved work; or achieve the most prodigious underground labours, and cut through walls of masonry, and saw iron bars and fetters; 'tis misfortune that awakens ingenuity, or fortitude, or endurance, in hearts where these qualities had never come to life but for the circumstance which gave them a being.

''Twas after Jason left her, no doubt,' Lady Castlewood once said with one of her smiles to young Esmond (who was reading to her a version of certain lines out of Euripides), 'that Medea became a learned woman and a great enchantress.'

'And she could conjure the stars out of Heaven,' the young tutor added, 'but she could not bring Jason back again.'

'What do you mean?' asked my lady, very angry.

'Indeed I mean nothing,' said the other, 'save what I've read in books. What should I know about such matters? I have seen no woman save you and little Beatrix, and the Parson's wife and my late mistress, and your ladyship's woman here.'

'The men who wrote your books,' says my lady, 'your Horaces, and Ovids, and Virgils, as far as I know of them, all thought ill of us, as all the heroes they wrote about used us basely. We were bred to be slaves always; and even of our own times, as you are still the only lawgivers, I think our sermons seem to say that the best woman is she who bears her master's chains most gracefully. 'Tis a pity there are no nunneries permitted by our church: Beatrix and I would fly to one, and end our days in peace there away from you.'

'And is there no slavery in a convent?' says Esmond.

'At least if women are slaves there, no one sees them,' answered the lady. 'They don't work in street-gangs with the public to jeer them: and if they suffer, suffer in private. Here comes my lord home from hunting. Take away the books. My lord does not love to see them. Lessons are over for to-day, Mr Tutor.' And with a curtsey and a smile she would end this sort of colloquy.

Indeed 'Mr Tutor', as my lady called Esmond, had now business enough on his hands in Castlewood House. He had three pupils, his lady and her two children, at whose lessons she would always be present; besides writing my lord's letters, and arranging his accompts for him – when these could be got from Esmond's indolent patron.

Of the pupils the two young people were but lazy scholars, and as my lady would admit no discipline such as was then in use, my lord's son only learned what he liked, which was but little, and never to his life's end could be got to construe more than six lines of Virgil. Mistress Beatrix chattered French prettily from a very early age; and sang sweetly, but this was from her mother's teaching – not Harry Esmond's, who could scarce distinguish between Green Sleeves and Lillabullero; although he had no greater delight in life than to hear the ladies sing. He sees them now, (will he ever forget them?) as they used to sit together of the summer evenings – the two golden heads over the page – the child's little hand and the mother's beating the time, with their voices rising and falling in unison.

But if the children were careless, 'twas a wonder how eagerly the mother learned from her young tutor – and taught him too. The happiest instinctive faculty was this lady's – a faculty for discerning latent beauties and hidden graces of books, especially books of poetry, as in a walk she would spy out field-flowers and make posies of them, such as no other hand could. She was a critic not by reason but by feeling; the sweetest commentator of those books they read together; and the happiest hours of young Esmond's life, perhaps, were those past in the company of this kind mistress and her children.

These happy days were to end soon, however; and it was by the Lady Castlewood's own decree that they were brought to a conclusion. It happened about Christmas-time, Harry Esmond being now past sixteen years of age, that his old comrade, adversary, and friend, Tom Tusher, returned from his school in London, a fair, well-grown, and sturdy lad, who was about to enter college, with an exhibition from his school, and a prospect of after promotion in the Church. Tom Tusher's talk was of nothing but Cambridge, now; and the boys, who were good friends, examined each other eagerly about their progress in books. Tom had learned some Greek and Hebrew, besides Latin, in which he was pretty well skilled, and also had given himself to mathematical studies under his father's guidance, who was a proficient in those sciences, of which Esmond knew nothing, nor could he write Latin so well as Tom, though he could talk it better, having been taught by his dear friend the Jesuit Father, for whose memory the lad ever retained the warmest affection, reading his books, keeping his swords clean in the little crypt where the Father had shown them to Esmond on the night of his visit; and often of a night sitting in the Chaplain's room, which he inhabited, over his books, his verses, and rubbish, with which the lad occupied himself, he would look up at the window, thinking he wished it might open and let in the good Father. He had come and passed away like a dream; but for the swords and books Harry might almost think the Father was an imagination of his mind – and for two letters which had come to him, one from abroad full of advice and affection, another soon after he had been confirmed by the Bishop of Hexton, in which Father Holt deplored his falling away. But Harry Esmond felt so confident now of his being in the right, and of his own powers as a casuist, that he thought he was able to face the Father himself in argument, and possibly convert him.

To work upon the faith of her young pupil, Esmond's kind mistress sent to the library of her father the Dean, who had been distinguished in the disputes of the late King's reign; and, an old soldier now, had hung up his weapons of controversy. These he took down from his shelves willingly for young Esmond, whom he benefited by his own personal advice and instruction. It did not require much persuasion to induce the boy to worship with his beloved mistress. And the good old nonjuring Dean flattered himself with a conversion which in truth was owing to a much gentler and fairer persuader.

Under her ladyship's kind eyes (my lord's being sealed in sleep pretty generally), Esmond read many volumes of the works of the famous British divines of the last age,[13] and was familiar with Wake and Sherlock, with Stillingfleet and Patrick. His mistress never tired to listen or to read, to pursue the text with fond comments, to urge those points which her fancy dwelt on most, or her reason deemed most important. Since the death of her father, the Dean, this lady hath admitted a certain latitude of theological reading, which her orthodox father would never have allowed; his favourite writers appealing more to reason and antiquity than to the passions or imaginations of their readers, so that the works of Bishop Taylor, nay, those of Mr Baxter and Mr Law, have in reality found more favour with my Lady Castlewood than the severer volumes of our great English schoolmen.

In later life, at the University, Esmond re-opened the controversy, and pursued it in a very different manner, when his patrons had determined for him that he was to embrace the ecclesiastical life. But though his mistress's heart was in this calling, his own never was much. After that first fervour of simple devotion, which his beloved Jesuit priest had inspired in him, speculative theology took but little hold upon the young man's mind. When his early credulity was disturbed, and his saints and virgins taken out of his worship, to rank little higher than the divinities of Olympus, his belief became acquiescence rather than ardour; and he made his mind up to assume the cassock and bands, as another man does to wear a breast-plate and jack-boots, or to mount a merchant's desk for a livelihood, and from obedience and necessity, rather than from choice. There were scores of such men in Mr Esmond's time at the universities, who were going to the Church with no better calling than his.

When Thomas Tusher was gone, a feeling of no small depression and disquiet fell upon young Esmond, of which, though he did not complain, his kind mistress must have divined the cause: for soon after she showed not only that she understood the reason of Harry's melancholy, but could provide a remedy for it. Her habit was thus to watch, unobservedly, those to whom duty or affection bound her, and to prevent their designs, or to fulfil them, when she had the power. It was this lady's disposition to think kindnesses, and devise silent bounties, and to scheme benevolence for those about her. We take such goodness, for the most part, as if it was our due; the Marys who bring ointment for our feet get but little thanks. Some of us never feel this devotion at all, or are moved by it to gratitude or acknowledgment; others only recall it years after, when the days are past in which those sweet kindnesses were spent on us, and we offer back our return for the debt by a poor tardy payment of tears. Then forgotten tones of love recur to us, and kind glances shine out of the past – O so bright and clear! – O so longed after! – because they are out of reach; as holiday music from withinside a prison wall – or sunshine seen through the bars; more prized because unattainable – more bright because of the contrast of present darkness and solitude, whence there is no escape.

All the notice, then, which Lady Castlewood seemed to take of Harry Esmond's melancholy, upon Tom Tusher's departure, was, by a gaiety unusual to her, to attempt to dispel his gloom. She made his three scholars (herself being the chief one) more cheerful than ever they had been before, and more docile too, all of them learning and reading much more than they had been accustomed to do. 'For who knows,' said the lady, 'what may happen, and whether we may be able to keep such a learned tutor long?'

Frank Esmond said he for his part did not want to learn any more, and cousin Harry might shut up his book whenever he liked, if he would come out a-fishing; and little Beatrix declared she would send for Tom Tusher, and *he* would be glad enough to come to Castlewood, if Harry chose to go away.

At last comes a messenger from Winchester one day, bearer of a letter with a great black seal from the Dean there, to say that his sister was dead, and had left her fortune of £2000 among her six nieces, the Dean's daughters; and many a time since has Harry Esmond recalled the flushed face and eager look where-with, after this intelligence, his kind lady regarded him. She did not pretend to any grief about the deceased relative, from whom she and her family had been many years parted.

When my lord heard of the news, he also did not make any very long face. 'The money will come very handy to furnish the music-room and the cellar, which is getting low, and buy your ladyship a coach and a couple of horses that will do indifferent to ride or for the coach. And Beatrix, you shall have a spinnet: and Frank, you shall have a little horse from Hexton Fair; and Harry, you shall have five pounds to buy some books,' said my lord, who was generous with his own, and indeed with other folks' money. 'I wish your aunt would die once a year, Rachel; we could spend your money, and all your sisters', too.'

'I have but one aunt – and – and I have another use for the money, my lord,' says my lady, turning very red.

'Another use, my dear; and what do you know about money?' cries my lord. 'And what the devil is there that I don't give you which you want?'

'I intend to give this money – can't you fancy how, my lord?'

My lord swore one of his large oaths that he did not know in the least what she meant.

'I intend it for Harry Esmond to go to college – Cousin Harry,' says my lady, 'you mustn't stay longer in this dull place, but make a name to yourself, and for us too, Harry.'

'D——n it, Harry's well enough here,' says my lord, for a moment looking rather sulky.

'Is Harry going away? You don't mean to say you will go away?' cry out Frank and Beatrix at one breath.

'But he will come back: and this will always be his home,' cries my lady, with blue eyes looking a celestial kindness; 'and his scholars will always love him; won't they?'

'By G——d, Rachel, you're a good woman!' says my lord, seizing my lady's hand, at which she blushed very much, and shrank back, putting her children before her. 'I wish you joy, my kinsman,' he continued, giving Harry Esmond a hearty slap on the shoulder. 'I won't baulk your luck. Go to Cambridge, boy; and when Tusher dies you shall have the living here, if you are not better provided by that time. We'll furnish the dining-room and buy the horses another year. I'll give thee a nag out of the stable: take any one except my hack and the bay gelding and the coach-horses; and God speed thee, my boy!'

'Have the sorrel, Harry; 'tis a good one. Father says 'tis the best in the stable,' says little Frank, clapping his hands, and jumping up. 'Let's come and see him in the stable.' And the other, in his delight and eagerness, was for leaving the room that instant to arrange about his journey.

The Lady Castlewood looked after him with sad penetrating glances. 'He wishes to be gone already, my lord,' said she to her husband.

The young man hung back abashed. 'Indeed, I would stay for ever if your ladyship bade me,' he said.

'And thou wouldst be a fool for thy pains, kinsman,' said my lord. 'Tut, tut, man. Go and see the world. Sow thy wild oats; and take the best luck that Fate sends thee. I wish I were a boy again that I might go to college, and taste the Trumpington ale.'

'Ours, indeed, is but a dull home,' cries my lady, with a little of sadness, and may be of satire, in her voice: 'an old glum house, half ruined, and the rest only half furnished; a woman and two children are but poor company for men that are accustomed to better. We are only fit to be your worship's hand-maids, and your pleasures must of necessity lie elsewhere than at home.'

'Curse me, Rachel, if I know now whether thou art in earnest or not,' said my lord.

'In earnest, my lord!' says she, still clinging by one of her children. 'Is there much subject here for joke?' And she made him a grand curtsey, and, giving a stately look to Harry Esmond, which seemed to say, 'Remember; you understand me, though he does not,' she left the room with her children.

'Since she found out that confounded Hexton business,' my lord said – 'and be hanged to them that told her! – she has not been the same woman. She, who used to be as humble as a milk-maid, is as proud as a princess,' says my lord. 'Take my counsel, Harry Esmond, and keep clear of women. Since I have had any-thing to do with the jades, they have given me nothing but disgust. I had a wife at Tangier, with whom, as she couldn't speak a word of my language, you'd have thought I might lead a quiet life. But she tried to poison me, because she was jealous of a Jew girl. There was your aunt, for aunt she is – Aunt Jezebel, a pretty life your father led with *her*, and here's my lady. When I saw her on a pillion riding behind the Dean her father, she looked and was such a baby, that a sixpenny doll might have pleased her. And now you see what she is – hands off, highty-tighty, high and mighty, an empress couldn't be grander. Pass us the tankard, Harry, my boy. A mug of beer and a toast at morn, says my host. A toast and a mug of beer at noon, says my dear. D——n it, Polly loves a mug of ale, too, and laced with brandy, by Jove!' Indeed, I suppose they drank it together; for my lord was often thick in his speech at mid-day dinner; and at night at supper, speechless altogether.

Harry Esmond's departure resolved upon, it seemed as if the Lady Castlewood, too, rejoiced to lose him; for more than once, when the lad, ashamed perhaps at his own secret eagerness to go away (at any rate stricken with sadness at the idea of leaving those from whom he had received so many proofs of love and kindness inestimable), tried to express to his mistress his sense of gratitude to her, and his sorrow at quitting those who had so sheltered and tended a nameless and houseless orphan, Lady Castlewood cut short his protests of love and his lamentations, and would hear of no grief, but only look forward to Harry's fame and prospects in life. 'Our little legacy will keep you for four years like a gentleman. Heaven's Providence, your own genius, industry, honour, must do the rest for you. Castlewood will always be a home for you; and these children, whom you have taught and loved, will not forget to love you. And Harry,' said she (and this was the only time when she spoke with a tear in her eye, or a tremor in her voice), 'it may happen in the course of nature that I shall be called away from them: and their father – and – and they will need true friends and protectors. Promise me that you will be true to them – as – as I think I have been to you – and a mother's fond prayer and blessing go with you.'

'So help me God, madam, I will,' said Harry Esmond, falling on his knees, and kissing the hand of his dearest mistress. 'If you will have me stay now, I will. What matters whether or no I make my way in life, or whether a poor bastard dies as unknown as he is now? 'Tis enough that I have your love and kindness surely; and to make you happy is duty enough for me.'

'Happy!' says she; 'but indeed I ought to be, with my children, and——'

'Not happy!' cried Esmond (for he knew what her life was, though he and his mistress never spoke a word concerning it). 'If not happiness, it may be ease. Let me stay and work for you – let me stay and be your servant.'

'Indeed, you are best away,' said my lady, laughing, as she put her hand on the boy's head for a moment. 'You shall stay in no such dull place. You shall go to college and distinguish yourself as becomes your name. That is how you shall please me best; and – and if my children want you, or I want you, you shall come to us; and I know we may count on you.'

'May Heaven forsake me if you may not,' Harry said, getting up from his knee.

'And my knight longs for a dragon this instant that he may fight,' said my lady, laughing; which speech made Harry Esmond start, and turn red; for indeed the very thought was in his mind, that he would like that some chance should immediately happen whereby he might show his devotion. And it pleased him to think that his lady had called him 'her knight,' and often and often he recalled this to his mind, and prayed that he might be her true knight, too.

My lady's bed-chamber window looked out over the country, and you could see from it the purple hills beyond Castlewood village, the green common betwixt that and the Hall, and the old bridge which crossed over the river. When Harry Esmond went away for Cambridge, little Frank ran alongside his horse as far as the bridge, and there Harry stopped for a moment, and looked back at the house where the best part of his life had been past. It lay before him with its grey familiar towers, a pinnacle or two shining in the sun, the buttresses and terrace walls casting great blue shades on the grass. And Harry remembered all his life after how he saw his mistress at the window looking out on him, in a white robe, the little Beatrix's chestnut curls resting at her mother's side. Both waved a farewell to him, and little Frank sobbed to leave him. Yes, he *would* be his lady's true knight, he vowed in his heart; he waved her an adieu with his hat. The village people had good-bye to say to him too. All knew that Master Harry was going to college, and most of them had a kind word and a look of farewell. I do not stop to say what adventures he began to imagine, or what career to devise for himself, before he had ridden three miles from home. He had not read Monsieur Galland's ingenious Arabian tales[14] as yet; but be sure that there are other folks who build castles in the air, and have fine hopes, and kick them down too, besides honest Alnaschar.

## Chapter 10

# I GO TO CAMBRIDGE, AND DO BUT
# LITTLE GOOD THERE

MY lord, who said he should like to revisit the old haunts of his youth, kindly accompanied Harry Esmond in his first journey to Cambridge. Their road lay through London, where my Lord Viscount would also have Harry stay a few days to show him the pleasures of the town, before he entered upon his university studies, and whilst here Harry's patron conducted the young man to my Lady Dowager's house at Chelsey near London: the kind lady at Castlewood having specially ordered that the young gentleman and the old should pay a respectful visit in that quarter.

Her ladyship the Viscountess Dowager occupied a handsome new house in Chelsey, with a garden behind it, and facing the river, always a bright and animated sight with its swarms of sailors, barges, and wherries. Harry laughed at recognising in the parlour the well-remembered old piece of Sir Peter Lely, wherein his father's widow was represented as a virgin huntress, armed with a gilt bow and arrow, and encumbered only with that small quantity of drapery which it would seem the virgins in King Charles's day were accustomed to wear.

My Lady Dowager had left off this peculiar habit of huntress when she married. But though she was now considerably past sixty years of age, I believe she thought that airy nymph of the picture could still be easily recognised in the venerable personage who gave an audience to Harry and his patron.

She received the young man with even more favour than she showed to the elder, for she chose to carry on the conversation in French, in which my Lord Castlewood was no great proficient, and expressed her satisfaction at finding that Mr Esmond could speak fluently in that language. ' 'Twas the only one fit for polite conversation,' she condescended to say, 'and suitable to persons of high breeding.'

My lord laughed afterwards, as the gentlemen went away,

at his kinswoman's behaviour. He said he remembered the time when she could speak English fast enough, and joked in his jolly way at the loss he had had of such a lovely wife as that.

My Lady Viscountess deigned to ask his lordship news of his wife and children; she had heard that Lady Castlewood had had the small-pox; she hoped she was not so *very* much disfigured as people said.

At this remark about his wife's malady, my Lord Viscount winced and turned red; but the Dowager, in speaking of the disfigurement of the young lady, turned to her looking-glass and examined her old wrinkled countenance in it with such a grin of satisfaction, that it was all her guests could do to refrain from laughing in her ancient face.

She asked Harry what his profession was to be; and my lord, saying that the lad was to take orders, and have the living of Castlewood when old Doctor Tusher vacated it; she did not seem to show any particular anger at the notion of Harry's becoming a Church of England clergyman, nay, was rather glad than otherwise, that the youth should be so provided for. She bade Mr Esmond not to forget to pay her a visit whenever he passed through London, and carried her graciousness so far as to send a purse with twenty guineas for him, to the tavern at which my lord put up (the Greyhound, in Charing Cross); and, along with this welcome gift for her kinsman, she sent a little doll for a present to my lord's little daughter Beatrix, who was growing beyond the age of dolls by this time, and was as tall almost as her venerable relative.

After seeing the town, and going to the plays, my Lord Castlewood and Esmond rode together to Cambridge, spending two pleasant days upon the journey. Those rapid new coaches were not established as yet, that performed the whole journey between London and the University in a single day; however, the road was pleasant and short enough to Harry Esmond, and he always gratefully remembered that happy holiday, which his kind patron gave him.

Mr Esmond was entered a pensioner of Trinity College in Cambridge, to which famous college my lord had also in his youth belonged. Doctor Montague[1] was master at this time, and

received my Lord Viscount with great politeness: so did Mr
Bridge, who was appointed to be Harry's tutor. Tom Tusher,
who was of Emmanuel College, and was by this time a junior
soph, came to wait upon my lord, and to take Harry under his
protection; and comfortable rooms being provided for him in
the great court close by the gate, and near to the famous Mr
Newton's[2] lodgings, Harry's patron took leave of him with
many kind words and blessings, and an admonition to him to
behave better at the University than my lord himself had ever
done.

'Tis needless in these memoirs to go at any length into the
particulars of Harry Esmond's college career. It was like that
of a hundred young gentlemen of that day. But he had the ill-
fortune to be older by a couple of years than most of his fellow-
students; and by his previous solitary mode of bringing up,
the circumstances of his life, and the peculiar thoughtfulness
and melancholy that had naturally engendered, he was, in a
great measure, cut off from the society of comrades who were
much younger and higher-spirited than he. His tutor, who had
bowed down to the ground, as he walked my lord over the
college grass-plats, changed his behaviour as soon as the
nobleman's back was turned, and was – at least Harry thought
so – harsh and overbearing. When the lads used to assemble in
their *grèges*[3] in hall, Harry found himself alone in the midst of
that little flock of boys; they raised a great laugh at him when
he was set on to read Latin, which he did with the foreign
pronunciation taught to him by his old master, the Jesuit, than
which he knew no other. Mr Bridge, the tutor, made him the
object of clumsy jokes, in which he was fond of indulging. The
young man's spirit was chafed, and his vanity mortified; and
he found himself, for some time, as lonely in this place as ever
he had been at Castlewood, whither he longed to return. His
birth was a source of shame to him, and he fancied a hundred
slights and sneers from young and old, who, no doubt, had
treated him better had he met them himself more frankly. And
as he looks back, in calmer days, upon this period of his life,
which he thought so unhappy, he can see that his own pride
and vanity caused no small part of the mortifications which he

attributed to others' ill-will. The world deals good-naturedly with good-natured people, and I never knew a sulky misanthropist who quarrelled with it, but it was he, and not it, that was in the wrong. Tom Tusher gave Harry plenty of good advice on this subject, for Tom had both good sense and good humour; but Mr Harry chose to treat his senior with a great deal of superfluous disdain and absurd scorn, and would by no means part from his darling injuries, in which, very likely, no man believed but himself. As for honest Doctor Bridge, the tutor found, after a few trials of wit with the pupil, that the younger man was an ugly subject for wit, and that the laugh was often turned against him. This did not make tutor and pupil any better friends; but had, so far, an advantage for Esmond, that Mr Bridge was induced to leave him alone; and so long as he kept his chapels, and did the college exercises required of him, Bridge was content not to see Harry's glum face in his class, and to leave him to read and sulk for himself in his own chamber.

A poem or two in Latin and English, which were pronounced to have some merit, and a Latin oration (for Mr Esmond could write that language better than pronounce it), got him a little reputation both with the authorities of the University and amongst the young men, with whom he began to pass for more than he was worth. A few victories over their common enemy Mr Bridge, made them incline towards him, and look upon him as the champion of their order against the seniors. Such of the lads as he took into his confidence, found him not so gloomy and haughty as his appearance led them to believe; and Don Dismallo, as he was called, became presently a person of some little importance in his college, and was, as he believes, set down by the seniors there as rather a dangerous character.

Don Dismallo was a stanch young Jacobite, like the rest of his family; gave himself many absurd airs of loyalty; used to invite young friends to Burgundy, and give the King's health on King James's birthday; wore black on the day of his abdication; fasted on the anniversary of King William's coronation; and performed a thousand absurd antics, of which he smiles now to think.

These follies caused many remonstrances on Tom Tusher's part, who was always a friend to the powers that be, as Esmond was always in opposition to them. Tom was a Whig, while Esmond was a Tory. Tom never missed a lecture, and capped the proctor with the profoundest of bows. No wonder he sighed over Harry's insubordinate courses, and was angry when the others laughed at him. But that Harry was known to have my Lord Viscount's protection, Tom no doubt would have broken, with him altogether. But honest Tom never gave up a comrade as long as he was the friend of a great man. This was not out of scheming on Tom's part, but a natural inclination towards the great. 'Twas no hypocrisy in him to flatter, but the bent of his mind, which was always perfectly good-humoured, obliging, and servile.

Harry had very liberal allowances, for his dear mistress of Castlewood not only regularly supplied him, but the Dowager at Chelsey made her donation annual, and received Esmond at her house near London every Christmas; but, in spite of these benefactions, Esmond was constantly poor; whilst 'twas a wonder with how small a stipend from his father, Tom Tusher contrived to make a good figure. 'Tis true that Harry both spent, gave, and lent his money very freely, which Thomas never did. I think he was like the famous Duke of Marlborough[4] in this instance, who, getting a present of fifty pieces, when a young man, from some foolish woman who fell in love with his good looks, showed the money to Cadogan in a drawer scores of years after, where it had lain ever since he had sold his beardless honour to procure it. I do not mean to say that Tom ever let out his good looks so profitably, for nature had not endowed him with any particular charms of person, and he ever was a pattern of moral behaviour, losing no opportunity of giving the very best advice to his younger comrade; with which article, to do him justice, he parted very freely. Not but that he was a merry fellow, too, in his way; he loved a joke, if by good fortune he understood it, and took his share generously of a bottle if another paid for it, and especially if there was a young lord in company to drink it. In these cases there was not a harder drinker in the University than Mr Tusher could be;

and it was edifying to behold him, fresh shaved and with smug face, singing out 'Amen!' at early chapel in the morning. In his reading, poor Harry permitted himself to go a-gadding after all the Nine Muses, and so very likely had but little favour from any one of them; whereas Tom Tusher, who had no more turn for poetry than a ploughboy, nevertheless, by a dogged perseverance and obsequiousness in courting the divine Calliope,[5] got himself a prize, and some credit in the University, and a fellowship at his college, as a reward for his scholarship. In this time of Mr Esmond's life, he got the little reading which he ever could boast of, and passed a good part of his days greedily devouring all the books on which he could lay hand. In this desultory way the works of most of the English, French, and Italian poets came under his eyes, and he had a smattering of the Spanish tongue likewise, besides the ancient languages, of which, at least of Latin, he was a tolerable master.

Then, about midway in his University career, he fell to reading for the profession to which worldly prudence rather than inclination called him, and was perfectly bewildered in theological controversy. In the course of his reading (which was neither pursued with that seriousness or that devout mind which such a study requires), the youth found himself, at the end of one month, a Papist, and was about to proclaim his faith; the next month a Protestant, with Chillingworth,[6] and the third a sceptic, with Hobbs[7] and Bayle.[8] Whereas honest Tom Tusher never permitted his mind to stray out of the prescribed University path, accepted the Thirty-nine Articles with all his heart, and would have signed and sworn to other nine-and-thirty with entire obedience. Harry's wilfulness in this matter, and disorderly thoughts and conversation, so shocked and afflicted his senior, that there grew up a coldness and estrangement between them, so that they became scarce more than mere acquaintances, from having been intimate friends when they came to college first. Politics ran high, too, at the University; and here, also, the young men were at variance. Tom professed himself, albeit a high churchman, a strong King William's-man; whereas Harry brought his family Tory politics to college with him, to which he must add a dangerous admiration for Oliver Cromwell, whose side, or King James's by turns, he often chose to take in the disputes which the young gentlemen used to hold in each other's rooms, where they debated on the state of the nation, crowned and deposed kings, and toasted past and present heroes or beauties in flagons of college ale.

Thus, either from the circumstances of his birth, or the natural melancholy of his disposition, Esmond came to live very much by himself during his stay at the University, having neither ambition enough to distinguish himself in the college career, nor caring to mingle with the mere pleasures and boyish frolics of the students, who were, for the most part, two or three years younger than he. He fancied that the gentlemen of the common room of his college slighted him on account of his birth, and hence kept aloof from their society. It may be that he made the ill-will, which he imagined came from them, by his own behaviour, which, as he looks back on it in after-life, he now sees was morose and haughty. At any rate, he was as tenderly grateful for kindness as he was susceptible of slight and wrong; and, lonely as he was generally, yet had one or two very warm friendships for his companions of those days.

One of these was a queer gentleman that resided in the University, though he was no member of it, and was the professor of a science scarce recognized in the common course of college education. This was a French refugee-officer, who had been driven out of his native country at the time of the Protestant persecutions there, and who came to Cambridge, where he taught the science of the small-sword, and set up a saloon-of-arms. Though he declared himself a Protestant, 'twas said Mr Moreau was a Jesuit in disguise; indeed, he brought very strong recommendations to the Tory party, which was pretty strong in that University, and very likely was one of the many agents whom King James had in this country. Esmond found this gentleman's conversation very much more agreeable, and to his taste, than the talk of the college divines in the common room; he never wearied of Moreau's stories of the wars of Turenne and Condé,[9] in which he had borne a part; and being familiar with the French tongue from his youth, and in a place

where but few spoke it, his company became very agreeable to
the brave old professor of arms, whose favourite pupil he was,
and who made Mr Esmond a very tolerable proficient in the
noble science of *escrime*.[10]

At the next term Esmond was to take his degree of Bachelor
of Arts, and afterwards, in proper season, to assume the cassock
and bands which his fond mistress would have him wear. Tom
Tusher himself was a parson and a fellow of his college by this
time; and Harry felt that he would very gladly cede his right
to the living of Castlewood to Tom, and that his own calling
was in no way the pulpit. But as he was bound, before all
things in the world, to his dear mistress at home, and knew
that a refusal on his part would grieve her, he determined to
give her no hint of his unwillingness to the clerical office; and
it was in this unsatisfactory mood of mind that he went to
spend the last vacation he should have at Castlewood before he
took orders.

## Chapter 11

### I COME HOME FOR A HOLIDAY TO
### CASTLEWOOD, AND FIND A SKELETON
### IN THE HOUSE

AT his third long vacation, Esmond came as usual to Castlewood, always feeling an eager thrill of pleasure when he found
himself once more in the house where he had passed so many
years, and beheld the kind familiar eyes of his mistress looking
upon him. She and her children (out of whose company she
scarce ever saw him) came to greet him. Miss Beatrix was
grown so tall that Harry did not quite know whether he might
kiss her or no; and she blushed and held back when he offered
that salutation, though she took it, and even courted it, when
they were alone. The young lord was shooting up to be like his
gallant father in look, though with his mother's kind eyes: the
Lady of Castlewood herself seemed grown, too, since Harry

saw her – in her look more stately, in her person fuller, in her face, still as ever most tender and friendly, a greater air of command and decision than had appeared in that guileless sweet countenance which Harry remembered so gratefully. The tone of her voice was so much deeper and sadder when she spoke and welcomed him, that it quite startled Esmond, who looked up at her surprised as she spoke, when she withdrew her eyes from him; nor did she ever look at him afterwards when his own eyes were gazing upon her. A something hinting at grief and secret, and filling his mind with alarm undefinable, seemed to speak with that low thrilling voice of hers, and look out of those clear sad eyes. Her greeting to Esmond was so cold that it almost pained the lad (who would have liked to fall on his knees and kiss the skirt of her robe, so fond and ardent was his respect and regard for her), and he faltered in answering the questions which she, hesitating on her side, began to put to him. Was he happy at Cambridge? Did he study too hard? She hoped not. He had grown very tall, and looked very well.

'He has got a moustache!' cries out Master Esmond.

'Why does he not wear a peruke like my Lord Mohun?' asked Miss Beatrix. 'My lord says that nobody wears their own hair.'

'I believe you will have to occupy your old chamber,' says my lady. 'I hope the housekeeper has got it ready.'

'Why, mamma, you have been there ten times these three days yourself!' exclaims Frank.

'And she cut some flowers which you planted in my garden – do you remember, ever so many years ago? – when I was quite a little girl,' cries out Miss Beatrix, on tiptoe. 'And mamma put them in your window.'

'I remember when you grew well after you were ill that you used to like roses,' said the lady, blushing like one of them. They all conducted Harry Esmond to his chamber; the children running before, Harry walking by his mistress hand-in-hand.

The old room had been ornamented and beautified not a little to receive him. The flowers were in the window in a china vase; and there was a fine new counterpane on the bed, which chatter-box Beatrix said mamma had made too. A fire was crackling on the hearth, although it was June. My lady thought the room wanted warming; everything was done to make him happy and welcome: 'And you are not to be a page any longer, but a gentleman and kinsman, and to walk with papa and mamma,' said the children. And as soon as his dear mistress and children had left him to himself, it was with a heart overflowing with love and gratefulness that he flung himself down on his knees by the side of the little bed, and asked a blessing upon those who were so kind to him.

The children, who are always house tell-tales, soon made him acquainted with the little history of the house and family. . Papa had been to London twice. Papa often went away now. Papa had taken Beatrix to Westlands, where she was taller than Sir George Harper's second daughter, though she was two years older. Papa had taken Beatrix and Frank both to Bellminster, where Frank had got the better of Lord Bellminster's son in a boxing-match – my lord, laughing, told Harry afterwards. Many gentlemen came to stop with papa, and papa had gotten a new game from London, a French game, called a billiard – that the French king played it very well: and the Dowager Lady Castlewood had sent Miss Beatrix a present; and papa had gotten a new chaise, with two little horses, which he drove himself, beside the coach, which mamma went in; and Doctor Tusher was a cross old plague, and they did not like to learn from him at all; and papa did not care about them learning, and laughed when they were at their books, but mamma liked them to learn, and taught them; and 'I don't think papa is fond of mamma,' said Miss Beatrix, with her great eyes. She had come quite close up to Harry Esmond by the time this prattle took place, and was on his knee, and had examined all the points of his dress, and all the good or bad features of his homely face.

'You shouldn't say that papa is not fond of mamma,' said the boy, at this confession. 'Mamma never said so; and mamma forbade you to say it, Miss Beatrix.'

'Twas this, no doubt, that accounted for the sadness in Lady Castlewood's eyes, and the plaintive vibrations of her voice. Who does not know of eyes, lighted by love once, where the flame shines no more? — of lamps extinguished, once properly trimmed and tended? Every man has such in his house. Such mementos make our splendidest chambers look blank and sad; such faces seen in a day cast a gloom upon our sunshine. So oaths mutually sworn, and invocations of Heaven, and priestly ceremonies, and fond belief, and love, so fond and faithful that it never doubted but that it should live forever, are all of no avail towards making love eternal: it dies, in spite of the banns and the priest; and I have often thought there should be a visitation of the sick for it, and a funeral service, and an extreme unction, and an *abi in pace*.[1] It has its course, like all mortal things — its beginnings, progress, and decay. It buds and it blooms out into sunshine, and it withers and ends. Strephon and Chloe languish apart; join in a rapture: and presently you hear that Chloe is crying, and Strephon has broken his crook across her back. Can you mend it so as to show no marks of rupture? Not all the priests of Hymen, not all the incantations to the gods, can make it whole!

Waking up from dreams, books, and visions of college honours, in which, for two years, Harry Esmond had been immersed, he found himself instantly, on his return home, in the midst of this actual tragedy of life, which absorbed and interested him more than all his tutor taught him. The persons whom he loved best in the world, and to whom he owed most, were living unhappily together. The gentlest and kindest of women was suffering ill-usage and shedding tears in secret: the man who made her wretched by neglect, if not by violence, was Harry's benefactor and patron. In houses where, in place of that sacred, inmost flame of love, there is discord at the centre, the whole household becomes hypocritical, and each lies to his neighbour. The husband (or it may be the wife) lies when the visitor comes in, and wears a grin of reconciliation before him. The wife lies (indeed, her business is to do that, and to smile, however much she is beaten), swallows her tears, and lies to her lord and master; lies in bidding little Jacky respect dear papa; lies in assuring grandpapa that she is perfectly happy. The servants lie, wearing grave faces behind their master's chair, and pretending to be unconscious of the fighting; and so, from morning till bed-time, life is passed in falsehood. And wiseacres call this a proper regard of morals, and point out Baucis and Philemon[2] as examples of a good life.

If my lady did not speak of her griefs to Harry Esmond, my lord was by no means reserved when in his cups, and spoke his mind very freely, bidding Harry in his coarse way, and with his blunt language, beware of all women as cheats, jades, jilts, and using other unmistakable monosyllables in speaking of them. Indeed, 'twas the fashion of the day as I must own; and there's not a writer of my time of any note, with the exception of poor Dick Steele, that does not speak of a woman as of a slave, and scorn and use her as such. Mr Pope, Mr Congreve,[3] Mr Addison, Mr Gay, every one of 'em, sing in this key, each according to his nature and politeness; and louder and fouler than all in abuse is Doctor Swift, who spoke of them as he treated them, worst of all.

Much of the quarrels and hatred which arise between married people come in my mind from the husband's rage and revolt at discovering that his slave and bedfellow, who is to minister to all his wishes, and is church-sworn to honour and obey him – is his superior; and that *he*, and not she, ought to be the subordinate of the twain; and in these controversies, I think, lay the cause of my lord's anger against his lady. When he left her, she began to think for herself, and her thoughts were not in his favour. After the illumination, when the love-lamp is put out that anon we spoke of, and by the common daylight we look at the picture, what a daub it looks! what a clumsy effigy! How many men and wives come to this knowledge, think you? And if it be painful to a woman to find herself mated for life to a boor, and ordered to love and honour a dullard; it is worse still for the man himself perhaps, whenever in his dim comprehension the idea dawns that his slave and drudge yonder is, in truth, his superior; that the woman who does his bidding, and submits to his humour, should be his lord; that she can think a thousand things beyond the power of his muddled brains; and that in yonder head, on the pillow opposite to him, lie a thousand feelings, mysteries of thought, latent scorns and rebellions, whereof he only dimly perceives the existence as they look out furtively from her eyes: treasures of love doomed to perish without a hand to gather them; sweet fancies and images of beauty that would grow and unfold themselves into flower; bright wit that would shine like diamonds could it be brought into the sun: and the tyrant in possession crushes the outbreak of all these, drives them back like slaves into the dungeon and darkness, and chafes without that his prisoner is rebellious, and his sworn subject undutiful and refractory. So the lamp was out in Castlewood Hall, and the lord and lady there saw each other as they were. With her illness and altered beauty my lord's fire for his wife disappeared; with his selfishness and faithlessness her foolish fiction of love and reverence was rent away. Love! – who is to love what is base and unlovely? Respect! – who is to respect what is gross and sensual? Not all the marriage oaths sworn before all the parsons, cardinals, ministers, muftis, and rabbins[4] in the world, can bind to that monstrous allegiance. This couple was living apart then; the woman happy to be allowed to love and tend her children (who were never of her own good-will away from her) and thankful to have saved such treasures as these out of the wreck in which the better part of her heart went down.

These young ones had had no instructors save their mother, and Doctor Tusher for their theology occasionally, and had made more progress than might have been expected under a tutor so indulgent and fond as Lady Castlewood. Beatrix could sing and dance like a nymph. Her voice was her father's delight after dinner. She ruled over the house with little imperial ways, which her parents coaxed and laughed at. She had long learned the value of her bright eyes, and tried experiments in coquetry, *in corpore vili*,[5] upon rustics and country squires, until she should prepare to conquer the world and the fashion. She put on a new ribbon to welcome Harry Esmond, made eyes at him, and directed her young smiles at him, not a little to the amusement of the young man, and the joy of her father, who laughed his great laugh, and encouraged her in her thousand antics. Lady Castlewood watched the child gravely and sadly: the little one was pert in her replies to her mother, yet eager in her protestations of love and promises of amendment; and as ready to cry (after a little quarrel brought on by her own giddiness) until she had won back her mamma's favour, as she was to risk the kind lady's displeasure by fresh outbreaks of restless vanity. From her mother's sad looks she fled to her father's chair and boozy laughter. She already set the one against the other: and the little rogue delighted in the mischief which she knew how to make so early.

The young heir of Castlewood was spoiled by father and mother both. He took their caresses as men do, and as if they were his right. He had his hawks and his spaniel dog, his little horse and his beagles. He had learned to ride and to drink, and to shoot flying: and he had a small court, the sons of the huntsman and woodman, as became the heir-apparent, taking after the example of my lord his father. If he had a headache, his mother was as much frightened as if the plague were in the house: my lord laughed and jeered in his abrupt way – (indeed, 'twas on the day after New Year's Day, and an excess of mince pie) – and said with some of his usual oaths – 'D——n it, Harry Esmond – you see how my lady takes on about Frank's megrim. She used to be sorry about me, my boy (pass the tankard, Harry), and to be frightened if I had a headache once. She don't care about my head now. They're like that – women are – all the same Harry, all jilts in their hearts. Stick to college – stick to punch and buttery ale: and never see a woman that's handsomer than an old cinder-faced bedmaker. That's my counsel.'

It was my lord's custom to fling out many jokes of this nature, in presence of his wife and children, at meals – clumsy sarcasms which my lady turned many a time, or which, sometimes, she affected not to hear, or which now and again would hit their mark and make the poor victim wince (as you could see by her flushing face and eyes filling with tears), or which again worked her up to anger and retort, when, in answer to one of these heavy bolts, she would flash back with a quivering reply. The pair were not happy; nor indeed was it happy to be with them. Alas that youthful love and truth should end in bitterness and bankruptcy! To see a young couple loving each other is no wonder; but to see an old couple loving each other is the best sight of all. Harry Esmond became the confidant of one and the other – that is, my lord told the lad all his griefs and wrongs (which were indeed of Lord Castlewood's own making), and Harry divined my lady's; his affection leading him easily to penetrate the hypocrisy under which Lady Castlewood generally chose to go disguised, and see her heart aching whilst her face wore a smile. 'Tis a hard task for women in life, that mask which the world bids them wear. But there is no greater crime than for a woman who is ill used and unhappy to show that she is so. The world is quite relentless about bidding her to keep a cheerful face; and our women, like the Malabar wives,⁶ are forced to go smiling and painted to sacrifice themselves with their husbands; their relations being the most eager to push them on to their duty, and, under their shouts and applauses, to smother and hush their cries of pain.

So, into the sad secret of his patron's household, Harry Esmond became initiated, he scarce knew how. It had passed under his eyes two years before, when he could not understand it; but reading, and thought, and experience of men, had oldened him; and one of the deepest sorrows of a life which had never, in truth, been very happy, came upon him now when he was compelled to understand and pity a grief which he stood quite powerless to relieve.

It hath been said my lord would never take the oath of allegiance, nor his seat as a peer of the kingdom of Ireland, where, indeed, he had but a nominal estate; and refused an English peerage which King William's government offered him as a bribe to secure his loyalty.

He might have accepted this, and would doubtless, but for the earnest remonstrances of his wife (who ruled her husband's opinions better than she could govern his conduct), and who being a simple-hearted woman, with but one rule of faith and right, never thought of swerving from her fidelity to the exiled family, or of recognising any other sovereign but King James; and, though she acquiesced in the doctrine of obedience to the reigning power, no temptation, she thought, could induce her to acknowledge the Prince of Orange as rightful monarch, nor to let her lord so acknowledge him. So my Lord Castlewood remained a nonjuror all his life nearly, though his self-denial caused him many a pang, and left him sulky and out of humour.

The year after the Revolution, and all through King William's life, 'tis known there were constant intrigues for the restoration of the exiled family; but if my Lord Castlewood took any share of these, as is probable, 'twas only for a short time, and when Harry Esmond was too young to be introduced into such important secrets.

But in the year 1695, when that conspiracy of Sir John Fenwick, Colonel Lowick, and others, was set on foot, for waylaying King William as he came from Hampton Court to London, and a secret plot was formed, in which a vast number of the nobility and people of honour were engaged; Father Holt appeared at Castlewood, and brought a young friend with him, a gentleman whom 'twas easy to see that both my lord and the Father treated with uncommon deference. Harry Esmond saw this gentleman, and knew and recognised him in after-life, as shall be shown in its place; and he has little doubt now that my Lord Viscount was implicated somewhat in the transactions which always kept Father Holt employed and travelling hither and thither under a dozen of different names and disguises. The Father's companion went by the name of Captain James; and it was under a very different name and appearance that Harry Esmond afterwards saw him.

It was the next year that the Fenwick conspiracy[7] blew up, which is a matter of public history now, and which ended in the execution of Sir John and many more, who suffered manfully for their treason, and who were attended to Tyburn by my lady's father Dean Armstrong, Mr Collier, and other stout nonjuring clergymen, who absolved them at the gallows-foot.

'Tis known that when Sir John was apprehended, discovery was made of a great number of names of gentlemen engaged in the conspiracy; when, with a noble wisdom and clemency, the Prince burned the list of conspirators furnished to him, and said he would know no more. Now it was, after this, that Lord Castlewood swore his great oath that he would never, so help him Heaven, be engaged in any transaction against that brave and merciful man; and so he told Holt when the indefatigable priest visited him, and would have had him engage in a farther conspiracy. After this my lord ever spoke of King William as he was – as one of the wisest, the bravest, and the greatest of men. My Lady Esmond (for her part) said she could never pardon the King, first, for ousting his father-in-law from his throne, and secondly, for not being constant to his wife, the Princess Mary. Indeed, I think if Nero were to rise again and be king of England, and a good family man, the ladies would pardon him. My lord laughed at his wife's objections – the standard of virtue did not fit him much.

The last conference which Mr Holt had with his lordship took place when Harry was come home for his first vacation from college (Harry saw his old tutor but for a half hour, and exchanged no private words with him), and their talk, whatever it might be, left my Lord Viscount very much disturbed in mind – so much so, that his wife, and his young kinsman, Henry Esmond, could not but observe his disquiet. After Holt was gone, my lord rebuffed Esmond, and again treated him with the greatest deference; he shunned his wife's questions and company, and looked at his children with such a face of gloom and anxiety, muttering 'Poor children – poor children!' in a way that could not but fill those whose life it was to watch him and obey him, with great alarm. For which gloom, each person interested in the Lord Castlewood, framed in his or her own mind an interpretation.

My lady, with a laugh of cruel bitterness, said, 'I suppose the person at Hexton has been ill, or has scolded him' (for my lord's infatuation about Mrs Marwood was known only too well). Young Esmond feared for his money affairs, into the condition of which he had been initiated; and that the expenses, always greater than his revenue, had caused Lord Castlewood disquiet.

One of the causes why my Lord Viscount had taken young Esmond into his special favour was a trivial one, that hath not before been mentioned, though it was a very lucky accident in Henry Esmond's life. A very few months after my lord's coming to Castlewood, in the winter time – the little boy, being a child in a petticoat, trotting about – it happened that little Frank was with his father after dinner, who fell asleep over his wine, heedless of the child, who crawled to the fire; and, as good fortune would have it, Esmond was sent by his mistress for the boy just as the poor little screaming urchin's coat was set on fire by a log; when Esmond, rushing forward, tore the dress off the infant, so that his own hands were burned more than the child's, who was frightened rather than hurt, by this accident. But certainly 'twas providential that a resolute person should have come in at that instant, or the child had been burned to death probably, my lord sleeping very heavily after drinking, and not waking so cool as a man should who had a danger to face.

Ever after this the father, loud in his expressions of remorse and humility for being a tipsy good-for-nothing, and of admiration for Harry Esmond, whom his lordship would style a hero for doing a very trifling service, had the tenderest regard for his son's preserver, and Harry became quite as one of the family. His burns were tended with the greatest care by his kind mistress, who said that Heaven had sent him to be the guardian of her children, and that she would love him all her life.

And it was after this, and from the very great love and tenderness which had grown up in this little household, rather than to the exhortations of Dean Armstrong (though these had no small weight with him), that Harry came to be quite of the religion of his house and his dear mistress, of which he has ever since been a professing member. As for Doctor Tusher's boasts that he was the cause of this conversion – even in these young days Mr Esmond had such a contempt for the Doctor, that had Tusher bade him believe anything (which he did not – never meddling at all), Harry would that instant have questioned the truth on't.

My lady seldom drank wine; but on certain days of the year, such as birthdays (poor Harry had never a one) and anniversaries, she took a little; and this day, the 29th December, was one. At the end, then, of this year, '96, it might have been a fortnight after Mr Holt's last visit, Lord Castlewood being still very gloomy in mind, and sitting at table – my lady bidding a servant bring her a glass of wine, and looking at her husband with one of her sweet smiles, said –

'My lord, will you not fill a bumper too, and let me call a toast?'

'What is it, Rachel?' says he, holding out his empty glass to be filled.

' 'Tis the 29th of December,' says my lady, with her fond look of gratitude: and 'my toast is, "Harry – and God bless him, who saved my boy's life!"'

My lord looked at Harry hard, and drank the glass, but clapped it down on the table in a moment, and, with a sort of groan, rose up, and went out of the room. What was the matter? We all knew that some great grief was over him.

Whether my lord's prudence had made him richer, or legacies had fallen to him, which enabled him to support a greater establishment than that frugal one which had been too much for his small means, Harry Esmond knew not; but the house of Castlewood was now on a scale much more costly than it had been during the first year of his lordship's coming to the title. There were more horses in the stable and more servants in the hall, and many more guests coming and going now than formerly, when it was found difficult enough by the strictest economy to keep the house as befitted one of his lordship's rank, and the estate out of debt. And it did not require very much penetration to find, that many of the new acquaintances at Castlewood were not agreeable to the lady there: not that she ever treated them or any mortal with anything but courtesy; but they were persons who could not be welcome to her; and whose society a lady so refined and reserved could scarce desire for her children. There came fuddling squires from the country round, who bawled their songs under her windows and drank themselves tipsy with my lord's punch and ale: there came officers from Hexton, in whose company our little lord was made to hear talk and to drink, and swear too in a way that made the delicate lady tremble for her son. Esmond tried to console her by saying what he knew of his college experience; that with this sort of company and conversation a man must fall in sooner or later in his course through the world: and it mattered very little whether he heard it at twelve years old or twenty – the youths who quitted mother's apron-strings the latest being not uncommonly the wildest rakes. But it was about her daughter that Lady Castlewood was the most anxious, and the danger which she thought menaced the little Beatrix from the indulgencies which her father gave her (it must be owned that my lord, since these unhappy domestic differences especially, was at once violent in his language to the children when angry, as he was too familiar, not to say coarse, when he was in a good humour), and from the company into which the careless lord brought the child.

Not very far off from Castlewood is Sark Castle, where the Marchioness of Sark lived, who was known to have been a mistress of the late King Charles – and to this house, whither indeed a great part of the country gentry went, my lord insisted upon going, not only himself, but on taking his little daughter and son, to play with the children there. The children were nothing loth, for the house was splendid and the welcome kind enough. But my lady, justly no doubt, thought that the children of such a mother as that noted Lady Sark had been, could be no good company for her two; and spoke her mind to her lord. His own language when he was thwarted was not indeed of the gentlest: to be brief, there was a family dispute on this, as there had been on many other points – and the lady was not only forced to give in, for the other's will was law – nor could she, on account of their tender age, tell her children what was the nature of her objection to their visit of pleasure, or indeed mention to them any objection at all – but she had the additional secret mortification, to find them returning delighted with their new friends, loaded with presents from them, and eager to be allowed to go back to a place of such delights as Sark Castle. Every year she thought the company there would be more dangerous to her daughter, as from a child Beatrix grew to a woman, and her daily-increasing beauty, and many faults of character too, expanded.

It was Harry Esmond's lot to see one of the visits which the old Lady of Sark paid to the lady of Castlewood Hall: whither she came in state with six chestnut horses and blue ribbons, a page on each carriage step, a gentleman of the horse, and armed servants riding before and behind her. And, but that it was unpleasant to see Lady Castlewood's face, it was amusing to watch the behaviour of the two enemies: the frigid patience of the younger lady, and the unconquerable good-humour of the elder – who would see no offence whatever her rival intended, and who never ceased to smile and to laugh, and to coax the children, and to pay compliments to every man, woman, child, nay dog, or chair and table, in Castlewood, so bent was she upon admiring everything there. She lauded the children, and wished – as indeed she well might – that her own family had been brought up as well as those cherubs. She had never seen such a complexion as dear Beatrix's – though to be sure she had a right to it from father and mother – Lady Castlewood's was indeed a wonder of freshness, and Lady Sark sighed to think she had not been born a fair woman; and remarking Harry Esmond, with a fascinating superannuated smile, she complimented him on his wit, which she said she could see from his eyes and forehead; and vowed that she would never have *him* at Sark until her daughter were out of the way.[8]

## Chapter 12

### MY LORD MOHUN COMES AMONG US FOR NO GOOD

THERE had ridden along with this old Princess's cavalcade, two gentlemen; her son, my Lord Firebrace, and his friend, my Lord Mohun,[1] who both were greeted with a great deal of cordiality by the hospitable Lord of Castlewood. My Lord Firebrace was but a feeble-minded and weak-limbed young nobleman, small in stature and limited in understanding – to judge from the talk young Esmond had with him; but the other was a person of a handsome presence, with the *bel air*, and a bright daring warlike aspect, which, according to the chronicle of those days, had already achieved for him the conquest of several beauties and toasts. He had fought and conquered in France, as well as in Flanders; he had served a couple of campaigns with the Prince of Baden on the Danube, and witnessed the rescue of Vienna from the Turk. And he spoke of his military exploits pleasantly, and with the manly freedom of a soldier, so as to delight all his hearers at Castlewood, who were little accustomed to meet a companion so agreeable.

On the first day this noble company came, my lord would not hear of their departure before dinner, and carried away the gentlemen to amuse them, whilst his wife was left to do the honours of her house to the old Marchioness and her daughter within. They looked at the stables, where my Lord Mohun praised the horses, though there was but a poor show there: they walked over the old house and gardens, and fought the siege of Oliver's time over again: they played a game of rackets in the old court, where my Lord Castlewood beat my Lord Mohun, who said he loved ball of all things, and would quickly come back to Castlewood for his revenge. After dinner they played bowls, and drank punch in the green alley; and when they parted they were sworn friends, my Lord Castlewood kissing the other lord before he mounted on horseback, and pronouncing him the best companion he had met for many a long day. All night long, over his tobacco-pipe, Castlewood did not cease to talk to Harry Esmond in praise of his new friend, and in fact did not leave off speaking of him until his lordship was so tipsy that he could not speak plainly any more.

At breakfast next day it was the same talk renewed; and when my lady said there was something free in the Lord Mohun's looks and manner of speech which caused her to mistrust him, her lord burst out with one of his laughs and oaths; said that he never liked man, woman, or beast, but what she was sure to be jealous of it; that Mohun was the prettiest fellow in England; that he hoped to see more of him whilst in the country; and that he would let Mohun know what my Lady Prude said of him.

'Indeed,' Lady Castlewood said, 'I liked his conversation well enough. 'Tis more amusing than that of most people I know. I thought it, I own, too free; not from what he said, as rather from what he implied.'

'Psha! your ladyship does not know the world,' said her

husband; 'and you have always been as squeamish as when you were a miss of fifteen.'

'You found no fault when I was a miss at fifteen.'

'Begad, madam, you are grown too old for a pinafore now; and I hold that 'tis for me to judge what company my wife shall see,' said my lord, slapping the table.

'Indeed, Francis, I never thought otherwise,' answered my lady, rising and dropping him a curtsey, in which stately action, if there was obedience, there was defiance too; and in which a bystander, deeply interested in the happiness of that pair as Harry Esmond was, might see how hopelessly separated they were; what a great gulf of difference and discord had run between them.

'By G——d! Mohun is the best fellow in England; and I'll invite him here, just to plague that woman. Did you ever see such a frigid insolence as it is, Harry? That's the way she treats me,' he broke out, storming, and his face growing red as he clenched his fists and went on. 'I'm nobody in my own house. I'm to be the humble servant of that parson's daughter. By Jove! I'd rather she should fling the dish at my head than sneer at me as she does. She puts me to shame before the children with her d——d airs; and, I'll swear, tells Frank and Beaty that papa's a reprobate, and that they ought to despise me.'

'Indeed and indeed, sir, I never heard her say a word but of respect regarding you,' Harry Esmond interposed.

'No, curse it! I wish she would speak. But she never does. She scorns me, and holds her tongue. She keeps off from me, as if I was a pestilence. By George! she was fond enough of her pestilence once. And when I came a-courting, you would see miss blush – blush red, by George! for joy. Why, what do you think she said to me, Harry? She said herself when I joked with her about her d——d smiling red cheeks: " 'Tis as they do at Saint James's; I put up my red flag when my king comes." I was the king, you see, she meant. But now, sir, look at her! I believe she would be glad if I was dead; and dead I've been to her these five years – ever since you all of you had the small-pox: and she never forgave me for going away.'

'Indeed, my lord, though 'twas hard to forgive, I think my mistress forgave it,' Harry Esmond said; 'and remember how eagerly she watched your lordship's return, and how sadly she turned away when she saw your cold looks.'

'Damme!' cries out my lord; 'would you have had me wait and catch the small-pox? Where the deuce had been the good of that? I'll bear danger with any man – but not useless danger – no, no. Thank you for nothing. And – you nod your head, and I know very well, Parson Harry, what you mean. There was the – the other affair to make her angry. But is a woman never to forgive a husband who goes a-tripping? Do you take me for a saint?'

'Indeed, sir, I do not,' says Harry, with a smile.

'Since that time my wife's as cold as the statue at Charing Cross. I tell thee she has no forgiveness in her, Henry. Her coldness blights my whole life, and sends me to the punch-bowl, or driving about the country. My children are not mine, but hers, when we are together. 'Tis only when she is out of sight with her abominable cold glances, that run through me, that they'll come to me, and that I dare to give them so much as a kiss; and that's why I take 'em and love 'em in other people's houses, Harry. I'm killed by the very virtue of that proud woman. Virtue! give me the virtue that can forgive; give me the virtue that thinks not of preserving itself, but of making other folks happy. Damme, what matters a scar or two if 'tis got in helping a friend in ill fortune?'

And my lord again slapped the table, and took a great draught from the tankard. Harry Esmond admired as he listened to him, and thought how the poor preacher of this self-sacrifice had fled from the small-pox, which the lady had borne so cheerfully, and which had been the cause of so much disunion in the lives of all in this house. 'How well men preach,' thought the young man, 'and each is the example in his own sermon. How each has a story in a dispute, and a true one, too, and both are right, or wrong, as you will!' Harry's heart was pained within him, to watch the struggles and pangs that tore the breast of this kind, manly, friend and protector.

'Indeed, sir,' said he, 'I wish to God that my mistress could hear you speak as I have heard you; she would know much that would make her life the happier, could she hear it.' But my lord flung away with one of his oaths, and a jeer; he said that Parson Harry was a good fellow; but that as for women, all women were alike – all jades, and heartless. So a man dashes a fine vase down and despises it for being broken. It may be worthless – true: but who had the keeping of it, and who shattered it?

Harry, who would have given his life to make his benefactress and her husband happy, bethought him, now that he saw what my lord's state of mind was, and that he really had a great deal of that love left in his heart, and ready for his wife's acceptance if she would take it, whether he could not be a means of reconciliation between these two persons, whom he revered the most in the world. And he cast about how he should break a part of his mind to his mistress, and warn her that in his, Harry's, opinion, at least, her husband was still her admirer, and even her lover.

But he found the subject a very difficult one to handle, when he ventured to remonstrate, which he did in the very gravest tone (for long confidence and reiterated proofs of devotion and loyalty had given him a sort of authority in the house, which he resumed as soon as ever he returned to it); and with a speech that should have some effect, as, indeed, it was uttered with the speaker's own heart, he ventured most gently to hint to his adored mistress, that she was doing her husband harm by her ill opinion of him, and that the happiness of all the family depended upon setting her right.

She, who was ordinarily calm and most gentle, and full of smiles and soft attentions, flushed up when young Esmond so spoke to her, and rose from her chair, looking at him with a haughtiness and indignation that he had never before known her to display. She was quite an altered being for that moment; and looked an angry Princess insulted by a vassal.

'Have you ever heard me utter a word in my lord's disparagement?' she asked hastily, hissing out her words, and stamping her foot.

'Indeed no,' Esmond said, looking down.

'Are you come to me as his ambassador – *you*?' she continued.

'I would sooner see peace between you than anything else in the world,' Harry answered, 'and would go of any embassy that had that end.'

'So *you* are my lord's go-between?' she went on, not regarding this speech. 'You are sent to bid me back into slavery again, and inform me that my lord's favour is graciously restored to his handmaid? He is weary of Covent Garden, is he, that he comes home and would have the fatted calf killed?'

'There's good authority for it, surely,' said Esmond.

'For a son, yes; but my lord is not my son. It was he who cast me away from him. It was he who broke our happiness down, and he bids me to repair it. It was he who showed himself to me at last, as he was, not as I had thought him. It is he who comes before my children stupid and senseless with wine – who leaves our company for that of frequenters of taverns and bagnios – who goes from his home to the city yonder and his friends there, and when he is tired of them returns hither, and expects that I shall kneel and welcome him. And he sends *you* as his chamberlain! What a proud embassy! Monsieur, I make you my compliment of the new place.'

'It would be a proud embassy, and a happy embassy too, could I bring you and my lord together,' Esmond replied.

'I presume you have fulfilled your mission now, sir. 'Twas a pretty one for you to undertake. I don't know whether 'tis your Cambridge philosophy, or time, that has altered your ways of thinking,' Lady Castlewood continued, still in a sarcastic tone. 'Perhaps you too have learned to love drink, and to hiccup over your wine or punch; – which is your worship's favourite liquor? Perhaps you too put up at the Rose on your way through London, and have your acquaintances in Covent Garden. My services to you, sir, to principal and ambassador, to master and – and lacquey.'

'Great Heavens! madam,' cried Harry, 'What have I done that thus, for a second time, you insult me? Do you wish me to blush for what I used to be proud of, that I lived on your bounty? Next to doing you a service (which my life would pay for), you know that to receive one from you is my highest pleasure.

What wrong have I done you that you should wound me so, cruel woman?'

'What wrong?' she said, looking at Esmond with wild eyes. 'Well, none – none that you know of, Harry, or could help. Why did you bring back the small-pox,' she added, after a pause, 'from Castlewood village? You could not help it, could you? Which of us knows whither fate leads us? But we were all happy, Henry, till then.' And Harry went away from this colloquy, thinking still that the estrangement between his patron and his beloved mistress was remediable, and that each had at heart a strong attachment to the other.

The intimacy between the Lords Mohun and Castlewood appeared to increase as long as the former remained in the country; and my Lord of Castlewood especially seemed never to be happy out of his new comrade's sight. They sported together, they drank, they played bowls and tennis: my Lord Castlewood would go for three days to Sark, and bring back my Lord Mohun to Castlewood, where indeed his lordship made himself very welcome to all persons, having a joke or a new game at romps for the children, all the talk of the town for my lord, and music and gallantry and plenty of the *beau langage* for my lady, and for Harry Esmond, who was never tired of hearing his stories of his campaigns and his life at Vienna, Venice, Paris, and the famous cities of Europe which he had visited both in peace and war. And he sang at my lady's harpsichord, and played cards or backgammon, or his new game of billiards with my lord (of whom he invariably got the better); always having a consummate good-humour, and bearing himself with a certain manly grace, that might exhibit somewhat of the camp and Alsatia perhaps, but that had its charm and stamped him a gentleman: and his manner to Lady Castlewood was so devoted and respectful, that she soon recovered from the first feelings of dislike which she had conceived against him – nay, before long, began to be interested in his spiritual welfare, and hopeful of his conversion, lending him books of piety, which he promised dutifully to study. With her my lord talked of reform, of settling into quiet life, quitting the Court and town, and buying some land in the neighbourhood – though it must be owned that, when the two lords were together over their Burgundy after dinner, their talk was very different, and there was very little question of conversion on my Lord Mohun's part. When they got to their second bottle, Harry Esmond used commonly to leave these two noble topers, who, though they talked freely enough, Heaven knows, in his presence (Good Lord, what a set of stories, of Alsatia and Spring Garden,[2] of the taverns and gaming-houses, of the ladies of the Court, and mesdames of the theatres, he can recall out of their godly conversation!) – although I say they talked before Esmond freely, yet they seemed pleased when he went away, and then they had another bottle, and then they fell to cards, and then my Lord Mohun came to her ladyship's drawing-room; leaving his boon companion to sleep off his wine.

'Twas a point of honour with the fine gentlemen of those days to lose or win magnificently at their horse-matches, or games of cards and dice – and you could never tell, from the demeanour of these two lords afterwards, which had been successful and which the loser at their games. And when my lady hinted to my lord that he played more than she liked, he dismissed her with a 'pish,' and swore that nothing was more equal than play betwixt gentlemen, if they did but keep it up long enough. And these kept it up long enough you may be sure. A man of fashion of that time often passed a quarter of his day at cards, and another quarter at drink: I have known many a pretty fellow, who was a wit too, ready of repartee, and possessed of a thousand graces, who would be puzzled if he had to write more than his name.

There is scarce any thoughtful man or woman, I suppose, but can look back upon his course of past life, and remember some point, trifling as it may have seemed at the time of occurrence, which has nevertheless turned and altered his whole career. 'Tis with almost all of us, as in M. Massillon's[3] magnificent image regarding King William, a *grain de sable*[4] that perverts or perhaps overthrows us; and so it was but a light word flung in the air, a mere freak of perverse child's temper, that brought down a whole heap of crushing woes upon that family whereof Harry Esmond formed a part.

Coming home to his dear Castlewood in the third year of his academical course (wherein he had now obtained some distinction, his Latin poem on the death of the Duke of Gloucester,[5] Princess Anne of Denmark's son, having gained him a medal, and introduced him to the society of the University wits), Esmond found his little friend and pupil Beatrix grown to be taller than her mother, a slim and lovely young girl, with cheeks mantling with health and roses: with eyes like stars shining out of azure, with waving bronze hair clustered about the fairest young forehead ever seen: and a mien and shape haughty and beautiful, such as that of the famous antique statue of the huntress Diana – at one time haughty, rapid, imperious, with eyes and arrows that dart and kill. Harry watched and wondered at this young creature, and likened her in his mind to Artemis with the ringing bow and shafts flashing death upon the children of Niobe; at another time she was coy and melting as Luna shining tenderly upon Endymion. This fair creature, this lustrous Phœbe, was only young as yet, nor had nearly reached her full splendour but crescent and brilliant, our young gentleman of the University, his head full of poetical fancies,[6] his heart perhaps throbbing with desires undefined, admired this rising young divinity; and gazed at her (though only as at some 'bright particular star,'[7] far above his earth) with endless delight and wonder. She had been a coquette from the earliest times almost, trying her freaks and jealousies, her wayward frolics and winning caresses, upon all that came within her reach; she set her women quarrelling in the nursery, and practised her eyes on the groom as she rode behind him on the pillion.

She was the darling and torment of father and mother. She intrigued with each secretly; and bestowed her fondness and withdrew it, plied them with tears, smiles, kisses, cajolements; – when the mother was angry, as happened often, flew to the father, and sheltering behind him, pursued her victim; when both were displeased, transferred her caresses to the domestics, or watched until she could win back her parents' good graces, either by surprising them into laughter and good-humour, or appeasing them by submission and artful humility. She was

*sævo læta negotio*, like that fickle goddess[8] Horace describes,
and of whose 'malicious joy' a great poet of our own has written
so nobly – who, famous and heroic as he was, was not strong
enough to resist the torture of women.

It was but three years before, that the child, then but ten
years old, had nearly managed to make a quarrel between
Harry Esmond and his comrade, good-natured, phlegmatic
Thomas Tusher, who never of his own seeking quarrelled with
anybody: by quoting to the latter some silly joke which Harry
had made regarding him – (it was the merest, idlest jest, though
it near drove two old friends to blows, and I think such a battle
would have pleased her) – and from that day Tom kept at a
distance from her; and she respected him, and coaxed him sedulously whenever they met. But Harry was much more easily
appeased, because he was fonder of the child: and when she
made mischief, used cutting speeches, or caused her friends
pain, she excused herself for her fault, not by admitting and
deploring it, but by pleading not guilty, and asserting innocence
so constantly, and with such seeming artlessness, that it was
impossible to question her plea. In her childhood, they were but
mischiefs then which she did; but her power became more fatal
as she grew older – as a kitten first plays with a ball, and then
pounces on a bird and kills it. 'Tis not to be imagined that
Harry Esmond had all this experience at this early stage of his
life, whereof he is now writing the history – many things here
noted were but known to him in later days. Almost everything
Beatrix did or undid seemed good, or at least pardonable, to
him then, and years afterwards.

It happened, then, that Harry Esmond came home to Castlewood for his last vacation, with good hopes of a fellowship at
his college, and a contented resolve to advance his fortune that
way. 'Twas in the first year of the present century, Mr Esmond
(as far as he knew the period of his birth) being then twenty-two
years old. He found his quondam pupil shot up into this beauty
of which we have spoken, and promising yet more: her brother,
my lord's son, a handsome high-spirited brave lad, generous
and frank, and kind to everybody, save perhaps his sister, with
whom Frank was at war (and not from his but her fault) –

adoring his mother, whose joy he was: and taking her side in the unhappy matrimonial differences which were now permanent, while of course Mistress Beatrix ranged with her father. When heads of families fall out, it must naturally be that their dependants wear the one or the other party's colour; and even in the parliaments in the servants' hall or the stables, Harry, who had an early observant turn, could see which were my lord's adherents and which my lady's, and conjecture pretty shrewdly how their unlucky quarrel was debated. Our laqueys sit in judgment on us. My lord's intrigues may be ever so stealthily conducted, but his valet knows them; and my lady's woman carries her mistress's private history to the servants' scandal-market, and exchanges it against the secrets of other abigails.[9]

## Chapter 13

### MY LORD LEAVES US AND HIS EVIL BEHIND HIM

My Lord Mohun (of whose exploits and fame some of the gentlemen of the University had brought down but ugly reports) was once more a guest at Castlewood, and seemingly more intimately allied with my lord even than before. Once in the spring those two noblemen had ridden to Cambridge from Newmarket, whither they had gone for the horse-racing, and had honoured Harry Esmond with a visit at his rooms; after which Doctor Montague, the master of the college, who had treated Harry somewhat haughtily, seeing his familiarity with these great folks, and that my Lord Castlewood laughed and walked with his hand on Harry's shoulder, relented to Mr Esmond, and condescended to be very civil to him; and some days after his arrival, Harry, laughing, told this story to Lady Esmond, remarking how strange it was that men famous for learning and renowned over Europe, should, nevertheless, so bow down to a title, and cringe to a nobleman ever so poor. At this, Mistress Beatrix flung up her head, and said, it became those of low origin to respect their betters; that the parsons made themselves a great deal too proud, she thought; and that she liked the way at Lady Sark's best, where the Chaplain, though he loved pudding, as all parsons do, always went away before the custard.

'And when I am a parson,' says Mr Esmond, 'will you give me no custard, Beatrix?'

'You – you are different,' Beatrix answered. 'You are of our blood.'

'My father was a parson, as you call him,'[1] said my lady.

'But mine is a peer of Ireland,' says Mistress Beatrix, tossing her head. 'Let people know their places. I suppose you will have me go down on my knees and ask a blessing of Mr Thomas Tusher, that has just been made a curate, and whose mother was a waiting-maid.'

And she tossed out of the room, being in one of her flighty humours then.

When she was gone, my lady looked so sad and grave, that Harry asked the cause of her disquietude. She said it was not merely what he said of Newmarket, but what she had remarked, with great anxiety and terror, that my lord, ever since his acquaintance with the Lord Mohun especially, had recurred to his fondness for play, which he had renounced since his marriage.

'But men promise more than they are able to perform in marriage,' said my lady, with a sigh. 'I fear he has lost large sums; and our property, always small, is dwindling away under this reckless dissipation. I heard of him in London with very wild company. Since his return letters and lawyers are constantly coming and going: he seems to me to have a constant anxiety, though he hides it under boisterousness and laughter. I looked through – through the door last night, and – and before,' said my lady, 'and saw them at cards after midnight; no estate will bear that extravagance, much less ours, which will be so diminished that my son will have nothing at all, and my poor Beatrix no portion!'

'I wish I could help you, madam,' said Harry Esmond, sighing, and wishing that unavailingly, and for the thousandth time in his life.

'Who can? Only God,' said Lady Esmond. 'only God, in whose hands we are.' And so it is, and for his rule over his family, and for his conduct to wife and children – subjects over whom his power is monarchical – any one who watches the world must think with trembling sometimes of the account which many a man will have to render. For in our society there's no law to control the King of the Fireside. He is master of property, happiness – life almost. He is free to punish, to make happy or unhappy – to ruin or to torture. He may kill a wife gradually, and be no more questioned than the Grand Seignior who drowns a slave at midnight. He may make slaves and hypocrites of his children; or friends and freemen; or drive them into revolt and enmity against the natural law of love. I have heard politicians and coffee-house wiseacres talking over the newspaper, and railing at the tyranny of the French King, and the Emperor, and wondered how these (who are monarchs, too, in their way) govern their own dominions at home, where each man rules absolute. When the annals of each little reign are shown to the Supreme Master, under whom we hold sovereignty, histories will be laid bare of household tyrants as cruel as Amurath, and as savage as Nero, and as reckless and dissolute as Charles.

If Harry Esmond's patron erred, 'twas in the latter way, from a disposition rather self-indulgent than cruel; and he might have been brought back to much better feelings, had time been given to him to bring his repentance to a lasting reform.

As my lord and his friend Lord Mohun were such close companions, Mistress Beatrix chose to be jealous of the latter; and the two gentlemen often entertained each other by laughing, in their rude boisterous way, at the child's freaks of anger and show of dislike. 'When thou art old enough, thou shalt marry Lord Mohun,' Beatrix's father would say: on which the girl would pout and say, 'I would rather marry Tom Tusher.' And because the Lord Mohun always showed an extreme gallantry to my Lady Castlewood, whom he professed to admire devotedly one day, in answer to this old joke of her father's, Beatrix said, 'I think my lord would rather marry mamma than marry me; and is waiting till you die to ask her.'

The words were said lightly and pertly by the girl one night before supper, as the family party were assembled near the great fire. The two lords, who were at cards, both gave a start; my lady turned as red as scarlet, and bade Mistress Beatrix go to her own chamber; whereupon the girl, putting on, as her wont was, the most innocent air, said, 'I am sure I meant no wrong; I am sure mamma talks a great deal more to Harry Esmond than she does to papa – and she cried when Harry went away, and she never does when papa goes away; and last night she talked to Lord Mohun for ever so long, and sent us out of the room, and cried when we came back, and——'

'D——n!' cried out my Lord Castlewood, out of all patience. 'Go out of the room, you little viper!' and he started up and flung down his cards.

'Ask Lord Mohun what I said to him, Francis,' her ladyship said, rising up with a scared face, but yet with a great and touching dignity and candour in her look and voice. 'Come away with me, Beatrix.' Beatrix sprung up too; she was in tears now.

'Dearest mamma, what have I done?' she asked. 'Sure I meant no harm.' And she clung to her mother, and the pair went out sobbing together.

'I will tell you what your wife said to me, Frank,' my Lord Mohun cried – 'Parson Harry may hear it; and, as I hope for heaven, every word I say is true. Last night, with tears in her eyes, your wife implored me to play no more with you at dice or at cards, and you know best whether what she asked was not for your good.'

'Of course it was, Mohun,' says my lord in a dry hard voice. 'Of course, you are a model of a man: and the world knows what a saint you are.'

My Lord Mohun was separated from his wife, and had had many affairs of honour: of which women as usual had been the cause.

'I am no saint, though your wife is – and I can answer for my actions as other people must for their words,' said my Lord Mohun.

'By G——, my lord, you shall,' cried the other starting up.

'We have another little account to settle first, my lord,' says Lord Mohun. Whereupon Harry Esmond, filled with alarm for the consequences to which this disastrous dispute might lead, broke out into the most vehement expostulations with his patron and his adversary. 'Gracious Heavens!' he said, 'my lord, are you going to draw a sword upon your friend in your own house? Can you doubt the honour of a lady who is as pure as heaven, and would die a thousand times rather than do you a wrong? Are the idle words of a jealous child to set friends at variance? Has not my mistress, as much as she dared do, besought your lordship, as the truth must be told, to break your intimacy with my Lord Mohun; and to give up the habit which may bring ruin on your family? But for my Lord Mohun's illness, had he not left you?'

' 'Faith, Frank, a man with a gouty toe can't run after other men's wives,' broke out my Lord Mohun, who indeed was in that way, and with a laugh and a look at his swathed limb so frank and comical, that the other, dashing his fist across his forehead was caught by that infectious good-humour and said, with his oath, '—— it, Harry, I believe thee,' and so this quarrel was over, and the two gentlemen, at swords drawn but just now, dropped their points, and shook hands.

*Beati pacifici.*[2] 'Go, bring my lady back,' said Harry's patron. Esmond went away only too glad to be the bearer of such good news. He found her at the door; she had been listening there, but went back as he came. She took both his hands; hers were marble cold. She seemed as if she would fall on his shoulder. 'Thank you, and God bless you, my dear brother Harry,' she said. She kissed his hand; Esmond felt her tears upon it: and leading her into the room, and up to my lord, the Lord Castlewood with an outbreak of feeling and affection, such as he had not exhibited for many a long day, took his wife to his heart, and bent over and kissed her and asked her pardon.

' 'Tis time for me to go to roost. I will have my gruel a-bed,' said my Lord Mohun: and limped off comically on Harry Esmond's arm. 'By George, that woman is a pearl!' he said; 'and 'tis only a pig that wouldn't value her. Have you seen the vulgar trapesing orange-girl[3] whom Esmond' – but here Mr

Esmond interrupted him, saying, that these were not affairs for him to know.

My lord's gentleman came in to wait upon his master, who was no sooner in his nightcap and dressing-gown than he had another visitor whom his host insisted on sending to him: and this was no other than the Lady Castlewood herself with the toast and gruel, which her husband bade her make and carry with her own hands in to her guest.

Lord Castlewood stood looking after his wife as she went on this errand, and as he looked, Harry Esmond could not but gaze on him, and remarked in his patron's face an expression of love, and grief, and care, which very much moved and touched the young man. Lord Castlewood's hands fell down at his sides, and his head on his breast, and presently he said –

'You heard what Mohun said, parson?'

'That my lady was a saint?'

'That there are two accounts to settle. I have been going wrong these five years, Harry Esmond. Ever since you brought that damned small-pox into the house, there has been a fate pursuing me, and I had best have died of it, and not run away from it like a coward. I left Beatrix with her relations, and went to London; and I fell among thieves, Harry, and I got back to confounded cards and dice, which I hadn't touched since my marriage – no, not since I was in the Duke's Guard, with those wild Mohocks.[4] And I have been playing worse and worse, and going deeper and deeper into it; and I owe Mohun two thousand pounds now; and when it's paid I am little better than a beggar. I don't like to look my boy in the face; he hates me, I know he does. And I have spent Beaty's little portion; and the Lord knows what will come if I live; the best thing I can do is to die, and release what portion of the estate is redeemable for the boy.'

Mohun was as much master at Castlewood as the owner of the Hall itself; and his equipages filled the stables, where, indeed, there was room in plenty for many more horses than Harry Esmond's impoverished patron could afford to keep. He had arrived on horseback with his people; but when his gout broke out my Lord Mohun sent to London for a light chaise he had, drawn by a pair of small horses, and running as swift, wherever roads were good, as a Laplander's sledge. When this carriage came, his lordship was eager to drive the Lady Castlewood abroad in it, and did so many times, and at a rapid pace, greatly to his companion's enjoyment, who loved the swift motion and the healthy breezes over the Downs which lie hard upon Castlewood, and stretch thence towards the sea. As this amusement was very pleasant to her, and her lord, far from showing any mistrust of her intimacy with Lord Mohun, encouraged her to be his companion; as if willing, by his present extreme confidence, to make up for any past mistrust which his jealousy had shown; the Lady Castlewood enjoyed herself freely in this harmless diversion, which, it must be owned, her guest was very eager to give her; and it seemed that she grew the more free with Lord Mohun, and pleased with his company, because of some sacrifice which his gallantry was pleased to make in her favour.

Seeing the two gentlemen constantly at cards still of evenings, Harry Esmond one day deplored to his mistress that this fatal infatuation of her lord should continue; and now they seemed reconciled together, begged his lady to hint to her husband that he should play no more.

But Lady Castlewood, smiling archly and gaily, said she would speak to him presently, and that, for a few nights more at least, he might be let to have his amusement.

'Indeed, madam,' said Harry, 'you know not what it costs you; and 'tis easy for any observer who knows the game, to see that Lord Mohun is by far the stronger of the two.'

'I know he is,' says my lady, still with exceeding good-humour; 'he is not only the best player, but the kindest player in the world.'

'Madam, madam,' Esmond cried, transported and provoked. 'Debts of honour must be paid some time or other; and my master will be ruined if he goes on.'

'Harry, shall I tell you a secret?' my lady replied, with kindness and pleasure still in her eyes. 'Francis will not be ruined if he goes on; he will be rescued if he goes on. I repent of having spoken and thought unkindly of the Lord Mohun when he was here in the past year. He is full of much kindness

and good; and 'tis my belief that we shall bring him to better
things. I have lent him Tillotson and your favourite Bishop
Taylor, and he is much touched, he says; and as a proof of his
repentance – (and herein lies my secret) – what do you think he
is doing with Francis? He is letting poor Frank win his money
back again. He hath won already at the last four nights; and
my Lord Mohun says that he will not be the means of injuring
poor Frank and my dear children.'

'And in God's name, what do you return him for this sacrifice?' asked Esmond, aghast; who knew enough of men, and of
this one in particular, to be aware that such a finished rake gave
nothing for nothing. 'How, in Heaven's name, are you to pay
him?'

'Pay him! With a mother's blessing and a wife's prayers!'
cries my lady, clasping her hands together. Harry Esmond did
not know whether to laugh, to be angry, or to love his dear
mistress more than ever for the obstinate innocency with which
she chose to regard the conduct of a man of the world, whose
designs he knew better how to interpret. He told the lady,
guardedly, but so as to make his meaning quite clear to her,
what he knew in respect of the former life and conduct of this
nobleman; of other women against whom he had plotted, and
whom he had overcome; of the conversation which he, Harry
himself, had had with Lord Mohun, wherein the lord made a
boast of his libertinism, and frequently avowed that he held all
women to be fair game (as his lordship styled this pretty sport),
and that they were all, without exception, to be won. And the
return Harry had for his entreaties and remonstrances was a fit
of anger on Lady Castlewood's part, who would not listen to
his accusations, she said, and retorted that he himself must be
very wicked and perverted, to suppose evil designs, where she
was sure none were meant. 'And this is the good meddlers get
of interfering,' Harry thought to himself with much bitterness;
and his perplexity and annoyance were only the greater, because
he could not speak to my Lord Castlewood himself upon a
subject of this nature, or venture to advise or warn him regarding
a matter so very sacred as his own honour, of which my lord
was naturally the best guardian.

But though Lady Castlewood would listen to no advice from her young dependant, and appeared indignantly to refuse it when offered, Harry had the satisfaction to find that she adopted the counsel which she professed to reject; for the next day she pleaded a headache, when my Lord Mohun would have had her drive out, and the next day the headache continued; and next day, in a laughing gay way she proposed that the children should take her place in his lordship's car, for they would be charmed with a ride of all things; and she must not have all the pleasure for herself. My lord gave them a drive with a very good grace, though I daresay with rage and disappointment inwardly – not that his heart was very seriously engaged in his designs upon this simple lady; but the life of such men is often one of intrigue, and they can no more go through the day without a woman to pursue, than a fox-hunter without his sport after breakfast.

Under an affected carelessness of demeanour, and though there was no outward demonstration of doubt upon his patron's part since the quarrel between the two lords, Harry yet saw that Lord Castlewood was watching his guest very narrowly; and caught signs of distrust and smothered rage (as Harry thought) which foreboded no good. On the point of honour Esmond knew how touchy his patron was; and watched him almost as a physician watches a patient, and it seemed to him that this one was slow to take the disease, though he could not throw off the poison when once it had mingled with his blood. We read in Shakespeare[5] (whom the writer for his part considers to be far beyond Mr Congreve, Mr Dryden, or any of the wits of the present period) that when jealousy is once declared, nor poppy, nor mandragora, nor all the drowsy syrups of the East, will ever soothe it or medicine it away.

In fine, the symptoms seemed to be so alarming to this young physician (who indeed young as he was had felt the kind pulses of all those dear kinsmen), that Harry thought it would be his duty to warn my Lord Mohun, and let him know that his designs were suspected and watched. So one day, when in rather a pettish humour, his lordship had sent to Lady Castle-wood, who had promised to drive with him, and now refused to come, Harry said – 'My lord, if you will kindly give me a place by your side I will thank you; I have much to say to you, and would like to speak to you alone.'

'You honour me by giving me your confidence, Mr Henry Esmond,' says the other, with a very grand bow. My lord was always a fine gentleman, and young as he was there was that in Esmond's manner which showed that he was a gentleman too, and that none might take a liberty with him – so the pair went out, and mounted the little carriage which was in waiting for them in the court, with its two little cream-coloured Hanoverian horses covered with splendid furniture and champing at the bit.

'My lord,' says Harry Esmond, after they were got into the country, and pointing to my Lord Mohun's foot, which was swathed in flannel, and put up rather ostentatiously on a cushion – 'my lord, I studied medicine at Cambridge.'

'Indeed, Parson Harry,' says he: 'and are you going to take out a diploma: and cure your fellow-students of the——' [6]

'Of the gout,' says Harry, interrupting him, and looking him hard in the face; 'I know a good deal about the gout.'

'I hope you may never have it. 'Tis an infernal disease,' says my lord, 'and its twinges are diabolical. Ah!' and he made a dreadful wry face, as if he just felt a twinge.

'Your lordship would be much better if you took off all that flannel – it only serves to inflame the toe,' Harry continued, looking his man full in the face.

'O! it only serves to inflame the toe, does it?' says the other, with an innocent air.

'If you took off that flannel, and flung that absurd slipper away, and wore a boot,' continues Harry.

'You recommend me boots, Mr Esmond?' asks my lord.

'Yes, boots and spurs. I saw your lordship three days ago run down the gallery fast enough,' Harry goes on. 'I am sure that taking gruel at night is not so pleasant as claret to your lordship; and besides it keeps your lordship's head cool for play, whilst my patron's is hot and flustered with drink.'

' 'Sdeath, sir, you dare not say that I don't play fair?' cries my lord, whipping his horses, which went away at a gallop.

'You are cool when my lord is drunk,' Harry continued;

'your lordship gets the better of my patron. I have watched you as I looked up from my books.'

'You young Argus!' says Lord Mohun, who liked Harry Esmond – and for whose company and wit, and a certain daring manner, Harry had a great liking too – 'You young Argus! you may look with all your hundred eyes and see we play fair. I've played away an estate of a night, and I've played my shirt off my back; and I've played away my periwig and gone home in a night-cap. But no man can say I ever took an advantage of him beyond the advantage of the game. I played a dice-cogging[7] scoundrel in Alsatia for his ears and won 'em, and have one of 'em in my lodging in Bow Street in a bottle of spirits. Harry Mohun will play any man for anything – always would.'

'You are playing awful stakes, my lord, in my patron's house,' Harry said, 'and more games than are on the cards.'

'What do you mean, sir?' cries my lord, turning round, with a flush on his face.

'I mean,' answers Harry, in a sarcastic tone, 'that your gout is well – if ever you had it.'

'Sir!' cried my lord, getting hot.

'And to tell the truth I believe your lordship has no more gout than I have. At any rate, change of air will do you good, my Lord Mohun. And I mean fairly that you had better go from Castlewood.'

'And were you appointed to give me this message?' cries the Lord Mohun. 'Did Frank Esmond commission you?'

'No one did. 'Twas the honour of my family that commissioned me.'

'And you are prepared to answer this?' cries the other, furiously lashing his horses.

'Quite, my lord: your lordship will upset the carriage if you whip so hotly.'

'By George, you have a brave spirit!' my lord cried out, bursting into a laugh. 'I suppose 'tis that infernal *botte de Jesuite*[8] that makes you so bold,' he added.

' 'Tis the peace of the family I love best in the world,' Harry Esmond said warmly – ' 'tis the honour of a noble benefactor – the happiness of my dear mistress and her children. I owe them everything in life, my lord; and would lay it down for any one of them. What brings you here to disturb this quiet household? What keeps you lingering month after month in the country? What makes you feign illness and invent pretexts for delay? Is it to win my poor patron's money? Be generous, my lord, and spare his weakness for the sake of his wife and children. Is it to practise upon the simple heart of a virtuous lady? You might as well storm the Tower single-handed. But you may blemish her name by light comments on it, or by lawless pursuits – and I don't deny that 'tis in your power to make her unhappy. Spare these innocent people, and leave them.'

'By the Lord, I believe thou hast an eye to the pretty Puritan thyself, Master Harry,' says my lord, with his reckless, good-humoured laugh, and as if he had been listening with interest to the passionate appeal of the young man. 'Whisper, Harry. Art thou in love with her thyself? Hath tipsy Frank Esmond come by the way of all flesh?'

'My lord, my lord,' cried Harry, his face flushing and his eyes filling as he spoke, 'I never had a mother, but I love this lady as one. I worship her as a devotee worships a saint. To hear her name spoken lightly seems blasphemy to me. Would you dare think of your own mother so, or suffer anyone so to speak of her! It is a horror to me to fancy that any man should think of her impurely. I implore you, I beseech you, to leave her. Danger will come out of it.'

'Danger, psha!' says my lord, giving a cut to the horses, which at this minute – for we were got on to the Downs – fairly ran off into a gallop that no pulling could stop. The rein broke in Lord Mohun's hands, and the furious beasts scampered madly forwards, the carriage swaying to and fro, and the persons within it holding on to the sides as best they might, until seeing a great ravine before them, where an upset was inevitable, the two gentlemen leapt for their lives, each out of his side of the chaise. Harry Esmond was quit for a fall on the grass, which was so severe that it stunned him for a minute; but he got up presently very sick, and bleeding at the nose, but with no other hurt. The Lord Mohun was not so fortunate; he fell on his head against a stone, and lay on the ground dead to all appearance.

This misadventure happened as the gentlemen were on their return homewards; and my Lord Castlewood, with his son and daughter, who were going out for a ride, met the ponies as they were galloping with the car behind, the broken traces entangling their heels, and my lord's people turned and stopped them. It was young Frank who spied out Lord Mohun's scarlet coat as he lay on the ground, and the party made up to that unfortunate gentleman and Esmond, who was now standing over him. His large periwig and feathered hat had fallen off, and he was bleeding profusely from a wound on the forehead, and looking, and being, indeed, a corpse.

'Great God! he's dead!' says my lord. 'Ride, some one: fetch a doctor – stay. I'll go home and bring back Tusher; he knows surgery,' and my lord, with his son after him, galloped away.

They were scarce gone when Harry Esmond, who was indeed but just come to himself, bethought him of a similar accident which he had seen on a ride from Newmarket to Cambridge, and taking off a sleeve of my lord's coat, Harry, with a penknife, opened a vein in his arm, and was greatly relieved, after a moment, to see the blood flow. He was near half-an-hour before he came to himself, by which time Doctor Tusher and little Frank arrived, and found my lord not a corpse indeed, but as pale as one.

After a time, and when he was able to bear motion, they put my lord upon a groom's horse, and gave the other to Esmond, the men walking on each side of my lord, to support him, if need were, and worthy Doctor Tusher with them. Little Frank and Harry rode together at a foot pace.

When we rode together home, the boy said: 'We met mamma, who was walking on the terrace with the Doctor, and papa frightened her, and told her you were dead – '

'That I was dead?' asks Harry.

'Yes. Papa says: "Here's poor Harry killed, my dear"; on which mamma gives a great scream; and oh, Harry! she drops down; and I thought she was dead, too. And you never saw such a way as papa was in: he swore one of his great oaths; and he turned pale; and then he began to laugh somehow, and he told the Doctor to take his horse, and me to follow him; and we left him. And I looked back, and saw him dashing water out of the fountain on to mamma. Oh, she was so frightened!'

Musing upon this curious history – for my Lord Mohun's name was Henry too, and they called each other Frank and Harry often – and not a little disturbed and anxious, Esmond rode home. His dear lady was on the terrace still, one of her women with her, and my lord no longer there. There are steps and a little door thence down into the road. My lord passed, looking very ghastly, with a handkerchief over his head, and without his hat and periwig, which a groom carried, but his politeness did not desert him, and he made a bow to the lady above.

'Thank Heaven you are safe,' she said.

'And so is Harry, too, mamma,' says little Frank, – 'huzzay!'

Harry Esmond got off the horse to run to his mistress, as did little Frank, and one of the grooms took charge of the two beasts, while the other, hat and periwig in hand, walked by my lord's bridle to the front gate, which lay half-a-mile away.

'Oh, my boy! what a fright you have given me!' Lady Castlewood said, when Harry Esmond came up, greeting him with one of her shining looks, and a voice of tender welcome; and she was so kind as to kiss the young man ('twas the second time she had so honoured him), and she walked into the house between him and her son, holding a hand of each.

## Chapter 14

### WE RIDE AFTER HIM TO LONDON

AFTER a repose of a couple of days, the Lord Mohun was so far recovered of his hurt as to be able to announce his departure for the next morning; when, accordingly, he took leave of Castlewood, proposing to ride to London by easy stages, and lie two nights upon the road. His host treated him with a studied and ceremonious courtesy, certainly different from my lord's usual frank and careless demeanour; but there was no

reason to suppose that the two lords parted otherwise than
good friends, though Harry Esmond remarked that my Lord
Viscount only saw his guest in company with other persons,
and seemed to avoid being alone with him. Nor did he ride any
distance with Lord Mohun, as his custom was with most of his
friends, whom he was always eager to welcome and unwilling
to lose; but contented himself, when his lordship's horses were
announced, and their owner appeared booted for his journey,
to take a courteous leave of the ladies of Castlewood, by following
the Lord Mohun downstairs to his horses, and by bowing and
wishing him a good-day, in the courtyard. 'I shall see you in
London before very long, Mohun,' my lord said, with a smile;
'when we will settle our accounts together.'

'Do not let them trouble you, Frank,' said the other good-
naturedly, and, holding out his hand, looked rather surprised
at the grim and stately manner in which his host received his
parting salutation: and so, followed by his people, he rode
away.

Harry Esmond was witness of the departure. It was very
different to my lord's coming, for which great preparation had
been made (the old house putting on its best appearance to
welcome its guest), and there was a sadness and constraint
about all persons that day, which filled Mr Esmond with gloomy
forebodings, and sad indefinite apprehensions. Lord Castlewood
stood at the door watching his guest and his people as they
went out under the arch of the outer gate. When he was there,
Lord Mohun turned once more, my Lord Viscount slowly
raised his beaver[1] and bowed. His face wore a peculiar livid
look, Harry thought. He cursed and kicked away his dogs,
which came jumping about him – then he walked up to the
fountain in the centre of the court, and leaned against a pillar
and looked into the basin. As Esmond crossed over to his own
room, late the Chaplain's, on the other side of the court, and
turned to enter in at the low door, he saw Lady Castlewood
looking through the curtains of the great window of the drawing-
room overhead, at my lord as he stood regarding the fountain.
There was in the court a peculiar silence somehow; and the
scene remained long in Esmond's memory: – the sky bright

overhead; the buttresses of the building and the sundial casting shadow over the gilt *memento mori* inscribed underneath; the two dogs, a black greyhound and a spaniel nearly white, the one with his face up to the sun, and the other snuffing amongst the grass and stones, and my lord leaning over the fountain, which was plashing audibly. 'Tis strange how that scene and the sound of that fountain remain fixed on the memory of a man who has beheld a hundred sights of splendour, and danger too, of which he has kept no account.

It was Lady Castlewood – she had been laughing all the morning, and especially gay and lively before her husband and his guest, who, as soon as the two gentlemen went together from her room, ran to Harry, the expression of her countenance quite changed now, and with a face and eyes full of care, and said, 'Follow them, Harry, I am sure something has gone wrong.' And so it was that Esmond was made an eavesdropper at this lady's orders: and retired to his own chamber, to give himself time in truth to try and compose a story which would soothe his mistress, for he could not but have his own apprehension that some serious quarrel was pending between the two gentlemen.

And now for several days the little company at Castlewood sate at table as of evenings: this care, though unnamed and invisible, being nevertheless present alway, in the minds of at least three persons there. My lord was exceeding gentle and kind. Whenever he quitted the room, his wife's eyes followed him. He behaved to her with a kind of mournful courtesy and kindness remarkable in one of his blunt ways and ordinary rough manner. He called her by her Christian name often and fondly, was very soft and gentle with the children, especially with the boy, whom he did not love, and being lax about church generally, he went thither and performed all the offices (down even to listening to Doctor Tusher's sermon) with great devotion.

'He paces his room all night; what is it? Henry, find out what it is,' Lady Castlewood said constantly to her young dependant. 'He has sent three letters to London,' she said, another day.

'Indeed, madam, they were to a lawyer,' Harry answered,

who knew of these letters, and had seen a part of the correspondence, which related to a new loan my lord was raising; and when the young man remonstrated with his patron, my lord said, 'he was only raising money to pay off an old debt on the property, which must be discharged.'

Regarding the money, Lady Castlewood was not in the least anxious. Few fond women feel money-distressed; indeed you can hardly give a woman a greater pleasure than to bid her pawn her diamonds for the man she loves; and I remember hearing Mr Congreve say of my Lord Marlborough, that the reason why my lord was so successful with women as a young man was, because he took money of them. 'There are few men who will make such a sacrifice for them,' says Mr Congreve, who knew a part of the sex pretty well.[2]

Harry Esmond's vacation was just over, and, as hath been said, he was preparing to return to the University for his last term before taking his degree and entering into the Church. He had made up his mind for this office, not indeed with that reverence which becomes a man about to enter upon a duty so holy, but with a worldly spirit of acquiescence in the prudence of adopting that profession for his calling. But his reasoning was that he owed all to the family of Castlewood, and loved better to be near them than anywhere else in the world; that he might be useful to his benefactors, who had the utmost confidence in him and affection for him in return; that he might aid in bringing up the young heir of the house and acting as his governor; that he might continue to be his dear patron's and mistress's friend and adviser, who both were pleased to say that they should ever look upon him as such: and so, by making himself useful to those he loved best, he proposed to console himself for giving up of any schemes of ambition which he might have had in his own bosom. Indeed, his mistress had told him that she would not have him leave her; and whatever she commanded was will to him.

The Lady Castlewood's mind was greatly relieved in the last few days of this well-remembered holiday time, by my lord's announcing one morning, after the post had brought him letters from London, in a careless tone, that the Lord Mohun was gone to Paris, and was about to make a great journey in Europe; and though Lord Castlewood's own gloom did not wear off, or his behaviour alter, yet this cause of anxiety being removed from his lady's mind, she began to be more hopeful and easy in her spirits, striving too, with all her heart, and by all the means of soothing in her power, to call back my lord's cheerfulness and dissipate his moody humour.

He accounted for it himself, by saying that he was out of health; that he wanted to see his physician; that he would go to London, and consult Doctor Cheyne.[3] It was agreed that his lordship and Harry Esmond should make the journey as far as London together; and of a Monday morning, the 10th of October, in the year 1700, they set forwards towards London on horseback. The day before being Sunday, and the rain pouring down, the family did not visit church; and at night my lord read the service to his family, very finely, and with a peculiar sweetness and gravity – speaking the parting benediction, Harry thought, as solemn as ever he heard it. And he kissed and embraced his wife and children before they went to their own chambers with more fondness than he was ordinarily wont to show, and with a solemnity and feeling of which they thought in after days with no small comfort.

They took horse the next morning (after adieux from the family as tender as on the night previous), lay that night on the road, and entered London at nightfall; my lord going to the Trumpet, in the Cockpit,[4] Whitehall, an house used by the military in his time as a young man, and accustomed by his lordship ever since.

An hour after my lord's arrival (which showed that his visit had been arranged before-hand), my lord's man of business arrived from Gray's Inn; and thinking that his patron might wish to be private with the lawyer, Esmond was for leaving them: but my lord said his business was short; introduced Mr Esmond particularly to the lawyer, who had been engaged for the family in the old lord's time; who said that he had paid the money, as desired that day, to my Lord Mohun himself, at his lodgings in Bow Street; that his lordship had expressed some surprise, as it was not customary to employ lawyers, he said, in such transactions between men of honour; but, nevertheless, he had returned my Lord Viscount's note of hand, which he held at his client's disposition.

'I thought the Lord Mohun had been in Paris!' cried Mr Esmond, in great alarm and astonishment.

'He is come back at my invitation,' said my Lord Viscount. 'We have accounts to settle together.'

'I pray Heaven they are over, sir,' says Esmond.

'Oh, quite,' replied the other, looking hard at the young man. 'He was rather troublesome about that money which I told you I had lost to him at play. And now 'tis paid, and we are quits on that score, and we shall meet good friends again.'

'My lord,' cried out Esmond, 'I am sure you are deceiving me, and that there is a quarrel between the Lord Mohun and you.'

'Quarrel – pish! We shall sup together this very night, and drink a bottle. Every man is ill-humoured who loses such a sum as I have lost. But now 'tis paid, and my anger is gone with it.'

'Where shall we sup, sir?' says Harry.

'*We!* Let some gentlemen wait till they are asked,' says my Lord Viscount with a laugh. 'You go to Duke Street, and see Mr Betterton.[5] You love the play, I know. Leave me to follow my own devices; and in the morning we'll breakfast together, with what appetite we may, as the play says.'

'By G——! my lord, I will not leave you this night,' says Harry Esmond. 'I think I know the cause of your dispute. I swear to you 'tis nothing. On the very day the accident befell Lord Mohun, I was speaking to him about it. I know that nothing has passed but idle gallantry on his part.'

'You know that nothing has passed but idle gallantry between Lord Mohun and my wife,' says my lord, in a thundering voice – 'you knew of this, and did not tell me?'

'I knew more of it than my dear mistress did herself, sir – a thousand times more. How was she, who was as innocent as a child, to know what was the meaning of the covert addresses of a villain?'

'A villain he is, you allow, and would have taken my wife away from me.'

'Sir, she is as pure as an angel,' cried young Esmond.

'Have I said a word against her?' shrieks out my lord. 'Did I ever doubt that she was pure? It would have been the last day of her life when I did. Do you fancy I think that *she* would go astray? No, she hasn't passion enough for that. She neither sins nor forgives. I know her temper – and now I've lost her: by Heaven I love her ten thousand times more than ever I did – yes, when she was young and as beautiful as an angel – when she smiled at me in her old father's house, and used to lie in wait for me there as I came from hunting – when I used to fling my head down on her little knees and cry like a child on her lap – and swear I would reform and drink no more, and play no more, and follow women no more; when all the men of the Court used to be following her – when she used to look with her child more beautiful, by George, than the Madonna in the Queen's Chapel. I am not good like her, I know it. Who is – by Heaven, who is? I tired and wearied her, I know that very well. I could not talk to her. You men of wit and books could do that, and I couldn't – I felt I couldn't. Why, when you was but a boy of fifteen I could hear you two together talking your poetry and your books till I was in such a rage that I was fit to strangle you. But you were always a good lad, Harry, and I loved you, you know I did. And I felt she didn't belong to me: and the children don't. And I besotted myself, and gambled, and drank, and took to all sorts of devilries out of despair and fury. And now comes this Mohun, and she likes him, I know she likes him.'

'Indeed, and on my soul, you are wrong, sir,' Esmond cried.

'She takes letters from him,' cries my lord – 'look here, Harry,' and he pulled out a paper with a brown stain of blood upon it. 'It fell from him that day he wasn't killed. One of the grooms picked it up from the ground and gave it me. Here it is in their d——d comedy jargon. "Divine Gloriana – Why look so coldly on your slave who adores you? Have you no compassion on the tortures you have seen me suffering? Do you vouchsafe no reply to billets that are written with the blood of my heart?" She had more letters from him.'

'But she answered none,' cries Esmond.

'That's not Mohun's fault,' says my lord, 'and I will be revenged on him, as God's in heaven, I will.'

'For a light word or two, will you risk your lady's honour and your family's happiness, my lord?' Esmond interposed beseechingly.

'Psha – there shall be no question of my wife's honour,' said my lord; 'we can quarrel on plenty of grounds beside. If I live, that villain will be punished; if I fall, my family will be only the better: there will only be a spendthrift the less to keep in the world: and Frank has better teaching than his father. My mind is made up, Harry Esmond, and whatever the event is I am easy about it. I leave my wife and you as guardians to the children.'

Seeing that my lord was bent upon pursuing this quarrel, and that no entreaties would draw him from it, Harry Esmond (then of a hotter and more impetuous nature than now, when care, and reflection, and grey hairs have calmed him) thought it was his duty to stand by his kind generous patron, and said – 'My lord, if you are determined upon war, you must not go into it alone. 'Tis the duty of our house to stand by its chief: and I should neither forgive myself nor you if you did not call me, or I should be absent from you at a moment of danger.'

'Why, Harry, my poor boy, you are bred for a parson,' says my lord, taking Esmond by the hand very kindly: 'and it were a great pity that you should meddle in the matter.'

'Your lordship thought of being a churchman once,' Harry answered, 'and your father's orders did not prevent him fighting at Castlewood against the Roundheads. Your enemies are mine, sir: I can use the foils, as you have seen, indifferently well, and don't think I shall be afraid when the buttons are taken off 'em.' And then Harry explained with some blushes and hesitation (for the matter was delicate, and he feared lest, by having put himself forward in the quarrel, he might have offended his patron), how he had himself expostulated with the Lord Mohun, and proposed to measure swords with him if need were, and he could not be got to withdraw peaceably in this dispute. 'And I should have beat him, sir,' says Harry, laughing. 'He never could parry that *botte* I brought from Cambridge. Let us have half-an-hour of it, and rehearse – I can teach it your lordship: 'tis the most delicate point in the world, and if you miss it your adversary's sword is through you.'

'By George, Harry! you ought to be the head of the house,' says my lord, gloomily. 'You had been better Lord Castlewood than a lazy sot like me,' he added, drawing his hand across his eyes, and surveying his kinsman with very kind and affectionate glances.

'Let us take our coats off and have half-an-hour's practice before nightfall,' says Harry, after thankfully grasping his patron's manly hand.

'You are but a little bit of a lad,' says my lord, good-humour-edly; 'but, in faith, I believe you could do for that fellow. No, my boy,' he continued, 'I'll have none of your feints and tricks of stabbing: I can use my sword pretty well too, and will fight my own quarrel my own way.'

'But I shall be by to see fair play,' cries Harry.

'Yes, God bless you – you shall be by.'

'When is it, sir?' says Harry, for he saw that the matter had been arranged privately, and before-hand, by my lord.

' 'Tis arranged thus: I sent off a courier to Jack Westbury to say that I wanted him specially. He knows for what, and will be here presently, and drink part of that bottle of sack. Then we shall go to the theatre in Duke Street, where we shall meet Mohun; and then we shall all go sup at the Rose or the Grey-hound. Then we shall call for cards, and there will be probably a difference over the cards – and then, God help us! – either a wicked villain and traitor shall go out of the world, or a poor worthless devil, that doesn't care to remain in it. I am better away, Hal – my wife will be all the happier when I am gone,' says my lord, with a groan, that tore the heart of Harry Esmond so that he fairly broke into a sob over his patron's kind hand.

'The business was talked over with Mohun before he left home – Castlewood I mean' – my lord went on. 'I took the letter into him, which I had read, and I charged him with his villainy, and he could make no denial of it, only he said that my wife was innocent.'

'And so she is; before Heaven, my lord, she is!' cries Harry.

'No doubt, no doubt. They always are,' says my lord. 'No doubt, when she heard he was killed, she fainted from accident.'

'But, my lord, *my* name is Harry,' cried out Esmond, burning red. 'You told my lady, "Harry was killed!" '

'Damnation! shall I fight you too?' shouts my lord in a fury. 'Are you, you little serpent, warmed by my fire, going to sting – *you*. – No, my boy, you're an honest boy; you are a good boy.' (And here he broke from rage into tears even more cruel to see.) 'You are an honest boy, and I love you; and, by Heavens, I am so wretched that I don't care what sword it is that ends me. Stop, here's Jack Westbury. Well, Jack! Welcome, old boy! This is my kinsman, Harry Esmond.'

'Who brought your bowls for you at Castlewood, sir,' says Harry, bowing; and the three gentlemen sate down and drank of that bottle of sack which was prepared for them.

'Harry is number three,' says my lord. 'You needn't be afraid of him, Jack.' And the Colonel gave a look, as much as to say, 'Indeed, he don't look as if I need.' And then my lord explained what he had only told by hints before. When he quarrelled with Lord Mohun he was indebted to his lordship in a sum of sixteen hundred pounds, for which Lord Mohun said he proposed to wait until my Lord Viscount should pay him. My lord had raised the sixteen hundred pounds and sent them to Lord Mohun that morning, and before quitting home had put his affairs into order, and was now quite ready to abide the issue of the quarrel.

When we had drunk a couple of bottles of sack, a coach was called, and the three gentlemen went to the Duke's Playhouse, as agreed. The play was one of Mr Wycherley's – 'Love in a Wood'.

Harry Esmond has thought of that play ever since with a kind of terror, and of Mrs Bracegirdle, the actress who performed the girl's part in the comedy. She was disguised as a page,[6] and came and stood before the gentlemen as they sate on the stage,[7] and looked over her shoulder with a pair of arch black eyes, and laughed at my lord, and asked what ailed the gentleman from the country, and had he had bad news from Bullock Fair?[8]

Between the acts of the play the gentlemen crossed over and conversed freely. There were two of Lord Mohun's party, Captain Macartney, in a military habit, and a gentleman in a suit of blue velvet and silver in a fair periwig, with a rich fall of point of Venice lace – my lord the Earl of Warwick and Holland. My lord had a paper of oranges, which he ate and offered to the actresses, joking with them. And Mrs Bracegirdle, when my Lord Mohun said something rude, turned on him, and asked him what he did there, and whether he and his friends had come to stab anybody else, as they did poor Will Mountford?[9] My lord's dark face grew darker at this taunt, and wore a mischievous fatal look. They that saw it remembered it, and said so afterward.

When the play was ended the two parties joined company; and my Lord Castlewood then proposed that they should go to a tavern and sup. Lockit's, the Greyhound, in Charing Cross, was the house selected. All six marched together that way; the three lords going ahead, Lord Mohun's Captain, and Colonel Westbury, and Harry Esmond, walking behind them. As they walked, Westbury told Harry Esmond about his old friend Dick the Scholar, who had got promotion, and was Cornet of the Guards, and had wrote a book called the 'Christian Hero', and had all the guards to laugh at him for his pains, for the Christian Hero[10] was breaking the commandments constantly, Westbury said, and had fought one or two duels[11] already. And, in a lower tone, Westbury besought young Mr Esmond to take no part in the quarrel. 'There was no need for more seconds than one,' said the Colonel, 'and the Captain or Lord Warwick might easily withdraw.' But Harry said no; he was bent on going through with the business. Indeed, he had a plan in his head, which, he thought, might prevent my Lord Viscount from engaging.

They went in at the bar of the tavern, and desired a private room and wine and cards, and when the drawer had brought these, they began to drink and call healths, and as long as the servants were in the room appeared very friendly.

Harry Esmond's plan was no other than to engage in talk with Lord Mohun, to insult him, and so get the first of the quarrel. So when cards were proposed he offered to play. 'Psha!' says my Lord Mohun (whether wishing to save Harry, or not choosing to try the *botte de Jesuite*, it is not to be known) – 'Young gentlemen from college should not play these stakes. You are too young.'

'Who dares say I am too young?' broke out Harry. 'Is your lordship afraid?'

'Afraid!' cries out Mohun.

But my good Lord Viscount saw the move – 'I'll play you for ten moidores, Mohun,' says he – 'You silly boy, we don't play for groats here as you do at Cambridge': and Harry, who had no such sum in his pocket (for his half-year's salary was always pretty well spent before it was due), fell back with rage and vexation in his heart that he had not money enough to stake.

'I'll stake the young gentleman a crown,' says the Lord Mohun's Captain.

'I thought crowns were rather scarce with the gentlemen of the army,' says Harry.

'Do they birch at college?' says the Captain.

'They birch fools,' says Harry, 'and they cane bullies, and they fling puppies into the water.'

'Faith, then, there's some escapes drowning,' says the Captain, who was an Irishman; and all the gentlemen began to laugh, and made poor Harry only more angry.

My Lord Mohun presently snuffed a candle. It was when the drawers brought in fresh bottles and glasses and were in the room – on which my Lord Viscount said – 'The Deuce take you, Mohun, how damned awkward you are. Light the candle, you drawer.'

'Damned awkward is a damned awkward expression, my lord,' says the other. 'Town gentlemen don't use such words – or ask pardon if they do.'

'I'm a country gentleman,' says my Lord Viscount.

'I see it by your manner,' says my Lord Mohun. 'No man shall say damned awkward to me.'

'I fling the words in your face, my lord,' says the other; 'shall I send the cards too?'

'Gentlemen, gentlemen! before the servants?' cry out Colonel Westbury and my Lord Warwick in a breath. The drawers go out of the room hastily. They tell the people below of the quarrel upstairs.

'Enough has been said,' says Colonel Westbury. 'Will your lordships meet to-morrow morning?'

'Will my Lord Castlewood withdraw his words?' asks the Earl of Warwick.

'My Lord Castlewood will be —— first,' says Colonel Westbury.

'Then we have nothing for it. Take notice, gentlemen, there have been outrageous words – reparation asked and refused.'

'And refused,' says my Lord Castlewood, putting on his hat. 'Where shall the meeting be? and when?'

'Since my lord refuses me satisfaction, which I deeply regret, there is no time so good as now,' says my Lord Mohun. 'Let us have chairs and go to Leicester Field.'

'Are your lordship and I to have the honour of exchanging a pass or two?' says Colonel Westbury, with a low bow to my Lord of Warwick and Holland.

'It is an honour for me,' says my lord with a profound congée, 'to be matched with a gentleman who has been at Mons and Namur.'[12]

'Will your Reverence permit me to give you a lesson?' says the Captain.

'Nay, nay, gentlemen, two on a side are plenty,' says Harry's patron. 'Spare the boy, Captain Macartney,' and he shook Harry's hand – for the last time, save one, in his life.

At the bar of the tavern all the gentlemen stopped, and my Lord Viscount said, laughing, to the barwoman, that those cards set people sadly a-quarrelling; but that the dispute was over now, and the parties were all going away to my Lord Mohun's house, in Bow Street, to drink a bottle more before going to bed.

A half-dozen of chairs[13] were now called, and the six gentlemen stepping into them, the word was privately given to the
chairmen to go to Leicester Field,[14] where the gentlemen were
set down opposite the Standard Tavern. It was midnight, and
the town was a-bed by this time, and only a few lights in the
windows of the houses; but the night was bright enough for
the unhappy purpose which the disputants came about; and so
all six entered into that fatal square, the chairmen standing
without the railing and keeping the gate, lest any persons should
disturb the meeting.

All that happened there hath been matter of public notoriety,
and is recorded, for warning to lawless men, in the annals of
our country. After being engaged for not more than a couple
of minutes, as Harry Esmond thought (though being occupied
at the time with his own adversary's point, which was active,
he may not have taken a good note of time), a cry from the
chairmen without, who were smoking their pipes, and leaning
over the railings of the field as they watched the dim combat
within, announced that some catastrophe had happened which
caused Esmond to drop his sword and look round, at which
moment his enemy wounded him in the right hand. But the
young man did not heed this hurt much, and ran up to the
place where he saw his dear master was down.

My Lord Mohun was standing over him.

'Are you much hurt, Frank?' he asked in a hollow voice.

'I believe I'm a dead man,' my lord said from the ground.

'No, no, not so,' says the other; 'and I call God to witness,
Frank Esmond, that I would have asked your pardon, had you
but given me a chance. In – in the first cause of our falling out,
I swear that no one was to blame but me, and – and that my
lady——'

'Hush!' says my poor Lord Viscount, lifting himself on his
elbow, and speaking faintly. ' 'Twas a dispute about the cards –
the cursed cards. Harry, my boy, are you wounded too? God
help thee! I loved thee, Harry, and thou must watch over my
little Frank – and – and carry this little heart to my wife.'

And here my dear lord felt in his breast for a locket he wore
there, and, in the act, fell back, fainting.

We were all at this terrified, thinking him dead; but Esmond and Colonel Westbury bade the chairmen to come into the field; and so my lord was carried to one Mr Aimes, a surgeon, in Long Acre,[15] who kept a bath, and there the house was wakened up, and the victim of this quarrel carried in.

My Lord Viscount was put to bed, and his wound looked to by the surgeon, who seemed both kind and skilful. When he had looked to my lord, he bandaged up Harry Esmond's hand (who, from loss of blood, had fainted too, in the house, and may have been some time unconscious); and when the young man came to himself, you may be sure he eagerly asked what news there were of his dear patron; on which the surgeon carried him to the room where the Lord Castlewood lay; who had already sent for a priest; and desired earnestly, they said, to speak with his kinsman. He was lying on a bed, very pale and ghastly, with that fixed, fatal look in his eyes, which betokens death; and faintly beckoning all the other persons away from him with his hand, and crying out 'Only Harry Esmond,' the hand fell powerless down on the coverlet, as Harry came forward, and knelt down and kissed it.

'Thou art all but a priest, Harry,' my Lord Viscount gasped out, with a faint smile, and pressure of his cold hand. 'Are they all gone? Let me make thee a death-bed confession.'

And with sacred Death waiting, as it were, at the bedfoot, as an awful witness of his words, the poor dying soul gasped out his last wishes in respect of his family; – his humble profession of contrition for his faults; – and his charity towards the world he was leaving. Some things he said concerned Harry Esmond as much as they astonished him. And my Lord Viscount, sinking visibly, was in the midst of these strange confessions, when the ecclesiastic for whom my lord had sent, Mr Atterbury,[16] arrived.

This gentleman had reached to no great church dignity as yet, but was only preacher at St Bride's, drawing all the town thither by his eloquent sermons. He was godson to my lord, who had been pupil to his father; had paid a visit to Castlewood from Oxford more than once; and it was by his advice, I think, that Harry Esmond was sent to Cambridge, rather than to

Oxford, of which place Mr Atterbury, though a distinguished member, spoke but ill.

Our messenger found the good priest already at his books, at five o'clock in the morning, and he followed the man eagerly to the house where my poor Lord Viscount lay, Esmond watching him, and taking his dying words from his mouth.

My lord, hearing of Mr Atterbury's arrival, and squeezing Esmond's hand, asked to be alone with the priest; and Esmond left them there for this solemn interview. You may be sure that his own prayers and grief accompanied that dying benefactor. My lord had said to him that which confounded the young man – informed him of a secret which greatly concerned him. Indeed, after hearing it, he had had good cause for doubt and dismay; for mental anguish as well as resolution. While the colloquy between Mr Atterbury and his dying penitent took place within, an immense contest of perplexity was agitating Lord Castlewood's young companion.

At the end of an hour – it may be more – Mr Atterbury came out of the room looking very hard at Esmond, and holding a paper.

'He is on the brink of God's awful judgment,' the priest whispered. 'He has made his breast clean to me. He forgives and believes, and makes restitution. Shall it be in public? Shall we call a witness to sign it?'

'God knows,' sobbed out the young man, 'my dearest lord has only done me kindness all his life.'

The priest put the paper into Esmond's hand. He looked at it. It swam before his eyes.

' 'Tis a confession,' he said.

' 'Tis as you please,' said Mr Atterbury.

There was a fire in the room, where the cloths were drying for the baths, and there lay a heap in a corner, saturated with the blood of my dear lord's body. Esmond went to the fire, and threw the paper into it. 'Twas a great chimney with glazed Dutch tiles. How we remember such trifles in such awful moments! – the scrap of the book that we have read in a great grief – the taste of that last dish that we have eaten before a duel, or some such supreme meeting or parting. On the Dutch tiles at the bagnio was a rude picture representing Jacob in hairy gloves, cheating Isaac of Esau's birthright. The burning paper lighted it up.

' 'Tis only a confession, Mr Atterbury,' said the young man. He leaned his head against the mantelpiece: a burst of tears came to his eyes. They were the first he had shed as he sate by his lord, scared by this calamity and more yet by what the poor dying gentleman had told him, and shocked to think that he should be the agent of bringing this double misfortune on those he loved best.

'Let us go to him,' said Mr Esmond. And accordingly they went into the next chamber, where, by this time, the dawn had broke, which showed my lord's poor pale face and wild appealing eyes, that wore that awful fatal look of coming dissolution. The surgeon was with him. He went into the chamber as Atterbury came out thence. My Lord Viscount turned round his sick eyes towards Esmond. It choked the other to hear that rattle in his throat.

'My Lord Viscount,' says Mr Atterbury, 'Mr Esmond wants no witnesses, and hath burned the paper.'

'My dearest master!' Esmond said, kneeling down, and taking his hand and kissing it.

My Lord Viscount sprang up in his bed, and flung his arms round Esmond. 'God bl—bless . . .' was all he said. The blood rushed from his mouth, deluging the young man. My dearest lord was no more. He was gone with a blessing on his lips, and love and repentance and kindness in his manly heart.

'*Benedicti benedicentes*,' says Mr Atterbury, and the young man kneeling at the bedside, groaned out an Amen.

'Who shall take the news to her?' was Mr Esmond's next thought. And on this he besought Mr Atterbury to bear the tidings to Castlewood. He could not face his mistress himself with those dreadful news. Mr Atterbury complying kindly, Esmond writ a hasty note on his table-book[17] to my lord's man, bidding him get the horses for Mr Atterbury, and ride with him, and send Esmond's own valise to the Gatehouse prison, whither he resolved to go and give himself up.

# BOOK II

## CONTAINS MR ESMOND'S MILITARY LIFE, AND OTHER MATTERS APPERTAINING TO THE ESMOND FAMILY

### Chapter 1

### I AM IN PRISON, AND VISITED, BUT NOT CONSOLED THERE

THOSE may imagine, who have seen death untimely strike down persons revered and beloved, and know how unavailing consolation is, what was Harry Esmond's anguish after being an actor in that ghastly midnight scene of blood and homicide. He could not, he felt, have faced his dear mistress, and told her that story. He was thankful that kind Atterbury consented to break the sad news to her; but, besides his grief, which he took into prison with him, he had that in his heart which secretly cheered and consoled him.

A great secret had been told to Esmond by his unhappy stricken kinsman, lying on his death-bed. Were he to disclose it, as in equity and honour he might do, the discovery would but bring greater grief upon those whom he loved best in the world, and who were sad enough already. Should he bring down shame and perplexity upon all those beings to whom he was attached by so many tender ties of affection and gratitude? degrade his father's widow? impeach and sully his father's and kinsman's honour? and for what? for a barren title, to be worn at the expense of an innocent boy, the son of his dearest benefactress. He had debated this matter in his conscience, whilst his poor lord was making his dying confession. On one side were ambition, temptation, justice even; but love, gratitude, and fidelity, pleaded on the other. And when the struggle was over in Harry's mind, a glow of righteous happiness filled it; and it was with grateful tears in his eyes that he returned thanks to God for that decision which he had been enabled to make.

'When I was denied by my own blood,' thought he, 'these dearest friends received and cherished me. When I was a nameless orphan myself, and needed a protector, I found one in yonder kind soul, who has gone to his account repenting of the innocent wrong he has done.'

And with this consoling thought he went away to give himself up at the prison, after kissing the cold lips of his benefactor.

It was on the third day after he had come to the Gatehouse prison, (where he lay in no small pain from his wound, which inflamed and ached severely); and with those thoughts and resolutions that have been just spoke of, to depress, and yet to console him, that H. Esmond's keeper came and told him that a visitor was asking for him, and though he could not see her face, which was enveloped in a black hood, her whole figure, too, being veiled and covered with the deepest mourning, Esmond knew at once that his visitor was his dear mistress.

He got up from his bed, where he was lying, being very weak; and advancing towards her, as the retiring keeper shut the door upon him and his guest in that sad place, he put forward his left hand (for the right was wounded and bandaged), and he would have taken that kind one of his mistress, which had done so many offices of friendship for him for so many years.

But the Lady Castlewood went back from him, putting back her hood, and leaning against the great stanchioned door which the gaoler had just closed upon them. Her face was ghastly white, as Esmond saw it, looking from the hood; and her eyes, ordinarily so sweet and tender, were fixed at him with such a tragic glance of woe and anger, as caused the young man, unaccustomed to unkindness from that person, to avert his own glances from her face.

'And this, Mr Esmond,' she said, 'is where I see you; and 'tis to this you have brought me!'

'You have come to console me in my calamity, madam,' said he (though, in truth, he scarce knew how to address her, his emotions at beholding her so overpowered him).

She advanced a little, but stood silent and trembling, looking out at him from her black draperies, with her small white hands clasped together, and quivering lips and hollow eyes.

'Not to reproach me,' he continued after a pause. 'My grief is sufficient as it is.'

'Take back your hand – do not touch me with it!' she cried. 'Look! there's blood on it!'

'I wish they had taken it all,' said Esmond, 'if you are unkind to me.'

'Where is my husband?' she broke out. 'Give me back my husband, Henry. Why did you stand by at midnight and see him murdered? Why did the traitor escape who did it? You, the champion of your house, who offered to die for us! You that he loved and trusted, and to whom I confided him – you that vowed devotion and gratitude, and I believed you – yes, I believed you – why are you here, and my noble Francis gone? Why did you come among us? You have only brought us grief and sorrow; and repentance, bitter, bitter repentance, as a return for our love and kindness. Did I ever do you a wrong, Henry? You were but an orphan child when I first saw you – when *he* first saw you, who was so good, and noble, and trusting. He would have had you sent away, but, like a foolish woman, I besought him to let you stay. And you pretended to love us, and we believed you – and you made our house wretched, and my husband's heart went from me: and I lost him through you – I lost him – the husband of my youth, I say. I worshipped him: you know I worshipped him – and he was changed to me. He was no more my Francis of old – my dear, dear soldier. He loved me before he saw you; and I loved him; O, God is my witness how I loved him! Why did he not send you from among us? 'Twas only his kindness, that could refuse me nothing then. And, young as you were – yes, and weak and alone – there was evil, I knew there was evil, in keeping you. I read it in your face and eyes. I saw that they boded harm to us – and it came, I knew it would. Why did you not die when you had the small-pox – and I came myself and watched you, and you didn't know me in your delirium – and you called out for me, though I was there at your side. All that has happened since, was a just judgment on my wicked heart – my wicked jealous heart. O, I am punished – awfully punished! My husband lies in his blood – murdered for defending me, my kind, kind, generous lord – and you were by, and you let him die, Henry!'

These words, uttered in the wildness of her grief, by one who was ordinarily quiet, and spoke seldom except with a gentle smile and a soothing tone, rung in Esmond's ear; and 'tis said that he repeated many of them in the fever into which he now fell from his wound, and perhaps from the emotion which such passionate, undeserved upbraidings caused him. It seemed as if his very sacrifices and love for this lady and her family were to turn to evil and reproach: as if his presence amongst them was indeed a cause of grief, and the continuance of his life but woe and bitterness to theirs. As the Lady Castlewood spoke bitterly, rapidly, without a tear, he never offered a word of appeal or remonstrance; but sate at the foot of his prison-bed, stricken only with the more pain at thinking it was that soft and beloved hand which should stab him so cruelly, and powerless against her fatal sorrow. Her words as she spoke struck the chords of all his memory, and the whole of his boyhood and youth passed within him; whilst this lady, so fond and gentle but yesterday – this good angel whom he had loved and worshipped – stood before him, pursuing him with keen words and aspect malign.

'I wish I were in my lord's place,' he groaned out. 'It was not my fault that I was not there, madam. But Fate is stronger than all of us, and willed what has come to pass. It had been better for me to have died when I had the illness.'

'Yes, Henry,' said she – and as she spoke she looked at him with a glance that was at once so fond and so sad, that the young man, tossing up his arms, wildly fell back, hiding his head in the coverlet of the bed. As he turned he struck against the wall with his wounded hand, displacing the ligature; and he felt the blood rushing again from the wound. He remembered feeling a secret pleasure at the accident – and thinking, 'Suppose I were to end now, who would grieve for me?'

This hemorrhage, or the grief and despair in which the luckless young man was at the time of the accident, must have brought on a deliquium[1] presently; for he had scarce any recollection afterwards, save of some one, his mistress probably, seizing his hand – and then of the buzzing noise in his ears as he awoke, with two or three persons of the prison around his bed, whereon he lay in a pool of blood from his arm.

It was now bandaged up again by the prison surgeon, who happened to be in the place; and the Governor's wife and servant, kind people both, were with the patient. Esmond saw his mistress still in the room when he awoke from his trance; but she went away without a word; though the Governor's wife told him that she sate in her room for some time afterward, and did not leave the prison until she heard that Esmond was likely to do well.

Days afterwards, when Esmond was brought out of a fever which he had, and which attacked him that night pretty sharply, the honest keeper's wife brought her patient a handkerchief fresh washed and ironed, and at the corner of which he recognized his mistress's well-known cypher and viscountess's crown. 'The lady had bound it round his arm when he fainted, and before she called for help,' the keeper's wife said. 'Poor lady; she took on sadly about her husband. He has been buried to-day, and a many of the coaches of the nobility went with him – my Lord Marlborough's and my Lord Sunderland's, and many of the officers of the Guards, in which he served in the old King's time; and my lady has been with her two children to the King at Kensington,[2] and asked for justice against my Lord Mohun, who is in hiding, and my lord the Earl of Warwick and Holland, who is ready to give himself up and take his trial.'

Such were the news, coupled with assertions about her own honesty and that of Molly her maid, who would never have stolen a certain trumpery gold sleeve-button of Mr Esmond's that was missing after his fainting fit, that the keeper's wife brought to her lodger. His thoughts followed to that untimely grave, the brave heart, the kind friend, the gallant gentleman, honest of word and generous of thought (if feeble of purpose, but are his betters much stronger than he?) who had given him bread and shelter when he had none; home and love when he needed them; and who, if he had kept one vital secret from him, had done that of which he repented ere dying – a wrong indeed, but one followed by remorse, and occasioned by almost irresistible temptation.

Esmond took his handkerchief when his nurse left him, and very likely kissed it, and looked at the bauble embroidered in the corner. 'It has cost thee grief enough,' he thought, 'dear lady, so loving and so tender. Shall I take it from thee and thy children? No, never! Keep it, and wear it, my little Frank, my pretty boy. If I cannot make a name for myself, I can die without one. Some day, when my dear mistress sees my heart, I shall be righted; or if not here or now, why, elsewhere; where Honour doth not follow us, but where Love reigns perpetual.'

'Tis needless to narrate here, as the reports of the lawyers already have chronicled them, the particulars or issue of that trial which ensued upon my Lord Castlewood's melancholy homicide. Of the two lords engaged in that said matter, the second, my lord the Earl of Warwick and Holland, who had been engaged with Colonel Westbury, and wounded by him, was found not guilty by his peers, before whom he was tried (under the presidence of the Lord Steward, Lord Somers); and the principal, the Lord Mohun, being found guilty of the manslaughter (which, indeed, was forced upon him, and of which he repented most sincerely), pleaded his clergy; and so was discharged without any penalty. The widow of the slain nobleman, as it was told us in prison, showed an extraordinary spirit; and, though she had to wait for ten years before her son was old enough to compass it, declared she would have revenge of her husband's murderer. So much and suddenly had grief, anger, and misfortune appeared to change her. But fortune, good or ill, as I take it, does not change men and women. It but develops their characters. As there are a thousand thoughts lying within a man that he does not know till he takes up the pen to write, so the heart is a secret even to him (or her) who has it in his own breast. Who hath not found himself surprised into revenge, or action, or passion, for good or evil; whereof the seeds lay within him, latent and unsuspected, until the occasion called them forth? With the death of her lord, a change seemed to come over the whole conduct and mind of Lady Castlewood; but of this we shall speak in the right season and anon.

The lords being tried then before their peers at Westminster, according to their privilege, being brought from the Tower with state processions and barges, and accompanied by lieutenants and axemen, the commoners engaged in that melancholy fray took their trial at Newgate, as became them; and, being all found guilty, pleaded likewise their benefit of clergy.[3] The sentence, as we all know, in these cases is, that the culprit lies a year in prison, or during the King's pleasure, and is burned in the hand, or only stamped with a cold iron; or this part of the punishment is altogether remitted at the grace of the Sovereign. So Harry Esmond found himself a criminal and a prisoner at two-and-twenty years old; as for the two Colonels, his comrades, they took the matter very lightly. Duelling was a part of their business; and they could not in honour refuse any invitations of that sort.

But the case was different with Mr Esmond. His life was changed by that stroke of the sword which destroyed his kind patron's. As he lay in prison, old Doctor Tusher fell ill and died; and Lady Castlewood appointed Thomas Tusher to the vacant living; about the filling of which she had a thousand times fondly talked to Harry Esmond: how they never should part; how he should educate her boy; how to be a country clergyman, like saintly George Herbert[4] or pious Doctor Ken,[5] was the happiest and greatest lot in life; how (if he were obstinately bent on it, though, for her part, she owned rather to holding Queen Bess's opinion, that a bishop should have no wife, and if not a bishop why a clergyman?) she would find a good wife for Harry Esmond: and so on, with a hundred pretty prospects told by fireside evenings, in fond prattle, as the children played about the hall. All these plans were overthrown now. Thomas Tusher wrote to Esmond, as he lay in prison, announcing that his patroness had conferred upon him the living his reverend father had held for many years; that she never, after the tragical events which had occurred (whereof Tom spoke with a very edifying horror), could see in the revered Tusher's pulpit, or at her son's table, the man who was answerable for the father's life; that her ladyship bade him to say that she prayed for her kinsman's repentance and his worldly happiness; that he was free to command her aid for any scheme of life which he might propose to himself; but that on this side of the grave she would see him no more. And Tusher, for his own part, added that Harry should have his prayers as a friend of his youth, and commended him whilst he was in prison to read certain works of theology, which his Reverence pronounced to be very wholesome for sinners in his lamentable condition.

And this was the return for a life of devotion – this the end of years of affectionate intercourse and passionate fidelity! Harry would have died for his patron, and was held as little better than his murderer; he had sacrificed, she did not know how much, for his mistress, and she threw him aside – he had endowed her family with all they had, and she talked about giving him alms as to a menial! The grief for his patron's loss; the pains of his own present position, and doubts as to the future: all these were forgotten under the sense of the consummate outrage which he had to endure, and overpowered by the superior pang of that torture.

He writ back a letter to Mr Tusher from his prison, congratulating his Reverence upon his appointment to the living of Castlewood; sarcastically bidding him to follow in the footsteps of his admirable father, whose gown had descended upon him – thanking her ladyship for her offer of alms, which he said he should trust not to need; and beseeching her to remember that, if ever her determination should change towards him, he would be ready to give her proofs of a fidelity which had never wavered, and which ought never to have been questioned by that house. 'And if we meet no more, or only as strangers in this world,' Mr Esmond concluded, 'a sentence against the cruelty and injustice of which I disdain to appeal; hereafter she will know who was faithful to her, and whether she had any cause to suspect the love and devotion of her kinsman and servant.'

After the sending of this letter, the poor young fellow's mind was more at ease than it had been previously. The blow had been struck, and he had borne it. His cruel goddess had shaken her wings and fled: and left him alone and friendless, but *virtute suâ*.[6] And he had to bear him up, at once the sense of his right and the feeling of his wrongs, his honour and his misfortune. As I have seen men waking and running to arms at a sudden trumpet, before emergency a manly heart leaps up resolute; meets the threatening danger with undaunted countenance; and, whether conquered or conquering, faces it always. Ah! no man knows his strength or his weakness, till occasion proves them. If there be some thoughts and actions of his life from the memory of which a man shrinks with shame, sure there are some which he may be proud to own and remember; forgiven injuries, conquered temptations (now and then), and difficulties vanquished by endurance.

It was these thoughts regarding the living, far more than any great poignancy of grief respecting the dead, which affected Harry Esmond whilst in prison after his trial: but it may be imagined that he could take no comrade of misfortune into the confidence of his feelings, and they thought it was remorse and sorrow for his patron's loss which affected the young man, in error of which opinion he chose to leave them. As a companion he was so moody and silent that the two officers, his fellow-sufferers, left him to himself mostly, liked little very likely what they knew of him, consoled themselves with dice, cards, and the bottle, and whiled away their own captivity in their own way. It seemed to Esmond as if he lived years in that prison and was changed and aged when he came out of it. At certain periods of life we live years of emotion in a few weeks – and look back on those times, as on great gaps between the old life and the new. You do not know how much you suffer in those critical maladies of the heart, until the disease is over and you look back on it afterwards. During the time, the suffering is at least sufferable. The day passes in more or less of pain, and the night wears away somehow. 'Tis only in after days that we see what the danger has been – as a man out a-hunting or riding for his life looks at a leap, and wonders how he should have survived the taking of it. O, dark months of grief and rage! of wrong and cruel endurance! He is old now who recalls you. Long ago he has forgiven and blest the soft hand that wounded him; but the mark is there, and the wound is cicatrized only – no time, tears, caresses, or repentance, can obliterate the scar. We are indocile to put up with grief, however. *Reficimus rates quassas*:[7] we tempt the ocean again and again, and try upon new ventures. Esmond thought of his early time as a noviciate, and of this past trial as an initiation before entering into life – as our young Indians undergo tortures silently before they pass to the rank of warriors in the tribe.

The officers, meanwhile, who were not let into the secret of the grief which was gnawing at the side of their silent young friend, and being accustomed to such transactions, in which one comrade or another was daily paying the forfeit of the sword, did not of course bemoan themselves very inconsolably about the fate of their late companion in arms. This one told stories of former adventures of love, or war, or pleasure, in which poor Frank Esmond had been engaged; t'other recollected how a constable had been bilked, or a tavern-bully beaten: whilst my lord's poor widow was sitting at his tomb worshipping him as an actual saint and spotless hero – so the visitors said who had news of Lady Castlewood; and Westbury and Macartney had pretty nearly had all the town to come and see them.

The duel, its fatal termination, the trial of the two peers and the three commoners concerned, had caused the greatest excitement in the town. The prints and News Letters were full of them. The three gentlemen in Newgate were almost as much crowded as the bishops in the Tower, or a highwayman before execution. We were allowed to live in the Governor's house, as hath been said, both before trial and after condemnation, waiting the King's pleasure; nor was the real cause of the fatal quarrel known, so closely had my lord and the two other persons who knew it kept the secret, but every one imagined that the origin of the meeting was a gambling dispute. Except fresh air, the prisoners had, upon payment, most things they could desire. Interest was made that they should not mix with the vulgar convicts, whose ribald choruses and loud laughter and curses could be heard from their own part of the prison, where they and the miserable debtors were confined pell-mell.

## Chapter 2

### I COME TO THE END OF MY CAPTIVITY, BUT NOT OF MY TROUBLE

AMONG the company which came to visit the two officers was an old acquaintance of Harry Esmond; that gentleman of the Guards, namely, who had been so kind to Harry when Captain Westbury's troop had been quartered at Castlewood more than seven years before. Dick the Scholar was no longer Dick the Trooper now, but Captain Steele of Lucas's Fusiliers, and secretary to my Lord Cutts, that famous officer of King William's, the bravest and most beloved man of the English army. The two jolly prisoners had been drinking with a party of friends (for our cellar and that of the keepers of Newgate, too, were supplied with endless hampers of Burgundy and Champagne that the friends of the Colonels sent in); and Harry, having no wish for their drink or their conversation, being too feeble in health for the one and too sad in spirits for the other, was sitting apart in his little room, reading such books as he had, one evening, when honest Colonel Westbury, flushed with liquor, and always good-humoured in and out of his cups, came laughing into Harry's closet, and said, 'Ho, young Killjoy! here's a friend come to see thee; he'll pray with thee, or he'll drink with thee; or he'll drink and pray turn about. Dick, my Christian hero, here's the little scholar of Castlewood.'

Dick came up and kissed Esmond on both cheeks, imparting a strong perfume of burnt sack along with his caress to the young man.

'What! is this the little man that used to talk Latin and fetch our bowls? How tall thou art grown! I protest I should have known thee anywhere. And so you have turned ruffian and fighter; and wanted to measure swords with Mohun, did you? I protest that Mohun said at the Guard dinner yesterday, where there was a pretty company of us, that the young fellow wanted to fight him, and was the better man of the two.'

'I wish we could have tried and proved it, Mr Steele,' says

Esmond, thinking of his dead benefactor, and his eyes filling
with tears.

With the exception of that one cruel letter which he had from
his mistress, Mr Esmond heard nothing from her, and she
seemed determined to execute her resolve of parting from him
and disowning him. But he had news of her, such as it was, which
Mr Steele assiduously brought him from the Prince's and
Princess's Court, where our honest Captain had been advanced
to the post of gentleman waiter.[1] When off duty there, Captain
Dick often came to console his friends in captivity; a good nature
and a friendly disposition towards all who were in ill-fortune no
doubt prompting him to make his visits, and good fellowship and
good wine to prolong them.

'Faith,' says Westbury, 'the little scholar was the first to begin
the quarrel – I mind me of it now – at Lockit's. I always hated
that fellow Mohun. What was the real cause of the quarrel
betwixt him and poor Frank? I would wager 'twas a woman.'

''Twas a quarrel about play – on my word, about play,' Harry
said. 'My poor lord lost great sums to his guest at Castlewood.
Angry words passed between them; and, though Lord Castlewood was the kindest and most pliable soul alive, his spirit was
very high; and hence that meeting which has brought us all
here,' says Mr Esmond, resolved never to acknowledge that
there had ever been any other cause but cards for the duel.

'I do not like to use bad words of a nobleman,' says Westbury; 'but if my Lord Mohun were a commoner, I would say,
'twas a pity he was not hanged. He was familiar with dice and
women at a time other boys are at school, being birched; he was
as wicked as the oldest rake, years ere he had done growing; and
handled a sword and a foil, and a bloody one too, before ever he
used a razor. He held poor Will Mountford in talk that night,
when bloody Dick Hill ran him through. He will come to a bad
end, will that young lord; and no end is bad enough for him,' says
honest Mr Westbury: whose prophecy was fulfilled twelve years
after, upon that fatal day when Mohun fell, dragging down one
of the bravest and greatest gentlemen in England in his fall.

From Mr Steele, then, who brought the public rumour, as
well as his own private intelligence, Esmond learned the move-

ments of his unfortunate mistress. Steele's heart was of very inflammable composition and the gentleman usher spoke in terms of boundless admiration both of the widow (that most beautiful woman, as he said) and of her daughter, who, in the Captain's eyes, was a still greater paragon. If the pale widow, whom Captain Richard, in his poetic rapture, compared to a Niobe in tears – to a Sigismunda – to a weeping Belvidera,[2] was an object the most lovely and pathetic which his eyes had ever beheld, or for which his heart had melted, even her ripened perfections and beauty were as nothing compared to the promise of that extreme loveliness which the good Captain saw in her daughter. It was *matre pulcra filia pulcrior*.[3] Steele composed sonnets whilst he was on duty in his Prince's antechamber, to the maternal and filial charms. He would speak for hours about them to Harry Esmond; and, indeed, he could have chosen few subjects more likely to interest the unhappy young man, whose heart was now as always devoted to these ladies; and who was thankful to all who loved them, or praised them, or wished them well.

Not that his fidelity was recompensed by any answering kindness, or show of relenting even, on the part of a mistress obdurate now after ten years of love and benefactions. The poor young man getting no answer, save Tusher's, to that letter which he had written, and being too proud to write more, opened a part of his heart to Steele, than whom no man, when unhappy, could find a kinder hearer or more friendly emissary; described (in words which were no doubt pathetic, for they came *imo pectore*, and caused honest Dick to weep plentifully) his youth, his constancy, his fond devotion to that household which had reared him; his affection how earned, and how tenderly requited until but yesterday, and (as far as he might) the circumstances and causes for which that sad quarrel had made of Esmond a prisoner under sentence, a widow and orphans of those whom in life he held dearest. In terms that might well move a harder-hearted man than young Esmond's confidant – for, indeed, the speaker's own heart was half broke as he uttered them – he described a part of what had taken place in that only sad interview which his mistress had granted him; how she had left him with anger and almost imprecation, whose words and thoughts until then had been only blessing and kindness; how she had accused him of the guilt of that blood, in exchange for which he would cheerfully have sacrificed his own (indeed, in this the Lord Mohun, the Lord Warwick, and all the gentlemen engaged, as well as the common rumour out of doors – Steele told him – bore out the luckless young man); and with all his heart, and tears, he besought Mr Steele to inform his mistress of her kinsman's unhappiness, and to deprecate that cruel anger she showed him. Half frantic with grief at the injustice done him, and contrasting it with a thousand soft recollections of love and confidence gone by, that made his present misery inexpressibly more bitter, the poor wretch passed many a lonely day and wakeful night in a kind of powerless despair and rage against his iniquitous fortune. It was the softest hand that struck him, the gentlest and most compassionate nature that persecuted him. 'I would as lief,' he said, 'have pleaded guilty to the murder, and have suffered for it like any other felon, as have to endure the torture to which my mistress subjects me.'

Although the recital of Esmond's story, and his passionate appeals and remonstrances, drew so many tears from Dick who heard them, they had no effect upon the person whom they were designed to move. Esmond's ambassador came back from the mission with which the poor young gentleman had charged him, with a sad blank face and a shake of the head, which told that there was no hope for the prisoner; and scarce a wretched culprit in that prison of Newgate ordered for execution, and trembling for a reprieve, felt more cast down than Mr Esmond, innocent and condemned.

As had been arranged between the prisoner and his counsel in their consultations, Mr Steele had gone to the Dowager's house in Chelsey, where it has been said the widow and her orphans were, had seen my Lady Viscountess and pleaded the cause of her unfortunate kinsman. 'And I think I spoke well, my poor boy,' says Mr Steele; 'for who would not speak well in such a cause, and before so beautiful a judge? I did not see the lovely Beatrix (sure her famous namesake of Florence was never half so beautiful), only the young Viscount was in the room with the

Lord Churchill, my Lord of Marlborough's eldest son. But these young gentlemen went off to the garden; I could see them from the window tilting at each other with poles in a mimic tournament (grief touches the young but lightly, and I remember that I beat a drum at the coffin of my own father). My Lady Viscountess looked out at the two boys at their game, and said – "You see, sir, children are taught to use weapons of death as toys, and to make a sport of murder"; and as she spoke she looked so lovely, and stood there in herself so sad and beautiful an instance of that doctrine whereof I am a humble preacher, that had I not dedicated my little volume of the Christian Hero (I perceive, Harry, thou hast not cut the leaves of it. The sermon is good, believe me, though the preacher's life may not answer it) – I say, hadn't I dedicated the volume to Lord Cutts, I would have asked permission to place her ladyship's name on the first page. I think I never saw such a beautiful violet as that of her eyes, Harry. Her complexion is of the pink of the blush-rose, she hath an exquisite turned wrist and dimpled hand, and I make no doubt——'

'Did you come to tell me about the dimples on my lady's hand?' broke out Mr Esmond, sadly.

'A lovely creature in affliction seems always doubly beautiful to me,' says the poor Captain, who indeed was but too often in a state to see double; and so checked he resumed the interrupted thread of his story. 'As I spoke my business,' Mr Steele said, 'and narrated to your mistress what all the world knows, and the other side hath been eager to acknowledge – that you had tried to put yourself between the two lords, and to take your patron's quarrel on your own point; I recounted the general praises of your gallantry, besides my Lord Mohun's particular testimony to it; I thought the widow listened with some interest, and her eyes – I have never seen such a violet, Harry – looked up at mine once or twice. But after I had spoken on this theme for a while she suddenly broke away with a cry of grief. "I would to God, sir," she said, "I had never heard that word gallantry which you use, or known the meaning of it. My lord might have been here but for that; my home might be happy; my poor boy have a father. It was what you gentlemen call gallantry came into my home, and drove my husband on to the cruel sword that killed him. You should not speak the word to a Christian woman, sir – a poor widowed mother of orphans, whose home was happy until the world came into it – the wicked godless world, that takes the blood of the innocent, and lets the guilty go free."

'As the afflicted lady spoke in this strain, sir,' Mr Steele continued, 'it seemed as if indignation moved her, even more than grief. "Compensation!" she went on passionately, her cheeks and eyes kindling; "what compensation does your world give the widow for her husband, and the children for the murder of their father? The wretch who did the deed has not even a punishment. Conscience! what conscience has he, who can enter the house of a friend, whisper falsehood and insult to a woman that never harmed him, and stab the kind heart that trusted him? My lord – my Lord Wretch, my Lord Villain's, my Lord Murderer's peers meet to try him, and they dismiss him with a word or two of reproof, and send him into the world again, to pursue women with lust and falsehood, and to murder unsuspecting guests[4] that harbour him. That day, my lord – my Lord Murderer – (I will never name him) – was let loose, a woman was executed at Tyburn for stealing in a shop. But a man may rob another of his life, or a lady of her honour, and shall pay no penalty! I take my child, run to the throne, and on my knees ask for justice, and the King refuses me. The King! he is no king of mine – he never shall be. He, too, robbed the throne from the King his father – the true King – and he has gone unpunished, as the great do."

'I then thought to speak for you,' Mr Steele continued, 'and I interposed by saying, "There was one, madam, who, at least, would have put his own breast between your husband's and my Lord Mohun's sword. Your poor young kinsman, Harry Esmond, hath told me that he tried to draw the quarrel on himself."

'"Are you come from *him*?" asked the lady' (so Mr Steele went on), 'rising up with a great severity and stateliness. "I thought you had come from the Princess. I saw Mr Esmond in his prison, and bade him farewell. He brought misery into my house. He never should have entered it."

'"Madam, madam, he is not to blame," I interposed,' continued Mr Steele.

'"Do I blame him to you, sir?" asked the widow. "If 'tis he who sent you, say that I have taken counsel, where" – she spoke with a very pallid cheek now, and a break in her voice – "where all who ask may have it; – and that it bids me to part from him, and to see him no more. We met in the prison for the last time – at least for years to come. It may be, in years hence, when – when our knees and our tears and our contrition have changed our sinful hearts, sir, and wrought our pardon, we may meet again – but not now. After what has passed, I could not bear to see him. I wish him well, sir; but I wish him farewell, too; and if he has that – that regard towards us which he speaks of, I beseech him to prove it by obeying me in this."

'"I shall break the young man's heart, madam, by this hard sentence,"' Mr Steele said.

'The lady shook her head,' continued my kind scholar. '"The hearts of young men, Mr Steele, are not so made," she said. "Mr Esmond will find other – other friends. The mistress of this house has relented very much towards the late lord's son," she added, with a blush, "and has promised me, that is, has promised that she will care for his fortune. Whilst I live in it, after the horrid horrid deed which has passed, Castlewood must never be a home to him – never. Nor would I have him write to me – except – no – I would have him never write to me, nor see him more. Give him if you will, my parting— Hush! not a word of this before my daughter."

'Here the fair Beatrix entered from the river, with her cheeks flushing with health, and looking only the more lovely and fresh for the mourning habiliments which she wore. And my Lady Viscountess said—

'"Beatrix, this is Mr Steele, gentleman-usher to the Prince's Highness. When does your new comedy appear, Mr Steele?" I hope thou wilt be out of prison for the first night, Harry.'

The sentimental captain concluded his sad tale, saying, 'Faith, the beauty of *Filia pulcrior* drove *pulcram matrem* out of my head; and yet as I came down the river, and thought about the pair, the pallid dignity and exquisite grace of the matron had the uppermost, and I thought her even more noble than the virgin!'

The party of prisoners lived very well in Newgate, and with comforts very different to those which were awarded to the poor wretches there (his insensibility to their misery, their gaiety still more frightful, their curses and blasphemy, hath struck with a kind of shame since – as proving how selfish, during his imprisonment, his own particular grief was, and how entirely the thoughts of it absorbed him); if the three gentlemen lived well under the care of the Warden of Newgate, it was because they paid well; and indeed the cost at the dearest ordinary or the grandest tavern in London could not have furnished a longer reckoning, than our host of the Handcuff Inn – as Colonel Westbury called it. Our rooms were the three in the gate over Newgate – on the second story looking up Newgate Street towards Cheapside and Paul's Church. And we had leave to walk on the roof, and could see thence Smithfield and the Bluecoat Boys' School, Gardens, and the Chartreux, where, as Harry Esmond remembered, Dick the Scholar, and his friend Tom Tusher, had had their schooling.

Harry could never have paid his share of that prodigious heavy reckoning which my landlord brought to his guests once a week: for he had but three pieces in his pockets that fatal night before the duel, when the gentlemen were at cards, and offered to play five. But whilst he was yet ill at the Gatehouse, after Lady Castlewood had visited him there, and before his trial, there came one in an orange-tawny coat and blue lace, the livery which the Esmonds always wore, and brought a sealed packet for Mr Esmond, which contained twenty guineas, and a note saying that a counsel had been appointed for him, and that more money would be forthcoming whenever he needed it.

'Twas a queer letter from the scholar as she was, or as she called herself: the Dowager Viscountess Castlewood; written in the strange barbarous French which she and many other fine ladies of that time – witness Her Grace of Portsmouth – employed. Indeed, spelling was not an article of general commodity in the world then, and my Lord Marlborough's letters[5] can show that he, for one, had but a little share of this part of grammar.

'Mong Coussin', my Lady Viscountess Dowager wrote, 'je scay que vous vous etes bravement batew et grievement bléssay – du costé de feu M. le Vicomte. M. le Compte de Varique[6] ne se playt qua parlay de vous: M. de Moon[7] auçy. Il di que vous avay voulew vous bastre avecque luy – que vous estes plus fort que luy fur l'ayscrimme – quil'y a surtout certaine Botte que vous scavay quil n'a jammay sceu pariay: et que c'en eut été fay de luy si vouseluy vous vous fussiay battews ansamb. Aincy ce pauv Vicompte est mort. Mort et peutayt – Mon coussin, mon coussin! jay dans la tayste que vous n'estes quung pety Monst – angcy que les Esmonds ong tousjours esté. La veuve est chay moy. J'ay recuilly cet' pauve famme. Elle est furieuse cont vous, allans tous les jours chercher le Roy (d'icy) démandant à gran cri revanche pour son Mary.[8] Elle ne veux voyre ni entende parlay de vous: pourtant elle ne say qu'en parlay milfoy par jour. Quand vous seray hor prison venay me voyre. J'auray soing de vous. Si cette petite Prude veut se défaire de song pety Monste (Hélas je craing quil ne soy trotar!) je m'en chargeray. J'ay encor quelqu interay et quelques escus de costay.[9]

'La Veuve se raccommode avec Miladi Marlboro qui est tout puiçante avecque la Pcesse Anne. Cet dam sentéraysent pour la petite prude; qui pourctant a un fi du mesme asge que vous savay.

'En sortant de prisong venez icy. Je ne puy vous recevoir chaymoy à cause des méchansetés du monde, may pre du moy vous aurez logement.

'ISABELLE VICOMPTESSE D'ESMOND'

Marchioness of Esmond this lady sometimes called herself, in virtue of that patent which had been given by the late King James to Harry Esmond's father; and in this state she had her train carried by a knight's wife, a cup and cover of assay[10] to drink from, and fringed cloth.[11]

He was of the same age as little Francis, whom we shall henceforth call Viscount Castlewood here, was H.R.H. the Prince of Wales,[12] born in the same year and month with Frank, and just proclaimed at Saint Germains, King of Great Britain, France, and Ireland.

## Chapter 3

## I TAKE THE QUEEN'S PAY IN QUIN'S
## REGIMENT

THE fellow in the orange-tawny livery with blue lace and facings was in waiting when Esmond came out of prison, and, taking the young gentleman's slender baggage, led the way out of that odious Newgate, and by Fleet Conduit, down to the Thames, where a pair of oars was called, and they went up the river to Chelsey. Esmond thought the sun had never shone so bright; nor the air felt so fresh and exhilarating. Temple Garden, as they rowed by, looked like the Garden of Eden to him, and the aspect of the quays, wharves, and buildings by the river, Somerset House, and Westminster (where the splendid new bridge[1] was just beginning), Lambeth tower and palace, and that busy shining scene of the Thames swarming with boats and barges, filled his heart with pleasure and cheerfulness – as well such a beautiful scene might to one who had been a prisoner so long, and with so many dark thoughts deepening the gloom of his captivity. They rowed up at length to the pretty village of Chelsey, where the nobility have many handsome country-houses; and so came to my Lady Viscountess's house, a cheerful new house in the row facing the river, with a handsome garden behind it, and a pleasant look-out both towards Surrey and Kensington, where stands the noble ancient palace of the Lord Warwick, Harry's reconciled adversary.

Here in her ladyship's saloon, the young man saw again some of those pictures which had been at Castlewood, and which she had removed thence on the death of her lord, Harry's father. Specially, and in the place of honour, was Sir Peter Lely's picture of the Honourable Mistress Isabella Esmond as Diana, in yellow satin, with a bow in her hand and a crescent in her forehead; and dogs frisking about her. 'Twas painted about the time when royal Endymions were said to find favour with this virgin huntress; and, as goddesses, have youth perpetual, this one believed to the day of her death that she never grew older:

and always persisted in supposing the picture was still like her.

After he had been shown to her room by the groom of the chamber, who filled many offices besides in her ladyship's modest household; and after a proper interval, his elderly goddess Diana vouchsafed to appear to the young man. A blackamoor in a Turkish habit, with red boots and a silver collar, on which the Viscountess's arms were engraven, preceded her and bore her cushion; then came her gentlewoman; a little pack of spaniels barking and frisking about preceded the austere huntress – then, behold, the Viscountess herself 'dropping odours'.[2] Esmond recollected from his childhood that rich aroma of musk which his mother-in-law (for she may be called so) exhaled. As the sky grows redder and redder towards sunset, so, in the decline of her years, the cheeks of my Lady Dowager blushed more deeply. Her face was illuminated with vermilion, which appeared the brighter from the white paint employed to set it off. She wore the ringlets which had been in fashion in King Charles's time; whereas the ladies of King William's had head-dresses like the towers of Cybèle.[3] Her eyes gleamed out from the midst of this queer structure of paint, dyes, and pomatums. Such was my Lady Viscountess, Mr Esmond's father's widow.

He made her such a profound bow as her dignity and relationship merited: and advanced with the greatest gravity, and once more kissed that hand, upon the trembling knuckles of which glittered a score of rings – remembering old times when that trembling hand made him tremble. 'Marchioness,' says he, bowing, and on one knee, 'is it only the hand I may have the honour of saluting?' For, accompanying that inward laughter, which the sight of such an astonishing old figure might well produce in the young man, there was goodwill too, and the kindness of consanguinity. She had been his father's wife, and was his grandfather's daughter. She had suffered him in old days, and was kind to him now after her fashion. And now that bar-sinister was removed from Esmond's thought, and that secret opprobrium no longer cast upon his mind, he was pleased to feel family ties and own them – perhaps secretly vain of the sacrifice he had made, and to think that he, Esmond, was really the chief of his house, and only prevented by his own magnanimity from advancing his claim.

At least, ever since he had learned that secret from his poor patron on his dying bed, actually as he was standing beside it, he had felt an independency which he had never known before, and which since did not desert him. So he called his old aunt Marchioness, but with an air as if he was the Marquis of Esmond who so addressed her.

Did she read in the young gentleman's eyes, which had now no fear of hers or their superannuated authority, that he knew or suspected the truth about his birth? She gave a start of surprise at his altered manner: indeed, it was quite a different bearing to that of the Cambridge student who had paid her a visit two years since, and whom she had dismissed with five pieces sent by the groom of the chamber. She eyed him, then trembled a little more than was her wont, perhaps, and said, 'Welcome, cousin,' in a frightened voice.

His resolution, as has been said before, had been quite different, namely, so to bear himself through life as if the secret of his birth was not known to him; but he suddenly and rightly determined on a different course. He asked that her ladyship's attendants should be dismissed, and when they were private – 'Welcome, nephew, at least, madam, it should be,' he said. 'A great wrong has been done to me and to you, and to my poor mother, who is no more.'

'I declare before Heaven that I was guiltless of it,' she cried out, giving up her cause at once. 'It was your wicked father who——'

'Who brought this dishonour on our family,' says Mr Esmond. 'I know it full well. I want to disturb no one. Those who are in present possession have been my dearest benefactors, and are quite innocent of intentional wrong to me. The late lord, my dear patron, knew not the truth until a few months before his death, when Father Holt brought the news to him.'

'The wretch! he had it in confession! He had it in confession!' cried out the Dowager Lady.

'Not so. He learned it elsewhere as well as in confession,' Mr

Esmond answered. 'My father, when wounded at the Boyne, told the truth to a French priest, who was in hiding after the battle, as well as to the priest there, at whose house he died. This gentleman did not think fit to divulge the story till he met with Mr Holt at Saint Omer's. And the latter kept it back for his own purpose, and until he had learned whether my mother was alive or no. She is dead years since: my poor patron told me with his dying breath; and I doubt him not. I do not know even whether I could prove a marriage. I would not if I could. I do not care to bring shame on our name, or grief upon those whom I love, however hardly they may use me. My father's son, madam, won't aggravate the wrong my father did you. Continue to be his widow, and give me your kindness. 'Tis all I ask from you; and I shall never speak of this matter again.'

'Mais vous etes un noble jeune homme!' breaks out my lady, speaking, as usual with her when she was agitated, in the French language.

'*Noblesse oblige*,' says Mr Esmond, making her a low bow. 'There are those alive to whom, in return for their love to me, I often fondly said I would give my life away. Shall I be their enemy now, and quarrel about a title? What matters who has it? 'Tis with the family still.'

'What can there be in that little prude of a woman, that makes men so *raffoler*⁴ about her?' cries out my Lady Dowager. 'She was here for a month petitioning the King. She is pretty, and well conserved; but she has not the *bel air*. In his late Majesty's Court all the men pretended to admire her; and she was no better than a little wax doll. She is better now, and looks the sister of her daughter; but what mean you all by bepraising her? Mr Steele, who was in waiting on Prince George, seeing her with her two children going to Kensington, writ a poem about her; and says he shall wear her colours, and dress in black for the future. Mr Congreve says he will write a Mourning Widow, that shall be better than his Mourning Bride.⁵ Though their husbands quarrelled and fought when that wretched Churchill deserted the King (for which he deserved to be hung), Lady Marlborough has again gone wild about the little widow; insulted me in my own drawing-room, by saying that 'twas not the *old* widow, but the young Viscountess, she had come to see. Little Castlewood and little Lord Churchill are to be sworn friends, and have boxed each other twice or thrice like brothers already. 'Twas that wicked young Mohun who, coming back from the provinces last year, where he had disinterred her, raved about her all the winter; said she was a pearl set before swine; and killed poor stupid Frank. The quarrel was all about his wife. I know 'twas all about her. Was there anything between her and Mohun, nephew? Tell me now; was there anything? About yourself, I do not ask you to answer questions.' Mr Esmond blushed up. 'My lady's virtue is like that of a saint in Heaven, madam,' he cried out.

'Eh! mon neveu. Many saints get to Heaven after having – a deal to repent of. I believe you are like all the rest of the fools, and madly in love with her.'

'Indeed, I loved and honoured her before all the world,' Esmond answered. 'I take no shame in that.'

'And she has shut her door on you – given the living to that horrid young cub, son of that horrid old bear, Tusher, and says she will never see you more. Monsieur mon neveu – we are all like that. When I was a young woman, I'm positive that a thousand duels were fought about me. And when poor Monsieur de Souchy drowned himself in the canal at Bruges because I danced with Count Springbock, I couldn't squeeze out a single tear, but danced till five o'clock the next morning. 'Twas the Count – no, 'twas my Lord Ormond that payed the fiddles, and his Majesty did me the honour of dancing all night with me. – How you are grown! You have got the *bel air*. You are a black man.[6] Our Esmonds are all black. The little prude's son is fair; so was his father – fair and stupid. You were an ugly little wretch when you came to Castlewood – you were all eyes, like a young crow. We intended you should be a priest. That awful Father Holt – how he used to frighten me when I was ill! I have a comfortable director now – the Abbé Douillette – a dear man. We make meagre on Fridays always. My cook is a devout pious man. You, of course, are of the right way of thinking. They say the Prince of Orange is very ill indeed.'

In this way the old Dowager rattled on remorselessly to Mr

Esmond, who was quite astounded with her present volubility, contrasting it with her former haughty behaviour to him. But she had taken him into favour for the moment, and chose not only to like him, as far as her nature permitted, but to be afraid of him; and he found himself to be as familiar with her now as a young man, as, when a boy, he had been timorous and silent. She was as good as her word respecting him. She introduced him to her company, of which she entertained a good deal – of the adherents of King James of course – and a great deal of loud intriguing took place over her card-tables. She presented Mr Esmond as her kinsman to many persons of honour; she supplied him not illiberally with money, which he had no scruple in accepting from her, considering the relationship which he bore to her, and the sacrifices which he himself was making in behalf of the family. But he had made up his mind to continue at no woman's apron-strings longer; and perhaps had cast about how he should distinguish himself, and make himself a name, which his singular fortune had denied him. A discontent with his former bookish life and quietude, – a bitter feeling of revolt at that slavery in which he had chosen to confine himself for the sake of those whose hardness towards him made his heart bleed, – a restless wish to see men and the world, – led him to think of the military profession: at any rate, to desire to see a few campaigns, and accordingly he pressed his new patroness to get him a pair of colours[7]; and one day had the honour of finding himself appointed an ensign in Colonel Quin's regiment of Fusileers on the Irish establishment.

Mr Esmond's commission was scarce three weeks old when that accident befell King William which ended the life of the greatest, the wisest, the bravest, and most clement sovereign whom England ever knew. 'Twas the fashion of the hostile party to assail this great prince's reputation during his life; but the joy which they and all his enemies in Europe showed at his death, is a proof of the terror in which they held him. Young as Esmond was, he was wise enough (and generous enough too, let it be said) to scorn that indecency of gratulation which broke out amongst the followers of King James in London, upon the death of this illustrious prince, this invincible warrior, this wise and moderate statesman. Loyalty to the exiled King's family was traditional, as has been said, in that house to which Mr Esmond belonged. His father's widow had all her hopes, sympathies, recollections, prejudices, engaged on King James's side; and was certainly as noisy a conspirator as ever asserted the King's rights, or abused his opponent's, over a quadrille[8] table or a dish of bohea.[9] Her ladyship's house swarmed with ecclesiastics, in disguise and out; with tale-bearers from St Germains; and quidnuncs[10] that knew the last news from Versailles; nay, the exact force and number of the next expedition which the French king was to send from Dunkirk, and which was to swallow up the Prince of Orange, his army, and his Court. She had received the Duke of Berwick when he landed here in '96. She kept the glass he drank from, vowing she never would use it till she drank King James the Third's health in it on his Majesty's return; she had tokens from the Queen, and relics of the saint who, if the story was true, had not always been a saint as far as she and many others were concerned. She believed in the miracles wrought at his tomb, and had a hundred authentic stories of wondrous cures effected by the blessed King's rosaries, the medals which he wore, the locks of his hair, or what not. Esmond remembered a score of marvellous tales which the credulous old woman told him. There was the Bishop of Autun, that was healed of a malady he had for forty years, and which left him after he said mass for the repose of the King's soul. There was M. Marais, a surgeon in Auvergne, who had a palsy in both his legs, which was cured through the King's intercession. There was Philip Pitet, of the Benedictines, who had a suffocating cough, which well nigh killed him, but he besought relief of Heaven through the merits and intercession of the blessed King, and he straightway felt a profuse sweat breaking out all over him, and was recovered perfectly. And there was the wife of Mons. Lepervier, dancing-master to the Duke of Saxe-Gotha, who was entirely eased of a rheumatism by the King's intercession, of which miracle there could be no doubt, for her surgeon and his apprentice had given their testimony, under oath, that they did not in any way contribute to the cure. Of these tales, and a thousand like them, Mr Esmond believed as much as he chose. His kinswoman's greater faith had swallow for them all.

The English High Church party did not adopt these legends. But truth and honour, as they thought, bound them to the exiled King's side; nor had the banished family any warmer supporter than the kind lady of Castlewood, in whose house Esmond was brought up. She influenced her husband, very much more perhaps than my lord knew, who admired his wife prodigiously though he might be inconstant to her, and who, adverse to the trouble of thinking himself, gladly enough adopted the opinions which she chose for him. To one of her simple and faithful heart, allegiance to any sovereign but the one was impossible. To serve King William for interest's sake would have been a monstrous hypocrisy and treason. Her pure conscience could no more have consented to it than to a theft, a forgery, or any other base action. Lord Castlewood might have been won over, no doubt, but his wife never could: and he submitted his conscience to hers in this case as he did in most others, when he was not tempted too sorely. And it was from his affection and gratitude most likely, and from that eager devotion for his mistress, which characterised all Esmond's youth, that the young man subscribed to this, and other articles of faith, which his fond benefactress set him. Had she been a Whig, he had been one; had she followed Mr Fox,[11] and turned Quaker, no doubt he would have abjured ruffles and a periwig, and have foresworn swords, lace coats, and clocked stockings. In the scholars' boyish disputes at the University, where parties ran very high, Esmond was noted as a Jacobite, and very likely from vanity as much as affection took the side of his family.

Almost the whole of the clergy of the country and more than a half of the nation were on this side. Ours is the most loyal people in the world surely; we admire our kings, and are faithful to them long after they have ceased to be true to us. 'Tis a wonder to any one who looks back at the history of the Stuart family to think how they kicked their crowns away from them; how they flung away chances after chances; what treasures of loyalty they dissipated, and how fatally they were bent on con-summating their own ruin. If ever men had fidelity, 'twas they;

if ever men squandered opportunity, 'twas they; and, of all the enemies they had, they themselves were the most fatal.*

When the Princess Anne succeeded, the wearied nation was glad enough to cry a truce from all these wars, controversies, and conspiracies, and to accept in the person of a Princess of the blood royal a compromise between the parties into which the country was divided. The Tories could serve under her with easy consciences; though a Tory herself, she represented the triumph of the Whig opinion. The people of England, always liking that their Princes should be attached to their own families were pleased to think the Princess was faithful to hers; and up to the very last day and hour of her reign, and but for that fatality which he inherited from his fathers along with their claims to the English crown, King James the Third might have worn it. But he neither knew how to wait an opportunity, nor to use it when he had it; he was venturesome when he ought to have been cautious, and cautious when he ought to have dared everything. 'Tis with a sort of rage at his inaptitude that one thinks of his melancholy story. Do the Fates deal more specially with kings than with common men? One is apt to imagine so, in considering the history of that royal race, in whose behalf so much fidelity, so much valour, so much blood were desperately and bootlessly expended.

The King dead then, the Princess Anne (ugly Anne Hyde's daughter,[13] our Dowager at Chelsey called her) was proclaimed by trumpeting heralds all over the town from Westminster to Ludgate Hill, amidst immense jubilations of the people.

Next week my Lord Marlborough was promoted to the Garter, and to be Captain-General of Her Majesty's forces at home and abroad. This appointment only inflamed the Dowager's rage, or, as she thought it, her fidelity to her rightful sovereign. 'The Princess is but a puppet in the hands of that fury of a woman,[14] who comes into my drawing-room and insults me to my face. What can come to a country that is given over to such a woman?' says the Dowager: 'As for that double-faced traitor, my Lord Marlborough, he has betrayed every man and

---

* Ω ποποι, οἱον δη νυ θεονς βροτοι αιτιοωνται
ἐξ ἡμεων γαρ φασι κακ' εμμεναι, οι δε και αντοι
σφησιν ατασθαλιησιν ὑπερ μορον αλγε' εχουσιν.[12]

every woman with whom he has had to deal, except his horrid wife, who makes him tremble. 'Tis all over with the country when it has got into the clutches of such wretches as these.'

Esmond's old kinswoman saluted the new powers in this way; but some good fortune at least occurred to a family which stood in great need of it, by the advancement of these famous personages who benefited humbler people that had the luck of being in their favour. Before Mr Esmond left England in the month of August, and being then at Portsmouth, where he had joined his regiment, and was busy at drill, learning the practice and mysteries of the musket and pike, he heard that a pension on the Stamp office[15] had been got for his late beloved mistress, and that the young Mistress Beatrix was also to be taken into Court. So much good, at least, had come of the poor widow's visit to London, not revenge upon her husband's enemies, but reconcilement to old friends, who pitied, and seemed inclined to serve her. As for the comrades in prison and the late misfortune; Colonel Westbury was with the Captain-General gone to Holland; Captain Macartney was now at Portsmouth, with his regiment of Fusileers and the force under command of his Grace the Duke of Ormond, bound for Spain it was said; my Lord Warwick was returned home; and Lord Mohun, so far from being punished for the homicide which had brought so much grief and change into the Esmond family, was gone in company of my Lord Macclesfield's splendid embassy[16] to the Elector of Hanover, carrying the Garter to his Highness, and a complimentary letter from the Queen.

## Chapter 4

### RECAPITULATIONS

FROM such fitful lights as could be cast upon his dark history by the broken narrative of his poor patron, torn by remorse and struggling in the last pangs of dissolution, Mr Esmond had been made to understand so far, that his mother was long since dead;

and so there could be no question as regarded her or her honour, tarnished by her husband's desertion and injury, to influence her son in any steps which he might take either for prosecuting or relinquishing his own just claims. It appeared from my poor lord's hurried confession, that he had been made acquainted with the real facts of the case only two years since, when Mr Holt visited him, and would have implicated him in one of those many conspiracies by which the secret leaders of King James's party in this country were ever endeavouring to destroy the Prince of Orange's life or power; conspiracies so like murder, so cowardly in the means used, so wicked in the end, that our nation has sure done well in throwing off all allegiance and fidelity to the unhappy family that could not vindicate its right except by such treachery – by such dark intrigue and base agents. There were designs against King William that were no more honourable than the ambushes of cut-throats and footpads. 'Tis humiliating to think that a great Prince, possessor of a great and sacred right, and upholder of a great cause, should have stooped to such baseness of assassination and treasons as are proved by the unfortunate King James's own warrant and sign-manual given to his supporters in this country. What he and they called levying war was, in truth, no better than instigating murder. The noble Prince of Orange burst magnanimously through those feeble meshes of conspiracy in which his enemies tried to envelop him: it seemed as if their cowardly daggers broke upon the breast of his undaunted resolution. After King James's death, the Queen and her people at St Germains – priests and women for the most part – continued their intrigues in behalf of the young Prince, James the Third, as he was called in France and by his party here (this Prince, or Chevalier de St George, was born in the same year with Esmond's young pupil Frank, my Lord Viscount's son): and the Prince's affairs, being in the hands of priests and women, were conducted as priests and women will conduct them, artfully, cruelly, feebly, and to a certain bad issue. The moral of the Jesuits' story I think as wholesome a one as ever was writ: the artfullest, the wisest, the most toilsome, and dexterous plot-builders in the world – there always comes a day when the roused public indignation kicks their flimsy edifice down, and sends its cowardly enemies a-flying. Mr Swift hath finely described that passion for intrigue, that love of secrecy, slander, and lying, which belongs to weak people, hangers-on of weak courts. 'Tis the nature of such to hate and envy the strong, and conspire their ruin; and the conspiracy succeeds very well, and everything presages the satisfactory overthrow of the great victim; until one day Gulliver rouses himself, shakes off the little vermin of an enemy, and walks away unmolested. Ah! the Irish soldiers might well say after the Boyne, 'Change kings with us, and we will fight it over again.' Indeed, the fight was not fair between the two. 'Twas a weak priest-ridden, woman-ridden man, with such puny allies and weapons as his own poor nature led him to choose, contending against the schemes, the generalship, the wisdom, and the heart of a hero.

On one of these many coward's errands, then (for, as I view them now, I can call them no less), Mr Holt had come to my lord at Castlewood, proposing some infallible plan for the Prince of Orange's destruction, in which my Lord Viscount, loyalist as he was, had indignantly refused to join. As far as Mr Esmond could gather from his dying words, Holt came to my lord with a plan of insurrection, and offer of the renewal, in his person, of that marquis's title which King James had conferred on the preceding Viscount; and on refusal of this bribe, a threat was made, on Holt's part, to upset my Lord Viscount's claim to his estate and title of Castlewood altogether. To back this astounding piece of intelligence, of which Henry Esmond's patron now had the first light, Holt came armed with the late lord's dying declaration, after the affair of the Boyne, at Trim, in Ireland, made both to the Irish priest and a French ecclesiastic of Holt's order, that was with King James's army. Holt showed, or pretended to show, the marriage certificate of the late Viscount Esmond with my mother, in the city of Brussels, in the year 1677, when the Viscount, then Thomas Esmond, was serving with the English army in Flanders; he could show, he said, that this Gertrude, deserted by her husband long since, was alive, and a professed nun in the year 1685, at Brussels, in which year Thomas Esmond married his uncle's daughter, Isabella, now called

Viscountess Dowager of Castlewood; and leaving him, for twelve hours, to consider this astounding news (so the poor dying lord said), disappeared with his papers in the mysterious way in which he came. Esmond knew how, well enough: by that window from which he had seen the father issue: – but there was no need to explain to my poor lord, only to gather from his parting lips the words which he would soon be able to utter no more.

Ere the twelve hours were over, Holt himself was a prisoner, implicated in Sir John Fenwick's conspiracy, and locked up at Hexton first, whence he was transferred to the Tower; leaving the poor Lord Viscount, who was not aware of the others being taken, in daily apprehension of his return, when (as my Lord Castlewood declared, calling God to witness, and with tears in his dying eyes) it had been his intention at once to give up his estate and his title to their proper owner, and to retire to his own house at Walcote with his family. 'And would to God I had done it,' the poor lord said; 'I would not be here now, wounded to death, a miserable, stricken man!'

My lord waited day after day, and, as may be supposed, no messenger came; but at a month's end Holt got means to convey to him a message out of the Tower, which was to this effect: that he should consider all unsaid that had been said, and that things were as they were.

'I had a sore temptation,' said my poor lord. 'Since I had come into this cursed title of Castlewood, which hath never prospered with me, I have spent far more than the income of that estate, and my paternal one, too. I calculated all my means down to the last shilling and found I never could pay you back, my poor Harry, whose fortune I had had for twelve years. My wife and children must have gone out of the house dishonoured, and beggars. God knows, it hath been a miserable one for me and mine. Like a coward I clung to that respite which Holt gave me. I kept the truth from Rachel and you. I tried to win money of Mohun, and only plunged deeper into debt; I scarce dared look thee in the face when I saw thee. This sword hath been hanging over my head these two years. I swear I felt happy when Mohun's blade entered my side.'

After lying ten months in the Tower, Holt, against whom

nothing could be found except that he was a Jesuit priest, known to be in King James's interest, was put on shipboard by the incorrigible forgiveness of King William, who promised him, however, a hanging if ever he should again set foot on English shore. More than once, whilst he was in prison himself, Esmond had thought where those papers could be, which the Jesuit had shown to his patron, and which had such an interest for himself. They were not found on Mr Holt's person when that Father was apprehended, for had such been the case my lords of the Council had seen them, and this family history had long since been made public. However, Esmond cared not to seek the papers. His resolution being taken; his poor mother dead; what matter to him that documents existed proving his right to a title which he was determined not to claim, and of which he vowed never to deprive that family which he loved best in the world? Perhaps he took a greater pride out of his sacrifice than he would have had in those honours which he was resolved to forgo. Again, as long as these titles were not forthcoming, Esmond's kinsman, dear young Francis, was the honourable and undisputed owner of the Castlewood estate and title. The mere word of a Jesuit could not overset Frank's right of occupancy, and so Esmond's mind felt actually at ease to think the papers were missing, and in their absence his dear mistress and her son the lawful lady and lord of Castlewood.

Very soon after his liberation, Mr Esmond made it his business to ride to that village of Ealing where he had passed his earliest years in this country, and to see if his old guardians were still alive and inhabitants of that place. But the only relique which he found of old M. Pastoureau was a stone in the church-yard, which told that Athanasius Pastoureau, a native of Flanders, lay there buried, aged 87 years. The old man's cottage, which Esmond perfectly recollected, and the garden (where in his childhood he had passed many hours of play and reverie, and had many a beating from his termagant of a foster-mother), were now in the occupation of quite a different family; and it was with difficulty that he could learn in the village what had come of Pastoureau's widow and children. The clerk of the parish recollected her – the old man was scarce altered in the

fourteen years that had passed since last Esmond set eyes on him.
It appeared she had pretty soon consoled herself after the death
of her old husband, whom she ruled over, by taking a new one
younger than herself, who spent her money and ill-treated her
and her children. The girl died; one of the boys 'listed; the other
had gone apprentice. Old Mr Rogers, the clerk, said he had
heard that Mrs Pastoureau was dead too. She and her husband
had left Ealing this seven year; and so Mr Esmond's hopes of
gaining any information regarding his parentage from this
family, were brought to an end. He gave the old clerk a crown-
piece for his news, smiling to think of the time when he and his
little playfellows had slunk out of the churchyard, or hidden
behind the gravestones, at the approach of this awful authority.

Who was his mother? What had her name been? When did
she die? Esmond longed to find some one who could answer
these questions to him, and thought even of putting them to his
aunt the Viscountess, who had innocently taken the name which
belonged of right to Henry's mother. But she knew nothing, or
chose to know nothing, on this subject, nor, indeed, could Mr
Esmond press her much to speak on it. Father Holt was the only
man who could enlighten him, and Esmond felt he must wait
until some fresh chance or new intrigue might put him face to
face with his old friend, or bring that restless indefatigable spirit
back to England again.

The appointment to his ensigncy, and the preparations necessary for the campaign, presently gave the young gentleman
other matters to think of. His new patroness treated him very
kindly and liberally; she promised to make interest and pay
money, too, to get him a company speedily; she bade him procure a handsome outfit, both of clothes and of arms, and was
pleased to admire him when he made his first appearance in his
laced scarlet coat, and to permit him to salute her on the occasion
of this interesting investiture. 'Red,' says she, tossing up her old
head, 'hath always been in the colour worn by the Esmonds.'
And so her ladyship wore it on her own cheeks very faithfully to
the last. She would have him be dressed, she said, as became his
father's son, and paid cheerfully for his five-pound beaver, his
black buckled periwig, and his fine holland shirts, and his

swords, and his pistols, mounted with silver. Since the day he was born, poor Harry had never looked such a fine gentleman: his liberal stepmother filled his purse with guineas, too, some of which Captain Steele and a few choice spirits helped Harry to spend in an entertainment which Dick ordered (and, indeed, would have paid for, but that he had no money when the reckoning was called for; nor would the landlord give him any more credit) at the Garter,[1] over against the gate of the Palace, in Pall Mall.

The old Viscountess, indeed, if she had done Esmond any wrong formerly, seemed inclined to repair it by the present kindness of her behaviour: she embraced him copiously at parting, wept plentifully, bade him write by every packet, and gave him an inestimable relic, which she besought him to wear round his neck – a medal, blessed by I know not what Pope, and worn by his late sacred Majesty King James. So Esmond arrived at his regiment with a better equipage than most young officers could afford. He was older than most of his seniors, and had a further advantage which belonged but to very few of the army gentlemen in his day – many of whom could do little more than write their names – that he had read much, both at home and at the University, was master of two or three languages, and had that further education which neither books nor years will give, but which some men get from the silent teaching of adversity. She is a great schoolmistress, as many a poor fellow knows, that hath held his hand out to her ferule, and whimpered over his lesson before her awful chair.

## Chapter 5

### I GO ON THE VIGO BAY EXPEDITION, TASTE SALT WATER, AND SMELL POWDER[1]

THE first expedition in which Mr Esmond had the honour to be engaged, rather resembled one of the invasions projected by the redoubted Captain Avory or Captain Kid, than a war between

crowned heads, carried on by generals of rank and honour. On
the 1st day of July, 1702, a great fleet, of a hundred and fifty sail,
set sail from Spithead, under the command of Admiral Shovell,
having on board 12,000 troops, with his Grace the Duke of
Ormond as the Capt.-General of the expedition. One of these
12,000 heroes having never been to sea before, or, at least, only
once in his infancy, when he made the voyage to England from
that unknown country where he was born – one of those 12,000 –
the junior ensign of Col. Quin's regiment of Fusileers – was in a
quite unheroic state of corporal prostration a few hours after
sailing; and an enemy, had he boarded the ship, would have had
easy work of him. From Portsmouth we put into Plymouth, and
took in fresh reinforcements. We were off Finisterre on the 31st
of July, so Esmond's table-book informs him; and on the 8th of
August made the rock of Lisbon. By this time the ensign was
grown as bold as an admiral, and a week afterwards had the
fortune to be under fire for the first time – and under water,
too – his boat being swamped in the surf in Toros Bay, where the
troops landed. The ducking of his new coat was all the harm the
young soldier got in this expedition, for, indeed, the Spaniards
made no stand before our troops, and were not in strength to
do so.

But the campaign, if not very glorious, was very pleasant.
New sights of nature, by sea and land – a life of action, beginning
now for the first time – occupied and excited the young man.
The many accidents, and the routine of ship-board – the
military duty – the new acquaintances, both of his comrades in
arms, and of the officers of the fleet – served to cheer and
occupy his mind, and waken it out of that selfish depression into
which his late unhappy fortunes had plunged him. He felt as if
the ocean separated him from his past care, and welcomed the
new era of life which was dawning for him. Wounds heal rapidly
in a heart of two-and-twenty; hopes revive daily; and courage
rallies, in spite of a man. Perhaps, as Esmond thought of his late
despondency and melancholy, and how irremediable it had
seemed to him, as he lay in his prison a few months back, he was
almost mortified in his secret mind at finding himself so
cheerful.

To see with one's own eyes men and countries, is better than reading all the books of travel in the world; and it was with extreme delight and exultation that the young man found himself actually on his grand tour, and in the view of people and cities which he had read about as a boy. He beheld war for the first time – the pride, pomp, and circumstance of it, at least, if not much of the danger. He saw actually, and with his own eyes, those Spanish cavaliers and ladies whom he had beheld in imagination in that immortal story of Cervantes, which had been the delight of his youthful leisure. 'Tis forty years since Mr Esmond witnessed those scenes, but they remain as fresh in his memory as on the day when first he saw them as a young man. A cloud, as of grief, that had lowered over him, and had wrapped the last years of his life in gloom, seemed to clear away from Esmond during this fortunate voyage and campaign. His energies seemed to awaken and to expand, under a cheerful sense of freedom. Was his heart secretly glad to have escaped from that fond but ignoble bondage at home? Was it that the inferiority to which the idea of his base birth had compelled him, vanished with the knowledge of that secret, which though, perforce, kept to himself, was yet enough to cheer and console him? At any rate, young Esmond of the army was quite a different being to the sad little dependant of the kind Castlewood household, and the melancholy student of Trinity Walks; discontented with his fate, and with the vocation into which that drove him, and thinking, with a secret indignation, that the cassock and bands, and the very sacred office with which he had once proposed to invest himself, were, in fact, but marks of a servitude which was to continue all his life long. For, disguise it as he might to himself, he had all along felt that to be Castlewood's Chaplain was to be Castlewood's inferior still, and that his life was but to be a long, hopeless servitude. So, indeed, he was far from grudging his old friend Tom Tusher's good fortune (as Tom, no doubt, thought it). Had it been a mitre and Lambeth which his friends offered him, and not a small living and a country parsonage, he would have felt as much a slave in one case as in the other, and was quite happy and thankful to be free.

The bravest man I ever knew in the army, and who had been

present in most of King William's actions, as well as in the campaigns of the great Duke of Marlborough, could never be got to tell us of any achievement of his, except that once Prince Eugene ordered him up a tree to reconnoitre the enemy, which feat he could not achieve on account of the horseman's boots he wore; and on another day that he was very nearly taken prisoner because of these jack-boots, which prevented him from running away. The present narrator shall imitate this laudable reserve, and doth not intend to dwell upon his military exploits, which were in truth not very different from those of a thousand other gentlemen. This first campaign of Mr Esmond's lasted but a few days; and as a score of books have been written concerning it, it may be dismissed very briefly here.

When our fleet came within view of Cadiz, our commander sent a boat with a white flag and a couple of officers to the Governor of Cadiz, Don Scipio de Brancaccio, with a letter from his Grace, in which he hoped that as Don Scipio had formerly served with the Austrians against the French in England, 'twas to be hoped that his Excellency would now declare himself against the French King and for the Austrian in the war between King Philip and King Charles. But his Excellency, Don Scipio, prepared a reply, in which he announced that, having served his former king with honour and fidelity, he hoped to exhibit the same loyalty and devotion towards his present sovereign, King Philip V; and by the time this letter was ready, the officers had been taken to see the town, and the alameda,[2] and the theatre, where bull-fights are fought, and the convents, where the admirable works of Don Bartholomew Murillo inspired one of them with a great wonder and delight – such as he had never felt before – concerning this divine art of painting; and these sights over, and a handsome refection and chocolate being served to the English gentlemen, they were accompanied back to their shallop with every courtesy, and were the only two officers of the English army that saw at that time that famous city.

The General tried the power of another proclamation on the Spaniards, in which he announced that we only came in the interest of Spain and King Charles, and for ourselves wanted to make no conquest nor settlement in Spain at all. But all this eloquence was lost upon the Spaniards, it would seem: the Captain-General of Andalusia would no more listen to us than the Governor of Cadiz; and in reply to his Grace's proclamation, the Marquis of Villadarias fired off another, which those who knew the Spanish thought rather the best of the two; and of this number was Harry Esmond, whose kind Jesuit in old days had instructed him, and now had the honour of translating for his Grace these harmless documents of war. There was a hard touch[3] for his Grace, and, indeed, for other generals in Her Majesty's service, in the concluding sentence of the Don: 'That he and his council had the generous example of their ancestors to follow, who had never yet sought their elevation in the blood or in the flight of their kings. "*Mori pro patria*" was his device, which the Duke might communicate to the Princess who governed England.'

Whether the troops were angry at this repartee or no, 'tis certain something put them in a fury; for, not being able to get possession of Cadiz, our people seized upon Port Saint Mary's and sacked it, burning down the merchant's store-houses, getting drunk with the famous wines there, pillaging and robbing quiet houses and convents, murdering and doing worse. And the only blood which Mr Esmond drew in this shameful campaign, was the knocking down an English sentinel with a half-pike, who was offering insult to a poor trembling nun. Is she going to turn out a beauty? or a princess? or perhaps Esmond's mother that he had lost and never seen? Alas no, it was but a poor wheezy old dropsical woman, with a wart on her nose. But having been early taught a part of the Roman religion, he never had the horror of it that some Protestants have shown, and seem to think to be a part of ours.

After the pillage and plunder of St Mary's, and an assault upon a fort or two, the troops all took shipping, and finished their expedition, at any rate, more brilliantly than it had begun. Hearing that the French fleet with a great treasure was in Vigo Bay, our Admirals, Rooke and Hopson, pursued the enemy thither; the troops landed and carried the forts that protected the bay, Hopson passing the boom first on board his ship the Torbay, and the rest of the ships, English and Dutch, following him.

Twenty ships were burned or taken in the Port of Redondilla, and a vast deal more plunder than was ever accounted for; but poor men before that expedition were rich afterwards, and so often was it found and remarked that the Vigo officers came home with pockets full of money, that the notorious Jack Shafto,[4] who made such a figure at the coffee-houses and gaming-tables in London, and gave out that he had been a soldier at Vigo, owned, when he was about to be hanged, that Bagshot Heath had been *his* Vigo, and that he only spoke of La Redondilla[5] to turn away people's eyes from the real place where the booty lay. Indeed, Hounslow or Vigo – which matters much? The latter was a bad business, though Mr Addison did sing its praises in Latin. That honest gentleman's muse had an eye to the main chance; and I doubt whether she saw much inspiration in the losing side.

But though Esmond, for his part, got no share of this fabulous booty, one great prize which he had out of the campaign was, that excitement of action and change of scene, which shook off a great deal of his previous melancholy. He learnt at any rate to bear his fate cheerfully. He brought back a browned face, a heart resolute enough, and a little pleasant store of knowledge and observation, from that expedition, which was over with the autumn, when the troops were back in England again; and Esmond giving up his post of secretary to General Lumley, whose command was over, and parting with that officer with many kind expressions of good-will on the General's side, had leave to go to London, to see if he could push his fortunes any way further, and found himself once more in his dowager aunt's comfortable quarters at Chelsey, and in greater favour than ever with the old lady. He propitiated her with a present of a comb, a fan, and a black mantle, such as the ladies of Cadiz wear, and which my Lady Viscountess pronounced became her style of beauty mightily. And she was greatly edified at hearing of that story of his rescue of the nun, and felt very little doubt but that her King James's relic, which he had always dutifully worn in his desk, had kept him out of danger, and averted the shot of the enemy. My lady made feasts for him, introduced him to more company, and pushed his fortunes with such enthusiasm and

success, that she got a promise of a company for him through the
Lady Marlborough's interest, who was graciously pleased to
accept of a diamond worth a couple of hundred guineas, which
Mr Esmond was enabled to present to her ladyship through his
aunt's bounty, and who promised that she would take charge of
Esmond's fortune. He had the honour to make his appearance at
the Queen's drawing-room occasionally, and to frequent my
Lord Marlborough's levees. That great man received the young
one with very especial favour, so Esmond's comrades said, and
deigned to say that he had received the best reports of Mr
Esmond, both for courage and ability, whereon you may be sure
the young gentleman made a profound bow, and expressed himself eager to serve under the most distinguished captain in the
world.

Whilst his business was going on thus prosperously, Esmond
had his share of pleasure, too, and made his appearance along
with other young gentlemen at the coffee-houses, the theatres,
and the Mall. He longed to hear of his dear mistress and her
family: many a time, in the midst of the gaieties and pleasures of
the town, his heart fondly reverted to them; and often as the
young fellows of his society were making merry at the tavern,
and calling toasts (as the fashion of that day was) over their wine,
Esmond thought of persons – of two fair women, whom he had
been used to adore almost, and emptied his glass with a sigh.

By this time the elder Viscountess had grown tired again of
the younger, and whenever she spoke of my lord's widow, 'twas
in terms by no means complimentary towards that poor lady;
the younger woman not needing her protection any longer, the
elder abused her. Most of the family quarrels that I have seen in
life (saving always those arising from money-disputes, when a
division of twopence-halfpenny will often drive the dearest
relatives into war and estrangement), spring out of jealousy and
envy. Jack and Tom, born of the same family and to the same
fortune, live very cordially together, not until Jack is ruined
when Tom deserts him, but until Tom makes a sudden rise in
prosperity, which Jack can't forgive. Ten times to one 'tis the
unprosperous man that is angry, not the other who is in fault.
'Tis Mrs Jack, who can only afford a chair, that sickens at Mrs

Tom's new coach-and-six, cries out against her sister's airs, and sets her husband against his brother. 'Tis Jack who sees his brother shaking hands with a lord (with whom Jack would like to exchange snuff-boxes himself), that goes home and tells his wife how poor Tom is spoiled, he fears, and no better than a sneak, parasite, and beggar on horseback. I remember how furious the coffee-house wits were with Dick Steele when he set up his coach, and fine house in Bloomsbury; they began to forgive him when the bailiffs were after him,[6] and abused Mr Addison for selling Dick's country house. And yet Dick in the spunging-house, or Dick in the Park, with his four mares and plated harness, was exactly the same gentle, kindly, improvident, jovial Dick Steele: and yet Mr Addison was perfectly right in getting the money which was his, and not giving up the amount of his just claim, to be spent by Dick upon champagne and fiddlers, laced clothes, fine furniture, and parasites, Jew and Christian, male and female, who clung to him. As, according to the famous maxim of Monsieur de Rochefoucault, 'in our friends' misfortunes there's something secretly pleasant to us'; so, on the other hand, their good fortune is disagreeable. If 'tis hard for a man to bear his own good luck, 'tis harder still for his friends to bear it for him; and but few of them ordinarily can stand that trial: whereas one of the 'precious uses'[7] of adversity is, that it is a great reconciler; that it brings back averted kindness, disarms animosity, and causes yesterday's enemy to fling his hatred aside, and hold out a hand to the fallen friend of old days. There's pity and love, as well as envy, in the same heart and towards the same person. The rivalry stops when the competitor tumbles; and, as I view it, we should look at these agreeable and disagreeable qualities of our humanity humbly alike. They are consequent and natural, and our kindness and meanness both manly.

So you may either read the sentence, that the elder of Esmond's two kinswomen pardoned the younger her beauty, when that had lost somewhat of its freshness, perhaps; and forgot most her grievances against the other, when the subject of them was no longer prosperous and enviable; or we may say more benevolently (but the sum comes to the same figures, worked either way), that Isabella repented of her unkindness towards Rachel, when Rachel was unhappy; and, bestirring herself in behalf of the poor widow and her children, gave them shelter and friendship. The ladies were quite good friends as long as the weaker one needed a protector. Before Esmond went away on his first campaign, his mistress was still on terms of friendship (though a poor little chit, a woman that had evidently no spirit in her, &c.) with the elder Lady ˙Castlewood; and Mistress[8] Beatrix was allowed to be a beauty.

But between the first year of Queen Anne's reign, and the second, sad changes for the worse had taken place in the two younger ladies, at least in the elder's description of them. Rachel, Viscountess Castlewood, had no more face than a dumpling, and Mrs Beatrix was grown quite coarse, and was losing all her beauty. Little Lord Blandford – (she never would call him Lord Blandford; his father was Lord Churchill – the King, whom he betrayed, had made him Lord Churchill, and he was Lord Churchill still) – might be making eyes at her; but his mother, that vixen of a Sarah Jennings,[9] would never hear of such a folly. Lady Marlborough had got her to be a maid of honour at Court to the Princess, but she would repent of it. The widow Francis (she was but Mrs Francis Esmond), was a scheming, artful, heartless hussy. She was spoiling her brat of a boy, and she would end by marrying her Chaplain.

'What, Tusher?' cried Mr Esmond, feeling a strange pang of rage and astonishment.

'Yes – Tusher, my maid's son; and who has got all the qualities of his father, the lacquey in black, and his accomplished mamma, the waiting-woman,' cries my lady. 'What, do you suppose that a sentimental widow, who will live down in that dingy dungeon of a Castlewood, where she spoils her boy, kills the poor with her drugs, has prayers twice a day and sees nobody but the chaplain – what do you suppose she can do, *mon cousin*, but let the horrid parson, with his great square toes, and hideous little green eyes, make love to her? *Cela c'est vu, mon cousin.* When I was a girl at Castlewood, all the chaplains fell in love with me – they've nothing else to do.'

My lady went on with more talk of this kind, though, in truth,

Esmond had no idea of what she said further, so entirely did her first words occupy his thought. Were they true? Not all, nor half, nor a tenth part of what the garrulous old woman said, was true. Could this be so? No ear had Esmond for anything else, though his patroness chattered on for an hour.

Some young gentlemen of the town, with whom Esmond had made acquaintance, had promised to present him to that most charming of actresses, and lively and agreeable of women, Mrs Bracegirdle,[10] about whom Harry's old adversary Mohun had drawn swords, a few years before my poor lord and he fell out. The famous Mr Congreve had stamped with his high approval, to the which there was no gainsaying, this delightful person; and she was acting in Dick Steele's comedies, and finally, and for twenty-four hours after beholding her, Mr Esmond felt himself, or thought himself, to be as violently enamoured of this lovely brunette, as were a thousand other young fellows about the city. To have once seen her was to long to behold her again; and to be offered the delightful privilege of her acquaintance, was a pleasure the very idea of which set the young lieutenant's heart on fire. A man cannot live with comrades under the tents without finding out that he too is five-and-twenty. A young fellow cannot be cast down by grief and misfortune ever so severe but some night he begins to sleep sound, and some day when dinner-time comes to feel hungry for a beefsteak. Time, youth, and good health, new scenes and the excitement of action and a campaign, had pretty well brought Esmond's mourning to an end; and his comrades said that Don Dismal, as they called him, was Don Dismal no more. So when a party was made to dine at the Rose, and go to the playhouse afterward, Esmond was as pleased as another to take his share of the bottle and the play.

How was it that the old aunt's news, or it might be scandal, about Tom Tusher, caused such a strange and sudden excitement in Tom's old playfellow? Hadn't he sworn a thousand times in his own mind that the lady of Castlewood, who had treated him with such kindness once, and then had left him so cruelly, was, and was to remain henceforth, indifferent to him for ever? Had his pride and his sense of justice not long since helped him to cure the pain of that desertion – was it even a pain to him now? Why, but last night as he walked across the fields and meadows to Chelsey from Pall Mall, had he not composed two or three stanzas of a song, celebrating Bracegirdle's brown eyes, and declaring them a thousand times more beautiful than the brightest blue ones that ever languished under the lashes of an insipid fair beauty! But Tom Tusher! Tom Tusher, the waiting-woman's son, raising up his little eyes to his mistress! Tom Tusher presuming to think of Castlewood's widow! Rage and contempt filled Mr Harry's heart at the very notion; the honour of the family, of which he was the chief, made it his duty to prevent so monstrous an alliance, and to chastise the upstart who could dare to think of such an insult to their house. 'Tis true Mr Esmond often boasted of republican principles, and could remember many fine speeches he had made at college and elsewhere, with *worth* and not *birth* for a text; but Tom Tusher to take the place of the noble Castlewood – faugh! 'twas as monstrous as King Hamlet's widow taking off her weeds for Claudius. Esmond laughed at all widows, all wives, all women; and were the banns about to be published, as no doubt they were, that very next Sunday at Walcote Church, Esmond swore that he would be present to shout No! in the face of the congregation, and to take a private revenge upon the ears of the bridegroom.

Instead of going to dinner then at the Rose that night, Mr Esmond bade his servant pack a portmanteau and get horses, and was at Farnham, half-way on the road to Walcote, thirty miles off, before his comrades had got to their supper after the play. He bade his man give no hint to my Lady Dowager's household of the expedition on which he was going; and as Chelsey was distant from London, the roads bad, and infested by footpads, and Esmond often in the habit, when engaged in a party of pleasure, of lying at a friend's lodging in town, there was no need that this old aunt should be disturbed at his absence – indeed, nothing more delighted the old lady than to fancy that *mon cousin*, the incorrigible young sinner, was abroad boxing the watch,[11] or scouring St Giles's.[12] When she was not at her books of devotion, she thought Etheridge and Sedley very good reading. She had a hundred pretty stories about Rochester,[13]

Harry Jermyn, and Hamilton; and if Esmond would but have run away with the wife even of a citizen, 'tis my belief she would have pawned her diamonds (the best of them went to our Lady of Chaillot [14]) to pay his damages.

My lord's little house of Walcote, which he inhabited before he took his title and occupied the house of Castlewood – lies about a mile from Winchester, and his widow had returned to Walcote after my lord's death as a place always dear to her, and where her earliest and happiest days had been spent, cheerfuller than Castlewood, which was too large for her straitened means, and giving her, too, the protection of the ex-Dean, her father. The young Viscount had a year's schooling at the famous college there, with Mr Tusher as his governor. [15] So much news of them Mr Esmond had had during the past year from the old Viscountess, his own father's widow; from the young one there had never been a word.

Twice or thrice in his benefactor's lifetime, Esmond had been to Walcote; and now, taking but a couple of hours rest only at the inn on the road, he was up again long before daybreak, and made such good speed that he was at Walcote by two o'clock of the day. He rid to the inn of the village, where he alighted and sent a man thence to Mr Tusher, with a message that a gentleman from London would speak with him on urgent business. The messenger came back to say the Doctor was in town, most likely at prayers in the Cathedral, My Lady Viscountess was there too; she always went to Cathedral prayers every day.

The horses belonged to the post-house at Winchester. Esmond mounted again, and rode on to the George; whence he walked, leaving his grumbling domestic at last happy with a dinner, straight to the Cathedral. The organ was playing; the winter's day was already growing grey, as he passed under the street-arch into the cathedral-yard, and made his way into the ancient solemn edifice.

## Chapter 6

### THE 29TH DECEMBER

THERE was scarce a score of persons in the Cathedral besides the Dean and some of his clergy, and the choristers, young and old, that performed the beautiful evening prayer. But Doctor Tusher was one of the officiants, and read from the eagle,[1] in an authoritative voice, and a great black periwig; and in the stalls, still in her black widow's hood, sate Esmond's dear mistress, her son by her side, very much grown, and indeed a noble-looking youth, with his mother's eyes, and his father's curling brown hair, that fell over his *point de Venise*[2] – a pretty picture such as Vandyke might have painted. Mons. Rigaud's[3] portrait of my Lord Viscount, done at Paris afterwards, gives but a French version of his manly, frank, English face. When he looked up there were two sapphire beams out of his eyes, such as no painter's palette has the colour to match, I think. On this day there was not much chance of seeing that particular beauty of my young lord's countenance; for the truth is, he kept his eyes shut for the most part, and, the anthem being rather long, was asleep.

But the music ceasing, my lord woke up, looking about him, and his eyes lighting on Mr Esmond, who was sitting opposite him, gazing with no small tenderness and melancholy upon two persons who had had so much of his heart for so many years; Lord Castlewood, with a start, pulled at his mother's sleeve (her face had scarce been lifted from her book), and said, 'Look, mother!' so loud, that Esmond could hear on the other side of the church, and the old Dean on his throned stall. Lady Castlewood looked for an instant as her son bade her, and held up a warning finger to Frank; Esmond felt his whole face flush, and his heart throbbing, as that dear lady beheld him once more. The rest of the prayers were speedily over: Mr Esmond did not hear them; nor did his mistress, very likely, whose hood went more closely over her face, and who never lifted her head again until the service was over, the blessing given, and

Mr Dean, and his procession of ecclesiastics, out of the inner chapel.

Young Castlewood came clambering over the stalls before the clergy were fairly gone, and, running up to Esmond, eagerly embraced him. 'My dear, dearest old Harry,' he said, 'are you come back? Have you been to the wars? You'll take me with you when you go again? Why didn't you write to us? Come to mother.'

Mr Esmond could hardly say more than a 'God bless you, my boy,' for his heart was very full and grateful at all this tenderness on the lad's part; and he was as much moved at seeing Frank, as he was fearful about that other interview which was now to take place; for he knew not if the widow would reject him as she had done so cruelly a year ago.

'It was kind of you to come back to us, Henry,' Lady Esmond said. 'I thought you might come.'

'We read of the fleet coming to Portsmouth. Why did you not come from Portsmouth?' Frank asked, or my Lord Viscount, as he now must be called.

Esmond had thought of that too. He would have given one of his eyes so that he might see his dear friends again once more; but believing that his mistress had forbidden him her house, he had obeyed her, and remained at a distance.

'You had but to ask, and you knew I would be here,' he said.

She gave him her hand, her little fair hand: there was only her marriage ring on it. The quarrel was all over. The year of grief and estrangement was passed. They never had been separated. His mistress had never been out of his mind all that time. No, not once. No, not in the prison; nor in the camp; nor on shore before the enemy; nor at sea under the stars of solemn midnight, nor as he watched the glorious rising of the dawn: not even at the table, where he sate carousing with friends, or at the theatre yonder, where he tried to fancy that other eyes were brighter than hers. Brighter eyes there might be, and faces more beautiful, but none so dear – no voice so sweet as that of his beloved mistress, who had been sister, mother, goddess to him during his youth – goddess now no

more, for he knew of her weaknesses; and by thought, by
suffering, and that experience it brings, was older now than
she; but more fondly cherished as woman perhaps than ever
she had been adored as divinity. What is it? Where lies it, the
secret which makes one little hand the dearest of all? Whoever
can unriddle that mystery? Here she was, her son by his side,
his dear boy. Here she was, weeping and happy. She took his
hand in both hers; he felt her tears. It was a rapture of reconciliation.

'Here comes Squaretoes,' says Frank. 'Here's Tusher.'

Tusher, indeed, now appeared, creaking on his great heels.
Mr Tom had divested himself of his alb or surplice, and came
forward habited in his cassock and great black periwig. How
had Harry Esmond ever been for a moment jealous of this
fellow?

'Give us thy hand, Tom Tusher,' he said. The Chaplain
made him a very low and stately bow. 'I am charmed to see
Captain Esmond,' says he. 'My lord and I have read the
*Reddas incolumen precor*,[4] and applied it, I am sure, to you.
You come back with Gaditanian laurels: when I heard you
were bound thither, I wished, I am sure, I was another Septi-
mius. My Lord Viscount, your lordship remembers *Septimi,
Gades aditure mecum*?'[5]

'There's an angle of earth that I love better than Gades,
Tusher,' says Mr Esmond. ' 'Tis that one where your Reverence
hath a parsonage, and where our youth was brought up.'

'A house that has so many sacred recollections to me,' says
Mr Tusher (and Harry remembered how Tom's father used to
flog him there) – 'a house near to that of my respected patron,
my most honoured patroness, must ever be a dear abode to me.
But, madam, the verger waits to close the gates on your ladyship.'

'And Harry's coming home to supper. Huzzay! huzzay!'
cries my lord. 'Mother, shall I run home and bid Beatrix put
her ribbons on? Beatrix is a maid of honour, Harry. Such a fine
set-up minx!'

'Your heart was never in the Church, Harry,' the widow
said, in her sweet low tone, as they walked away together. (Now,
it seemed they had never been parted, and again, as if they had

been ages asunder.) 'I always thought you had no vocation that way; and that 'twas a pity to shut you out from the world. You would but have pined and chafed at Castlewood: and 'tis better you should make a name for yourself. I often said so to my dear lord. How he loved you! 'Twas my lord that made you stay with us.'

'I asked no better than to stay near you always,' said Mr Esmond.

'But to go was best, Harry. When the world cannot give peace, you will know where to find it; but one of your strong imagination and eager desires must try the world first before he tires of it. 'Twas not to be thought of, or if it once was, it was only by my selfishness that you should remain as Chaplain to a country gentleman and tutor to a little boy. You are of the blood of the Esmonds, kinsman; and that was always wild in youth. Look at Francis. He is but fifteen, and I scarce can keep him in my nest. His talk is all of war and pleasure, and he longs to serve in the next campaign. Perhaps he and the young Lord Churchill shall go the next. Lord Marlborough has been good to us. You know how kind they were in my misfortune. And so was your – your father's widow. No one knows how good the world is, till grief comes to try us. 'Tis through my Lady Marlborough's goodness that Beatrix hath her place at Court; and Frank is under my Lord Chamberlain. And the Dowager Lady, your father's widow, has promised to provide for you – has she not?'

Esmond said, 'Yes. As far as present favour went, Lady Castlewood was very good to him. And should her mind change,' he added gaily, 'as ladies' minds will, I am strong enough to bear my own burden, and make my way somehow. Not by the sword very likely. Thousands have a better genius for that than I, but there are many ways in which a young man of good parts and education can get on in the world; and I am pretty sure, one way or other, of promotion!' Indeed, he had found patrons already in the army, and amongst persons very able to serve him, too; and told his mistress of the flattering aspect of fortune. They walked as though they had never been parted, slowly, with the grey twilight closing round them.

'And now we are drawing near to home,' she continued, 'I knew you would come, Harry, if – if it was but to forgive me for having spoken unjustly to you after that horrid – horrid misfortune. I was half frantic with grief then when I saw you. And I know now – they have told me. That wretch, whose name I can never mention, even has said it: how you tried to avert the quarrel, and would have taken it on yourself, my poor child: but it was God's will that I should be punished, and that my dear lord should fall.'

'He gave me his blessing on his death-bed,' Esmond said. 'Thank God for that legacy!'

'Amen, amen! dear Henry,' says the lady, pressing his arm. 'I knew it. Mr Atterbury, of St Bride's, who was called to him, told me so. And I thanked God, too, and in my prayers ever since remembered it.'

'You had spared me many a bitter night, had you told me sooner,' Mr Esmond said.

'I know it, I know it,' she answered, in a tone of such sweet humility, as made Esmond repent that he should ever have dared to reproach her. 'I know how wicked my heart has been; and I have suffered too, my dear. I confessed to Mr Atterbury – I must not tell any more. He – I said I would not write to you or go to you – and it was better even that, having parted, we should part. But I knew you would come back – I own that. That is no one's fault. And to-day, Henry, in the anthem, when they sang it, "When the Lord turned the captivity of Zion, we were like them that dream," I thought, yes, like them that dream – them that dream. And then it went, "They that sow in tears shall reap in joy; and he that goeth forth and weepeth, shall doubtless come home again with rejoicing, bringing his sheaves with him"; I looked up from the book, and saw you. I was not surprised when I saw you. I knew you would come, my dear, and saw the gold sunshine round your head.'

She smiled an almost wild smile as she looked up at him. The moon was up by this time, glittering keen in the frosty sky. He could see, for the first time now clearly, her sweet careworn face.

'Do you know what day it is?' she continued. 'It is the 29th of December – it is your birthday! But last year we did not drink it – no, no. My lord was cold, and my Harry was likely to die; and my brain was in a fever; and we had no wine. But now – now you are come again, bringing your sheaves with you, my dear.' She burst into a wild flood of weeping as she spoke; she laughed and sobbed on the young man's heart, crying out wildly, 'bringing your sheaves with you – your sheaves with you!'

As he had sometimes felt, gazing up from the deck at midnight into the boundless starlit depths overhead, in a rapture of devout wonder at that endless brightness and beauty – in some such a way now, the depth of this pure devotion (which was, for the first time, revealed to him quite) smote upon him, and filled his heart with thanksgiving. Gracious God, who was he, weak and friendless creature, that such a love should be poured out upon him? Not in vain, not in vain has he lived – hard and thankless should he be to think so – that has such a treasure given him. What is ambition compared to that, but selfish vanity? To be rich, to be famous? What do these profit a year hence, when other names sound louder than yours, when you lie hidden away under the ground, along with the idle titles engraven on your coffin? But only true love lives after you – follows your memory with secret blessing – or precedes you, and intercedes for you. *Non omnis moriar* [6] – if dying, I yet live in a tender heart or two; nor am lost and hopeless living, if a sainted departed soul still loves and prays for me.

'If – if 'tis so, dear lady,' Mr Esmond said, 'why should I ever leave you? If God hath given me this great boon – and near or far from me, as I know now – the heart of my dearest mistress follows me; let me have that blessing near me, nor ever part with it till life separate us. Come away – leave this Europe, this place which has so many sad recollections for you. Begin a new life in a new world. My good lord often talked of visiting that land in Virginia which King Charles gave us – gave his ancestor. Frank will give us that. No man there will ask if there is a blot on my name, or inquire in the woods what my title is.'

'And my children – and my duty – and my good father, Henry?' she broke out. 'He has none but me now; for soon my sister will leave him, and the old man will be alone. He has conformed[7] since the new Queen's reign; and here in Winchester, where they love him, they have found a church for him. When the children leave me, I will stay with him. I cannot follow them into the great world, where their way lies – it scares me. They will come and visit me; and you will, sometimes, Henry – yes, sometimes, as now, in the Holy Advent season, when I have seen and blessed you once more.'

'I would leave all to follow you,' said Mr Esmond; 'and can you not be as generous for me, dear lady?'

'Hush, boy!' she said, and it was with a mother's sweet plaintive tone and look that she spoke. 'The world is beginning for you. For me, I have been so weak and sinful that I must leave it, and pray out an expiation, dear Henry. Had we houses of religion as there were once, and many divines of our church would have them again, I often think I would retire to one and pass my life in penance. But I would love you still – yes, there is no sin in such a love as mine now; and my dear lord in heaven may see my heart; and knows the tears that have washed my sin away – and now – now my duty is here, by my children whilst they need me, and by my poor old father, and——'

'And not by me?' Henry said.

'Hush!' she said again, and raised her hand up to his lip. 'I have been your nurse. You could not see me, Harry, when you were in the small-pox, and I came and sate by you. Ah! I prayed that I might die, but it would have been in sin, Henry. Oh, it is horrid to look back to that time. It is over now and past, and it has been forgiven me. When you need me again I will come ever so far. When your heart is wounded, then come to me, my dear. Be silent! let me say all. You never loved me, dear Henry – no, you do not now, and I thank Heaven for it. I used to watch you, and knew by a thousand signs that it was so. Do you remember how glad you were to go away to college! 'Twas I sent you. I told my papa that, and Mr Atterbury too, when I spoke to him in London. And they both gave me absolution – both – and they are godly men, having authority to bind and to loose. And they forgave me, as my dear lord forgave me before he went to heaven.'

'I think the angels are not all in heaven,' Mr Esmond said. And as a brother folds a sister to his heart; and as a mother cleaves to her son's breast – so for a few moments Esmond's beloved mistress came to him and blessed him.

## Chapter 7

### I AM MADE WELCOME AT WALCOTE

As they came up to the house at Walcote, the windows from within were lighted up with friendly welcome; the supper-table was spread in the oak-parlour; it seemed as if forgiveness and love were awaiting the returning prodigal. Two or three familiar faces of domestics were on the look-out at the porch – the old housekeeper was there, and young Lockwood from Castlewood in my lord's livery of tawny and blue. His dear mistress pressed his arm as they passed into the hall. Her eyes beamed out on him with affection indescribable. 'Welcome,' was all she said: as she looked up, putting back her fair curls and black hood. A sweet rosy smile blushed on her face: Harry thought he had never seen her look so charming. Her face was lighted with a joy that was brighter than beauty – she took a hand of her son who was in the hall waiting his mother – she did not quit Esmond's arm.

'Welcome, Harry!' my young lord echoed after her. 'Here, we are all come to say so. Here's old Pincot, hasn't she grown handsome?' and Pincot, who was older, and no handsomer than usual, made a curtsey to the Captain, as she called Esmond, and told my lord to 'Have done, now.'

'And here's Jack Lockwood. He'll make a famous grenadier Jack; and so shall I; we'll both 'list under you, cousin. As soon as I am seventeen, I go to the army – every gentleman goes to the army. Look! who comes here – ho, ho!' he burst into a laugh. ' 'Tis Mistress Trix, with a new ribbon; I knew she would put one on as soon as she heard a Captain was coming to supper.'

This laughing colloquy took place in the hall of Walcote House: in the midst of which is a staircase that leads from an open gallery, where are the doors of the sleeping chambers: and from one of these, a wax candle in her hand, and illuminating her, came Mistress Beatrix – the light falling indeed upon the scarlet ribbon which she wore, and upon the most brilliant white neck in the world.

Esmond had left a child and found a woman, grown beyond the common height; and arrived at such a dazzling completeness of beauty, that his eyes might well show surprise and delight at beholding her. In hers there was a brightness so lustrous and melting, that I have seen a whole assembly follow her as if by an attraction irresistible: and that night the great Duke was at the playhouse after Ramillies, every soul turned and looked (she chanced to enter at the opposite side of the theatre at the same moment) at her, and not at him. She was a brown beauty: that is, her eyes, hair, and eyebrows and eyelashes, were dark: her hair curling with rich undulations, and waving over her shoulders; but her complexion was as dazzling white as snow in sunshine; except her cheeks, which were a bright red, and her lips, which were of a still deeper crimson. Her mouth and chin, they said, were too large and full, and so they might be for a goddess in marble, but not for a woman whose eyes were fire, whose look was love, whose voice was the sweetest low song, whose shape was perfect symmetry, health, decision, activity, whose foot as it planted itself on the ground, was firm but flexible, and whose motion, whether rapid or slow, was always perfect grace – agile as a nymph, lofty as a queen – now melting, now imperious, now sarcastic: there was no single movement of hers but was beautiful. As he thinks of her, he who writes feels young again, and remembers a paragon.

So she came holding her dress with one fair rounded arm, and her taper before her, tripping down the stair to greet Esmond.

'She hath put on her scarlet stockings and white shoes,' says my lord, still laughing. 'O, my fine mistress! is this the way you set your cap at the Captain!' She approached, shining smiles upon Esmond, who could look at nothing but her eyes.

She advanced holding forward her head, as if she would have him kiss her as he used to do when she was a child.

'Stop,' she said, 'I am grown too big! Welcome, cousin Harry,' and she made him an arch curtsey, sweeping down to the ground almost, with the most gracious bend, looking up the while with the brightest eyes and sweetest smile. Love seemed to radiate from her. Harry eyed her with such a rapture as the first lover is described as having by Milton.

'*N'est ce pas?*' says my lady, in a low, sweet voice, still hanging on his arm.

Esmond turned round with a start and a blush, as he met his mistress's clear eyes. He had forgotten her, rapt in admiration of the *filia pulcrior*.

'Right foot forward, toe turned out, so: now drop the curtsey, and show the red stockings, Trix. They've silver clocks, Harry. The Dowager sent 'em. She went to put 'em on,' cries my lord.

'Hush, you stupid child!' says Miss, smothering her brother with kisses; and then she must come and kiss her mamma, looking all the while at Harry, over his mistress's shoulder. And if she did not kiss him, she gave him both her hands, and then took one of his in both hands, and said, 'Oh, Harry, we're so, *so* glad you're come!'

'There are woodcocks for supper,' says my lord: 'Huzzay! It was such a hungry sermon.'

'And it is the 29th of December; and our Harry has come home.'

'Huzzay, old Pincot!' again says my lord; and my dear lady's lips looked as if they were trembling with a prayer. She would have Harry lead in Beatrix to the supper-room, going herself with my young Lord Viscount; and to this party came Tom Tusher directly, whom four at least out of the company of five wished away. Away he went, however, as soon as the sweetmeats were put down, and then, by the great crackling fire, his mistress or Beatrix, with her blushing graces, filling his glass for him, Harry told the story of his campaign, and passed the most delightful night his life had ever known. The sun was up long ere he was, so deep, sweet, and refreshing was his slumber. He woke as if angels had been watching at his bed

all night. I daresay one that was as pure and loving as an angel
had blest his sleep with her prayers.

Next morning the Chaplain read prayers to the little household
at Walcote, as the custom was; Esmond thought Mistress
Beatrix did not listen to Tusher's exhortation much: her eyes
were wandering everywhere during the service, at least whenever
he looked up he met them. Perhaps he also was not very attentive
to his Reverence the Chaplain. 'This might have been my life,'
he was thinking; 'this might have been my duty from now till
old age. Well, were it not a pleasant one to be with these dear
friends and part from 'em no more? Until – until the destined
lover comes and takes away pretty Beatrix' – and the best part
of Tom Tusher's exposition, which may have been very learned
and eloquent, was quite lost to poor Harry by this vision of the
destined lover, who put the preacher out.

All the while of the prayers, Beatrix knelt a little way before
Harry Esmond. The red stockings were changed for a pair of
grey, and black shoes, in which her feet looked to the full as
pretty. All the roses of spring could not vie with the brightness
of her complexion; Esmond thought he had never seen anything like the sunny lustre of her eyes. My Lady Viscountess
looked fatigued, as if with watching, and her face was pale.

Miss Beatrix remarked these signs of indisposition in her
mother, and deplored them. 'I am an old woman,' says my
lady, with a kind smile; 'I cannot hope to look as young as you
do, my dear.'

'She'll never look as good as you do if she lives till she's a
hundred,' says my lord, taking his mother by the waist, and
kissing her hand.

'Do I look very wicked, cousin?' says Beatrix, turning full
round on Esmond, with her pretty face so close under his
chin, that the soft perfumed hair touched it. She laid her
finger-tips on his sleeve as she spoke; and he put his other
hand over hers.

'I'm like your looking-glass,' says he, 'and that can't flatter
you.'

'He means that you are always looking at him, my dear,'
says her mother, archly. Beatrix ran away from Esmond at

this, and flew to her mamma, whom she kissed, stopping my lady's mouth with her pretty hand.

'And Harry is very good to look at,' says my lady, with her fond eyes regarding the young man.

'If 'tis good to see a happy face,' says he, 'you see that.' My lady said Amen, with a sigh; and Harry thought the memory of her dead lord rose up and rebuked her back again into sadness; for her face lost the smile, and resumed its look of melancholy.

'Why, Harry, how fine we look in our scarlet and silver, and our black periwig,' cries my lord. 'Mother, I am tired of my own hair. When shall I have a peruke? Where did you get your steenkirk,[1] Harry?'

'It's some of my Lady Dowager's lace,' says Harry; 'she gave me this and a number of other fine things.'

'My Lady Dowager isn't such a bad woman,' my lord continued.

'She's not so – so red as she's painted,' says Miss Beatrix.

Her brother broke into a laugh. 'I'll tell her you said so; by the Lord, Trix, I will,' he cries out.

'She'll know that you hadn't the wit to say it, my lord,' says Miss Beatrix.

'We won't quarrel the first day Harry's here, will we, mother?' said the young lord. 'We'll see if we can get on to the new year without a fight. Have some of this Christmas pie? and here comes the tankard; no, it's Pincot with the tea.'

'Will the Captain choose a dish?' asks Mistress Beatrix.

'I say, Harry,' my lord goes on, 'I'll show thee my horses after breakfast; and we'll go a bird-netting to-night, and on Monday there's a cock-match at Winchester – do you love cock-fighting,[2] Harry? – between the gentlemen of Sussex and the gentlemen of Hampshire, at ten pound the battle, and fifty pound the odd battle to show one-and-twenty cocks.'

'And what will you do, Beatrix, to amuse our kinsman?' asks my lady.

'I'll listen to him,' says Beatrix; 'I am sure he has a hundred things to tell us. And I'm jealous already of the Spanish ladies. Was that a beautiful nun at Cadiz that you rescued from the

soldiers? Your man talked of it last night in the kitchen, and
Mrs Betty told me this morning as she combed my hair. And
he says you must be in love, for you sate on deck all night, and
scribbled verses all day in your table-book.' Harry thought if
he had wanted a subject for verses yesterday, to-day he had
found one: and not all the Lindamiras and Ardelias of the poets
were half so beautiful as this young creature; but he did not
say so, though someone did for him.

This was his dear lady who, after the meal was over, and the
young people were gone, began talking of her children with
Mr Esmond, and of the characters of one and the other, and
of her hopes and fears for both of them. ' 'Tis not while they
are at home,' she said, 'and in their mother's nest, I fear for
them – 'tis when they are gone into the world, whither I shall
not be able to follow them. Beatrix will begin her service next
year. You may have heard a rumour about – about my Lord
Blandford. They were both children; and it is but idle talk. I
know my kinswoman would never let him make such a poor
marriage as our Beatrix would be. There's scarce a princess in
Europe that she thinks is good enough for him or for her
ambition.'

'There's not a princess in Europe to compare with her,' says
Esmond.

'In beauty? No, perhaps not,' answered my lady. 'She is
most beautiful, isn't she? 'Tis not a mother's partiality that
deceives me. I marked you yesterday when she came down the
stair: and read it in your face. We look when you don't fancy
us looking, and see better than you think, dear Harry: and just
now when they spoke about your poems – you writ pretty lines
when you were but a boy – you thought Beatrix was a pretty
subject for verse, did not you, Harry?' (The gentleman could
only blush for a reply.) 'And so she is – nor are you the first
her pretty face has captivated. 'Tis quickly done. Such a pair
of bright eyes as hers learn their power very soon, and use it
very early.' And, looking at him keenly with hers, the fair widow
left him.

And so it is – a pair of bright eyes with a dozen glances
suffice to subdue a man; to enslave him and inflame him; to

make him even forget; they dazzle him so that the past becomes straightway dim to him; and he so prizes them that he would give all his life to possess 'em. What is the fond love of dearest friends compared to this treasure? Is memory as strong as expectancy? fruition, as hunger? gratitude, as desire? I have looked at royal diamonds in the jewel-rooms in Europe, and thought how wars have been made about 'em: Mogul sovereigns deposed and strangled for them, or ransomed with them: millions expended to buy them; and daring lives lost in digging out the little shining toys that I value no more than the button in my hat. And so there are other glittering baubles (of rare water too) for which men have been set to kill and quarrel ever since mankind began; and which last but for a score of years, when their sparkle is over. Where are those jewels now that beamed under Cleopatra's forehead, or shone in the sockets of Helen?

The second day after Esmond's coming to Walcote, Tom Tusher had leave to take a holiday, and went off in his very best gown and bands to court the young woman whom his Reverence desired to marry, and who was not a viscount's widow, as it turned out, but a brewer's relict at Southampton, with a couple of thousand pounds to her fortune: for honest Tom's heart was under such excellent control, that Venus herself without a portion would never have caused it to flutter. So he rode away on his heavy-paced gelding to pursue his jog-trot loves, leaving Esmond to the society of his dear mistress and her daughter, and with his young lord for a companion, who was charmed not only to see an old friend, but to have the tutor and his Latin books put out of the way.

The boy talked of things and people, and not a little about himself, in his frank artless way. 'Twas easy to see that he and his sister had the better of their fond mother, for the first place in whose affections, though they fought constantly, and though the kind lady persisted that she loved both equally, 'twas not difficult to understand that Frank was his mother's darling and favourite. He ruled the whole household (always excepting rebellious Beatrix) not less now than when he was a child marshalling the village boys in playing at soldiers, and caning them lustily too, like the sturdiest corporal. As for Tom Tusher, his Reverence treated the young lord with that politeness and deference which he always showed for a great man, whatever his age or his stature was. Indeed, with respect to this young one, it was impossible not to love him, so frank and winning were his manners, his beauty, his gaiety, the ring of his laughter, and the delightful tone of his voice. Wherever he went, he charmed and domineered. I think his old grandfather, the Dean, and the grim old housekeeper, Mrs Pincot, were as much his slaves as his mother was: and as for Esmond, he found himself presently submitting to a certain fascination thé boy had, and slaving it like the rest of the family. The pleasure which he had in Frank's mere company and converse exceeded that which he ever enjoyed in the society of any other man, however delightful in talk, or famous for wit. His presence brought sunshine into a room, his laugh, his prattle, his noble beauty and brightness of look cheered and charmed indescribably. At the least tale of sorrow, his hands were in his purse, and he was eager with sympathy and bounty. The way in which women loved and petted him, when, a year or two afterwards, he came upon the world, yet a mere boy, and the follies which they did for him (as indeed he for them), recalled the career of Rochester,[3] and outdid the successes of Grammont.[4] His very creditors loved him; and the hardest usurers, and some of the rigid prudes of the other sex too, could deny him nothing. He was no more witty than another man, but what he said, he said and looked as no man else could say or look it. I have seen the women at the comedy at Bruxelles crowd round him in the lobby: and as he sate on the stage more people looked at him than at the actors, and watched him; and I remember at Ramillies,[5] when he was hit and fell, a great big red-haired Scotch sergeant flung his halbert down, burst out a-crying like a woman, seizing him up as if he had been an infant, and carrying him out of the fire. This brother and sister were the most beautiful couple ever seen; though after he winged away from the maternal nest this pair were seldom together.

Sitting at dinner two days after Esmond's arrival (it was the

last day of the year), and so happy a one to Harry Esmond, that
to enjoy it was quite worth all the previous pain which he had
endured and forgot: my young lord, filling a bumper, and
bidding Harry take another, drank to his sister, saluting her
under the title of 'Marchioness'.

'Marchioness!' says Harry, not without a pang of wonder,
for he was curious and jealous already.

'Nonsense, my lord,' says Beatrix, with a toss of her head.
My Lady Viscountess looked up for a moment at Esmond, and
cast her eyes down.

'The Marchioness of Blandford,' says Frank, 'don't you
know – hath not Rouge Dragon told you?' (My lord used to
call the Dowager at Chelsea by this and other names.) 'Blandford has a lock of her hair: the Duchess found him on his
knees to Mistress Trix, and boxed his ears, and said Doctor
Hare[6] should whip him.'

'I wish Mr Tusher would whip you too,' says Beatrix.

My lady only said: 'I hope you will tell none of these silly
stories elsewhere than at home, Francis.'

' 'Tis true, on my word,' continues Frank: 'look at Harry
scowling, mother, and see how Beatrix blushes as red as the
silver-clocked stockings.'

'I think we have best leave the gentlemen to their wine and
their talk,' says Mistress Beatrix, rising up with the air of a
young queen, tossing her rustling, flowing draperies about her,
and quitting the room, followed by her mother.

Lady Castlewood again looked at Esmond, as she stooped
down and kissed Frank. 'Do not tell those silly stories, child,'
she said: 'do not drink much wine, sir; Harry never loved to
drink wine.' And she went away, too, in her black robes, looking
back on the young man with her fair, fond face.

'Egad! it's true,' says Frank, sipping his wine with the air
of a lord. 'What think you of this Lisbon – real Collares? 'Tis
better than your heady port: we got it out of one of the Spanish
ships that came from Vigo last year: my mother bought it
at Southampton, as the ship was lying there – the Rose, Captain
Hawkins.'

'Why, I came home in that ship,' says Harry.

'And it brought home a good fellow and good wine,' says my lord. 'I say, Harry, I wish thou hadst not that cursed bar sinister.'

'And why not the bar sinister,' asks the other.

'Suppose I go to the army and am killed – every gentleman goes to the army – who is to take care of the women? Trix will never stop at home; mother's in love with you, – yes, I think mother's in love with you. She was always praising you, and always talking about you; and when she went to Southampton, to see the ship, I found her out. But you see it is impossible: we are of the oldest blood in England; we came in with the Conqueror; we were only baronets, – but what then? we were forced into that. James the First forced our great-grandfather. We are above titles; we old English gentry don't want 'em; the Queen can make a duke any day. Look at Blandford's father, Duke Churchill, and Duchess Jennings; what were they, Harry? Damn it, sir, what are they, to turn up their noses at us? Where were they, when our ancestor rode with King Henry at Agincourt, and filled up the French King's cup after Poictiers? 'Fore George, sir, why shouldn't Blandford marry Beatrix? By G——! he *shall* marry Beatrix, or tell me the reason why. We'll marry with the best blood of England, and none but the best blood of England. You are an Esmond, and you can't help your birth, my boy. Let's have another bottle. What! no more? I've drunk three parts of this myself. I had many a night with my father; you stood to him like a man, Harry. You backed your blood; you can't help your misfortune, you know, – no man can help that.'

The elder said he would go in to his mistress's tea-table. The young lad, with a heightened colour and voice, began singing a snatch of a song, and marched out of the room. Esmond heard him presently calling his dogs about him, and cheering and talking to them; and by a hundred of his looks and gestures, tricks of voice and gait, was reminded of the dead lord, Frank's father.

And so, the sylvester[7] night passed away; the family parted long before midnight, Lady Castlewood remembering, no doubt, former New Year's Eves, when healths were drunk, and laughter went round in the company of him, to whom years past, and present, and future, were to be as one; and so cared not to sit with her children and hear the Cathedral bells ringing the birth of the year 1703. Esmond heard the chimes as he sat in his own chamber, ruminating by the blazing fire there, and listened to the last notes of them, looking out from his window towards the city, and the great grey towers of the Cathedral lying under the frosty sky, with the keen stars shining above.

The sight of these brilliant orbs no doubt made him think of other luminaries. 'And so her eyes have already done execution,' thought Esmond – 'on whom? – who can tell me?' Luckily his kinsman was by, and Esmond knew he would have no difficulty in finding out Mistress Beatrix's history from the simple talk of the boy.

## Chapter 8

### FAMILY TALK

WHAT Harry admired and submitted to in the pretty lad, his kinsman, was (for why should he resist it?) the calmness of patronage which my young lord assumed, as if to command was his undoubted right, and all the world (below his degree) ought to bow down to Viscount Castlewood.

'I know my place, Harry,' he said. 'I'm not proud – the boys at Winchester College say I'm proud: but I'm not proud. I am simply Francis James Viscount Castlewood in the peerage of Ireland. I might have been (do you know that?) Francis James Marquis and Earl of Esmond in that of England. The late lord refused the title which was offered to him by my godfather, his late Majesty. You should know that – you are of our family, you know – you cannot help your bar sinister, Harry, my dear fellow; and you belong to one of the best families in England, in spite of that; and you stood by my father, and by G——! I'll stand by you. You shall never want a friend, Harry, while Francis James Viscount Castlewood has a shilling. It's now

1703 – I shall come of age in 1709. I shall go back to Castlewood; I shall live at Castlewood; I shall build up the house. My property will be pretty well restored by then. The late Viscount mismanaged my property, and left it in a very bad state. My mother is living close, as you see, and keeps me in a way hardly befitting a peer of these realms; for I have but a pair of horses, a governor, and a man that is valet and groom. But when I am of age, these things will be set right, Harry. Our house will be as it should be. You'll always come to Castlewood, won't you? You shall always have your two rooms in the court kept for you; and if anybody slights you, d—— them! let them have a care of *me*. I shall marry early – Trix will be a duchess by that time, most likely; for a cannon-ball may knock over his Grace any day, you know.'

'How?' says Harry.

'Hush, my dear!' says my Lord Viscount. 'You are of the family – you are faithful to us, by George, and I tell you everything. Blandford will marry her – or' – and here he put his little hand on his sword – 'you understand the rest. Blandford knows which of us two is the best weapon. At small-sword, or back-sword,[1] or sword and dagger, if he likes: I can beat him. I have tried him, Harry; and begad, he knows I am a man not to be trifled with.'

'But you do not mean,' says Harry, concealing his laughter, but not his wonder, 'that you can force my Lord Blandford, the son of the first man of this kingdom, to marry your sister at sword's point?'

'I mean to say that we are cousins by the mother's side, though that's nothing to boast of. I mean to say that an Esmond is as good as a Churchill; and when the King comes back, the Marquis of Esmond's sister may be a match for any nobleman's daughter in the kingdom. There are but two marquises in all England, William Herbert, Marquis of Powis, and Francis James, Marquis of Esmond; and hark you, Harry, now swear you'll never mention this. Give me your honour as a gentleman, for you *are* a gentleman, though you are a ——'

'Well, well,' says Harry, a little impatient.

'Well, then, when after my late Viscount's misfortune, my

mother went up with us to London, to ask for justice against you all (as for Mohun, I'll have his blood, as sure as my name is Francis Viscount Esmond), we went to stay with our cousin my Lady Marlborough, with whom we had quarrelled for ever so long. But when misfortune came, she stood by her blood: – so did the Dowager Viscountess stand by her blood, – so did you. Well, sir, whilst my mother was petitioning the late Prince of Orange – for I will never call him King – and while you were in prison, we lived at my Lord Marlborough's house, who was only a little there, being away with the army in Holland. And then . . . I say, Harry, you won't tell, now?'

Harry again made a vow of secrecy.

'Well, there used to be all sorts of fun, you know: my Lady Marlborough was very fond of us, and she said I was to be her page; and she got Trix to be a maid of honour, and while she was up in her room crying, we used to be always having fun, you know; and the Duchess used to kiss me, and so did her daughters, and Blandford fell tremendous in love with Trix, and she liked him; and one day he – he kissed her behind a door – he did though, – and the Duchess caught him, and she banged such a box of the ear both to Trix and Blandford –you should have seen it! And then she said that we must leave directly, and abused my mamma, who was cognizant of the business; but she wasn't – never thinking about anything but father. And so we came down to Walcote; Blandford being locked up, and not allowed to see Trix. But *I* got at him. I climbed along the gutter, and in through the window, where he was crying.

'"Marquis," says I, when he had opened it and helped me in, "you know I wear a sword," for I had brought it.

'"O, Viscount," says he – "O, my dearest Frank!" and he threw himself into my arms and burst out a-crying. "I do love Mistress Beatrix so, that I shall die if I don't have her."

'"My dear Blandford," says I, "you are young to think of marrying"; for he was but fifteen, and a young fellow of that age can scarce do so, you know.

'"But I'll wait twenty years, if she'll have me," says he. "I'll never marry – no never, never, never, marry anybody but

her. No, not a princess, though they would have me do it ever
so. If Beatrix will wait for me, her Blandford swears he will be
faithful." And he wrote a paper (it wasn't spelt right, for he
wrote "I'm ready to *sine with my blode*," which you know, Harry,
isn't the way of spelling it), and vowing that he would marry
none other but the Honourable Mistress Gertrude Beatrix
Esmond, only sister of his dearest friend Francis James, fourth
Viscount Esmond. And so I gave him a locket of her hair.'

'A locket of her hair!' cries Esmond.

— 'Yes. Trix gave me one after the fight with the Duchess
that very day. I am sure I didn't want it; and so I gave it him,
and we kissed at parting, and said – "Good-bye, brother." And
I got back through the gutter; and we set off home that very
evening. And he went to King's College, in Cambridge, and
*I'm* going to Cambridge soon; and if he doesn't stand to his
promise (for he's only wrote once), – he knows I wear a sword,
Harry. Come along, and let's go see the cocking-match at
Winchester.'

'... But I say,' he added, laughing, after a pause, 'I don't
think Trix will break her heart about him. Law bless you!
Whenever she sees a man, she makes eyes at him; and young
Sir Wilmot Crawley of Queen's Crawley, and Anthony Henley
of Alresford, were at swords drawn about her, at the Winchester
Assembly, a month ago.'

That night Mr Harry's sleep was by no means so pleasant
or sweet as it had been on the first two evenings after his arrival
at Walcote. 'So the bright eyes have been already shining on
another,' thought he, 'and the pretty lips, or the cheeks at any
rate, have begun the work which they were made for. Here's a
girl not sixteen, and one young gentleman is already whimpering
over a lock of her hair, and two country squires are ready to cut
each other's throats that they may have the honour of a dance
with her. What a fool am I to be dallying about this passion
and singeing my wings in this foolish flame. Wings! – why not
say crutches? There is but eight years' difference between us,
to be sure; but in life I am thirty years older. How could I ever
hope to please such a sweet creature as that, with my rough ways
and glum face? Say that I have merit ever so much, and won

myself a name, could she ever listen to me? She must be my Lady Marchioness, and I remain a nameless bastard. Oh! my master, my master!' (Here he fell to thinking with a passionate grief of the vow which he had made to his poor dying lord.) 'Oh! my mistress, dearest and kindest, will you be contented with the sacrifice which the poor orphan makes for you, whom you love, and who so loves you?'

And then came a fiercer pang of temptation. 'A word from me,' Harry thought, 'a syllable of explanation, and all this might be changed; but no, I swore it over the dying bed of my benefactor. For the sake of him and his; for the sacred love and kindness of old days; I gave my promise to him, and may kind Heaven enable me to keep my vow!'

The next day, although Esmond gave no sign of what was going on in his mind, but strove to be more than ordinarily gay and cheerful when he met his friends at the morning meal, his dear mistress, whose clear eyes it seemed no emotion of his could escape, perceived that something troubled him, for she looked anxiously towards him more than once during the breakfast, and when he went up to his chamber afterwards she presently followed him, and knocked at his door.

As she entered, no doubt the whole story was clear to her at once, for she found our young gentleman packing his valise, pursuant to the resolution which he had come to overnight of making a brisk retreat out of this temptation.

She closed the door very carefully behind her, and then leant against it, very pale, her hands folded before her, looking at the young man, who was kneeling over his work of packing. 'Are you going so soon?' she said.

He rose up from his knees, blushing, perhaps, to be so discovered, in the very act, as it were, and took one of her fair little hands – it was that which had her marriage ring on – and kissed it.

'It is best that it should be so, dearest lady,' he said.

'I knew you were going, at breakfast. I – I thought you might stay. What has happened? Why can't you remain longer with us? What has Frank told you – you were talking together late last night?'

'I had but three days' leave from Chelsea,' Esmond said, as gaily as he could. 'My aunt – she lets me call her aunt – is my mistress now; I owe her my lieutenancy and my laced coat. She has taken me into high favour; and my new general is to dine at Chelsea to-morrow – General Lumley, madam – who has appointed me his aide-de-camp, and on whom I must have the honour of waiting. See, here is a letter from the Dowager; the post brought it last night; and I would not speak of it, for fear of disturbing our last merry meeting.'

My lady glanced at the letter, and put it down with a smile that was somewhat contemptuous. 'I have no need to read the letter,' says she – (indeed, 'twas as well she did not; for the Chelsea missive, in the poor Dowager's usual French jargon, permitted him a longer holiday than he said. '*Je vous donne,*' quoth her ladyship, '*oui jour, pour vous fatigay parfaitement de vos parens fatigans*') – 'I have no need to read the letter,' says she. 'What was it Frank told you last night?'

'He told me little I did not know,' Mr Esmond answered. 'But I have thought of that little, and here's the result: I have no right to the name I bear, dear lady; and it is only by your sufferance that I am allowed to keep it. If I thought for an hour of what has perhaps crossed your mind too——'

'Yes, I did, Harry,' said she; 'I thought of it; and think of it. I would sooner call you my son than the greatest prince in Europe – yes, than the greatest prince. For who is there so good and so brave, and who would love her as you would? But there are reasons a mother can't tell.'

'I know them,' said Mr Esmond, interrupting her with a smile. 'I know there's Sir Wilmot Crawley of Queen's Crawley, and Mr Anthony Henley of the Grange, and my Lord Marquis of Blandford, that seems to be the favoured suitor. You shall ask me to wear my Lady Marchioness's favours and to dance at her ladyship's wedding.'

'Oh! Harry, Harry, it is none of these follies that frighten me,' cried out Lady Castlewood. 'Lord Churchill is but a child, his outbreak about Beatrix was a mere boyish folly. His parents would rather see him buried than married to one below him in rank. And do you think that I would stoop to sue for a husband for Francis Esmond's daughter; or submit to have my girl smuggled into that proud family to cause a quarrel between son and parents, and to be treated only as an inferior? I would disdain such a meanness. Beatrix would scorn it. Ah! Henry, 'tis not with you the fault lies, 'tis with her. I know you both, and love you: need I be ashamed of that love now? No, never, never, and 'tis not you, dear Harry, that is unworthy. 'Tis for my poor Beatrix I tremble – whose headstrong will frightens me; whose jealous temper (they say I was jealous too, but, pray God, I am cured of that sin) and whose vanity no words or prayers of mine can cure – only suffering, only experience, and remorse afterwards. Oh! Henry, she will make no man happy who loves her. Go away, my son: leave her: love us always, and think kindly of us: and for me, my dear, you know that these walls contain all that I love in the world.'

In after life, did Esmond find the words true which his fond mistress spoke from her sad heart? Warning he had: but I doubt others had warning before his time, and since: and he benefited by it as most men do.

My young Lord Viscount was exceeding sorry when he heard that Harry could not come to the cock-match with him, and must go to London, but no doubt my lord consoled himself when the Hampshire cocks won the match; and he saw every one of the battles, and crowed properly over the conquered Sussex gentlemen.

As Esmond rode towards town his servant, coming up to him, informed him with a grin, that Mistress Beatrix had brought out a new gown and blue stockings for that day's dinner, in which she intended to appear, and had flown into a rage and given her maid a slap on the face soon after she heard he was going away. Mistress Beatrix's woman, the fellow said, came down to the servants' hall, crying, and with the mark of a blow still on her cheek: but Esmond peremptorily ordered him to fall back and be silent, and rode on with thoughts enough of his own to occupy him – some sad ones, some inexpressibly dear and pleasant.

His mistress, from whom he had been a year separated, was his dearest mistress again. The family from which he had been parted, and which he loved with the fondest devotion, was his family once more. If Beatrix's beauty shone upon him, it was with a friendly lustre, and he could regard it with much such a delight as he brought away after seeing the beautiful pictures of the smiling Madonnas in the convent at Cadiz, when he was despatched thither with a flag: and as for his mistress, 'twas difficult to say with what a feeling he regarded her. 'Twas happiness to have seen her: 'twas no great pang to part; a filial tenderness, a love that was at once respect and protection, filled his mind as he thought of her; and near her or far from her, and from that day until now, and from now till death is past, and beyond it, he prays that sacred flame may ever burn.

## Chapter 9

### I MAKE THE CAMPAIGN OF 1704 [1]

MR ESMOND rode up to London then, where, if the Dowager had been angry at the abrupt leave of absence he took, she was mightily pleased at his speedy return.

He went immediately and paid his court to his new general, General Lumley,[2] who received him graciously, having known his father, and also, he was pleased to say, having had the very best accounts of Mr Esmond from the officer whose aide-de-camp he had been at Vigo. During this winter Mr Esmond was gazetted to a lieutenancy in Brigadier Webb's regiment of Fusileers, then with their colonel in Flanders; but being now attached to the suite of Mr Lumley, Esmond did not join his own regiment until more than a year afterwards, and after his return from the campaign of Blenheim, which was fought the next year. The campaign began very early, our troops marching out of their quarters before the winter was almost over, and investing the city of Bonn, on the Rhine, under the Duke's command. His Grace joined the army in deep grief of mind, with crape on his sleeve, and his household in mourning; and the very same packet which brought the Commander-in-Chief over, brought letters to the forces which preceded him, and one from his dear mistress to Esmond, which interested him not a little.

The young Marquis of Blandford, his Grace's son, who had been entered in King's College in Cambridge (whither my Lord Viscount had also gone, to Trinity, with Mr Tusher as his governor), had been seized with small-pox, and was dead at sixteen years of age, and so poor Frank's schemes for his sister's advancement were over, and that innocent childish passion nipped in the birth.

Esmond's mistress would have had him return, at least her letters hinted as much; but in the presence of the enemy this was impossible, and our young man took his humble share in the siege, which need not be described here, and had the good luck to escape without a wound of any sort, and to drink his General's health after the surrender. He was in constant military duty this year, and did not think of asking for a leave of absence, as one or two of his less fortunate friends did, who were cast away in that tremendous storm which happened towards the close of November, that 'which of late o'er pale Britannia past' (as Mr Addison sang of it),[3] and in which scores of our greatest ships and 15,000 of our seamen went down. .

They said that our Duke was quite heart-broken by the calamity which had befallen his family; but his enemies found that he could subdue them, as well as master his grief. Successful as had been this great General's operations in the past year, they were far enhanced by the splendour of his victory in the ensuing campaign. His Grace the Captain-General went to England after Bonn, and our army fell back into Holland, where, in April 1704, his Grace again found the troops embarking from Harwich and landing at Maesland Sluys: thence his Grace came immediately to the Hague, where he received the foreign ministers, general-officers, and other people of quality. The greatest honours were paid to his Grace everywhere – at the Hague, Utrecht, Ruremonde, and Maestricht; the civic authorities coming to meet his coaches: salvos of cannon saluting him, canopies of state being erected for him where he stopped, and feasts prepared for the numerous gentlemen following in his suite. His Grace reviewed the troops of the States-General between Liège and Maestricht, and afterwards the English forces, under the command of General Churchill, near Bois-le-Duc. Every preparation was made for a long march; and the army heard, with no small elation, that it was the Commander-in-Chief's intention to carry the war out of the Low Countries, and to march on the Mozelle. Before leaving our camp at Maestricht, we heard that the French, under the Marshall Villeroy, were also bound towards the Mozelle.

Towards the end of May, the army reached Coblentz; and next day, his Grace, and the generals accompanying him, went to visit the Elector of Treves at his Castle of Ehrenbreitstein, the Horse and Dragoons passing the Rhine whilst the Duke was entertained at a grand feast by the Elector. All as yet was novelty, festivity, and splendour – a brilliant march of a great and glorious army through a friendly country, and sure through some of the most beautiful scenes of nature which I ever witnessed.

The Foot and Artillery, following after the Horse as quick as possible, crossed the Rhine under Ehrenbreitstein, and so to Castel, over against Mayntz, in which city his Grace, his generals, and his retinue were received at the landing-place by the Elector's coaches, carried to his Highness's palace amidst the thunder of cannon, and then once more magnificently entertained. Gidlingen, in Bavaria, was appointed as the general rendezvous of the army, and thither, by different routes, the whole forces of English, Dutch, Danes, and German auxiliaries took their way. The Foot and Artillery under General Churchill passed the Neckar, at Heidelberg; and Esmond had an opportunity of seeing that city and palace, once so famous and beautiful (though shattered and battered by the French, under Turenne, in the late war), where his grandsire, had served the beautiful and unfortunate Electress-Palatine, the first King Charles's sister.

At Mindelsheim, the famous Prince of Savoy[4] came to visit our commander, all of us crowding eagerly to get a sight of that brilliant and intrepid warrior; and our troops were drawn up in battalia before the Prince, who was pleased to express his admiration of this noble English army. At length we came in sight of the enemy between Dillingen and Lawingen, the Brentz lying between the two armies. The Elector, judging that Donauwort would be the point of his Grace's attack, sent a strong detachment of his best troops to Count Darcos, who was posted at Schellenberg, near that place, where great intrenchments were thrown up, and thousands of pioneers employed to strengthen the position.

On the 2nd of July, his Grace stormed the post, with what success on our part need scarce be told. His Grace advanced with six thousand Foot, English and Dutch, thirty squadrons, and three regiments of Imperial Cuirassiers, the Duke crossing the river at the head of the Cavalry. Although our troops made the attack with unparalleled courage and fury – rushing up to the very guns of the enemy, and being slaughtered before their works – we were driven back many times, and should not have carried them, but that the Imperialists came up under the Prince of Baden, when the enemy could make no head against us: we pursued him into the trenches, making a terrible slaughter there, and into the very Danube, where a great part of his troops, following the example of their generals, Count Darcos and the Elector himself, tried to save themselves by swimming. Our army entered Donauwort, which the Bavarians evacuated; and where 'twas said the Elector purposed to have given us a warm reception, by burning us in our beds; the cellars of the houses, when we took possession of them, being found stuffed with straw. But though the links⁵ were there, the link-boys had run away. The townsmen saved their houses, and our General took possession of the enemy's ammunition in the arsenals, his stores, and magazines. Five days afterwards a great 'Te Deum' was sung in Prince Lewis's army, and a solemn day of thanksgiving held in our own; the Prince of Savoy's compliments coming to his Grace the Captain-General during the day's religious ceremony, and concluding, as it were, with an amen.

And now, having seen a great military march through a friendly country; the pomps and festivities of more than one German court; the severe struggle of a hotly-contested battle, and the triumph of victory; Mr Esmond beheld another part of military duty; our troops entering the enemy's territory, and putting all around them to fire and sword; burning farms, wasted fields, shrieking women, slaughtered sons and fathers, and drunken soldiery, cursing and carousing in the midst of tears, terror, and murder. Why does the stately Muse of History, that delights in describing the valour of heroes and the grandeur of conquest, leave out these scenes, so brutal, mean, and degrading, that yet form by far the greater part of the drama of war? You, gentlemen of England, who live at home at ease, and compliment yourselves in the songs of triumph with which our chieftains are bepraised – you pretty maidens, that come tumbling down the stairs when the fife and drum call you, and huzzah for the British Genadiers – do you take account that these items go to make up the amount of the triumph you admire, and form part of the duties of the heroes you fondle? Our chief, whom England and all Europe, saving only the Frenchmen, worshipped almost, had this of the godlike in him, that he was impassible before victory, before danger, before defeat. Before the greatest obstacle or the most trivial ceremony; before a hundred thousand men drawn in battalia, or a peasant slaughtered at the door of his burning hovel; before a carouse of drunken German lords, or a monarch's court, or a cottage-table, where his plans were laid, or an enemy's battery, vomiting flame and death, and strewing corpses round about him; – he was always cold, calm, resolute, like fate. He performed a treason or a court-bow, he told a falsehood as black as Styx, as easily as he paid a compliment or spoke about the weather. He took a mistress, and left her; he betrayed his benefactor, and supported him, or would have murdered him, with the same calmness always, and having no more remorse than Clotho when she weaves the thread or Lachesis when she cuts it.[6] In the hour of battle I have heard the Prince of Savoy's officers say, the Prince became possessed with a sort of warlike fury; his eyes lighted up; he rushed hither and thither, raging; he shrieked curses and encouragement, yelling and harking his bloody war-dogs on, and himself always at the first of the hunt. Our Duke was as calm at the mouth of the cannon as at the door of a drawing-room. Perhaps he could not have been the great man he was, had he had a heart either for love or hatred, or pity or fear, or regret or remorse. He achieved the highest deed of daring, or deepest calculation of thought, as he performed the very meanest action of which a man is capable; told a lie, or cheated a fond woman, or robbed a poor beggar of a half-penny, with a like awful serenity and equal capacity of the highest and lowest acts of our nature.

His qualities were pretty well known in the army, where there were parties of all politics, and of plenty of shrewdness and wit; but there existed such a perfect confidence in him, as the first captain of the world, and such a faith and admiration in his prodigious genius and fortune, that the very men whom he notoriously cheated of their pay, the chiefs whom he used and injured – (for he used all men, great and small, that came near him, as his instruments alike, and took something of theirs, either some quality or some property – the blood of a soldier, it might be, or a jewelled hat, or a hundred thousand crowns from a king, or a portion out of a starving sentinel's three farthings; or [when he was young] a kiss from a woman, and the gold chain off her neck, taking all he could from woman or man, and having, as I have said, this of the godlike in him, that he could see a hero perish or a sparrow fall, with the same amount of sympathy for either. Not that he had no tears; he could always order up this reserve at the proper moment to battle; he could draw upon tears or smiles alike, and whenever need was for using this cheap coin. He would cringe to a shoe-black, as he would flatter a minister or a monarch; be haughty, be humble, threaten, repent, weep, grasp your hand, or stab you whenever he saw occasion) – But yet those of the army, who knew him best and had suffered most from him, admired him most of all: and as he rode along the lines to battle or galloped up in the nick of time to a battalion reeling from before the enemy's charge or shot, the fainting men and officers got new courage as they saw the splendid calm of his face, and felt that his will made them irresistible.

After the great victory of Blenheim[7] the enthusiasm of the army for the Duke, even of his bitterest personal enemies in it, amounted to a sort of rage – nay, the very officers who cursed him in their hearts, were among the most frantic to cheer him. Who could refuse his meed of admiration to such a victory and such a victor? Not he who writes: a man may profess to be ever so much a philosopher; but he who fought on that day must feel a thrill of pride as he recalls it.

The French right was posted near to the village of Blenheim, on the Danube, where the Marshal Tallard's quarters were; their line extending through, it may be a league and a half, before Lutzingen and up to a woody hill, round the base of which, and acting against the Prince of Savoy, were forty of his squadrons. Here was a village that the Frenchmen had burned, the wood being, in fact, a better shelter and easier of guard than any village.

Before these two villages and the French lines ran a little stream, not more than two foot broad, through a marsh (that was mostly dried up from the heats of the weather), and this stream was the only separation between the two armies – ours coming up and ranging themselves in line of battle before the French, at six o'clock in the morning; so that our line was quite visible to theirs; and the whole of this great plain was black and swarming with troops for hours before the cannonading began.

On one side and the other this cannonading lasted many hours, the French guns being in position in front of their line, and doing severe damage among our Horse especially, and on our right wing of Imperialists under the Prince of Savoy, who could neither advance his artillery nor his lines, the ground before him being cut up by ditches, morasses, and very difficult of passage for the guns.

It was past mid-day when the attack began on our left, where Lord Cutts commanded, the bravest and most beloved officer in the English army. And now, as if to make his experience in war complete, our young aide-de-camp having seen two great armies facing each other in line of battle, and had the honour of riding with orders from one end to other of the line, came in for a not uncommon accompaniment of military glory, and was knocked on the head, along with many hundred of brave fellows, almost at the very commencement of this famous day of Blenheim.[8] A little after noon, the disposition for attack being completed with much delay and difficulty, and under a severe fire from the enemy's guns, that were better posted and more numerous than ours, a body of English and Hessians, with Major-General Wilkes commanding at the extreme left of our line, marched upon Blenheim, advancing with great gallantry, the Major-General on foot, with his officers, at the head of the column, and marching, with his hat off, intrepidly in the face of the enemy, who was pouring in a tremendous fire from his guns and musketry, to which our people were instructed not to reply, except with pike and bayonet when they reached the French palisades. To these Wilkes walked intrepidly, and struck the wood-work with his sword before our people charged it. He was shot down at the instant, with his colonel, major, and several officers; and our troops cheering and huzzaing, and coming on, as they did, with immense resolution and gallantry, were nevertheless stopped by the murderous fire from behind the enemy's defences, and then attacked in flank by a furious charge of French Horse which swept out of Blenheim, and cut down our men in great numbers. Three fierce and desperate assaults of our Foot were made and repulsed by the enemy; so that our columns of Foot were quite shattered, and fell back, scrambling over the little rivulet, which we had crossed so resolutely an hour before, and pursued by the French cavalry, slaughtering us and cutting us down.

And now the conquerors were met by a furious charge of English Horse under Esmond's general, General Lumley, behind whose squadrons the flying Foot found refuge, and formed again, whilst Lumley drove back the French Horse, charging up to the village of Blenheim and the palisades where Wilkes, and many hundred more gallant Englishmen, lay in slaughtered heaps. Beyond this moment, and of this famous victory, Mr Esmond knows nothing; for a shot brought down his horse and our young gentleman on it, who fell crushed and stunned under the animal; and came to his senses he knows not how long after, only to lose them again from pain and loss of blood. A dim sense, as of people groaning round about him, a wild incoherent thought or two for her who occupied so much of his heart now, and that here his career, and his hopes, and misfortunes were ended, he remembers in the course of these hours. When he woke up it was with a pang of extreme pain, his breastplate was taken off, his servant was holding his head up, the good and faithful lad of Hampshire* was blubbering over his master, whom he found and had thought dead, and a surgeon was probing a wound in the shoulder, which he must have got at the same moment when his horse was shot and fell over him. The battle was over at this end of the field, by this time: the village was in possession of the English, its brave defenders prisoners, or fled, or drowned, many of them, in the neighbouring waters of Donau. But for honest Lockwood's faithful search after his master, there had no doubt been an end of Esmond here, and of this his story. The marauders were out rifling the bodies as they lay on the field, and Jack had brained one of these gentry with the club-end of his musket, who had eased Esmond of his hat and periwig, his purse, and fine silver-mounted pistols which the Dowager gave him, and was fumbling in his pockets for further treasure, when Jack Lockwood came up and put an end to the scoundrel's triumph.

Hospitals for our wounded were established at Blenheim, and here for several weeks Esmond lay in very great danger of his life; the wound was not very great from which he suffered, and the ball extracted by the surgeon on the spot where our young gentleman received it; but a fever set in next day, as he was lying in hospital, and that almost carried him away. Jack Lockwood said he talked in the wildest manner during his delirium; that he called himself the Marquis of Esmond, and seizing one of the surgeon's assistants who came to dress his wounds, swore that he was Madam Beatrix, and that he would make her a duchess if she would but say yes. He was passing the days in these crazy fancies, and *vana somnia*, whilst the army was singing Te Deum for the victory, and those famous festivities were taking place at which our Duke, now made a Prince of the Empire, was entertained by the King of the Romans⁹ and his nobility. His Grace went home by Berlin and Hanover and Esmond lost the festivities which took place at those cities,

*My mistress before I went this campaign sent me John Lockwood out of Walcote, who hath ever since remained with me. – H. E.

and which his general shared in company of the other general officers who travelled with our great captain. When he could move it was by the Duke of Wirtemburg's city of Stuttgard that he made his way homewards, revisiting Heidelberg again, whence he went to Manheim, and hence had a tedious but, easy water journey down the river of Rhine, which he had thought a delightful and beautiful voyage indeed, but that his heart was longing for home, and something far more beautiful and delightful.

As bright and welcome as the eyes almost of his mistress shone the lights of Harwich, as the packet came in from Holland. It was not many hours ere he, Esmond, was in London, of that you may be sure, and received with open arms by the old Dowager of Chelsey, who vowed, in her jargon of French and English, that he had the *air noble*, that his pallor embellished him, that he was an Amadis [10] and deserved a Gloriana; and, oh! flames and darts! what was his joy at hearing that his mistress was come into waiting, and was now with her Majesty at Kensington! Although Mr Esmond had told Jack Lockwood to get horses and they would ride for Winchester that night; when he heard this news he countermanded the horses at once; his business lay no longer in Hants; all his hope and desire lay within a couple of miles of him in Kensington Park wall. Poor Harry had never looked in the glass before so eagerly to see whether he had the *bel air*, and his paleness really did become him; he never took such pains about the curl of his periwig, and the taste of his embroidery and point-lace, as now, before Mr Amadis presented himself to Madam Gloriana. Was the fire of the French lines half so murderous as the killing glances from her ladyship's eyes? Oh! darts and raptures, how beautiful were they!

And as, before the blazing sun of morning, the moon fades away in the sky almost invisible; Esmond thought, with a blush perhaps, of another sweet pale face, sad and faint, and fading out of sight, with its sweet fond gaze of affection; such a last look it seemed to cast as Eurydice might have given, yearning after her lover, when fate and Pluto summoned her, and she passed away into the shades.

## Chapter 10

### AN OLD STORY ABOUT A FOOL AND A WOMAN

ANY taste for pleasure which Esmond had (and he liked to *desipere in loco*,[1] neither more nor less than most young men of his age) he could now gratify to the utmost extent, and in the best company which the town afforded. When the army went into winter quarters abroad, those of the officers who had interest or money easily got leave of absence, and found it much pleasanter to spend their time in Pall Mall and Hyde Park, than to pass the winter away behind the fortifications of the dreary old Flanders towns, where the English troops were gathered. Yatches and packets passed daily between the Dutch and Flemish ports and Harwich; the roads thence to London and the great inns were crowded with army gentlemen; the taverns and ordinaries of the town swarmed with red-coats; and our great Duke's levees at St James's were as thronged as they had been at Ghent and Brussels, where we treated him, and he us, with the grandeur and ceremony of a sovereign. Though Esmond had been appointed to a lieutenancy in the Fusileer regiment of which that celebrated officer, Brigadier John Richmond Webb,[2] was colonel, he had never joined the regiment, nor been introduced to its excellent commander, though they had made the same campaign together, and been engaged in the same battle. But being aide-de-camp to General Lumley, who commanded the division of Horse, and the army marching to its point of destination on the Danube by different routes, Esmond had not fallen in, as yet, with his commander and future comrades of the fort; and it was in London, in Golden Square, where Major-General Webb lodged, that Captain Esmond had the honour of first paying his respects to his friend, patron, and commander of after days.

Those who remember this brilliant and accomplished gentleman may recollect his character, upon which he prided himself, I think, not a little, of being the handsomest man in the army;

a poet who writ a dull copy of verses upon the battle of Oudenarde three years after, describing Webb, says:—

> 'To noble danger Webb conducts the way,
>   His great example all his troops obey;
>   Before the front the General sternly rides,
>   With such an air as Mars to battle strides:
>   Propitious Heaven must sure a hero save,
>   Like Paris handsome, and like Hector brave.'

Mr Webb thought these verses quite as fine as Mr Addison's
on the Blenheim campaign, and, indeed, to be Hector *à la
mode de Paris*, was part of this gallant gentleman's ambition. It
would have been difficult to find an officer in the whole army,
or amongst the splendid courtiers and cavaliers of the Maison
du Roy,[3] that fought under Vendosme and Villeroy in the army
opposed to ours, who was a more accomplished soldier and
perfect gentleman, and either braver or better-looking. And, if
Mr Webb believed of himself what the world said of him, and
was deeply convinced of his own indisputable genius, beauty,
and valour, who has a right to quarrel with him very much?
This self-content of his kept him in general good-humour, of
which his friends and dependants got the benefit.

He came of a very ancient Wiltshire family, which he respected above all families in the world: he could prove a lineal
descent from King Edward the First, and his first ancestor,
Roaldus de Richmond, rode by William the Conqueror's side
on Hastings field. 'We were gentlemen, Esmond,' he used to
say, 'when the Churchills were horseboys.' He was a very tall
man, standing in his pumps six feet three inches (in his great
jack-boots, with his tall, fair periwig, and hat and feather, he
could not have been less than eight feet high). 'I am taller than
Churchill,' he would say, surveying himself in the glass, 'and
I am a better made man; and if the women won't like a man that
hasn't a wart on his nose,[4] faith, I can't help myself, and
Churchill has the better of me there.' Indeed, he was always
measuring himself with the Duke, and always asking his friends
to measure them. And talking in this frank way, as he would do,
over his cups, wags would laugh and encourage him; friends

would be sorry for him; schemers and flatterers would egg him on, and tale-bearers carry the stories to headquarters, and widen the difference which already existed there between the great captain and one of the ablest and bravest lieutenants he ever had.

His rancour against the Duke was so apparent, that one saw it in the first half-hour's conversation with General Webb; and his lady, who adored her General, and thought him a hundred times taller, handsomer, and braver than a prodigal nature had made him, hated the great Duke with such an intensity as it becomes faithful wives to feel against their husbands' enemies. Not that my Lord Duke was so yet; Mr Webb had said a thousand things against him, which his superior had pardoned; and his Grace, whose spies were everywhere, had heard a thousand things more that Webb had never said. But it cost this great man no pains to pardon; and he passed over an injury or a benefit alike easily.

Should any child of mine take the pains to read these, his ancestor's, memoirs, I would not have him judge of the great Duke* by what a contemporary has written of him. No man hath been so immensely lauded and decried as this great statesman and warrior; as, indeed, no man ever deserved better the very greatest praise and the strongest censure. If the present writer joins with the latter faction, very likely a private pique of his own may be the cause of his ill-feeling.

On presenting himself at the Commander-in-Chief's levee, his Grace had not the least remembrance of General Lumley's aide-de-camp, and though he knew Esmond's family perfectly well, having served with both lords (my Lord Francis and the Viscount, Esmond's father) in Flanders, and in the Duke of York's Guard, the Duke of Marlborough, who was friendly and serviceable to the (so-styled) legitimate representatives of the Viscount Castlewood, took no sort of notice of the poor lieutenant who bore their name. A word of kindness or acknowledgment, or a single glance of approbation, might have changed Esmond's opinion of the great man; and instead of a satire,

*This passage in the Memoirs of Esmond is written on a leaf inserted into the MS. book, and dated 1744, probably after he had heard of the Duchess's death.

which his pen cannot help writing, who knows but that the humble historian might have taken the other side of panegyric? We have but to change the point of view, and greatest action looks mean; as we turn the perspective-glass, and a giant appears a pigmy. You may describe, but who can tell whether your sight is clear or not, or your means of information accurate? Had the great man said but a word of kindness to the small one (as he would have stepped out of his gilt chariot to shake hands with Lazarus in rags and sores, if he thought Lazarus could have been of any service to him), no doubt Esmond would have fought for him with pen and sword to the utmost of his might; but my lord the lion did not want master mouse at this moment, and so Muscipulus went off and nibbled in opposition.

So it was, however, that a young gentleman, who, in the eyes of his family, and in his own, doubtless, was looked upon as a consummate hero, found that the great hero of the day took no more notice of him that of the smallest drummer in his Grace's army. The Dowager at Chelsey was furious against this neglect of her family, and had a great battle with Lady Marlborough (as Lady Castlewood insisted on calling the Duchess). Her Grace was now Mistress of the Robes to her Majesty, and one of the greatest personages in this kingdom, as her husband was in all Europe, and the battle between the two ladies took place in the Queen's drawing-room.

The Duchess, in reply to my aunt's eager clamour, said haughtily, that she had done her best for the legitimate branch of the Esmonds, and could not be expected to provide for the bastard brats of the family.

'Bastards,' says the Viscountess, in a fury, 'there are bastards amongst the Churchills, as your Grace knows, and the Duke of Berwick is provided for well enough.'

'Madam,' says the Duchess, 'you know whose fault it is that there are no such dukes in the Esmond family too, and how that little scheme of a certain lady miscarried.'

Esmond's friend, Dick Steele, who was in waiting on the Prince, heard the controversy between the ladies at Court. 'And faith,' says Dick, 'I think, Harry, thy kinswoman had the worst of it.'

He could not keep the story quiet; 'twas all over the coffee-houses ere night; it was printed in a News Letter before a month was over, and 'The Reply of her Grace the Duchess of M-rlb-r-gh, to a Popish Lady of the Court, once a favourite of the Late K—— J-m-s' was printed in half-a-dozen places, with a note stating that 'this Duchess, when the head of this lady's family came by his death lately in a fatal duel, never rested until she got a pension for the orphan heir, and widow, from her Majesty's bounty.' The squabble did not advance poor Esmond's promotion much, and indeed made him so ashamed of himself that he dared not show his face at the Commander-in-Chief's levees again.

During those eighteen months which had passed since Esmond saw his dear mistress, her good father, the old Dean, quitted this life, firm in his principles to the very last, and enjoining his family always to remember that the Queen's brother, King James the Third, was their rightful sovereign. He made a very edifying end, as his daughter told Esmond, and, not a little to her surprise, after his death (for he had lived always very poorly) my lady found that her father had left no less a sum than £3000 behind him, which he bequeathed to her.

With this little fortune Lady Castlewood was enabled, when her daughter's turn at Court came, to come to London, where she took a small genteel house at Kensington, in the neighbourhood of the Court, bringing her children with her, and here it was that Esmond found his friends.

As for the young lord, his university career had ended rather abruptly. Honest Tusher, his governor, had found my young gentleman quite ungovernable. My lord worried his life away with tricks; and broke out, as home-bred lads will, into a hundred youthful extravagancies, so that Doctor Bentley, the new master of Trinity, thought fit to write to the Viscountess Castlewood, my lord's mother, and beg her to remove the young nobleman from a college where he declined to learn, and where he only did harm by his riotous example. Indeed, I believe he nearly set fire to Nevil's Court,[5] that beautiful new quadrangle of our college, which Sir Christopher Wren had lately built. He knocked down a proctor's man that wanted to arrest him in a midnight prank; he gave a dinner party on the Prince of Wales's birthday, which was within a fortnight of his own, and the twenty young gentlemen then present sallied out after their wine, having toasted King James's health with open windows, and sung cavalier songs, and shouted 'God save the King!' in the great court, so that the master came out of his lodge at midnight, and dissipated the riotous assembly.

This was my lord's crowning freak, and the Rev. Thomas Tusher, domestic chaplain to the Right Honourable the Lord Viscount Castlewood, finding his prayers and sermons of no earthly avail to his lordship, gave up his duties of governor; went and married his brewer's widow at Southampton, and took her and her money to his parsonage-house at Castlewood.

My lady could not be angry with her son for drinking King James's health, being herself a loyal Tory, as all the Castlewood family were, and acquiesced with a sigh, knowing, perhaps, that her refusal would be of no avail to the young lord's desire for a military life. She would have liked him to be in Mr Esmond's regiment, hoping that Harry might act as guardian and adviser to his wayward young kinsman; but my young lord would hear of nothing but the Guards, and a commission was got for him in the Duke of Ormond's regiment; so Esmond found my lord, ensign and lieutenant, when he returned from Germany after the Blenheim campaign.

The effect produced by both Lady Castlewood's children when they appeared in public was extraordinary, and the whole town speedily rang with their fame; such a beautiful couple, it was declared, never had been seen; the young maid of honour was toasted at every table and tavern, and as for my young lord, his good looks were even more admired than his sister's. A hundred songs were written about the pair, and as the fashion of that day was, my young lord was praised in these Anacreontics[6] as warmly as Bathyllus.[7] You may be sure that he accepted very complacently the town's opinion of him, and acquiesced with that frankness and charming good-humour he always showed in the idea that he was the prettiest fellow in all London.

The old Dowager at Chelsea, though she could never be got to acknowledge that Mrs Beatrix was any beauty at all (in which opinion, as it may be imagined, a vast number of the ladies agreed with her), yet, on the very first sight of young Castlewood, she owned she fell in love with him; and Henry Esmond, on his return to Chelsea, found himself quite superseded in her favour by her younger kinsman. That feat of drinking the King's health at Cambridge would have won her heart, she said, if nothing else did. 'How had the dear young fellow got such beauty?' she asked. 'Not from his father – certainly not from his mother. How had he come by such noble manners, and the perfect *bel air*. That countrified Walcote widow could never have taught him.' Esmond had his own opinion about the countrified Walcote widow, who had a quiet grace, and serene kindness, that had always seemed to him the perfection of good breeding, though he did not try to argue this point with his aunt. But he could agree in most of the praises which the enraptured old Dowager bestowed on my Lord Viscount, than whom he never beheld a more fascinating and charming gentleman. Castlewood had not wit so much as enjoyment. 'The lad looks good things,' Mr Steele used to say; 'and his laugh lights up a conversation as much as ten repartees from Mr Congreve. I would as soon sit over a bottle with him as with Mr Addison; and rather listen to his talk than hear Nicolini.[8] Was ever a man so gracefully drunk as my Lord Castlewood? I would give anything to carry my wine' (though indeed, Dick bore his very kindly, and plenty of it, too) 'like this incomparable young man. When he is sober he is delightful; and when tipsy, perfectly irresistible.' And referring to his favourite, Shakespeare (who was quite out of fashion until Steele brought him back into the mode), Dick compared Lord Castlewood to Prince Hal, and was pleased to dub Esmond as ancient Pistol.

The Mistress of the Robes, the greatest lady in England after the Queen, or even before her Majesty, as the world said, though she never could be got to say a civil word to Beatrix, whom she had promoted to her place as maid of honour, took her brother into instant favour. When young Castlewood, in his new uniform, and looking like a prince out of a fairy-tale, went to pay his duty to her Grace, she looked at him for a minute in silence, the young man blushing and in confusion before her, then fairly burst out a-crying, and kissed him before her daughters and company. 'He was my boy's friend,' she said, through her sobs. 'My Blandford might have been like him.' And everybody saw, after this mark of the Duchess's favour, that my young lord's promotion was secure, and people crowded round the favourite's favourite, who became vainer and gayer, and more good-humoured than ever.

Meanwhile Madam Beatrix was making her conquests on her own side, and amongst them was one poor gentleman, who had been shot by her young eyes two years before, and had never been quite cured of that wound; he knew, to be sure, how hopeless any passion might be, directed in that quarter, and had taken that best, though ignoble, *remedium amoris*, a speedy retreat from before the charmer, and a long absence from her; and not being dangerously smitten in the first instance, Esmond pretty soon got the better of his complaint, and if he had it still, did not know he had it, and bore it easily. But when he returned after Blenheim, the young lady of sixteen, who had appeared the most beautiful object his eyes had ever looked on two years back, was now advanced to a perfect ripeness and perfection of beauty, such as instantly enthralled the poor devil, who had already been a fugitive from her charms. Then he had seen her but for two days, and fled; now he beheld her day after day, and when she was at Court, watched after her; when she was at home, made one of the family party; when she went abroad, rode after her mother's chariot; when she appeared in public places, was in the box near her, or in the pit looking at her; when she went to church was sure to be there, though he might not listen to the sermon, and be ready to hand her to her chair if she deigned to accept of his services, and select him from a score of young men who were always hanging round about her. When she went away, accompanying her Majesty to Hampton Court, a darkness fell over London. Gods, what nights has Esmond passed, thinking of her, rhyming about her, talking about her! His friend Dick

Steele was at this time courting the young lady, Mrs Scurlock,[9] whom he married; she had a lodging in Kensington Square, hard by my Lady Castlewood's house there. Dick and Harry, being on the same errand, used to meet constantly at Kensington. They were always prowling about that place, or dismally walking thence, or eagerly running thither. They emptied scores of bottles at the King's Arms, each man prating of his love, and allowing the other to talk on condition that he might have his own turn as a listener. Hence arose an intimacy between them, though to all the rest of their friends they must have been insufferable. Esmond's verses to 'Gloriana at the Harpsichord,' to 'Gloriana's Nosegay,' to 'Gloriana at Court,' appeared this year in the 'Observator'. Have you never read them? They were thought pretty poems, and attributed by some to Mr Prior.

This passion did not escape – how should it? – the clear eyes of Esmond's mistress: he told her all; what will a man not do when frantic with love? To what baseness will he not demean himself? What pangs will he not make others suffer, so that he may ease his selfish heart of a part of its own pain? Day after day he would seek his dear mistress, pour insane hopes, supplications, rhapsodies, raptures, into her ear. She listened, smiled, consoled, with untiring pity and sweetness. Esmond was the eldest of her children, so she was pleased to say; and as for her kindness, who ever had or would look for aught else from one who was an angel of goodness and pity? After what has been said, 'tis needless almost to add that poor Esmond's suit was unsuccessful. What was a nameless, penniless lieutenant to do, when some of the greatest in the land were in the field? Esmond never so much as thought of asking permission to hope so far above his reach as he knew this prize was – and passed his foolish, useless life in mere abject sighs and impotent longing. What nights of rage, what days of torment, of passionate unfulfilled desire, of sickening jealousy, can he recall! Beatrix thought no more of him than of the lacquey that followed her chair. His complaints did not touch her in the least; his raptures rather fatigued her; she cared for his verses no more than for Dan Chaucer's,[10] who's dead these ever so many hundred years; she did not hate him; she rather despised him, and just suffered him.

One day, after talking to Beatrix's mother, his dear, fond, constant mistress – for hours – for all day along – pouring out his flame and his passion, his despair and rage, returning again and again to the theme, pacing the room, tearing up the flowers on the table, twisting and breaking into bits the wax out of the stand-dish,[11] and performing a hundred mad freaks of passionate folly; seeing his mistress at last quite pale and tired out with sheer weariness of compassion, and watching over his fever for the hundredth time, Esmond seized up his hat, and took his leave. As he got into Kensington Square, a sense of remorse came over him for the wearisome pain he had been inflicting upon the dearest and kindest friend ever man had. He went back to the house, where the servant still stood at the open door, ran up the stairs, and found his mistress where he had left her in the embrasure of the window, looking over the fields towards Chelsey. She laughed, wiping away at the same time the tears which were in her kind eyes; he flung himself down on his knees, and buried his head in her lap. She had in her hand the stalk of one of the flowers, a pink, that he had torn to pieces. 'Oh, pardon me, pardon me, my dearest and kindest,' he said: 'I am in hell, and you are the angel that brings me a drop of water.'

'I am your mother, you are my son, and I love you always,' she said, holding her hands over him; and he went away comforted and humbled in mind, as he thought of that amazing and constant love and tenderness with which this sweet lady ever blessed and pursued him.

## Chapter 11

### THE FAMOUS MR JOSEPH ADDISON[1]

THE gentlemen ushers had a table at Kensington, and the Guard a very splendid dinner daily at St James's, at either of which ordinaries Esmond was free to dine. Dick Steele liked the Guard table better than his own at the gentlemen ushers', where there was less wine and more ceremony; and Esmond had many a jolly afternoon in company of his friend, and a hundred times at least saw Dick into his chair. If there is verity in wine, according to the old adage, what an amiable-natured character Dick's must have been! In proportion as he took in wine he overflowed with kindness. His talk was not witty so much as charming. He never said a word that could anger anybody, and only became the more benevolent the more tipsy he grew. Many of the wags derided the poor fellow in his cups, and chose him as a butt for their satire; but there was a kindness about him, and a sweet playful fancy, that seemed to Esmond far more charming than the pointed talk of the brightest wits, with their elaborate repartees and affected severities. I think Steele shone rather than sparkled. Those famous *beaux-esprits* of the coffee-houses (Mr William Congreve,[2] for intance, when his gout and his grandeur permitted him to come among us) would make many brilliant hits – half-a-dozen in a night some-times – but, like sharpshooters, when they had fired their shot, they were obliged to retire under cover till their pieces were loaded again, and wait till they got another chance at their enemy; whereas Dick never thought that his bottle-companion was a butt to aim at – only a friend to shake by the hand. The poor fellow had half the town in his confidence; everybody knew everything about his loves and his debts, his creditors' or his mistress's obduracy. When Esmond first came on to the town, honest Dick was all flames and raptures for a young lady, a West India fortune, whom he married. In a couple of years the lady was dead, the fortune was all but spent, and the honest widower was as eager in pursuit of a new paragon of beauty as if he had never courted and married and buried the last one.

Quitting the Guard table on one sunny afternoon, when by chance Dick had a sober fit upon him, he and his friend were making their way down Germain Street, and Dick all of a sudden left his companion's arm, and ran after a gentleman who was poring over a folio volume at the book-shop near to St James's Church. He was a fair, tall man, in a snuff-coloured suit, with a plain sword, very sober, and almost shabby in appearance – at least when compared to Captain Steele, who loved to adorn his

jolly round person with the finest of clothes, and shone in
scarlet and gold lace. The Captain rushed up, then, to the
student of the bookstall, took him in his arms, hugged him, and
would have kissed him – for Dick was always hugging and
bussing his friends – but the other stepped back with a flush
on his pale face, seeming to decline this public manifestation of
Steele's regard.

'My dearest Joe, where hast thou hidden thyself this age?'
cries the Captain, still holding both his friend's hands; 'I have
been languishing for thee this fortnight.'

'A fortnight is not an age, Dick,' says the other, very good-
humouredly. (He had light-blue eyes, extraordinary bright,
and a face perfectly regular and handsome, like a tinted statue.)
'And I have been hiding myself – where do you think?'

'What! not across the water,³ my dear Joe?' says Steele,
with a look of great alarm: 'thou knowest I have always——'

'No,' says his friend, interrupting him with a smile: 'we are
not come to such straits as that, Dick. I have been hiding, sir,
at a place where people never think of finding you – at my own
lodgings, whither I am going to smoke a pipe now and drink a
glass of sack; will your honour come?'

'Harry Esmond, come hither,' cries out Dick. 'Thou hast
heard me talk over and over again of my dearest Joe, my
guardian angel.'

'Indeed,' says Mr Esmond, with a bow, 'it is not from you
only that I have learnt to admire Mr Addison. We loved good
poetry at Cambridge, as well as at Oxford; and I have some of
yours by heart, though I have put on a red coat ... "*O, qui
canoro blandius Orpheo vocale ducis carmen*";⁴ shall I go on, sir?'
says Mr Esmond, who indeed had read and loved the charming
Latin poems of Mr Addison, as every scholar of that time knew
and admired them.

'This is Captain Esmond, who was at Blenheim,' says Steele.

'Lieutenant Esmond,' says the other, with a low bow; 'at
Mr Addison's service.'

'I have heard of you,' says Mr Addison, with a smile; as,
indeed, everybody about town had heard that unlucky story
about Esmond's dowager aunt and the Duchess.

'We were going to the George, to take a bottle before the play,' says Steele; 'wilt thou be one, Joe?'

Mr Addison said his own lodgings were hard by, where he was still rich enough to give a good bottle of wine to his friends; and invited the two gentlemen to his apartment in the Haymarket, whither we accordingly went.

'I shall get credit with my landlady,' says he, with a smile, 'when she sees two such fine gentlemen as you come up my stair.' And he politely made his visitors welcome to his apartment, which was indeed but a shabby one, though no grandee of the land could receive his guests with a more perfect and courtly grace than this gentleman. A frugal dinner, consisting of a slice of meat and a penny loaf, was awaiting the owner of the lodgings. 'My wine is better than my meat,' says Mr Addison; 'my Lord Halifax[5] sent me the Burgundy.' And he set a bottle and glasses before his friends, and ate his simple dinner in a very few minutes, after which the three fell to, and began to drink. 'You see,' says Mr Addison, pointing to his writing-table, whereon was a map of the action at Hochstedt, and several other gazettes and pamphlets relating to the battle, 'that I, too, am busy about your affairs, Captain. I am engaged as a poetical gazetteer, to say truth, and am writing a poem on the campaign.'

So Esmond, at the request of his host, told him what he knew about the famous battle, drew the river on the table, *aliquo mero*, and with the aid of some bits of tobacco-pipe, showed the advance of the left wing, where he had been engaged.

A sheet or two of the verses lay already on the table beside our bottles and glasses, and Dick having plentifully refreshed himself from the latter, took up the pages of manuscript, writ out with scarce a blot or correction, in the author's slim, neat handwriting, and began to read therefrom with great emphasis and volubility. At pauses of the verse the enthusiastic reader stopped and fired off a great salvo of applause.

Esmond smiled at the enthusiasm of Addison's friend. 'You are like the German Burghers,' says he, 'and the Princes on the Mozelle; when our army came to a halt, they always sent a deputation to compliment the chief, and fired a salute with all their artillery from their walls.'

'And drunk the great chief's health afterward, did not they?' says Captain Steele, gaily filling up a bumper; – he never was tardy at that sort of acknowledgment of a friend's merit.

'And the Duke, since you will have me act his Grace's part,' says Mr Addison, with a smile and something of a blush, 'pledged his friends in return. Most serene Elector of Covent Garden, I drink to your Highness's health,' and he filled himself a glass. Joseph required scarce more pressing than Dick to that sort of amusement; but the wine never seemed at all to fluster Mr Addison's brains; it only unloosed his tongue, whereas Captain Steele's head and speech were quite overcome by a single bottle.

No matter what the verses were, and, to say truth, Mr Esmond found some of them more than indifferent, Dick's enthusiasm for his chief never faltered, and in every line from Addison's pen, Steele found a master-stroke. By the time Dick had come to that part of the poem, wherein the bard describes as blandly as though he were recording a dance at the opera, or a harmless bout of bucolic cudgelling at a village fair, that bloody and ruthless part of our campaign, with the remembrance whereof every soldier who bore a part in must sicken with shame – when we were ordered to ravage and lay waste the Elector's country; and with fire and murder, slaughter and crime, a great part of his dominions was overrun; – when Dick came to the lines:

> 'In vengeance roused the soldier fills his hand
> With sword and fire, and ravages the land.
> In crackling flames a thousand harvests burn,
> A thousand villages to ashes turn.
> To the thick woods the woolly flocks retreat,
> And mixed with bellowing herds confusedly bleat.
> Their trembling lords the common shade partake,
> And cries of infants found in every brake.
> The listening soldier fixed in sorrow stands,
> Loth to obey his leader's just commands.
> The leader grieves, by generous pity swayed,
> To see his just commands so well obeyed:'[6]

by this time wine and friendship had brought poor Dick to a perfectly maudlin state, and he hiccupped out the last line with a tenderness that set one of his auditors a-laughing.

'I admire the licence of you poets,' says Esmond to Mr Addison. (Dick, after reading of the verses, was fain to go off, insisting on kissing his two dear friends before his departure, and reeling away with his periwig over his eyes.) 'I admire your art: the murder of the campaign is done to military music, like a battle at the opera, and the virgins shriek in harmony, as our victorious grenadiers march into their villages. Do you know what a scene it was?' (By this time, perhaps, the wine had warmed Mr Esmond's head too.) 'What a triumph you are celebrating? what scenes of shame and horror were enacted, over which the commander's genius presided, as calm as though he didn't belong to our sphere? You talk of the "listening soldier fixed in sorrow," the "leader's grief swayed by generous pity"; to my belief the leader cared no more for bleating flocks than he did for infants' cries, and many of our ruffians butchered one or the other with equal alacrity. I was ashamed of my trade when I saw those horrors perpetrated, which came under every man's eyes. You hew out of your polished verses a stately image of smiling victory; I tell you 'tis an uncouth, distorted, savage idol; hideous, bloody, and barbarous. The rites performed before it are shocking to think of. You great poets should show it as it is – ugly and horrible, not beautiful and serene. Oh, sir, had you made the campaign, believe me, you never would have sung it so.'

During this little outbreak, Mr Addison was listening, smoking out of his long pipe, and smiling very placidly. 'What would you have?' says he. 'In our polished days, and according to the rules of art, 'tis impossible that the Muse should depict tortures or begrime her hands with the horrors of war. These are indicated rather than described; as in the Greek tragedies that, I dare say, you have read (and sure there can be no more elegant specimens of composition); Agamemnon is slain, or Medea's children[7] destroyed, away from the scene; – the chorus occupying the stage and singing of the action to pathetic music. Something of this I attempt, my dear sir, in my humble way:

'tis a panegyric I mean to write, and not a satire. Were I to sing as you would have me, the town would tear the poet in pieces, and burn his book by the hands of the common hangman. Do you not use tobacco? Of all the weeds grown on earth, sure the nicotian is the most soothing and salutary. We must paint our great Duke,' Mr Addison went on, 'not as a man, which no doubt he is, with weaknesses like the rest of us, but as a hero. 'Tis in a triumph, not a battle, that your humble servant is riding his sleek Pegasus. We college-poets trot, you know, on very easy nags; it hath been, time out of mind, part of the poet's profession to celebrate the actions of heroes in verse, and to sing the deeds which you men of war perform. I must follow the rules of my art, and the composition of such a strain as this must be harmonious and majestic, not familiar, or too near the vulgar truth. *Si parva licet*:[8] if Virgil could invoke the divine Augustus, a humbler poet from the banks of the Isis may celebrate a victory and a conqueror of our own nation, in whose triumphs every Briton has a share, and whose glory and genius contributes to every citizen's individual honour. When hath there been, since our Henrys' and Edwards' days, such a great feat of arms as that from which you yourself have brought away marks of distinction? If 'tis in my power to sing that song worthily, I will do so, and be thankful to my Muse. If I fail as a poet, as a Briton at least I will show my loyalty, and fling up my cap and huzzah for the conqueror:

> "————*Rheni pacator et Istri*
> *Omnis in hoc uno variis discordia cessit*
> *Ordinibus; lætatur eques, plauditque senator,*
> *Votaque patricio certant plebeia favori.*"[9]

'There were as brave men on that field,' says Mr Esmond (who never could be made to love the Duke of Marlborough, nor to forget those stories which he used to hear in his youth regarding that great chief's selfishness and treachery) ' – there were men at Blenheim as good as the leader, whom neither knights nor senators applauded, nor voices plebeian or patrician favoured, and who lie there forgotten, under the clods. What poet is there to sing them?'

'To sing the gallant souls of heroes sent to Hades!'[10] says Mr Addison, with a smile: 'Would you celebrate them all? If I may venture to question anything in such an admirable work, the catalogue of the ships in Homer hath always appeared to me as somewhat wearisome; what had the poem been, supposing the writer had chronicled the names of captains, lieutenants, rank and file? One of the greatest of a great man's qualities is success; 'tis the result of all the others; 'tis a latent power in him which compels the favour of the gods, and subjugates fortune. Of all his gifts I admire that one in the great Marlborough. To be brave? every man is brave. But in being victorious, as he is, I fancy there is something divine. In presence of the occasion, the great soul of the leader shines out, and the god is confessed. Death itself respects him, and passes by him to lay others low. War and carnage flee before him to ravage other parts of the field, as Hector from before the divine Achilles. You say he hath no pity; no more have the gods, who are above it, and superhuman. The fainting battle gathers, strength at his aspect; and, wherever he rides, victory charges with him.'

A couple of days after, when Mr Esmond revisited his poetic friend, he found this thought, struck out in the fervour of conversation, improved and shaped into those famous lines,[11] which are in truth the noblest in the poem of the 'Campaign'. As the two gentlemen sat engaged in talk, Mr Addison solacing himself with his customary pipe; the little maid-servant that waited on his lodging came up, preceding a gentleman in fine laced clothes, that had evidently been figuring at Court, or a great man's levee. The courtier coughed a little at the smoke of the pipe, and looked round the room curiously, which was shabby enough, as was the owner in his worn snuff-coloured[12] suit and plain tie-wig.[13]

'How goes on the *magnum opus*, Mr Addison?' says the Court gentleman on looking down at the papers that were on the table.

'We were but now over it,' says Addison (the greatest courtier in the land could not have a more splendid politeness, or greater dignity of manner); 'here is the plan,' says he, 'on the table: *hac ibat Simois*,[14] here ran the little river Nebel: *hic est Sigeia tellus*,[15] here are Tallard's quarters, at the bowl of this pipe, at the attack of which Captain Esmond was present. I have the honour to introduce him to Mr Boyle; and Mr Esmond was but now depicting *aliquo prœlia mixta mero*,[16] when you came in.' In truth the two gentlemen had been so engaged when the visitor arrived, and Addison, in his smiling way, speaking of Mr Webb, colonel of Esmond's regiment (who commanded a brigade in the action, and greatly distinguished himself there), was lamenting that he could find never a suitable rhyme for Webb, otherwise the brigade should have had a place in the poet's verses. 'And for you, you are just a lieutenant,' says Addison, 'and the Muse can't occupy herself with any gentleman under the rank of a field-officer.'

Mr Boyle was all impatient to hear, saying that my Lord Treasurer[17] and my Lord Halifax were equally anxious; and Addison, blushing, began reading of his verses, and, I suspect, knew their weak parts as well as the most critical hearer. When he came to the lines describing the angel, that he read with great animation, looking at Esmond, as much as

'Inspired repulsed battalions to engage,
And taught the doubtful battle where to rage,'

to say, 'You know where that simile came from – from our talk, and our bottle of Burgundy, the other day.'

The poet's two hearers were caught with enthusiasm, and applauded the verses with all their might. The gentleman of the Court sprang up in great delight. 'Not a word more, my dear sir,' says he. 'Trust me with the papers – I'll defend them with my life. Let me read them over to my Lord Treasurer, whom I am appointed to see in half-an-hour. I venture to promise, the verses shall lose nothing by my reading, and then, sir, we shall see whether Lord Halifax has a right to complain that his friend's pension is no longer paid.'[18] And without more ado, the courtier in lace seized the manuscript pages, placed them in his breast with his ruffled hand over his heart, executed a most gracious wave of the hat with the disengaged hand, and smiled and bowed out of the room, leaving an odour of pomander behind him.

'Does not the chamber look quite dark?' says Addison surveying it, 'after the glorious appearance and disappearance of that gracious messenger? Why, he illuminated the whole room. Your scarlet, Mr Esmond, will bear any light; but this threadbare old coat of mine, how very worn it looked under the glare of that splendour! I wonder whether they will do anything for me,' he continued. 'When I came out of Oxford into the world, my patrons promised me great things; and you see where their promises have landed me, in a lodging up two pair of stairs, with a sixpenny dinner from the cook's shop. Well, I suppose this promise will go after the others, and fortune will jilt me, as the jade has been doing any time these seven years. "I puff the prostitute away,"[19]' says he, smiling, and blowing a cloud out of his pipe. 'There is no hardship in poverty, Esmond, that is not bearable; no hardship even in honest dependence that an honest man may not put up with. I came out of the lap of Alma Mater, puffed up with her praises of me, and thinking to make a figure in the world with the parts and learning which had got me no small name in our college. The world is the ocean, and Isis and Charwell are but little drops, of which the sea takes no account. My reputation ended a mile beyond Maudlin Tower; no one took note of me; and I learned this, at least, to bear up against evil fortune with a cheerful heart. Friend Dick hath made a figure in the world, and has passed me in the race long ago. What matters a little name or a little fortune? There is no fortune that a philosopher cannot endure. I have been not unknown as a scholar, and yet forced to live by turning bear-leader[20] and teaching a boy to spell. What then? The life was not pleasant, but possible – the bear was bearable. Should this venture fail, I will go back to Oxford; and some day, when you are a general, you shall find me a curate in a cassock and bands, and I shall welcome your honour to my cottage in the country, and to a mug of penny ale. 'Tis not poverty that's the hardest to bear, or the least happy lot in life,' says Mr Addison, shaking the ash out of his pipe. 'See, my pipe is smoked out. Shall we have another bottle? I have still a couple in the cupboard, and of the right sort. No more? – let us go abroad and take a turn on the Mall, or look in at the theatre and see Dick's comedy. 'Tis not a masterpiece of wit; but Dick is a good fellow, though he doth not set the Thames on fire.'

Within a month after this day, Mr Addison's ticket had come up a prodigious prize in the lottery of life. All the town was in an uproar of admiration of his poem, the 'Campaign', which Dick Steele was spouting at every coffee-house in Whitehall and Covent Garden. The wits on the other side of Temple Bar saluted him at once as the greatest poet the world had seen for ages; the people huzza'ed for Marlborough and for Addison, and, more than this, the party in power provided for the meritorious poet, and Mr Addison got the appointment of Commissioner of Excise,[21] which the famous Mr Locke vacated, and rose from this place to other dignities and honours; his prosperity from henceforth to the end of his life being scarce ever interrupted. But I doubt whether he was not happier in his garret in the Haymarket, than ever he was in his splendid palace at Kensington; and I believe the fortune that came to him in the shape of the countess his wife, was no better than a shrew and a vixen.[22]

Gay as the town was, 'twas but a dreary place for Mr Esmond, whether his charmer was in it or out of it, and he was glad when his general gave him notice that he was going back to his division of the army which lay in winter-quarters at Bois-le-Duc. His dear mistress bade him farewell with a cheerful face; her blessing he knew he had always, and wheresoever fate carried him. Mrs Beatrix was away in attendance on her Majesty at Hampton Court, and kissed her fair finger-tips to him, by way of adieu, when he rode thither to take his leave. She received her kinsman in a waiting-room where there were half-a-dozen more ladies of the Court, so that his high-flown speeches, had he intended to make any (and very likely he did), were impossible; and she announced to her friends that her cousin was going to the army, in as easy a manner as she would have said he was going to a chocolate-house. He asked with a rather rueful face, if she had any orders for the army? and she was pleased to say that she would like a mantle of Mechlin lace. She made him a saucy curtsey in reply to his own dismal bow. She deigned to kiss her finger-tips from the window, where she stood laughing with the other ladies, and chanced to see him as he made his way to the Toy. The Dowager at Chelsey was not sorry to part with him this time. '*Mon cher, vous êtes triste comme un sermon,*' she did him the honour to say to him; indeed, gentlemen in his condition are by no means amusing companions, and besides, the fickle old woman had now found a much more amiable favourite, and *raffolé*'d for her darling lieutenant of the Guard. Frank remained behind for a while, and did not join the army till later, in the suite of his Grace the Commander-in-Chief. His dear mother, on the last day before Esmond went away, and when the three dined together, made Esmond promise to befriend her boy, and besought Frank to take the example of his kinsman as of a loyal gentleman and brave soldier, so she was pleased to say; and at parting, betrayed not the least sign of faltering or weakness, though, God knows, that fond heart was fearful enough when others were concerned, though so resolute in bearing its own pain.

Esmond's general embarked at Harwich. 'Twas a grand sight to see Mr Webb dressed in scarlet on the deck, waving his hat as our yacht put off, and the guns saluted from the shore. Harry did not see his Viscount again, until three months after, at Bois-le-Duc, when his Grace the Duke came to take the command, and Frank brought a budget of news from home: how he had supped with this actress, and got tired of that; how he had got the better of Mr St John,[23] both over the bottle, and with Mrs Mountford,[24] of the Haymarket Theatre, (a veteran charmer of fifty, with whom the young scapegrace chose to fancy himself in love); how his sister was always at her tricks, and had jilted a young baron for an old earl. 'I can't make out Beatrix,' he said; 'she cares for none of us – she only thinks about herself; she is never happy unless she is quarrelling; but as for my mother – my mother, Harry, is an angel.' Harry tried to impress on the young fellow the necessity of doing everything in his power to please that angel; not to drink too much; not to go into debt; not to run after the pretty Flemish girls, and so forth, as became a senior speaking to a lad. 'But Lord bless thee!' the boy said; 'I may do what I like, and I know she will love me all the same'; and so, indeed, he did what he liked. Everybody spoiled him, and his grave kinsman as much as the rest.


*Chapter 12*

### I GET A COMPANY IN THE CAMPAIGN OF 1706

ON Whit-Sunday, the famous 23rd of May, 1706, my young lord first came under the fire of the enemy, whom we found posted in order of battle, their lines extending three miles or more, over the high ground behind the little Gheet river, and having on his left the little village of Anderkirk or Autre-église, and on his right Ramillies,[1] which has given its name to one of the most brilliant and disastrous days of battle that history ever hath recorded.

Our Duke here once more met his old enemy of Blenheim, the Bavarian Elector and the Mareschal Villeroy, over whom the Prince of Savoy had gained the famous victory of Chiari.[2] What Englishman or Frenchman doth not know the issue of that day? Having chosen his own ground, having a force superior to the English, and besides the excellent Spanish and Bavarian troops, the whole Maison-du-Roy with him, the most splendid body of Horse in the world – in an hour (and in spite of the prodigious gallantry of the French Royal Household, who charged through the centre of our line and broke it), this magnificent army of Villeroy was utterly routed by troops that had been marching for twelve hours, and by the intrepid skill of a commander, who did, indeed, seem in the presence of the enemy to be the very genius of victory.

I think it was more from conviction than policy, though that policy was surely the most prudent in the world, that the great Duke always spoke of his victories with an extraordinary

modesty, and as if it was not so much his own admirable genius
and courage which achieved these amazing successes, but as if
he was a special and fatal instrument in the hands of Providence,
that willed irresistibly the enemy's overthrow. Before his actions
he always had the church service read solemnly, and professed
an undoubting belief that our Queen's arms were blessed and
our victory sure. All the letters which he writ after his battles
show awe rather than exultation; and he attributes the glory of
these achievements, about which I have heard mere petty
officers and men bragging with a pardonable vain-glory, in no
wise to his own bravery or skill, but to the superintending
protection of Heaven, which he ever seemed to think was our
especial ally. And our army got to believe so, and the enemy
learnt to think so too; for we never entered into a battle without
a perfect confidence that it was to end in a victory; nor did the
French, after the issue of Blenheim, and that astonishing
triumph of Ramillies, ever meet us without feeling that the game
was lost before it was begun to be played, and that our general's
fortune was irresistible. Here, as at Blenheim, the Duke's
charger was shot, and 'twas thought for a moment he was dead.
As he mounted another, Binfield, his master of the Horse,
kneeling to hold his Grace's stirrup, had his head shot away
by a cannon-ball. A French gentleman of the Royal Household,
that was a prisoner with us, told the writer that at the time of
the charge of the Household, when their Horse and ours were
mingled, an Irish officer recognised the Prince-Duke, and
calling out – 'Marlborough, Marlborough!' fired his pistol at
him *à bout-portant*,[3] and that a score more carbines and pistols
were discharged at him. Not one touched him: he rode through
the French Cuirassiers sword-in-hand, and entirely unhurt,
and calm and smiling rallied the German Horse, that was
reeling before the enemy, brought these and twenty squadrons
of Orkney's back upon them, and drove the French across the
river again – leading the charge himself, and defeating the only
dangerous move the French made that day.

Major-General Webb commanded on the left of our line,
and had his own regiment under the orders of their beloved
colonel. Neither he nor they belied their character for gallantry

on this occasion; but it was about his dear young lord that Esmond was anxious, never having sight of him save once, in the whole course of the day, when he brought an order from the Commander-in-Chief to Mr Webb. When our Horse, having charged round the right flank of the enemy by Overkirk, had thrown him into entire confusion, a general advance was made, and our whole line of Foot, crossing the little river and the morass, ascended the high ground where the French were posted, cheering as they went, the enemy retreating before them. 'Twas a service of more glory than danger, the French battalions never waiting to exchange push of pike or bayonet with ours; and the gunners flying from their pieces which our line left behind us as they advanced, and the French fell back.

At first it was a retreat orderly enough; but presently the retreat became a rout, and a frightful slaughter of the French ensued on this panic; so that an army of sixty thousand men was utterly crushed and destroyed in the course of a couple of hours. It was as if a hurricane had seized a compact and numerous fleet, flung it all to the winds, shattered, sunk, and annihilated it; *afflavit Deus, et dissipati sunt,*[4] The French army of Flanders was gone, their artillery, their standards, their treasure, provisions, and ammunition were all left behind them: the poor devils had even fled without their soup-kettles, which are as much the palladia of the French infantry as of the Grand Signor's Janissaries, and round which they rally even more than round their lilies.

The pursuit, and a dreadful carnage which ensued (for the dregs of a battle, however brilliant, are ever a base residue of rapine, cruelty, and drunken plunder), was carried far beyond the field of Ramillies.

Honest Lockwood, Esmond's servant, no doubt wanted to be among the marauders himself and take his share of the booty; for when, the action over, and the troops got to their ground for the night, the Captain bade Lockwood get a horse, he asked, with a very rueful countenance, whether his honour would have him come too; but his honour only bade him go about his own business, and Jack hopped away quite delighted as soon as he saw his master mounted. Esmond made his way, and not without danger and difficulty, to his Grace's head-quarters, and found for himself very quickly where the aides-de-camp's quarters were, in an out-building of a farm, where several of these gentlemen were seated, drinking and singing, and at supper. If he had any anxiety about his boy, 'twas relieved at once. One of the gentlemen was singing a song to a tune that Mr Farquhar and Mr Gay both had used in their admirable comedies, and very popular in the army of that day; after the song came a chorus, 'Over the hills and far away'; and Esmond heard Frank's fresh voice soaring, as it were, over the songs of the rest of the young men – a voice that had always a certain artless, indescribable pathos with it, and indeed which caused Mr Esmond's eyes to fill with tears now, out of thankfulness to God the child was safe and still alive to laugh and sing.

When the song was over Esmond entered the room, where he knew several of the gentlemen present, and there sat my young lord, having taken off his cuirass, his waistcoast open, his face flushed, his long yellow hair hanging over his shoulders, drinking with the rest; the youngest, gayest, handsomest there. As soon as he saw Esmond, he clapped down his glass, and running towards his friend, put both his arms round him and embraced him. The other's voice trembled with joy as he greeted the lad; he had thought but now as he stood in the courtyard under the clear-shining moonlight; 'Great God! what a scene of murder is here within a mile of us; what hundreds and thousands have faced danger to-day; and here are these lads singing over their cups, and the same moon that is shining over yonder horrid field is looking down on Walcote very likely, while my lady sits and thinks about her boy that is at the war.' As Esmond embraced his young pupil now, 'twas with the feel-ing of quite religious thankfulness, and an almost paternal pleasure that he beheld him.

Round his neck was a star with a striped ribbon, that was made of small brilliants and might be worth a hundred crowns. 'Look,' says he, 'won't that be a pretty present for mother!'

'Who gave you the Order?' says Harry, saluting the gentle-man: 'did you win it in battle?'

'I won it,' cried the other, 'with my sword and my spear. There was a mousquetaire that had it round his neck – such a big mousquetaire, as big as General Webb, I called out to him to surrender, and that I'd give him quarter: he called me a *petit polisson*,[5] and fired his pistol at me, and then sent it at my head with a curse. I rode at him, sir, drove my sword right under his arm-hole, and broke it in the rascal's body. I found a purse in his holster with sixty-five Louis in it, and a bundle of love-letters, and a flask of Hungary-water. *Vive la guerre*, there are the ten pieces you lent me. I should like to have a fight every day'; and he pulled at his little moustache and bade a servant bring a supper to Captain Esmond.

Harry fell to with a very good appetite; he had tasted nothing since twenty hours ago, at early dawn. Master Grandson, who read this, do you look for the history of battles and sieges? Go, find them in the proper books; this is only the story of your grandfather and his family. Far more pleasant to him than the victory, though for that too he may say *meminisse juvat*,[6] it was to find that the day was over, and his dear young Castlewood was unhurt.

And would you, sirrah, wish to know how it was that a sedate Captain of Foot, a studious and rather solitary bachelor of eight or nine and twenty years of age, who did not care very much for the jollities which his comrades engaged in, and was never known to lose his heart in any garrison-town – should you wish to know why such a man had so prodigious a tenderness, and tended so fondly a boy of eighteen, wait, my good friend, until thou art in love with thy school-fellow's sister, and then see how mighty tender thou wilt be towards him. Esmond's general and his Grace the Prince-Duke were notoriously at variance, and the former's friendship was in no wise likely to advance any man's promotion, of whose services Webb spoke well; but rather likely to injure him, so the army said, in the favour of the greater man. However, Mr Esmond had the good fortune to be mentioned very advantageously by Major-General Webb in his report after the action; and the major of his regiment and two of the captains having been killed upon the day of Ramillies, Esmond, who was second of the lieutenants, got his company, and had the honour of serving as Captain Esmond in the next campaign.

My lord went home in the winter, but Esmond was afraid to follow him. His dear mistress wrote him letters more than once, thanking him, as mothers know how to thank, for his care and protection of her boy, extolling Esmond's own merits with a great deal more praise than they deserved; for he did his duty no better than any other officer; and speaking sometimes, though gently and cautiously, of Beatrix. News came from home of at least half-a-dozen grand matches that the beautiful maid of honour was about to make. She was engaged to an earl, our gentlemen of St James's[7] said, and then jilted him for a duke, who, in his turn, had drawn off. Earl or duke it might be who should win this Helen, Esmond knew she would never bestow herself on a poor captain. Her conduct, it was clear, was little satisfactory to her mother, who scarcely mentioned her, or else the kind lady thought it was best to say nothing, and leave time to work out its cure. At any rate, Harry was best away from the fatal object which always wrought him so much mischief; and so he never asked for leave to go home, but remained with his regiment that was garrisoned in Brussels, which city fell into our hands when the victory of Ramillies drove the French out of Flanders.

## Chapter 13

### I MEET AN OLD ACQUAINTANCE
### IN FLANDERS, AND FIND MY MOTHER'S
### GRAVE AND MY OWN CRADLE THERE

BEING one day in the Church of St Gudule, at Brussels, admiring the antique splendour of the architecture (and always entertaining a great tenderness and reverence for the Mother Church, that hath been as wickedly persecuted in England as ever she herself persecuted in the days of her prosperity), Esmond saw kneeling at a side altar, an officer in a green uniform coat, very deeply engaged in devotion. Something familiar in the figure and posture of the kneeling man struck Captain Esmond, even before he saw the officer's face. As he rose up, putting away into his pocket a little black breviary, such as priests use, Esmond beheld a countenance so like that of his friend and tutor of early days, Father Holt, that he broke out into an exclamation of astonishment and advanced a step towards the gentleman, who was making his way out of church. The German officer too looked surprised when he saw Esmond, and his face from being pale grew suddenly red. By this mark of recognition, the Englishman knew that he could not be mistaken; and though the other did not stop, but on the contrary rather hastily walked away towards the door, Esmond pursued him and faced him once more, as the officer, helping himself to holy water, turned mechanically towards the altar to bow to it ere he quitted the sacred edifice.

'My Father!' says Esmond in English.

'Silence! I do not understand. I do not speak English,' says the other in Latin.

Esmond smiled at this sign of confusion, and replied in the same language. 'I should know my Father in any garment, black or white, shaven or bearded': for the Austrian officer was habited quite in the military manner, and had as warlike a moustachio as any Pandour.[1]

He laughed – we were on the church steps by this time, passing through the crowd of beggars that usually is there holding up little trinkets for sale and whining for alms. 'You speak Latin,' says he, 'in the English way, Harry Esmond; you have forsaken the old true Roman tongue you once knew.' His tone was very frank, and friendly quite; the kind voice of fifteen years back; he gave Esmond his hand as he spoke.

'Others have changed their coats too, my Father,' says Esmond, glancing at his friend's military decoration.

'Hush! I am Mr or Captain von Holtz, in the Bavarian Elector's service, and on a mission to his Highness the Prince of Savoy. You can keep a secret I know from old times.'

'Captain von Holtz,' says Esmond, 'I am your very humble servant.'

'And you, too, have changed your coat,' continues the other in his laughing way; 'I have heard of you at Cambridge and afterwards: we have friends everywhere; and I am told that Mr Esmond at Cambridge was as good a fencer as he was a bad theologian.' (So, thinks Esmond, my old *maître d'armes* was a Jesuit as they said.)

'Perhaps you are right,' says the other, reading his thoughts quite as he used to do in old days: 'you were all but killed at Hochstedt of a wound in the left side. You were before that at Vigo, aide-de-camp to the Duke of Ormonde. You got your company the other day after Ramillies; your general and the Prince-Duke are not friends; he is of the Webbs of Lydiard Tregoze, in the county of York, a relation of my Lord St John. Your cousin, M. de Castlewood, served his first campaign this year in the Guard; yes, I do know a few things as you see.'

Captain Esmond laughed in his turn. 'You have indeed a curious knowledge,' he says. A foible of Mr Holt's, who did know more about books and men than, perhaps, almost any person Esmond had ever met, was omniscience; thus in every point he here professed to know, he was nearly right, but not quite. Esmond's wound was in the right side, not the left; his first general was General Lumley; Mr Webb came out of Wiltshire, not out of Yorkshire; and so forth. Esmond did not think fit to correct his old master in these trifling blunders, but they served to give him a knowledge of the other's character, and he smiled to think that this was his oracle of early days; only now no longer infallible or divine.

'Yes,' continues Father Holt, or Captain von Holtz, 'for a man who has not been in England these eight years, I know what goes on in London very well. The old Dean is dead, my Lady Castlewood's father. Do you know that your recusant bishops[2] wanted to consecrate him Bishop of Southampton, and that Collier[3] is Bishop of Thetford by the same imposition? The Princess Anne has the gout and eats too much; when the King returns, Collier will be an archbishop.'

'Amen!' says Esmond, laughing; 'and I hope to see your eminence no longer in jack-boots, but red stockings, at Whitehall.'

'You are always with us – I know that – I heard of that when you were at Cambridge; so was the late lord; so is the young Viscount.'

'And so was my father before me,' said Mr Esmond, looking calmly at the other, who did not, however, show the least sign of intelligence in his impenetrable grey eyes – how well Harry remembered them and their look! only crows' feet were wrinkled round them – marks of black old Time had settled there.

Esmond's face chose to show no more sign of meaning than the Father's. There may have been on the one side and the other just the faintest glitter of recognition, as you see a bayonet shining out of an ambush; but each party fell back, when everything was again dark.

'And you, mon capitaine, where have you been?' says Esmond, turning away the conversation from this dangerous ground, where neither chose to engage.

'I may have been in Pekin,' says he, 'or I may have been in Paraguay— who knows where? I am now Captain von Holtz, in the service of his Electoral Highness, come to negotiate exchange of prisoners with his Highness of Savoy.'

'Twas well known that very many officers in our army were well affected towards the young King at St Germains, whose right to the throne was undeniable, and whose accession to it, at the death of his sister, by far the greater part of the English people would have preferred, to the having a petty German prince for a sovereign, about whose cruelty, rapacity, boorish manners, and odious foreign ways, a thousand stories were current. It wounded our English pride to think, that a shabby High-Dutch duke, whose revenues were not a tithe as great as those of many of the princes of our ancient English nobility, who could not speak a word of our language, and whom we chose to represent as a sort of German boor, feeding on train-oil and sour-crout, with a bevy of mistresses in a barn, should come to reign over the proudest and most polished people in the world. Were we, the conquerors of the Grand Monarch, to submit to that ignoble domination? What did the Hanoverian's Protestantism matter to us? Was it not notorious (we were told and led to believe so) that one of the daughters of this Protestant hero was

being bred up with no religion at all, as yet, and ready to be made
Lutheran or Roman, according as the husband might be, whom
her parents should find for her? This talk, very idle and abusive
much of it was, went on at a hundred mess-tables in the army;
there was scarce an ensign that did not hear it, or join in it, and
everybody knew, or affected to know, that the Commander-in-
Chief himself had relations with his nephew, the Duke of
Berwick[4] ('twas by an Englishman, thank God, that we were
beaten at Almanza), and that his Grace was most anxious to
restore the royal race of his benefactors, and to repair his
former treason.

This is certain, that for a considerable period no officer in the
Duke's army lost favour with the Commander-in-Chief for
entertaining or proclaiming his loyalty towards the exiled family.
When the Chevalier de St George, as the King of England called
himself, came with the dukes of the French blood royal, to join
the French army under Vendosme, hundreds of ours saw him
and cheered him, and we all said he was like his father in this,
who, seeing the action of La Hogue[5] fought between the French
ships and ours, was on the side of his native country during the
battle. But this, at least, the Chevalier knew, and every one
knew, that, however well our troops and their general might be
inclined towards the Prince personally, in the face of the
enemy there was no question at all. Wherever my Lord Duke
found a French army, he would fight and beat it, as he did at
Oudenarde, two years after Ramillies, where his Grace achieved
another of his transcendent victories; and the noble young
Prince, who charged gallantly along with the magnificent
Maison-du-Roy, sent to compliment his conquerors after the
action.

In this battle, where the young Electoral Prince of Hanover[6]
behaved himself very gallantly, fighting on our side, Esmond's
dear General Webb distinguished himself prodigiously, exhibit-
ing consummate skill and coolness as a general, and fighting with
the personal bravery of a common soldier. Esmond's good-luck
again attended him; he escaped without a hurt, although more
than a third of his regiment was killed, had again the honour to
be favourably mentioned in his commander's report, and was

advanced to the rank of major. But of this action there is little need to speak, as it hath been related in every Gazette, and talked of in every hamlet in this country. To return from it to the writer's private affairs, which here, in his old age, and at a distance, he narrates for his children who come after him. Before Oudenarde, and after that chance rencontre with Captain von Holtz at Brussels, a space of more than a year elapsed, during which the captain of Jesuits and the captain of Webb's Fusileers were thrown very much together. Esmond had no difficulty in finding out (indeed, the other made no secret of it to him, being assured from old times of his pupil's fidelity), that the negotiator of prisoners was an agent from St Germains, and that he carried intelligence between great personages in our camp and that of the French. 'My business,' said he, 'and I tell you, both because I can trust you, and your keen eyes have already discovered it, is between the King of England and his subjects, here engaged in fighting the French King. As between you and them, all the Jesuits in the world will not prevent your quarrelling: fight it out, gentlemen. St George for England, I say – and you know who says so, wherever he may be.'

I think Holt loved to make a parade of mystery, as it were, and would appear and disappear at our quarters as suddenly as he used to return and vanish in the old days at Castlewood. He had passes between both armies, and seemed to know (but with that inaccuracy which belonged to the good Father's omniscience) equally well what passed in the French camp and in ours. One day he would give Esmond news of a great feste that took place in the French quarters, of a supper of Monsieur de Rohan's, where there was play and violins, and then dancing and masques: the King drove thither in Marshal Villar's own guinguette.[7] Another day he had the news of his Majesty's ague; the King had not had a fit these ten days, and might be said to be well. Captain Holtz made a visit to England during this time, so eager was he about negotiating prisoners; and 'twas on returning from this voyage that he began to open himself more to Esmond, and to make him, as occasion served, at their various meetings, several of those confidences which are here set down all together.

The reason of his increased confidence was this: upon going to

London, the old director of Esmond's aunt, the Dowager, paid her ladyship a visit at Chelsey, and there learnt from her that Captain Esmond was acquainted with the secret of his family, and was determined never to divulge it. The knowledge of this fact raised Esmond in his old tutor's eyes, so Holt was pleased to say, and he admired Harry very much for his abnegation.

'The family at Castlewood have done far more for me than my own ever did,' Esmond said. 'I would give my life for them. Why should I grudge the only benefit that 'tis in my power to confer on them?' The good Father's eyes filled with tears at this speech, which to the other seemed very simple; he embraced Esmond, and broke out into many admiring expressions; he said he was a *noble coeur*, that he was proud of him, and fond of him as his pupil and friend – regretted more than ever that he had lost him, and been forced to leave him in those early times, when he might have had an influence over him, have brought him into that only true church, to which the Father belonged, and enlisted him in the noblest army in which a man ever engaged – meaning his own Society of Jesus, which numbers (says he) in its troops the greatest heroes the world ever knew; – warriors, brave enough to dare or endure anything, to encounter any odds, to die any death; – soldiers that have won triumphs a thousand times more brilliant than those of the greatest general; that have brought nations on their knees to their sacred banner, the Cross; that have achieved glories and palms incomparably brighter than those awarded to the most splendid earthly conquerors – crowns of immortal light, and seats in the high places of Heaven.

Esmond was thankful for his old friend's good opinion, however little he might share the Jesuit Father's enthusiasm. 'I have thought of that question, too,' says he, 'dear Father,' and he took the other's hand— 'thought it out for myself, as all men must, and contrive to do the right, and trust to Heaven as devoutly in my way as you in yours. Another six months of you as a child, and I had desired no better. I used to weep upon my pillow at Castlewood as I thought of you, and I might have been a brother of your order; and who knows,' Esmond added, with a smile, 'a priest in full orders, and with a pair of moustachios, and a Bavarian uniform.'

'My son,' says Father Holt, turning red, 'in the cause of religion and loyalty all disguises are fair.'

'Yes,' broke in Esmond, 'all disguises are fair, you say; and all uniforms, say I, black or red, – a black cockade or a white one[8] – or a laced hat, or a sombrero, with a tonsure under it. I cannot believe that St Francis Xavier sailed over the sea in a cloak, or raised the dead – I tried; and very nearly did once, but cannot. Suffer me to do the right, and to hope for the best in my own way.'

Esmond wished to cut short the good Father's theology, and succeeded; and the other, sighing over his pupil's invincible ignorance, did not withdraw his affection from him, but gave him his utmost confidence – as much, that is to say, as a priest can give: more than most do; for he was naturally garrulous, and too eager to speak.

Holt's friendship encouraged Captain Esmond to ask, what he long wished to know, and none could tell him, some history of the poor mother whom he had often imagined in his dreams, and whom he never knew. He described to Holt those circumstances which are already put down in the first part of this story – the promise he had made to his dear lord, and that dying friend's confession; and he besought Mr Holt to tell him what he knew regarding the poor woman from whom he had been taken.

'She was of this very town,' Holt said, and took Esmond to see the street where her father lived, and where, as he believed, she was born. 'In 1676, when your father came hither in the retinue of the late King, then Duke of York, and banished hither in disgrace,[9] Captain Thomas Esmond became acquainted with your mother, pursued her, and made a victim of her; he hath told me in many subsequent conversations, which I felt bound to keep private then, that she was a woman of great virtue and tenderness, and in all respects a most fond, faithful creature. He called himself Captain Thomas, having good reason to be ashamed of his conduct towards her, and hath spoken to me many times with sincere remorse for that, as with fond love for her many amiable qualities. He owned to having treated her very ill; and that at this time his life was one of profligacy, gambling, and poverty. She became with child of you; was cursed by her own parents at that discovery; though she never upbraided, except by her involuntary tears, and the misery depicted on her countenance, the author of her wretchedness and ruin.

'Thomas Esmond – Captain Thomas, as he was called – became engaged in a gaming-house brawl, of which the consequence was a duel, and a wound so severe that he never – his surgeon said – could outlive it. Thinking his death certain, and touched with remorse, he sent for a priest of the very Church of St Gudule where I met you; and on the same day, after his making submission to our church, was married to your mother a few weeks before you were born. My Lord Viscount Castlewood, Marquis of Esmond, by King James's patent, which I myself took to your father, your lordship was christened at St Gudule by the same curé who married your parents, and by the name of Henry Thomas, son of E. Thomas, officier Anglois, and Gertrude Maes. You see you belong to us from your birth, and why I did not christen you when you became my dear little pupil at Castlewood.

'Your father's wound took a favourable turn – perhaps his conscience was eased by the right he had done – and to the surprise of the doctors he recovered. But as his health came back, his wicked nature, too, returned. He was tired of the poor girl, whom he had ruined; and receiving some remittance from his uncle, my lord the old viscount then in England, he pretended business, promised return, and never saw your poor mother more.

'He owned to me, in confession first, but afterwards in talk before your aunt, his wife, else I never could have disclosed what I now tell you, that on coming to London he writ a pretended confession to poor Gertrude Maes – Gertrude Esmond – of his having been married in England previously, before uniting himself with her; said that his name was not Thomas; that he was about to quit Europe for the Virginia plantations, where, indeed, your family had a grant of land from King Charles the First; sent her a supply of money, the half of the last hundred guineas he had, entreated her pardon, and bade her farewell.

'Poor Gertrude never thought that the news in this letter might be untrue as the rest of your father's conduct to her.

But though a young man of her own degree, who knew her history, and whom she liked before she saw the English gentleman who was the cause of all her misery, offered to marry her, and to adopt you as his own child, and give you his name, she refused him. This refusal only angered her father, who had taken her home; she never held up her head there, being the subject of constant unkindness after her fall; and some devout ladies of her acquaintance offering to pay a little pension for her, she went into a convent, and you were put out to nurse.

'A sister of the young fellow, who would have adopted you as his son, was the person who took charge of you. Your mother and this person were cousins. She had just lost a child of her own, which you replaced, your own mother being too sick and feeble to feed you; and presently your nurse grew so fond of you, that she even grudged letting you visit the convent where your mother was, and where the nuns petted the little infant, as they pitied and loved its unhappy parent. Her vocation became stronger every day, and at the end of two years she was received as a sister of the house.

'Your nurse's family were silk-weavers out of France, whither they returned to Arras in French Flanders, shortly before your mother took her vows, carrying you with them, then a child of three years old. 'Twas a town, before the late vigorous measures of the French King, full of Protestants, and here your nurse's father, old Pastoureau, he with whom you afterwards lived at Ealing, adopted the reformed doctrines, perverting all his house with him. They were expelled thence by the edict of his Most Christian Majesty, and came to London, and set up their looms in Spittlefields. The old man brought a little money with him, and carried on his trade, but in a poor way. He was a widower; by this time his daughter, a widow too, kept house for him, and his son and he laboured together at their vocation. Meanwhile your father had publicly owned his conversion just before King Charles's death (in whom our church had much such another convert), was reconciled to my Lord Viscount Castlewood, and married, as you know, to his daughter.

'It chanced that the younger Pastoureau, going with a piece of brocade to the mercer, who employed him, on Ludgate Hill, met his old rival coming out of an ordinary there. Pastoureau knew your father at once, seized him by the collar, and upbraided him as a villain, who had seduced his mistress, and afterwards deserted her and her son. Mr Thomas Esmond also recognized Pastoureau at once, besought him to calm his indignation, and not to bring a crowd round about them; and bade him to enter into the tavern, out of which he had just stepped, when he would give him any explanation. Pastoureau entered, and heard the landlord order the drawer to show Captain Thomas to a room; it was by his Christian name that your father was familiarly called at his tavern haunts, which, to say the truth, were none of the most reputable.

'I must tell you that Captain Thomas, or my Lord Viscount afterwards, was never at a loss for a story, and could cajole a woman or a dun with a volubility, and an air of simplicity at the same time, of which many a creditor of his has been the dupe. His tales used to gather verisimilitude as he went on with them. He strung together fact after fact with a wonderful rapidity and coherence. It required, saving your presence, a very long habit of acquaintance with your father to know when his lordship was l——, – telling the truth or no.

'He told me with rueful remorse when he was ill – for the fear of death set him instantly repenting, and with shrieks of laughter when he was well, his lordship having a very great sense of humour – how in half-an-hour's time, and before a bottle was drunk, he had completely succeeded in biting[10] poor Pastoureau. The seduction he owned too: that he could not help; he was quite ready with tears at a moment's warning, and shed them profusely to melt his credulous listener. He wept for your mother even more than Pastoureau did, who cried very heartily, poor fellow, as my lord informed me; he swore upon his honour that he had twice sent money to Brussels, and mentioned the name of the merchant with whom it was lying for poor Gertrude's use. He did not even know whether she had a child or no, or whether she was alive or dead; but got these facts easily out of honest Pastoureau's answers to him. When he heard that she was in a convent, he said he hoped to end his days in one himself, should he survive his wife, whom he hated, and had been

forced by a cruel father to marry; and when he was told that
Gertrude's son was alive, and actually in London, "I started,"
says he; "for then, damme, my wife was expecting to lie-in, and
I thought should this old Put,[11] my father-in-law, run rusty,[12]
here would be a good chance to frighten him."

'He expressed the deepest gratitude to the Pastoureau family
for their care of the infant: you were now near six years old; and
on Pastoureau bluntly telling him, when he proposed to go that
instant and see the darling child, that they never wished to see
his ill-omened face again within their doors; that he might have
the boy, though they should all be very sorry to lose him; and
that they would take his money, they being poor, if he gave it; or
bring him up, by God's help, as they had hitherto done, without:
he acquiesced in this at once, with a sigh, said, "Well, 'twas
better that the dear child should remain with friends who had
been so admirably kind to him"; and in his talk to me afterwards,
honestly praised and admired the weaver's conduct and spirit;
owned that the Frenchman was a right fellow, and he, the Lord
have mercy upon him, a sad villain.

'Your father,' Mr Holt went on to say, 'was good-natured
with his money when he had it; and having that day received a
supply from his uncle, gave the weaver ten pieces with perfect
freedom, and promised him further remittances. He took down
eagerly Pastoureau's name and place of abode in his table-book,
and when the other asked him for his own, gave, with the utmost
readiness, his name as Captain Thomas, New Lodge, Penzance,
Cornwall; he said he was in London for a few days only on
business connected with his wife's property; described her as a
shrew, though a woman of kind disposition; and depicted his
father as a Cornish squire, in an infirm state of health, at whose
death he hoped for something handsome, when he promised
richly to reward the admirable protector of his child, and to
provide for the boy. "And by Gad, sir," he said to me in his
strange laughing way, "I ordered a piece of brocade of the very
same pattern as that which the fellow was carrying, and presented it to my wife for a morning wrapper, to receive company
after she lay-in of our little boy."

'Your little pension was paid regularly enough; and when

your father became Viscount Castlewood on his uncle's demise, I was employed to keep a watch over you, and 'twas at my instance that you were brought home. Your foster-mother was dead; her father made acquaintance with a woman whom he married, who quarrelled with his son. The faithful creature came back to Brussels to be near the woman he loved, and died, too, a few months before her. Will you see her cross in the convent cemetery? The Superior is an old penitent of mine, and remembers Sœur Marie Madeleine fondly still.'

Esmond came to this spot in one sunny evening of spring, and saw, amidst a thousand black crosses, casting their shadows across the grassy mounds, that particular one which marked his mother's resting-place. Many more of those poor creatures that lay there had adopted that same name, with which sorrow had rebaptized her, and which fondly seemed to hint their individual story of love and grief. He fancied her in tears and darkness, kneeling at the foot of her cross, under which her cares were buried. Surely he knelt down, and said his own prayer there, not in sorrow so much as in awe (for even his memory had no recollection of her), and in pity for the pangs which the gentle soul in life had been made to suffer. To this cross she brought them; for this heavenly bridegroom she exchanged the husband who had wooed her, the traitor who had left her. A thousand such hillocks lay round about, the gentle daisies springing out of the grass over them, and each bearing its cross and requiescat. A nun, veiled in black, was kneeling hard by, at a sleeping sister's bedside (so fresh made, that the spring had scarce had time to spin a coverlid for it); beyond the cemetery walls you had glimpses of life and the world, and the spires and gables of the city. A bird came down from a roof opposite, and lit first on a cross, and then on the grass below it, whence it flew away presently with a leaf in its mouth: then came a sound as of chanting, from the chapel of the sisters hard by; others had long since filled the place, which poor Mary Magdalene once had there, were kneeling at the same stall, and hearing the same hymns and prayers in which her stricken heart had found consolation. Might she sleep in peace – might she sleep in peace; and we, too, when our struggles and

pains are over! But the earth is the Lord's as the heaven is; we
are alike His creatures here and yonder. I took a little flower off
the hillock, and kissed it, and went my way, like the bird that had
just lighted on the cross by me, back into the world again. Silent
receptacle of death! tranquil depth of calm, out of reach of
tempest and trouble! I felt as one who had been walking below
the sea, and treading amidst the bones of shipwrecks.

## Chapter 14

### THE CAMPAIGN OF 1707, 1708

DURING the whole of the year which succeeded that in which
the glorious battle of Ramillies had been fought, our army made
no movement of importance, much to the disgust of very many
of our officers remaining inactive in Flanders, who said that his
Grace the Captain-General had had fighting enough, and was
all for money now, and the enjoyment of his five thousand a year
and his splendid palace at Woodstock,[1] which was now being
built. And his Grace had sufficient occupation fighting his
enemies at home this year, where it begun to be whispered that
his favour was decreasing, and his Duchess losing her hold on the
Queen, who was transferring her royal affections to the famous
Mrs Masham,[2] and Mrs Masham's humble servant, Mr Harley. Against their intrigues, our Duke passed a great part of
his time intriguing. Mr Harley was got out of office, and his
Grace, in so far, had a victory. But her Majesty, convinced
against her will, was of that opinion still, of which the poet says[3]
people are when so convinced, and Mr Harley before long had
his revenge.

Meanwhile the business of fighting did not go on any way to
the satisfaction of Marlborough's gallant lieutenants. During all
1707, with the French before us, we had never so much as a
battle; our army in Spain was utterly routed at Almanza by the
gallant Duke of Berwick; and we of Webb's, which regiment the
young Duke had commanded before his father's abdication,

were a little proud to think that it was our colonel who had
achieved this victory. 'I think if I had had Galway's place, and
my Fusileers,' says our general, 'we would not have laid down
our arms, even to our old colonel, as Galway did'; and Webb's
officers swore if we had had Webb, at least we would not have
been taken prisoners. Our dear old general talked incautiously of
himself and of others; a braver or a more brilliant soldier never
lived than he; but he blew his honest trumpet rather more
loudly than became a commander of his station, and, mighty man
of valour as he was, shook his great spear, and blustered before
the army too fiercely.

Mysterious Mr Holtz went off on a secret expedition in the
early part of 1708, with great elation of spirits, and a prophecy to
Esmond that a wonderful something was about to take place.
This secret came out on my friend's return to the army, whither
he brought a most rueful and dejected countenance, and owned
that the great something he had been engaged upon had failed
utterly. He had been indeed with that luckless expedition of the
Chevalier de St George, who was sent by the French King with
ships and an army from Dunkirk, and was to have invaded and
conquered Scotland. But that ill wind which ever opposed all the
projects upon which the Prince ever embarked, prevented the
Chevalier's invasion of Scotland,[4] as 'tis known, and blew poor
Monsieur von Holtz back into our camp again, to scheme and
foretell, and to pry about as usual. The Chevalier (the King of
England, as some of us held him) went from Dunkirk to the
French army to make the campaign against us. The Duke of
Burgundy had the command this year, having the Duke of Berry
with him, and the famous Mareschal Vendosme and the Duke of
Matignon to aid him in the campaign. Holtz, who knew everything that was passing in Flanders and France (and the Indies
for what I know), insisted that there would be no more fighting
in 1708 than there had been in the previous year, and that our
commander had reasons for keeping him quiet. Indeed,
Esmond's general, who was known as a grumbler, and to have a
hearty mistrust of the great Duke, and hundreds more officers
besides, did not scruple to say that these private reasons came to
the Duke in the shape of crown-pieces from the French King, by

whom the Generalissimo was bribed to avoid a battle. There were plenty of men in our lines, quidnuncs, to whom Mr Webb listened only too willingly, who could specify the exact sums the Duke got, how much fell to Cadogan's[5] share, and what was the precise fee given to Doctor Hare.

And the successes with which the French began the campaign of 1708, served to give strength to these reports of treason, which were in everybody's mouth. Our general allowed the enemy to get between us and Ghent, and declined to attack him, though for eight and forty hours the armies were in presence of each other. Ghent was taken, and on the same day Monsieur de la Mothe summoned[6] Bruges; and these two great cities fell into the hands of the French without firing a shot. A few days afterwards La Mothe seized upon the fort of Plashendall: and it began to be supposed that all Spanish Flanders, as well as Brabant, would fall into the hands of the French troops; when the Prince Eugene arrived from the Mozelle, and then there was no more shillyshallying.

The Prince of Savoy always signalised his arrival at the army by a great feast (my Lord Duke's entertainments were both seldom and shabby): and I remember our general returning from his dinner with the two Commanders-in-Chief; his honest head a little excited by wine, which was dealt out much more liberally by the Austrian than by the English commander: – 'Now,' says my general, slapping the table, with an oath, 'he must fight; and when he is forced to it, d—— it, no man in Europe can stand up against Jack Churchill.' Within a week the battle of Oudenarde was fought, when, hate each other as they might, Esmond's general and the Commander-in-Chief were forced to admire each other, so splendid was the gallantry of each upon this day.

The brigade commanded by Major-General Webb gave and received about as hard knocks as any that were delivered in that action, in which Mr Esmond had the fortune to serve at the head of his own company in his regiment, under the command of their own colonel as Major-General; and it was his good luck to bring the regiment out of action as commander of it, the four senior officers above him being killed in the prodigious slaughter which

happened on that day. I like to think that Jack Haythorn, who
sneered at me for being a bastard and a parasite of Webb's, as he
chose to call me, and with whom I had had words, shook hands
with me the day before the battle begun. Three days before, poor
Brace, our lieutenant-colonel, had heard of his elder brother's
death, and was heir to a baronetcy in Norfolk, and four thousand
a year. Fate, that had left him harmless through a dozen campaigns, seized on him just as the world was worth living for, and
he went into action, knowing, as he said, that the luck was going
to turn against him. The major had just joined us – a creature of
Lord Marlborough, put in much to the dislike of the other
officers, and to be a spy upon us, as it was said. I know not
whether the truth was so, nor who took the tattle of our mess to
head-quarters, but Webb's regiment, as its colonel, was known to
be in the Commander-in-Chief's black books: 'And if he did not
dare to break it up at home,' our gallant old chief used to say,
'he was determined to destroy it before the enemy'; so that poor
Major Proudfoot was put into a post of danger.

Esmond's dear young Viscount, serving as aide-de-camp to
my Lord Duke, received a wound, and won an honourable name
for himself in the Gazette; and Captain Esmond's name was sent
in for promotion by his general, too, whose favourite he was. It
made his heart beat to think that certain eyes at home, the
brightest in the world, might read the page on which his humble
services were recorded; but his mind was made up steadily to
keep out of their dangerous influence, and to let time and
absence conquer that passion he had still lurking about him.
Away from Beatrix, it did not trouble him; but he knew as
certain that if he returned home, his fever would break out again,
and avoided Walcote as a Lincolnshire-man avoids returning to
his fens, where he is sure that the ague is lying in wait for him.

We of the English party in the army, who were inclined to
sneer at everything that came out of Hanover, and to treat as
little better than boors and savages the Elector's Court and
family, were yet forced to confess that, on the day of Oudenarde,
the young Electoral Prince, then making his first campaign, conducted himself with the spirit and courage of an approved
soldier. On this occasion his Electoral Highness had better luck

than the King of England, who was with his cousins in the enemy's camp, and had to run with them at the ignominious end of the day. With the most consummate generals in the world before them, and an admirable commander on their own side, they chose to neglect the counsels, and to rush into a combat with the former, which would have ended in the utter annihilation of their army but for the great skill and bravery of the Duke of Vendosme, who remedied, as far as courage and genius might, the disasters occasioned by the squabbles and follies of his kinsmen, the legitimate princes of the blood royal.[7]

'If the Duke of Berwick had but been in the army, the fate of the day would have been very different,' was all that poor Mr von Holtz could say; 'and you would have seen that the hero of Almanza was fit to measure swords with the conqueror of Blenheim.'

The business relative to the exchange of prisoners was always going on, and was at least that ostensible one which kept Mr Holtz perpetually on the move between the forces of the French and the Allies. I can answer for it, that he was once very near hanged as a spy by Major-General Wayne, when he was released and sent on to head-quarters by a special order of the Commander-in-Chief. He came and went, always favoured, wherever he was, by some high though occult protection. He carried messages between the Duke of Berwick and his uncle, our Duke. He seemed to know as well what was taking place in the Prince's quarter as our own: he brought the compliments of the King of England to some of our officers, the gentlemen of Webb's among the rest, for their behaviour on that great day; and after Wynendael, when our general was chafing at the neglect of our Commander-in-Chief, he said he knew how that action was regarded by the chiefs of the French army, and that the stand made before Wynendael wood was the passage by which the Allies entered Lille.

'Ah,' says Holtz (and some folks were very willing to listen to him), 'if the King came by his own, how changed the conduct of affairs would be! His Majesty's very exile has this advantage, that he is enabled to read England impartially, and to judge honestly of all the eminent men. His sister is always in the hand of one greedy favourite or another, through whose eyes she sees, and to whose flattery or dependants she gives away everything. Do you suppose that his Majesty, knowing England so well as he does, would neglect such a man as General Webb? He ought to be in the House of Peers as Lord Lydiard. The enemy and all Europe know his merit; it is that very reputation which certain great people, who hate all equality and independence, can never pardon.' It was intended that these conversations should be carried to Mr Webb. They were welcome to him, for great as his services were, no man could value them more than John Richmond Webb did himself, and the differences between him and Marlborough being notorious, his Grace's enemies in the army and at home began to court Webb, and set him up against the all-grasping, domineering chief. And soon after the victory of Oudenarde, a glorious opportunity fell into General Webb's way, which that gallant warrior did not neglect, and which gave him the means of immensely increasing his reputation at home.

After Oudenarde, and against the counsels of Marlborough, it was said, the Prince of Savoy sat down before Lille, the capital of French Flanders, and commenced that siege, the most celebrated of our time, and almost as famous as the siege of Troy itself, for the feats of valour performed in the assault and the defence. The enmity of that Prince of Savoy against the French King was a furious personal hate, quite unlike the calm hostility of our great English general, who was no more moved by the game of war than that of billiards, and pushed forward his squadrons, and drove his red battalions hither and thither as calmly as he would combine a stroke or make a cannon with the balls. The game over (and he played it so as to be pretty sure to win it), not the least animosity against the other party remained in the breast of this consummate tactician. Whereas between the Prince of Savoy and the French it was *guerre à mort*. Beaten off in one quarter, as he had been at Toulon in the last year,[8] he was back again on another frontier of France, assailing it with his indefatigable fury. When the Prince came to the army, the smouldering fires of war were lighted up and burst out into a flame. Our phlegmatic Dutch allies were made to advance at a quick march – our calm Duke forced into action. The Prince was

an army in himself against the French; the energy of his hatred
prodigious, indefatigable – infectious over hundreds of thousands
of men. The Emperor's general was repaying, and with a vengeance, the slight[9] the French King had put upon the fiery little
Abbé of Savoy. Brilliant and famous as a leader himself, and
beyond all measure daring and intrepid, and enabled to cope
with almost the best of those famous men of war who commanded the armies of the French King, Eugene had a weapon,
the equal of which could not be found in France, since the
cannon-shot of Sasbach laid low the noble Turenne, and could
hurl Marlborough at the heads of the French host, and crush
them as with a rock, under which all the gathered strength of
their strongest captains must go down.

The English Duke took little part in that vast siege of Lille,
which the Imperial Generalissimo pursued with all his force and
vigour, further than to cover the besieging lines from the Duke
of Burgundy's army, between which and the Imperialists our
Duke lay. Once, when Prince Eugene was wounded, our Duke
took his Highness's place in the trenches; but the siege was with
the Imperialists, not with us. A division under Webb and
Rantzau was detached into Artois and Picardy upon the most
painful and odious service that Mr Esmond ever saw in the
course of his military life. The wretched towns of the defenceless
provinces, whose young men had been drafted away into the
French armies, which year after year the insatiable war devoured,
were left at our mercy; and our orders were to show them none.
We found places garrisoned by invalids, and children and
women: poor as they were, and as the costs of this miserable war
had made them, our commission was to rob these almost starving
wretches – to tear the food out of their granaries, and strip them
of their rags. 'Twas an expedition of rapine and murder we were
sent on: our soldiers did deeds such as an honest man must blush
to remember. We brought back money and provisions in
quantity to the Duke's camp; there had been no one to resist us,
and yet who dares to tell with what murder and violence, with
what brutal cruelty, outrage, insult, that ignoble booty had been
ravished from the innocent and miserable victims of the war?

Meanwhile, gallantly as the operations before Lille had been conducted, the Allies had made but little progress, and 'twas said when we returned to the Duke of Marlborough's camp, that the siege would never be brought to a satisfactory end, and that the Prince of Savoy would be forced to raise it. My Lord Marlborough gave this as his opinion openly; those who mistrusted him, and Mr Esmond owns himself to be of the number, hinted that the Duke had his reasons why Lille should not be taken, and that he was paid to that end by the French King. If this was so, and I believe it, General Webb had now a remarkable opportunity of gratifying his hatred of the Commander-in-Chief, of baulking that shameful avarice, which was one of the basest and most notorious qualities of the famous Duke, and of showing his own consummate skill as a commander. And when I consider all the circumstances preceding the event which will now be related, that my Lord Duke was actually offered certain millions of crowns provided that the siege of Lille should be raised; that the Imperial army before it was without provisions and ammunition, and must have decamped but for the supplies that they received; that the march of the convoy destined to relieve the siege was accurately known to the French; and that the force covering it was shamefully inadequate to that end, and by six times inferior to Count de la Mothe's army, which was sent to intercept the convoy; when 'tis certain that the Duke of Berwick, De la Mothe's chief, was in constant correspondence with his uncle,[10] the English Generalissimo: I believe on my conscience that 'twas my Lord Marlborough's intention to prevent those supplies, of which the Prince of Savoy stood in absolute need, from ever reaching his Highness; that he meant to sacrifice the little army which covered this convoy, and to betray it as he had betrayed Tollemache at Brest,[11] as he betrayed every friend he had, to further his own schemes of avarice or ambition. But for the miraculous victory which Esmond's general won over an army six or seven times greater than his own, the siege of Lille must have been raised; and it must be remembered that our gallant little force was under the command of a general whom Marlborough hated, that he was furious with the conqueror, and tried by the most open and shameless injustice afterwards to rob him of the credit of his victory.

## Chapter 15

### GENERAL WEBB WINS THE BATTLE OF WYNENDAEL[1]

By the besiegers and besieged of Lille, some of the most brilliant feats of valour were performed that ever illustrated any war. On the French side (whose gallantry was prodigious, the skill and bravery of Marshal Boufflers actually eclipsing those of his conqueror, the Prince of Savoy) may be mentioned that daring action of Messieurs de Luxembourg and Tournefort, who, with a body of Horse and dragoons, carried powder into the town, of which the besieged were in extreme want, each soldier bringing a bag with forty pounds of powder behind him; with which perilous provision they engaged our own Horse, faced the fire of the Foot brought out to meet them; and though half of the men were blown up in the dreadful errand they rode on, a part of them got into the town with the succours of which the garrison was so much in want. A French officer, Monsieur du Bois, performed an act equally daring, and perfectly successful. The Duke's great army lying at Helchin, and covering the siege, and it being necessary for M. de Vendosme to get news of the condition of the place, Captain du Bois performed his famous exploit: not only passing through the lines of the siege, but swimming afterwards no less than seven moats and ditches: and coming back the same way, swimming with his letters in his mouth.

By these letters Monsieur de Boufflers said that he could undertake to hold the place till October; and that, if one of the convoys of the Allies could be intercepted, they must raise the siege altogether.

Such a convoy as hath been said was now prepared at Ostend, and about to march for the siege; and on the 27th September, we (and the French too) had news that it was on its way. It was composed of 700 waggons, containing ammunition of all sorts, and was escorted out of Ostend by 2000 infantry and 300 horse. At the same time M. de la Mothe quitted Bruges, having with him five and thirty battalions, and upwards of sixty squadrons, and forty guns in pursuit of the convoy.

Major-General Webb had meanwhile made up a force of twenty battalions, and three squadrons of dragoons, at Turout, whence he moved to cover the convoy and pursue La Mothe: with whose advanced guard ours came up upon the great plain of Turout, and before the little wood and castle of Wynendael; behind which the convoy was marching.

As soon as they came in sight of the enemy, our advanced troops were halted, with the wood behind them, and the rest of our force brought up as quickly as possible, our little body of Horse being brought forward to the opening of the plain, as our general said, to amuse the enemy. When M. la Mothe came up he found us posted in two lines in front of the wood; and formed his own army in battle facing ours, in eight lines, four of infantry in front, and dragoons and cavalry behind.

The French began the action, as usual, with a cannonade which lasted three hours, when they made their attack, advancing in twelve lines, four of Foot and four of Horse, upon the allied troops in the wood where we were posted. Their infantry behaved ill; they were ordered to charge with the bayonet, but, instead, began to fire, and almost at the very first discharge from our men, broke and fled. The cavalry behaved better; with these alone, who were three or four times as numerous as our whole force, Monsieur de la Mothe might have won victory: but only two of our battalions were shaken in the least; and these speedily rallied: nor could the repeated attacks of the French Horse cause our troops to budge an inch from the position in the wood in which our general had placed them.

After attacking for two hours, the French retired at nightfall entirely foiled. With all the loss we had inflicted upon him, the enemy was still three times stronger than we; and it could not be supposed that our general could pursue M. de la Mothe, or do much more than hold our ground about the wood, from which the Frenchman had in vain attempted to dislodge us. La Mothe retired behind his forty guns, his cavalry protecting them better than it had been enabled to annoy us; and meanwhile the convoy, which was of more importance than all our little force, and the safe passage of which we would have dropped to the last man to accomplish, marched away in perfect safety during the action, and joyfully reached the besieging camp before Lille.

Major-General Cadogan, my Lord Duke's Quartermaster-General (and between whom and Mr Webb there was no love lost), accompanied the convoy, and joined Mr Webb with a couple of hundred Horse just as the battle was over, and the enemy in full retreat. He offered, readily enough, to charge with his Horse upon the French as they fell back; but his force was too weak to inflict any damage upon them; and Mr Webb, commanding as Cadogan's senior, thought enough was done in holding our ground before an enemy that might still have overwhelmed us had we engaged him in the open territory, and in securing the safe passage of the convoy. Accordingly, the Horse brought up by Cadogan did not draw a sword; and only prevented, by the good countenance they showed, any disposition the French might have had to renew the attack on us. And no attack coming, at nightfall General Cadogan drew off with his squadron, being bound for head-quarters, the two generals at parting grimly saluting each other.

'He will be at Roncq[2] time enough to lick my Lord Duke's trenchers at supper,' says Mr Webb.

Our own men lay out in the woods of Wynendael that night, and our general had his supper in the little castle there.

'If I was Cadogan, I would have a peerage for this day's work,' General Webb said; 'and Harry, thou shouldst have a regiment. Thou hast been reported in the last two actions: thou wert near killed in the first. I shall mention thee in my despatch to his Grace the Commander-in-Chief, and recommend thee to poor Dick Harwood's vacant majority. Have you ever a hundred guineas to give Cardonnel? Slip them into his hand to-morrow, when you go to head-quarters with my report.'

In this report the Major-General was good enough to mention Captain Esmond's name with particular favour; and that gentleman carried the despatch to head-quarters the next day, and was not a little pleased to bring back a letter by his Grace's secretary, addressed to Lieutenant-General Webb.[3] The Dutch officer despatched by Count Nassau Woudenbourg, Vælt-Mareschal Auverquerque's son, brought back also a complimentary letter to his commander, who had seconded Mr Webb in the action with great valour and skill.

Esmond, with a low bow and a smiling face, presented his despatch, and saluted Mr Webb as Lieutenant-General, as he gave it in. The gentlemen round about him – he was riding with his suite on the road to Menin as Esmond came up with him – gave a cheer, and he thanked them, and opened the despatch with rather a flushed eager face.

He slapped it down on his boot in a rage after he had read it. ''Tis not even writ with his own hand. Read it out, Esmond.' And Esmond read it out: –

'Sir – Mr Cadogan is just now come in, and has acquainted me with the success of the action you had yesterday in the afternoon against the body of troops commanded by M. de la Mothe, at Wynendael, which must be attributed chiefly to your good conduct and resolution. You may be sure I shall do you justice at home, and be glad on all occasions to own the service you have done in securing this convoy. – Yours, &c., M.'

'Two lines by that d——d Cardonnel,[4] and no more, for the taking of Lille – for beating five times our number – for an action as brilliant as the best he ever fought,' says poor Mr Webb. 'Lieutenant-General! That's not his doing. I was the oldest major-general. By ——, I believe he had been better pleased if I had been beat.'

The letter to the Dutch officer was in French, and longer and more complimentary than that to Mr Webb.

'And this is the man,' he broke out, 'that's gorged with gold – that's covered with titles and honours that we won for him – and that grudges even a line of praise to a comrade in arms! Hasn't he enough? Don't we fight that he may roll in riches? Well, well, wait for the Gazette, gentlemen. The Queen and the country will do us justice if his Grace denies it us.' There were tears of rage in the brave warrior's eyes as he spoke; and he dashed them off his face on to his glove. He shook his fist in the air. 'Oh, by the Lord!' says he, 'I know what I had rather have than a peerage!'

'And what is that, sir?' some of them asked.

'I had rather have a quarter of an hour with John Churchill, on a fair green field, and only a pair of rapiers between my shirt and his——'

'Sir!' interposes one.

'Tell him so! I know that's what you mean. I know every word goes to him that's dropped from every general officer's mouth. I don't say he's not brave. Curse him! he's brave enough; but we'll wait for the Gazette, gentlemen. God save her Majesty! she'll do us justice.'

The Gazette did not come to us till a month afterwards; when my general and his officers had the honour to dine with Prince Eugene in Lille; his Highness being good enough to say that we had brought the provisions, and ought to share in the banquet. 'Twas a great banquet. His Grace of Marlborough was on his Highness's right, and on his left the Mareschal de Boufflers,[5] who had so bravely defended the place. The chief officers of either army were present; and you may be sure Esmond's general was splendid this day: his tall noble person, and manly beauty of face, made him remarkable anywhere; he wore, for the first time, the star of the Order of Generosity, that his Prussian Majesty had sent to him for his victory. His Highness, the Prince of Savoy, called a toast to the conqueror of Wynendael. My Lord Duke drank it with rather a sickly smile. The aides-de-camp were present; and Harry Esmond and his dear young lord were together, as they always strove to be when duty would permit: they were over against the table where the generals were, and could see all that passed pretty well. Frank laughed at my Lord Duke's glum face: the affair of Wynendael, and the Captain-General's conduct to Webb, had been the talk of the whole army. When his Highness spoke, and gave–'Le vainqueur de Wynendael; son armée et sa victoire,' adding 'qui nous font diner à Lille aujourd'huy' – there was a great cheer through the hall; for Mr Webb's bravery, generosity, and very weaknesses of character caused him to be beloved in the army.

'Like Hector, handsome, and like Paris, brave!' whispers Frank Castlewood. 'A Venus, an elderly Venus, couldn't refuse him a pippin. Stand up, Harry. See, we are drinking the army of Wynendael. Ramillies is nothing to it. Huzzay! huzzay!'

At this very time, and just after our general had made his acknowledgment, some-one brought in an English Gazette – and was passing it from hand to hand down the table. Officers were eager enough to read it; mothers and sisters at home must have sickened over it. There scarce came out a Gazette for six years that did not tell of some heroic death or some brilliant achievement.

'Here it is – Action of Wynendael – here you are, General,' says Frank, seizing hold of the little dingy paper that soldiers love to read so; and, scrambling over from our bench, he went to where the General sat, who knew him, and had seen many a time at his table his laughing, handsome face, which everybody loved who saw. The generals in their great perukes made way for him. He handed the paper over General Dohna's buff coat to our General on the opposite side.

He came hobbling back, and blushing at his feat: 'I thought he'd like it, Harry,' the young fellow whispered. 'Didn't I like to read my name after Ramillies, in the "London Gazette" – Viscount Castlewood serving a volunteer – I say, what's yonder?'

Mr Webb, reading the Gazette, looked very strange – slapped it down on the table – then sprung up in his place, and began – 'Will your Highness please to——'

His Grace the Duke of Marlborough here jumped up too – 'There's some mistake, my dear General Webb.'

'Your Grace had better rectify it,' says Mr Webb, holding out the letter; but he was five off his Grace the Prince-Duke, who, besides, was higher than the General (being seated with the Prince of Savoy, the Electoral Prince of Hanover, and the envoys of Prussia and Denmark, under a baldaquin [6]), and Webb could not reach him, tall as he was.

'Stay,' says he, with a smile, as if catching at some idea, and then, with a perfect courtesy, drawing his sword, he ran the Gazette through with the point, and said, 'Permit me to hand it to your Grace.'

The Duke looked very black. 'Take it,' says he, to his Master of the Horse, who was waiting behind him.

The Lieutenant-General made a very low bow, and retired and finished his glass. The Gazette in which Mr Cardonnel, the Duke's secretary, gave an account of the victory of Wynendael, mentioned Mr Webb's name, but gave the sole praise and conduct of the action to the Duke's favourite, Mr Cadogan.

There was no little talk and excitement occasioned by this

strange behaviour of General Webb, who had almost drawn a sword upon the Commander-in-Chief, but the General, after the first outbreak of his anger, mastered it outwardly altogether; and, by his subsequent behaviour, had the satisfaction of even more angering the Commander-in-Chief, than he could have done by any public exhibition of resentment.

On returning to his quarters, and consulting with his chief adviser, Mr Esmond, who was now entirely in the General's confidence, and treated by him as a friend, and almost a son, Mr Webb writ a letter to his Grace the Commander-in-Chief, in which he said: –

'Your Grace must be aware that the sudden perusal of the "London Gazette",' in which your Grace's secretary, Mr Cardonnel, hath mentioned Major-General Cadogan's name, as the officer commanding in the late action of Wynendael, must have caused a feeling of anything but pleasure to the General who fought that action.

'Your Grace must be aware that Mr Cadogan was not even present at the battle, though he arrived with squadrons of Horse at its close, and put himself under the command of his superior officer. And as the result of the battle of Wynendael, in which Lieutenant-General Webb had the good fortune to command, was the capture of Lille, the relief of Brussels, then invested by the enemy under the Elector of Bavaria, the restoration of the great cities of Ghent and Bruges, of which the enemy (by treason within the walls) had got possession in the previous year: Mr Webb cannot consent to forego the honours of such a success and service, for the benefit of Mr Cadogan, or any other person.

'As soon as the military operations of the year are over, Lieutenant-General Webb will request permission to leave the army, and return to his place in Parliament, where he gives notice to his Grace the Commander-in-Chief, that he shall lay his case before the House of Commons, the country, and her Majesty the Queen.

'By his eagerness to rectify that false statement of the Gazette, which had been written by his Grace's secretary, Mr Cardonnel, Mr Webb, not being able to reach his Grace the Commander-in-Chief on account of the gentlemen seated between them, placed the paper containing the false statement on his sword, so that it might more readily arrive in the hands of his Grace the Duke of Marlborough, who surely would wish to do justice to every officer of his army.

'Mr Webb knows his duty too well to think of insubordination to his superior officer, or of using his sword in a campaign against any but the enemies of her Majesty. He solicits permission to return to England immediately the military duties will permit, and take with him to England Captain Esmond, of his regiment, who acted as his aide-de-camp, and was present during the entire action, and noted by his watch the time when Mr Cadogan arrived at its close.'

The Commander-in-Chief could not but grant this permission, nor could he take notice of Webb's letter, though it was couched in terms the most insulting. Half the army believed that the cities of Ghent and Bruges were given up by a treason, which some in our army very well understood; that the Commander-in-Chief would not have relieved Lille if he could have helped himself; that he would not have fought that year had not the Prince of Savoy forced him. When the battle once began, then, for his own renown, my Lord Marlborough would fight as no man in the world ever fought better; and no bribe on earth could keep him from beating the enemy.*

---

*Our grandfather's hatred of the Duke of Malborough appears all through his account of these campaigns. He always persisted that the Duke was the greatest traitor and soldier history ever told of: and declared that he took bribes on all hands during the war. My Lord Marquis (for so we may call him here, though he never went by any other name than Colonel Esmond) was in the habit of telling many stories which he did not set down in his memoirs, and which he had from his friend the Jesuit, who was not always correctly informed, and who persisted that Marlborough was looking for a bribe of two millions of crowns before the campaign of Ramillies.

And our grandmother used to tell us children, that on his first presentation to my Lord Duke, the Duke turned his back upon my grandfather; and said to the Duchess, who told my Lady Dowager at Chelsey, who afterwards told Colonel Esmond – 'Tom Esmond's bastard has been to my levee; he has the hang-dog look of his rogue of a father' – an expression which my grandfather never forgave. He was as constant in his dislikes as in his attachments; and exceedingly partial to Webb, whose side he took against the more celebrated general. We have General Webb's portrait now at Castlewood, Va.

But the matter was taken up by the subordinates; and half the army might have been by the ears, if the quarrel had not been stopped. General Cadogan sent an intimation to General Webb to say that he was ready if Webb liked, and would meet him. This was a kind of invitation our stout old general was always too ready to accept, and 'twas with great difficulty we got the General to reply that he had no quarrel with Mr Cadogan, who had behaved with perfect gallantry, but only with those at head-quarters, who had belied him. Mr Cardonnel offered General Webb reparation; Mr Webb said he had a cane at the service of Mr Cardonnel, and the only satisfaction he wanted from him was one he was not likely to get, namely, the truth. The officers in our staff of Webb's, and those in the immediate suite of the General, were ready to come to blows; and hence arose the only affair in which Mr Esmond ever engaged as principal, and that was from a revengeful wish to wipe off an old injury.

My Lord Mohun, who had a troop in Lord Macclesfield's regiment of the Horse Guards, rode this campaign with the Duke. He had sunk by this time to the very worst reputation; he had had another fatal duel in Spain; he had married, and for-saken his wife; he was a gambler, a profligate, and debauchee. He joined just before Oudenarde; and, as Esmond feared, as soon as Frank Castlewood heard of his arrival, Frank was for seeking him out, and killing him. The wound my lord got at Oudenarde prevented their meeting, but that was nearly healed, and Mr Esmond trembled daily lest any chance should bring his boy and this known assassin together. They met at the mess-table of Handyside's regiment at Lille; the officer commanding not knowing of the feud between the two noblemen.

Esmond had not seen the hateful handsome face of Mohun for nine years, since they had met on that fatal night in Leicester Field. It was degraded with crime and passion now; it wore the anxious look of a man who has three deaths – and who knows how many hidden shames, and lusts, and crimes – on his con-science. He bowed with a sickly low bow, and slunk away when our host presented us round to one another. Frank Castlewood had not known him till then, so changed was he. He knew the boy well enough.

'Twas curious to look at the two – especially the young man, whose face flushed up when he heard the hated name of the other; and who said in his bad French and his brave boyish voice – 'He had long been anxious to meet my Lord Mohun.' The other only bowed, and moved away from him. I do him justice, he wished to have no quarrel with the lad.

Esmond put himself between them at table. 'D—— it,' says Frank, 'why do you put yourself in the place of a man who is above you in degree? My Lord Mohun should walk after me. I want to sit by my Lord Mohun.'

Esmond whispered to Lord Mohun, that Frank was hurt in the leg at Oudenarde; and besought the other to be quiet. Quiet enough he was for some time; disregarding the many taunts which young Castlewood flung at him, until after several healths, when my Lord Mohun got to be rather in liquor.

'Will you go away, my lord?' Mr Esmond said to him, imploring him to quit the table.

'No, by G——,' says my Lord Mohun. 'I'll not go away for any man'; he was quite flushed with wine by this time.

The talk got round to the affairs of yesterday. Webb had offered to challenge the Commander-in-Chief: Webb had been ill-used: Webb was the bravest, handsomest, vainest man in the army. Lord Mohun did not know that Esmond was Webb's aide-de-camp. He began to tell some stories against the General, which, from t'other side of Esmond, young Castlewood contradicted.

'I can't bear any more of this,' says my Lord Mohun.

'Nor can I, my lord,' says Mr Esmond, starting up. 'The story my Lord Mohun has told respecting General Webb is false, gentlemen – false, I repeat,' and making a low bow to Lord Mohun, and without a single word more, Esmond got up and left the dining-room. These affairs were common enough among the military of those days. There was a garden behind the house, and all the party turned instantly into it; and the two gentlemen's coats were off and their points engaged within two minutes after Esmond's words had been spoken. If Captain Esmond had put Mohun out of the world, as he might, a villain would have been punished and spared further villainies – but who is one man to

punish another? I declare upon my honour that my only thought
was to prevent Lord Mohun from mischief with Frank, and the
end of this meeting was, that after half-a-dozen passes my lord
went home with a hurt which prevented him from lifting his
right arm for three months.

'O Harry! why didn't you kill the villain?' young Castlewood
asked. 'I can't walk without a crutch: but I could have met him
on horseback with sword and pistol.' But Harry Esmond said,
''Twas best to have no man's life on one's conscience, not even
that villain's'; and this affair, which did not occupy three
minutes, being over, the gentlemen went back to their wine, and
my Lord Mohun to his quarters, where he was laid up with a
fever which had spared mischief had it proved fatal. And very
soon after this affair Harry Esmond and his General left the
camp for London; whither a certain reputation had preceded the
Captain, for my Lady Castlewood of Chelsey received him as if
he had been a conquering hero. She gave a great dinner to Mr
Webb, where the General's chair was crowned with laurels; and
her ladyship called Esmond's health in a toast, to which my kind
General was graciously pleased to bear the strongest testimony;
and took down a mob of at least forty coaches to cheer our
General as he came out of the House of Commons, the day when
he received the thanks of Parliament for his action. The mob
huzza'd and applauded him, as well as the fine company: it was
splendid to see him waving his hat, and bowing, and laying his
hand upon his Order of Generosity. He introduced Mr Esmond
to Mr St John and the Right Honourable Robert Harley,
Esquire, as he came out of the House walking between them; and
was pleased to make many flattering observations regarding Mr
Esmond's behaviour during the three last campaigns.

Mr St John (who had the most winning presence of any man I
ever saw, excepting always my peerless young Frank Castlewood) said he had heard of Mr Esmond before from Captain
Steele, and how he had helped Mr Addison to write his famous
poem of the 'Campaign.'

''Twas as great an achievement as the victory of Blenheim
itself,' Mr Harley said, who was famous as a judge and patron of
letters; and so, perhaps, it may be – though for my part I think

there are twenty beautiful lines, but all the rest is commonplace, and Mr Addison's hymn worth a thousand such poems.

All the town was indignant at my Lord Duke's unjust treatment of General Webb, and applauded the vote of thanks[8] which the House of Commons gave to the General for his victory at Wynendael. 'Tis certain that the capture of Lille was the consequence of that lucky achievement, and the humiliation of the old French King, who was said to suffer more at the loss of this great city, than from any of the former victories our troops had won over him. And, I think, no small part of Mr Webb's exultation at his victory, arose from the idea that Marlborough had been disappointed of a great bribe the French King had promised him, should the siege be raised. The very sum of money offered to him was mentioned by the Duke's enemies; and honest Mr Webb chuckled at the notion, not only of beating the French, but of beating Marlborough too, and intercepting a convoy of three millions of French crowns, that were on their way to the Generalissimo's insatiable pockets. When the General's lady went to the Queen's drawing-room, all the Tory women crowded round her with congratulations, and made her a train greater than the Duchess of Marlborough's own. Feasts were given to the General by all the chiefs of the Tory party, who vaunted him as the Duke's equal in military skill; and perhaps used the worthy soldier as their instrument, whilst he thought they were but acknowledging his merits as a commander. As the General's aide-de-camp, and favourite officer, Mr Esmond came in for a share of his chief's popularity, and was presented to her Majesty, and advanced to the rank of Lieutenant-Colonel, at the request of his grateful chief.

We may be sure there was one family in which any good fortune that happened to Esmond, caused such a sincere pride and pleasure, that he, for his part, was thankful he could make them so happy. With these fond friends, Blenheim and Oudenarde seemed to be mere trifling incidents of the war; and Wynendael was its crowning victory. Esmond's mistress never tired to hear accounts of the battle; and I think General Webb's lady grew jealous of her, for the General was for ever at Kensington, and talking on that delightful theme. As for his aide-de-camp,

though, no doubt, Esmond's own natural vanity was pleased at
the little share of reputation which his good fortune had won
him, yet it was chiefly precious to him (he may say so, now that
he hath long since outlived it) because it pleased his mistress,
and, above all, because Beatrix valued it.

As for the old Dowager of Chelsey, never was an old woman in
all England more delighted nor more gracious than she. Esmond
had his quarters in her ladyship's house, where the domestics
were instructed to consider him as their master. She bade him
give entertainments, of which she defrayed the charges, and was
charmed when his guests were carried away tipsy in their
coaches. She must have his picture taken; and accordingly he
was painted by Mr Jervas,[9] in his red coat, and smiling upon a
bomb-shell, which was bursting at the corner of the piece. She
vowed that unless he made a great match, she should never die
easy, and was for ever bringing young ladies to Chelsey, with
pretty faces and pretty fortunes, at the disposal of the Colonel.
He smiled to think how times were altered with him, and of the
early days in his father's lifetime, when a trembling page he
stood before her, with her ladyship's basin and ewer, or crouched
in her coach-step. The only fault she found with him was, that he
was more sober than an Esmond ought to be; and would neither
be carried to bed by his valet, nor lose his heart to any beauty,
whether of St James's or Covent Garden.

What is the meaning of fidelity in love, and whence the birth
of it? 'Tis a state of mind that men fall into, and depending on
the man rather than the woman. We love being in love, that's the
truth on't. If we had not met Joan, we would have met Kate, and
adored her. We know our mistresses are no better than many
other women, nor no prettier, nor no wiser, nor no wittier. 'Tis
not for these reasons we love a woman, or for any special quality
or charm I know of; we might as well demand that a lady should
be the tallest woman in the world, like the Shropshire giantess,*
as that she should be a paragon in any other character, before we
began to love her. Esmond's mistress had a thousand faults
beside her charms: he knew both perfectly well! She was

---

*'Tis not thus *woman loves*: Col. E. hath owned to this folly for a *score of
women* besides. – R.

imperious, she was light-minded, she was flighty, she was false, she had no reverence in her character; she was in everything, even in beauty, the contrast of her mother, who was the most devoted and the least selfish of women. Well, from the very first moment he saw her on the stairs at Walcote, Esmond knew he loved Beatrix. There might be better women – he wanted that one. He cared for none other. Was it because she was gloriously beautiful? Beautiful as she was, he had heard people say a score of times in their company, that Beatrix's mother looked as young, and was the handsomer of the two. Why did her voice thrill in his ear so? She could not sing near so well as Nicolini or Mrs Tofts,[10] nay, she sang out of tune, and yet he liked to hear her better than St Cecilia. She had not a finer complexion than Mrs Steele (Dick's wife, whom he had now got, and who ruled poor Dick with a rod of pickle), and yet to see her dazzled Esmond; he would shut his eyes, and the thought of her dazzled him all the same. She was brilliant and lively in talk, but not so incomparably witty as her mother, who, when she was cheerful, said the finest things; but yet to hear her, and to be with her, was Esmond's greatest pleasure. Days passed away between him and these ladies, he scarce knew how. He poured his heart out to them, so as he never could in any other company, where he hath generally passed for being moody, or supercilious and silent. This society* was more delightful than that of the greatest wits to him. May Heaven pardon him the lies he told the Dowager at Chelsey, in order to get a pretext for going away to Kensington; the business at the Ordnance[11] which he invented; the interview with his General, the Courts and statesman's levees which he *didn't* frequent and describe; who wore a new suit on Sunday at Saint James's or at the Queen's birth-day; how many coaches filled the street at Mr Harley's levee, how many bottles he had had the honour to drink overnight with Mr St John at the Cocoa-Tree,[12] or at the Garter with Mr Walpole and Mr Steele.

Mistress Beatrix Esmond had been a dozen times on the point of making great matches, so the Court scandal said; but for his part Esmond never would believe the stories against her; and

*And, indeed, so was his to them, a thousand thousand times more charming, for where was his equal? – R.

came back, after three years' absence from her, not so frantic as he had been perhaps, but still hungering after her and no other; still hopeful, still kneeling, with his heart in his hand for the young lady to take. We were now got to 1709. She was near twenty-two years old, and three years at Court, and without a husband.

''Tis not for want of being asked,' Lady Castlewood said, looking into Esmond's heart, as she could, with that perceptiveness affection gives. 'But she will make no mean match, Harry: she will not marry as I would have her; the person whom I should like to call my son, and Henry Esmond knows who that is, is best served by my not pressing his claim. Beatrix is so wilful, that what I would urge on her, she would be sure to resist. The man who would marry her will not be happy with her, unless he be a great person, and can put her in a great position. Beatrix loves admiration more than love; and longs, beyond all things, for command. Why should a mother speak so of her child? You are my son, too, Harry. You should know the truth about your sister. I thought you might cure yourself of your passion,' my lady added, fondly. 'Other people can cure themselves of that folly, you know. But I see you are still as infatuated as ever. When we read your name in the Gazette, I pleaded for you, my poor boy. Poor boy, indeed! You are growing a grave old gentleman now, and I am an old woman. She likes your fame well enough, and she likes your person. She says you have wit, and fire, and good breeding, and are more natural than the fine gentlemen of the Court. But this is not enough. She wants a commander-in-chief, and not a colonel. Were a duke to ask her, she would leave an earl whom she had promised. I told you so before. I know not how my poor girl is so worldly.'

'Well,' says Esmond, 'a man can but give his best and his all. She has that from me. What little reputation I have won, I swear I cared for it because I thought Beatrix would be pleased with it. What care I to be a colonel or a general? Think you 'twill matter a few score years hence, what our foolish honours to-day are? I would have had a little fame, that she might wear it in her hat. If I had anything better, I would endow her with it. If she wants my life, I would give it her. If she marries another, I will say God bless him. I make no boast, nor no complaint. I think my fidelity is folly, perhaps. But so it is. I cannot help myself. I love her. You are a thousand times better: the fondest, the fairest, the dearest, of women. Sure, my dear lady, I see all Beatrix's faults as well as you do. But she is my fate. 'Tis endurable. I shall not die for not having her. I think I should be no happier if I won her. *Que voulez-vous?* as my Lady of Chelsey would say. *Je l'aime.*'

'I wish she would have you,' said Harry's fond mistress, giving a hand to him. He kissed the fair hand ('twas the prettiest dimpled little hand in the world, and my Lady Castlewood, though now almost forty years old, did not look to be within ten years of her age). He kissed and kept her fair hand, as they talked together.

'Why,' says he, 'should she hear me? She knows what I would say. Far or near, she knows I'm her slave. I have sold myself for nothing, it may be. Well, 'tis the price I choose to take. I am worth nothing, or I am worth all.'

'You are such a treasure,' Esmond's mistress was pleased to say, 'that the woman who has your love, shouldn't change it away against a kingdom, I think. I am a country-bred woman, and cannot say but the ambitions of the town seem mean to me. I never was awe-stricken by my Lady Duchess's rank and finery, or afraid,' she added, with a sly laugh, 'of anything but her temper. I hear of Court ladies who pine because her Majesty looks cold on them; and great noblemen who would give a limb that they might wear a garter on the other. This worldliness, which I can't comprehend, was born with Beatrix, who, on the first day of her waiting, was a perfect courtier. We are like sisters, and she the eldest sister, somehow. She tells me I have a mean spirit. I laugh, and say she adores a coach-and-six. I cannot reason her out of her ambition. 'Tis natural to her, as to me to love quiet, and be indifferent about rank and riches. What are they, Harry? and for how long do they last? Our home is not here.' She smiled as she spoke, and looked like an angel that was only on earth on a visit. 'Our home is where the just are, and where our sins and sorrows enter not. My father used to rebuke me, and say that I was too hopeful about Heaven. But I cannot help my nature, and grow obstinate as I grow to be an old woman; and as I love my children so, sure our Father loves us with a thousand and a thousand times greater love. It must be that we shall meet yonder, and be happy. Yes, you – and my children, and my dear lord. Do you know, Harry, since his death, it has always seemed to me as if his love came back to me, and that we are parted no more. Perhaps he is here now, Harry – I think he is. Forgiven I am sure he is: even Mr Atterbury absolved him, and he died forgiving. O, what a noble heart he had! How generous he was! I was but fifteen, and a child when he married me. How good he was to stoop to me! He was always good to the poor and humble.' She stopped, then presently, with a peculiar expression, as if her eyes were looking into Heaven, and saw my lord there, she smiled, and gave a little laugh. 'I laugh to see you, sir,' she says; 'when you come, it seems as if you never were away.' One may put her words down, and remember them, but how describe her sweet tones, sweeter than music.

My young lord did not come home at the end of the campaign, and wrote that he was kept at Bruxelles on military duty. Indeed, I believe he was engaged in laying siege to a certain lady, who was of the suite of Madame de Soissons, the Prince of Savoy's mother, who was just dead, and who, like the Flemish fortresses, was taken and retaken a great number of times during the war, and occupied by French, English, and Imperialists. Of course, Mr Esmond did not think fit to enlighten Lady Castlewood regarding the young scapegrace's doings; nor had he said a word about the affair with Lord Mohun, knowing how abhorrent that man's name was to his mistress. Frank did not waste much time or money on pen and ink; and, when Harry came home with his General, only writ two lines to his mother, to say his wound in the leg was almost healed, that he would keep his coming of age next year – that the duty aforesaid would keep him at Bruxelles, and that Cousin Harry would tell all the news.

But from Bruxelles, knowing how the Lady Castlewood always liked to have a letter about the famous 29th of December, my lord writ her a long and full one, and in this he must have described the affair with Mohun; for when Mr Esmond came to visit his mistress one day, early in the new year, to his great wonderment, she and her daughter both came up and saluted him, and after them the Dowager of Chelsea, too, whose chairman had just brought her ladyship from her village to Kensington across the fields. After this honour, I say, from the two ladies of Castlewood, the Dowager came forward in great state, with her grand tall headdress of King James's reign, that she never forsook, and said, 'Cousin Henry, all our family have met; and we thank you, cousin, for your noble conduct towards the head of our house.' And pointing to her blushing cheek, she made Mr Esmond aware that he was to enjoy the rapture of an embrace there. Having saluted one cheek, she turned to him the other. 'Cousin Harry,' said both the other ladies, in a little chorus, 'we thank you for your noble conduct'; and then Harry became aware that the story of the Lille affair had come to his kinswomen's ears. It pleased him to hear them all saluting him as one of their family.

The tables of the dining-room were laid for a great entertainment; and the ladies were in gala dresses – my Lady of Chelsea in her highest *tour*, my Lady Viscountess out of black, and looking fair and happy, *à ravir ;* and the Maid of Honour attired with that splendour which naturally distinguished her, and wearing on her beautiful breast the French officer's star which Frank had sent home after Ramillies.

'You see, 'tis a gala day with us,' says she, glancing down to the star complacently, 'and we have our orders on. Does not mamma look charming? 'Twas I dressed her!' Indeed, Esmond's dear mistress, blushing as he looked at her, with her beautiful fair hair and an elegant dress, according to the *mode*, appeared to have the shape and complexion of a girl of twenty.

On the table was a fine sword, with a red velvet scabbard, and a beautiful chased silver handle, with a blue riband for a swordknot. 'What is this?' says the Captain, going up to look at this pretty piece.

Mrs Beatrix advanced towards it. 'Kneel down,' says she: 'we dub you our knight with this' – and she waved the sword over his head – 'my Lady Dowager hath given the sword; and I give the riband, and mamma hath sewn on the fringe.'

'Put the sword on him, Beatrix,' says her mother. 'You are our knight, Harry – our true knight. Take a mother's thanks and prayers for defending her son, my dear, dear friend.' She could say no more, and even the Dowager was affected, for a couple of rebellious tears made sad marks down those wrinkled old roses which Esmond had just been allowed to salute.

'We had a letter from dearest Frank,' his mother said, 'three days since, whilst you were on your visit to your friend Captain Steele, at Hampton. He told us all that you had done, and how nobly you had put yourself between him and that – that wretch.'

'And I adopt you from this day,' says the Dowager; 'and I wish I was richer, for your sake, son Esmond,' she added with a wave of her hand; and as Mr Esmond dutifully went down on his knee before her ladyship, she cast her eyes up to the ceiling (the gilt chandelier, and the twelve wax candles in it, for the party was numerous), and invoked a blessing from that quarter upon the newly adopted son.

'Dear Frank,' says the other Viscountess, 'how fond he is of his military profession! He is studying fortification very hard, I wish he were here. We shall keep his coming of age at Castlewood next year.'

'If the campaign permit us,' says Mr Esmond.

'I am never afraid when he is with you,' cries the boy's mother. 'I am sure my Henry will always defend him.'

'But there will be a peace before next year; we know it for certain,' cries the Maid of Honour. 'Lord Marlborough will be dismissed, and that horrible Duchess turned out of all her places. Her Majesty won't speak to her now. Did you see her at Bushy,[13] Harry? she is furious, and she ranges about the park like a lioness, and tears people's eyes out.'

'And the Princess Anne will send for somebody,' says my Lady of Chelsey, taking out her medal and kissing it.

'Did you see the King at Oudenarde, Harry?' his mistress asked. She was a staunch Jacobite, and would no more have thought of denying her King than her God.

'I saw the young Hanoverian only': Harry said, 'The Chevalier de St George——'

'The King, sir, the King!' said the ladies and Miss Beatrix; and she slapped her pretty hands, and cried 'Vive le Roy.'

By this time there came a thundering knock, that drove in the doors of the house almost. It was three o'clock, and the company were arriving; and presently the servant announced Captain Steele and his lady.

Captain and Mrs Steele, who were the first to arrive, had driven to Kensington from their country-house, the Hovel at Hampton Wick.[14] 'Not from our mansion in Bloomsbury Square,' as Mrs Steele took care to inform the ladies. Indeed Harry had ridden away from Hampton that very morning, leaving the couple by the ears; for from the chamber where he lay, in a bed that was none of the cleanest, and kept awake by the company which he had in his own bed, and the quarrel which was going on in the next room, he could hear both night and morning the curtain lecture[15] which Mrs Steele was in the habit of administering to poor Dick.

At night it did not matter so much for the culprit; Dick was fuddled, and when in that way no scolding could interrupt his benevolence. Mr Esmond could hear him coaxing and speaking in that maudlin manner, which punch and claret produce, to his beloved Prue, and beseeching her to remember that there was a *distiwisht officer ithe nex roob*, who would overhear her. She went on, nevertheless, calling him a drunken wretch, and was only interrupted in her harangues by the Captain's snoring.

In the morning, the unhappy victim awoke to a headache and consciousness, and the dialogue of the night was resumed. 'Why do you bring captains home to dinner when there's not a guinea in the house? How am I to give dinners when you leave me without a shilling? How am I to go trapesing to Kensington in my yellow satin sack before all the fine company? I've nothing fit to put on; I never have': and so the dispute went on – Mr Esmond interrupting the talk when it seemed to be growing too intimate by blowing his nose as loudly as ever he could, at the sound of which trumpet there came a lull. But Dick was charming, though his wife was odious, and 'twas to give Mr Steele pleasure, that the ladies of Castlewood, who were ladies of no small fashion, invited Mrs Steele.

Beside the Captain and his lady, there was a great and notable assemblage of company: my Lady of Chelsey having sent her lacqueys and liveries to aid the modest attendance at Kensington. There was Lieutenant-General Webb, Harry's kind patron, of whom the Dowager took possession, and who resplended in velvet and gold lace; there was Harry's new acquaintance, the Right Honourable Henry St John, Esquire, the General's kinsman, who was charmed with the Lady Castlewood, even more than with her daughter; there was one of the greatest noblemen in the kingdom, the Scots Duke of Hamilton, just created Duke of Brandon in England; and two other noble lords of the Tory party, my Lord Ashburnham, and another I have forgot; and for ladies, her Grace the Duchess of Ormonde and her daughters, the Lady Mary and the Lady Betty, the former one of Mistress Beatrix's colleagues in waiting on the Queen.

'What a party of Tories!' whispered Captain Steele to Esmond, as we were assembled in the parlour before dinner. Indeed, all the company present, save Steele, were of that faction.

Mr St John made his special compliments to Mrs Steele, and so charmed her that she declared she would have Steele a Tory too.

'Or will you have me a Whig?' says Mr St John. 'I think, madam, you could convert a man to anything.'

'If Mr St John ever comes to Bloomsbury Square I will teach him what I know,' says Mrs Steele, dropping her handsome eyes. 'Do you know Bloomsbury Square?'

'Do I know the Mall? Do I know the Opera? Do I know the reigning toast? Why, Bloomsbury is the very height of the mode,' says Mr St John. ''Tis *rus in urbe*. You have gardens all the way to Hampstead, and palaces round about you – Southampton House and Montague House.'

'Where you wretches go and fight duels,' cries Mrs Steele.

'Of which the ladies are the cause!' says her entertainer. 'Madam, is Dick a good swordsman? How charming the Tatler is! We all recognised your portrait in the 49th number, and I have been dying to know you ever since I read it. "Aspasia must be allowed to be the first of the beauteous order of love." Doth not the passage run so? "In this accomplished lady love is the constant effect, though it is never the design; yet though her mien carries much more invitation than command, to behold her is an immediate check to loose behaviour, and to love her is a liberal education."[16]

'Oh indeed!' says Mrs Steele, who did not seem to understand a word of what the gentleman was saying.

'Who could fail to be accomplished under such a mistress?' says Mr St John, still gallant and bowing.

'Mistress! upon my word, sir!' cries the lady. 'If you mean me, sir, I would have you know that I am the Captain's wife.'

'Sure we all know it,' answers Mr St John, keeping his countenance very gravely; and Steele broke in, saying, ''Twas not about Mrs Steele I writ that paper – though I am sure she is worthy of any compliment I can pay her – but of the Lady Elizabeth Hastings.'

'I hear Mr Addison is equally famous as a wit and a poet,' says Mr St John. 'Is it true that his hand is to be found in your Tatler, Mr Steele?'

'Whether 'tis the sublime or the humorous, no man can come near him,' cries Steele.

'A fig, Dick, for your Mr Addison!' cries out his lady: 'a gentleman who gives himself such airs and holds his head so high now. I hope your ladyship thinks as I do: I can't bear those very fair men with white eyelashes – a black man for me.' (All the black men at table applauded, and made Mrs Steele a bow for this compliment.) 'As for this Mr Addison,' she went on, 'he comes to dine with the Captain sometimes, never says a word to me, and then they walk upstairs, both tipsy, to a dish of tea. I remember your Mr Addison when he had but one coat to his back, and that with a patch at the elbow.'

'Indeed – a patch at the elbow! You interest me,' says Mr St John. ''Tis charming to hear of one man of letters from the charming wife of another.'

'Law, I could tell you ever so much about 'em,' continues the voluble lady. 'What do you think the Captain has got now? – a little hunchback fellow – a little hop-o'-my-thumb creature that he calls a poet – a little Popish brat!'

'Hush, there are two in the room,' whispers her companion.

'Well, I call him Popish because his name is Pope,' says the lady. ''Tis only my joking way. And this little dwarf of a fellow has wrote a pastoral poem[17] – all about shepherds and shepherdesses, you know.'

'A shepherd should have a little crook,' says my mistress, laughing from her end of the table: on which Mrs Steele said, 'She did not know, but the Captain brought home this queer little creature when she was in bed with her first boy, and it was a mercy he had come no sooner; and Dick raved about his *genus*, and was always raving about some nonsense or other.'

'Which of the Tatlers do you prefer, Mrs Steele?' asked Mr St John.

'I never read but one, and think it all a pack of rubbish, sir,' says the lady. 'Such stuff about Bickerstaffe, and Distaff, and Quarterstaff,[18] as it all is! There's the Captain going on still with the Burgundy – I know he'll be tipsy before he stops – Captain Steele!'

'I drink to your eyes, my dear,' says the Captain, who seemed to think his wife charming, and to receive as genuine all the satiric compliments which Mr St John paid her.

All this while the Maid of Honour had been trying to get Mr Esmond to talk, and no doubt voted him a dull fellow. For, by some mistake, just as he was going to pop into the vacant place, he was placed far away from Beatrix's chair, who sate between his Grace and my Lord Ashburnham, and shrugged her lovely white shoulders, and cast a look as if to say, 'Pity me,' to her cousin. My Lord Duke and his young neighbour were presently in a very animated and close conversation. Mrs Beatrix could no more help using her eyes than the sun can help shining, and setting those it shines on a-burning. By the time the first course was done the dinner seemed long to Esmond: by the time the soup came he fancied they must have been hours at table: and as for the sweets and jellies he thought they never would be done.

At length the ladies rose, Beatrix throwing a Parthian glance at the duke as she retreated; a fresh bottle and glasses were fetched, and toasts were called. Mr St John asked his Grace the Duke of Hamilton and the company to drink to the health of his

Grace the Duke of Brandon. Another lord gave General Webb's health, 'and may he get the command the bravest officer in the world deserves.' Mr Webb thanked the company, complimented his aide-de-camp, and fought his famous battle over again.

'*Il est fatiguant*,' whispers Mr St John, '*avec sa trompette de Wynendael.*'

Captain Steele, who was not of our side, loyally gave the health of the Duke of Marlborough, the greatest general of the age.

'I drink to the greatest general with all my heart,' says Mr Webb; 'there can be no gainsaying that character of him. My glass goes to the General, and not to the Duke, Mr Steele.' And the stout old gentleman emptied his bumper; to which Dick replied by filling and emptying a pair of brimmers, one for the General and one for the Duke.

And now his Grace of Hamilton, rising up, with flashing eyes (we had all been drinking pretty freely), proposed a toast to the lovely, to the incomparable Mrs Beatrix Esmond; we all drank it with cheers, and my Lord Ashburnham especially, with a shout of enthusiasm.

'What a pity there is a Duchess of Hamilton,' whispers St John, who drank more wine and yet was more steady than most of the others, and we entered the drawing-room where the ladies were at their tea. As for poor Dick, we were obliged to leave him alone at the dining-table, where he was hiccupping out the lines from the 'Campaign,' in which the greatest poet had celebrated the greatest general in the world; and Harry Esmond found him, half an hour afterwards, in a more advanced stage of liquor, and weeping about the treachery of Tom Boxer.[19]

The drawing-room was all dark to poor Harry, in spite of the grand illumination. Beatrix scarce spoke to him. When my Lord Duke went away, she practised upon the next in rank, and plied my young Lord Ashburnham with all the fire of her eyes and the fascinations of her wit. Most of the party were set to cards, and Mr St John, after yawning in the face of Mrs Steele, whom he did not care to pursue any more; and talking in his most brilliant animated way to Lady Castlewood, whom he pronounced to be beautiful, of a far higher order of beauty than her daughter, presently took his leave, and went his way. The rest of the company speedily followed, my Lord Ashburnham the last, throwing fiery glances at the smiling young temptress, who had bewitched more hearts than his in her thrall.

No doubt, as a kinsman of the house, Mr Esmond thought fit to be the last of all in it; he remained after the coaches had rolled away – after his dowager aunt's chair and flambeaux had marched off in the darkness towards Chelsey, and the towns-people had gone to bed, who had been drawn into the square to gape at the unusual assemblage of chairs and chariots, lacqueys and torch-men. The poor mean wretch lingered yet for a few minutes, to see whether the girl would vouchsafe him a smile, or a parting word of consolation. But her enthusiasm of the morning was quite died out, or she chose to be in a different mood. She fell to joking about the dowdy appearance of Lady Betty, and mimicked the vulgarity of Mrs Steele; and then she put up her little hand to her mouth and yawned, lighted a taper, and shrugged her shoulders, and dropping Mr Esmond a saucy curtsey, sailed off to bed.

'The day began so well, Henry, that I had hoped it might have ended better,' was all the consolation that poor Esmond's fond mistress could give him; and as he trudged home through the dark alone, he thought, with bitter rage in his heart, and a feeling of almost revolt against the sacrifice he had made: – 'She would have me,' thought he, 'had I but a name to give her. But for my promise to her father, I might have my rank and my mistress too.'

I suppose a man's vanity is stronger than any other passion in him; for I blush, even now, as I recall the humiliation of those distant days, the memory of which still smarts, though the fever of baulked desire has passed away more than a score of years ago. When the writer's descendants come to read this memoir, I wonder will they have lived to experience a similar defeat and shame? Will they ever have knelt to a woman, who has listened to them, and played with them, and laughed at them – who beckoning them with lures and caresses and with Yes, smiling from her eyes, has tricked them on to their knees, and turned her back and left them? All this shame Mr Esmond had to undergo; and he submitted, and revolted, and presently came crouching back for more.

After this feste, my young Lord Ashburnham's coach was for ever rolling in and out of Kensington Square; his lady mother came to visit Esmond's mistress, and at every assembly in the town, wherever the Maid of Honour made her appearance, you might be pretty sure to see the young gentleman in a new suit every week, and decked out in all the finery that his tailor or embroiderer could furnish for him. My lord was for ever paying Mr Esmond compliments: bidding him to dinner, offering him horses to ride, and giving him a thousand uncouth marks of respect and good-will. At last, one night at the coffee-house, whither my lord came considerably flushed and excited with drink, he rushes up to Mr Esmond, and cries out – 'Give me joy, my dearest Colonel; I am the happiest of men.'

'The happiest of men needs no dearest colonel to give him joy,' says Mr Esmond. 'What is the cause of this supreme felicity?'

'Haven't you heard?' says he. 'Don't you know? I thought the family told you everything: the adorable Beatrix hath promised to be mine.'

'What!' cries out Mr Esmond, who had spent happy hours with Beatrix that very morning – had writ verses for her, that she had sung at the harpsichord.

'Yes,' says he: 'I waited on her to-day. I saw you walking towards Knightsbridge as I passed in my coach; and she looked so lovely, and spoke so kind, that I couldn't help going down on my knees, and – and – sure I'm the happiest of men in all the world; and I'm very young; but she says I shall get older: and you know I shall be of age in four months; and there's very little difference between us; and I'm so happy. I should like to treat the company to something. Let us have a bottle – a dozen bottles – and drink the health of the finest woman in England.'

Esmond left the young lord tossing off bumper after bumper, and strolled away to Kensington to ask whether the news was true. 'Twas only too sure: his mistress's sad, compassionate face told him the story; and then she related what particulars of it she knew, and how my young lord had made his offer, half-an-hour after Esmond went away that morning, and in the very room where the song lay yet on the harpsichord, which Esmond had writ, and they had sung together.

# BOOK III

## CONTAINING THE END OF MR ESMOND'S ADVENTURES IN ENGLAND

### Chapter 1

### I COME TO AN END OF MY BATTLES AND BRUISES

THAT feverish desire to gain a little reputation which Esmond had had, left him now perhaps that he had attained some portion of his wish, and the great motive of his ambition was over. His desire for military honour was that it might raise him in Beatrix's eyes. 'Twas next to nobility and wealth the only kind of rank she valued. It was the stake quickest won or lost too; for law is a very long game that requires a life to practise; and to be distinguished in letters or the Church would not have forwarded the poor gentleman's plans in the least. So he had no suit to play but the red one, and he played it; and this, in truth, was the reason of his speedy promotion; for he exposed himself more than most gentlemen do, and risked more to win more. Is he the only man that hath set his life against a stake which may be not worth the winning? Another risks his life (and his honour, too, sometimes) against a bundle of bank-notes, or a yard of blue riband,[1] or a seat in Parliament; and some for the mere pleasure and excitement of the sport; as a field of a hundred huntsmen will do, each out-bawling and out-galloping the other at the tail of a dirty fox, that is to be the prize of the foremost happy conqueror.

When he heard this news of Beatrix's engagement in marriage, Colonel Esmond knocked under[2] to his fate, and resolved to surrender his sword, that could win him nothing now he cared for; and in this dismal frame of mind he determined to retire from the regiment, to the great delight of the captain next in rank to him, who happened to be a young gentlemen of good fortune, who eagerly paid Mr Esmond a thousand guineas for his majority in Webb's regiment, and was knocked on the head the next campaign. Perhaps Esmond would not have been sorry to share his fate. He was more the Knight of the Woful Countenance than ever he had been. His moodiness must have made him perfectly odious to his friends under the tents, who like a jolly fellow, and laugh at a melancholy warrior always sighing after Dulcinea at home.

Both the ladies of Castlewood approved of Mr Esmond quitting the army, and his kind General coincided in his wish of retirement, and helped in the transfer of his commission, which brought a pretty sum into his pocket. But when the Commander-in-Chief came home, and was forced, in spite of himself, to appoint Lieutenant-General Webb to the command of a division of the army in Flanders, the Lieutenant-General prayed Colonel Esmond so urgently to be his aide-de-camp and military secretary, that Esmond could not resist his kind patron's entreaties, and again took the field, not attached to any regiment, but under Webb's orders. What must have been the continued agonies of fears* and apprehensions which racked the gentle breasts of wives and matrons in those dreadful days, when every Gazette brought accounts of deaths and battles, and when the present anxiety over, and the beloved person escaped, the doubt still remained that a battle might be fought, possibly, of which the next Flanders letter would bring the account; so they, the poor tender creatures, had to go on sickening and trembling through the whole campaign. Whatever these terrors were on the part of Esmond's mistress (and that tenderest of women must have felt them most keenly for both her sons, as she called them), she never allowed them outwardly to appear, but hid her apprehension as she did her charities and devotion. 'Twas only by chance that Esmond, wandering in Kensington, found his mistress coming out of a mean cottage there, and heard that she had a score of poor retainers, whom she visited and comforted in their sickness and poverty, and who blessed her daily. She attended the early church daily (though of a Sunday especially, she encouraged and advanced all sorts of cheerfulness and innocent

* What indeed? Psm. xci, 2, 3, 7. – R.E.

gaiety in her little household): and by notes entered into a table-book of hers at this time, and devotional compositions writ with a sweet artless fervour, such as the best divines could not surpass, showed how fond her heart was, how humble and pious her spirit, what pangs of apprehension she endured silently, and with what a faithful reliance she committed the care of those she loved to the awful Dispenser of death and life.

As for her ladyship at Chelsey, Esmond's newly-adopted mother, she was now of an age when the danger of any second party doth not disturb the rest much. She cared for trumps more than for most things in life. She was firm enough in her own faith, but no longer very bitter against ours. She had a very good-natured, easy French director, Monsieur Gauthier by name, who was a gentleman of the world, and would take a hand of cards with Dean Atterbury, my lady's neighbour at Chelsey, and was well with all the High Church party. No doubt Monsieur Gauthier[3] knew what Esmond's peculiar position was, for he corresponded with Holt, and always treated Colonel Esmond with particular respect and kindness; but for good reasons the Colonel and the Abbé never spoke on this matter together, and so they remained perfect good friends.

All the frequenters of my Lady of Chelsey's house were of the Tory and High Church party. Madame Beatrix was as frantic about the King as her elderly kinswoman: she wore his picture on her heart; she had a piece of his hair; she vowed he was the most injured, and gallant, and accomplished, and unfortunate, and beautiful of princes. Steele, who quarrelled with very many of his Tory friends, but never with Esmond, used to tell the Colonel that his kinswoman's house was a rendezvous of Tory intrigues; that Gauthier was a spy; that Atterbury was a spy; that letters were constantly going from that house to the Queen at St Germains; on which Esmond, laughing, would reply, that they used to say in the army the Duke of Marlborough was a spy too, and as much in correspondence with that family as any Jesuit. And without entering very eagerly into the controversy, Esmond had frankly taken the side of his family. It seemed to him that King James the Third was undoubtedly King of England by right: and at his sister's death it would be better to have him than a foreigner over us. No man admired King William more; a hero and a conqueror, the bravest, justest, wisest of men – but 'twas by the sword he conquered the country, and held and governed it by the very same right that the great Cromwell held it, who was truly and greatly a sovereign. But that a foreign despotic prince, out of Germany, who happened to be descended from King James the First, should take possession of this empire, seemed to Mr Esmond a monstrous injustice – at least, every Englishman had a right to protest, and the English Prince, the heir-at-law, the first of all. What man of spirit with such a cause would not back it? What man of honour with such a crown to win would not fight for it? But that race was destined. That Prince had himself against him, an enemy he could not overcome. He never dared to draw his sword, though he had it. He let his chances slip by as he lay in the lap of opera-girls, or snivelled at the knees of priests asking pardon; and the blood of heroes, and the devotedness of honest hearts, and endurance, courage, fidelity, were all spent for him in vain.[4]

But let us return to my Lady of Chelsey, who, when her son Esmond announced to her ladyship that he proposed to make the ensuing campaign, took leave of him with perfect alacrity, and was down to piquet with her gentlewoman before he had well quitted the room on his last visit. 'Tierce to a king,' were the last words he ever heard her say: the game of life was pretty nearly over for the good lady, and three months afterwards she took to her bed, where she flickered out without any pain, so the Abbé Gauthier wrote over to Mr Esmond, then with his General on the frontier of France. The Lady Castlewood was with her at her ending, and had written too, but these letters must have been taken by a privateer in the packet that brought them; for Esmond knew nothing of their contents until his return to England.

My Lady Castlewood had left everything to Colonel Esmond, 'as a reparation for the wrong done to him'; 'twas writ in her will. But her fortune was not much, for it never had been large, and the honest Viscountess had wisely sunk most of the money she had upon an annuity which terminated with her life. However, there was the house and furniture, plate and pictures at Chelsey, and a sum of money lying at her merchant's, Sir Josiah

Child, which altogether would realize a sum of near three hundred pounds per annum, so that Mr Esmond found himself, if not rich, at least easy for life. Likewise, there were the famous diamonds which had been said to be worth fabulous sums, though the goldsmith pronounced they would fetch no more than four thousand pounds. These diamonds, however, Colonel Esmond reserved, having a special use for them: but the Chelsey house, plate, goods, &c., with the exception of a few articles which he kept back, were sold by his orders; and the sums resulting from the sale invested in the public securities so as to realize the aforesaid annual income of three hundred pounds.

Having now something to leave, he made a will, and despatched it home. The army was now in presence of the enemy; and a great battle expected every day. 'Twas known that the General-in-Chief was in disgrace, and the parties at home strong against him; and there was no stroke this great and resolute player would not venture to recall his fortune when it seemed desperate. Frank Castlewood was with Colonel Esmond; his General having gladly taken the young nobleman on to his staff. His studies of fortifications at Bruxelles were over by this time. The fort he was besieging had yielded, I believe, and my lord had not only marched in with flying colours, but marched out again. He used to tell his boyish wickednesses with admirable humour, and was the most charming young scapegrace in the army.

'Tis needless to say that Colonel Esmond had left every penny of his little fortune to this boy. It was the Colonel's firm conviction that the next battle would put an end to him: for he felt aweary of the sun, and quite ready to bid that and the earth farewell. Frank would not listen to his comrade's gloomy forebodings, but swore they would keep his birthday at Castlewood that autumn, after the campaign. He had heard of the engagement at home. 'If Prince Eugene goes to London,' says Frank, 'and Trix can get hold of him, she'll jilt Ashburnham for his Highness. I tell you, she used to make eyes at the Duke of Marlborough, when she was only fourteen and ogling poor little Blandford. *I* wouldn't marry her, Harry, no, not if her eyes were twice as big. I'll take my fun. I'll enjoy for the next three years every possible pleasure. I'll sow my wild oats then, and marry some quiet, steady, modest, sensible Viscountess; hunt my harriers; and settle down at Castlewood. Perhaps I'll represent the county – no, damme, *you* shall represent the county. You have the brains of the family. By the Lord, my dear old Harry, you have the best head and the kindest heart in all the army; and every man says so – and when the Queen dies, and the King comes back, why shouldn't you go to the House of Commons and be a minister, and be made a peer, and that sort of thing? *You* be shot in the next action! I wager a dozen of Burgundy you are not touched. Mohun is well of his wound. He is always with Corporal John[5] now. As soon as ever I see his ugly face I'll spit in it. I took lessons of Father – of Captain Holtz at Bruxelles. What a man that is! He knows everything.' Esmond bade Frank have a care; that Father Holt's knowledge was rather dangerous; not, indeed, knowing as yet how far the Father had pushed his instructions with his young pupil.

The gazetteers and writers, both of the French and English side, have given accounts sufficient of that bloody battle of Blarignies or Malplaquet, which was the last and the hardest-earned of the victories of the great Duke of Marlborough. In that tremendous combat, near upon two hundred and fifty thousand men were engaged, more than thirty thousand of whom were slain or wounded (the Allies lost twice as many men as they killed of the French, whom they conquered): and this dreadful slaughter very likely took place because a great General's credit was shaken at home, and he thought to restore it by a victory. If such were the motives which induced the Duke of Marlborough to venture that prodigious stake, and desperately sacrifice thirty thousand brave lives, so that he might figure once more in a Gazette, and hold his places and pensions a little longer, the event defeated the dreadful and selfish design, for the victory was purchased at a cost which no nation, greedy of glory as it may be, would willingly pay for any triumph. The gallantry of the French was as remarkable as the furious bravery of their assailants. We took a few score of their flags, and a few pieces of their artillery; but we left twenty thousand of the bravest soldiers of the world round about the intrenched lines, from which the enemy was driven. He retreated in perfect good order; the panic-spell seemed to be broken, under which the French had laboured ever since the disaster of Hochstedt; and, fighting now on the threshold of their country, they showed an heroic ardour of resistance, such as had never met us in the course of their aggressive war. Had the battle been more successful, the conqueror might have got the price for which he waged it. As it was (and justly, I think), the party adverse to the Duke in England were indignant at the lavish extravagance of slaughter, and demanded more eagerly than ever the recall of a chief, whose cupidity and desperation might urge him further still. After this bloody fight of Malplaquet, I can answer for it, that in the Dutch quarters and our own, and amongst the very regiments and commanders, whose gallantry was most conspicuous upon this frightful day of carnage, the general cry was, that there was enough of the war. The French were driven back into their own boundary, and all their conquests and booty of Flanders disgorged. As for the Prince of Savoy, with whom our Commander-in-Chief, for reasons of his own, consorted more closely than ever, 'twas known that he was animated not merely by a political hatred, but by personal rage against the old French King: the Imperial Generalissimo never forgot the slight put by Lewis upon the Abbé de Savoie,[6] and in the humiliation or ruin of His Most Christian Majesty, the Holy Roman Emperor found his account. But what were these quarrels to us, the free citizens of England and Holland? Despot as he was, the French monarch was yet the chief of European civilisation, more venerable in his age and misfortunes than at the period of his most splendid successes; whilst his opponent was but a semi-barbarous tyrant, with a pillaging murderous horde of Croats and Pandours, composing a half of his army, filling our camp with their strange figures, bearded like the miscreant Turks their neighbours, and carrying into Christian warfare their native heathen habits of rapine, lust, and murder. Why should the best blood in England and France be shed in order that the Holy Roman and Apostolic master of these ruffians should have his revenge over the Christian King? And it was to this end we were fighting; for this that every village and family in England was deploring the death of beloved sons and fathers. We dared not speak to each other, even at table, of Malplaquet, so frightful were the gaps left in our army by the cannon of that bloody action. 'Twas heart-rending, for an officer who had a heart, to look down his line on a parade-day afterwards, and miss hundreds of faces of comrades – humble or of high rank – that had gathered but yesterday full of courage and cheerfulness round the torn and blackened flags. Where were our friends? As the great Duke reviewed us, riding along our lines with his fine suite of prancing aides-de-camp and generals, stopping here and there to thank an officer with those eager smiles and bows of which his Grace was always lavish, scarce a huzzah could be got for him, though Cadogan, with an oath, rode up and cried – 'D——n you, why don't you cheer?' But the men had no heart for that: not one of them but was thinking, 'Where's my comrade? – where's my brother that fought by me, or my dear captain that led me yesterday?' 'Twas the most gloomy pageant I ever looked on; and the 'Te Deum,' sung by our chaplains, the most woeful and dreary satire.

Esmond's General added one more to the many marks of honour which he had received in the front of a score of battles, and got a wound in the groin, which laid him on his back; and you may be sure he consoled himself by abusing the Commander-in-Chief, as he lay groaning– 'Corporal John's as fond of me,' he used to say, 'as King David was of General Uriah; and so he always gives me the post of danger.' He persisted, to his dying day, in believing that the Duke intended he should be beat at Wynendael, and sent him purposely with a small force, hoping that he might be knocked on the head there. Esmond and Frank Castlewood both escaped without hurt, though the division which our General commanded suffered even more than any other, having to sustain not only the fury of the enemy's cannonade, which was very hot and well-served, but the furious and repeated charges of the famous Maison du Roy, which we had to receive and beat off again and again, with volleys of shot and hedges of iron, and our four lines of musketeers and pikemen. They said the King of England charged us no less than twelve times that day, along with the French Household. Esmond's late regiment, General Webb's own Fusileers, served in the division which their Colonel commanded. The General was thrice in the centre of the square of the Fusileers, calling the fire at the French charges; and, after the action, his Grace the Duke of Berwick sent his compliments to his old regiment and their Colonel for their behaviour on the field.

We drank my Lord Castlewood's health and majority, the 25th of September, the army being then before Mons: and here Colonel Esmond was not so fortunate as he had been in actions much more dangerous, and was hit by a spent ball just above the place where his former wound was, which caused the old wound to open again, fever, spitting of blood, and other ugly symptoms, to ensue; and, in a word, brought him near to death's door. The kind lad, his kinsman, attended his elder comrade with a very praiseworthy affectionateness and care until he was pronounced out of danger by the doctors, when Frank went off, passed the winter at Bruxelles, and besieged, no doubt, some other fortress there. Very few lads would have given up their pleasures so long and so gaily as Frank did; his cheerful prattle soothed many long days of Esmond's pain and languor. Frank was supposed to be still at his kinsman's bedside for a month after he had left it, for letters came from his mother at home full of thanks to the younger gentleman for his care of his elder brother (so it pleased Esmond's mistress now affectionately to style him); nor was Mr Esmond in a hurry to undeceive her, when the good young fellow was gone for his Christmas holiday. It was as pleasant to Esmond on his couch to watch the young man's pleasure at the idea of being free, as to note his simple efforts to disguise his satisfaction on going away. There are days when a flask of champagne at a cabaret, and a red-cheeked partner to share it, are too strong temptations for any young fellow of spirit. I am not going to play the moralist, and cry 'Fie.' For ages past, I know how old men preach, and what young men practise; and that patriarchs have had their weak moments, too, long since Father Noah toppled over after discovering the vine. Frank went off, then, to his pleasures at Bruxelles, in which capital many young fellows of our army declared they found infinitely greater diversion even than in London: and Mr Henry Esmond remained in his sick-room, where he writ a fine comedy, that his mistress pronounced to be sublime, and that was acted no less than three successive nights in London in the next year.

Here, as he lay nursing himself, ubiquitous Mr Holtz reappeared, and stopped a whole month at Mons, where he not only won over Colonel Esmond to the King's side in politics (that side being always held by the Esmond family); but where he endeavoured to re-open the controversial question between the Churches once more, and to recall Esmond to that religion in which, in his infancy, he had been baptised. Holtz was a casuist, both dexterous and learned, and presented the case between the English Church and his own in such a way that those who granted his premises ought certainly to allow his conclusions. He touched on Esmond's delicate state of health, chance of dissolution, and so forth; and enlarged upon the immense benefits that the sick man was likely to forego – benefits which the Church of England did not deny to those of the Roman communion, as how should she, being derived from that Church, and only an offshoot from it. But Mr Esmond said that his Church was the Church of his country, and to that he chose to remain faithful: other people were welcome to worship and to subscribe any other set of articles, whether at Rome or at Augsburg.[7] But if the good Father meant that Esmond should join the Roman communion for fear of consequences, and that all England ran the risk of being damned for heresy, Esmond, for one, was perfectly willing to take his chance of the penalty along with the countless millions of his fellow countrymen, who were bred in the same faith, and along with some of the noblest, the truest, the purest, the wisest, the most pious and learned men and women in the world.

As for the political question, in that Mr Esmond could agree with the Father much more readily, and had come to the same conclusion, though, perhaps, by a different way. The right-divine, about which Doctor Sacheverel[8] and the High Church party in England were just now making a bother, they were welcome to hold as they chose. If Richard Cromwell and his father before him, had been crowned and anointed (and bishops enough would have been found to do it), it seemed to Mr Esmond that they would have had the right-divine just as much as any

Plantagenet, or Tudor, or Stuart. But the desire of the country being unquestionably for an hereditary monarchy, Esmond thought an English king out of St Germains was better and fitter than a German prince from Herrenhausen, and that if he failed to satisfy the nation, some other Englishman might be found to take his place; and so, though with no frantic enthusiasm, or worship of that monstrous pedigree which the Tories chose to consider divine, he was ready to say, 'God save King James!' when Queen Anne went the way of kings and commoners.

'I fear, Colonel, you are no better than a republican at heart,' says the priest with a sigh.

'I am an Englishman,' says Harry, 'and take my country as I find her. The will of the nation being for Church and King, I am for Church and King, too; but English Church, and English King; and that is why your Church isn't mine, though your King is.'

Though they lost the day at Malplaquet, it was the French who were elated by that action, whilst the conquerors were dispirited by it; and the enemy gathered together a larger army than ever, and made prodigious efforts for the next campaign. Marshal Berwick was with the French this year; and we heard that Mareschal Villars was still suffering of his wound, was eager to bring our Duke to action, and vowed he would fight us in his coach. Young Castlewood came flying back from Bruxelles, as soon as he heard that fighting was to begin; and the arrival of the Chevalier de St George was announced about May. 'It's the King's third campaign, and it's mine,' Frank liked saying. He was come back a greater Jacobite than ever, and Esmond suspected that some fair conspirators at Bruxelles had been inflaming the young man's ardour. Indeed, he owned that he had a message from the Queen, Beatrix's godmother, who had given her name[9] to Frank's sister the year before he and his sovereign were born.

However desirous Marshal Villars might be to fight, my Lord Duke did not seem disposed to indulge him this campaign. Last year his Grace had been all for the Whigs and Hanoverians; but finding, on going to England, his country cold towards himself, and the people in a ferment of High Church loyalty, the Duke comes back to his army cooled towards the Hanoverians, cautious with the Imperialists, and particularly civil and polite towards the Chevalier de St George. 'Tis certain that messengers and letters were continually passing between his Grace and his brave nephew, the Duke of Berwick, in the opposite camp. No man's caresses were more opportune than his Grace's, and no man ever uttered expressions of regard and affection more generously. He professed to Monsieur de Torcy, so Mr St John told the writer, quite an eagerness to be cut in pieces for the exiled Queen and her family; nay more, I believe, this year he parted with a portion of the most precious part of himself – his money – which he sent over to the royal exiles. Mr Tunstal, who was in the Prince's service, was twice or thrice in and out of our camp; the French, in theirs of Arlieu and about Arras. A little river, the Canihe, I think 'twas called (but this is writ away from books and Europe; and the only map the writer hath of these scenes of his youth, bears no mark of this little stream), divided our picquets from the enemy's. Our sentries talked across the stream, when they could make themselves understood to each other, and when they could not, grinned, and handed each other their brandy-flasks or their pouches of tobacco. And one fine day of June, riding thither with the officer who visited the outposts (Colonel Esmond was taking an airing on horseback, being too weak for military duty), they came to this river, where a number of English and Scots were assembled, talking to the good-natured enemy on the other side.

Esmond was especially amused with the talk of one long fellow, with a great curling red moustache, and blue eyes, that was half a dozen inches taller than his swarthy little comrades on the French side of the stream, and being asked by the Colonel, saluted him, and said that he belonged to the Royal Cravats.

From his way of saying 'Royal Cravat,' Esmond at once knew that the fellow's tongue had first wagged on the banks of the Liffey, and not the Loire; and the poor soldier – a deserter probably – did not like to venture very deep into French conversation, lest his unlucky brogue should peep out. He chose to restrict himself to such few expressions in the French language as he thought he had mastered easily; and his attempt at disguise was infinitely amusing. Mr Esmond whistled Lillibullero, at which Teague's[10] eyes began to twinkle, and then flung him a dollar, when the poor boy broke out with a 'God bless – that is, Dieu bénisse votre honor,' that would infallibly have sent him to the Provost-Marshal had he been on our side of the river.

Whilst this parley was going on, three officers on horseback, on the French side, appeared at some little distance, and stopped as if eyeing us, when one of them left the other two, and rode close up to us who were by the stream. 'Look, look!' says the Royal Cravat, with great agitation, 'pas lui, that's he; not him, l'autre,' and pointed to the distant officer on a chestnut horse, with a cuirass shining in the sun, and over it a broad blue ribbon.

'Please to take Mr Hamilton's services to my Lord Marlborough – my Lord Duke,' says the gentleman in English; and, looking to see that the party were not hostilely disposed, he added, with a smile, 'There's a friend of yours, gentlemen, yonder; he bids me to say that he saw some of your faces on the 11th of September last year.'[11]

As the gentleman spoke, the other two officers rode up, and came quite close. We knew at once who it was. It was the King, then two-and-twenty years old, tall and slim, with deep brown eyes, that looked melancholy, though his lips wore a smile. We took off our hats and saluted him. No man, sure, could see for the first time, without emotion, the youthful inheritor of so much fame and misfortune. It seemed to Mr Esmond that the Prince was not unlike young Castlewood, whose age and figure he resembled. The Chevalier de St George acknowledged the salute, and looked at us hard. Even the idlers on our side of the river set up a hurrah. As for the Royal Cravat, he ran to the Prince's stirrup, knelt down and kissed his boot, and bawled and looked a hundred ejaculations and blessings. The Prince bade the aide-de-camp give him a piece of money; and when the party saluting us had ridden away, Cravat spat upon the piece of gold by way of benediction, and swaggered away, pouching his coin and twirling his honest carroty moustache.

The officer in whose company Esmond was, the same little captain of Handyside's regiment, Mr Sterne,[12] who had proposed the garden at Lille, when my Lord Mohun and Esmond had their affair, was an Irishman too, and as brave a little soul as ever wore a sword. 'Bedad,' says Roger Sterne, 'that long fellow spoke French so beautiful that I shouldn't have known he wasn't a foreigner, till he broke out with his hulla-ballooing, and only an Irish calf can bellow like that.' – And Roger made another remark in his wild way, in which there was sense as well as absurdity – 'If that young gentleman,' says he, 'would but ride to our camp instead of Villars's, toss up his hat and say, "Here am I, the King, who'll follow me?" by the Lord, Esmond, the whole army would rise and carry him home again, and beat Villars, and take Paris by the way.'

The news of the Prince's visit was all through the camp quickly, and scores of ours went down in hopes to see him. Major Hamilton, whom we had talked with, sent back by a trumpet several silver pieces for officers with us. Mr Esmond received one of these; and that medal, and a recompense not uncommon amongst princes, were the only rewards he ever had from a royal person, whom he endeavoured not very long after to serve.

Esmond quitted the army almost immediately after this, following his General home; and, indeed, being advised to travel in the fine weather and attempt to take no further part in the campaign. But he heard from the army, that of the many who crowded to see the Chevalier de St George, Frank Castlewood had made himself most conspicuous: my Lord Viscount riding across the little stream bareheaded to where the Prince was, and dismounting and kneeling before him to do him homage. Some said that the Prince had actually knighted him, but my lord denied that statement, though he acknowledged the rest of the story, and said: – 'From having been out of favour with Corporal John,' as he called the Duke, 'before, his Grace warned him not to commit those follies, and smiled on him cordially ever after.'

'And he was so kind to me,' Frank writ,[13] 'that I thought I would put in a good word for Master Harry, but when I mentioned your name he looked as black as thunder, and said he had never heard of you.'

## Chapter 2

### I GO HOME, AND HARP ON THE OLD STRING

AFTER quitting Mons and the army, and as he was waiting for a packet at Ostend, Esmond had a letter from his young kinsman Castlewood at Bruxelles, conveying intelligence whereof Frank besought him to be the bearer to London, and which caused Colonel Esmond no small anxiety.

The young scapegrace, being one-and-twenty years old, and being anxious to sow his 'wild otes,' as he wrote, had married Mademoiselle de Wertheim, daughter of Count de Wertheim, Chamberlain to the Emperor, and having a post in the household of the Governor of the Netherlands. 'P.S.,' – the young gentleman wrote: 'Clotilda is *older than me*, which perhaps may be objected to her: but I am so *old a raik* that the age makes no difference, and I am *determined* to reform. We were married at St Gudule, by Father Holt. She is heart and soul for the *good cause*. And here the cry is *Vif-le-Roy*, which my mother will *join in*, and Trix *too*. Break this news to 'em gently: and tell Mr Finch, my agent, to press the people for their rents, and send me the *ryno*[1] anyhow. Clotilda sings, and plays on the spinet *beautifully*. She is a fair beauty. And if it's as on, you shall stand *Godfather*. I'm going to leave the army, having had *enuf of soldering*; and my Lord Duke *recommends* me. I shall pass the winter here: and stop at least until Clo's lying-in. I call her *old Clo*, but nobody else shall. She is the cleverest woman in all Bruxelles: understanding painting, music, poetry, and perfect at *cookery and puddens*. I borded with the Count, that's how I came to know her. There are four Counts her brothers. One an Abbey – three with the Prince's army. They have a lawsuit for *an immense fortune*: but are now in *a pore way*. Break this to mother, who'll take anything from *you*. And write, and bid Finch write *amediately*. Hostel de l'Aigle Noire, Bruxelles, Flanders.'

So Frank had married a Roman Catholic lady, and an heir

was expected, and Mr Esmond was to carry this intelligence to his mistress at London. 'Twas a difficult embassy; and the Colonel felt not a little tremor as he neared the capital.

He reached his inn late, and sent a messenger to Kensington to announce his arrival and visit the next morning. The messenger brought back news that the Court was at Windsor, and the fair Beatrix absent and engaged in her duties there. Only Esmond's mistress remained in her house at Kensington. She appeared in Court but once in the year; Beatrix was quite the mistress and ruler of the little mansion, inviting the company thither, and engaging in every conceivable frolic of town pleasure. Whilst her mother, acting as the young lady's protectress and elder sister, pursued her own path, which was quite modest and secluded.

As soon as ever Esmond was dressed (and he had been awake long before the town), he took a coach for Kensington, and reached it so early that he met his dear mistress coming home from morning prayers. She carried her prayer-book, never allowing a footman to bear it, as everybody else did: and it was by this simple sign Esmond knew what her occupation had been. He called to the coachman to stop, and jumped out as she looked towards him. She wore her hood as usual, and she turned quite pale when she saw him. To feel that kind little hand near to his heart seemed to give him strength. They soon were at the door of her ladyship's house – and within it.

With a sweet sad smile she took his hand and kissed it.

'How ill you have been: how weak you look, my dear Henry,' she said.

'Tis certain the Colonel did look like a ghost, except that ghosts do not look very happy, 'tis said. Esmond always felt so on returning to her after absence, indeed whenever he looked in her sweet kind face.

'I am come back to be nursed by my family,' says he. 'If Frank had not taken care of me after my wound, very likely I should have gone altogether.'

'Poor Frank, good Frank!' says his mother. 'You'll always be kind to him, my lord,' she went on. 'The poor child never knew he was doing you a wrong.'

'My lord!' cries out Colonel Esmond. 'What do you mean, dear lady?'

'I am no lady,' says she; 'I am Rachel Esmond, Francis Esmond's widow, my lord. I cannot bear that title. Would we never had taken it from him who has it now. But we did all in our power, Henry: we did all in our power; and my lord and I – that is——'

'Who told you this tale, dearest lady?' asked the Colonel.

'Have you not had the letter I writ you? I writ to you at Mons directly I heard it,' says Lady Esmond.

'And from whom?' again asked Colonel Esmond – and his mistress then told him that on her death-bed the Dowager Countess, sending for her, had presented her with this dismal secret as a legacy. ' 'Twas very malicious of the Dowager,' Lady Esmond said, 'to have had it so long, and to have kept the truth from me. "Cousin Rachel," she said,' and Esmond's mistress could not forbear smiling as she told the story, ' "Cousin Rachel," cries the Dowager, "I have sent for you, as the doctors say I may go off any day in this dysentery; and to ease my conscience of a great load that has been on it. You always have been a poor creature and unfit for great honour, and what I have to say won't, therefore, affect you so much. You must know, Cousin Rachel, that I have left my house, plate, and furniture, three thousand pounds in money, and my diamonds that my late revered Saint and Sovereign, King James, presented me with, to my Lord Viscount Castlewood."

' "To my Frank?" says Lady Castlewood. "I was in hopes——"

' "To Viscount Castlewood, my dear, Viscount Castlewood, and Baron Esmond of Shandon in the kingdom of Ireland, Earl and Marquis of Esmond under patent of his Majesty King James the Second, conferred upon my husband the late Marquis – for I am Marchioness of Esmond before God and man."

' "And have you left poor Harry nothing, dear Marchioness?" asks Lady Castlewood' (she hath told me the story completely since with her quiet arch way; the most charming any woman ever had: and I set down the narrative here a

length so as to have done with it). ' "And have you left poor
Harry nothing," ' asks my dear lady: 'for you know, Henry,'
she says with her sweet smile, 'I used always to pity Esau – and
I think I am on his side – though papa tried very hard to convince me the other way.'

' "Poor Harry!" says the old lady. "So you want something
left to poor Harry: he, he! (Reach me the drops, cousin).
Well then my dear, since you want poor Harry to have a fortune,
you must understand that ever since the year 1691, a week
after the battle of the Boyne, where the Prince of Orange
defeated his royal sovereign and father, for which crime he is
now suffering in flames (ugh, ugh), Francis Esmond hath been
Marquis of Esmond and Earl of Castlewood in the United
Kingdom, and Baron and Viscount Castlewood of Shandon in
Ireland, and a Baronet – and his eldest son will be – by courtesy,
styled Earl of Castlewood – he! he! What do think of that, my
dear?"

' "Gracious mercy! how long have you known this?" ' cries
the other lady (thinking perhaps that the old Marchioness was
wandering in her wits).

' "My husband, before he was converted, was a wicked
wretch," the sick sinner continued. "When he was in the Low
Countries he seduced a weaver's daughter; and added to his
wickedness by marrying her. And then he came to this country
and married me – a poor girl – a poor innocent young thing – I
say," though she was past forty, you know, Harry, when she
married: and as for being innocent – "Well," she went on, "I
knew nothing of my lord's wickedness for three years after our
marriage, and after the burial of our poor little boy I had it
done over again, my dear, I had myself married by Father Holt
in Castlewood chapel, as soon as ever I heard the creature was
dead – and having a great illness then, arising from another sad
disappointment I had, the priest came and told me that my
lord had a son before our marriage, and that the child was at
nurse in England; and I consented to let the brat be brought
home, and a queer little melancholy child it was when it came.

' "Our intention was to make a priest of him: and he was
bred for this, until you perverted him from it, you wicked

woman. And I had again hopes of giving an heir to my lord, when he was called away upon the King's business, and died fighting gloriously at the Boyne water.

' "Should I be disappointed – I owed your husband no love, my dear, for he had jilted me in the most scandalous way; and I thought there would be time to declare the little weaver's son for the true heir. But I was carried off to prison, where your husband was so kind to me – urging all his friends to obtain my release, and using all his credit in my favour – that I relented towards him, especially as my director counselled me to be silent; and that it was for the good of the King's service that the title of our family should continue with your husband the late Viscount, whereby his fidelity would be always secured to the King. And a proof of this, is that a year before your husband's death, when he thought of taking a place under the Prince of Orange, Mr Holt went to him, and told him what the state of the matter was, and obliged him to raise a large sum for his Majesty; and engaged him in the true cause so heartily, that we were sure of his support on any day when it should be considered advisable to attack the usurper. Then his sudden death came; and there was a thought of declaring the truth. But 'twas determined to be best for the King's service to let the title still go with the younger branch; and there's no sacrifice a Castlewood wouldn't make for that cause, my dear.

' "As for Colonel Esmond, he knew the truth already." (and then, Harry,' my mistress said, 'she told me of what had happened at my dear husband's deathbed). "He doth not intend to take the title, though it belongs to him. But it eases my conscience that you should know the truth, my dear. And your son is lawfully Viscount Castlewood so long as his cousin doth not claim the rank." '

This was the substance of the Dowager's revelation. Dean Atterbury had knowledge of it, Lady Castlewood said, and Esmond very well knows how: that divine being the clergyman for whom the late lord had sent on his death-bed: and when Lady Castlewood would instantly have written to her son, and conveyed the truth to him, the Dean's advice was that a letter should be writ to Colonel Esmond rather; that the matter should be submitted to his decision, by which alone the rest of the family were bound to abide.

'And can my dearest lady doubt what that will be?' says the Colonel.

'It rests with you, Harry, as the head of our house.'

'It was settled twelve year since, by my dear lord's bed-side,' says Colonel Esmond. 'The children must know nothing of this. Frank and his heirs after him must bear our name.' 'Tis his rightfully; I have not even a proof of that marriage of my father and mother, though my poor lord, on his death-bed, told me that Father Holt had brought such a proof to Castle-wood. I would not seek it when I was abroad. I went and looked at my poor mother's grave in her convent. What matter to her now? No court of law on earth, upon my mere word, would deprive my Lord Viscount and set me up. I am the head of the house, dear lady; but Frank is Viscount of Castlewood still. And rather than disturb him, I would turn monk, or disappear in America.'

As he spoke so to his dearest mistress, for whom he would have been willing to give up his life, or to make any sacrifice any day, the fond creature flung herself down on her knees before him, and kissed both his hands in an outbreak of passion-ate love and gratitude, such as could not but melt his heart, and make him feel very proud and thankful that God had given him the power to show his love for her, and to prove it by some little sacrifice on his own part. To be able to bestow benefits or happiness on those one loves is sure the greatest blessing conferred upon a man – and what wealth or name, or gratifica-tion of ambition or vanity, could compare with the pleasure Esmond now had of being able to confer some kindness upon his best and dearest friends?

'Dearest saint,' says he – 'purest soul, that has had so much to suffer, that has blest the poor lonely orphan with such a treasure of love. 'Tis for me to kneel, not for you: 'tis for me to be thankful that I can make you happy. Hath my life any other aim? Blessed be God that I can serve you! What pleasure, think you, could all the world give me compared to that?'

'Don't raise me,' she said, in a wild way, to Esmond, who

would have lifted her. 'Let me kneel – let me kneel, and – and – worship you.'

Before such a partial judge, as Esmond's dear mistress owned herself to be, any cause which he might plead was sure to be given in his favour; and accordingly he found little difficulty in reconciling her to the news whereof he was bearer, of her son's marriage to a foreign lady, Papist though she was. Lady Castlewood never could be brought to think so ill of that religion as other people in England thought of it: she held that ours was undoubtedly a branch of the Church Catholic, but that the Roman was one of the main stems on which, no doubt, many errors had been grafted (she was, for a woman, extraordinarily well versed in this controversy, having acted, as a girl, as secretary to her father, the late Dean, and written many of his sermons, under his dictation); and if Frank had chosen to marry a lady of the Church of south Europe, as she would call the Roman communion, that was no need why she should not welcome her as a daughter-in-law: and accordingly she writ to her new daughter a very pretty, touching letter (as Esmond thought, who had cognisance of it before it went), in which the only hint of reproof was a gentle remonstrance that her son had not written to herself, to ask a fond mother's blessing for that step which he was about taking. 'Castlewood knew very well,' so she wrote to her son, 'that she never denied him anything in her power to give, much less would she think of opposing a marriage that was to make his happiness, as she trusted, and keep him out of wild courses, which had alarmed her a good deal: and she besought him to come quickly to England, to settle down in his family house of Castlewood ("It is his family house," says she, to Colonel Esmond, "though only his own house by your forbearance"), and to receive the accompt of her stewardship during his ten years' minority.' By care and frugality, she had got the estate into a better condition than ever it had been since the Parliamentary wars; and my lord was now master of a pretty, small income, not encumbered of debts, as it had been, during his father's ruinous time. 'But in saving my son's fortune,' says she, 'I fear I have lost a great

part of my hold on him.' And, indeed, this was the case; her
ladyship's daughter complaining that their mother did all for
Frank, and nothing for her; and Frank himself being dissatisfied at the narrow, simple way of his mother's living at
Walcote, where he had been brought up more like a poor
parson's son, than a young nobleman that was to make a figure
in the world. 'Twas this mistake in his early training, very
likely, that set him so eager upon pleasure when he had it in
his power; nor is he the first lad that has been spoiled by the
over-careful fondness of women. No training is so useful for
children, great or small, as the company of their betters in rank
or natural parts; in whose society they lose the overweening
sense of their own importance, which stay-at-home people very
commonly learn.

But, as a prodigal that's sending in a schedule of his debts
to his friends, never puts all down, and, you may be sure, the
rogue keeps back some immense swingeing bill, that he doesn't
dare to own; so the poor Frank had a very heavy piece of news
to break to his mother, and which he hadn't the courage to
introduce into his first confession. Some misgivings Esmond
might have, upon receiving Frank's letter, and knowing into
what hands the boy had fallen; but whatever these misgivings
were, he kept them to himself, not caring to trouble his mistress
with any fears that might be groundless.

However, the next mail which came from Bruxelles, after
Frank had received his mother's letters there, brought back a
joint composition from himself and his wife, who could spell
no better than her young scapegrace of a husband, full of
expressions of thanks, love, and duty to the Dowager Viscountess, as my poor lady now was styled; and along with this letter
(which was read in a family council, namely, the Viscountess,
Mistress Beatrix, and the writer of this memoir, and which was
pronounced to be vulgar by the maid of honour, and felt to be
so by the other two), there came a private letter for Colonel
Esmond from poor Frank, with another dismal commission for
the Colonel to execute, at his best opportunity; and this was to
announce that Frank had seen fit, 'by the exhortation of Mr
Holt, the influence of his Clotilda, and the blessing of Heaven

and the saints,' says my lord, demurely, 'to change his religion, and be received into the bosom of that Church of which his sovereign, many of his family, and the greater part of the civilised world, were members.' And his lordship added a postscript, of which Esmond knew the inspiring genius very well, for it had the genuine twang of the seminary, and was quite unlike poor Frank's ordinary style of writing and thinking; in which he reminded Colonel Esmond that he too was, by birth, of that Church; and that his mother and sister should have his lordship's prayers to the saints (an inestimable benefit, truly!) for their conversion.

If Esmond had wanted to keep this secret he could not; for a day or two after receiving this letter, a notice from Bruxelles appeared in the 'Post-Boy' and other prints, announcing that 'a young Irish lord, the Viscount C—stlew—d, just come to his majority, and who had served the last campaigns with great credit, as aide-de-camp to his Grace the Duke of Marlborough, had declared for the Popish religion at Bruxelles, and had walked in a procession barefoot, with a wax-taper in his hand.' The notorious Mr Holt, who had been employed as a Jacobite agent during the last reign, and many times pardoned by King William, had been, the 'Post Boy' said, the agent of this conversion.

The Lady Castlewood was as much cast down by this news as Miss Beatrix was indignant at it. 'So,' says she, 'Castlewood is no longer a home for us, mother. Frank's foreign wife will bring her confessor, and there will be frogs for dinner; and all Tusher's and my grandfather's sermons are flung away upon my brother. I used to tell you that you killed him with the catechism, and that he would turn wicked as soon as he broke from his mammy's leading-strings. O, mother, you would not believe that the young scapegrace was playing you tricks, and that sneak of a Tusher was not a fit guide for him. O, those parsons! I hate 'em all,' says Mistress Beatrix, clapping her hands together; 'yes, whether they wear cassocks and buckles, or beards and bare feet. There's a horrid Irish wretch who never misses a Sunday at Court,[2] and who pays me compliments there, the horrible man; and if you want to know what parsons are, you should see his behaviour, and hear him talk of his own cloth. They're all the same, whether they're bishops or bonzes, or Indian fakirs. They try to domineer, and they frighten us with kingdom come; and they wear a sanctified air in public, and expect us to go down on our knees and ask their blessing; and they intrigue, and they grasp, and they backbite, and they slander worse than the worst courtier or the wickedest old woman. I heard this Mr Swift sneering at my Lord Duke of Marlborough's courage the other day. He! that Teague from Dublin! because his Grace is not in favour, dares to say this of him; and he says this that it may get to her Majesty's ear, and to coax and wheedle Mrs Masham. They say the Elector of Hanover has a dozen of mistresses in his court at Herrenhausen, and if he comes to be king over us, I wager that the bishops and Mr Swift, that wants to be one, will coax and wheedle them. O, those priests and their grave airs! I'm sick of their square toes and their rustling cassocks. I should like to go to a country where there was not one, or turn Quaker, and get rid of 'em; and I would, only the dress is not becoming, and I've much too pretty a figure to hide it. Haven't I, cousin?' and here she glanced at her person and the looking-glass, which told her rightly that more beautiful shape and face never were seen.

'I made that onslaught on the priests,' says Miss Beatrix, afterwards, 'in order to divert my poor dear mother's anguish about Frank. Frank is as vain as a girl, cousin. Talk of us girls being vain, what are *we* to you? It was easy to see that the first woman who chose would make a fool of him, or the first robe – I count a priest and a women all the same. We are always caballing; we are not answerable for the fibs we tell; we are always cajoling and coaxing, or threatening; and we are always making mischief, Colonel Esmond – mark my word for that, who know the world, sir, and have to make my way in it. I see as well as possible how Frank's marriage hath been managed. The Count, our papa-in-law, is always away at the coffee-house. The Countess, our mother, is always in the kitchen looking after the dinner. The Countess, our sister, is at the spinet. When my lord comes to say he is going on the campaign, the lovely Clotilda bursts into tears and faints so; he catches her in his arms – no, sir, keep your distance, cousin, if you please – she cries on his shoulder, and he says, "O, my divine, my adored, my beloved Clotilda, are you sorry to part with me?" "O, my Francisco," says she, "oh, my lord?" and at this very instant mamma and a couple of young brothers, with moustachios and long rapiers, come in from the kitchen, where they have been eating bread and onions. Mark my word, you will have all this woman's relations at Castlewood three months after she has arrived there. The old Count and Countess, and the young counts and all the little countesses her sisters. Counts! every one of these wretches says he is a count. Guiscard,[3] that stabbed Mr Harvy, said he was a count; and I believe he was a barber. All Frenchmen are barbers – Fiddle-dee! don't contradict me – or else dancing-masters, or else priests'; and so she rattled on.

'Who was it taught *you* to dance, Cousin Beatrix?' says the colonel.

She laughed out the air of a minuet, and swept a low curtsey, coming up to the recover[4] with the prettiest little foot in the world pointed out. Her mother came in as she was in this attitude; my lady had been in her closet, having taken poor Frank's conversion in a very serious way; the madcap girl ran up to her mother, put her arms round her waist, kissed her, tried to make her dance, and said: 'Don't be silly, you kind little mamma, and cry about Frank turning Papist. What a figure he must be, with a white sheet and a candle walking in a procession barefoot!' And she kicked off her little slippers (the wonderfullest little shoes with wonderful tall red heels; Esmond pounced upon one as it fell close beside him), and she put on the drollest little *moue*, and marched up and down the room holding Esmond's cane by way of taper. Serious as her mood was, Lady Castlewood could not refrain from laughing; and as for Esmond, he looked on with that delight with which the sight of this fair creature always inspired him: never had he seen any woman so arch, so brilliant, and so beautiful.

Having finished her march, she put out her foot for her slipper. The Colonel knelt down: 'If you will be Pope, I will turn Papist,' says he; and her Holiness gave him gracious leave to kiss the little stockinged foot before he put the slipper on.

Mamma's feet began to pat on the floor during this operation, and Beatrix, whose bright eyes nothing escaped, saw that little mark of impatience. She ran up and embraced her mother, with her usual cry of, 'O, you silly little mamma: your feet are quite as pretty as mine,' says she: 'they are, cousin, though she hides 'em; but the shoemaker will tell you that he makes for both off the same last.'

'You are taller than I am, dearest,' says her mother, blushing over her whole sweet face – 'and – and it is your hand, my dear, and not your foot he wants you to give him,' and she said it with a hysteric laugh, that had more of tears than laughter in it; laying her head on her daughter's fair shoulder, and hiding it there. They made a very pretty picture together, and looked like a pair of sisters – the sweet simple matron seeming younger than her years, and her daughter, if not older, yet somehow, from a commanding manner and grace which she possessed above most women, her mother's superior and protectress.

'But, O,' cries my mistress, recovering herself after this scene, and returning to her usual sad tone, ' 'tis a shame that we should laugh and be making merry on a day when we ought to be down on our knees and asking pardon.'

'Asking pardon for what?' says saucy Mrs Beatrix – 'because Frank takes it into his head to fast on Fridays, and worship images? You know if you had been born a Papist, mother, a Papist you would have remained to the end of your days. 'Tis the religion of the King and some of the best quality. For my part, I'm no enemy to it, and think Queen Bess was not a penny better than Queen Mary.'

'Hush, Beatrix! Do not jest with sacred things, and remember of what parentage you come,' cries my lady. Beatrix was ordering her ribbons, and adjusting her tucker,[5] and performing a dozen provoking pretty ceremonies, before the glass. The girl was no hypocrite at least. She never at that time could be brought to think but of the world and her beauty; and seemed to have no more sense of devotion than some people have of music, that cannot distinguish one air from another. Esmond saw this fault in her, as he saw many others – a bad wife would Beatrix Esmond

make, he thought, for any man under the degree of a prince.
She was born to shine in great assemblies, and to adorn palaces,
and to command everywhere – to conduct an intrigue of politics,
or to glitter in a queen's train. But to sit at a homely table, and
mend the stockings of a poor man's children! that was no fitting
duty for her, or at least one that she wouldn't have broke her
heart in trying to do. She was a princess, though she had scarce
a shilling to her fortune; and one of her subjects – the most
abject and devoted wretch, sure, that ever drivelled at a woman's
knees – was this unlucky gentleman; who bound his good
sense, and reason, and independence, hand and foot; and
submitted them to her.

And who does not know how ruthlessly women will tyranise
when they are let to domineer? and who does not know how
useless advice is? I could give good counsel to my descendants,
but I know they'll follow their own way, for all their grandfather's sermon. A man gets his own experience about women,
and will take nobody's hearsay; nor, indeed, is the young fellow
worth a fig that would. 'Tis I that am in love with my mistress,
not my old grandmother that counsels me; 'tis I that have fixed
the value of the thing I would have, and know the price I would
pay for it. It may be worthless to you, but 'tis all my life to me.
Had Esmond possessed the Great Mogul's crown and all his
diamonds, or all the Duke of Marlborough's money, or all the
ingots sunk at Vigo, he would have given them all for this
woman. A fool he was, if you will; but so is a sovereign a fool,
that will give half a principality for a little crystal as big as a
pigeon's egg, and called a diamond: so is a wealthy nobleman
a fool, that will face danger or death, and spend half his life,
and all his tranquillity, caballing for a blue riband: so is a Dutch
merchant a fool, that hath been known to pay ten thousand
crowns for a tulip.[6] There's some particular prize we all of us
value, and that every man of spirit will venture his life for.
With this, it may be to achieve a great reputation for learning;
with that, to be a man of fashion, and the admiration of the
town; with another, to consummate a great work of art or poetry,
and go to immortality that way; and with another, for a certain
time of his life, the sole object and aim is a woman.

Whilst Esmond was under the domination of this passion, he remembers many a talk he had with his intimates, who used to rally Our Knight of the Rueful Countenance at his devotion, whereof he made no disguise, to Beatrix; and it was with replies such as the above he met his friends' satire. 'Granted, I am a fool,' says he, 'and no better than you; but you are not better than I. You have your folly you labour for; give me the charity of mine. What flatteries do you, Mr St John, stoop to whisper in the ears of a queen's favourite? What nights of labour doth not the laziest man in the world endure, foregoing his bottle, and his boon companions, foregoing Lais, in whose lap he would like to be yawning, that he may prepare a speech full of lies, to cajole three hundred stupid country-gentlemen in the House of Commons, and get the hiccuping cheers of the October Club!⁷ What days will you spend in your jolting chariot!' (Mr Esmond often rode to Windsor, and especially, of later days, with the Secretary). 'What hours will you pass on your gouty feet – and how humbly will you kneel down to present a despatch – you, the proudest man in the world, that has not knelt to God since you were a boy, and in that posture whisper, flatter, adore almost, a stupid woman, that's often boozy with two much meat and drink, when Mr Secretary goes for his audience! If my pursuit is vanity, sure yours is too.' And then the Secretary would fly out in such a rich flow of eloquence, as this pen cannot pretend to recall; advocating his scheme of ambition, showing the great good he would do for his country when he was the undisputed chief of it; backing his opinion with a score of pat sentences from Greek and Roman authorities (of which kind of learning he made rather an ostentatious display), and scornfully vaunting the very arts and meannesses by which fools were to be made to follow him, opponents to be bribed or silenced, doubters converted, and enemies overawed.

'I am Diogenes,'⁸ says Esmond, laughing, 'that is taken up for a ride in Alexander's⁹ chariot. I have no desire to vanquish Darius or to tame Bucephalus. I do not want what you want, a great name or a high place: to have them would bring me no pleasure. But my moderation is taste, not virtue; and I know that what I do want, is as vain as that which you long after. Do not grudge me my vanity, if I allow yours; or rather, let us laugh at both indifferently, and at ourselves, and at each other.'

'If your charmer holds out,' says St John, 'at this rate, she may keep you twenty years besieging her, and surrender by the time you are seventy, and she is old enough to be a grandmother. I do not say the pursuit of a particular woman is not as pleasant a pastime as any other kind of hunting,' he added; 'only, for my part, I find the game won't run long enough. They knock under too soon – that's the fault I find with 'em.'

'The game which you pursue is in the habit of being caught, and used to being pulled down,' says Mr Esmond.

'But Dulcinea del Toboso is peerless, eh?' says the other. 'Well, honest Harry, go and attack windmills – perhaps thou art not more mad than other people,' St John added, with a sigh.

## Chapter 3

### A PAPER OUT OF THE SPECTATOR

DOTH any young gentleman of my progeny, who may read his old grandfather's papers, chance to be presently suffering under the passion of Love? There is a humiliating cure, but one that is easy and almost specific for the malady – which is, to try an alibi.[1] Esmond went away from his mistress and was cured a half dozen times; he came back to her side, and instantly fell ill again of the fever. He vowed that he could leave her and think no more of her, and so he could pretty well, at least, succeed in quelling that rage and longing he had whenever he was with her; but as soon as he returned he was as bad as ever again. Truly a ludicrous and pitiable object, at least exhausting everybody's pity but his dearest mistress's, Lady Castlewood's, in whose tender breast he reposed all his dreary confessions, and who never tired of hearing him and pleading for him.

Sometimes Esmond would think there was hope. Then

again he would be plagued with despair, at some impertinence or coquetry of his mistress. For days they would be like brother and sister, or the dearest friends – she, simple, fond, and charming – he, happy beyond measure at her good behaviour. But this would all vanish on a sudden. Either he would be too pressing, and hint his love, when she would rebuff him instantly, and give his vanity a box on the ear: or he would be jealous, and with perfect good reason, of some new admirer that had sprung up, or some rich young gentleman newly arrived in the town, that this incorrigible flirt would set her nets and baits to draw in. If Esmond remonstrated, the little rebel would say – 'Who are you? I shall go my own way, sirrah, and that way is towards a husband, and I don't want *you* on the way. I am for your betters, Colonel, for your betters: do you hear that? You might do if you had an estate and were younger; only eight years older than I, you say! pish, you are a hundred years older. You are an old, old Graveairs, and I should make you miserable, that would be the only comfort I should have in marrying you. But you have not money enough to keep a cat decently after you have paid your man his wages, and your landlady her bill. Do you think I'm going to live in a lodging, and turn the mutton at a string whilst your honour nurses the baby? Fiddlestick, and why did you not get this nonsense knocked out of your head when you were in the wars? You are come back more dismal and dreary than ever. You and mamma are fit for each other. You might be Darby and Joan, and play cribbage to the end of your lives.'

'At least you own to your worldliness, my poor Trix,' says her mother.

'Worldliness – O my pretty lady! Do you think that I am a child in the nursery, and to be frightened by Bogey? Worldliness, to be sure; and pray, madam, where is the harm of wishing to be comfortable? When you are gone, you dearest old woman, or when I am tired of you and have run away from you, where shall I go? Shall I go and be head nurse to my Popish sister-in-law, take the children their physic, and whip 'em, and put 'em to bed when they are naughty? Shall I be Castlewood's upper servant, and perhaps marry Tom Tusher? *Merci*, I have been

long enough Frank's humble servant. Why am I not a man? I
have ten times his brains, and had I worn the – well, don't let
your ladyship be frightened – had I worn a sword and periwig
instead of this mantle and commode, to which nature has
condemned me – (though 'tis a pretty stuff, too – cousin Esmond! you will go to the Exchange[2] tomorrow, and get the exact
counterpart of this riband, sir, do you hear) – I would have
made our name talked about. So would Graveairs here have
made something out of our name if he had represented it. My
Lord Graveairs would have done very well. Yes, you have a
very pretty way, and would have made a very decent, grave
speaker'; and here she began to imitate Esmond's way of
carrying himself, and speaking to his face, and so ludicrously
that his mistress burst out a-laughing, and even he himself
could see there was some likeness in the fantastical malicious
caricature.

'Yes,' says she, 'I solemnly vow, own, and confess, that I
want a good husband. Where's the harm of one? My face is
my fortune. Who'll come? – buy, buy, buy! I cannot toil,
neither can I spin, but I can play twenty-three games on the
cards. I can dance the last dance, I can hunt the stag, and I
think I could shoot flying.[3] I can talk as wicked as any woman
of my years, and know enough stories to amuse a sulky husband
for at least one thousand and one nights. I have a pretty taste
for dress, diamonds, gambling, and old china. I love sugar
plums, Malines lace (that you brought me, cousin, is very
pretty), the opera, and everything that is useless and costly. I
have got a monkey and a little black boy – Pompey, sir, go and
give a dish of chocolate to Colonel Graveairs – and a parrot
and a spaniel, and I must have a husband. Cupid, you
hear?'

'Iss, Missis,' says Pompey, a little grinning negro Lord
Peterborow gave her, with a bird of paradise in his turbant,
and a collar with his mistress's name on it.

'Iss, Missis!' says Beatrix, imitating the child. 'And if
husband not come, Pompey must go fetch one.'

And Pompey went away grinning with his chocolate tray, as
Miss Beatrix ran up to her mother and ended her sally of

mischief in her common way, with a kiss – no wonder that upon paying such a penalty her fond judge pardoned her.

When Mr Esmond came home, his health was still shattered; and he took a lodging near to his mistress's, at Kensington, glad enough to be served by them, and to see them day after day. He was enabled to see a little company – and of the sort he liked best. Mr Steele and Mr Addison both did him the honour to visit him: and drank many a flask of good claret at his lodging, whilst their entertainer, through his wound, was kept to diet drink and gruel. These gentlemen were Whigs, and great admirers of my Lord Duke of Marlborough; and Esmond was entirely of the other party. But their different views of politics did not prevent the gentlemen from agreeing in private, nor from allowing, on one evening when Esmond's kind old patron, Lieutenant-General Webb, with a stick and a crutch, hobbled up to the Colonel's lodging (which was prettily situate at Knightsbridge, between London and Kensington, and looking over the Gardens), that the Lieutenant-General was a noble and gallant soldier – and even that he had been hardly used in the Wynendael affair. He took his revenge in talk, that must be confessed; and if Mr Addison had had a mind to write a poem about Wynendael, he might have heard from the commander's own lips the story a hundred times over.

Mr Esmond, forced to be quiet, betook himself to literature for a relaxation, and composed his comedy, whereof the prompter's copy lieth in my walnut escrutoire, sealed up and docketed 'The Faithful Fool, a Comedy, as it was performed by her Majesty's Servants.' 'Twas a very sentimental piece; and Mr Steele, who had more of that kind of sentiment than Mr Addison, admired it, whilst the other rather sneered at the performance; though he owned that, here and there, it contained some pretty strokes. He was bringing out his own play of 'Cato' at the time, the blaze of which quite extinguished Esmond's farthing candle: and his name was never put to the piece, which was printed as by a Person of Quality. Only nine copes were sold, though Mr Dennis, the great critic,[4] praised it, and said 'twas a work of great merit; and Colonel Esmond had the whole impression burned one day in a rage, by Jack Lockwood, his man.

All this comedy was full of bitter satiric strokes against a certain young lady. The plot of the piece was quite a new one. A young woman was represented with a great number of suitors, selecting a pert fribble of a peer, in place of the hero; (but ill-acted, I think, by Mr Wilks,[5] the Faithful Fool), who persisted in admiring her. In the fifth act, Teraminta was made to discover the merits of Eugenio[6] (the F. F.), and to feel a partiality for him too late; for he announced that he had bestowed his hand and estate upon Rosaria, a country lass, endowed with every virtue. But it must be owned that the audience yawned through the play; and that it perished on the third night, with only half-a-dozen persons to behold its agonies. Esmond and his two mistresses came to the first night, and Miss Beatrix fell asleep; whilst her mother, who had not been to a play since King James the Second's time, thought the piece, though not brilliant, had a very pretty moral.

Mr Esmond dabbled in letters, and wrote a deal of prose and verse at this time of leisure. When displeased with the conduct of Miss Beatrix, he would compose a satire, in which he relieved his mind. When smarting under the faithlessness of women, he dashed off a copy of verses, in which he held the whole sex up to scorn. One day, in one of these moods, he made a little joke, in which (swearing him to secrecy) he got his friend Dick Steele to help him; and, composing a paper, he had it printed exactly like Steele's paper, and by his printer, and laid on his mistress's breakfast-table the following:—

'SPECTATOR[7]

'No. 341                                        'Tuesday, April 1, 1712

Mutato nomine de te Fabula narratur. – HORACE
Thyself the moral of the Fable see. – CREECH

'Jocasta is known as a woman of learning and fashion, and as one of the most amiable persons of this Court and country. She is at home two mornings of the week, and all the wits and a few of the beauties of London flock to her assemblies. When she goes abroad to Tunbridge or the Bath,[8] a retinue of adorers rides the journey with her; and, besides the London beaux, she has a crowd of admirers at the Wells, the polite amongst the natives of Sussex and Somerset pressing round her tea-tables, and being anxious for a nod from her chair. Jocasta's acquaintance is thus very numerous. Indeed, 'tis one smart writer's work to keep her visiting-book — a strong footman is engaged to carry it; and it would require a much stronger head, even than Jocasta's own, to remember the names of all her dear friends.

'Either at Epsom Wells or at Tunbridge (for of this important matter Jocasta cannot be certain) it was her ladyship's fortune to become acquainted with a young gentleman, whose conversation was so sprightly, and manners amiable, that she invited the agreeable young spark to visit her if ever he came to London, where her house in Spring Garden should be open to him. Charming as he was, and without any manner of doubt a pretty fellow, Jocasta hath such a regiment of the like continually marching round her standard that 'tis no wonder her attention is distracted amongst them. And so, though this gentleman made a considerable impression upon her, and touched her heart for at least three-and-twenty minutes, it must be owned that she has forgotten his name. He is a dark man, and may be eight-and-twenty years old. His dress is sober, though of rich materials. He has a mole on his forehead over his left eye; has a blue ribbon to his cane and sword, and wears his own hair.

'Jocasta was much flattered by beholding her admirer (for that everybody admires who sees her is a point which she never can for a moment doubt) in the next pew to her at Saint James's Church last Sunday; and the manner in which he appeared to go to sleep during the sermon – though from under his fringed eyelids it was evident he was casting glances of respectful rapture towards Jocasta – deeply moved and interested her. On coming out of church, he found his way to her chair, and made her an elegant bow as she stepped into it. She saw him at Court afterwards, where he carried himself with a most distinguished air, though none of her acquaintances knew his name; and the next night he was at the play, where her ladyship was pleased to acknowledge him from the side-box.

'During the whole of the comedy she racked her brains so to remember his name, that she did not hear a word of the piece: and having the happiness to meet him once more in the lobby of the playhouse, she went up to him in a flutter, and bade him remember that she kept two nights in the week, and that she longed to see him at Spring Garden.

'He appeared on Tuesday, in a rich suit, showing a very fine taste both in the tailor and wearer; and though a knot of us were gathered round the charming Jocasta, fellows who pretended to know every face upon the town, not one could tell the gentleman's name in reply to Jocasta's eager inquiries, flung to the right and left of her as he advanced up the room with a bow that would become a duke.

'Jocasta acknowledged this salute with one of those smiles and curtseys of which that lady hath the secret. She curtseys with a languishing air, as if to say, "You are come at last. I have been pining for you": and then she finishes her victim with a killing look, which declares: "O Philander! I have no eyes but for you." Camilla [9] hath as good a curtsey perhaps, and Thalestris [10] much such another look; but the glance and the curtsey together belong to Jocasta of all the English beauties alone.

' "Welcome to London, sir," says she. "One can see you are from the country by your looks." She would have said "Epsom," or "Tunbridge," had she remembered rightly at which place she had met the stranger; but, alas! she had forgotten.

'The gentleman said, "he had been in town but three days; and one of his reasons for coming hither was to have the honour of paying his court to Jocasta."

'She said, "the waters had agreed with her but indifferently."

' "The waters were for the sick," the gentleman said: "the young and beautiful come but to make them sparkle. And, as the clergyman read the service on Sunday," he added, "your ladyship reminded me of the angel that visited the pool." [11] A murmur of approbation saluted this sally. Manilio, [12] who is a wit when he is not at cards, was in such a rage that he revoked when he heard it.

'Jocasta was an angel visiting the waters; but at which of the Bethesdas? She was puzzled more and more; and, as her way always is, looked the more innocent and simple, the more artful her intentions were.

' "We were discoursing," says she, "about spelling of names and words when you came. Why should we say goold and write gold, and call china chayny, and Cavendish Candish, and Cholmondeley Chumley? If we call Pulteney Poltney, why shouldn't we call poultry pultry – and——"

' "Such an enchantress as your ladyship," says he, "is mistress of all sorts of spells." But this was Doctor Swift's pun, and we all knew it.[13]

' "And – and how do you spell your name?" says she, coming to the point, at length; for this sprightly conversation had lasted much longer than is here set down, and been carried on through at least three dishes of tea.

' "O, madam," says he, "*I spell my name with the y.*" And laying down his dish, my gentleman made another elegant bow, and was gone in a moment.

'Jocasta hath had no sleep since this mortification, and the stranger's disappearance. If baulked in anything, she is sure to lose her health and temper; and we, her servants, suffer, as usual, during the angry fits of our Queen. Can you help us, Mr Spectator, who know everything, to read this riddle for her, and set at rest all our minds? We find in her list, Mr Berty, Mr Smith, Mr Pike, Mr Tyler – who may be Mr Bertie, Mr Smyth, Mr Pyke, Mr Tiler, for what we know. She hath turned away the clerk of her visiting-book, a poor fellow with a great family of children. Read me this riddle, good Mr Shortface,[14] and oblige your admirer – ŒDIPUS.'

'*The Trumpet Coffee-house, Whitehall*

'MR SPECTATOR – I am a gentleman but little acquainted with the town, though I have had a university education, and passed some years serving my country abroad, where my name is better known than in the coffee-houses and St James's.

'Two years since my uncle died, leaving a pretty estate in the county of Kent; and being at Tunbridge Wells last summer, after my mourning was over, and on the look-out, if truth must be told, for some young lady who would share with me the solitude of my great Kentish house, and be kind to my tenantry (for whom a woman can do a great deal more good than the best-intentioned man can), I was greatly fascinated by a young lady of London, who was the toast of all the company at the Wells. Everyone knows Saccharissa's beauty; and I think, Mr Spectator, no one better than herself.

'My table-book informs me that I danced no less than seven-and-twenty sets with her at the Assembly. I treated her to the fiddles twice.[15] I was admitted on several days to her lodging, and received by her with a great deal of distinction, and, for a time, was entirely her slave. It was only when I found, from common talk of the company at the Wells, and from narrowly watching one, who I once thought of asking the most sacred question a man can put to a woman, that I became aware how unfit she was to be a country gentleman's wife; and that this fair creature was but a heartless worldly jilt, playing with affections that she never meant to return, and, indeed, incapable of returning them. 'Tis admiration such women want, not love that touches them; and I can conceive, in her old age, no more wretched creature than this lady will be, when her beauty hath deserted her, when her admirers have left her, and she hath neither friendship nor religion to console her.

'Business calling me to London, I went to St James's Church last Sunday, and there opposite me sat my beauty of the Wells. Her behaviour during the whole service was so pert, languishing, and absurd; she flirted her fan, and ogled and eyed me in a manner so indecent, that I was obliged to shut my eyes, so as actually not to see her, and whenever I opened them beheld hers (and very bright they are) still staring at me. I fell in with her afterwards at Court, and at the playhouse; and here nothing would satisfy her but she must elbow through the crowd and speak to me, and invite me to the assembly which she holds at her house, not very far from Ch—r—ng Cr—ss.

'Having made her a promise to attend, of course I kept my promise; and found the young widow in the midst of a half-dozen of card-tables, and a crowd of wits and admirers. I made the best bow I could, and advanced towards her; and saw by a peculiar puzzled look in her face, though she tried to hide her perplexity, that she had forgotten even my name.

'Her talk, artful as it was, convinced me that I had guessed aright. She turned the conversation most ridiculously upon the spelling of names and words; and I replied with as ridiculous, fulsome compliments as I could pay her: indeed, one in which I compared her to an angel visiting the sick wells, went a little too far, nor should I have employed it, but that the allusion came from the Second Lesson last Sunday, which we both had heard, and I was pressed to answer her.

'Then she came to the question, which I knew was awaiting me, me, and asked how I *spelt* my name? "Madam," says I, turning on my heel, "I spell it with the y". And so I left her, wondering at the light-heartedness of the townpeople, who forget and make friends so easily, and resolved to look elsewhere for a partner for your constant reader, CYMON WYLDOATS.

'You know my real name, Mr Spectator, in which there is no such a letter as *hupsilon*. But if the lady, whom I have called Saccharissa, wonders that I appear no more at the tea-tables, she is hereby respectfully informed the reason *y*.'

The above is a parable, whereof the writer will now expound the meaning. Jocasta was no other than Miss Esmond, Maid of Honour to her Majesty. She had told Mr Esmond this little story of having met a gentleman, somewhere, and forgetting his name, when the gentleman, with no such malicious intentions as those of 'Cymon' in the above fable, made the answer simply as above; and we all laughed to think how little Mistress Jocasta-Beatrix had profited by her artifice and precautions.

As for Cymon, he was intended to represent yours and her very humble servant, the writer of the apologue and of this story, which we had printed on a 'Spectator' paper at Mr Steele's office, exactly as those famous journals were printed, and which was laid on the table at breakfast in place of the real newspaper. Mistress Jocasta, who had plenty of wit, could not live without her 'Spectator' to her tea; and this sham 'Spectator' was intended to convey to the young woman that she herself was a flirt, and that Cymon was a gentleman of honour and resolution, seeing all her faults, and determined to break the chains once and for ever.

For though enough hath been said about this love-business already – enough, at least, to prove to the writer's heirs what a silly fond fool their old grandfather was, who would like them to consider him as a very wise old gentleman yet; not near all has been told concerning this matter, which, if it were allowed to take in Esmond's journal the space it occupied in his time, would weary his kinsmen and women of a hundred years' time beyond all endurance; and from such a diary of folly and drivelling, raptures and rage, as no man of ordinary vanity would like to leave behind him.

The truth is, that, whether she laughed at him or encouraged him; whether she smiled or was cold, and turned her smiles on another – worldly and ambitious as he knew her to be; hard and careless, as she seemed to grow with her Court life, and a hundred admirers that came to her and left her; Esmond, do what he would, never could get Beatrix out of his mind; thought of her constantly at home or away. If he read his name in a Gazette, or escaped the shot of a cannon-ball or a greater danger in the campaign, as has happened to him more than once, the instant thought after the honour achieved or the danger avoided, was 'What will *she* say of it? Will this distinction or the idea of this peril elate her or touch her, so as to be better inclined towards me?' He could no more help this passionate fidelity of temper than he could help the eyes he saw with – one or the other seemed a part of his nature; and knowing every one of her faults as well as the keenest of her detractors, and the folly of an attachment to such a woman, of which the fruition could never bring him happiness for above a week, there was yet a charm about this Circe from which the poor deluded gentleman could not free himself; and for a much longer period than Ulysses (another middle-aged officer, who had travelled much, and been in the foreign wars), Esmond felt himself enthralled and besotted by the wiles of this enchantress. Quit her! He could no more quit her, as the Cymon of this story was made to quit his false one, than he could lose his consciousness of yesterday. She had but to raise her finger, and he would come back from ever so far; she had but to say I have discarded such and such an adorer, and the poor infatuated wretch would be sure to come and *rôder*[16] about her mother's house, willing to be put on the ranks of suitors, though he knew he might be cast off the next week. If he were like Ulysses in his folly at least, she was in so far like Penelope, that she had a crowd of suitors, and undid day after day and night after night the handiwork of fascination and the web of coquetry with which she was wont to allure and entertain them.

Part of her coquetry may have come from her position about the Court, where the beautiful Maid of Honour was the light about which a thousand beaux came and fluttered; where she was sure to have a ring of admirers round her, crowding to listen to her repartees as much as to admire her beauty; and where she spoke and listened to much free talk, such as one never would have thought the lips or ears of Rachel Castlewood's daughter would have uttered or heard. When in waiting at Windsor or Hampton, the Court ladies and gentlemen would be making riding parties together; Mrs Beatrix in a horseman's coat and hat, the foremost after the stag-hounds and over the park fences, a crowd of young fellows at her heels. If the English country ladies at this time were the most pure and modest of any ladies in the world – the English town and Court ladies permitted themselves words and behaviour that were neither modest nor pure; and claimed, some of them, a freedom which those who love that sex most would never wish to grant them. The gentlemen of my family that follow after me (for I don't encourage the ladies to pursue any such studies) may read in the works of Mr Congreve, and Doctor Swift, and others, what was the conversation and what the habits of our time.

The most beautiful woman in England in 1712, when Esmond returned to this country, a lady of high birth, and though of no fortune to be sure, with a thousand fascinations of wit and manners – Beatrix Esmond – was now six-and-twenty years old, and Beatrix Esmond still. Of her hundred adorers she had not chosen one for a husband; and those who had asked had been jilted by her; and more still had left her. A succession of near ten years' crops of beauties had come up since her time, and had been reaped by proper *husbandmen*, if we may make an agricultural simile, and had been housed comfortably long ago. Her own contemporaries were sober mothers by this time; girls with not a tithe of her charms, or her wit, having made good matches, and now claiming precedence over the spinster who but lately had derided and outshone them. The young beauties were beginning to look down on Beatrix as an old maid, and sneer, and call her one of Charles II's ladies, and ask whether her portrait was not in the Hampton Court Gallery? But still she reigned, at least in one man's opinion, superior over all the little misses that were the toasts of the young lads; and in Esmond's eyes was ever perfectly lovely and young.

Who knows how many were nearly made happy by possessing her, or, rather, how many were fortunate in escaping this siren? 'Tis a marvel to think that her mother was the purest and simplest woman in the whole world, and that this girl should have been born from her. I am inclined to fancy, my mistress, who never said a harsh word to her children (and but twice or thrice only to one person), must have been too fond and pressing with the maternal authority; for her son and her daughter both revolted early; nor after their first flight from the nest could they ever be brought back quite to the fond mother's bosom. Lady Castlewood, and perhaps it was as well, knew little of her daughter's life and real thoughts. How was she to apprehend what passed in Queens' antechambers and at Court tables? Mrs Beatrix asserted her own authority so resolutely that her mother quickly gave in. The Maid of Honour had her own equipage; went from home and came back at her own will: her mother was alike powerless to resist her or to lead her, or to command or to persuade her.

She had been engaged once, twice, thrice, to be married, Esmond believed. When he quitted home, it hath been said, she was promised to my Lord Ashburnham, and now, on his return, behold his lordship was just married to Lady Mary Butler, the Duke of Ormonde's daughter, and his fine houses, and twelve thousand a year of fortune, for which Miss Beatrix had rather coveted him, was out of her power. To her Esmond could say nothing in regard to the breaking of this match; and, asking his mistress about it, all Lady Castlewood answered was: 'Do not speak to me about it, Harry. I cannot tell you how or why they parted, and I fear to inquire. I have told you before, that with all her kindness, and wit, and generosity, and that sort of splendour of nature she has; I can say but little good of poor Beatrix, and look with dread at the marriage she will form. Her mind is fixed on ambition only, and making a great figure: and, this achieved, she will tire of it as she does of everything. Heaven help her husband, whoever he shall be! My Lord

Ashburnham was a most excellent young man, gentle and yet manly, of very good parts, so they told me, and as my little conversation would enable me to judge: and a kind temper – kind and enduring I'm sure he must have been, from all that he had to endure. But he quitted her at last, from some crowning piece of caprice or tyranny of hers; and now he has married a young woman that will make him a thousand times happier than my poor girl ever could.'

The rupture, whatever its cause was (I heard the scandal, but indeed shall not take pains to repeat at length in this diary the trumpery coffee-house story), caused a good deal of low talk; and Mr Esmond was present at my lord's appearance at the Birthday with his bride, over whom the revenge that Beatrix took was to look so imperial and lovely that the modest downcast young lady could not appear beside her, and Lord Ashburnham, who had his reasons for wishing to avoid her, slunk away quite shamefaced, and very early. This time his Grace the Duke of Hamilton,[17] whom Esmond had seen about her before, was constant at Miss Beatrix's side: he was one of the most splendid gentlemen of Europe, accomplished by books, by travel, by long command of the best company, distinguished as a statesman, having been ambassador in King William's time, and a noble speaker in the Scots' Parliament, where he had led the party that was against the Union, and though now five or six and forty years of age, a gentleman so high in stature, accomplished in wit, and favoured in person, that he might pretend to the hand of any princess in Europe.

'Should you like the Duke for a cousin?' says Mr Secretary St John, whispering to Colonel Esmond in French; 'it appears that the widower consoles himself.'

But to return to our little Spectator paper and the conversation which grew out of it. Miss Beatrix at first was quite *bit* [18] (as the phrase of that day was) and did not 'smoke' the authorship of the story: indeed Esmond had tried to imitate as well as he could Mr Steele's manner (as for the other author of the Spectator, his prose style I think is altogether inimitable); and Dick, who was the idlest and best-natured of men, would have let the piece pass into his journal and go to posterity as one of his own lucubrations, but that Esmond did not care to have a lady's name whom he loved sent forth to the world in a light so unfavourable. Beatrix pished and psha'd over the paper; Colonel Esmond watching with no little interest her countenance as she read it.

'How stupid your friend Mr Steele becomes!' cries Miss Beatrix. 'Epsom and Tunbridge! Will he never have done with Epsom and Tunbridge, and with beaux at church, and Jocastas and Lindamiras? Why does he not call women Nelly and Betty, as their godfathers and godmothers did for them in their baptism?'

'Beatrix, Beatrix!' says her mother, 'speak gravely of grave things.'

'Mamma thinks the Church Catechism came from Heaven, I believe,' says Beatrix, with a laugh, 'and was brought down by a bishop from a mountain. O how I used to break my heart over it! Besides, I had a Popish godmother, mamma; why did you give me one?'

'I gave you the Queen's name,' says her mother, blushing. 'And a very pretty name it is,' said somebody else.

Beatrix went on reading – 'Spell my name with a y – why, you wretch,' says she, turning round to Colonel Esmond, 'you have been telling my story to Mr Steele – or stop – you have written the paper yourself to turn me into ridicule. For shame, sir!'

Poor Mr Esmond felt rather frightened, and told a truth, which was nevertheless an entire falsehood. 'Upon my honour,' says he, 'I have not even read the Spectator of this morning,' Nor had he, for that was not the Spectator, but a sham newspaper put in its place.

She went on reading: her face rather flushed as she read. 'No,' she says, 'I think you couldn't have written it. I think it must have been Mr Steele when he was drunk – and afraid of his horrid vulgar wife. Whenever I see an enormous compliment to a woman, and some outrageous panegyric about female virtue, I always feel sure that the Captain and his better half have fallen out over-night, and that he has been brought home tipsy, or has been found out in——'

'Beatrix!' cries the Lady Castlewood.

'Well, mamma! Do not cry out before you are hurt. I am not going to say anything wrong. I won't give you more annoyance than you can help, you pretty kind mamma. Yes, and your little Trix is a naughty little Trix, and she leaves undone those things which she ought to have done, and does those things which she ought not to have done, and there's——well now – I won't go on. Yes I will, unless you kiss me.' And with this the young lady lays aside her paper, and runs up to her mother and performs a variety of embraces with her ladyship, saying as plain as eyes could speak to Mr Esmond, 'There, sir: would not *you* like to play the very same pleasant game?'

'Indeed, madam, I would,' says he.

'Would what?' asked Miss Beatrix.

'What you meant when you looked at me in that provoking way,' answers Esmond.

'What a confessor!' cries Beatrix, with a laugh.

'What is it Henry would like, my dear?' asks her mother, the kind soul, who was always thinking what we would like, and how she could please us.

The girl runs up to her – 'O you silly kind mamma,' she says, kissing her again, 'that's what Harry would like'; and she broke out into a great joyful laugh: and Lady Castlewood blushed as bashful as a maid of sixteen.

'Look at her, Harry,' whispers Beatrix running up, and speaking in her sweet low tones. 'Doesn't the blush become her? Isn't she pretty? She looks younger than I am, and I am sure she is a hundred million thousand times better.'

Esmond's kind mistress left the room, carrying her blushes away with her.

'If we girls at Court could grow such roses as that,' continues Beatrix with her laugh, 'what wouldn't we do to preserve 'em? We'd clip their stalks and put 'em in salt and water. But those flowers don't bloom at Hampton Court and Windsor, Henry.' She paused for a minute, and the smile fading away from her April face, gave place to a menacing shower of tears: 'O how good she is, Harry,' Beatrix went on to say. 'O what a saint she is! Her goodness frightens me. I'm not fit to live with her. I

should be better I think if she were not so perfect. She has had
a great sorrow in her life, and a great secret; and repented of it.
It could not have been my father's death. She talks freely about
that; nor could she have loved him very much – though who
knows what we women do love, and why?'

'What, and why, indeed,' says Mr Esmond.

'No one knows,' Beatrix went on, without noticing this
interruption except by a look, 'what my mother's life is. She
hath been at early prayer this morning: she passes hours in
her closet; if you were to follow her thither, you would find her
at prayers now. She tends the poor of the place – the horrid
dirty poor! She sits through the curate's sermons – O those
dreary sermons! And you see, *on a beau dire*; but good as they
are, people like her are not fit to commune with us of the
world. There is always, as it were, a third person present, even
when I and my mother are alone. She can't be frank with me
quite; who is always thinking of the next world, and of her
guardian angel, perhaps that's in company. O, Harry, I'm
jealous of that guardian angel!' here broke out Mistress Beatrix.
'It's horrid, I know; but my mother's life is all for Heaven,
and mine – all for earth. We can never be friends quite; and then,
she cares more for Frank's little finger than she does for me – I
know she does: and she loves you, sir, a great deal too much;
and I hate you for it. I would have had her all to myself; but
she wouldn't. In my childhood, it was my father she loved – (O,
how could she? I remember him kind and handsome, but so
stupid, and not being able to speak after drinking wine). And
then, it was Frank; and now, it is Heaven and the clergyman.
How I would have loved her! From a child I used to be in a
rage that she loved anybody but me; but she loved you all
better – all, I know she did. And now, she talks of the blessed
consolation of religion. Dear soul! She thinks she is happier
for believing, as she must, that we are all of us wicked and
miserable sinners; and this world is only a *pied à terre* for the
good, where they stay for a night, as we do, coming from
Walcote, at that great, dreary, uncomfortable Hounslow Inn, in
those horrid beds. O, do you remember those horrid beds? – and
the chariot comes and fetches them to Heaven the next morning.'

'Hush, Beatrix,' says Mr Esmond.

'Hush, indeed. You are a hypocrite, too, Henry, with your grave airs and your glum face. We are all hypocrites. Oh dear me! We are all alone, alone, alone,' says poor Beatrix, her fair breast heaving with a sigh.

'It was I that writ every line of that paper, my dear,' says Mr Esmond. 'You are not so worldly as you think yourself, Beatrix, and better than we believe you. The good we have in us we doubt of; and the happiness that's to our hand we throw away. You bend your ambition on a great marriage and establishment – and why? You'll tire of them when you win them; and be no happier with a coronet on your coach——'

'Than riding pillion with Lubin[19] to market,' says Beatrix. 'Thank you, Lubin!'

'I'm a dismal shepherd, to be sure,' answers Esmond, with a blush; 'and require a nymph that can tuck my bed-clothes up, and make me water-gruel. Well, Tom Lockwood can do that. He took me out of the fire upon his shoulders, and nursed me through my illness as love will scarce ever do. Only good wages, and a hope of my clothes, and the contents of my portmanteau. How long was it that Jacob served an apprenticeship for Rachel?'

'For mamma!' says Beatrix. 'Is it mamma your honour wants, and that I should have the happiness of calling you papa?'

Esmond blushed again. 'I spoke of a Rachel that a shepherd courted five thousand years ago; when shepherds were longer lived than now. And my meaning was, that since I saw you first after our separation – a child you were then . . .'

'And I put on my best stockings to captivate you, I remember, sir . . .'

'You have had my heart ever since then, such as it was; and such as you were, I cared for no other woman. What little reputation I have won, it was that you might be pleased with it: and, indeed, it is not much; and I think a hundred fools in the army have got and deserved quite as much. Was there something in the air of that dismal old Castlewood that made us all gloomy, and dissatisfied, and lonely under its ruined old roof?

We were all so, even when together and united, as it seemed, following our separate schemes, each as we sat round the table.'

'Dear, dreary old place!' cries Beatrix. 'Mamma hath never had the heart to go back thither since we left it, when – never mind how many years ago,' and she flung back her curls, and looked over her fair shoulder at the mirror superbly, as if she said, 'Time, I defy you.'

'Yes,' says Esmond, who had the art, as she owned, of divining many of her thoughts. 'You can afford to look in the glass still; and only be pleased by the truth it tells you. As for me, do you know what my scheme is? I think of asking Frank to give me the Virginia estate King Charles gave our grandfather.' (She gave a superb curtsey, as much as to say, 'Our grandfather, indeed! Thank you, Mr Bastard.') 'Yes, I know you are thinking of my bar-sinister, and so am I. A man cannot get over it in this country; unless, indeed, he wears it across a king's arms, when 'tis a highly honourable coat; and I am thinking of retiring into the plantations, and building myself a wigwam in the woods, and perhaps, if I want company, suiting myself with a squaw. We will send your ladyship furs over for the winter; and, when you are old, we'll provide you with tobacco. I am not quite clever enough, or not rogue enough – I know not which – for the old world. I may make a place for myself in the new, which is not so full; and found a family there. When you are a mother yourself, and a great lady, perhaps I shall send you over from the plantation some day a little barbarian that is half Esmond half Mohock, and you will be kind to him for his father's sake, who was, after all, your kinsman; and whom you loved a little.'

'What folly you are talking, Harry,' says Miss Beatrix, looking with her great eyes.

' 'Tis sober earnest,' says Esmond. And, indeed, the scheme had been dwelling a good deal in his mind for some time past, and especially since his return home, when he found how hopeless, and even degrading to himself, his passion was. 'No,' says he, then, 'I have tried half-a-dozen times now, I can bear being away from you well enough; but being with you is intolerable' (another low curtsey on Miss Beatrix's part), 'and I will go. I have enough to buy axes and guns for my men, and beads and blankets for the savages; and I'll go and live amongst them.'

'*Mon ami*,' she says, quite kindly, and taking Esmond's hand, with an air of great compassion. 'You can't think that in our position anything more than our present friendship is possible. You are our elder brother – as such we view you, pitying your misfortune, not rebuking you with it. Why, you are old enough and grave enough to be our father. I always thought you a hundred years old, Harry, with your solemn face and grave air. I feel as a sister to you, and can no more. Isn't that enough, sir?' And she put her face quite close to his – who knows with what intention?

'It's too much,' says Esmond, turning away. 'I can't bear this life, and shall leave it. I shall stay, I think, to see you married, and then freight a ship, and call it the Beatrix, and bid you all . . . '

Here the servant, flinging the door open, announced his Grace the Duke of Hamilton, and Esmond started back with something like an imprecation on his lips, as the nobleman entered, looking splendid in his star and green riband. He gave Mr Esmond just that gracious bow which he would have given to a lacquey who fetched him a chair or took his hat, and seated himself by Miss Beatrix, as the poor Colonel went out of the room with a hang-dog look.

Esmond's mistress was in the lower room as he passed downstairs. She often met him as he was coming away from Beatrix; and she beckoned him into the apartment.

'Has she told you, Harry?' Lady Castlewood said.

'She has been very frank – very,' says Esmond.

'But – but about what is going to happen?'

'What is going to happen?' says he, his heart beating.

'His Grace the Duke of Hamilton has proposed to her,' says my lady. 'He made his offer yesterday. They will marry as soon as his mourning is over; and you have heard his Grace is appointed Ambassador to Paris; and the Ambassadress goes with him.'

## Chapter 4

## BEATRIX'S NEW SUITOR

THE gentleman whom Beatrix had selected was, to be sure, twenty years older than the Colonel, with whom she quarrelled for being too old; but this one was but a nameless adventurer, and the other the greatest duke in Scotland, with pretensions even to a still higher title. My Lord Duke of Hamilton had, indeed, every merit belonging to a gentleman, and he had had the time to mature his accomplishments fully, being upwards of fifty years old when Madam Beatrix selected him for a bridegroom. Duke Hamilton, then Earl of Arran, had been educated at the famous Scottish university of Glasgow, and, coming to London, became a great favourite of Charles the Second, who made him a lord of his bedchamber, and afterwards appointed him Ambassador to the French King, under whom the Earl served two campaigns as his Majesty's aide-de-camp; and he was absent on this service when King Charles died.

King James continued my lord's promotion – made him Master of the Wardrobe, and Colonel of the Royal Regiment of Horse; and his lordship adhered firmly to King James, being of the small company that never quitted that unfortunate monarch till his departure out of England; and then it was, in 1688, namely, that he made the friendship with Colonel Francis Esmond, that had always been, more or less, maintained in the two families.

The Earl professed a great admiration for King William always, but never could give him his allegiance; and was engaged in more than one of the plots in the late great King's reign, which always ended in the plotters' discomfiture, and generally in their pardon, by the magnanimity of the King. Lord Arran was twice prisoner in the Tower during this reign, undauntedly saying, when offered his release, upon parole not to engage against King William, that he would not give his word, because 'he was sure he could not keep it'; but, nevertheless, he was both times discharged without any trial; and the King bore this noble enemy so little malice, that when his mother, the Duchess of Hamilton, of her own right, resigned her claim on her husband's death, the Earl was, by patent signed at Loo, 1690, created Duke of Hamilton, Marquis of Clydesdale, and Earl of Arran, with precedency from the original creation. His Grace took the oaths and his seat in the Scottish Parliament in 1700: was famous there for his patriotism and eloquence, especially in the debates about the Union Bill, which Duke Hamilton opposed with all his strength, though he would not go the length of the Scottish gentry, who were for resisting it by force of arms. 'Twas said he withdrew his opposition all of a sudden, and in consequence of letters from the King at St Germains, who entreated him on his allegiance not to thwart the Queen, his sister, in this measure; and the Duke, being always bent upon effecting the King's return to his kingdom through a reconciliation between his Majesty and Queen Anne, and quite averse to his landing with arms and French troops, held aloof, and kept out of Scotland during the time when the Chevalier de St George's descent from Dunkirk was projected, passing his time in England in his great estate of Staffordshire.

When the Whigs went out of office in 1710, the Queen began to show his Grace the very greatest marks of her favour. He was created Duke of Brandon and Baron of Dutton in England; having the Thistle already originally bestowed on him by King James the Second, his Grace was now promoted to the honour of the Garter – a distinction so great and illustrious, that no subject hath ever borne them hitherto together. When this objection was made to her Majesty, she was pleased to say, 'Such a subject as the Duke of Hamilton has a pre-eminent claim to every mark of distinction which a crowned head can confer. I will henceforth wear both orders myself.'

At the Chapter held at Windsor in October, 1712, the Duke and other knights, including Lord-Treasurer, the new-created Earl of Oxford and Mortimer, were installed; and a few days afterwards his Grace was appointed Ambassador-Extraordinary to France, and his equipages, plate, and liveries commanded, of the most sumptuous kind, not only for his Excellency the Ambassador, but for her Excellency the Ambassadress, who was to accompany him. Her arms were already quartered on the coach panels, and her brother was to hasten over on the appointed day to give her away.

His lordship was a widower, having married, in 1698, Elizabeth daughter of Digby Lord Gerard, by which marriage great estates came into the Hamilton family; and out of these estates came, in part, that tragic quarrel which ended the Duke's career.

From the loss of a tooth to that of a mistress there's no pang that is not bearable. The apprehension is much more cruel than the certainty; and we make up our mind to the misfortune when 'tis irremediable, part with the tormentor, and mumble our crust on t'other side of the jaws. I think Colonel Esmond was relieved when a ducal coach and six came and whisked his charmer away out of his reach, and placed her in a higher sphere. As you have seen the nymph in the opera-machine go up to the clouds at the end of the piece where Mars, Bacchus, Apollo, and all the divine company of Olympians are seated, and quaver out her last song as a goddess: so when this portentous elevation was accomplished in the Esmond family, I am not sure that every one of us did not treat the divine Beatrix with special honours; at least, the saucy little beauty carried her head with a toss of supreme authority, and assumed a touch-me-not air, which all her friends very good-humouredly bowed to.

An old army acquaintance of Colonel Esmond's, honest Tom Trett, who had sold his company, married a wife, and turned merchant in the city, was dreadfully gloomy for a long time, though living in a fine house on the river, and carrying on a great trade to all appearance. At length Esmond saw his friend's name in the Gazette as a bankrupt; and a week after this circumstance my bankrupt walks into Mr Esmond's lodging with a face perfectly radiant with good-humour, and as jolly and careless as when they had sailed from Southampton ten years before for Vigo. 'This bankruptcy,' says Tom, 'has been hanging over my head these three years; the thought hath prevented my sleeping, and I have looked at poor Polly's head on t'other pillow, and then towards my razor on the table, and thought to put an end to myself, and so give my woes the slip. But now we are bankrupts: Tom Trett pays as many shillings in the pound as he can; his wife has a little cottage at Fulham, and her fortune secured to herself. I am afraid neither of bailiff nor of creditor; and for the last six nights have slept easy.' So it was that when Fortune shook her wings and left him, honest Tom cuddled himself up in his ragged virtue, and fell asleep.

Esmond did not tell his friend how much his story applied to Esmond too; but he laughed at it, and used it; and having fairly struck his docket in this love transaction, determined to put a cheerful face on his bankruptcy. Perhaps Beatrix was a little offended at his gaiety. 'Is this the way, sir, that you receive, the announcement of your misfortune,' says she, 'and do you come smiling before me as if you were glad to be rid of me?'

Esmond would not be put off from his good-humour, but told her the story of Tom Trett and his bankruptcy. 'I have been hankering after the grapes on the wall,' says he, 'and lost my temper because they were beyond my reach; was there any wonder? They're gone now, and another has them – a taller man than your humble servant has won them.' And the Colonel made his cousin a low bow.

'A taller man, cousin Esmond!' says she. 'A man of spirit would have scaled the wall, sir, and seized them! A man of courage would have fought for 'em, not gaped for 'em.'

'A duke has but to gape and they drop into his mouth,' says Esmond, with another low bow.

'Yes, sir,' says she, 'a duke *is* a taller man than you. And why should I not be grateful to one such as his Grace, who gives me his heart and his great name? It is a great gift he honours me with; I know 'tis a bargain between us; and I accept it, and will do my utmost to perform my part of it. 'Tis no question of sighing and philandering between a nobleman of his Grace's age and a girl who hath little of that softness in her nature. Why should I not own that I am ambitious, Harry Esmond; and if it be no sin in a man to covet honour, why should a woman too not desire it? Shall I be frank with you, Harry, and say that if you had not been down on your knees, and so humble, you might have fared better with me? A woman of my spirit, cousin, is to be won by gallantry, and not by sighs and rueful faces. All the time you are worshipping and singing hymns to me, I know very well I am no goddess, and grow weary of the incense. So would you have been weary of the goddess too – when she was called Mrs Esmond, and got out of humour because she had not pin-money enough, and was forced to go about in an old gown. Eh! cousin, a goddess in a mob-cap, that has to make her husband's gruel, ceases to be divine – I am sure of it. I should have been sulky and scolded; and of all the proud wretches in the world Mr Esmond is the proudest, let me tell him that. You never fall into a passion; but you never forgive, I think. Had you been a great man, you might have been good-humoured; but being nobody, sir, you are too great a man for me; and I'm afraid of you, cousin – there; and I won't worship you, and you'll never be happy except with a woman who will. Why, after I belonged to you, and after one of my tantrums, you would have put the pillow over my head some night, and smothered me, as the black man does the woman in the play that you're so fond of. What's the creature's name? – Desdemona. You would, you little black-eyed Othello!'

'I think I should, Beatrix,' says the Colonel.

'And I want no such ending. I intend to live to be a hundred, and to go to ten thousand routes and balls, and to play cards every night of my life till the year eighteen hundred. And I like to be the first of my company, sir; and I like flattery and compliments, and you give me none; and I like to be made to laugh, sir, and who's to laugh at *your* dismal face I should like to know; and I like a coach-and-six or a coach-and-eight; and I like diamonds, and a new gown every week; and people to say, "That's the Duchess – How well her Grace looks – Make way for Madame l'Ambassadrice d'Angleterre – Call her Excellency's people" – that's what I like. And as for you, you want a woman to bring your slippers and cap, and to sit at your feet, and cry "O caro! O bravo!" whilst you read your Shakes-

peares, and Miltons, and stuff. Mamma would have been the
wife for you, had you been a little older, though you look ten
years older than she does – you do, you glum-faced, blue-
bearded, little old man! You might have sat, like Darby and
Joan, and flattered each other; and billed and cooed like a pair
of old pigeons on a perch. I want my wings and to use them,
sir.' And she spread out her beautiful arms, as if indeed she
could fly off like the pretty 'Gawrie,' whom the man in the
story was enamoured of.

'And what will your Peter Wilkins[1] say to your flight?' says
Esmond, who never admired this fair creature more than when
she rebelled and laughed at him.

'A duchess knows her place,' says she, with a laugh. 'Why,
I have a son already made for me, and thirty years old (my
Lord Arran), and four daughters. How they will scold, and
what a rage they will be in, when I come to take the head of
the table! But I give them only a month to be angry; at the end
of that time they shall love me every one, and so shall Lord
Arran, and so shall all his Grace's Scots vassals and followers
in the Highlands. I'm bent on it; and, when I take a thing in
my head, 'tis done. His Grace is the greatest gentleman in
Europe, and I'll try and make him happy; and, when the King
comes back, you may count on my protection, cousin Esmond –
for come back the King will and shall: and I'll bring him back
from Versailles, if he comes under my hoop.'

'I hope the world will make you happy, Beatrix,' says Esmond
with a sigh. 'You'll be Beatrix till you are my Lady Duchess –
will you not? I shall then make your Grace my very lowest
bow.'

'None of these sighs and this satire, cousin,' she says. 'I take
his Grace's great bounty thankfully – yes, thankfully; and will
wear his honours becomingly. I do not say he hath touched my
heart; but he has my gratitude, obedience, admiration – I have
told him that, and no more; and with that his noble heart is
content. I have told him all – even the story of that poor creature
that I was engaged to – and that I could not love; and I gladly
gave his word back to him, and jumped for joy to get back my
own. I am twenty-five years old.'

'Twenty-six, my dear,' says Esmond.

'Twenty-five, sir – I choose to be twenty-five; and, in eight years, no man hath ever touched my heart. Yes – you did once, for a little, Harry, when you came back after Lille, and engaging with that murderer, Mohun, and saving Frank's life. I thought I could like you; and mamma begged me hard, on her knees, and I did – for a day. But the old chill came over me, Henry, and the old fear of you and your melancholy; and I was glad when you went away, and engaged with my Lord Ashburnham, that I might hear no more of you, that's the truth. You are too good for me somehow. I could not make you happy, and should break my heart in trying, and not being able to love you. But if you had asked me when we gave you the sword, you might have had me, sir, and we both should have been miserable by this time. I talked with that silly lord all night just to vex you and mamma, and I succeeded, didn't I? How frankly we can talk of these things! It seems a thousand years ago: and, though we are here sitting in the same room, there's a great wall between us. My dear, kind, faithful, gloomy old cousin! I can like you now, and admire you too, sir, and say that you are brave, and very kind, and very true, and a fine gentleman for all – for all your little mishap at your birth,' says she, wagging her arch head.

'And now, sir,' says she, with a curtsey, 'we must have no more talk except when mamma is by, as his Grace is with us; for he does not half like you, cousin, and is as jealous as the black man in your favourite play.'

Though the very kindness of the words stabbed Mr Esmond with the keenest pang, he did not show his sense of the wound by any look of his (as Beatrix, indeed, afterwards owned to him), but said, with a perfect command of himself and an easy smile, 'The interview must not end yet, my dear, until I have had my last word. Stay, here comes your mother' (indeed she came in here with her sweet anxious face, and Esmond, going up, kissed her hand respectfully). 'My dear lady may hear, too, the last words, which are no secrets, and are only a parting benediction accompanying a present for your marriage from an old gentleman your guardian; for I feel as if I was the guardian

of all the family, and an old old fellow that is fit to be the grandfather of you all; and in this character let me make my Lady
Duchess her wedding present. They are the diamonds my
father's widow left me. I had thought Beatrix might have had
them a year ago; but they are good enough for a duchess,
though not bright enough for the handsomest woman in the
world.' And he took the case out of his pocket in which the
jewels were, and presented them to his cousin.

She gave a cry of delight, for the stones were indeed very
handsome, and of great value; and the next minute the necklace
was where Belinda's cross[2] is in Mr Pope's admirable poem,
and glittering on the whitest and most perfectly-shaped neck
in all England.

The girl's delight at receiving these trinkets was so great,
that after rushing to the looking-glass and examining the effect
they produced upon that fair neck which they surrounded,
Beatrix was running back with her arms extended, and was
for paying her cousin with a price, that he would have liked no
doubt to receive from those beautiful rosy lips of hers, but at
this moment the door opened, and his Grace the bridegroom
elect was announced.

He looked very black upon Mr Esmond, to whom he made a
very low bow indeed, and kissed the hand of each lady in his
most ceremonious manner. He had come in his chair from the
palace hard by, and wore his two stars of the Garter and the
Thistle.

'Look, my Lord Duke,' says Mrs Beatrix, advancing to him,
and showing the diamonds on her breast.

'Diamonds,' says his Grace. 'Hm! they seem pretty.'

'They are a present on my marriage,' says Beatrix.

'From her Majesty?' asks the Duke. 'The Queen is very good.'

'From my cousin Henry – from our cousin Henry' – cry
both the ladies in a breath.

'I have not the honour of knowing the gentleman. I thought
that my Lord Castlewood had no brother: and that on your
ladyship's side there were no nephews.'

'From our cousin, Colonel Henry Esmond, my lord,' says
Beatrix, taking the Colonel's hand very bravely – 'who was left

guardian to us by our father, and who has a hundred times shown his love and friendship for our family.'

'The Duchess of Hamilton receives no diamonds but from her husband, madam,' says the Duke – 'may I pray you to restore these to Mr Esmond?'

'Beatrix Esmond may receive a present from our kinsman and benefactor, my Lord Duke,' says Lady Castlewood, with an air of great dignity. 'She is my daughter yet: and if her mother sanctions the gift – no one else hath the right to question it.'

'Kinsman and benefactor!' says the Duke. 'I know of no kinsman: and I do not choose that my wife should have for benefactor a——'

'My lord,' says Colonel Esmond.

'I am not here to bandy words,' says his Grace: 'frankly I tell you that your visits to this house are too frequent, and that I choose no presents for the Duchess of Hamilton from gentlemen that bear a name they have no right to.'

'My lord!' breaks out Lady Castlewood, 'Mr Esmond hath the best right to that name of any man in the world: and 'tis as old and as honourable was your Grace's.'

My Lord Duke smiled, and looked as if Lady Castlewood was mad, that was so talking to him.

'If I called him benefactor,' said my mistress, 'it is because he has been so to us – yes, the noblest, the truest, the bravest, the dearest of benefactors. He would have saved my husband's life from Mohun's sword. He did save my boy's, and defended him from that villain. Are those no benefits!'

'I ask Colonel Esmond's pardon,' says his Grace, if possible more haughty than before; 'I would say not a word that should give him offence, and thank him for his kindness to your ladyship's family. My Lord Mohun and I are connected,[3] you know, by marriage – though neither by blood nor friendship; but I must repeat what I said, that my wife can receive no presents from Colonel Esmond.'

'My daughter may receive presents from the Head of our House: my daughter may thankfully take kindness from her father's, her mother's, her brother's dearest friend; and be grateful for one more benefit besides the thousand we owe him,' cries Lady Esmond. 'What is a string of diamond stones compared to that affection he hath given us – our dearest preserver and benefactor? We owe him not only Frank's life, but our all – yes, our all,' says my mistress, with a heightened colour and a trembling voice. 'The title we bear is his, if he would claim it. 'Tis we who have no right to our name: not he that's too great for it. He sacrificed his name at my dying lord's bedside – sacrificed it to my orphan children; gave up rank and honour because he loved us so nobly. His father was Viscount of Castlewood and Marquis of Esmond before him; and he is his father's lawful son and true heir, and we are the recipients of his bounty, and he the chief of a house that's as old as your own. And if he is content to forego his name that my child may bear it, we love him and honour him and bless him under whatever name he bears' – and here the fond and affectionate creature would have knelt to Esmond again, but that he prevented her; and Beatrix, running up to her with a pale face and a cry of alarm, embraced her and said, 'Mother, what is this?'

' 'Tis a family secret, my Lord Duke,' says Colonel Esmond: 'poor Beatrix knew nothing of it: nor did my lady till a year ago. And I have as good a right to resign my title as your Grace's mother to abdicate hers to you.'

'I should have told everything to the Duke of Hamilton,' said my mistress, 'had his Grace applied to me for my daughter's hand, and not to Beatrix. I should have spoken with you this very day in private, my lord, had not your words brought about this sudden explanation – and now 'tis fit Beatrix should hear it; and know, as I would have all the world know, what we owe to our kinsman and patron.'

And then in her touching way, and having hold of her daughter's hand, and speaking to her rather than my Lord Duke, Lady Castlewood told the story which you know already – lauding up to the skies her kinsman's behaviour. On his side Mr Esmond explained the reasons that seemed quite sufficiently cogent with him, why the succession in the family, as at present it stood, should not be disturbed; and he should remain, as he was, Colonel Esmond.

'And Marquis of Esmond, my lord,' says his Grace, with a low bow. 'Permit me to ask your lordship's pardon for words that were uttered in ignorance; and to beg for the favour of your friendship. To be allied to you, sir, must be an honour under whatever name you are known' (so his Grace was pleased to say): 'and in return for the splendid present you make my wife, your kinswoman, I hope you will please to command any service that James Douglas can perform. I shall never be easy until I repay you a part of my obligations at least; and ere very long, and with the mission her Majesty hath given me,' says the Duke, 'that may perhaps be in my power. I shall esteem it as a favour, my lord, if Colonel Esmond will give away the bride.'

'And if he will take the usual payment in advance, he is welcome,' says Beatrix, stepping up to him; and as Esmond kissed her, she whispered, 'O, why didn't I know you before?'

My Lord Duke was as hot as a flame at this salute, but said never a word: Beatrix made him a proud curtsey, and the two ladies quitted the room together.

'When does your Excellency go for Paris?' asks Colonel Esmond.

'As soon after the ceremony as may be,' his Grace answered. ''Tis fixed for the first of December: it cannot be sooner. The equipage will not be ready till then. The Queen intends the embassy should be very grand – and I have law business to settle. That ill-omened Mohun has come, or is coming, to London again: we are in a lawsuit about my late Lord Gerard's property; and he hath sent to me to meet him.'

## Chapter 5

### MOHUN APPEARS FOR THE LAST TIME IN THIS HISTORY

BESIDES my Lord Duke of Hamilton and Brandon, who, for family reasons, had kindly promised his protection and patronage to Colonel Esmond, he had other great friends in power now, both able and willing to assist him, and he might, with such allies, look forward to as fortunate advancement in civil life at home as he had got rapid promotion abroad. His Grace was magnanimous enough to offer to take Mr Esmond as secretary on his Paris embassy, but no doubt he intended that proposal should be rejected; at any rate, Esmond could not bear the thoughts of attending his mistress farther than the church-door after her marriage, and so declined that offer which his generous rival made him.

Other gentlemen in power were liberal at least of compliments and promises to Colonel Esmond. Mr Harley, now become my Lord Oxford and Mortimer, and installed Knight of the Garter on the same day as his Grace of Hamilton had received the same honour, sent to the Colonel to say that a seat in Parliament should be at his disposal presently, and Mr St John held out many flattering hopes of advancement to the Colonel when he should enter the House. Esmond's friends were all successful, and the most successful and triumphant of all was his dear old commander, General Webb, who was now appointed Lieutenant-General of the Land Forces, and received with particular honour by the ministry, by the Queen, and the people out of doors, who huzza'd the brave chief when they used to see him in his chariot, going to the House or to the Drawing-room, or hobbling on foot to his coach from St Stephen's upon his glorious old crutch and stick, and cheered him as loud as they had ever done Marlborough.

That great Duke was utterly disgraced,[1] and honest old Webb dated all his Grace's misfortunes from Wynendael, and vowed that Fate served the traitor right. Duchess Sarah had also gone to ruin; she had been forced to give up her keys, and her places, and her pensions: – 'Ah, ah!' says Webb, 'she would have locked up three millions of French crowns with her keys had I but been knocked on the head, but I stopped that convoy at Wynendael.' Our enemy Cardonnel was turned out of the House of Commons (along with Mr Walpole) for malversation of public money. Cadogan lost his place of Lieutenant of the Tower. Marlborough's daughters resigned their posts of ladies of the bed-chamber; and so complete was the

Duke's disgrace, that his son-in-law, Lord Bridgewater, was absolutely obliged to give up his lodging at St James's, and had his half-pension, as Master of the Horse, taken away. But I think the lowest depth of Marlborough's fall was when he humbly sent to ask General Webb when he might wait upon him; he who had commanded the stout old General, who had injured him and sneered at him, who had kept him dangling in his ante-chamber, who could not even after his great service condescend to write him a letter in his own hand. The nation was as eager for peace, as ever it had been hot for war. The Prince of Savoy came amongst us, had his audience of the Queen, and got his famous Sword of Honour,[2] and strove with all his force to form a Whig party together, to bring over the young Prince of Hanover – to do anything which might prolong the war, and consummate the ruin of the old sovereign whom he hated so implacably. But the nation was tired of the struggle; so completely wearied of it that not even our defeat at Denain[3] could rouse us into any anger, though such an action so lost two years before, would have set all England in a fury. 'Twas easy to see that the great Marlborough was not with the army. Eugene was obliged to fall back in a rage, and forego the dazzling revenge of his life. 'Twas in vain the Duke's side asked, 'Would we suffer our arms to be insulted? Would we not send back the only champion who could repair our honour?' The nation had had its bellyful of fighting; nor could taunts or outcries goad up our Britons any more.

For a statesman, that was always prating of liberty, and had the grandest philosophic maxims in his mouth, it must be owned that Mr St John sometimes rather acted like a Turkish than a Greek philosopher, and especially fell foul of one unfortunate set of men, the men of letters, with a tyranny a little extraordinary in a man who professed to respect their calling so much. The literary controversy at this time was very bitter; the government side was the winning one, the popular one, and I think might have been the merciful one. 'Twas natural that the opposition should be peevish and cry out; some men did so from their hearts, admiring the Duke of Marlborough's prodigious talents, and deploring the disgrace of the greatest general the world ever knew: 'twas the stomach that caused other patriots to grumble, and such men cried out because they were poor, and paid to do so. Against these my Lord Bolingbroke never showed the slightest mercy,[4] whipping a dozen into prison or into the pillory without the least commiseration.

From having been a man of arms Mr Esmond had now come to be a man of letters, but on a safer side than that in which the above-cited poor fellows ventured their liberties and ears. There was no danger on ours, which was the winning side; besides, Mr Esmond pleased himself by thinking that he writ like a gentleman if he did not always succeed as a wit.

Of the famous wits of that age, who have rendered Queen Anne's reign illustrious, and whose works will be in all Englishmen's hands in ages yet to come, Mr Esmond saw many, but at public places chiefly; never having a great intimacy with any of them, except with honest Dick Steele and Mr Addison, who parted company with Esmond, however, when that gentleman became a declared Tory, and lived on close terms with the leading persons of that party. Addison kept himself to a few friends, and very rarely opened himself except in their company. A man more upright and conscientious than he, it was not possible to find in public life, and one whose conversation was so various, easy, and delightful. Writing now in my mature years, I own that I think Addison's politics were the right, and were my time to come over again, I would be a Whig in England and not a Tory; but with people that take a side in politics, 'tis men rather than principles that commonly bind them. A kindness or a slight puts a man under one flag or the other, and he marches with it to the end of the campaign. Esmond's master in war was injured by Marlborough, and hated him: and the lieutenant fought the quarrels of his leader. Webb coming to London was used as a weapon by Marlborough's enemies (and true steel he was, that honest chief); nor was his aide-de-camp, Mr Esmond, an unfaithful or unworthy partisan. 'Tis strange here, and on a foreign soil, and in a land that is independent in all but the name (for that the North American colonies shall remain dependants on yonder little island for twenty years more, I never can think), to remember how the nation at home seemed to give itself up to the domination of one or other aristocratic party, and took a Hanoverian king, or a French one, according as either prevailed. And while the Tories, the October Club gentlemen, the High Church parsons that held by the Church of England, were for having a Papist king, for whom many of their Scottish and English leaders, firm churchmen all, laid down their lives with admirable loyalty and devotion; they were governed by men who had notoriously no religion at all, but used it as they would use any opinion for the purpose of forwarding their own ambition. The Whigs, on the other hand, who professed attachment to religion and liberty too, were compelled to send to Holland or Hanover for a monarch around whom they could rally. A strange series of compromises is that English history; compromise of principle, compromise of party, compromise of worship! The lovers of English freedom and independence submitted their religious consciences to an Act of Parliament; could not consolidate their liberty without sending to Zell or the Hague for a king to live under; and could not find amongst the proudest people in the world a man speaking their own language, and understanding their laws, to govern them. The Tory and High Church patriots were ready to die in defence of a Papist family that had sold us to France; the great Whig nobles, the sturdy Republican recusants who had cut off Charles Stuart's head for treason, were fain to accept a king whose title came to him through a royal grandmother, whose own royal grandmother's head had fallen under Queen Bess's hatchet. And our proud English nobles sent to a petty German town for a monarch to come and reign in London; and our prelates kissed the ugly hands of his Dutch mistresses, and thought it no dishonour. In England you can but belong to one party or t'other, and you take the house you live in with all its encumbrances, its retainers, its antique discomforts, and ruins even; you patch up, but you never build up anew. Will we of the new world submit much longer, even nominally, to this antient British superstition? There are signs of the times which make me think that ere long we shall care as little about King George here, and peers temporal and peers spiritual, as we do for King Canute or the Druids.

This chapter began about the wits, my grandson may say, and hath wandered very far from their company. The pleasantest of the wits I knew were the Doctors Garth[5] and Arbuthnot, and Mr Gay,[6] the author of 'Trivia', the most charming kind soul that ever laughed at a joke or cracked a bottle. Mr Prior[7] I saw, and he was the earthen pot swimming with the pots of brass down the stream, and always and justly frightened lest he should break in the voyage. I met him both at London and Paris, where he was performing piteous congees to the Duke of Shrewsbury, not having courage to support the dignity which his undeniable genius and talent had won him, and writing coaxing letters to Secretary St John, and thinking about his plate and his place, and what on earth should become of him should his party go out. The famous Mr Congreve I saw a dozen times at Button's,[8] a splendid wreck of a man, magnificently attired, and though gouty, and almost blind, bearing a brave face against fortune.

The great Mr Pope (of whose prodigious genius I have no words to express my admiration) was quite a puny lad at this time, appearing seldom in public places. There were hundreds of men, wits, and pretty fellows frequenting the theatres and coffee-houses of that day – whom 'nunc prescribere longum est.' Indeed I think the most brilliant of that sort I ever saw was not till fifteen years afterwards, when I paid my last visit in England, and met young Harry Fielding, son of the Fielding that served in Spain and afterwards in Flanders with us, and who for fun and humour seemed to top them all. As for the famous Doctor Swift, I can say of him, 'vidi tantum.'[9] He was in London all these years up to the death of the Queen; and in a hundred public places where I saw him, but no more; he never missed Court of a Sunday, where once or twice he was pointed out to your grandfather. He would have sought me out eagerly enough had I been a great man with a title to my name, or a star on my coat. At Court the Doctor had no eyes but for the very greatest. Lord Treasurer and St John used to call him Jonathan; and they paid him with this cheap coin for the service they took of him. He writ their lampoons, fought their enemies, flogged and bullied in their service, and it must be owned with a consummate skill and fierceness. 'Tis said he hath lost his intellect now, and forgotten his wrongs and his rage against mankind. I have always thought of him and of Marlborough as the two greatest men of that age. I have read his books (who doth not know them?) here in our calm woods, and imagine a giant to myself as I think of him, a lonely fallen Prometheus, groaning as the vulture tears him. Prometheus I saw, but when first I ever had any words with him, the giant stepped out of a sedan chair in the Poultry, whither he had come with a tipsy Irish servant parading before him, who announced him, bawling out his Reverence's name, whilst his master below was as yet haggling with the chairman. I disliked this Mr Swift, and heard many a story about him, of his conduct to men, and his words to women. He could flatter the great as he could bully the weak; and Mr Esmond, being younger and hotter in that day than now, was determined, should he ever meet this dragon, not to run away from his teeth and his fire.

Men have all sorts of motives which carry them onwards in life, and are driven into acts of desperation, or it may be of distinction, from a hundred different causes. There was one comrade of Esmond's, an honest little Irish lieutenant of Handyside's, who owed so much money to a camp suttler, that he began to make love to the man's daughter, intending to pay his debt that way; and at the battle of Malplaquet, flying away from the debt and lady too, he rushed so desperately on the French lines, that he got his company; and came a captain out of the action, and had to marry the suttler's daughter after all, who brought him his cancelled debt to her father as poor Roger's fortune. To run out of the reach of bill and marriage, he ran on the enemy's pikes; and as these did not kill him he was thrown back upon t'other horn of his dilemma. Our great Duke at the same battle was fighting, not the French, but the Tories in England; and risking his life and the army's, not for his country but for his pay and places; and for fear of his wife at home, that only being in life whom he dreaded. I have asked about men in my own company (new drafts of poor country boys were perpetually coming over to us during the wars, and brought from the ploughshare to the sword), and found that a half of them under the flags were driven thither on account of a woman: one fellow was jilted by his mistress and took the shilling in despair; another jilted the girl, and fled from her and the parish to the tents where the law could not disturb him. Why go on particularising? What can the sons of Adam and Eve expect, but to continue in that course of love and trouble their father and mother set out on? O my grandson! I am drawing nigh to the end of that period of my history, when I was acquainted with the great world of England and Europe; my years are past the Hebrew poet's limit, and I say unto thee all my troubles and joys too, for that matter, have come from a woman; as thine will when thy destined course begins. 'Twas a woman that made a soldier of me, that set me intriguing afterwards; I believe I would have spun smocks for her had she so bidden me; what strength I had in my head I would have given her; hath not every man in his degree had his Omphale[10] and Delilah? Mine befooled me on the banks of the Thames, and in dear old England; thou mayest find thine own by Rappahannoc.

To please that woman then I tried to distinguish myself as a soldier, and afterwards as a wit and a politician; as to please another I would have put on a black cassock and a pair of bands, and had done so but that a superior fate intervened to defeat that project. And I say, I think the world is like Captain Esmond's company I spoke of anon; and, could you see every man's career in life, you would find a woman clogging him; or clinging round his march and stopping him; or cheering him and goading him; or beckoning him out of her chariot, so that he goes up to her, and leaves the race to be run without him; or bringing him the apple, and saying, 'Eat'; or fetching him the daggers and whispering 'Kill! yonder lies Duncan, and a crown, and an opportunity.'

Your grandfather fought with more effect as a politician than as a wit; and having private animosities and grievances of his own and his General's against the great Duke in command of the army, and more information on military matters than most writers, who had never seen beyond the fire of a tobacco-pipe at Wills's, he was enabled to do good service for that cause which he embarked in, and for Mr St John and his party. But he disdained the abuse in which some of the Tory writers indulged; for instance, Doctor Swift, who actually chose to doubt the Duke of Marlborough's courage,[11] and was pleased to hint that his Grace's military capacity was doubtful: nor were Esmond's performances worse for the effect they were intended to produce (though no doubt they could not injure the Duke of Marlborough nearly so much in the public eyes as the malignant attacks of Swift did, which were carefully directed so as to blacken and degrade him), because they were writ openly and fairly by Mr Esmond, who made no disguise of them, who was now out of the army, and who never attacked the prodigious courage and talents, only the selfishness and rapacity, of the chief.

The Colonel then, having writ a paper for one of the Tory journals, called the 'Post-Boy' (a letter upon Bouchain,[12] that the town talked about for two whole days, when the appearance of an Italian singer supplied a fresh subject for conversation), and having business at the Exchange, where Mrs Beatrix wanted a pair of gloves or a fan very likely, Esmond went to correct his paper, and was sitting at the printer's, when the famous Doctor Swift came in, his Irish fellow with him that used to walk before his chair, and bawled out his master's name with great dignity.

Mr Esmond was waiting for the printer too, whose wife had gone to the tavern to fetch him, and was meantime engaged in drawing a picture of a soldier on horseback for a dirty little pretty boy of the printer's wife, whom she had left behind her.

'I presume you are the editor of the "Post-Boy", sir?' says the Doctor, in a grating voice that had an Irish twang; and he looked at the Colonel from under his two bushy eyebrows with a pair of very clear blue eyes. His complexion was muddy, his figure rather fat, his chin double. He wore a shabby cassock, and a shabby hat over his black wig, and he pulled out a great gold watch, at which he looks very fierce.

'I am but a contributor, Doctor Swift,' says Esmond, with the little boy still on his knee. He was sitting with his back in the window, so that the Doctor could not see him.

'Who told you I was Doctor Swift?' says the Doctor, eyeing the other very haughtily.

'Your Reverence's valet bawled out your name,' says the Colonel. 'I should judge you brought him from Ireland.'

'And pray, sir, what right have you to judge whether my servant came from Ireland or no? I want to speak with your employer, Mr Leach.[13] I'll thank ye go fetch him.'

'Where's your papa, Tommy?' asks the Colonel of the child, a smutty little wretch in a frock.

Instead of answering, the child begins to cry; the Doctor's appearance had no doubt frightened the poor little imp.

'Send that squalling little brat about his business, and do what I bid ye, sir,' says the Doctor.

'I must finish the picture first for Tommy,' says the Colonel, laughing. 'Here, Tommy, will you have your Pandour with whiskers or without?'

'Whisters,' says Tommy, quite intent on the picture.

'Who the devil are ye, sir?' cries the Doctor; 'are ye a printer's man or are ye not?' (he pronounced it like *naught*.)

'Your Reverence needn't raise the devil to ask who I am,' says Colonel Esmond. 'Did you ever hear of Doctor Faustus, little Tommy? or Friar Bacon, who invented gunpowder, and set the Thames on fire?'

Mr Swift turned quite red, almost purple. 'I did not intend any offence, sir,' says he.

'I daresay, sir, you offended without meaning,' says the other, drily.

'Who are ye, sir? Do you know who I am, sir? You are one of the pack of Grub Street scribblers that my friend Mr Secretary hath laid by the heels. How dare ye, sir, speak to me in this tone?' cries the Doctor in a great fume.

'I beg your honour's humble pardon if I have offended your honour,' says Esmond in a tone of great humility. 'Rather than be sent to the Compter,[14] or be put in the pillory, there's nothing I wouldn't do. But Mrs Leach, the printer's lady, told me to mind Tommy whilst she went for her husband to the tavern, and I daren't leave the child lest he should fall into the fire; but if your Reverence will hold him——'

'I take the little beast!' says the Doctor, starting back. 'I am engaged to your betters, fellow. Tell Mr Leach that when he makes an appointment with Doctor Swift he had best keep it, do ye hear? And keep a respectful tongue on your head, sir, when you address a person like me.'

'I'm but a poor broken-down soldier,' says the Colonel, 'and I've seen better days, though I am forced now to turn my hand to writing. We can't help our fate, sir.'

'You're the person that Mr Leach hath spoken to me of, I presume. Have the goodness to speak civilly when you are spoken to – and tell Leach to call at my lodgings in Bury Street, and bring the papers with him to-night at ten o'clock. And the next time you see me, you'll know me, and be civil, Mr Kemp.'

Poor Kemp, who had been a lieutenant at the beginning of the war, and fallen into misfortune, was the writer of the 'Post-Boy', and now took honest Mr Leach's pay in place of her Majesty's. Esmond had seen this gentleman, and a very ingenious, hard-working honest fellow he was, toiling to give bread to a great family, and watching up many a long winter night to keep the wolf from his door. And Mr St John, who had liberty always on his tongue, had just sent a dozen of the opposition writers into prison, and one actually into the pillory, for what he called libels, but libels not half so violent as those writ on our side. With regard to this very piece of tyranny, Esmond had remonstrated strongly with the Secretary, who laughed and said, the rascals were served quite right; and told Esmond a joke of Swift's regarding the matter. Nay, more, this Irishman, when St John was about to pardon a poor wretch condemned to death for rape, absolutely prevented the Secretary from exercising this act of good-nature, and boasted that he had had the man hanged; and great as the Doctor's genius might be, and splendid his ability, Esmond for one would affect no love for him, and never desired to make his acquaintance. The Doctor was at Court every Sunday assiduously enough, a place the Colonel frequented but rarely, though he had a great inducement to go there in the person of a fair maid of honour of her Majesty's; and the airs and patronage Mr Swift gave himself, forgetting gentlemen of his country whom he knew perfectly, his loud talk at once insolent and servile, nay, perhaps his very intimacy with Lord Treasurer and the Secretary, who indulged all his freaks and called him Jonathan, you may be sure, were remarked by many a person of whom the proud priest himself took no note, during that time of his vanity and triumph.

'Twas but three days after the 15th of November, 1712 (Esmond minds him well of the date), that he went by invitation to dine with his General, the foot of whose table he used to take on these festive occasions, as he had done at many a board, hard and plentiful, during the campaign. This was a great feast, and of the latter sort; the honest old gentleman loved to treat his friends splendidly: his Grace of Ormonde, before he joined his army as Generalissimo, my Lord Viscount Bolingbroke, one of her Majesty's Secretaries of State, my Lord Orkney, that had served with us abroad, being of the party. His Grace of Hamilton, Master of the Ordnance, and in whose honour the feast had been given, upon his approaching departure as Ambassador to Paris, had sent an excuse to General Webb at two o'clock, but an hour before the dinner: nothing but the most immediate business, his Grace said, should have prevented him having the pleasure of drinking a parting glass to the health of General Webb. His absence disappointed Esmond's old chief, who suffered much from his wounds besides; and though the company was grand, it was rather gloomy. St John came last, and brought a friend with him:– 'I'm sure,' says my General, bowing very politely, 'my table hath always a place for Doctor Swift.'

Mr Esmond went up to the Doctor with a bow and a smile:– 'I gave Doctor Swift's message,' says he, 'to the printer: I hope he brought your pamphlet to your lodgings in time.' Indeed poor Leach had come to his house very soon after the Doctor left it, being brought away rather tipsy from the tavern by his thrifty wife; and he talked of Cousin Swift in a maudlin way, though of course Mr Esmond did not allude to this relationship. The Doctor scowled, blushed, and was much confused, and said scarce a word during the whole of dinner. A very little stone will sometimes knock down these Goliaths of wit; and this one was often discomfited when met by a man

of any spirit; he took his place sulkily, put water in his wine
that the others drank plentifully, and scarce said a word.

The talk was about the affairs of the day, or rather about
persons than affairs: my Lady Marlborough's fury, her daughters in old clothes and mob-caps[15] looking out from their
windows and seeing the company pass to the Drawing-room;
the gentleman-usher's horror when the Prince of Savoy was
introduced to her Majesty in a tie-wig,[16] no man out of a full-
bottomed periwig ever having kissed the royal hand before;
about the Mohawks and the damage they were doing, rushing
through the town, killing and murdering. Some one said the
ill-omened face of Mohun had been seen at the theatre the
night before, and Macartney and Meredith with him. Meant to
be a feast, the meeting, in spite of drink and talk, was as dismal
as a funeral. Every topic started subsided into gloom. His
Grace of Ormonde went away because the conversation got
upon Denain, where we had been defeated in the last campaign.
Esmond's General was affected at the allusion to this action
too, for his comrade of Wynendael, the Count of Nassau
Woudenberg, had been slain there. Mr Swift, when Esmond
pledged him, said he drank no wine, and took his hat from the
peg and went away, beckoning my Lord Bolingbroke to follow
him; but the other bade him take his chariot and save his coach-
hire – he had to speak with Colonel Esmond; and when the rest
of the company withdrew to cards, these two remained behind
in the dark.

Bolingbroke always spoke freely when he had drunk freely.
His enemies could get any secret out of him in that condition;
women were even employed to ply him, and take his words
down. I have heard that my Lord Stair,[17] three years after,
when the Secretary fled to France and became the Pretender's
minister, got all the information he wanted by putting female
spies over St John in his cups. He spoke freely now:– 'Jonathan
knows nothing of this for certain, though he suspects it, and by
George, Webb will take an Archbishopric, and Jonathan a – no,
damme – Jonathan will take an Archbishopric from James, I
warrant me, gladly enough. Your Duke hath the string of the
whole matter in his hand,' the Secretary went on. 'We have

that which will force Marlborough to keep his distance, and he goes out of London in a fortnight. Prior hath his business; he left me this morning, and mark me, Harry, should fate carry off our august, our beloved, our most gouty and plethoric Queen, and Defender of the Faith, *la bonne cause triomphera. A la santé de la bonne cause*, Everything good comes from France. Wine comes from France; give us another bumper to the *bonne cause*.' We drank it together.

'Will the *bonne cause* turn Protestant?' asked Mr Esmond.

'No, hang it,' says the other, 'he'll defend our Faith as in duty bound, but he'll stick by his own. The Hind and the Panther[18] shall run in the same car, by Jove. Righteousness and peace shall kiss each other; and we'll have Father Massillon to walk down the aisle of St Paul's, cheek by jowl, with Doctor Sacheverel. Give us more wine; here's a health to the *bonne cause*, kneeling – damme, let's drink it kneeling.' He was quite flushed and wild with wine as he was talking.

'And suppose,' says Esmond, who always had this gloomy apprehension, 'the *bonne cause* should give us up to the French, as his father and uncle did before him.'

'Give us up to the French!' starts up Bolingbroke; 'is there any English gentleman that fears that? You who have seen Blenheim and Ramillies, afraid of the French! Your ancestors and mine, and brave old Webb's yonder, have met them in a hundred fields, and our children will be ready to do the like. Who's he that wishes for more men from England? My Cousin Westmoreland?[19] Give us up to the French, pshaw!'

'His uncle did,' says Mr Esmond.

'And what happened to his grandfather?' broke out St John, filling out another bumper. 'Here's to the greatest monarch England ever saw; here's to the Englishman that made a kingdom of her. Our great King came from Huntingdon, not Hanover,[20] our fathers didn't look for a Dutchman to rule us. Let him come and we'll keep him, and we'll show him White-hall. If he's a traitor let us have him here to deal with him; and then there are spirits here as great as any that have gone before. There are men here that can look at danger in the face and not be frightened at it. Traitor, treason! what names are these to scare you and me? Are all Oliver's men dead, or his glorious name forgotten in fifty years? Are there no men equal to him, think you, as good – aye, as good? God save the King! and, if the monarchy fails us, God save the British Republic!'

He filled another great bumper, and tossed it up and drained it wildly, just as the noise of rapid carriage-wheels approaching was stopped at our door, and after a hurried knock and a moment's interval, Mr Swift came into the hall, ran upstairs to the room we were dining in, and entered it with a perturbed face. St John, excited with drink, was making some wild quotation out of Macbeth, but Swift stopped him.

'Drink no more, my lord, for God's sake,' says he, 'I come with the most dreadful news.'

'Is the Queen dead?' cries out Bolingbroke, seizing on a water-glass.

'No, Duke Hamilton is dead;[21] he was murdered an hour ago by Mohun and Macartney; they had a quarrel this morning; they gave him not so much time as to write a letter. He went for a couple of his friends, and he is dead, and Mohun, too, the bloody villain, who was set on him. They fought in Hyde Park just before sunset; the Duke killed Mohun, and Macartney came up and stabbed him, and the dog is fled. I have your chariot below; send to every part of the country and apprehend that villain; come to the Duke's house and see if any life be left in him.'

'O Beatrix, Beatrix,' thought Esmond, 'and here ends my poor girl's ambition!'

## Chapter 6

### POOR BEATRIX

THERE had been no need to urge upon Esmond the necessity of a separation between him and Beatrix: Fate had done that completely; and I think from the very moment poor Beatrix had accepted the Duke's offer, she began to assume the majestic air of a Duchess, nay, Queen Elect, and to carry herself as one sacred and removed from us common people. Her mother and kinsman both fell into her ways, the latter scornfully perhaps, and uttering his usual gibes at her vanity and his own. There was a certain charm about this girl of which neither Colonel Esmond nor his fond mistress could forego the fascination; in spite of her faults and her pride and wilfulness, they were forced to love her; and, indeed, might be set down as the two chief flatterers of the brilliant creature's court.

Who, in the course of his life, hath not been so bewitched, and worshipped some idol or another? Years after this passion hath been dead and buried, along with a thousand other worldly cares and ambitions, he who felt it can recall it out of its grave, and admire, almost as fondly as he did in his youth, that lovely queenly creature. I invoke that beautiful spirit from the shades and love her still; or rather I should say such a past is always present to a man; such a passion once felt forms a part of his whole being, and cannot be separated from it; it becomes a portion of the man to-day, just as any great faith or conviction, the discovery of poetry, the awakening of religion, ever afterward influence him; just as the wound I had at Blenheim, and of which I wear the scar, hath become part of my frame and influenced my whole body, nay, spirit subsequently, though 'twas got and healed forty years ago. Parting and forgetting! What faithful heart can do these? Our great thoughts, our great affections, the Truths of our life, never leave us. Surely, they cannot separate from our consciousness; shall follow it whithersoever that shall go; and are of their nature divine and immortal.

With the horrible news of this catastrophe, which was confirmed by the weeping domestics at the Duke's own door, Esmond rode homewards as quick as his lazy coach would carry him, devising all the time how he should break the intelligence to the person most concerned in it; and if a satire upon human vanity could be needed, that poor soul afforded it in the altered company and occupations in which Esmond found her. For days before, her chariot had been rolling the street from mercer to toyshop – from goldsmith to laceman: her taste was perfect, or at least the fond bridegroom had thought so, and had given entire

authority over all tradesmen, and for all the plate, furniture, and
equipages, with which his Grace the Ambassador wished to
adorn his splendid mission. She must have her picture by
Kneller, a duchess not being complete without a portrait, and a
noble one he made, and actually sketched in, on a cushion, a
coronet which she was about to wear. She vowed she would wear
it at King James the Third's coronation, and never a princess in
the land would have become ermine better. Esmond found the
ante-chamber crowded with milliners and toyshop women,
obsequious goldsmiths with jewels, salvers, and tankards; and
mercers' men with hangings, and velvets, and brocades. My
Lady Duchess Elect was giving audience to one famous silver-
smith from Exeter Change, who brought with him a great chased
salver, of which he was pointing out the beauties as Colonel
Esmond entered. 'Come,' says she, 'Cousin, and admire the taste
of this pretty thing.' I think Mars and Venus were lying in the
golden bower, that one gilt Cupid carried off the war-god's
casque – another his sword – another his great buckler, upon
which my Lord Duke Hamilton's arms with ours were to be
engraved – and a fourth was kneeling down to the reclining
goddess with the ducal coronet in his hands, God help us! The
next time Mr Esmond saw that piece of plate, the arms were
changed, the ducal coronet had been replaced by a viscount's; it
formed part of the fortune of the thrifty goldsmith's own
daughter, when she married my Lord Viscount Squanderfield
two years after.

'Isn't this a beautiful piece?' says Beatrix, examining it, and
she pointed out the arch graces of the Cupids, and the fine
carving of the languid prostrate Mars. Esmond sickened as he
thought of the warrior dead in his chamber, his servants and
children weeping around him; and of this smiling creature attiring
herself, as it were, for that nuptial deathbed. ''Tis a pretty
piece of vanity,' says he, looking gloomily at the beautiful creature:
there were flambeaux in the room lighting up the brilliant
mistress of it. She lifted up the great gold salver with her fair arms.

'Vanity!' says she, haughtily, 'What is vanity in you, sir, is
propriety in me. You ask a Jewish price for it, Mr Graves; but
have it I will, if only to spite Mr Esmond.'

'O Beatrix, lay it down!' says Mr Esmond. 'Herodias! you know not what you carry in the charger.'

She dropped it with a clang; the eager goldsmith running to seize his fallen ware. The lady's face caught the fright from Esmond's pale countenance, and her eyes shone out like beacons of alarm: – 'What is it, Henry?' says she, running to him, and seizing both his hands, 'What do you mean by your pale face and gloomy tones?'

'Come away, come away!' says Esmond, leading her: she clung frightened to him, and he supported her upon his heart, bidding the scared goldsmith leave them. The man went into the next apartment, staring with surprise, and hugging his precious charger.

'O my Beatrix, my sister!' says Esmond, still holding in his arms the pallid and affrighted creature, 'you have the greatest courage of any woman in the world; prepare to show it now, for you have a dreadful trial to bear.'

She sprang away from the friend who would have protected her: – 'Hath he left me?' says she. 'We had words this morning: he was very gloomy, and I angered him: but he dared not, he dared not!' As she spoke a burning blush flushed over her whole face and bosom. Esmond saw it reflected in the glass by which she stood, with clenched hands, pressing her swelling heart.

'He has left you,' says Esmond, wondering that rage rather than sorrow was in her looks.

'And he is alive,' cries Beatrix, 'and you bring me this commission! He has left me, and you haven't dared to avenge me! You, that pretend to be the champion of our house, have let me suffer this insult! Where is Castlewood? I will go to my brother.'

'The Duke is not alive, Beatrix,' said Esmond.

She looked at her cousin wildly, and fell back to the wall as though shot in the breast: – 'And you come here, and – and – you killed him?'

'No; thank Heaven,' her kinsman said, 'the blood of that noble heart doth not stain my sword! In its last hour it was faithful to thee, Beatrix Esmond. Vain and cruel woman! kneel and thank the awful Heaven which awards life and death, and chastises pride, that the noble Hamilton died true to you; at least that 'twas not your quarrel, or your pride, or your wicked vanity, that drove him to his fate. He died by the bloody sword which already had drank your own father's blood. O woman, O sister! to that sad field where two corpses are lying – for the murderer died too by the hand of the man he slew – can you bring no mourners but your revenge and your vanity? God help and pardon thee, Beatrix, as he brings this awful punishment to your hard and rebellious heart.'

Esmond had scarce done speaking, when his mistress came in. The colloquy between him and Beatrix had lasted but a few minutes, during which time Esmond's servant had carried the disastrous news through the household. The army of Vanity-Fair, waiting without, gathered up all their fripperies and fled aghast. Tender Lady Castlewood had been in talk above with Dean Atterbury, the pious creature's almoner and director; and the Dean had entered with her as a physician whose place was at a sick-bed. Beatrix's mother looked at Esmond and ran towards her daughter, with a pale face and open heart and hands, all kindness and pity. But Beatrix passed her by, nor would she have any of the medicaments of the spiritual physician. 'I am best in my own room and by myself,' she said. Her eyes were quite dry; nor did Esmond ever see them otherwise, save once, in respect to that grief. She gave him a cold hand as she went out: 'Thank you, brother,' she said, in a low voice, and with a simplicity more touching than tears; 'all you have said is true and kind, and I will go away and ask pardon.' The three others remained behind, and talked over the dreadful story. It affected Doctor Atterbury more even than us, as it seemed. The death of Mohun, her husband's murderer, was more awful to my mistress than even the Duke's unhappy end. Esmond gave at length what particulars he knew of their quarrel, and the cause of it. The two noblemen had long been at war with respect to the Lord Gerard's property, whose two daughters my Lord Duke and Mohun had married. They had met by appointment that day at the lawyer's in Lincoln's Inn Fields; had words which, though they appeared very trifling to those who heard them, were not so to men exasperated by long and previous enmity. Mohun asked my Lord Duke where he could see his Grace's friends, and within an hour had sent two of his own to arrange this deadly duel. It was pursued with such fierceness, and sprung from so trifling a cause, that all men agreed at the time that there was a party, of which these three notorious brawlers were but agents, who desired to take Duke Hamilton's life away. They fought three on a side, as in that tragic meeting twelve years back, which hath been recounted already, and in which Mohun performed his second murder. They rushed in, and closed upon each other at once without any feints or crossing of swords even, and stabbed one at the other desperately, each receiving many wounds; and Mohun having his death-wound, and my Lord Duke lying by him, Macartney came up and stabbed his Grace as he lay on the ground, and gave him the blow of which he died. Colonel Macartney denied this, of which the horror and indignation of the whole kingdom would nevertheless have him guilty, and fled the country, whither he never returned.

What was the real cause of the Duke Hamilton's death? – a paltry quarrel that might easily have been made up, and with a ruffian so low, base, profligate, and degraded with former crimes and repeated murders, that a man of such a renown and princely rank as my Lord Duke might have disdained to sully his sword with the blood of such a villain. But his spirit was so high that those who wished his death knew that his courage was like his charity, and never turned any man away; and he died by the hands of Mohun, and the other two cut-throats that were set on him. The Queen's Ambassador to Paris died, the loyal and devoted servant of the House of Stuart, and a Royal Prince of Scotland himself, and carrying the confidence, the repentance of Queen Anne along with his own open devotion, and the good-will of millions in the country more, to the Queen's exiled brother and soverign.

That party to which Lord Mohun belonged had the benefit of his service, and now were well rid of such a ruffian. He, and Meredith, and Macartney, were the Duke of Marlborough's men; and the two colonels had been broke but the year before for drinking perdition to the Tories. His Grace was a Whig now and a Hanoverian, and as eager for war as Prince Eugene himself. I say not that he was privy to Duke Hamilton's death, I say that his party profited by it; and that three desperate and bloody instruments were found to effect that murder.

As Esmond and the Dean walked away from Kensington discoursing of this tragedy, and how fatal it was to the cause which they both had at heart, the street-criers were already out with their broadsides, shouting through the town the full, true, and horrible account of the death of Lord Mohun and Duke Hamilton in a duel. A fellow had got to Kensington, and was crying it in the square there at very early morning, when Mr Esmond happened to pass by. He drove the man from under Beatrix's very window, whereof the casement had been set open. The sun was shining though 'twas November: he had seen the market-carts rolling into London, the guard relieved at the Palace, the labourers trudging to their work in the gardens between Kensington and the City – the wandering merchants and hawkers filling the air with their cries. The world was going to its business again, although dukes lay dead and ladies mourned for them; and kings, very likely, lost their chances. So night and day pass away, and to-morrow comes, and our place knows us not. Esmond thought of the courier, now galloping on the North road to inform him, who was Earl of Arran yesterday, that he was Duke of Hamilton to-day, and of a thousand great schemes, hopes, ambitions, that were alive in the gallant heart, beating a few hours since, and now in a little dust quiescent.

## Chapter 7

### I VISIT CASTLEWOOD ONCE MORE

THUS, for a third time, Beatrix's ambitious hopes were circumvented, and she might well believe that a special malignant fate watched and pursued her, tearing her prize out of her hand just as she seemed to grasp it, and leaving her with only rage and grief for her portion. Whatever her feelings might have been of anger or of sorrow (and I fear me that the former emotion was that which most tore her heart), she would take no confidant, as people of softer natures would have done under such a calamity; her mother and her kinsman knew that she would disdain their pity, and that to offer it would be but to infuriate the cruel wound which fortune had inflicted. We knew that her pride was fully humbled and punished by this sudden and terrible blow; she wanted no teaching of ours to point out the sad moral of her story. Her fond mother could give but her prayers, and her kinsman his faithful friendship and patience to the unhappy, stricken creature; and it was only by hints, and a word or two uttered months afterwards, that Beatrix showed she understood their silent commiseration, and on her part was secretly thankful for their forbearance. The people about the Court said there was that in her manner which frightened away scoffing and condolence: she was above their triumph and their pity, and acted her part in that dreadful tragedy greatly and courageously; so that those who liked her least were yet forced to admire her. We, who watched her after her disaster, could not but respect the indomitable courage and majestic calm with which she bore it. 'I would rather see her tears than her pride,' her mother said, who was accustomed to bear her sorrows in a very different way, and to receive them as the stroke of God, with an awful submission and meekness. But Beatrix's nature was different to that tender parent's; she seemed to accept her grief, and to defy it; nor would she allow it (I believe not even in private, and in her own chamber) to extort from her the confession of even a tear of humiliation or a cry of pain. Friends and children of our race, who come after me, in which way will you bear your trials? I know one that prays God will give you love rather than pride, and that the Eye all-seeing shall find you in the humble place. Not that we should judge proud spirits otherwise than charitably. 'Tis nature hath fashioned some for ambition and dominion, as it hath formed others for obedience and gentle submission. The leopard follows his nature as the lamb does, and acts after leopard law; she can neither help her beauty, nor her courage, nor her cruelty; not a single spot on her shining coat; nor the conquering spirit which impels her; nor the shot which brings her down.

During that well-founded panic the Whigs had, lest the Queen should forsake their Hanoverian Prince, bound by oaths and treaties as she was to him, and recall her brother, who was allied to her by yet stronger ties of nature and duty, the Prince of Savoy, and the boldest of that party of the Whigs, were for bringing the young Duke of Cambridge[1] over, in spite of the Queen and the outcry of her Tory servants, arguing that the Electoral Prince, a peer and prince of the blood-royal of this realm too, and in the line of succession to the crown, had a right to sit in the Parliament whereof he was a member, and to dwell in the country which he one day was to govern. Nothing but the strongest ill-will expressed by the Queen, and the people about her, and menaces of the Royal resentment, should this scheme be persisted in, prevented it from being carried into effect.

The boldest on our side were, in like manner, for having our Prince into the country. The undoubted inheritor of the right divine; the feelings of more than half the nation, of almost all the clergy, of the gentry of England and Scotland with him; entirely innocent of the crime for which his father suffered – brave, young, handsome, unfortunate – who in England would dare to molest the Prince should he come among us, and fling himself upon British generosity, hospitality, and honour? An invader with an army of Frenchmen behind him, Englishmen of spirit would resist to the death, and drive back to the shores whence he came; but a prince, alone, armed with his right only, and relying on the loyalty of his people, was sure, many of his friends argued, of welcome, at least of safety, among us. The hand of his sister the Queen, of the people his subjects, never could be raised to do him a wrong. But the Queen was timid by nature, and the successive ministers she had, had private causes for their irresolution. The bolder and honester men, who had at heart the illustrious young exile's cause, had no scheme of interest of their own to prevent them from seeing the right done, and, provided only he came as an Englishman, were ready to venture their all to welcome and defend him.

St John and Harley both had kind words in plenty for the Prince's adherents, and gave him endless promises of future support: but hints and promises were all they could be got to give; and some of his friends were for measures much bolder, more efficacious, and more open. With a party of these, some of whom are yet alive, and some whose names Mr Esmond has no right to mention, he found himself engaged the year after that miserable death of Duke Hamilton, which deprived the Prince of his most courageous ally in this country. Dean Atterbury[2] was one of the friends whom Esmond may mention, as the brave bishop is now beyond exile and persecution, and to him, and one or two more, the Colonel opened himself of a scheme of his own, that, backed by a little resolution on the Prince's part, could not fail of bringing about the accomplishment of their dearest wishes.

My young Lord Viscount Castlewood had not come to England to keep his majority, and had now been absent from the country for several years. The year when his sister was to be married and Duke Hamilton died, my lord was kept at Bruxelles by his wife's lying-in. The gentle Clotilda could not bear her husband out of her sight; perhaps she mistrusted the young scapegrace should he ever get loose from her leading-strings; and she kept him by her side to nurse the baby and administer posset to the gossips.[3] Many a laugh poor Beatrix had had about Frank's uxoriousness: his mother would have gone to Clotilda when her time was coming, but that the mother-in-law was already in possession, and the negotiations for poor Beatrix's marriage were begun. A few months after the horrid catastrophe in Hyde Park, my mistress and her daughter retired to Castlewood, where my lord, it was expected, would soon join them. But, to say truth, their quiet household was little to his taste; he could be got to come to Walcote but once after his first campaign; and then the young rogue spent more than half his time in London, not appearing at Court or in public under his own name and title, but frequenting plays, bagnios, and the very worst company, under the name of Captain Esmond (whereby his innocent kinsman got more than once into trouble); and so under various pretexts, and in pursuit of all sorts of pleasures, until he plunged into the lawful one of marriage, Frank Castlewood had remained away from this country, and was unknown, save amongst the gentlemen of the army, with whom he had served abroad. The fond heart of his mother was pained by this long absence. 'Twas all that Henry Esmond could do to soothe her natural mortification, and find excuses for his kinsman's levity.

In the autumn of the year 1713, Lord Castlewood thought of returning home. His first child had been a daughter; Clotilda was in the way of gratifying his lordship with a second, and the pious youth thought that, by bringing his wife to his ancestral home, by prayers to St Philip of Castlewood, and what not, Heaven might be induced to bless him with a son this time, for whose coming the expectant mamma was very anxious.

The long-debated peace had been proclaimed this year at the end of March, and France was open to us. Just as Frank's poor mother had made all things ready for Lord Castlewood's reception, and was eagerly expecting her son, it was by Colonel Esmond's means that the kind lady was disappointed of her longing, and obliged to defer once more the darling hope of her heart.

Esmond took horses to Castlewood. He had not seen its ancient grey towers and well-remembered woods for nearly fourteen years, and since he rode thence with my lord, to whom his mistress with her young children by her side waved an adieu; what ages seem to have passed since then, what years of action and passion, of care, love, hope, disaster! The children were grown up now, and had stories of their own. As for Esmond, he felt to be a hundred years old; his dear mistress only seemed unchanged; she looked and welcomed him quite as of old. There was the fountain in the court babbling its familiar music, the old hall and its furniture, the carved chair my late lord used, the very flagon he drank from. Esmond's mistress knew he would like to sleep in the little room he used to occupy; 'twas made ready for him, and wall-flowers and sweet herbs set in the adjoining chamber, the chaplain's room.

In tears of not unmanly emotion, with prayers of submission to the awful Dispenser of death and life, of good and evil fortune, Mr Esmond passed a part of that first night at Castlewood, lying awake for many hours as the clock kept tolling (in tones so well remembered), looking back, as all men will, that revisit their home of childhood, over the great gulf of time, and surveying himself on the distant bank yonder, a sad little melancholy boy, with his lord still alive – his dear mistress, a girl yet, her children sporting around her. Years ago, a boy on that very bed, when she had blessed him and called him her knight, he had made a vow to be faithful and never desert her dear service. Had he kept that fond boyish promise? Yes, before Heaven; yes, praise be to God! His life had been hers; his blood, his fortune, his name, his whole heart ever since had been hers and her children's. All night long he was dreaming his boyhood over again, and waking fitfully; he half fancied he heard Father Holt calling to him from the next chamber, and that he was coming in and out from the mysterious window.

Esmond rose up before the dawn, passed into the next room, where the air was heavy with the odour of the wallflowers; looked into the brazier where the papers had been burnt, into the old presses where Holt's books and papers had been kept, and tried the spring, and whether the window worked still. The spring had not been touched for years, but yielded at length, and the whole fabric of the window sank down. He lifted it and it relapsed into its frame; no one had ever passed thence since Holt used it sixteen years ago.

Esmond remembered his poor lord saying, on the last day of his life, that Holt used to come in and out of the house like a ghost, and knew that the Father liked these mysteries, and practised such secret disguises, entrances, and exits: this was the way the ghost came and went, his pupil had always conjectured. Esmond closed the casement up again as the dawn was rising over Castlewood village; he could hear the clinking at the black-smith's forge yonder among the trees, across the green, and past the river, on which a mist still lay sleeping.

Next Esmond opened that long cupboard over the wood-work of the mantelpiece, big enough to hold a man, and in which Mr Holt used to keep sundry secret properties of his. The two swords he remembered so well as a boy, lay actually there still, and Esmond took them out and wiped them, with a strange curiosity of emotion. There were a bundle of papers here, too, which no doubt had been left at Holt's last visit to the place, in my Lord Viscount's life, that very day when the priest had been arrested and taken to Hexham[4] Castle. Esmond made free with these papers, and found treasonable matter to King William's reign, the names of Charnock and Perkins, Sir John Fenwick and Sir John Friend, Rookwood and Lodwick, Lords Montgomery and Ailesbury, Clarendon and Yarmouth, that had all been engaged in plots against the usurper; a letter from the Duke of Berwick too, and one from the King at St Germains, offering to confer upon his trusty and well-beloved Francis Viscount Castlewood the titles of Earl and Marquis of Esmond, bestowed by patent royal, and in the fourth year of his reign, upon Thomas Viscount Castlewood and the heirs-male of his body, in default of which issue the ranks and dignities were to pass to Francis aforesaid.

This was the paper, whereof my lord had spoken, which Holt showed him the very day he was arrested, and for an answer to which he would come back in a week's time. I put these papers hastily into the crypt whence I had taken them, being interrupted by a tapping of a light finger at the ring of the chamber-door; 'twas my kind mistress, with her face full of love and welcome. She, too, had passed the night wakefully, no doubt; but neither asked the other how the hours had been spent. There are things we divine without speaking, and know though they happen out of our sight. This fond lady hath told me that she knew both days when I was wounded abroad. Who shall say how far sympathy reaches, and how truly love can prophesy? 'I looked into your room,' was all she said; 'the bed was vacant, the little old bed! I knew I should find you here.' And tender and blushing faintly with a benediction in her eyes, the gentle creature kissed him.

They walked out, hand-in-hand, through the old court, and to the terrace-walk, where the grass was glistening with dew, and the birds in the green woods above were singing their delicious choruses under the blushing morning sky. How well all things were remembered! The ancient towers and gables of the Hall darkling against the east, the purple shadows on the green slopes, the quaint devices and carvings of the dial, the forest-crowned heights, the fair yellow plain cheerful with crops and corn, the shining river rolling through it towards the pearly hills beyond; all these were before us, along with a thousand beautiful memories of our youth, beautiful and sad, but as real and vivid in our minds as that fair and always-remembered scene our eyes beheld once more. We forget nothing. The memory sleeps, but wakens again; I often think how it shall be when, after the last sleep of death, the *réveillée* shall arouse us for ever, and the past in one flash of self-consciousness rush back, like the soul, revivified.

The house would not be up for some hours yet (it was July, and the dawn was only just awake), and here Esmond opened himself to his mistress, of the business he had in hand, and what part Frank was to play in it. He knew he could confide anything to her, and that the fond soul would die rather than reveal it; and bidding her keep the secret from all, he laid it entirely before his mistress (always as staunch a little loyalist as any in the kingdom), and indeed was quite sure that any plan of his was secure of her applause and sympathy. Never was such a glorious scheme to her partial mind, never such a devoted knight to execute it. An hour or two may have passed whilst they were having their colloquy. Beatrix came out to them just as their talk was over; her tall beautiful form robed in sable (which she wore without ostentation ever since last year's catastrophe), sweeping over the green terrace, and casting its shadows before her across the grass.

She made us one of her grand curtseys smiling, and called us 'the young people.' She was older, paler, and more majestic than in the year before; her mother seemed the youngest of the two. She never once spoke of her grief, Lady Castlewood told Esmond, or alluded, save by a quiet word or two, to the death of her hopes.

When Beatrix came back to Castlewood she took to visiting all the cottages and all the sick. She set up a school of children, and taught singing to some of them. We had a pair of beautiful old organs[5] in Castlewood Church, on which she played admirably, so that the music there became to be known in the country for many miles round, and no doubt people came to see the fair organist as well as to hear her. Parson Tusher and his wife were established at the vicarage, but his wife had brought him no children wherewith Tom might meet his enemies at the gate.

Honest Tom took care not to have many such; his great shovel-hat was in his hand for everybody. He was profuse of bows and compliments. He behaved to Esmond as if the Colonel had been a Commander-in-Chief; he dined at the Hall that day, being Sunday, and would not partake of pudding except under extreme pressure. He deplored my lord's perversion, but drank his lordship's health very devoutly; and an hour before at church sent the Colonel to sleep, with a long, learned, and refreshing sermon.

Esmond's visit home was but for two days; the business he had in hand calling him away and out of the country. Ere he went, he saw Beatrix but once alone, and then she summoned him out of the long tapestry room, where he and his mistress were sitting, quite as in old times, into the adjoining chamber, that had been Viscountess Isabel's sleeping apartment, and where Esmond perfectly well remembered seeing the old lady sitting up in the bed, in her night-rail, that morning when the troop of guard came to fetch her. The most beautiful woman in England lay in that bed now, whereof the great damask hangings were scarce faded since Esmond saw them last.

Here stood Beatrix in her black robes, holding a box in her hand; 'twas that which Esmond had given her before her marriage, stamped with a coronet which the disappointed girl was never to wear; and containing his aunt's legacy of diamonds.

'You had best take these with you, Harry,' says she; 'I have no need of diamonds any more.' There was not the least token of emotion in her quiet low voice. She held out the black shagreen-case with her fair arm, that did not shake in the least. Esmond saw she wore a black velvet bracelet on it, with my Lord Duke's picture in enamel; he had given it her but three days before he fell.

Esmond said the stones were his no longer, and strove to turn off that proffered restoration with a laugh: 'Of what good,' says he, 'are they to me? The diamond loop to his hat did not set off Prince Eugene,[6] and will not make my yellow face look any handsomer.'

'You will give them to your wife, cousin,' says she. 'My cousin, your wife has a lovely complexion and shape.'

'Beatrix,' Esmond burst out, the old fire flaming out as it

would at times, 'will you wear those trinkets at your marriage? You whispered once you did not know me: you know me better now: how I fought, what I have sighed for, for ten years, what forgone!'

'A price for your constancy, my lord!' says she; 'such a *preux chevalier* wants to be paid. O fie, cousin!'

'Again,' Esmond spoke out, 'if I do something you have at heart; something worthy of me and you; something that shall make me a name with which to endow you; will you take it? There was a chance for me once, you said; is it impossible to recall it? Never shake your head, but hear me: say you will hear me a year hence. If I come back to you and bring you fame, will that please you? If I do what you desire most – what he who is dead desired most – will that soften you?'

'What is it, Henry,' says she, her face lighting up; 'what mean you?'

'Ask no questions,' he said, 'wait, and give me but time; if I bring back that you long for, that I have a thousand times heard you pray for, will you have no reward for him who has done you that service? Put away those trinkets, keep them: it shall not be at my marriage, it shall not be at yours, but if man can do it, I swear a day shall come when there shall be a feast in your house, and you shall be proud to wear them. I say no more now; put aside these words, and lock away yonder box until the day when I shall remind you of both. All I pray of you now is, to wait and to remember.'

'You are going out of the country?' says Beatrix, in some agitation.

'Yes, tomorrow,' says Esmond.

'To Lorraine,⁷ cousin?' says Beatrix, laying her hand on his arm; 'twas the hand on which she wore the Duke's bracelet. 'Stay, Harry!' continued she, with a tone that had more despondency in it than she was accustomed to show. 'Hear a last word. I do love you, I do admire you – who would not, that has known such love as yours has been for us all? But I think I have no heart; at least, I have never seen the man that could touch it; and, had I found him, I would have followed him in rags had he been a private soldier, or to sea, like one of those buccaneers you

used to read to us about when we were children. I would do anything for such a man, bear anything for him: but I never found
one. You were ever too much of a slave to win my heart; even
my Lord Duke could not command it. I had not been happy had
I married him. I knew that three months after our engagement –
and was too vain to break it. O Harry! I cried once or twice, not
for him, but with tears of rage because I could not be sorry for
him. I was frightened to find I was glad of his death; and were I
joined to you, I should have the same sense of servitude, the
same longing to escape. We should both be unhappy, and you
the most, who are as jealous as the Duke was himself. I tried to
love him; I tried, indeed I did: affected gladness when he came:
submitted to hear when he was by me, and tried the wife's part I
thought I was to play for the rest of my days. But half-an-hour
of that complaisance wearied me, and what would a lifetime be?
My thoughts were away when he was speaking; and I was thinking, O that this man would drop my hand, and rise up from
before my feet! I knew his great and noble qualities, greater and
nobler than mine a thousand times, as yours are, cousin, I tell
you, a million and a million times better. But 'twas not for these
I took him. I took him to have a great place in the world, and I
lost it. I lost it, and do not deplore him – and I often thought, as
I listened to his fond vows and ardent words, O, if I yield to this
man, and meet *the other*, I shall hate him and leave him! I am not
good, Harry: my mother is gentle and good like an angel. I
wonder how she should have had such a child. She is weak, but
she would die rather than do a wrong; I am stronger than she,
but I would do it out of defiance. I do not care for what the
parsons tell me with their droning sermons: I used to see them at
Court as mean and as worthless as the meanest woman there.
O, I am sick and weary of the world! I wait but for one thing,
and when 'tis done, I will take Frank's religion and your poor
mother's, and go into a nunnery, and end like her. Shall I wear
the diamonds then? – they say the nuns wear their best trinkets the
day they take the veil. I will put them away as you bid me; farewell, cousin, mamma is pacing the next room, racking her little
head to know what we have been saying. She is jealous; all women
are. I sometimes think that is the only womanly quality I have.'

'Farewell. Farewell, brother!' She gave him her cheek as a brotherly privilege. The cheek was as cold as marble.

Esmond's mistress showed no signs of jealousy when he returned to the room where she was. She had schooled herself so as to look quite inscrutably, when she had a mind. Amongst her other feminine qualities she had that of being a perfect dissembler.

He rid away from Castlewood to attempt the task he was bound on, and stand or fall by it; in truth his state of mind was such, that he was eager for some outward excitement to counteract that gnawing malady which he was inwardly enduring.

## Chapter 8

### I TRAVEL TO FRANCE AND BRING HOME A PORTRAIT OF RIGAUD

MR ESMOND did not think fit to take leave at Court, or to inform all the world of Pall Mall and the coffee-houses, that he was about to quit England; and chose to depart in the most private manner possible. He procured a pass as for a Frenchman, through Doctor Atterbury, who did that business for him, getting the signature even from Lord Bolingbroke's office, without any personal application to the Secretary. Lockwood, his faithful servant, he took with him to Castlewood, and left behind there: giving out ere he left London that he himself was sick, and gone to Hampshire for country air, and so departed as silently as might be upon his business.

As Frank Castlewood's aid was indispensable for Mr Esmond's scheme, his first visit was to Bruxelles (passing by way of Antwerp, where the Duke of Marlborough was in exile), and in the first-named place Harry found his dear young Benedick,[1] the married man, who appeared to be rather out of humour with his matrimonial chain, and clogged with the obstinate embraces which Clotilda kept round his neck. Colonel Esmond was not presented to her; but Monsieur Simon was, a gentleman of the

Royal Cravat (Esmond bethought him of the regiment of his honest Irishman, whom he had seen that day after Malplaquet, when he first set eyes on the young King); and Monsieur Simon was introduced to the Viscountess Castlewood, née Comptesse Wertheim; to the numerous counts, the Lady Clotilda's tall brothers; to her father the chamberlain; and to the lady his wife, Frank's mother-in-law, a tall and majestic person of large proportions, such as became the mother of such a company of grenadiers as her warlike sons formed. The whole race were at free quarters in the little castle nigh to Bruxelles which Frank had taken; rode his horses; drank his wine; and lived easily at the poor lad's charges. Mr Esmond had always maintained a perfect fluency in the French, which was his mother tongue; and if this family (that spoke French with the twang which the Flemings use) discovered any inaccuracy in Mr Simon's pronunciation, 'twas to be attributed to the latter's long residence in England, where he had married and remained ever since he was taken prisoner at Blenheim. His story was perfectly pat; there were none there to doubt it save honest Frank, and he was charmed with his kinsman's scheme, when he became acquainted with it; and, in truth, always admired Colonel Esmond with an affectionate fidelity, and thought his cousin the wisest and best of all cousins and men. Frank entered heart and soul into the plan, and liked it the better as it was to take him to Paris, out of reach of his brothers, his father, and his mother-in-law, whose attentions rather fatigued him.

Castlewood, I have said, was born in the same year as the Prince of Wales; had not a little of the Prince's air, height, and figure; and, especially since he had seen the Chevalier de St George on the occasion before-named, took no small pride in his resemblance to a person so illustrious; which likeness he increased by all means in his power, wearing fair brown periwigs, such as the Prince wore, and ribbons, and so forth, of the Chevalier's colour.

This resemblance was, in truth, the circumstance on which Mr Esmond's scheme was founded; and, having secured Frank's secrecy and enthusiasm, he left him to continue his journey, and see the other personages on whom its success depended. The place whither Mr Simon next travelled was Bar, in Lorraine, where that merchant arrived with a consignment of broadcloths, valuable laces from Malines, and letters for his correspondent there.

Would you know how a prince, heroic from misfortunes, and descended from a line of kings, whose race seemed to be doomed like the Atridæ[2] of old – would you know how he was employed when the envoy who came to him through danger and difficulty beheld him for the first time? The young King, in a flannel jacket, was at tennis with the gentlemen of his suite, crying out after the balls, and swearing like the meanest of his subjects. The next time Mr Esmond saw him, 'twas when Monsieur Simon took a packet of laces to Miss Oglethorpe,[3] the Prince's ante-chamber in those days, at which ignoble door men were forced to knock for admission to his Majesty. The admission was given, the envoy found the King and the mistress together; the pair were at cards, and his Majesty was in liquor. He cared more for three honours than three kingdoms; and a half-dozen glasses of ratafia made him forget all his woes and his losses, his father's crown, and his grandfather's head.

Mr Esmond did not open himself to the Prince then. His Majesty was scarce in a condition to hear him; and he doubted whether a king who drank so much could keep a secret in his fuddled head; or whether a hand that shook so was strong enough to grasp at a crown. However at last, and after taking counsel with the Prince's advisers, amongst whom were many gentlemen, honest and faithful, Esmond's plan was laid before the King, and her actual Majesty Queen Oglethorpe, in council. The Prince liked the scheme well enough; 'twas easy and daring, and suited to his reckless gaiety and lively youthful spirit. In the morning after he had slept his wine off, he was very gay, lively, and agreeable. His manner had an extreme charm of archness, and a kind simplicity; and, to do her justice, her Oglethorpean Majesty was kind, acute, resolute, and of good counsel; she gave the Prince much good advice that he was too weak to follow, and loved him with a fidelity which he returned with an ingratitude quite royal.

Having his own forebodings regarding his scheme should it

ever be fulfilled, and his usual sceptic doubts as to the benefit which might accrue to the country by bringing a tipsy young monarch back to it, Colonel Esmond had his audience of leave, and quiet Monsieur Simon took his departure. At any rate the youth at Bar was as good as the older Pretender at Hanover; if the worst came to the worst, the Englishman could be dealt with as easy as the German. Monsieur Simon trotted on that long journey from Nancy to Paris, and saw that famous town, stealthily and like a spy, as in truth he was; and where, sure, more magnificence and more misery is heaped together, more rags and lace, more filth and gilding, than in any city in this world. Here he was put in communication with the King's best friend, his half brother, the famous Duke of Berwick; Esmond recognised him as the stranger who had visited Castlewood now near twenty years ago. His Grace opened to him when he found that Mr Esmond was one of Webb's brave regiment, that had once been his Grace's own. He was the sword and buckler indeed of the Stuart cause: there was no stain on his shield except the bar across it, which Marlborough's sister left him. Had Berwick been his father's heir, James the Third had assuredly sat on the English throne. He could dare, endure, strike, speak, be silent. The fire and genius, perhaps, he had not (that were given to baser men), but except these he had some of the best qualities of a leader. His Grace knew Esmond's father and history; and hinted at the latter in such a way as made the Colonel to think he was aware of the particulars of that story. But Esmond did not choose to enter on it, nor did the Duke press him. Mr Esmond said, 'No doubt he should come by his name if ever greater people came by theirs.'

What confirmed Esmond in his notion that the Duke of Berwick knew of his case was, that when the Colonel went to pay his duty at St Germains, her Majesty once addressed him by the title of Marquis. He took the Queen the dutiful remembrances of her goddaughter, and the lady whom, in the days of her prosperity, her Majesty had befriended. The Queen remembered Rachel Esmond perfectly well, had heard of my Lord Castlewood's conversion, and was much edified by that act of Heaven in his favour. She knew that others of that family had been of the only true Church too: 'Your father and your mother, Monsieur le Marquis,' her Majesty said (that was the only time she used the phrase). Monsieur Simon bowed very low, and said he had found other parents than his own who had taught him differently; but these had only one king: on which her Majesty was pleased to give him a medal blessed by the Pope, which had been found very efficacious in cases similar to his own, and to promise she would offer up prayers for his conversion and that of the family: which no doubt this pious lady did, though up to the present moment, and after twenty-seven years, Colonel Esmond is bound to say that neither the medal nor the prayers have had the slightest known effect upon his religious convictions.

As for the splendour of Versailles, Monsieur Simon, the merchant, only beheld them as a humble and distant spectator, seeing the old King but once, when he went to feed his carps; and asking for no presentation at his Majesty's Court.

By this time my Lord Viscount Castlewood was got to Paris, where, as the London prints presently announced, her ladyship was brought to bed of a son and heir. For a long while afterwards she was in a delicate state of health, and ordered by the physicians not to travel; otherwise 'twas well known that the Viscount Castlewood proposed returning to England, and taking up his residence at his own seat.

Whilst he remained at Paris, my Lord Castlewood had his picture done by the famous French painter Monsieur Rigaud, a present for his mother in London; and this piece Monsieur Simon took back with him when he returned to that city, which he reached about May, in the year 1714, very soon after which time my Lady Castlewood and her daughter, and their kinsman, Colonel Esmond, who had been at Castlewood all this time, likewise returned to London; her ladyship occupying her house at Kensington, Mr Esmond returning to his lodgings at Knightsbridge, nearer the town, and once more making his appearance at all public places, his health greatly improved by his long stay in the country.

The portrait of my lord, in a handsome gilt frame, was hung up in the place of honour in her ladyship's drawing-room. His lordship was represented in his scarlet uniform of Captain of the

Guard, with a light-brown periwig, a cuirass under his coat, a blue ribbon, and a fall of Bruxelles lace. Many of her ladyship's friends admired the piece beyond measure, and flocked to see it; Bishop Atterbury, Mr Lesly, good old Mr Collier, and others amongst the clergy, were delighted with the performance, and many among the first quality examined and praised it; only I must own that Doctor Tusher happened to come up to London, and seeing the picture (it was ordinarily covered by a curtain, but on this day Miss Beatrix happened to be looking at it when the Doctor arrived), the Vicar of Castlewood vowed he could not see any resemblance in the piece to his old pupil, except, perhaps, a little about the chin and the periwig; but we all of us convinced him, that he had not seen Frank for five years or more; that he knew no more about the Fine Arts than a ploughboy, and that he must be mistaken; and we sent him home assured that the piece was an excellent likeness. As for my Lord Bolingbroke, who honoured her ladyship with a visit occasionally, when Colonel Esmond showed him the picture he burst out laughing, and asked what devilry he was engaged on? Esmond owned simply that the portrait was not that of Viscount Castlewood, besought the Secretary on his honour to keep the secret, said that the ladies of the house were enthusiastic Jacobites, as was well known; and confessed that the picture was that of the Chevalier St George.

The truth is, that Mr Simon, waiting upon Lord Castlewood one day at Monsieur Rigaud's, whilst his lordship was sitting for his picture, affected to be much struck with a piece representing the Chevalier, whereof the head only was finished, and purchased it of the painter for a hundred crowns. It had been intended, the artist said, for Miss Oglethorpe, the Prince's mistress, but that young lady quitting Paris, had left the work on the artist's hands; and taking this piece home, when my lord's portrait arrived, Colonel Esmond, alias Monsieur Simon, had copied the uniform and other accessories from my lord's picture to fill up Rigaud's incomplete canvas: the Colonel all his life having been a practitioner of painting, and especially followed it during his long residence in the cities of Flanders, among the masterpieces of Vandyck and Rubens. My grandson hath the piece, such as it is, in Virginia now.

At the commencement of the month of June, Miss Beatrix Esmond, and my lady Viscountess, her mother, arrived from Castlewood; the former to resume her service at Court, which had been interrupted by the fatal catastrophe of Duke Hamilton's death. She once more took her place, then, in her Majesty's suite and at the maid's table, being always a favourite with Mrs Masham, the Queen's chief woman, partly perhaps on account of her bitterness against the Duchess of Marlborough, whom Miss Beatrix loved no better than her rival did. The gentlemen about the Court, my Lord Bolingbroke amongst others, owned that the young lady had come back handsomer than ever, and that the serious and tragic air, which her face now involuntarily wore, became her better than her former smiles and archness.

All the old domestics at the little house of Kensington Square were changed; the old steward that had served the family any time these five-and-twenty years, since the birth of the children of the house, was despatched into the kingdom of Ireland to see my lord's estate there: the housekeeper, who had been my lady's woman time out of mind, and the attendant of the young children, was sent away grumbling to Walcote, to see to the new painting and preparing of that house, which my Lady Dowager intended to occupy for the future, giving up Castlewood to her daughter-in-law, that might be expected daily from France. Another servant the Viscountess had was dismissed too – with a gratuity – on the pretext that her ladyship's train of domestics must be diminished; so, finally, there was not left in the household a single person who had belonged to it during the time my young Lord Castlewood was yet at home.

For the plan which Colonel Esmond had in view, and the stroke he intended, 'twas necessary that the very smallest number of persons should be put in possession of his secret. It scarce was known, except to three or four out of his family, and it was kept to a wonder.

On the 10th of June, 1714, there came by Mr Prior's messenger from Paris, a letter from my Lord Viscount Castlewood to his mother, saying that he had been foolish in regard of money matters, that he was ashamed to own he had lost at play, and by other extravagancies; and that instead of having great entertainments as he had hoped at Castlewood this year, he must live as quiet as he could, and make every effort to be saving. So far every word of poor Frank's letter was true, nor was there a doubt that that he and his tall brothers-in-law had spent a great deal more than they ought, and engaged the revenues of the Castlewood property, which the fond mother had husbanded and improved so carefully during the time of her guardianship.

His 'Clotilda,' Castlewood went on to say, 'was still delicate, and the physicians thought her lying-in had best take place at Paris. He should come without her ladyship, and be at his mother's house about the 17th or 18th day of June, proposing to take horse from Paris immediately, and bringing but a single servant with him; and he requested that the lawyers of Grey's Inn might be invited to meet him with their account, and the land-steward come from Castlewood with his, so that he might settle with them speedily, raise a sum of money whereof he stood in need, and be back to his Viscountess by the time of her lying-in.' Then his lordship gave some of the news of the town, sent his remembrance to kinsfolk, and so the letter ended. 'Twas put in the common post, and no doubt the French police and the English there had a copy of it, to which they were exceeding welcome.

Two days after, another letter was despatched by the public post of France, in the same open way, and this, after giving news of the fashion at Court there, ended by the following sentences, in which, but for those that had the key, 'twould be difficult for any man to find any secret lurked at all: –

'(The King will take) medicine on Thursday. His Majesty is better than he hath been of late, though incommoded by indigestion from his too great appetite. Madame Maintenon continues well. They have performed a play of Mons. Racine at St Cyr. The Duke of Shrewsbury and Mr Prior, our envoy, and all the English nobility here were present at it. (The Viscount Castlewood's passports) were refused to him, 'twas said; his lordship being sued by a goldsmith for *Vaisselle plate*, and a pearl necklace supplied to Mademoiselle Meruel of the French Comedy. 'Tis a pity such news should get abroad (and travel to England) about our young nobility here. Mademoiselle Meruel has been sent to the Fort l'Evesque; they say she has ordered not only plate, but furniture, and a chariot and horses (under that lord's name), of which extravagance his unfortunate Viscountess knows nothing.

'(His Majesty will be) eighty-two years of age on his next birthday. The Court prepares to celebrate it with a great feast. Mr Prior is in a sad way about their refusing at home to send him his plate. All here admired my Lord Viscount's portrait, and said it was a masterpiece of Rigaud. Have you seen it? It is (at the Lady Castlewood's house in Kensington Square). I think no English painter could produce such a piece.

'Our poor friend the Abbé hath been at the Bastile, but is now transported to the Conciergerie (where his friends may visit him. They are to ask for) a remission of his sentence soon. Let us hope the poor rogue will have repented in prison.

'(The Lord Castlewood) has had the affair of the plate made up, and departs for England.

'Is not this a dull letter? I have a cursed headache with drinking with Mat and some more over-night, and tipsy or sober am

'Thine ever ——.'

All this letter, save some dozen of words which I have put above between brackets, was mere idle talk, though the substance of the letter was as important as any letter well could be. It told those that had the key, that *the King will take the Viscount Castlewood's passports and travel to England under that lord's name. His Majesty will be at the Lady Castlewood's house in Kensington Square, where his friends may visit him; they are to ask for the Lord Castlewood.* This note may have passed under Mr Prior's eyes, and those of our new allies the French, and taught them nothing; though it explains sufficiently to persons in London what the event was which was about to happen, as 'twill show those who read my memoirs a hundred years hence, what was that errand on which Colonel Esmond of late had been busy. Silently and swiftly to do that about which others were conspiring, and thousands of Jacobites all over the country, clumsily caballing; alone to effect that which the leaders here were only talking about; to bring the Prince of Wales into the country openly in the face of all, under Bolingbroke's very eyes, the walls placarded with the proclamation signed with the Secretary's name, and offering five hundred pounds reward[4] for his apprehension: this was a stroke, the playing and winning of which might well give any adventurous spirit pleasure: the loss of the stake might involve a heavy penalty, but all our family were eager to risk that for the glorious chance of winning the game.

Nor should it be called a game, save perhaps with the chief player, who was not more or less sceptical than most public men with whom he had acquaintance in that age. (Is there ever a public man in England that altogether believes in his party? Is there one, however doubtful, that will not fight for it?) Young Frank was ready to fight without much thinking; he was a Jacobite as his father before him was; all the Esmonds were Royalists. Give him but the word, he would cry, 'God save King James!' before the palace guard, or at the Maypole in the Strand; and with respect to the women, as is usual with them, 'twas not a question of party but of faith; their belief was a passion; either Esmond's mistress or her daughter would have died for it cheerfully. I have laughed often, talking of King William's reign, and said I thought Lady Castlewood was disappointed the King did not persecute the family more; and those who know the nature of women may fancy for themselves, what needs not here be written down, the rapture with which these neophytes received the mystery when made known to them; the eagerness with which they looked forward to its completion; the reverence which they paid the minister who initiated them into that secret Truth, now known only to a few, but presently to reign over the world. Sure there is no bound to the trustingness of women. Look at Arria[5] worshipping the drunken clodpate of a husband who beats her; look at Cornelia treasuring as a jewel in her maternal heart the oaf her son; I have known a woman preach Jesuit's bark, and afterwards Doctor Berkeley's tar-water,[6] as though to swallow them were a divine decree, and to refuse them no better than blasphemy.

On his return from France Colonel Esmond put himself at the head of this little knot of fond conspirators. No death or torture he knew would frighten them out of their constancy. When he detailed his plan for bringing the King back, his elder mistress thought that that Restoration was to be attributed under Heaven to the Castlewood family and to its chief, and she worshipped and loved Esmond, if that could be, more than ever she had done. She doubted not for one moment of the success of his scheme, to mistrust which would have seemed impious in her eyes. And as for Beatrix, when she became acquainted with the plan, and joined it, as she did with all her heart, she gave Esmond one of her searching bright looks; 'Ah, Harry,' says she, 'why were you not head of our house? You are the only one fit to raise it; why do you give that silly boy the name and the honour? But 'tis so in the world; those get the prize that don't deserve or care for it. I wish I could give you *your* silly prize, cousin, but I can't; I have tried and I can't.' And she went away, shaking her head mournfully, but always, it seemed to Esmond, that her liking and respect for him was greatly increased, since she knew what capability he had both to act and bear; to do and to forego.

## Chapter 9

### THE ORIGINAL OF THE PORTRAIT
### COMES TO ENGLAND

'TWAS announced in the family that my Lord Castlewood would arrive, having a confidential French gentleman in his suite, who acted as a secretary to his lordship, and who, being a Papist, and a foreigner of good family, though now in rather a menial place, would have his meals served in his chamber, and not with the domestics of the house. The Viscountess gave up her bedchamber contiguous to her daughter's, and having a large convenient closet attached to it, in which a bed was put up, ostensibly for Monsieur Baptiste, the Frenchman; though 'tis needless to say, when the doors of the apartments were locked, and the two guests retired within it, the young Viscount became the servant of the illustrious Prince whom he entertained, and gave up gladly the more convenient and airy chamber and bed to his master. Madam Beatrix also retired to the upper region, her chamber being converted into a sitting-room for my lord. The better to carry the deceit, Beatrix affected to grumble before the servants, and to be jealous that she was turned out of her chamber to make way for my lord.

No small preparations were made, you may be sure, and no slight tremor of expectation caused the hearts of the gentle ladies of Castlewood to flutter, before the arrival of the personages who were about to honour their house. The chamber was ornamented with flowers; the bed covered with the very finest of linen; the two ladies insisting on making it themselves, and kneeling down at the bedside and kissing the sheets out of respect for the web that was to hold the sacred person of the king. The toilet was of silver and crystal; there was a copy of Eikon Basilike[1] laid on the writing-table; a portrait of the martyred King hung always over the mantel, having a sword of my poor Lord Castlewood underneath it, and a little picture or emblem which the widow loved always to have before her eyes on waking, and in which the hair of her lord and her two children was worked together. Her books of private devotions, as they were all of the English Church, she carried away with her to the upper apartment which she destined for herself. The ladies showed Mr Esmond, when they were completed, the fond preparations they had made. 'Twas then Beatrix knelt down and kissed the linen sheets. As for her mother Lady Castlewood made a curtsey at the door, as she would have done to the altar on entering a church, and owned that she considered the chamber in a manner sacred.

The company in the servant's hall never for a moment supposed that these preparations were made for any other person than the young Viscount, the lord of the house, whom his fond mother had been for so many years without seeing. Both ladies were perfect housewives, having the greatest skill in the making of confections, scented waters, &c., and keeping a notable superintendence over the kitchen. Calves enough were killed to feed an army of prodigal sons, Esmond thought, and laughed when he came to wait on the ladies, on the day when the guests were to arrive, to find two pairs of the finest and roundest arms to be seen in England (my Lady Castlewood was remarkable for this beauty of her person), covered with flour up above the elbows, and preparing paste, and turning rolling-pins in the housekeeper's closet. The guests would not arrive till supper-time, and my lord would prefer having that meal in his own chamber. You may be sure the brightest plate of the house was laid out there, and can understand why it was that the ladies insisted that they alone would wait upon the young chief of the family.

Taking horse, Colonel Esmond rode rapidly to Rochester, and there awaited the King in that very town where his father had last set his foot on the English shore. A room had been provided at an inn there for my Lord Castlewood and his servant; and Colonel Esmond timed his ride so well that he scarce had been half an hour in the place, and was looking over the balcony into the yard of the inn, when two travellers rode in at the inn-gate, and the Colonel running down, the next moment embraced his dear young lord.

My lord's companion, acting the part of a domestic, dismounted, and was for holding the Viscount's stirrup; but Colonel Esmond, calling to his own man, who was in the court bade him take the horses and settle with the lad who had ridden the post along with the two travellers, crying out in a cavalier tone in the French language to my lord's companion, and affecting to grumble that my lord's fellow was a Frenchman, and did not know the money or habits of the country: – 'My man will see to the horses, Baptiste,' says Colonel Esmond: 'do you understand English?' 'Very leetle.' ' So, follow my lord and wait upon him at dinner in his own room.' The landlord and his people came up presently bearing the dishes; 'twas well they made a noise and stir in the gallery, or they might have found Colonel Esmond on his knee before Lord Castlewood's servant, welcoming his Majesty to his kingdom, and kissing the hand of the King. We told the landlord that the Frenchman would wait on his master; and Esmond's man was ordered to keep sentry in the gallery without the door. The Prince dined with a good appetite, laughing and talking very gaily, and condescendingly bidding his two companions to sit with him at the table. He was in better spirits than poor Frank Castlewood, who Esmond thought might be wobegone on account of parting with his divine Clotilda; but the Prince wishing to take a short siesta after dinner, and retiring to an inner chamber where there was a bed, the cause of poor

Harry's[2] discomfiture came out; and bursting into tears, with many expressions of fondness, friendship, and humiliation, the faithful lad gave his kinsman to understand that he now knew all the truth, and the sacrifices which Colonel Esmond had made for him.

Seeing no good in acquainting poor Frank with that secret, Mr Esmond had entreated his mistress also not to reveal it to her son. The Prince had told the poor lad all as they were riding from Dover: 'I had as lief he had shot me, cousin,' Frank said: 'I knew you were the best, and the bravest, and the kindest of all men' (so the enthusiastic young fellow went on); 'but I never thought I owed you what I do, and can scarce bear the weight of the obligation.'

'I stand in the place of your father,' says Mr Esmond kindly, 'and sure a father may dispossess himself in favour of his son. I abdicate the twopenny crown, and invest you with the kingdom of Brentford,[3] don't be a fool and cry; you make a much taller and handsomer viscount than ever I could.' But the fond boy with oaths and protestations, laughter and incoherent outbreaks of passionate emotion, could not be got, for some little time, to put up with Esmond's raillery; wanted to kneel down to him, and kissed his hand; asked him and implored him to order something, to bid Castlewood give his own life up or take somebody else's; anything, so that he might show his gratitude for the generosity Esmond showed him.

'The K——, *he* laughed,' Frank said, pointing to the door where the sleeper was, and speaking in a low tone. 'I don't think he should have laughed as he told me the story. As we rode along from Dover, talking in French, he spoke about you, and your coming to him at the bar; he called you "*le grand sérieux*," Don Bellianis of Greece, and I don't know what names; mimicking your manner' (here Castlewood laughed himself) – 'and he did it very well. He seems to sneer at everything. He is not like a king: somehow, Harry, I fancy you are like a king. He does not seem to think what a stake we are all playing. He would have stopped at Canterbury to run after a barmaid there, had I not implored him to come on. He hath a house at Chaillot where he used to go and **bury himself away from the Queen, and with all sorts of bad** company,' says Frank, with a demure look; 'you may smile, but I am not the wild fellow I was; no, no, I have been taught better,' says Castlewood devoutly, making a sign on his breast.

'Thou art my dear brave boy,' says Colonel Esmond, touched at the young fellow's simplicity, 'and there will be a noble gentleman at Castlewood so long as my Frank is there.'

The impetuous young lad was for going down on his knees again, with another explosion of gratitude, but that we heard the voice from the next chamber of the august sleeper, just waking, calling out: – '*Eh, La Fleur,*[4] *un verre d'eau*'; his Majesty came out yawning: – 'A pest,' says he, 'upon your English ale, 'tis so strong that, *ma foi*, it hath turned my head.'

The effect of the ale was like a spur upon our horses, and we rode very quickly to London, reaching Kensington at nightfall. Mr Esmond's servant was left behind at Rochester, to take care of the tired horses, whilst we had fresh beasts provided along the road. And galloping by the Prince's side the Colonel explained to the Prince of Wales what his movements had been; who the friends were that knew of the expedition; whom, as Esmond conceived, the Prince should trust; entreating him, above all, to maintain the very closest secrecy until the time should come when his Royal Highness should appear. The town swarmed with friends of the Prince's cause; there were scores of correspondents with St Germains; Jacobites known and secret; great in station and humble; about the Court and the Queen; in the Parliament, Church, and among the merchants in the City. The Prince had friends numberless in the army, in the Privy Council, and the Officers of State. The great object, as it seemed, to the small band of persons who had concerted that bold stroke, who had brought the Queen's brother into his native country, was, that his visit should remain unknown until the proper time came, when his presence should surprise friends and enemies alike; and the latter should be found so unprepared and disunited, that they should not find time to attack him. We feared more from his friends than from his enemies. The lies, and tittle-tattle sent over to St Germain's by the Jacobite agents about London, had done an incalculable mischief to his cause, and wofully misguided him, and it was from these especially, that the persons engaged in the present venture were anxious to defend the chief actor in it.*

The party reached London by nightfall, leaving their horses at the Posting House over against Westminster, and being ferried over the water, where Lady Esmond's coach was already in waiting. In another hour we were all landed at Kensington, and the mistress of the house had the satisfaction which her heart had yearned after for many years, once more to embrace her son, who on his side, with all his waywardness, ever retained a most tender affection for his parent.

She did not refrain from this expression of her feeling, though the domestics were by, and my Lord Castlewood's attendant stood in the hall. Esmond had to whisper to him in French to take his hat off. Monsieur Baptiste was constantly neglecting his part with an inconceivable levity: more than once on the ride to London, little observations of the stranger, light remarks, and words betokening the greatest ignorance of the country the Prince came to govern, had hurt the susceptibility of the two gentlemen forming his escort; nor could either help owning in his secret mind that they would have had his behaviour otherwise, and that the laughter and the lightness, not to say license, which characterized his talk, scarce befitted such a great Prince, and such a solemn occasion. Not but that he could act at proper times with spirit and dignity. He had behaved, as we all knew, in a very courageous manner on the field. Esmond had seen a copy of the letter the Prince writ with his own hand when urged by his friends in England to abjure his religion, and admired that manly and magnanimous reply by which he refused to yield to the temptation[5] Monsieur Baptiste took off his hat, blushing at the hint Colonel Esmond ventured to give him, and said: – '*Tenez, elle est jolie, la petite mère; Foi-de-Chevalier! elle est charmante; mais l'autre, qui est cette nymphe, cet astre qui*

---

*The managers were the Bishop, who cannot be hurt by having his name mentioned, a very active and loyal Nonconformist Divine, a lady in the highest favour at Court, with whom Beatrix Esmond had communication, and two noblemen of the greatest rank, and a member of the House of Commons, who was implicated in more transactions than one in behalf of the Stuart family.[6]

*brille, cette Diane qui descend sur nous ?*' And he started back, and pushed forward, as Beatrix was descending the stair. She was in colours for the first time at her own house; she wore the diamonds Esmond gave her; it had been agreed between them, that she should wear these brilliants on the day when the King should enter the house, and a Queen she looked, radiant in charms, and magnificent and imperial in beauty.

Castlewood himself was startled by that beauty and splendour; he stepped back and gazed at his sister as though he had not been aware before (nor was he very likely) how perfectly lovely she was, and I thought blushed as he embraced her. The Prince could not keep his eyes off her; he quite forgot his menial part, though he had been schooled to it, and a little light portmanteau prepared expressly that he should carry it. He pressed forward before my Lord Viscount. 'Twas lucky the servants' eyes were busy in other directions, or they must have seen that this was no servant, or at least a very insolent and rude one.

Again Colonel Esmond was obliged to cry out 'Baptiste,' in a loud imperious voice, 'have a care to the valise'; at which hint the wilful young man ground his teeth together with something very like a curse between them, and then gave a brief look of anything but pleasure to his mentor. Being reminded, however, he shouldered the little portmanteau, and carried it up the stair, Esmond preceding him, and a servant with lighted tapers. He flung down his burden sulkily in the bed-chamber: – 'A Prince that will wear a crown must wear a mask,' says Mr Esmond, in French.

'*Ah, peste!* I see how it is ,' says Monsieur Baptiste, continuing the talk in French. 'The Great Serious is seriously –'

'– alarmed for Monsieur Baptiste,' broke in the Colonel. Esmond neither liked the tone with which the Prince spoke of the ladies, nor the eyes with which he regarded them.

The bed-chamber and the two rooms adjoining it, the closet and the apartment which was to be called my lord's parlour, were already lighted and awaiting their occupier; and the collation laid for my lord's supper. Lord Castlewood and his mother and sister came up the stair a minute afterwards, and, so soon as the domestics had quitted the apartment, Castlewood and

Esmond uncovered, and the two ladies went down on their knees before the Prince, who graciously gave a hand to each. He looked his part of Prince much more naturally than that of servant, which he had just been trying, and raised them both with a great deal of nobility, as well as kindness in his air. 'Madam,' says he, 'my mother will thank your ladyship for your hospitality to her son; for you, madam,' turning to Beatrix, 'I cannot bear to see so much beauty in such a posture. You will betray Monsieur Baptiste if you kneel to him; sure 'tis his place rather to kneel to you.'

A light shone out of her eyes; a gleam bright enough to kindle passion in any breast. There were times when this creature was so handsome, that she seemed, as it were, like Venus revealing herself a goddess in a flash of brightness. She appeared so now; radiant, and with eyes bright with a wonderful lustre. A pang, as of rage and jealousy, shot through Esmond's heart, as he caught the look she gave the Prince; and he clenched his hand involuntarily and looked across to Castlewood, whose eyes answered his alarm-signal, and were also on the alert. The Prince gave his subjects an audience of a few minutes, and then the two ladies and Colonel Esmond quitted the chamber. Lady Castlewood pressed his hand as they descended the stair, and the three went down to the lower rooms, where they waited awhile till the travellers above should be refreshed and ready for their meal.

Esmond looked at Beatrix, blazing with her jewels on her beautiful neck. 'I have kept my word,' says he: 'And I mine,' says Beatrix, looking down on the diamonds.

'Were I the Mogul Emperor,' says the Colonel, 'you should have all that were dug out of Golconda.'

'These are a great deal too good for me,' says Beatrix, dropping her head on her beautiful breast, 'so are you all, all': and and when she looked up again, as she did in a moment, and after a sigh, her eyes, as they gazed at her cousin, wore that melancholy and inscrutable look which 'twas always impossible to sound.

When the time came for the supper, of which we were advertised by a knocking overhead, Colonel Esmond and the two ladies went to the upper apartment, where the Prince already was, and by his side the young Viscount, of exactly the same age, shape, and with features not dissimilar, though Frank's were the handsomer of the two. The Prince sat down, and bade the ladies sit. The gentlemen remained standing: there was, indeed, but one more cover laid at the table: – 'Which of you will take it?' says he.

'The head of our house,' says Lady Castlewood, taking her son's hand, and looking towards Colonel Esmond with a bow and a great tremor of the voice; 'the Marquis of Esmond will have the honour of serving the King.'

'I shall have the honour of waiting on his Royal Highness,' says Colonel Esmond, filling a cup of wine, and, as the fashion of that day was, he presented it to the King on his knee.

'I drink to my hostess and her family,' says the Prince, with no very well-pleased air; but the cloud passed immediately off his face, and he talked to the ladies in a lively, rattling strain, quite undisturbed by poor Mr Esmond's yellow countenance, that I dare say looked very glum.

When the time came to take leave, Esmond marched homewards to his lodgings, and met Mr Addison on the road that night, walking to a cottage he had at Fulham, the moon shining on his handsome serene face: – 'What cheer, brother?' says Addison, laughing; 'I thought it was a footpad advancing in the dark, and behold 'tis an old friend. We may shake hands, Colonel, in the dark, 'tis better than fighting by daylight. Why should we quarrel, because I am a Whig and thou art a Tory? Turn thy steps and walk with me to Fulham, where there is a nightingale still singing in the garden, and a cool bottle in a cave I know of; you shall drink to the Pretender if you like, and I will drink my liquor my own way: I have had enough of good liquor? no, never. There is no such word as enough as a stopper for good wine. Thou wilt not come? Come any day, come soon. You know I remember *Simois* and the *Sigeia tellus*, and the *prœlia mixta mero, mixta mero*,' he repeated, with ever so slight a touch of *merum* in his voice, and walked back a little way on the road with Esmond, bidding the other remember he was always his friend, and indebted to him for his aid in the 'Campaign' poem. And very likely Mr Under-Secretary would have stepped in and taken t'other bottle at the Colonel's lodging, had the latter invited him, but Esmond's mood was none of the gayest, and he bade his friend an inhospitable good-night at the door.

'I have done the deed,' thought he, sleepless, and looking out into the night; 'he is here, and I have brought him; he and Beatrix are sleeping under the same roof now. Whom did I mean to serve in bringing him? Was it the Prince, was it Henry Esmond? Had I not best have joined the manly creed of Addison yonder, that scouts the old doctrine of right divine, that boldly declares that Parliament and people consecrate the Sovereign, not bishops, nor genealogies, nor oils, nor coronations.' The eager gaze of the young Prince, watching every movement of Beatrix, haunted Esmond and pursued him. The Prince's figure appeared before him in his feverish dreams many times that night. He wished the deed undone, for which he had laboured so. He was not the first that has regretted his own act, or brought about his own undoing. Undoing? Should he write that word in his late years? No, on his knees before Heaven, rather be thankful for what he then deemed his misfortune, and which hath caused the whole subsequent happiness of his life.

Esmond's man, honest John Lockwood, had served his master and the family all his life, and the Colonel knew that he could answer for John's fidelity as for his own. John returned with the horses from Rochester betimes the next morning, and the Colonel gave him to understand that on going to Kensington, where he was free of the servants' hall, and indeed courting Mrs Beatrix's maid, he was to ask no questions, and betray no surprise, but to vouch stoutly that the young gentleman he should see in a red coat there was my Lord Viscount Castlewood, and that his attendant in grey was Monsieur Baptiste, the Frenchman. He was to tell his friends in the kitchen such stories as he remembered of my Lord Viscount's youth at Castlewood; what a wild boy he was; how he used to drill Jack and cane him, before ever he was a soldier; everything, in fine, he knew respecting my Lord Viscount's early days. Jack's ideas of painting had not been much cultivated during his residence in Flanders with his master; and before my young lord's return, he had been easily got to believe that the picture brought over from Paris, and now hanging in

Lady Castlewood's drawing-room, was a perfect likeness of her son, the young lord. And the domestics having all seen the picture many times, and catching but a momentary imperfect glimpse of the two strangers on the night of their arrival, never had a reason to doubt the fidelity of the portrait; and next day, when they saw the original of the piece habited exactly as he was represented in the painting, with the same periwig, ribands, and uniform of the Guard, quite naturally addressed the gentleman as my Lord Castlewood, my Lady Viscountess's son.[8]

The secretary of the night previous was now the Viscount; the Viscount wore the secretary's grey frock; and John Lockwood was instructed to hint to the world below stairs that my lord being a Papist, and very devout in that religion, his attendant might be no other than his chaplain from Bruxelles; hence, if he took his meals in my lord's company there was little reason for surprise. Frank was further cautioned to speak English with a foreign accent, which task he performed indifferently well, and this caution was the more necessary because the Prince himself scarce spoke our language like a native of the island; and John Lockwood laughed with the folks below stairs at the manner in which my lord, after five years abroad, sometimes forgot his own tongue and spoke it like a Frenchman. 'I warrant,' says he, 'that with the English beef and beer, his lordship will soon get back the proper use of his mouth'; and, to do his new lordship justice, he took to beer and beef very kindly.

The Prince drank so much, and was so loud and impudent in his talk after drink, that Esmond often trembled for him. His meals were served as much as possible in his own chamber, though frequently he made his appearance in Lady Castlewood's parlour and drawing-room, calling Beatrix 'sister,' and her ladyship 'mother,' or 'madam,' before the servants. And, choosing to act entirely up to the part of brother and son, the Prince sometimes saluted Mrs Beatrix and Lady Castlewood with a freedom which his secretary did not like, and which, for his part, set Colonel Esmond tearing with rage.

The guests had not been three days in the house when poor Jack Lockwood came with a rueful countenance to his master

and said: 'My lord – that is, the gentleman – has been tampering
with Mrs Lucy' (Jack's sweetheart), 'and given her guineas and
a kiss.' I fear that Colonel Esmond's mind was rather relieved
than otherwise, when he found that the ancillary beauty was the
one whom the Prince had selected. His royal tastes were known to
lie that way, and continued so in after life. The heir of one of the
greatest names, of the greatest kingdoms, and of the greatest misfortunes in Europe, was often content to lay the dignity of his
birth and grief at the wooden shoes of a French chambermaid,
and to repent afterwards (for he was very devout) in ashes taken
from the dustpan. 'Tis for mortals such as these that nations
suffer, that parties struggle, that warriors fight and bleed. A year
afterwards gallant heads were falling, and Nithsdale in escape,
and Derwentwater on the scaffold; whilst the heedless ingrate,
for whom they risked and lost all, was tippling with his seraglio
of mistresses in his *petite maison* of Chaillot.

Blushing to be forced to bear such an errand, Esmond had to
go to the Prince and warn him that the girl whom his Highness
was bribing, was John Lockwood's sweetheart, an honest resolute man, who had served in six campaigns, and feared nothing,
and who knew that the person, calling himself Lord Castlewood,
was not his young master: and the Colonel besought the Prince
to consider what the effect of a single man's jealousy might be,
and to think of other designs he had in hand, more important
than the seduction of a waiting-maid, and the humiliation of a
brave man.

Ten times, perhaps, in the course of as many days, Mr
Esmond had to warn the royal young adventurer of some imprudence or some freedom. He received these remonstrances
very testily, save perhaps in this affair of poor Lockwood's,
when he deigned to burst out a-laughing, and said, 'What! The
*soubrette*[9] has peached to the *amoureux*, and Crispin[10] is angry,
and Crispin has served, and Crispin has been a corporal, has he?
Tell him we will reward his valour with a pair of colours, and
recompense his fidelity.'

Colonel Esmond ventured to utter some other words of en-
treaty, but the Prince, stamping imperiously, cried out, '*Assez,
milord; je m'ennuye à la prêche;* I am not come to London to go

to the sermon.' And he complained afterwards to Castlewood, that '*le petit jaune, le noir Colonel, le Marquis Misantrope*' (by which facetious names his Royal Highness was pleased to designate Colonel Esmond), 'fatigued him with his grand airs and virtuous homilies.'

The Bishop of Rochester, and other gentlemen engaged in the transaction which had brought the Prince over, waited upon his Royal Highness, constantly asking for my Lord Castlewood on their arrival at Kensington, and being openly conducted to his Royal Highness in that character, who received them either in my lady's drawing-room below, or above in his own apartment; and all implored him to quit the house as little as possible, and to wait there till the signal should be given for him to appear. The ladies entertained him at cards, over which amusement he spent many hours in each day and night. He passed many hours more in drinking, during which time he would rattle and talk very agreeably, and especially if the Colonel was absent, whose presence seemed to frighten him; and the poor 'Colonel Noir' took that hint as a command accordingly, and seldom intruded his black face upon the convivial hours of this august young prisoner. Except for those few persons of whom the porter had the list, Lord Castlewood was denied to all friends of the house who waited on his lordship. The wound he had received had broke out again from his journey on horseback, so the world and the domestics were informed. And Doctor A——,* his physician, (I shall not mention his name, but he was physician to the Queen, of the Scots nation, and a man remarkable for his benevolence as well as his wit), gave orders that he should be kept perfectly quiet until the wound should heal. With this gentleman, who was one of the most active and influential of our party, and the others before spoken of, the whole secret lay; and it was kept with so much faithfulness, and the story we told so simple and natural, that there was no likelihood of a discovery except from the imprudence of the Prince himself, and an adventurous levity that we had the greatest difficulty to control. As for Lady Castlewood, although she scarce spoke a word, 'twas easy to gather from her

---

*There can be very little doubt that the Doctor, mentioned by my dear father, was the famous Doctor Arbuthnot. – R. E. W.

demeanour, and one or two hints she dropped, how deep her mortification was at finding the hero whom she had chosen to worship all her life (and whose restoration had formed almost the most sacred part of her prayers), no more than a man, and not a good one. She thought misfortune might have chastened him; but that instructress had rather rendered him callous than humble. His devotion, which was quite real, kept him from no sin he had a mind to. His talk showed good-humour, gaiety, even wit enough; but there was a levity in his acts and words that he had brought from among those libertine devotees with whom he had been bred, and that shocked the simplicity and purity of the English lady, whose guest he was. Esmond spoke his mind to Beatrix pretty freely about the Prince, getting her brother to put in a word of warning. Beatrix was entirely of their opinion; she thought he was very light, very light and reckless; she could not even see the good looks Colonel Esmond had spoken of. The Prince had bad teeth, and a decided squint.' How could we say he did not squint? His eyes were fine, but there was certainly a cast in them. She rallied him at table with wonderful wit; she spoke of him invariably as of a mere boy; she was more fond of Esmond than ever; praised him to her brother, praised him to the Prince, when his Royal Highness was pleased to sneer at the Colonel, and warmly espoused his cause: 'And if your Majesty does not give him the Garter his father had, when the Marquis of Esmond comes to your Majesty's Court, I will hang myself in my own garters, or will cry my eyes out.' 'Rather than lose those,' says the Prince, 'he shall be made Archbishop and Colonel of the Guard' (it was Frank Castlewood who told me of this conversation over their supper).

'Yes,' cries she, with one of her laughs – I fancy I hear it now. Thirty years afterwards I hear that delightful music; 'yes, he shall be Archbishop of Esmond and Marquis of Canterbury.'

'And what will your ladyship be?' says the Prince; 'you have but to choose your place.'

'I,' says Beatrix, 'will be mother of the maids to the Queen of his Majesty King James the Third – Vive le Roy!' and she made him a great curtsey, and drank a part of a glass of wine in his honour.

'The Prince seized hold of the glass and drank the last drop of it,' Castlewood said, 'and my mother, looking very anxious, rose up and asked leave to retire. But that Trix is my mother's daughter, Harry,' Frank continued, 'I don't know what a horrid fear I should have of her. I wish – I wish this business were over. You are older than I am, and wiser, and better, and I owe you everything, and would die for you – before George I would; but I wish the end of this were come.'

Neither of us very likely passed a tranquil night; horrible doubts and torments racked Esmond's soul; 'twas a scheme of personal ambition, a daring stroke for a selfish end – he knew it. What cared he, in his heart, who was king? Were not his very sympathies and secret convictions on the other side – on the side of People, Parliament, Freedom? And here was he, engaged for a prince, that had scarce heard the word liberty; that priests and women, tyrants by nature both, made a tool of. The misanthrope was in no better humour after hearing that story, and his grim face more black and yellow than ever.

## Chapter 10

### WE ENTERTAIN A VERY DISTINGUISHED GUEST AT KENSINGTON

SHOULD any clue be found to the dark intrigues at the latter end of Queen Anne's time, or any historian be inclined to follow it, 'twill be discovered, I have little doubt, that not one of the great personages about the Queen had a defined scheme of policy, independent of that private and selfish interest which each was bent on pursuing; St John was for St John, and Harley for Oxford, and Marlborough for John Churchill, always; and according as they could get help from St Germains or Hanover, they sent over proffers of allegiance to the princes there, or betrayed one to the other: one cause, or one sovereign, was as good as another to them, so that they could hold the best place under him; and like Lockit and Peachum,[1] the Newgate chiefs in the Rogues' Opera Mr Gay wrote afterwards, had each in his hand documents and proofs of treason which would hang the other, only he did not dare to use the weapon, for fear of that one which his neighbour also carried in his pocket. Think of the great Marlborough, the greatest subject in all the world, a conqueror of princes, that had marched victorious over Germany, Flanders, and France, that had given the law to sovereigns abroad, and been worshipped as a divinity at home, forced to sneak out of England – his credit, honours, places, all taken from him; his friends in the army broke and ruined; and flying before Harley, as abject and powerless as a poor debtor before a bailiff with a writ. A paper, of which Harley got possession, and showing beyond doubt that the Duke was engaged with the Stuart family, was the weapon with which the Treasurer drove Marlborough out of the kingdom. He fled to Antwerp, and began intriguing instantly on the other side, and came back to England, as all know, a Whig and a Hanoverian.

Though the Treasurer turned out of the army and office every man, military or civil, known to be the Duke's friend, and gave the vacant posts among the Tory party, he, too, was playing the double game between Hanover and St Germains, awaiting the expected catastrophe of the Queen's death to be Master of the State, and offer it to either family that should bribe him best, or that the nation should declare for. Whichever the King was, Harley's object was to reign over him; and to this end he supplanted the former famous favourite, decried the actions of the war which had made Marlborough's name illustrious, and disdained no more than the great fallen competitor of his, the meanest arts, flatteries, intimidations, that would secure his power. If the greatest satirist the world ever hath seen had writ against Harley, and not for him, what a history had he left behind of the last years of Queen Anne's reign! But Swift, that scorned all mankind, and himself not the least of all, had this merit of a faithful partisan, that he loved those chiefs who treated him well, and stuck by Harley bravely in his fall, as he gallantly had supported him in his better fortune.

Incomparably more brilliant, more splendid, eloquent, accomplished, than his rival, the great St John could be as selfish as Oxford was, and could act the double part as skilfully as ambidextrous Churchill. He whose talk was always of liberty, no more shrunk from using persecution and the pillory against his opponents, than if he had been at Lisbon and Grand Inquisitor. This lofty patriot was on his knees at Hanover and St Germains too; notoriously of no religion, he toasted Church and Queen as boldly as the stupid Sacheverel, whom he used and laughed at; and to serve his turn, and to overthrow his enemy, he could intrigue, coax, bully, wheedle, fawn on the Court favourite, and creep up the back-stair as silently as Oxford, who supplanted Marlborough, and whom he himself supplanted. The crash of my Lord Oxford happened at this very time whereat my history is now arrived. He was come to the very last days of his power, and the agent whom he employed to overthrow the conqueror of Blenheim, was now engaged to upset the conqueror's conqueror, and hand over the staff of government to Bolingbroke, who had been panting to hold it.

In expectation of the stroke that was now preparing, the Irish regiments in the French service were all brought round about Boulogne in Picardy, to pass over if need were with the Duke of Berwick; the soldiers of France no longer, but subjects of James the Third of England and Ireland King. The fidelity of the great mass of the Scots (though a most active, resolute, and gallant Whig party, admirably and energetically ordered and disciplined, was known to be in Scotland too) was notoriously unshaken in their King. A very great body of Tory clergy, nobility, and gentry, were public partisans of the exiled Prince; and the indifferents might be counted on to cry King George or King James, according as either should prevail. The Queen, especially in her latter days, inclined towards her own family. The Prince was lying actually in London, within a stone's-cast of his sister's palace; the first minister toppling to his fall, and so tottering that the weakest push of a woman's finger would send him down; and as for Bolingbroke, his successor, we know on whose side his power and his splendid eloquence would be on the day when the Queen should appear openly before her Council and say:– 'This, my lords, is my brother; here is my father's heir, and mine after me.'

During the whole of the previous year the Queen had had many and repeated fits of sickness, fever, and lethargy, and her death had been constantly looked for by all her attendants. The Elector of Hanover had wished to send his son, the Duke of Cambridge – to pay his court to his cousin the Queen, the Elector said; – in truth, to be on the spot when death should close her career. Frightened perhaps to have such a *memento mori* under her royal eyes, her Majesty had angrily forbidden the young Prince's coming into England. Either she desired to keep the chances for her brother open yet; or the people about her did not wish to close with the Whig candidate till they could make terms with him. The quarrels of her ministers before her face at the Council board, the pricks of conscience very likely, the importunities of her ministers, and constant turmoil and agitation round about her, had weakened and irritated the Princess extremely; her strength was giving way under these continual trials of her temper, and from day to day it was expected she must come to a speedy end of them. Just before Viscount Castlewood and his companion came from France, her Majesty was taken ill. The St Anthony's fire[2] broke out on the royal legs; there was no hurry for the presentation of the young lord at Court, or that person who should appear under his name; and my Lord's Viscount's wound breaking out opportunely, he was kept conveniently in his chamber until such time as his physician should allow him to bend his knee before the Queen. At the commencement of July, that influential lady, with whom it has been mentioned that our party had relations, came frequently to visit her young friend, the maid of honour, at Kensington, and my Lord Viscount (the real or supposititious), who was an invalid at Lady Castlewood's house.

On the 27th day of July, the lady in question, who held the most intimate post about the Queen, came in her chair from the Palace hard by, bringing to the little party in Kensington Square, intelligence of the very highest importance. The final blow had been struck, and my Lord of Oxford and Mortimer was no longer Treasurer. The staff was as yet given to no successor, though my Lord Bolingbroke would undoubtedly be the man. And now the time was come, the Queen's Abigail[3] said: and now my Lord Castlewood ought to be presented to the Sovereign.

After that scene which Lord Castlewood witnessed and described to his cousin, who passed such a miserable night of mortification and jealousy as he thought over the transaction; no doubt the three persons who were set by nature as protectors over Beatrix came to the same conclusion, that she must be removed from the presence of a man whose desires towards her were expressed only too clearly; and who was no more scrupulous in seeking to gratify them than his father had been before him. I suppose Esmond's mistress, her son, and the Colonel himself, had been all secretly debating this matter in their minds, for when Frank broke out, in his blunt way, with:– 'I think Beatrix had best be anywhere but here,' – Lady Castlewood said:– 'I thank you, Frank, I have thought so too'; and Mr Esmond, though he only remarked that it was not for him to speak, showed plainly, by the delight on his countenance, how very agreeable that proposal was to him.

'One sees that you think with us, Henry,' says the Viscountess with ever so little of sarcasm in her tone: 'Beatrix is best out of this house whilst we have our guest in it, and as soon as this morning's business is done, she ought to quit London.'

'What morning's business?' asked Colonel Esmond, not knowing what had been arranged, though in fact the stroke next in importance to that of bringing the Prince, and of having him acknowledged by the Queen, was now being performed at the very moment we three were conversing together.

The Court lady with whom our plan was concerted, and who was a chief agent in it, the Court physician, and the Bishop of Rochester, who were the other two most active participators in our plan, had held many councils in our house at Kensington and elsewhere, as to the means best to be adopted for presenting our young adventurer to his sister the Queen. The simple and easy plan proposed by Colonel Esmond had been agreed to by all parties, which was that on some rather private day, when there were not many persons about the Court, the Prince should appear there as my Lord Castlewood, should be greeted by his sister-in-waiting, and led by that other lady into the closet of the Queen. And according to her Majesty's health or humour, and the circumstances that might arise during the interview, it was to be left to the discretion of those present at it, and to the Prince himself, whether he should declare that it was the Queen's own brother, or the brother of Beatrix Esmond, who kissed her royal hand. And this plan being determined on, we were all waiting in very much anxiety for the day and signal of execution.

Two mornings after that supper, it being the 27th day of July, the Bishop of Rochester breakfasting with Lady Castle-wood and her family, and the meal scarce over, Doctor A.'s coach drove up to our house at Kensington, and the Doctor appeared amongst the party there, enlivening a rather gloomy company; for the mother and daughter had had words in the morning in respect to the transactions of that supper, and other adventures perhaps, and on the day succeeding. Beatrix's haughty spirit brooked remonstrances from no superior, much less from her mother, the gentlest of creatures, whom the girl commanded rather than obeyed. And feeling she was wrong, and that by a thousand coquetries (which she could no more help exercising on every man that came near her, than the sun can help shining on great and small) she had provoked the Prince's dangerous admiration, and allured him to the expression of it, she was only the more wilful and imperious the more she felt her error.

To this party, the Prince being served with chocolate in his bedchamber, where he lay late sleeping away the fumes of his wine, the Doctor came, and by the urgent and startling nature of his news, dissipated instantly that private and minor unpleasantry under which the family of Castlewood was labouring.

He asked for the guest; the guest was above in his own apartment: he bade *Monsieur Baptiste* go up to his master instantly, and requested that *My Lord Viscount Castlewood* would straightway put his uniform on, and come away in the Doctor's coach now at the door.

He then informed Madam Beatrix what her part of the comedy was to be:– 'In half-an-hour,' says he, 'her Majesty and her favourite lady will take the air in the cedar walk behind the new Banqueting House. Her Majesty will be drawn in a garden-chair, Madam Beatrix Esmond, and *her brother, my Lord Viscount Castlewood*, will be walking in the private garden (here is Lady Masham's key), and will come unawares upon the royal party. The man that draws the chair will retire, and leave the Queen, the favourite, and the maid of honour and her brother, together; Mrs Beatrix will present her brother, and then! – and then, my Lord Bishop will pray for the result of the interview, and his Scots clerk will say Amen! Quick, put on your hood, Madam Beatrix; why doth not his Majesty come down? Such another chance may not present itself for months again.'

The Prince was late and lazy, and indeed had all but lost that chance through his indolence. The Queen was actually about to leave the garden just when the party reached it; the Doctor, the Bishop, the maid of honour and her brother went off together in the physician's coach, and had been gone half-an-hour when Colonel Esmond came to Kensington Square.

The news of this errand, on which Beatrix was gone, of course for a moment put all thoughts of private jealousy out of Colonel Esmond's head. In half-an-hour more the coach returned; the Bishop descended from it first, and gave his arm to Beatrix, who now came out. His lordship went back into the carriage again, and the maid of honour entered the house alone. We were all gazing at her from the upper window, trying to read from her countenance the result of the interview from which she had just come.

She came into the drawing-room in a great tremour and very pale; she asked for a glass of water as her mother went to meet her, and after drinking that and putting off her hood, she began to speak:– 'We may all hope for the best,' says she; 'it has cost the Queen a fit. Her Majesty was in her chair in the cedar walk, accompanied by Lady ———,[4] when we entered by the private wicket from the west side of the garden, and turned towards her, the Doctor following us. They waited in a side-walk hidden by the shrubs, as we advanced towards the chair. My heart throbbed so I scarce could speak; but my Prince whispered, "Courage, Beatrix," and marched on with a steady step. His face was a little flushed, but he was not afraid of the danger. He who fought so bravely at Malplaquet fears nothing.' Esmond and Castlewood looked at each other at this compliment neither liking the sound of it.

'The Prince uncovered,' Beatrix continued, 'and I saw the Queen turning round to Lady Masham, as if asking who these two were. Her Majesty looked very pale and ill, and then flushed up; the favourite made us a signal to advance, and I went up, leading my Prince by the hand, quite close to the chair: "Your Majesty will give my Lord Viscount your hand to kiss," says her lady, and the Queen put out her hand, which the Prince kissed, kneeling on his knee, he who should kneel to no mortal man or woman.

' "You have been long from England, my lord," says the Queen: "why were you not here to give a home to your mother and sister?"

' "I am come, madam, to stay now, if the Queen desires me," says the Prince, with another low bow.

' "You have taken a foreign wife, my lord, and a foreign religion; was not that of England good enough for you?"

' "In returning to my father's Church," says the Prince, "I do not love my mother the less, nor am I the less faithful servant of your Majesty."

'Here,' says Beatrix, 'the favourite gave me a little signal with her hand to fall back, which I did, though I died to hear what should pass; and whispered something to the Queen, which made her Majesty start and utter one or two words in a hurried manner, looking towards the Prince, and catching hold with her hand of the arm of her chair. He advanced still nearer towards it; he began to speak very rapidly; I caught the words, "Father, blessing, forgiveness," – and then presently the Prince fell on his knees; took from his breast a paper he had there, handed it to the Queen, who, as soon as she saw it, flung up both her arms with a scream, and took away that hand nearest the Prince, and which he endeavoured to kiss. He went on speaking with great animation of gesture, now clasping his hands together on his heart, now opening them as though to say: "I am here, your brother, in your power." Lady Masham ran round on the other side of the chair, kneeling too, and speaking with great energy. She clasped the Queen's hand on her side, and picked up the paper her Majesty had let fall. The Prince rose and made a further speech as though he would go; the favourite on the other hand urging her mistress, and then, running back to the Prince, brought him back once more close to the chair. Again he knelt down and took the Queen's hand, which she did not withdraw, kissing it a hundred times; my lady all the time, with sobs and supplications, speaking over the chair. This while the Queen sat with a stupefied look, crumpling the paper with one hand, as my Prince embraced the other; then of a sudden she uttered several piercing shrieks, and burst into a great fit of hysteric tears and laughter. "Enough, enough, sir, for this time," I heard Lady Masham say; and the chairman, who had withdrawn round the Banqueting-room, came back, alarmed by the cries. "Quick," says Lady Masham, "get some help," and I ran towards the Doctor, who, with the Bishop of Rochester, came up instantly. Lady Masham whispered the Prince he might hope for the very best; and to be ready to-morrow; and he hath gone away to the Bishop of Rochester's house, to meet several of his friends there. And so the great stroke is struck,' says Beatrix, going down on her knees, and clasping her hands, 'God save the King: God save the King!'

Beatrix's tale told, and the young lady herself calmed somewhat of her agitation, we asked with regard to the Prince, who was absent with Bishop Atterbury, and were informed that 'twas likely he might remain abroad the whole day. Beatrix's three kinsfolk looked at one another at this intelligence; 'twas clear the same thought was passing through the minds of all.

But who should begin to break the news? Monsieur Baptiste, that is, Frank Castlewood, turned very red, and looked towards Esmond; the Colonel bit his lips, and fairly beat a retreat into the window: it was Lady Castlewood that opened upon Beatrix with the news which we knew would do anything but please her.

'We are glad,' says she, taking her daughter's hand, and speaking in a gentle voice, 'that the guest is away.'

Beatrix drew back in an instant, looking round her at us three, and as if divining a danger. 'Why glad?' says she, her breast beginning to heave; 'are you so soon tired of him?'

'We think one of us devilishly too fond of him,' cries out Frank Castlewood.

'And which is it – you, my lord, or is it mamma, who is jealous because he drinks my health? or is it the head of the family' (here she turned with an imperious look towards Colonel Esmond), 'who has taken of late to preach the King sermons?'

'We do not say you are too free with his Majesty.'

'I thank you, madam,' says Beatrix, with a toss of the head and a curtsey.

But her mother continued, with very great calmness and dignity – 'At least we have not said so, though we might, were it possible for a mother to say such words to her own daughter, your father's daughter.'

'*Eh, mon père*,' breaks out Beatrix, 'was no better than other persons' fathers'; and again she looked towards the Colonel.

We all felt a shock as she uttered those two or three French words; her manner was exactly imitated from that of our foreign guest.

'You had not learned to speak French a month ago, Beatrix,' says her mother, sadly, 'nor to speak ill of your father.'

Beatrix, no doubt, saw that slip she had made in her flurry, for she blushed crimson: 'I have learnt to honour the King,' says she, drawing up, 'and 'twere as well that others suspected neither his Majesty nor me.'

'If you respected your mother a little more,' Frank said, 'Trix, you would do yourself no hurt.'

'I am no child,' says she, turning round on him; 'we have lived very well these five years without the benefit of your advice or example, and I intend to take neither now. Why does not the head of the house speak?' she went on; 'he rules everything here. When his chaplain has done singing the psalms, will his lordship deliver the sermon? I am tired of the psalms.' The Prince had used almost the very same words, in regard to Colonel Esmond, that the imprudent girl repeated in her wrath.

'You show yourself a very apt scholar, madam,' says the Colonel; and, turning to his mistress, 'Did your guest use these words in your ladyship's hearing, or was it to Beatrix in private that he was pleased to impart his opinion regarding my tiresome sermon?'

'Have you seen him alone?' cries my lord, starting up with an oath: 'by God, have you seen him alone?'

'Were he here, you wouldn't dare so to insult me; no, you would not dare!' cries Frank's sister. 'Keep your oaths, my lord, for your wife; we are not used here to such language. Till you came, there used to be kindness between me and mamma, and I cared for her when you never did, when you were away for years with your horses, and your mistress, and your Popish wife.'

'By ——,' says my lord, rapping out another oath, 'Clotilda is an angel; how dare you say a word against Clotilda?'

Colonel Esmond could not refrain from a smile, to see how easy Frank's attack was drawn off by that feint:– 'I fancy Clotilda is not the subject in hand,' says Mr Esmond, rather scornfully; 'her ladyship is at Paris, a hundred leagues off, preparing baby-linen. It is about my Lord Castlewood's sister, and not his wife, the question is.'

'He is not my Lord Castlewood,' says Beatrix, 'and he knows he is not; he is Colonel Francis Esmond's son, and no more, and he wears a false title; and he lives on another man's land, and he knows it.' Here was another desperate sally of the poor beleaguered garrison, and an *alerte* in another quarter. 'Again, I beg your pardon,' says Esmond. 'If there are no proofs of my claim, I have no claim. If my father acknowledged no heir, yours was his lawful successor, and my Lord Castlewood hath as good a right to his rank and small estate as any man in England. But that again is not the question, as you know very well: let us bring our talk back to it, as you will have me meddle in it. And I will give you frankly my opinion, that a house where a Prince lies all day, who respects no woman, is no

house for a young unmarried lady; that you were better in the
country than here; that he is here on a great end, from which
no folly should divert him; and that having nobly done your
part of this morning, Beatrix, you should retire off the scene
awhile, and leave it to the other actors of the play.'

As the Colonel spoke with a perfect calmness and politeness,
such as 'tis to be hoped he hath always shown to women,* his
mistress stood by him on one side of the table, and Frank
Castlewood on the other, hemming in poor Beatrix, that was
behind it, and, as it were, surrounding her with our approaches.

Having twice sallied out and been beaten back, she now, as I
expected, tried the *ultima ratio* of women, and had recourse to
tears. Her beautiful eyes filled with them; I never could bear
in her, nor in any woman, that expression of pain:- 'I am alone,'
sobbed she; 'you are three against me – my brother, my mother,
and you. What have I done, that you should speak and look so
unkindly at me? Is it my fault that the Prince should, as you
say, admire me? Did I bring him here? Did I do aught but
what you bade me, in making him welcome? Did you not tell me
that our duty was to die for him? Did you not teach me, mother,
night and morning, to pray for the King, before even ourselves?
What would you have of me, cousin, for you are the chief of
the conspiracy against me; I know you are, sir, and that my
mother and brother are acting but as you bid them; whither
would you have me go?'

'I would but remove from the Prince,' says Esmond, gravely,

---

*My dear father saith quite truly, that his manner towards our sex was
uniformly courteous. From my infancy upwards, he treated me with an
extreme gentleness, as though I was a little lady. I can scarce remember
(though I tried him often) ever hearing a rough word from him, nor was he
less grave and kind in his manner to the humblest negresses on his estate. He
was familiar with no one except my mother, and it was delightful to witness
up to the very last days the confidence between them. He was obeyed eagerly
by all under him; and my mother and all her household lived in a constant
emulation to please him, and quite a terror lest in any way they should
offend him. He was the humblest man, with all this; the least exacting, the
most easily contented; and Mr Benson, our minister at Castlewood, who
attended him at the last, ever said – 'I know not what Colonel Esmond's
doctrine was, but his life and death were those of a devout Christian.' –
R. E. W.

'a dangerous temptation; Heaven forbid I should say you would yield: I would only have him free of it. Your honour needs no guardian, please God, but his imprudence doth. He is so far removed from all women by his rank, that his pursuit of them cannot but be unlawful. We would remove the dearest and fairest of our family from the chance of that insult, and that is why we would have you go, dear Beatrix.'

'Harry speaks like a book,' says Frank, with one of his oaths, 'and, by ——, every word he saith is true. You can't help being handsome, Trix; no more can the Prince help following you. My counsel is that you go out of harm's way; for, by the Lord, were the Prince to play any tricks with you, King as he is, or is to be, Harry Esmond and I would have justice of him.'

'Are not two such champions enough to guard me?' says Beatrix, something sorrowfully; 'sure, with you two watching, no evil could happen to me.'

'In faith, I think not, Beatrix,' says Colonel Esmond; 'nor if the Prince knew us would he try.'

'But does he know you?' interposed Lady Esmond, very quiet: 'he comes of a country where the pursuit of kings is thought no dishonour to a woman. Let us go, dearest Beatrix. Shall we go to Walcote or to Castlewood? We are best away from the city; and when the Prince is acknowledged, and our champions have restored him, and he hath his own house at Saint James's or Windsor, we can come back to ours here. Do you not think so, Harry and Frank?'

Frank and Harry thought with her, you may be sure.

'We will go, then,' says Beatrix, turning a little pale; 'Lady Masham is to give me warning to-night how her Majesty is, and to-morrow——'

'I think we had best go to-day, my dear,' says my Lady Castlewood; 'we might have the coach and sleep at Hounslow, and reach home to-morrow. 'Tis twelve o'clock; bid the coach, cousin, be ready at one.'

'For shame!' burst out Beatrix, in a passion of tears and mortification. 'You disgrace me by your cruel precautions; my own mother is the first to suspect me, and would take me away as my gaoler. I will not go with you, mother; I will go as no one's prisoner. If I wanted to deceive, do you think I could find no means of evading you? My family suspects me. As those mistrust me that ought to love me most, let me leave them; I will go, but I will go alone: to Castlewood, be it. I have been unhappy there and lonely enough; let me go back, but spare me at least the humiliation of setting a watch over my misery, which is a trial I can't bear. Let me go when you will, but alone, or not at all. You three can stay and triumph over my unhappiness, and I will bear it as I have borne it before. Let my gaoler-in-chief go order the coach that is to take me away. I thank you, Henry Esmond for your share in the conspiracy. All my life long I'll thank you, and remember you; and you, brother, and you, mother, how shall I show my gratitude to you for your careful defence of my honour?'

She swept out of the room with the air of an empress, flinging glances of defiance at us all, and leaving us conquerors of the field, but scared, and almost ashamed of our victory. It did indeed seem hard and cruel that we three should have conspired the banishment and humiliation of that fair creature. We looked at each other in silence; 'twas not the first stroke by many of our actions in that unlucky time, which, being done, we wished undone. We agreed it was best she should go alone, speaking stealthily to one another, and under our breaths, like persons engaged in an act they felt ashamed in doing.

In a half-hour, it might be, after our talk she came back, her countenance wearing the same defiant air which it had borne when she left us. She held a shagreen case in her hand; Esmond knew it as containing his diamonds which he had given to her for her marriage with Duke Hamilton, and which she had worn so splendidly on the inauspicious night of the Prince's arrival. 'I have brought back,' says she, 'to the Marquis of Esmond the present he deigned to make me in days when he trusted me better than now. I will never accept a benefit or a kindness from Henry Esmond more, and I give back these family diamonds, which belonged to one king's mistress, to the gentleman that suspected I would be another. Have you been upon your message of coach-caller, my Lord Marquis? Will you send your valet to see that I do not run away?' We were right, yet, by her manner, she had put us all in the wrong; we were conquerors, yet the honours of the day seemed to be with the poor oppressed girl.

That luckless box containing the stones had first been ornamented with a baron's coronet, when Beatrix was engaged to the young gentleman from whom she parted, and afterwards the gilt crown of a duchess figured on the cover, which also poor Beatrix was destined never to wear. Lady Castlewood opened the case mechanically and scarce thinking what she did; and behold, besides the diamonds, Esmond's present, there lay in the box the enamelled miniature of the late Duke, which Beatrix had laid aside with her mourning when the King came into the house; and which the poor heedless thing very likely had forgotten.

'Do you leave this, too, Beatrix?' says her mother, taking the miniature out and with a cruelty she did not very often show; but there are some moments when the tenderest women are cruel, and some triumphs which angels can't forego. *

Having delivered this stab, Lady Esmond was frightened at the effect of her blow. It went to poor Beatrix's heart; she flushed up and passed a handkerchief across her eyes, and kissed the miniature, and put it into her bosom:– 'I had forgot it,' says she; 'my injury made me forget my grief; my mother has recalled both to me. Farewell, mother; I think I never can forgive you; something hath broke between us that no tears nor years can repair. I always said I was alone; you never loved me, never – and were jealous of me from the time I sat on my father's knee. Let me go away, the sooner the better; I can bear to be with you no more.'

'Go, child,' says her mother, still very stern; 'go and bend your proud knees and ask forgiveness; go, pray in solitude for humility and repentance. 'Tis not your reproaches that make me unhappy, 'tis your hard heart, my poor Beatrix; may God soften it, and teach you one day to feel for your mother!'

*This remark shows how unjustly and contemptuously even the best of men will sometimes judge of our sex. Lady Esmond had no intention of triumphing over her daughter; but from a sense of duty alone pointed out her deplorable wrong. – R. E.

If my mistress was cruel, at least she never could be got to own as much. Her haughtiness quite overtopped Beatrix's; and, if the girl had a proud spirit, I very much fear it came to her by inheritance.

## Chapter 11

### OUR GUEST QUITS US AS NOT BEING HOSPITABLE ENOUGH

BEATRIX'S departure took place within an hour, her maid going with her in the post-chaise, and a man armed on the coach-box to prevent any danger of the road. Esmond and Frank thought of escorting the carriage, but she indignantly refused their company, and another man was sent to follow the coach, and not to leave it till it had passed over Hounslow Heath on the next day. And these two forming the whole of Lady Castlewood's male domestics, Mr Esmond's faithful John Lockwood came to wait on his mistress during their absence, though he would have preferred to escort Mrs Lucy, his sweetheart, on her journey into the country.

We had a gloomy and silent meal; it seemed as if a darkness was over the house, since the bright face of Beatrix had been withdrawn from it. In the afternoon came a message from the favourite to relieve us somewhat from this despondency. 'The Queen hath been much shaken,' the note said; 'she is better now, and all things will go well. Let *my Lord Castlewood* be ready against we send for him.'

At night there came a second billet: 'There hath been a great battle in Council; Lord Treasurer hath broke his staff,[1] and hath fallen never to rise again; no successor is appointed. Lord B—— receives a great Whig company to-night at Golden Square. If he is trimming, others are true; the Queen hath no more fits, but is a-bed now, and more quiet. Be ready against morning, when I still hope all will be well.'

The Prince came home shortly after the messenger who bore

this billet had left the house. His Royal Highness was so much the better for the Bishop's liquor, that to talk affairs to him now was of little service. He was helped to the royal bed; he called Castlewood familiarly by his own name; he quite forgot the part upon the acting of which his crown, his safety, depended. 'Twas lucky that my Lady Castlewood's servants were out of the way, and only those heard him who would not betray him. He inquired after the adorable Beatrix, with a royal hiccup in his voice; he was easily got to bed, and in a minute or two plunged in that deep slumber and forgetfulness with which Bacchus rewards the votaries of that god. We wished Beatrix had been there to see him in his cups. We regretted, perhaps, that she was gone.

One of the party at Kensington Square was fool enough to ride to Hounslow that night, *coram latronibus*,[2] and to the inn which the family used ordinarily in their journeys out of London. Esmond desired my landlord not to acquaint Madam Beatrix with his coming, and had the grim satisfaction of passing by the door of the chamber where she lay with her maid, and of watching her chariot set forth in the early morning. He saw her smile and slip money into the man's hand who was ordered to ride behind the coach as far as Bagshot. The road being open, and the other servant armed, it appeared she dispensed with the escort of a second domestic; and this fellow, bidding his young mistress adieu with many bows, went and took a pot of ale in the kitchen, and returned in company with his brother servant, John Coachman, and his horses, back to London.

They were not a mile out of Hounslow when the two worthies stopped for more drink, and here they were scared by seeing Colonel Esmond gallop by them. The man said in reply to Colonel Esmond's stern question, that his young mistress had sent her duty; only that, no other message: she had had a very good night, and would reach Castlewood by nightfall. The Colonel had no time for further colloquy, and galloped on swiftly to London, having business of great importance there, as my reader very well knoweth. The thought of Beatrix riding away from the danger soothed his mind not a little. His horse was at Kensington Square (honest Dapple knew the way thither well enough) before the tipsy guest of last night was awake and sober.

The account of the previous evening was known all over the town early next day. A violent altercation had taken place before the Queen in the Council Chamber; and all the coffee-houses had their version of the quarrel. The news brought my Lord Bishop early to Kensington Square, where he awaited the waking of his royal master above stairs, and spoke confidently of having him proclaimed as Prince of Wales and heir to the throne before that day was over. The Bishop had entertained on the previous afternoon certain of the most influential gentlemen of the true British party. His Royal Highness had charmed all, both Scots and English, Papists and Churchmen: 'Even Quakers,' says he, 'were at our meeting; and, if the stranger took a little too much British punch and ale, he will soon grow more accustomed to those liquors; and my Lord Castlewood,' says the Bishop with a laugh, 'must bear the cruel charge of having been for once in his life a little tipsy. He toasted your lovely sister a dozen times, at which we all laughed,' says the Bishop, 'admiring so much fraternal affection. – Where is that charming nymph, and why doth she not adorn your ladyship's tea-table with her bright eyes?'

Her ladyship said, drily, that Beatrix was not at home that morning; my Lord Bishop was too busy with great affairs to trouble himself much about the presence or absence of any lady, however beautiful.

We were yet at table when Doctor A—— came from the Palace with a look of great alarm; the shocks the Queen had had the day before had acted on her severely; he had been sent for, and had ordered her to be blooded. The surgeon of Long Acre had come to cup the Queen, and her Majesty was now more easy and breathed more freely. What made us start at the name of Mr Aymé? '*Il faut être aimable pour être aimé*,' says the merry Doctor; Esmond pulled his sleeve, and bade him hush. It was to Aymé's house, after his fatal duel, that my dear Lord Castlewood, Frank's father, had been carried to die.

No second visit could be paid to the Queen on that day at

any rate; and when our guest above gave his signal that he was awake, the Doctor, the Bishop, and Colonel Esmond waited upon the Prince's levee, and brought him their news, cheerful or dubious. The Doctor had to go away presently, but promised to keep the Prince constantly acquainted with what was taking place at the Palace hard by. His counsel was, and the Bishop's, that as soon as ever the Queen's malady took a favourable turn, the Prince should be introduced to her bedside; the Council summoned; the guard at Kensington and St James's, of which two regiments were to be entirely relied on, and one known not to be hostile, would declare for the Prince, as the Queen would before the Lords of her Council, designating him as the heir to her throne.

With locked doors, and Colonel Esmond acting as secretary, the Prince and his Lordship of Rochester passed many hours of this day composing Proclamations and Addresses to the Country, to the Scots, to the Clergy, to the People of London and England; announcing the arrival of the exile descendant of three sovereigns, and his acknowledgement by his sister as heir to the throne. Every safeguard for their liberties, the Church and people could ask, was promised to them. The Bishop could answer for the adhesion of very many prelates, who besought of their flocks and brother ecclesiastics to recognize the sacred right of the future sovereign, and to purge the country of the sin of rebellion.

During the composition of these papers, more messengers than one came from the Palace regarding the state of the august patient there lying. At mid-day she was somewhat better; at evening the torpor again seized her, and she wandered in her mind. At night Doctor A—— was with us again, with a report rather more favourable: no instant danger at any rate was apprehended. In the course of the last two years her Majesty had had many attacks similar, but more severe.

By this time we had finished a half-dozen of proclamations, (the wording of them so as to offend no parties, and not to give umbrage to Whigs or Dissenters, required very great caution), and the young Prince, who had indeed shown, during a long day's labour, both alacrity at seizing the information given him, and ingenuity and skill in turning the phrases which were to go out signed by his name, here exhibited a good-humour and thoughtfulness that ought to be set down to his credit.

'Were these papers to be mislaid,' says he, 'or our scheme to come to mishap, my Lord Esmond's writing would bring him to a place where I heartily hope never to see him; and so, by your leave, I will copy the papers myself, though I am not very strong in spelling; and if they are found they will implicate none but the person they most concern'; and so, having carefully copied the proclamations out, the Prince burned those in Colonel Esmond's hand-writing: 'And now, and now, gentlemen,' says he, 'let us go to supper, and drink a glass with the ladies. My Lord Esmond, you will sup with us to-night; you have given us of late too little of your company.'

The Prince's meals were commonly served in the chamber which had been Beatrix's bedroom, adjoining that in which he slept. And the dutiful practice of his entertainers was to wait until their royal guest bade them take their places at table before they sat down to partake of the meal. On this night, as you may suppose, only Frank Castlewood and his mother were in waiting when the supper was announced to receive the Prince; who had passed the whole of the day in his own apartment, with the Bishop as his Minister of State, and Colonel Esmond officiating as Secretary of his Council.

The Prince's countenance wore an expression by no means pleasant, when looking towards the little company assembled, and waiting for him, he did not see Beatrix's bright face there as usual to greet him. He asked Lady Esmond for his fair introducer of yesterday: her ladyship only cast her eyes down, and said quietly, Beatrix could not be of the supper that night; nor did she show the least sign of confusion, whereas Castlewood turned red, and Esmond was no less embarrassed. I think women have an instinct of dissimulation; they know by nature how to disguise their emotions far better than the most consummate male courtiers can do. Is not the better part of the life of many of them spent in hiding their feelings, in cajoling their tyrants, in masking over with fond smiles and artful gaiety their doubt, or their grief, or their terror?

Our guest swallowed his supper very sulky; it was not till the second bottle his Highness began to rally. When Lady Castlewood asked leave to depart, he sent a message to Beatrix, hoping she would be present at the next day's dinner, and applied himself to drink, and to talk afterwards, for which there was subject in plenty.

The next day, we heard from our informer at Kensington that the Queen was somewhat better, and had been up for an hour, though she was not well enough yet to receive any visitor.

At dinner a single cover was laid for his Royal Highness; and the two gentlemen alone waited on him. We had had a consultation in the morning with Lady Castlewood, in which it had been determined that, should his Highness ask further questions about Beatrix, he should be answered by the gentlemen of the house.

He was evidently disturbed and uneasy, looking towards the door constantly, as if expecting someone. There came, however, nobody, except honest John Lockwood, when he knocked with a dish, which those within took from him; so the meals were always arranged, and I believe the council in the kitchen were of opinion that my young lord had brought over a priest, who had converted us all into Papists, and that Papists were like Jews, eating together, and not choosing to take their meals in the sight of Christians.

The Prince tried to cover his displeasure; he was but a clumsy dissembler at that time, and when out of humour could with difficulty keep a serene countenance; and having made some foolish attempts at trivial talk, he came to his point presently, and in as easy a manner as he could, saying to Lord Castlewood, he hoped, he requested, his lordship's mother and sister would be of the supper that night. As the time hung heavy on him, and he must not go abroad, would not Miss Beatrix hold him company at a game of cards?

At this, looking up at Esmond, and taking the signal from him, Lord Castlewood informed his Royal Highness * that his

* In London we addressed the Prince as Royal Highness invariably; though the women persisted in giving him the title of King.

sister Beatrix was not at Kensington; and that her family had
thought it best she should quit the town.

'Not at Kensington!' says he; 'is she ill? she was well
yesterday; wherefore should she quit the town? Is it at your
orders, my lord, or Colonel Esmond's, who seems the master
of this house?'

'Not of this, sir,' says Frank very nobly, 'only of our
house in the country, which he hath given to us. This is my
mother's house, and Walcote is my father's, and the Marquis
of Esmond knows he hath but to give his word, and I return his
to him.'

'The Marquis of Esmond! – the Marquis of Esmond,' says
the Prince, tossing off a glass, 'meddles too much with my
affairs, and presumes on the service he hath done me. If you
want to carry your suit with Beatrix, my lord, by blocking her
up in gaol, let me tell you that is not the way to win a woman.'

'I was not aware, sir, that I had spoken of my suit to Madam
Beatrix to your Royal Highness.'

'Bah, bah, Monsieur! we need not be a conjurer to see that.
It makes itself seen at all moments. You are jealous, my lord,
and the maid of honour cannot look at another face without
yours beginning to scowl. That which you do is unworthy,
Monsieur; is inhospitable – is, is *lâche*, yes *lâche*': (he spoke
rapidly in French, his rage carrying him away with each phrase):
'I come to your house; I risk my life; I pass it in ennui; I
repose myself on your fidelity; I have no company but your
lordship's sermons or the conversations of that adorable young
lady, and you take her from me; and you, you rest! *Merci,
Monsieur!* I shall thank you when I have the means; I shall
know to recompense a devotion a little importunate, my lord –
a little importunate. For a month past your airs of protector
have annoyed me beyond measure. You deign to offer me the
crown, and bid me take it on my knees like King John: Eh! I
know my history, Monsieur, and mock myself of frowning
barons. I admire your mistress, and you send her to a Bastille
of the province; I enter your house, and you mistrust me. I
will leave it, Monsieur; from to-night I will leave it. I have
other friends whose loyalty will not be so ready to question

mine. If I have garters to give away, 'tis to noblemen who are not so ready to think evil. Bring me a coach and let me quit this place, or let the fair Beatrix return to it. I will not have your hospitality at the expense of the freedom of that fair creature.'

This harangue was uttered with rapid gesticulations such as the French use, and in the language of that nation; the Prince striding up and down the room; his face flushed, and his hands trembling with anger. He was very thin and frail from repeated illness and a life of pleasure. Either Castlewood or Esmond could have broke him across their knee, and in half a minute's struggle put an end to him; and here he was insulting us both, and scarce deigning to hide from the two, whose honour it most concerned, the passion he felt for the young lady of our family. My Lord Castlewood replied to the Prince's tirade very nobly and simply.

'Sir,' says he, 'your Royal Highness is pleased to forget that others risk their lives, and for your cause. Very few Englishmen, please God, would dare to lay hands on your sacred person, though none would ever think of respecting ours. Our family's lives are at your service, and everything we have except our honour.'

'Honour! bah, sir, who ever thought of hurting your honour?' says the Prince with a peevish air.

'We implore your Royal Highness never to think of hurting it,' says Lord Castlewood with a low bow. The night being warm, the windows were open both towards the Gardens and the Square. Colonel Esmond heard through the closed door the voice of the watchman calling the hour, in the Square on the other side. He opened the door communicating with the Prince's room; Martin, the servant that had rode with Beatrix to Hounslow, was just going out of the chamber as Esmond entered it, and when the fellow was gone, and the watchman again sang his cry of 'Passed ten o'clock, and a star-light night,' Esmond spoke to the Prince in a low voice, and said – 'Your Royal Highness hears that man?'

'*Après, Monsieur?*' says the Prince.

'I have but to beckon him from the window, and send him

fifty yards, and he returns with a guard of men, and I deliver up to him the body of the person calling himself James the Third, for whose capture Parliament hath offered a reward of £5000, as your Royal Highness saw on our ride from Rochester. I have but to say the word, and, by the Heaven that made me, I would say it if I thought the Prince, for his honour's sake, would not desist from insulting ours. But the first gentleman of England knows his duty too well to forget himself with the humblest, or peril his crown for a deed that were shameful if it were done.'

'Has your lordship anything to say,' says the Prince, turning to Frank Castlewood, and quite pale with anger: 'any threat or any insult, with which you would like to end this agreeable night's entertainment?'

'I follow the head of our house,' says Castlewood, bowing gravely. 'At what time shall it please the Prince that we should wait upon him in the morning?'

'You will wait on the Bishop of Rochester early, you will bid him bring his coach hither; and prepare an apartment for me in his own house, or in a place of safety. The King will reward you handsomely, never fear, for all you have done in his behalf. I wish you a good night, and shall go to bed, unless it pleases the Marquis of Esmond to call his colleague, the watchman, and that I should pass the night with the Kensington guard. Fare you well, be sure I will remember you. My Lord Castlewood, I can go to bed to-night without need of a chamberlain.' And the Prince dismissed us with a grim bow, locking one door as he spoke, that into the supping-room, and the other through which we passed, after us. It led into the small chamber which Frank Castlewood or *Monsieur Baptiste* occupied, and by which Martin entered when Colonel Esmond but now saw him in the chamber.

At an early hour next morning the Bishop arrived, and was closeted for some time with his master in his own apartment, where the Prince laid open to his counsellor the wrongs which, according to his version, he had received from the gentlemen of the Esmond family. The worthy prelate came out from the conference with an air of great satisfaction; he was a man full of resources, and of a most assured fidelity, and possessed of genius, and a hundred good qualities; but captious and of a most jealous temper, that could not help exulting at the downfall of any favourite; and he was pleased in spite of himself to hear that the Esmond ministry was at an end.

'I have soothed your guest,' says he, coming out to the two gentlemen and the widow, who had been made acquainted with somewhat of the dispute of the night before. (By the version we gave her, the Prince was only made to exhibit anger because we doubted of his intentions in respect to Beatrix; and to leave us, because we questioned his honour.) 'But I think, all things considered, 'tis as well he should leave this house; and then, my Lady Castlewood,' says the Bishop, 'my pretty Beatrix may come back to it.'

'She is quite as well at home at Castlewood,' Esmond's mistress said, 'till everything is over.'

'You shall have your title, Esmond, that I promise you,' says the good Bishop, assuming the airs of a Prime Minister. 'The Prince hath expressed himself most nobly in regard of the little difference of last night, and I promise you he hath listened to my sermon, as well as to that of other folks,' says the Doctor archly; 'he hath every great and generous quality, with perhaps a weakness for the sex which belongs to his family, and hath been known in scores of popular sovereigns from King David downwards.'

'My lord, my lord,' breaks out Lady Esmond, 'the levity with which you speak of such conduct towards our sex shocks me, and what you call weakness I call deplorable sin.'

'Sin it is, my dear creature,' says the Bishop with a shrug, taking snuff; 'but consider what a sinner King Solomon was, and in spite of a thousand of wives too.'

'Enough of this, my lord,' says Lady Castlewood with a fine blush, and walked out of the room very stately.

The Prince entered it presently with a smile on his face, and if he felt any offence against us on the previous night, at present exhibited none. He offered a hand to each gentleman with great courtesy. 'If all your bishops preach so well as Doctor Atterbury,' says he, 'I don't know, gentlemen, what may happen to me. I spoke very hastily, my lords, last night, and ask pardon of both of you. But I must not stay any longer,' says he, 'giving umbrage to good friends, or keeping pretty girls away from their homes. My Lord Bishop hath found a safe place for me, hard by at a curate's house, whom the Bishop can trust, and whose wife is so ugly as to be beyond all danger; we will decamp into those new quarters, and I leave you, thanking you for a hundred kindnesses here. Where is my hostess, that I may bid her farewell; to welcome her in a house of my own, soon, I trust, where my friends shall have no cause to quarrel with me.'

Lady Castlewood arrived presently, blushing with great grace, and tears filling her eyes as the Prince graciously saluted her. She looked so charming and young, that the Doctor, in his bantering way, could not help speaking of her beauty to the Prince; whose compliment made her blush, and look more charming still.

## Chapter 12

### A GREAT SCHEME, AND WHO BAULKED IT

As characters written with a secret ink come out with the application of fire, and disappear again and leave the paper white, so soon as it is cool; a hundred names of men, high in repute and favour in the Prince's cause, that were writ in our private lists, would have been visible enough on the great roll of the conspiracy, had it ever been laid open under the sun. What crowds would have pressed forward, and subscribed their names and protested their loyalty, when the danger was over! What a number of Whigs, now high in place and creatures of the all-powerful minister, scorned Mr Walpole then![1] If ever a match was gained by the manliness and decision of a few at a moment of danger; if ever one was lost by the treachery and imbecility of those that had the cards in their hands, and might have played them, it was in that momentous game which was enacted in the next three days, and of which the noblest crown in the world was the stake.

From the conduct of my Lord Bolingbroke, those who were interested in the scheme we had in hand, saw pretty well that he was not to be trusted. Should the Prince prevail, it was his lordship's gracious intention to declare for him: should the Hanoverian party bring in their sovereign, who more ready to go on his knee, and cry God save King George? And he betrayed the one Prince and the other; but exactly at the wrong time. When he should have struck for King James, he faltered and coquetted with the Whigs; and having committed himself by the most monstrous professions of devotion, which the Elector rightly scorned, he proved the justness of their contempt for him by flying and taking renegado service with St Germains, just when he should have kept aloof: and that Court despised him, as the manly and resolute men who established the Elector in England had before done. He signed his own name to every accusation of insincerity his enemies made against him; and the King and the Pretender alike could show proofs of St John's treachery under his own hand and seal.

Our friends kept a pretty close watch upon his motions, as on those of the brave and hearty Whig party, that made little concealment of theirs. They would have in the Elector, and used every means in their power to effect their end. My Lord Marlborough was now with them. His expulsion from power by the Tories had thrown that great captain at once on the Whig side. We heard he was coming from Antwerp; and in fact, on the day of the Queen's death, he once more landed on English shore. A great part of the army was always with their illustrious leader; even the Tories in it were indignant at the injustice of the persecution which the Whig officers were made to undergo. The chiefs of these were in London, and at the head of them one of the most intrepid men in the world, the Scots Duke of Argyle, whose conduct, on the second day after that to which I have now brought down my history, ended, as such honesty and bravery deserved to end, by establishing the present royal race on the English throne.

Meanwhile there was no slight difference of opinion amongst

the councillors surrounding the Prince, as to the plan his Highness should pursue. His female minister at Court, fancying she saw some amelioration in the Queen, was for waiting a few days, or hours it might be, until he could be brought to her bedside, and acknowledged as her heir. Mr Esmond was for having him march thither, escorted by a couple of troops of Horse Guards, and openly presenting himself to the Council. During the whole of the night of the 29th–30th July, the Colonel was engaged with gentlemen of the military profession, whom 'tis needless here to name; suffice it to say that several of them had exceeding high rank in the army, and one of them in especial was a general, who, when he heard the Duke of Marlborough was coming on the other side, waved his crutch over his head with a huzzah, at the idea that he should march out and engage him. Of the three Secretaries of State, we knew that one was devoted to us. The Governor of the Tower was ours: the two companies on duty at Kensington barrack were safe; and we had intelligence, very speedy and accurate, of all that took place at the Palace within.

At noon, on the 30th of July, a message came to the Prince's friends that the Committee of Council was sitting at Kensington Palace, their Graces of Ormonde and Shrewsbury, the Archbishop of Canterbury and the three Secretaries of State, being there assembled. In an hour afterwards, hurried news was brought that the two great Whig Dukes, Argyle and Somerset, had broke into the Council-chamber without a summons, and taken their seat at table. After holding a debate there, the whole party proceeded to the chamber of the Queen, who was lying in great weakness, but still sensible, and the lords recommended his Grace of Shrewsbury as the fittest person to take the vacant place of Lord Treasurer; her Majesty gave him the staff, as all know. 'And now,' writ my messenger from Court, '*now or never is the time.*'

Now or never was the time indeed. In spite of the Whig Dukes, our side had still the majority in the Council, and Esmond, to whom the message had been brought (the personage at Court not being aware that the Prince had quitted his lodging in Kensington Square), and Esmond's gallant young aide-de-camp, Frank Castlewood, putting on sword and uniform, took a brief leave of their dear lady, who embraced and blessed them both; and went to her chamber to pray for the issue of the great event which was then pending.

Castlewood sped to the barrack to give warning to the captain of the guard there; and then went to the King's Arms tavern at Kensington, where our friends were assembled, having come by parties of twos and threes, riding or in coaches, and were got together in the upper chamber, fifty-three of them; their servants, who had been instructed to bring arms likewise, being below in the garden of the tavern, where they were served with drink. Out of this garden is a little door that leads into the road of the Palace, and through this it was arranged that masters and servants were to march, when that signal was given, and that personage appeared, for whom all were waiting. There was in our company the famous officer next in command to the Captain-General of the Forces, his Grace the Duke of Ormonde, who was within at the Council. There were with him two more generals, nine major-generals and brigadiers, seven colonels, eleven Peers of Parliament, and twenty-one members of the House of Commons. The Guard was with us within and without the Palace: the Queen was with us; the Council (save the two Whig Dukes, that must have succumbed); the day was our own, and with a beating heart Esmond walked rapidly to the Mall of Kensington, where he had parted with the Prince on the night before. For three nights the Colonel had not been to bed: the last had been passed summoning the Prince's friends together, of whom the great majority had no sort of inkling of the transaction pending until they were told that he was actually on the spot, and were summoned to strike the blow. The night before and after the altercation with the Prince, my gentleman, having suspicions of his Royal Highness, and fearing lest he should be minded to give us the slip, and fly off after his fugitive beauty, had spent, if the truth must be told, at the Greyhound tavern, over against my Lady Esmond's house in Kensington Square, with an eye on the door, lest the Prince should escape from it. The night before that he had passed in his boots at the Crown at Hounslow, where he must watch forsooth all night, in order to get one moment's glimpse of Beatrix in the morning. And fate had decreed that he was to have a fourth night's ride and wakefulness before his business was ended.

He ran to the curate's house in Kensington Mall, and asked for Mr Bates, the name the Prince went by. The curate's wife said Mr Bates had gone abroad very early in the morning in his boots, saying he was going to the Bishop of Rochester's house at Chelsey. But the Bishop had been at Kensington himself two hours ago to seek for Mr Bates, and had returned in his coach to his own house, when he heard that the gentleman was gone thither to seek him.

This absence was most unpropitious, for an hour's delay might cost a kingdom; Esmond had nothing for it but to hasten to the King's Arms, and tell the gentlemen there assembled that Mr George (as we called the Prince there) was not at home, but that Esmond would go fetch him; and taking a general's coach that happened to be there, Esmond drove across the country to Chelsey, to the Bishop's house there.

The porter said two gentlemen were with his lordship, and Esmond ran past this sentry up to the locked door of the Bishop's study, at which he rattled, and was admitted presently. Of the Bishop's guests one was a brother prelate, and the other the Abbé G——.

'Where is Mr George?' says Mr Esmond; 'now is the time.' The Bishop looked scared; 'I went to his lodging,' he said, 'and they told me he was come hither. I returned as quick as coach would carry me; and he hath not been here.'

The Colonel burst out with an oath; that was all he could say to their reverences; ran down the stairs again, and bidding the coachman, an old friend and fellow-campaigner, drive as if he was charging the French with his master at Wynendael – they were back at Kensington in half-an-hour.

Again Esmond went to the curate's house. Mr George had not returned. The Colonel had to go with this blank errand to the gentlemen at the King's Arms, that were grown very impatient by this time.

Out of the window of the tavern, and looking over the garden wall, you can see the green before Kensington Palace, the Palace gate (round which the ministers' coaches were standing), and the barrack building. As we were looking out from this window in gloomy discourse, we heard presently trumpets blowing, and some of us ran to the window of the front room, looking into the High Street of Kensington, and saw a regiment of Horse coming.

'It's Ormonde's Guards,' says one.

'No, by God, it's Argyle's old regiment!' says my General, clapping down his crutch.

It was, indeed, Argyle's regiment that was brought from Westminster, and that took the place of the regiment at Kensington on which we could rely.

'O, Harry!' says one of the generals there present, 'you were born under an unlucky star; I begin to think that there's no Mr George, nor Mr Dragon either. 'Tis not the peerage I care for, for our name is so ancient and famous, that merely to be called Lord Lydiard would do me no good; but 'tis the chance you promised me of fighting Marlborough.'

As we were talking, Castlewood entered the room with a disturbed air.

'What news, Frank?' says the Colonel. 'Is Mr George coming at last?'

'Damn him, look here!' says Castlewood, holding out a paper. 'I found it in the book – the what you call it, 'Eikum Basilikum', – that villain Martin put it there – he said his young mistress bade him. It was directed to me, but it was meant for him I know, and I broke the seal and read it.'

The whole assembly of officers seemed to swim away before Esmond's eyes as he read the paper; all that was written on it was:– 'Beatrix Esmond is sent away to prison, to Castlewood, where she will pray for happier days.'

'Can you guess where he is?' says Castlewood.

'Yes,' says Colonel Esmond. He knew full well, Frank knew full well: our instinct told whither that traitor had fled.

He had courage to turn to the company and say, 'Gentlemen, I fear very much that Mr George will not be here to-day;

something hath happened – and – and – I very much fear some accident may befall him, which must keep him out of the way. Having had your noon's draught, you had best pay the reckoning and go home; there can be no game where there is no one to play it.'

Some of the gentlemen went away without a word, others called to pay their duty to her Majesty and ask for her health. The little army disappeared into the darkness out of which it had been called; there had been no writings, no paper to implicate any man. Some few officers and Members of Parliament had been invited over-night to breakfast at the King's Arms, at Kensington; and they had called for their bill and gone home.

## Chapter 13

### AUGUST 1, 1714

'DOES my mistress know of this?' Esmond asked of Frank, as they walked along.

'My mother found the letter in the book, on the toilet-table. She had writ it ere she had left home,' Frank said. 'Mother met her on the stairs, with her hand upon the door, trying to enter, and never left her after that till she went away. He did not think of looking at it there, nor had Martin the chance of telling him. I believe the poor devil meant no harm, though I half killed him; he thought 'twas to Beatrix's brother he was bringing the letter.'

Frank never said a word of reproach to me, for having brought the villain amongst us. As we knocked at the door I said, 'When will the horses be ready?' Frank pointed with his cane; they were turning the street that moment.

We went up and bade adieu to our mistress; she was in a dreadful state of agitation by this time, and that Bishop was with her whose company she was so fond of.

'Did you tell him, my lord,' says Esmond, 'that Beatrix was

at Castlewood?' The Bishop blushed and stammered: 'Well,' says he, 'I . . .'

'You served the villain right,' broke out Mr Esmond, 'and he has lost a crown by what you told him.'

My mistress turned quite white. 'Henry, Henry,' says she, 'do not kill him.'

'It may not be too late,' says Esmond; 'he may not have gone to Castlewood; pray God it is not too late.' The Bishop was breaking out with some *banales* phrases about loyalty and the sacredness of the Sovereign's person; but Esmond sternly bade him hold his tongue, burn all papers, and take care of Lady Castlewood; and in five minutes he and Frank were in the saddle, John Lockwood behind them, riding towards Castlewood at a rapid pace.

We were just got to Alton, when who should meet us but old Lockwood, the porter from Castlewood, John's father, walking by the side of the Hexham flying-coach, who slept the night at Alton. Lockwood said his young mistress had arrived at home on Wednesday night, and this morning, Friday, had despatched him with a packet for my lady at Kensington, saying the letter was of great importance.

We took the freedom to break it, while Lockwood stared with wonder, and cried out his Lord bless me's, and Who'd 'a thought it's, at the sight of his young lord, whom he had not seen these seven years.

The packet from Beatrix contained no news of importance at all. It was written in a jocular strain, affecting to make light of her captivity. She asked whether she might have leave to visit Mrs Tusher, or to walk beyond the court and the garden wall. She gave news of the peacocks, and a fawn she had there. She bade her mother send her certain gowns and smocks by old Lockwood; she sent her duty to a certain person, if certain other persons permitted her to take such a freedom; how that, as she was not able to play cards with him, she hoped he would read good books, such as Doctor Atterbury's sermons and Eikon Basilike: she was going to read good books: she thought her pretty mamma would like to know she was not crying her eyes out.

'Who is in the house besides you, Lockwood?' says the Colonel.

'There be the laundry-maid, and the kitchen-maid, Madam Beatrix's maid, the man from London, and that be all; and he sleepeth in my lodge away from the maids,' says old Lockwood.

Esmond scribbled a line with a pencil on the note, giving it to the old man, and bidding him go on to his lady. We knew why Beatrix had been so dutiful on a sudden, and why she spoke of Eikon Basilike. She writ this letter to put the Prince on the scent, and the porter out of the way.

'We have a fine moonlight night for riding on,' says Esmond; 'Frank, we may reach Castlewood in time yet.' All the way along they made inquiries at the post-houses, when a tall young gentleman in a grey suit, with a light-brown periwig, just the colour of my lord's, had been seen to pass. He had set off at six that morning, and we at three in the afternoon. He rode almost as quickly as we had done; he was seven hours ahead of us still when we reached the last stage.

We rode over Castlewood Downs before the breaking of dawn. We passed the very spot where the car was upset fourteen years since, and Mohun lay. The village was not up yet, nor the forge lighted, as we rode through it, passing by the elms, where the rooks were still roosting, and by the church, and over the bridge. We got off our horses at the bridge and walked up to the gate.

'If she is safe,' says Frank, trembling, and his honest eyes filling with tears, 'a silver statue to Our Lady!' He was going to rattle at the great iron knocker on the oak gate; but Esmond stopped his kinsman's hand. He had his own fears, his own hopes, his own despairs and griefs, too; but he spoke not a word of these to his companion, or showed any signs of emotion.

He went and tapped at the little window at the porter's lodge, gently, but repeatedly, until the man came to the bars.

'Who's there?' says he, looking out; it was the servant from Kensington.

'My Lord Castlewood and Colonel Esmond,' we said, from below. 'Open the gate and let us in without any noise.'

'My Lord Castlewood?' says the other; 'my lord's here, and in bed.'

'Open, d——n you,' says Castlewood, with a curse.

'I shall open to no one,' says the man, shutting the glass window as Frank drew a pistol. He would have fired at the porter, but Esmond again held his hand.

'There are more ways than one,' says he, 'of entering such a great house as this.' Frank grumbled that the west gate was half a mile round. 'But I know of a way that's not a hundred yards off,' says Mr Esmond; and leading his kinsman close along the wall, and by the shrubs, which had now grown thick on what had been an old moat about the house, they came to the buttress, at the side of which the little window was, which was Father Holt's private door. Esmond climbed up to this easily, broke a pane that had been mended, and touched the spring inside, and the two gentlemen passed in that way, treading as lightly as they could; and so going through the passage into the court, over which the dawn was now reddening, and where the fountain plashed in the silence.

They sped instantly to the porter's lodge, where the fellow had not fastened his door that led into the court; and pistol in hand came upon the terrified wretch, and bade him be silent. Then they asked (Esmond's head reeled, and he almost fell as he spoke) when Lord Castlewood had arrived? He said on the previous evening, about eight of the clock. – 'And what then?' – His lordship supped with his sister. – 'Did the man wait?' – Yes, he and my lady's maid both waited: the other servants made the supper; and there was no wine, and they could give his lordship but milk, at which he grumbled; and – and Madam Beatrix kept Miss Lucy always in the room with her. And there being a bed across the court in the chaplain's room, she had arranged my lord was to sleep there. Madam Beatrix had come downstairs laughing with the maids, and had locked herself in, and my lord had stood for a while talking to her through the door, and she laughing at him. And then he paced the court awhile, and she came again to the upper window; and my lord implored her to come down and walk in the room; but she would not, and laughed at him again, and shut the window;

and so my lord uttering what seemed curses, but in a foreign language, went to the chaplain's room to bed.

'Was this all?' – 'All,' the man swore upon his honour; 'all as he hoped to be saved. – Stop, there was one thing more. My lord, on arriving, and once or twice during supper, did kiss his sister as was natural, and she kissed him.' At this Esmond ground his teeth with rage, and well nigh throttled the amazed miscreant who was speaking, whereas Castlewood, seizing hold of his cousin's hand, burst into a great fit of laughter.

'If it amuses thee,' says Esmond in French, 'that your sister should be exchanging of kisses with a stranger, I fear poor Beatrix will give thee plenty of sport.' – Esmond darkly thought, how Hamilton, Ashburnham, had before been masters of those roses that the young Prince's lips were now feeding on. He sickened at that notion. Her cheek was desecrated, her beauty tarnished; shame and honour stood between it and him. The love was dead within him; had she a crown to bring him with her love, he felt that both would degrade him.

But this wrath against Beatrix did not lessen the angry feelings of the Colonel against the man who had been the occasion if not the cause of the evil. Frank sat down on a stone bench in the courtyard, and fairly fell asleep, while Esmond paced up and down the court, debating what should ensue. What mattered how much or how little had passed between the Prince and the poor faithless girl? They were arrived in time perhaps to rescue her person, but not her mind; had she not instigated the young Prince to come to her; suborned servants, dismissed others, so that she might communicate with him? The treacherous heart within her had surrendered, though the place was safe; and it was to win this that he had given a life's struggle and devotion; this, that she was ready to give away for the bribe of a coronet or a wink of the Prince's eye.

When he had thought his thoughts out he shook up poor Frank from his sleep, who rose yawning, and said he had been dreaming of Clotilda. 'You must back me,' says Esmond, 'in what I am going to do. I have been thinking that yonder scoundrel may have been instructed to tell that story, and that the whole of it may be a lie; if it be, we shall find it out from the gentleman who is asleep yonder. See if the door leading to my lady's rooms' (so we called the rooms at the north-west angle of the house), 'see if the door is barred as he saith.' We tried, it was indeed as the lacquey had said, closed within.

'It may have been open and shut afterwards,' says poor Esmond; 'the foundress of our family let our ancestor in in that way.'

'What will you do, Harry, if – if what that fellow saith should turn out untrue?' The young man looked scared and frightened into his kinsman's face; I dare say it wore no very pleasant expression.

'Let us first go see whether the two stories agree,' says Esmond; and went in at the passage and opened the door into what had been his own chamber now for well nigh five-and-twenty years. A candle was still burning, and the Prince asleep dressed on the bed – Esmond did not care for making a noise. The Prince started up in his bed, seeing two men in his chamber; '*Qui est là?*' says he, and took a pistol from under his pillow.

'It is the Marquis of Esmond,' says the Colonel, 'come to welcome his Majesty to his house of Castlewood, and to report of what hath happened in London. Pursuant to the King's orders, I passed the night before last, after leaving his Majesty, in waiting upon the friends of the King. It is a pity that his Majesty's desire to see the country and to visit our poor house should have caused the King to quit London without notice yesterday, when the opportunity happened which in all human probability may not occur again; and had the King not chosen to ride to Castlewood, the Prince of Wales might have slept at St James's.'

' 'Sdeath! gentlemen,' says the Prince, starting off his bed, whereon he was lying in his clothes, 'the Doctor was with me yesterday morning, and after watching by my sister all night, told me I might not hope to see the Queen.'

'It would have been otherwise,' says Esmond with another bow; 'as, by this time, the Queen may be dead in spite of the Doctor. The Council was met, a new Treasurer was appointed,

the troops were devoted to the King's cause; and fifty loyal
gentlemen of the greatest names of this kingdom were assembled
to accompany the Prince of Wales, who might have been the
acknowledged heir of the throne, or the possessor of it by this
time, had your Majesty not chosen to take the air. We were
ready; there was only one person that failed us, your Majesty's
gracious——'

'*Morbleu, Monsieur*, you give me too much Majesty,' said
the Prince; who had now risen up and seemed to be looking
to one of us to help him to his coat. But neither stirred.

'We shall take care,' says Esmond, 'not much oftener to
offend in that particular.'

'What mean you, my lord?' says the Prince, and muttered
something about a *guet-à-pens*, which Esmond caught up.

'The snare, sir,' said he, 'was not of our laying; it is not we
that invited you. We came to avenge, and not to compass, the
dishonour of our family.'

'Dishonour! *Morbleu*, there has been no dishonour,' says the
Prince, turning scarlet, 'only a little harmless playing.'

'That was meant to end seriously.'

'I swear,' the Prince broke out impetuously, 'upon the
honour of a gentleman, my lords——'

'That we arrived in time. No wrong hath been done, Frank,'
says Colonel Esmond, turning round to young Castlewood,
who stood at the door as the talk was going on. 'See! here is a
paper whereon his Majesty hath deigned to commence some
verses in honour, or dishonour, of Beatrix. Here is "Madame"
and "Flamme," "Cruelle" and "Rebelle," and "Amour" and
"Jour," in the royal writing and spelling. Had the gracious lover
been happy, he had not passed his time in sighing.' In fact, and
actually as he was speaking, Esmond cast his eyes down towards
the table, and saw a paper on which my young Prince had been
scrawling a madrigal, that was to finish his charmer on the
morrow.

'Sir,' says the Prince, burning with rage (he had assumed his
royal coat unassisted by this time), 'did I come here to receive
insults?'

'To confer them, may it please your Majesty,' says the

Colonel, with a very low bow, 'and the gentlemen of our family are come to thank you.'

'*Malédiction*,' says the young man, tears starting into his eyes with helpless rage and mortification. 'What will you with me, gentlemen?'

'If your Majesty will please to enter the next apartment,' says Esmond, preserving his grave tone, 'I have some papers there which I would gladly submit to you, and by your permission I will lead the way'; and, taking the taper up, and backing before the Prince with very great ceremony, Mr Esmond passed into the little chaplain's room, through which we had just entered into the house:– 'Please to set a chair for his Majesty, Frank,' says the Colonel to his companion, who wondered almost as much at this scene, and was as much puzzled by it, as the other actor in it. Then going to the crypt over the mantel-piece, the Colonel opened it, and drew thence the papers which so long had lain there.

'Here, may it please your Majesty,' says he, 'is the Patent of Marquis sent over by your royal father at St Germains to Viscount Castlewood, my father: here is the witnessed certificate of my father's marriage to my mother, and of my birth and christening; I was christened of that religion of which your sainted sire gave all through life so shining example. These are my titles, dear Frank, and this what I do with them: here go Baptism and Marriage, and here the Marquisate and the August Sign-Manual, with which your predecessor was pleased to honour our race.' And as Esmond spoke he set the papers burning in the brazier. 'You will please, sir, to remember,' he continued, 'that our family hath ruined itself by fidelity to yours: that my grandfather spent his estate, and gave his blood and his son to die for your service; that my dear lord's grand-father[1] (for lord you are now, Frank, by right and title too) died for the same cause; that my poor kinswoman, my father's second wife, after giving away her honour to your wicked perjured race, sent all her wealth to the King; and got in return that precious title that lies in ashes, and this inestimable yard of blue riband. I lay this at your feet and stamp upon it: I draw this sword, and break it and deny you; and, had you completed the wrong you designed us, by Heaven I would have driven it through your heart, and no more pardoned you than your father pardoned Monmouth. Frank will do the same, won't you, cousin?'

Frank, who had been looking on with a stupid air at the papers as they flamed in the old brazier, took out his sword and broke it, holding his head down:– 'I go with my cousin,' says he, giving Esmond a grasp of the hand. 'Marquis or not, by ——, I stand by him any day. I beg your Majesty's pardon for swearing; that is – that is – I'm for the Elector of Hanover, It's all your Majesty's own fault. The Queen's dead most likely by this time. And you might have been King if you hadn't come dangling after Trix.'

'Thus to lose a crown,' says the young Prince, starting up, and speaking French in his eager way; 'to lose the loveliest woman in the world; to lose the loyalty of such hearts as yours, is not this, my lords, enough of humiliation? – Marquis, if I go on my knees will you pardon me? – No, I can't do that, but I can offer your reparation, that of honour, that of gentlemen. Favour me by crossing the sword with mine: yours is broke – see, yonder in the armoire are two'; and the Prince took them out as eager as a boy, and held them towards Esmond:– 'Ah! you will? *Merci, monsieur, merci!*'

Extremely touched by this immense mark of condescension and repentance for wrong done, Colonel Esmond bowed down so low as almost to kiss the gracious young hand that conferred on him such an honour, and took his guard in silence. The swords were no sooner met, than Castlewood knocked up Esmond's with the blade of his own, which he had broke off short at the shell; and the Colonel falling back a step dropped his point with another very low bow, and declared himself perfectly satisfied.

'*Eh bien, Vicomte,*' says the young Prince, who was a boy, and a French boy, '*il ne nous reste qu'une chose à faire*': he placed his sword upon the table, and the fingers of his two hands upon his breast:– 'We have one more thing to do,' says he; 'you do not divine it?' He stretched out his arms:– '*Embrassons nous!*'

The talk was scarce over when Beatrix entered the room:—what came she to seek there? She started and turned pale at the sight of her brother and kinsman, drawn swords, broken sword-blades, and papers yet smouldering in the brazier.

'Charming Beatrix,' says the Prince, with a blush which became him very well, 'these lords have come a-horseback from London, where my sister lies in a despaired state, and where her successor makes himself desired. Pardon me for my escapade of last evening. I had been so long a prisoner, that I seized the occasion of a promenade on horseback, and my horse naturally bore me towards you. I found you a queen in your little court, where you deigned to entertain me. Present my homages to your maids of honour. I sighed as you slept, under the window of your chamber, and then retired to seek rest in my own. It was there that these gentlemen agreeably roused me. Yes, milords, for that is a happy day that makes a Prince acquainted, at whatever cost to his vanity, with such a noble heart as that of the Marquis of Esmond. Mademoiselle, may we take your coach to town? I saw it in the hangar, and this poor Marquis must be dropping with sleep.'

'Will it please the King to breakfast before he goes?' was all Beatrix could say. The roses had shuddered out of her cheeks; her eyes were glaring; she looked quite old. She came up to Esmond and hissed out a word or two:— 'If I did not love you before, cousin,' says she, 'think how I love you now.' If words could stab, no doubt she would have killed Esmond; she looked at him as if she could.

But her keen words gave no wound to Mr Esmond; his heart was too hard. As he looked at her, he wondered that he could ever have loved her. His love of ten years was over; it fell down dead on the spot, at the Kensington Tavern, where Frank brought him the note out of Eikon Basilike. The Prince blushed and bowed low, as she gazed at him, and quitted the chamber. I have never seen her from that day.

Horses were fetched and put to the chariot presently. My lord rode outside, and as for Esmond he was so tired that he was no sooner in the carriage than he fell asleep, and never woke till night, as the coach came into Alton.

As we drove to the Bell Inn comes a mitred coach with our old friend Lockwood beside the coachman. My Lady Castlewood and the Bishop were inside; she gave a little scream when she saw us. The two coaches entered the inn almost together; the landlord and people coming out with lights to welcome the visitors.

We in our coach sprang out of it, as soon as ever we saw the dear lady, and above all, the Doctor in his cassock. What was the news? Was there yet time? Was the Queen alive? These questions were put hurriedly, as Boniface[2] stood waiting before his noble guests to bow them up the stair.

'Is she safe?' was what Lady Castlewood whispered in a flutter to Esmond.

'All's well, thank God,' says he, as the fond lady took his hand and kissed it, and called him her preserver and her dear. *She* wasn't thinking of queens and crowns.

The Bishop's news was reassuring: at least all was not lost; the Queen yet breathed or was alive when they left London, six hours since. ('It was Lady Castlewood who insisted on coming,' the Doctor said.) Argyle had marched up regiments from Portsmouth, and sent abroad for more; the Whigs were on the alert, a pest on them (I am not sure but the Bishop swore as he spoke), and so too were our people. And all might be saved, if only the Prince could be at London in time. We called for horses, instantly to return to London. We never went up poor crestfallen Boniface's stairs, but into our coaches again. The Prince and his Prime Minister in one, Esmond in the other, with only his dear mistress as a companion.

Castlewood galloped forwards on horseback to gather the Prince's friends, and warn them of his coming. We travelled through the night, Esmond discoursing to his mistress of the events of the last twenty-four hours; of Castlewood's ride and his; of the Prince's generous behaviour and their reconciliation. The night seemed short enough; and the starlit hours passed away serenely in that fond company.

So we came along the road; the Bishop's coach heading ours; and, with some delays in procuring horses, we got to Hammersmith about four o'clock on Sunday morning, the first of August, and half-an-hour after, it being then bright day, we rode by my Lady Warwick's house, and so down the street of Kensington.

Early as the hour was, there was a bustle in the street, and many people moving to and fro. Round the gate leading to the Palace, where the guard is, there was especially a great crowd. And the coach ahead of us stopped, and the Bishop's man got down to know what the concourse meant.

There presently came from out of the gate, Horse Guards with their trumpets, and a company of heralds with their tabards. The trumpets blew, and the herald-at-arms came forward and proclaimed GEORGE, by the grace of God, of Great Britain, France, and Ireland, King, Defender of the Faith. And the people shouted God save the King!

Among the crowd shouting and waving their hats, I caught sight of one sad face, which I had known all my life, and seen under many disguises. It was no other than poor Mr Holt's, who had slipped over to England to witness the triumph of the good cause; and now beheld its enemies victorious, amidst the acclamations of the English people. The poor fellow had forgot to huzza or to take his hat off, until his neighbours in the crowd remarked his want of loyalty, and cursed him for a Jesuit in disguise, when he ruefully uncovered and began to cheer. Sure he was the most unlucky of men: he never played a game but he lost it; or engaged in a conspiracy but 'twas certain to end in defeat. I saw him in Flanders after this, whence he went to Rome to the headquarters of his Order; and actually reappeared among us in America, very old, and busy, and hopeful. I am not sure that he did not assume the hatchet and moccasins there; and, attired in a blanket and war-paint, skulk about a missionary amongst the Indians. He lies buried in our neighbouring province of Maryland now, with a cross over him, and a mound of earth above him; under which that unquiet spirit is for ever at peace.

With the sound of King George's trumpets, all the vain hopes of the weak and foolish young Pretender were blown away; and with that music, too, I may say, the drama of my own life was ended. That happiness, which hath subsequently crowned it, cannot be written in words; 'tis of its nature sacred and secret, and not to be spoken of, though the heart be ever so full of thankfulness, save to Heaven and the One Ear alone – to one fond being, the truest and tenderest and purest wife ever man was blessed with. As I think of the immense happiness which was in store for me, and of the depth and intensity of that love which, for so many years, hath blessed me, I own to a transport of wonder and gratitude for such a boon – nay, am thankful to have been endowed with a heart capable of feeling and knowing the immense beauty and value of the gift which God hath bestowed upon me. Sure, love *vincit omnia*; is immeasurably above all ambition, more precious than wealth, more noble than name. He knows not life who knows not that: he hath not felt the highest faculty of the soul who hath not enjoyed it. In the name of my wife I write the completion of hope, and the summit of happiness. To have such a love is the one blessing, in comparison of which all earthly joy is of no value; and to think of her, is to praise God.

It was at Bruxelles, whither we retreated after the failure of our plot – our Whig friends advising us to keep out of the way – that the great joy of my life was bestowed upon me, and that my dear mistress became my wife. We had been so accustomed to an extreme intimacy and confidence, and had lived so long and tenderly together, that we might have gone on to the end without thinking of a closer tie; but circumstances brought about that event which so prodigiously multiplied my happiness and hers (for which I humbly thank Heaven), although a calamity befell us, which, I blush to think, hath occurred more than once in our house. I know not what infatuation of ambition urged the beautiful and wayward woman, whose name hath occupied so many of these pages, and who was served by me with ten years of such a constant fidelity and passion; but ever after that day at Castlewood, when we rescued her, she persisted in holding all her family as her enemies, and left us, and escaped to France, to what a fate I disdain to tell. Nor was her son's house a home for my dear mistress; my poor Frank was weak, as perhaps all our race hath been, and led by women. Those around him were imperious, and in a terror of his mother's influence over him, lest he should recant, and deny the creed which he had adopted by their persuasion. The difference of their religion separated the son and the mother: my dearest mistress felt that she was severed from her children and alone in the world – alone but for one constant servant on whose fidelity, praised be Heaven, she could count. 'Twas after a scene of ignoble quarrel on the part of Frank's wife and mother (for the poor lad had been made to marry the whole of that German family with whom he had connected himself), that I found my mistress one day in tears, and then besought her to confide herself to the care and devotion of one who, by God's help, would never forsake her. And then the tender matron, as beautiful in her autumn, and as pure as virgins in their spring, with blushes of love and 'eyes of meek surrender,'[3] yielded to my respectful importunity, and consented to share my home. Let the last words I write thank her, and bless her who hath blessed it.

By the kindness of Mr Addison,[4] all danger of prosecution, and every obstacle against our return to England, was removed; and my son Frank's gallantry in Scotland[5] made his peace with the King's government. But we two cared no longer to live in England; and Frank formally and joyfully yielded over to us the possession of that estate which we now occupy, far away from Europe and its troubles, on the beautiful banks of the Potomac, where we have built a new Castlewood, and think with grateful hearts of our old home. In our transatlantic country we have a season, the calmest and most delightful of the year, which we call the Indian summer: I often say the autumn of our life resembles that happy and serene weather, and am thankful for its rest and its sweet sunshine. Heaven hath blessed us with a child, which each parent loves for her resemblance to the other. Our diamonds are turned into ploughs and axes for our plantations; and into negroes, the happiest and merriest, I think, in all this country: and the only jewel by which my wife sets any store, and from which she hath never parted, is that gold button she took from my arm on the day when she visited me in prison, and which she wore ever after, as she told me, on the tenderest heart in the world.

# NOTES

THE pernicious respectability of the historical novel for school study and examination has rendered *Henry Esmond* the most edited and annotated of Thackeray's novels. Dryasdust commentary can, however, spoil a work much of whose charm is a brilliant, but often very thin, period veneer. It is no service to Thackeray or his reader to show the author blatantly lifting from his sources, to emphasize in the reading of it the *pastiche* of the style or to offer incidental historical essays. Thackeray did not believe with George Eliot that carelessness was 'a mortal sin in authorship', consequently there are a lot of small errors and discrepancies – hair is in one place brown, another fair; Walcote is near to Winchester and then Wells; non-jurors attend court, etc. The absorbed reader ignores these, but it is easy to assume a spurious editorial ascendancy. Notes are therefore offered; where the reference may be obscure; where Thackeray assumes a greater historical literacy in his reader than can reasonably be expected (though sometimes undeniably Thackeray wants to blind him); where there are significant errors or where interesting insight into working methods and opinion is given. I am indebted, especially in guidance to the numerous classical quotations, to the most thorough edition of *Henry Esmond*, that by T. C. and W. Snow (Oxford, 1915).

1. p.36. The *Dedication* also imitates the manners and language of the period. See, for example, the first dedication of the *Spectator*. William Bingham Baring, Lord Ashburton (1799–1864) was in his time a statesman and a patron of letters. His wife, Lady Harriet, made her home a salon for, among others, Thackeray and Carlyle. Thackeray and his daughters had in fact stayed at the Grange with Carlyle just as *Henry Esmond* was getting under way, which perhaps explains the compliment and the anti-Carlylean opening chapter (the two literary men seem to have fallen out). Thackeray left England in November 1852 for a lecturing tour in America, just as *Henry Esmond* was coming out.

## PREFACE

1. p.37. *My dear mother*: A number of references in the narrative date the time of Esmond's writing his memoirs as after 1740, and at the end of the novel Rachel Esmond is obviously still alive (see the last paragraph). Thackeray is not chronologically consistent about, for example, the age of his characters, about the exact merging of fiction into historical setting or even the synchronization of separate events in his own narrative, but never so wildly inconsistent as to disturb the reader. Discrepancies of this kind will not, therefore, be given undue emphasis in the notes.

2. p.38. The Comte de *Rochambeau* commanded the French troops who fought on the American side in the War of Independence.

3. p.38. *glorious war of independence:* Main elements of *The Virginians* are already present in Thackeray's mind – the pugnacious character of Madam Esmond and the 'fatal differences' which separated her sons in politics. The fact that she is apparently a republican here and a staunch loyalist in the later work is probably an attempt by Thackeray to bring her into unanimity with Esmond's disgust at royal ingratitude and the old world's political and religious factionalism.

4. p.40. *Lord Bolingbroke:* Bolingbroke retired to Dawley in 1724 on his return from exile.

5. p.40. *Sachem:* a chief.

6. p.40. *Bishop Tusher's lady* is Beatrix. Technically this preface should be read, as it was obviously written, after the novel, or better still after the sequel *The Virginians*.


## BOOK ONE

1. p.45. *the Tragic Muse:* Thackeray's elaborate comparison is between Melpomene, the muse of tragedy, and Clio, the muse of history.

2. p.45. *Queen Medea:* The allusion, the first of many in the novel, is to Euripedes' *Medea*. She helped her lover Jason to the Golden Fleece and slew their children when he later deserted her.

3. p.45. *Mr Dryden's words:* in fact, the words of Shakespeare, in *Twelfth Night*, and of Pope, in his *Ode on Saint Cecilia's Day*.

4. p.45. *cothurnus:* The 'cothurnus' is the boot with the massive sole which, with the mask, enhanced the stature of the Greek tragedian. As well as ceremonial history, they suggest the periwig and red high-heels of Louis.

5. p.46. *a hot, red-faced woman:* The image and the tone of this are Swift's, in his *Journal to Stella*, 31 July 1711, 'she hunts in a chaise with one horse, which she drives herself, and drives furiously, like Jehu, and is a mighty hunter, like Nimrod'. The statue referred to is the one by Bird which was raised in 1712 and replaced in 1885.

6. p.47. *Prayer-Book:* Until 1859 the Anglican prayer book contained a service of thanksgiving for the return of Charles II.

7. p.47. *sold his country* refers to the clandestine treaty of Dover with France, 1670, by which Charles II involved England in war with her 'ally' Holland. In return Charles was underwritten by Louis.

8. p.47. *Cato:* Addison's heroic play *Cato*, performed in 1713 – an expression of the Whig playwright's 'manly creed' of public liberty, which eventually becomes Esmond's. Cato's banishment is ironically likened to that of the House of Stuart.

9. p.47. *Ostade or Mieris:* Dutch genre painters of the seventeenth century.

10. p.47. *Kneller* and *Le Brun:* English and French court painters respectively of the same period.

11. p.47. *to claim Olympus:* i.e. divinity, and with it the divine right to succession.

12. p.48. *Tyburn Jack:* Thackeray is thinking of the last three plates of Hogarth's series *Industry and Idleness*.
13. p.48. *Hounslow Heath:* Hounslow Heath, like Bagshot mentioned subsequently, was on the main road to London from the west and notorious for highwaymen; thus in *The Beaux Stratagem* Farquhar names the highwayman and his two accomplices Gibbet, Hounslow and Bagshot. Since Castlewood is in Hampshire, the route, and the hazard, appear often in the novel.

## BOOK ONE: 1

1. p.48. *An Account of The Family of Esmond:* It has been a universally perpetuated error, as the Snow edition points out, to transpose the titles of the first and second chapters. Obviously the reverse order is the correct one.
2. p.48. *Van Dyke, Dobson* and *Lely:* three generations of fashionable court painters. Sir Peter Lely (1618–80), a Dutchman, painted the allegorical series of 'Beauties' of the court of Charles II, which inspired much of the Restoration court's reputation for immorality, of which in this novel Isabella Castlewood is a living relic. By a slip of the pen Thackeray later refers to the Dowager's representation as Diana herself (see p. 143).
3. p.49. *Dea certè:* 'Surely a goddess'. The exclamation of Aeneas on first seeing his mother Venus.
4. p.53. *when the sweetmeats were brought:* Dr Tusher is not unduly reticent, as it was proper for clergymen to retire at this stage of the meal. Much of the social observation of the first volume of *Henry Esmond* is drawn from, or from the same sources possibly, as the famous third chapter of Macaulay's *History*.

## BOOK ONE: 2

1. p.53. *com.:* i.e. 'comitatus', modern Latin for county.
2. p.54. *23 Eliz.:* i.e. the twenty-third year of Elizabeth's reign. The narrative momentarily mimics legal jargon.
3. p.54. *Francis:* Sir Francis fought on the losing side in the Thirty Years War, for Frederick, the Elector Palatinate, against the Imperialists under Ferdinand. James would be likely to reward him, since his daughter had married the 'unfortunate Prince'.
4. p.54. *banneret:* a title, obsolete even in Esmond's day, awarded for gallantry performed in the presence of the sovereign on the field of battle.
5. p.55. *Breda:* a town in Holland where the exiled king stayed from 1656–1658.
6. p.56. *Jack Churchill:* Frank Esmond insults Jack Churchill, later Duke of Marlborough, by an offensive allusion to his sister Arabella, mistress of the Duke of York and mother by him of the subsequent Duke of Berwick. His change of heart towards Isabella has been brought about by

the discovery that she may have been similarly honoured. Tangier came into English possession as part of the dowry of Catherine of Braganza when she married Charles II in 1662. The sentence beginning 'Jack Churchill, Frank Esmond's lieutenant . . .' is, for Thackeray, surprisingly slipshod in syntax, and suggests that his normally elastic style may have been feeling the strain of stuffing this chapter so full of family and national history.

7. p. 57. *Alsatia and the Friars:* the district of Whitefriars which offered sanctuary to debtors and criminals. Its name was by analogy with the buffer state in Europe, and its immunity derived from the convent of Carmelites which existed there until the sixteenth century. The immunity was abolished in 1697.

8. p. 57. *toy-shops:* Toyshops at this date were shops which sold women's things, such as cosmetics.

9. p. 57. *Sybil:* In calling her Sybil, Thomas Killigrew (1612–83), a court wit and dramatist, is ascribing to Isabel the age, not the wisdom, of the Greek prophetess.

10. p. 58. *his twopenny ordinary:* a tavern offering a standard twopenny meal.

11. p. 58. *touched by his Majesty:* touched by the monarch to be cured of scrofula, the 'king's evil'. The practice was discontinued by William and revived, finally, by Anne.

12. p. 59. *Esther . . . Vashti:* Esther the Jewess replaced Vashti in the favour of Ahasuerus (see *Book of Esther*, ch. 2). Lady Dorchester was in fact the daughter of Sir Charles Sedley.

13. p. 61. *fantastic:* i.e. in the Johnson Dictionary's fourth sense: 'capricious; humorous; unsteady; irregular'.

## BOOK ONE: 3

1. p. 62. *a whole colony of Frenchmen:* The Edict of Nantes, which protected Protestants, was revoked by Louis in 1685 as part of a general persecution. A large number of Huguenot refugees fled to England, many of whom set up in silk manufacture at Spitalfields.

2. p. 64. *the great lions and bears in the moats:* Harry goes on a standard tour, to the playhouse, the old London Bridge, and the Tower with its menagerie that was there until 1834. Swift took Lord Shelburn's children on a similar tour 'and saw all the sights, lions etc., then to Bedlam . . . and concluded the night at the puppet show.'

3. p. 67. *tower of lace:* The tower, or tour, is a high headdress kept erect by a wire frame, elsewhere in the novel called a commode. It went out of fashion about 1710.

4. p. 67. *clocks:* Clocks are hand-embroidered designs in coloured silk, gold or silver thread, on stockings.

5. p. 67. *pantofles* are slippers, and *red heels* were fashionable from the Restoration until well into the eighteenth century.

6. p.69. *The English household divines often marry the waiting-women*: something of a standing joke in the period. See Swift's directions to the waiting maid: 'but if you happen to be young with child by my lord, you must take up with the chaplain'.

7. p.70. *a new Castlewood*: i.e. Castlewood in Virginia, where Esmond, like Aeneas in Italy, finally settles and nostalgically applies the names of his childhood to his new surroundings.

8. p.71. *many private visitors*: James II has acceded to the throne, hence the freer social life of the Catholic Castlewoods. The Jesuits, who exercised special power with the king, are therefore more active.

## BOOK ONE: 4

1. p.74. *The French wit*: Montaigne. It is a favourite motto of Thackeray, and of Carlyle.

2. p.76. *News Letter*: a primitive fore-runner of the newspaper.

3. p.76. *Artamène, ou le grand Cyrus*: 1649. A fashionable and romantic French *roman à clef*, by Madame de Scudery.

4. p.76. *tric-trac*: backgammon.

5. p.76. '*The bishops forever*': In 1688 James II ordered a Declaration of Indulgence, removing all restrictions against Catholics and dissenters, to be read in all the churches. General opposition was led by seven Bishops, including the Archbishop of Canterbury, who petitioned the king against it. Foolishly James persecuted them. They were tried for sedition, amidst national protest, and acquitted, making James's position untenable.

## BOOK ONE: 5

1. p.80. *Job Lockwood, the porter's son*: variously Job, John, Jack and Tom Lockwood, later Esmond's man. Some editions rationalize this.

2. p.81. *famuli*: attendants.

3. p.81. *We are to be tolerated*: by the Toleration Act, 1689. In this scene and generally Thackeray draws extensively on Macaulay's picture of the Jesuits (ch. 6, *History of England*), for the subtle and indefatigable Father Holt.

4. p.82. *buffet*: low stool.

5. p.83. *Chrysostom*: 347–407. A Bishop of Constantinople, and also a notable exile, which may have suggested him to Holt.

6. p.84. *cured him of an ague with quinquina*: Cinchona, Peruvian Bark. It contained quinine and would therefore be genuinely medicinal for malaria (ague). Later Thackeray refers to it by another name, Jesuit's Bark, which he may have thought too obvious for this context.

7. p.86. *the Churchills – the Judases*: At Salisbury soon after William's arrival, 6 November 1688, James was delayed from immediate resistance by a violent nose-bleed. During the delay Churchill and others, as

part of an army conspiracy, went over to the invader. It was the turning-point for James.

8. p.88. *Sir Wilmot Crawley, of Queen's Crawley:* the progenitor of the *Vanity Fair* Crawleys, establishing the family traditions.

9. p.90. *Newbury:* There was no uprising at Newbury in July 1690. But Ginkel, a Dutch general, had suppressed similar uprisings and there was general ferment. A plot in Scotland *was* planned for William's absence in Ireland, where James was gathering French and Irish Catholic support for an invasion of England. Thackeray, incidentally, is pushing along the historical pace (chapter 4 finishes in November 1688).

## BOOK ONE: 6

1. p.94. *nightrail:* a loose wrap.

2. p.95. *this conspiracy:* ambiguous, since Thackeray is obviously aware from other references that Fenwick suffered death for a conspiracy five years later (see page 158). Coplestone is evidently an invention.

3. p.96. *which proved so fatal to many concerned in it:* the reader will ponder over the syntax of this sentence in vain. The manuscript shows that Thackeray left it half-corrected, obviously intending to return to it, but forgot.

4. p.97. *Dick the Scholar:* Richard Steele, later Sir Richard, (1672–1729). Thackeray has advanced his career a couple of years to get him into this stage of the plot as a guardsman. He was, of course, the famous man of letters.

5. p.98. *a sermon of Mr Cudworth's:* Ralph Cudworth, (1617–88), an English Divine. The extract is from his most famous sermon, on toleration, preached before the House of Commons in 1647.

6. p.100. *education at a famous school:* Charterhouse, or the Chartreux, where Thackeray himself was educated, and where, thinly disguised as Grey Friars, he sent Pendennis, Clive Newcome and Philip.

7. p.100. *a young gentleman of Edinburgh:* presumably Thomas Aikenhead, 'a well conducted youth of nineteen' at the University of Edinburgh, who was condemned and hanged in 1696 for, among other similar offences, suggesting that the Old Testament was written by Ezra. It is, of course, an anachronism here.

8. p.100. *Ridley's fire,* etc. the first of the set-piece parodies in the novel. Steele's catalogue is a typically conciliatory one of alternate Catholic and Protestant martyrs to persecution. Ridley was the Protestant Bishop, Campion and Southwell were Jesuit priests, and Sympson a Quaker preacher.

9. p.100. *Monsieur Rycaut:* Sir Paul Rycaut wrote *The Present State of the Ottoman Empire,* which appeared in 1669.

10. p.101. *deteriora sequi:* Ovid, *Metamorphoses,* 7.20. 'I see and approve the better course: I follow the worse.' In Thackeray's version it is the key to Steele's, and most Irishmen's, characters.

11. p.103. *the fatal battle of the Boyne:* a decisive defeat, 1 July 1690, for James, who left the field early.

12. p.104. *'He said what I don't care to repeat':* Thackeray is obviously working from memory here. It was a 'young gentleman' who called Harry bastard and Colonel Esmond who in fact separated them from fighting. It was in talking to Holt that the Colonel used the term 'bastard'.

13. p.105. *unicum filium suum dilectissimum:* his only and most beloved son.

14. p.106. *I remember ... never come to us again:* This speech is a passage from Steele's *Memories of his Childhood, Tatler* 181, with only slight variation. Thackeray would have known it well as one of the pathetic climaxes from his own lecture on Steele.

## BOOK ONE: 7

1. p.106. *maxima debetur pueris reverentia:* The greatest consideration is due to children (Juvenal, 14, 47). A favourite motto of Thackeray's as well.

2. p.106. *Saccharissa:* the sweetest one. A poetic eponym used seriously by Waller, and facetiously by Steele in a number of *Tatler* papers.

3. p.107. *a silver pocket-piece:* a piece of money kept as a good-luck charm.

4. p.111. *vacuæ sedes et inania arcana:* When Pompeius broke into the Holy of Holies at Jerusalem he found 'the shrines and the secret chamber empty' (Tacitus, *History*, 5, 9).

5. p.112. *shooting at a mark and flying:* shooting at a fixed target, and at birds on the wing.

6. p.112. *riding at the ring:* riding with a lance or spear to enter a ring target.

7. p.112. *ball and billiards:* tennis or rackets, and billiards, two separate games. Readers will note that Thackeray tends to introduce historical detail in clusters. In so doing he is not always careful about his expression. The 'to perfection' in this sentence makes nonsense of that in the previous.

## BOOK ONE: 8

1. p.114. *the custom of inoculation:* Lady Mary Wortly Montagu (1684–1762), while her husband was Ambassador at Constantinople, observed the practice there, and had her son inoculated. She was generally original in in the spread of inoculation, after 1720, against smallpox in England. The disease was prevalent in 1694. Among others Mary, William's Queen, died of it.

2. p.117. *a main:* a match at cockfighting.

3. p.122. *tambour-frame:* a round frame on which cloth was stretched for embroidery.

## BOOK ONE: 9

1. p.124. *a mole-hill . . . can upset an empire:* In February 1701 William's horse tripped on a molehill. The King fell, and later died of the injuries.
2. p.126. *Mr Prior's pretty poem:* The Garland, stanza 9.

> At Dawn poor Stella danced and sung,
> The amorous youth around her bowed.
> At night the fatal knell was rung,
> I saw and kissed her in her shroud.

3. p.128. '*The are both very fat and smelt of brandy*': the popular image of the Royal pair. Trevelyan quotes the doggerel;

> King William thinks all,
> Queen Mary talks all,
> Prince George drinks all,
> And Princess Anne eats all.

Anne married Prince George of Denmark in 1683.
4. p.129. *Mr Thomas Parr:* Old Parr's fabulous life span was 1483–1635.
5. p.130. *Ovid's epistles:* Esmond has been translating Ovid's *Heroides*, the plaints of lovelorn heroines, among which was one by Oenone to Paris, and Medea to Jason.
6. p.130. *chopped up the dean:* This is a fanciful reference to another part of the Medea myth. Pelias had banished Jason. His daughters asked Medea to restore him to youth. In revenge she showed them how, by cutting up and boiling a ram, it could be rejuvenated. When the daughters tried this on their father they found, however, that she had neglected to tell them the vital charm which would restore him to life.
7. p.131. *on 'Change:* the Royal Exchange.
8. p.131. *indocilis pauperiem pati:* not schooled to suffer poverty. Horace, *Odes*, I. I. 18. Like Thackeray, Esmond's Horatian cast of mind is indicated by frequent quotation.
9. p.131. *Corderius and Lily* were the standard Latin text-book and grammar.
10. p.132. *pudet hœc opprobria dicere nobis:* It is shameful to tell us such shocking things. Ovid, *Metamorphoses*, I, 758–9.
11. p.133. *the lady of Mr Addison's opera:* The allusive pattern is quite complex. Rosamund was Henry II's mistress, who lived in a forest (maze or labyrinth), and was killed by the king's jealous wife. The Viscount's paramour is an actress, and suggests the story of Addison's opera *Rosamund* (1706), in which the heroine is consistently referred to as 'fair', and which, ironically in this context, ends with a tribute to married fidelity:

> Who to forbidden joys would rove,
> Who knows the sweets of married love.

12. p.133. *Billingsgate:* Billingsgate was proverbial for the violence of the fishwives' language. One of Steele's *Tatler* papers is on it (number 204).

13. p.136. *famous British divines of the last age:* The allusion being drawn, with multiple illustration, is between academic and popular theology. The implication is that, in spite of her station and upbringing, Rachel is inclined to the low church and to latitudinarianism. Law and Baxter were Nonconformists, the others high-church dignitaries. Since she is Tory and Jacobite, she should also be high church. The tense of the verb 'have found' suggests that her change of opinion may have been parallel with Esmond's change to Whig and anti-Jacobite principles.

14. p.142. *Galland's ingenious Arabian tales:* Antoine Galland's (1646–1715) translations would not have been available until the first decade of the eighteenth century. Alnaschar was the pedlar who, carried away in a daydream of riches, kicked and broke the glassware by which he was to make his fortune.

## BOOK ONE: 10

1. p.144. *Dr Montague*, Master of Trinity, 1683–99, was the precursor of the better-known Bentley.

2. p.145. *famous Mr Newton* is, of course, the famous mathematician later Sir Isaac. Trinity was Thackeray's own college, and he seems to have given Esmond his own rooms.

3. p.145. *grèges:* groups. This, like *junior soph* (second year man), is college jargon.

4. p.147. *the famous Duke of Marlborough:* This is from one of Spence's *Anecdotes*, which is worth quoting in its original form for the light it sheds on Thackeray/Esmond's partisan opinions:

> This mean passion of that great man operated very strongly in him in the very beginning of his life, and continued to the very end of it. One day, as he was looking over some papers in his scrutoire with Lord Cadogan, he opened one of the little drawers, took out a green purse, and turned some broadpieces out of it. After viewing them for some time with a satisfaction that appeared very visibly on his face, 'Cadogan', says he, 'observe these pieces well. They deserve to be observed. There are just forty of them. 'Tis the very first *sum* I ever got in my life, and I have kept it always unbroken from that very time to this day'.

Thackeray has extended the meanness to something worse, and incorporated in it the unflattering fact that Marlborough received, while still a page at court, a gift of £5,000 from the Duchess of Cleveland (one of Charles II's mistresses), which he invested and which was said to have made his fortunes.

5. p.148. *Calliope:* the muse of epic poetry.

6. p.148. *Chillingworth:* (1602–44), a protestant divine who wrote *The Religion of Protestants, A Safe Way to Salvation.*

7. p.148. Thomas *Hobbs*: (1588–1679), the materialist philosopher.

8. p.148 Pierre *Bayle*: (1647–1706), the compiler of the famous Dictionary (1697).

9. p.149. *Turenne and Condé*: mid-seventeenth-century French Generals, involved variously and on different sides in the civil wars of the Fronde, and in the French war with Spain.

10. p.150. *escrime*: fencing.


## BOOK ONE: II

1. p.153. *abi in pace*: Go in peace; the final blessing given by a Catholic priest.

2. p.154. *Baucis and Philemon*: here ironically representative of the happy married life. They were offered a wish by the Gods and chose to die together.

3. p.154. *Mr Pope, Mr Congreve*, etc.: a parade of the English humourists on whom Thackeray had lectured. This passage and the page or so following is more in Thackeray's usual style than most of the novel.

4. p.155. *muftis, and rabbins*: Mohammedan and Jewish priests.

5. p.155. *in corpore vili*: on a worthless body.

6. p.157. *the Malabar wives*: The allusion, a favourite one with Thackeray in his attacks on the subjugation of women in marriage, is to Suttee, the immolation of the living wife on the funeral pyre of her dead husband, formerly practised by certain Hindus.

7. p.158. *the Fenwick conspiracy*: This may be taken as a model example of the way in which Thackeray adapts historical sources. It is finely worked into the narrative, but liberties are taken with fact. In what Thackeray calls the 'Fenwick conspiracy' Sir George Barclay, who landed from France in 1690, was the moving spirit. The 'young friend' he brought with him was the Duke of Berwick (James Fitzjames, hence Captain James), who was to stir up the Jacobite aristocracy. The plan was to ambush William on his return to Kensington from hunting in Richmond. A series of leaks and confessions, and the lucky chance of bad weather on the day when the crime was set up, saved William. Charnock and Keyes were the first to be executed. Jeremy Collier (1650–1726), a non-juring divine, attended Friend and Perkyns to Tyburn, where they were hanged next, and absolved them. Fenwick was beheaded on Tower Hill a year later. In Thackeray's version there are obvious discrepancies – Hampton Court for hunting in Richmond, the dates are slightly out, Barclay is not mentioned and the suggestion is that the conspirators were all executed in a lump at the gallows and absolved by Collier. Collier was originally to have played a much larger part in the novel.

8. p.163. *until her daughter were out of the way*: On the face of it, Thackeray gets very muddled up in this chapter. Esmond comes home for his last summer vacation, which suddenly changes to his first Christmas break. Crossings out in the manuscript reveal that the novelist originally wrote

a much longer account of his hero's life at Cambridge, discarded it, then when he was over a third of the way through the present chapter 11 reintroduced those sections which contained information vital to the plot (i.e. the fact of Harry's legitimacy). The joins were not made very neatly, the time settings were not assimilated, and as a result the chapter is both discontinuous and repetitive. It also makes the chronology of this part of the narrative quite unreliable (when, for example, did the Viscount discover the truth of Harry's birth, in 1696 as it is implied on p. 233, or in 1700 as is stated on p. 224?).

## BOOK ONE: 12

1. p.163. *my Lord Mohun:* Charles Mohun (1675–1712), 'a particularly fast nobleman' as Thackeray calls him in his essay on Steele. In the novel he is made somewhat older than he actually was, and his name is changed to Harry.

2. p.170. *Spring Garden:* later Vauxhall Gardens.

3. p.170. *M. Massillon:* (1663–1742), Bishop of Clermont, the greatest French preacher of his day.

4. p.170. *a grain de sable:* Snow's edition points out that this should properly be Pascal on Cromwell, since Pascal believed that Cromwell was killed by a grain of sand's obstructing his urethra.

5. p.171. *the death of the Duke of Gloucester:* The Duke was the only one of Anne's fifteen or so children to survive childhood. He died in 1700 at the age of eleven, thus causing the crisis of succession, which is important later in the novel.

6. p.171. *poetical fancies:* In this passage old Esmond parodies his younger self's 'poetical fancies'. *Diana, Artemis, Luna* and *Phoebe* are all connected by identification with the moon. The dozen children of Niobe were slain by Apollo and Artemis because of a slight against their mother, who had but two. Luna fell in love with Endymion and, in order to kiss him eternally, entranced him for ever in sleep.

7. p.171. *'bright particular star':* Shakespeare, *All's Well*, I.1.

8. p.172. *that fickle goddess:* Fortune is the goddess referred to. See Dryden's paraphrase of Horace:

> Fortune, that with malicious joy
> Does man, her slave, oppress,
> Proud of her office to destroy,
> Is seldom pleased to bless.

Legend has it that Dryden himself was unhappily married.

9. p.173. *abigails:* handmaidens, hence serving-maids. From Abigail, the wife of Nabal.

## BOOK ONE: 13

1. p.174. *a parson, as you call him:* The term strikes Lady Esmond as slightly offensive, since to her it would suggest merely a rector (and her father was a dean), and was only gradually coming to mean a clergyman in a more general sense.

2. p.177. *Beati pacifici:* Blessed are the peacemakers.

3. p.177. *the vulgar, trapesing orange-girl:* a euphemism, see *The Spectator*, 5 May 1712 (No. 380), where an orange-girl complains of a Jew who slipped a guinea into her hand 'and told me plainly, that he gave me the guinea for no other Intent but to purchase my Person for an Hour'.

4. p.178. *those wild Mohocks:* from Mohawks. 'Dissolute young gentlemen', in Macaulay's description, who would 'swagger about the town, breaking windows, upsetting sedans, beating quiet men, and offering rude caresses to pretty women' (*History*, chapter 3). In fact, the term did not become current until some ten years later.

5. p.181. *Shakespeare:* the reference to poppy, mandragora and all the drowsy syrups of the East comes from *Othello*, III. iii. 31. Esmond, like Steele, is unfashionably admiring of Shakespeare.

6. p.182. *'cure your fellow-students of the ———:* Mohun, of course, is about to say 'pox'. One of the most cunning aspects of *Henry Esmond* is the way in which Thackeray suggests licentiousness without actually producing it.

7. p.183. *dice-cogging:* to cog dice is to load them.

8. p.183. *botte de Jesuite:* Jesuit's thrust or stroke, which Henry could have learned from Holt or Moreau.

## BOOK ONE: 14

1. p.187. *beaver:* beaver hat.

2. p.189. *Mr Congreve, who knew a part of the sex pretty well:* On his death in 1729 Congreve left £10,000 to the Duchess of Marlborough. This would be evidence enough for Esmond's dark allusion.

3. p.190. *Dr Cheyne:* George Cheyne (1671–1743), a Scot and one of the best-known doctors of the period, with a reputation for conviviality.

4. p.190. *the Cockpit:* an area in Whitehall, derived from the cockpit there.

5. p.191. *You go to Duke Street and see Mr Betterton:* Thomas Betterton (1635–1710). Thackeray gets slightly mixed up here. Betterton earlier in his career had been associated with the Duke's Company. At this time he was in the United Company with Mrs Bracegirdle (1663–1748) in Little Lincoln's Inn Fields. Duke Street is an irrelevant association. There is also some contradiction in the Viscount's trying to get Harry out of the way by sending him to the same theatre where he is to meet Mohun.

6. p.195. *She was disguised as a page.* The play Thackeray is thinking of is

*The Plain Dealer*, where Fidelia impersonates a page. *Love in a Wood* was anyway a bad choice, as when it was produced in 1718 the bill bore the heading 'Acted but once these 30 years'.

7. p.196. *the gentlemen as they sat on the stage:* People of quality were allowed to sit on the stage, often, as here, to the irritation of the actors.

8. p.196. *Bullock Fair:* a somewhat jumbled version of *Henry IV*, II. iii. 2., a jibe at the Lord's long residence out of town.

9. p.196. *poor Will Mountford:* Mrs Bracegirdle's taunt at Mohun refers to the murder by him and Richard Hill of Will Mountford, an actor, who was supposed by the jealous Hill to be her favourite. Mohun was tried by his peers and acquitted.

10. p.196. *The Christian Hero:* This work was written by Steele, and published in 1701. 'Principally,' he wrote, 'to fix upon his own mind a strong Impression of Virtue and Religion in opposition to a stronger Propensity towards unwarrantable Pleasures.' By this time Steele was also writing comedies.

11. p.196. *one or two duels:* Steele fought a duel in 1700, and became an opponent of the practice for the rest of his life.

12. p.198. *Mons and Namur:* towns in the Low Countries, where engagements were fought in William III's campaign against Louis XIV.

13. p.199. *chairs:* sedan chairs.

14. p.199. *Leicester Field:* this stood near the site of the present Leicester Square. The duel is fought according to the older practice of having a battle between two teams rather than between individual opponents.

15. p.200. *Mr Aimes, a surgeon, in Long Acre:* This detail, with most of the rest of the duel, is taken from the account of the duel between Mohun and Coote (1698) in Howell's State Trials. Thackeray gives a vivid sketch of it in his essay of Steele in the *English Humourists*. Mr Aimes appears later in the novel, when his name is twisted to Aymé for the purpose of a pun.

16. p.200. *Mr Atterbury:* Francis Atterbury (1662-1732), later in the novel he is Dean of Christ Church and Bishop of Rochester. He was a Jacobite and influential with Queen Anne.

17. p.202. *table-book:* a pocket book.


BOOK TWO: I

1. p.206. *deliquium:* a fainting fit.

2. p.207. *the King at Kensington:* The King moved to Kensington for his health, because Whitehall was too foggy and Hampton Court too far.

3. p.209. *benefit of clergy:* The two lords availed themselves of the right of being tried by the House of Lords, their 'peers'. 'Benefit of clergy' was originally the right of the clergy to evade trial by a secular court. For certain offences, manslaughter, for example, it came to be available for anyone who was literate, with the advantages that Esmond describes. It was finally abolished in 1827.

4. p.209. *saintly George Herbert:* (1593–1633), the metaphysical poet. Lady Esmond thinks of him principally as the author of *The Country Parson.*

5. p.209. *pious Dr Ken:* Thomas Ken (1637–1711), Bishop of Bath and Wells, non-juror and philanthropist, one of the Seven Bishops.

6. p.210. *virtute suâ:* with his own strength.

7. p.211. *Reficimus rates quassas:* Let us repair our battered craft. Horace, *Odes,* I. i. 17.

## BOOK TWO: 2

1. p.214. *the post of gentleman waiter:* Steele was appointed as 'gentleman waiter' to Prince George, Queen Anne's husband, with the payment of £100 p.a., in 1706.

2. p.215. *a Niobe in tears, to a Sigismonda, to a weeping Belvidera:* images of suffering womanhood. In Dryden's *Sigismonda and Guiscardo* the heroine rinses her murdered lover's heart with her tears before killing herself. Belvidera, the heroine of Otway's *Venice Preserved,* is forced to betray her husband to save the state, runs distracted and dies.

3. p.215. *matre pulchra filia pulchrior:* lovely mother, lovelier daughter. Horace, *Odes,* I.xvi.1.

4. p.218. *guests:* In her distraction Rachel says 'guests' when she means 'hosts'.

5. p.220. *my Lord Marlborough's letters:* The Duke of Marlborough and Louise de Kerouaille, Duchess of Portsmouth and mistress of Charles II, were both bad spellers, and not uncommonly so in their age, but Thackeray is less interested in social history than in indulging the vein of comic illiteracy, with which he gained early popularity, in *The Yellow-plush Papers,* and which he enjoyed to the end of his writing career.

6. p.221. *Varique:* Warwick.

7. p.221. *Moon:* Mohun.

8. p.221. *Mary:* mari, i.e. husband.

9. p.221. *escus de costay:* ecus de côté, i.e. crowns on the side.

10. p.221. *assay:* ceremonial furniture, a cup for the taster.

11. p.221. *fringed cloth:* her 'cloth of estate', which would be over her chair or possibly her canopy.

12. p.221. *the Prince of Wales:* James Francis Edward was proclaimed James III of England in September 1701. It was one of the French provocations which led to the War of the Spanish Succession. Esmond calls him Prince of Wales, here and elsewhere, since that was his title when he left England with his father.

## BOOK TWO: 3

1. p.222. *the splendid new bridge:* Westminster Bridge was in fact not begun until 1739.

2. p.223. *'dropping odours':* Comus, II. 105–6.

> Braid your locks with rosy twine,
> Dropping odours, dropping wine.

3. p.223. *Cybèle:* the mother of the Olympian gods, whose crown was in the shape of a city wall. Later the Lady Dowager is described as having gone over to the more modish 'tower' or 'tour' (see p. 347). Isaac Disraeli in his *Curiosities* writes, 'a fashionable lady of that day much resembles the mythological figure of Cybèle, the mother of the gods, with three towers on her head'.

4. p.225. *raffoler:* rave.

5. p.225. *Mourning Bride:* Congreve turns a complimentary pun on the title of his tragedy *The Mourning Bride* (1697).

6. p.226. *a black man:* In the eighteenth century this meant a dark-complexioned man, not a blackamoor, though it may account for Esmond's affinity with Othello, who is also a 'black man' (see p. 181).

7. p.227. *a pair of colours:* i.e. get a commission, which would have to be bought. Regiments at this time were still known by their commanding Colonel's name.

8. p.228. *quadrille:* a card game.

9. p.228. *a dish of bohea:* China tea. Until the nineteenth century all tea came from China.

10. p.228. *quidnuncs:* gossips.

11. p.229. *Mr Fox:* George Fox, (1624–91). Founder of the Quaker movement.

12. p.230. The footnote: *The Odyssey.*i.32.

> 'Look how vainly men do blame the Gods, for of us they say comes evil, when they even of themselves through the blindness of their own hearts, have sorrows beyond that which is ordained' (Butcher and Lang).

13. p.230. *ugly Anne Hyde's daughter:* Anne's mother, Anne Hyde (1637–71), first wife of the Duke of York, later James II. Anne succeeded to the throne in 1701.

14. p.230. *that fury of a woman* is Lady Marlborough, at this time the new Queen's favourite. The Dowager refuses to call Anne Queen or William King because she recognizes James III.

15. p.231. *a pension on the Stamp Office:* At this time pensions could be awarded, as this one is, directly from sources of Royal revenue.

16. p. 231. *Lord Macclesfield's splendid embassy:* In 1701 Lord Macclesfield went to the Hannoverian Court to present the Act of Succession, by which Parliament debarred the Stuarts from ever succeeding to the English throne. Mohun was related to Macclesfield by marriage.

### BOOK TWO: 4

1. p.237. *the Garter:* About half the taverns and coffee-houses that Esmond mentions, like this, The Star and Garter in Pall Mall, were actual; though Thackeray is also prone to make up a likely sounding name if there is no convenient historical one to hand.

### BOOK TWO: 5

1. p.237. *THE VIGO BAY EXPEDITION:* In 1702 England formally declared war and entered in alliance with the United Provinces and the Holy Roman Empire on the War of the Spanish Succession, and some general historical framework might help place the close-ups which Thackeray offers in the following chapters.

When Charles II of Spain was obviously seen to be dying there were three contenders for his throne. One of these predeceased him. Since the the French would not agree to partition (the principle which was finally adopted by the peace-making Treaty of Utrecht in 1713), the succession became a straight fight between Charles, the Allies' candidate, and Philip, the French one. The English saw their trade and European interests threatened by French expansionist policy, but the *casus belli* was Louis putting his relative Philip on the Spanish throne when it fell vacant. As it is shown in *Henry Esmond* the war is followed on two fronts: Marlborough's inexorable advance over his continental enemies, and his gradual defeat at home by the Tories. At this early stage in the war Marlborough was in a strong position, and his wife was the Queen's favourite and Godolphin, a Whig and his relative by marriage, at the head of the Queen's Government.

One of the first movements of the French was into Spanish Flanders, hence the battles that follow in the Low Countries, but it was realized that it was essential to gain a Mediterranean port. This was the aim of the venture in which Esmond was concerned, and which might better be termed the Cadiz expedition. It was, through timourousness, incompetence and rapacity, the terrible failure that Esmond describes. It was, however, redeemed by the 'piracy', as Esmond calls it, when the Spanish treasure fleet and its French escort were destroyed and plundered in the Bay of Vigo.

In Esmond's account there are small errors of fact, for example, Shovell did not join the fleet until later, and some errors of bias, for example, Ormonde, the military commander, is not criticized, since he was, for the whole of the war, the Tories', and therefore the hero's, favoured alternative to Marlborough. But in general the novel's gazetteering is accurate enough to make annotation superfluous.

2. p.240. *the alameda:* the avenue or grove.

3. p.241. *a hard touch:* This refers to Ormonde's going over to William at the same time as Churchill.

4. p.242. *the notorious Jack Shafto:* Shafto is fictitious, but 'Vigo' did become a synonym for highway robbery, see Farquhar's *Beaux Stratagem*, where Gibbet talks of a prospective robbery as 'a galleon, a Vigo business'.

5. p.242. *La Redondilla:* the harbour at Vigo.

6. p.244. *the bailiffs were after him:* Addison at one time lent Steele £100, and Steele did not trouble himself to repay such a trivial amount. Addison, who as Johnson says, 'seems to have had other notions of £100', reclaimed his money by sending in the bailiffs.

7. p.244. *the 'precious uses' of adversity: As You Like It,* II.i.12.

8. p.245. *Mistress:* 'Mrs' was used indifferently with 'Miss' for unmarried women, hence 'Mistress Beatrix' is normal.

9. p.245. *Sarah Jennings:* With the Duke of Marlborough's elevation, his only son became Lord Blandford. Sarah Jennings was the maiden name of Lady Marlborough.

10. p.246. *Mrs Bracegirdle:* a real actress. It was, says Colley Cibber in his *Apology*, 'a fashion among the gay and young, to have a taste or *tendre* for Mrs Bracegirdle'. William Congreve (1670–1729) was said to have had a liaison with her, and wrote leading parts for her in his plays.

11. p.247. *boxing the watch:* not fisticuffs, but the mischievous habit of overturning the watch in their boxes.

12. p.247. *scouring St Giles's:* 'scouring' in the eighteenth-century sense of raising hell.

13. p.247. *Rochester,* etc. A company of Restoration wits and writers.

14. p.248. *our Lady of Chaillot:* On his death in France, James II's body was dismembered. His brain was bequeathed to the Scottish College at Paris; his bowels were divided between the English College at St Omer and the parish church of St Germain; his heart was deposited at the convent at Chaillot, hence the Dowager's pious donation.

15. p.248. *governor:* As a young nobleman Frank would have a private tutor in attendance, in this case Tusher.

## BOOK TWO: 6

1. p.249. *eagle:* a lectern in the form of an eagle.

2. p.249. *point de Venise:* finely worked lace collar.

3. p.249. *Rigaud:* Hyacinthe Rigaud (1659–1743), official painter to the French royalty. This portrait plays a large part in the climax of the novel.

4. p.251. *Reddas incolumen precor:* Give him back safe I pray. Horace, *Odes.* I.iii.7.

5. p.251. *Septimi, Gades aditure mecum:* Septimius, who would go with me to Cadiz. Horace, *Odes,* II.6. Septimius was a friend of Horace,

and in view of Esmond's feelings towards Tusher on his return from Cadiz, Tusher's compliment is unconsciously ironic.

6. p.254. *Non omnis moriar:* I shall not die completely. Horace, *Odes*, III.xxx.6.

7. p.255. *He has conformed:* After his long protest Rachel's father has at last sworn allegiance to the sovereign, and has therefore been given a living.

## BOOK TWO: 7

1. p.260. *steenkirk:* an affectedly casual but decorative collar. Originally a French fashion inspired by the disarray in which the French officers went into the Battle of Steinkirk, 1692.

2. p.260. *cock-fighting:* i.e. ten pounds for single victories, fifty pounds for the overall victory between two teams of twenty-one cocks.

3. p.263. *Rochester:* Earl of Rochester (1647–80), Restoration rake and poet.

4. p.263. *Grammont:* (1621–1707). On the banishment from Versailles, he became one of the luminaries of the Restoration court.

5. p.263. *Ramillies:* This is a small slip. Frank was wounded at Oudenarde.

6. p.264. *Dr Hare:* Francis Hare (1671–1740), his tutor at King's College Cambridge, and a friend of the Marlboroughs.

7. p.265. *sylvester:* New Year's Eve.

## BOOK TWO: 8

1. p.267. *back-sword:* a sword with one cutting edge.

## BOOK TWO: 9

1. p.273. *THE CAMPAIGN OF 1704:* This, and the following campaigns, took place in the summer. In the winter Marlborough would gather his forces. In general, this account stands by itself, the annotation being provided by Thackeray. He did not perhaps emphasize sufficiently the length and daring of Marlborough's march, which carried the war out of the Low Countries into Bavaria and the Danube. And there are the usual distortions, for example, he makes it seem as if Prince Lewis's secondary assault on the Schellenberg (the vast fortified hill by Donauwort) rescued Marlborough in the nick of time, whereas in fact it was planned. The ravaging of Bavaria, between the assault on Donauwort and the Battle of Blenheim, was intended to coerce Max Emmanuel either into submission or alliance. To his credit Marlborough does not seem to have been proud of it, and it is one of the few war crimes which can be brought against him. Needless to say, Esmond paints it as typical.

2. p.273. *General Lumley:* Either Lumley is being arch or Thackeray has forgotten that Esmond was the General's secretary at Vigo (see p. 242).

3. p.274. (*as Mr Addison sang of it*): in *The Campaign*. The terrible storm of 1703 ravaged the south of England, and damaged vast amounts of shipping.

4. p.275. *the famous Prince of Savoy*: Eugene (1663-1736), Commander of the Imperial Armies, and Marlborough's great partner in the war.

5. p.276. *the links*: These were the tow and pitch torches used to illuminate the London streets by nights, and carried by *link-boys*.

6. p.277. *Clotho* and *Lachesis*, with Atropos (who in fact cuts), the three Fates.

7. p.278. *the great victory of Blenheim*: Thackeray claimed to have had a 'second sight' in describing the scene of Blenheim, though in general his military descriptions are the least interesting parts of the novel. Blenheim was about ten miles along the river from previous engagement, and a month afterwards, which Thackeray overleaps with his digression on Marlborough's character. For this battle Marlborough shared command not with Lewis but with the more congenial Eugene. The victory of Blenheim freed Germany from the French and made Marlborough the darling of the Whigs.

8. p.279. *this famous day of Blenheim*: It was for factual chapters like this one that Thackeray used his amanuenses. Dictation, however, does not seem to have improved his syntax or his paragraph structure. This sentence and the one that follows are typically confusing.

9. p.281. *the King of the Romans*: the heir apparent to the Empire, Joseph.

10. p.282. *Amadis*: the hero of the romance, whose love was in fact called Oriana.

### BOOK TWO: 10

1. p.283. *desipere in loco*: relax upon occasion. Quoted with variations in a number of places in Horace's *Odes*.

2. p.283. John Richmond *Webb*: (1667-1724), distantly related to Thackeray.

3. p.284. *the Maison du Roy*: the French royal Household Troops.

4. p.284. *a wart on his nose*: referring, in fact, to the wart on Marlborough's lip.

5. p.287. *Nevil's Court*: Thackeray is thinking of the Library which Wren designed and which was completed at this period, not the Court. Dr Bentley, the famous classical scholar and controversialist, replaced Montague in 1700.

6. p.288. *Anacreontics*: poems in praise of love and wine.

7. p.288. *Bathyllus* was a youth beloved by Anacreon.

8. p.289. *Nicolini*: Nicolino Grimaldi, the famous Neopolitan singer, who came to England in 1708.

9. p.291. *the young lady Mrs Scurlock*: The first Mrs Steele died in 1706. Mrs Scurlock became the second on 9 September 1707.

10. p.291. *Dan Chaucer*: Spenser's dutiful title for the older poet (Dan = Master).

11. p..292 *stand-dish:* This should be 'standish'. Thackeray's version is a speculation as to its etymology. A dish containing writing and sealing materials.

## BOOK TWO: 11

1. p.292. *THE FAMOUS MR JOSEPH ADDISON:* The germ of this chapter is the alleged remark by Pope to Harte, on walking through the Haymarket, that it was in a garret there that Addison had composed his famous poem *The Campaign*. Dr Johnson also retails the story that Godolphin lamented to Halifax, Addison's patron, that Blenheim had not been adequately celebrated and, on Halifax's naming Addison as the man to do it, Henry Boyle was sent to commission the work; when the poem was no further advanced than the simile of the angel, Addison was rewarded with the place of Commissioner of Appeals, which Locke had vacated, and his garret days were over.

2. p.293. *Mr William Congreve:* Congreve was not an old man at this date, but after *The Way of the World* he withdrew from public life, and was a martyr to the gout and failing eyesight.

3. p.294. *Not across the water:* I guess from an entry in Partridge's *Dictionary of Slang* that this means not in the King's Bench Prison, which was on the other side of the river, for debt.

4. p.294. *O, qui canoro blandius Orpheo vocale ducis carmen:* the first line of Addison's Latin poem to Dr Hannes: O, you who sing as sweetly as Orpheus.

5. p.295. *my Lord Halifax:* the Earl of Halifax, Charles Montague (1661–1715), Whig statesman and patron of letters.

6. p.295. *In vengeance roused the soldier fills his hand,* etc.: Lines 227–38 of *The Campaign* (1705), rather inaccurately transcribed – which might be Thackeray's carelessness or a subtle intimation that this is an uncorrected draft.

7. p.297. *Medea's children:* Horace, *Ars Poetica.*

> Let not *Medea* draw her murth'ring Knife,
> And spill her Children's Blood upon the Stage.

Roscommon's translation as quoted by Addison in *The Spectator*, number 44.

8. p.298. *Si parva licet:* If the smaller may be compared to the greater.

9. p.298. '—— *Rheni pacator et Istri,* etc.: One of the epigraphs from Claudian to *The Campaign*. Geographically appropriate and yet flattering to Marlborough.

He conquered the Rhine and Danube, all dissension ceases in this man's presence. Soldiers, politicians, common people and nobles join in their praise.

10. p.299. *heroes sent to Hades:* This, and the following references in the paragraph, allude to Homer's *Iliad*.

11. p.299. *those famous lines:* the image of Marlborough as the angel of the storm (mentioned earlier on p. 298). Thackeray has coolly credited Esmond with inspiring what is agreed to be the best part of the poem.

12. p.299. *snuff-coloured suit:* brownish.

13. p.299. *plain tie-wig:* an informal wig in which the hair is tied into a queue. Addison was renowned for his tie-wig.

14. p.300. *hic ibat Simois:* here flowed the Simois.

15. p.300. *hic est Sigeia tellus:* here is the land of Sigeum.

16. p.300. *aliquo prœlia mixta mero:* battles engaged in with wine.

17. p.300. *my Lord Treasurer:* Sidney Godolphin (1645–1712). The Lord Treasurer, although nominally equivalent to our Chancellor of the Exchequer, was in fact the highest minister of the Crown.

18. p300.. *his friend's pension is no longer paid:* Addison's pension, which awarded in 1699, stopped with the change of government on Anne's succession.

19. p.301. '*I puff the prostitute away*': Dryden's paraphrase of Horace's *Odes,* III.29.

20. p.301. *bear-leader:* tutor. Johnson, in his *Lives of the Poets,* claims that he was 'compelled to become tutor of a travelling squire because his pension was not remitted'.

21. p.302. *Commissioner of Excise:* in fact, of Appeals. Thackeray does not make the same mistake in his *English Humourists,* and the Locke referred to is the philosopher.

22. p.302. *no better than a shrew and a vixen:* Addison married the Countess of Warwick in 1716. Tradition had it that she was as Macaulay says, in his essay on Addison, 'an arrogant and imperious woman'.

23. p.303. *Mr St John:* Henry St John (1678–1751), later referred to as Mr Secretary (i.e. Secretary of State), and Viscount Bolingbroke.

24. p.303. *Mrs Mountford:* the widow of the actor killed by Mohun.

## BOOK TWO: 12

1. p.304. *Ramillies:* Thackeray's account of this battle is again tight-packed. It took place against the background of a French recovery which made the victory all the more impressive. The account of Marlborough's near capture is a true one; characteristically Esmond emphasizes the general's good luck rather than his courage.

2. p.€04. *Chiari:* in the 1701–2 campaign.

3. p.305. *à bout-portant:* at point-blank.

4. p.306. *afflavit Deus, et dissipati sunt:* God breathed and they were scattered. From the medal struck on the victory over the Armada.

5. p.308. *petit polisson:* little blackguard.

6. p.308. *meminisse juvat:* it is pleasant to remember.

7. p.309. *our gentleman of St James's:* viz: Frank, a guardsman and therefore a member of the royal household of St James.

## BOOK TWO: 13

1. p.310. *Pandour:* Originally a Serbo-Croatian soldier, here it implies a blood-thirsty and brutal one.

2. p.311. *your recusant bishops:* those who refused to recognize William III.

3. p.311. *Collier is* means 'Collier would be'.

4. p.313. *the Duke of Berwick:* the Duke of Berwick was the illegitimate son of James II, and one of Louis's greatest generals. He defeated Lord Galway at Almanza, in 1707.

5. p.313. *La Hogue:* It was alleged that, when Louis' attempt to invade England in spring 1692, was repulsed, James watched the battle from La Hogue and rejoiced in the victory against his own side.

6. p.313. *the young Electoral Prince of Hanover:* later George II. Thackeray expatiates on the exploit in his *Four Georges*.

7. p.314. *Marshal Villar's own guinguette:* The Duc de Villars was Louis's most successful general. By 'guinguette' Thackeray obviously intends to mean 'gig', though, on the face of it, it means 'country house'.

8. p.316. *a black cockade or a white one:* black for the Hanoverian, white for the Jacobite cause.

9. p.316. *banished hither in disgrace:* It had been considered by Charles prudent for the Duke of York to leave the country for a while in 1679, to let Parliament cool down. The dates do not quite fit, but it is an interesting example of Thackeray knitting up Esmond's story with the larger historical scheme.

10. p.319. *biting:* cheating.

11. p.320. *old Put:* blockhead.

12. p.320. *run rusty:* cut up rough.

## BOOK TWO: 14

1. p.322. *his five thousand a year and his splendid palace at Woodstock:* As rewards from a grateful nation Marlborough had been given a pension of £5,000 p.a. in 1702, and later Blenheim Palace was built at public expense for him and his heirs.

2. p.322. *Mrs Masham:* (Abigail Hill), succeeded her relative, Lady Marlborough, as the Queen's favourite. She was instrumental in Harley's campaign against the Whig junto and Godolphin. When they succeeded, with the Tory victory in 1710, it was the beginning of the end for Marlborough.

3. p.322. *the poet says:* Butler, *Hudibras*, III.iii.547–8.

> A man convinced against his will
> Is of the same opinion still.

**The popular misquotation; it should be 'He that complies . . .'**

4. p.323. *the Chevalier's invasion of Scotland:* The abortive attempt to invade through Scotland in March 1708, which was frustrated by English naval action and bad weather.

5. p.324. *Cadogan:* William Cadogan (1675–1726), Marlborough's Quartermaster General.

6. p.324. *summoned:* called upon to surrender.

7. p.326. *the legitimate princes of the blood royal:* The syntax is somewhat perplexing in this sentence. The sense can be more easily grasped when it is realized that Vendosme had a claim of the throne through his illegitimate grandfather, whereas the Dukes of Burgundy and Berry were legitimate princes, sons of the Dauphin. Esmond, not unnaturally since he has to bear the stigma, stands up for bastards like Berwick and Vendosme.

8. p.327. *at Toulon in the last year:* In 1707 an ambitious attack on Toulon under Eugene had failed because of lack of enthusiasm and mal-coordination between the allies.

9. p.328. *the slight:* The slight, as retailed in Eugene's Memoirs, was Louis' refusing him a commission on the grounds that his constitution was too weak, and that he was better suited to be an 'abbé'.

10. p.329. *correspondence with his uncle:* It was true that Marlborough had corresponded with his nephew. He had also refused a number of vast bribes. In England scurrilous Tory allegations that Marlborough had been bribed to fail at Lille were current.

11. p.329. *Tollemache at Brest:* In 1694 Tollemache had been sent to capture Brest. Forewarned by Churchill and others, the French had repulsed the attack and Tollemache was killed. This accusation was made much of by Macaulay. It was denied by Marlborough's official biographer, Winston Churchill. From his letters it appears that, at the time of writing *Esmond*, Thackeray believed that Marlborough had planned something similar for his kinsman Webb.

## BOOK TWO: 15

1. p.330. *THE BATTLE OF WYNENDAEL:* better known to historians as the 'skirmish of Wynendael', though naturally Esmond's view is again biased. The Wynendael action was significant not simply as a defeat of vastly superior French forces but because it saved from attack the convoy of supplies on which the continuation of the seige of Lille depended.

2. p.332. *Roncq:* This was where Marlborough's headquarters were.

3. p.332. *Lieutenant-General Webb:* Lieutenant-General is a higher rank than Major-General. Webb had been promoted.

4. p.333. *that d——d Cardonnel:* Adam Cardonnel was Marlborough's civilian secretary. The note is much as Thackeray gives it. The manuscript shows he would leave gaps for such items and fill them in when his secretary, presumably, had looked them up. In the first edition

Thackeray wrote 'damned Cardonnel', which he afterwards removed, 'to save ears polite'.

5. p.334. *Mareschal de Boufflers, who had so bravely defended the place:* In the attention given to the Wynendael affair, Esmond has not informed the reader that Lille fell on 9 December. Boufflers was given the full honours of war by the allies, who could afford to be generous.

6. p.335. *a baldaquin:* a ceremonial canopy.

7. p.336. *the London Gazette:* The *London Gazette,* the official military record, did print on two occasions a false version of the Wynendael action, in which Cadogan was given credit for the victory. This was almost immediately corrected by the true version, and by Webb's own account. Marlborough almost certainly did not mean to slight Webb.

8. p.341. *the vote of thanks:* on 13 December. The Whigs applauded the victory; the Tories applauded a victor other than Marlborough.

9. p.342. *Mr Jervas:* Charles Jervas (1675–1739), the fashionable painter.

10. p.343. *Mrs Tofts* was a singer and an actress.

11. p.343. *the Ordnance:* i.e. military business.

12. p.343. *the Cocoa-Tree:* This was a Tory stronghold; and the Garter a coffee-house. The Walpole referred to is Robert Walpole (1676–1745).

13. p.348. *Bushy:* now Bushey, near Hampton Court. The Duchess referred to is, of course, the Duchess of Marlborough.

14. p.349. *the Hovel at Hampton Wick:* Steele's facetious name for his house.

15. p.349. *curtain lecture:* i.e. she nagged him in bed.

16. p.351. *to love her is a liberal education:* In his essay on Steele in the *English Humourists* Thackeray calls this 'the finest compliment to a woman that perhaps ever was offered'.

17. p.352. *a pastoral poem:* Pope's Pastorals were published in 1709. Pope was a Catholic and deformed, hence Mrs Steele's heavy-handed jokes.

18. p.352. *Bickerstaffe, and Distaff, and Quarterstaff:* Mrs Steele has read paper 11, the genealogy of the Bickerstaffs. Isaac Bickerstaff, originally a Swiftian butt, was a Tatlerian authorial *persona.*

19. p.353. *the treachery of Tom Boxer:* This hanging end is the result of a clumsy excision from the first edition. Between the paragraph ending 'Lady Elizabeth Hastings' and before that beginning 'I hear Mr Addison', came this:

'I always thought that paper was Mr Congreve's,' cries Mr St John, showing that he knew more about the subject than he pretended to Mr Steele, and who was the original Mr Bickerstaff drew.

'Tom Boxer said so in his *Observator.* But Tom's oracle is always making blunders,' cries Steele.

'Mr Boxer and my husband were friends once, and when the Captain was ill with the fever, no man could be kinder than Mr Boxer, who used to come to his bedside every day, and actually brought Dr Arbuthnot who cured him,' whispered Mrs Steele.

'Indeed, madam! How very interesting,' says Mr St John.

'But when the captain's last comedy came out, Mr Boxer took no notice of it – you know he is Mr Congreve's man, and won't ever give a word to the other house – and this made my husband angry.'

'Oh! Mr Boxer is Mr Congreve's man!' says Mr St John.

'Mr Congreve has wit enough of his own,' cries out Mr Steele. 'No one ever heard me grudge him or any other man his share.'

In his edition of the letters Gordon Ray explains this obscure passage. In his hostile review of Thackeray's lectures in the *Examiner* John Forster (the biographer of Dickens) wrongly ascribed a quotation from the forty-ninth *Spectator* paper to Congreve. Thackeray took this opportunity to correct him, he also alludes to Forster's kindness to him during the serious illness which interrupted *Pendennis*. The passage was irrelevant six years later when the Revised Edition was brought out, and Thackeray removed it. The manuscript shows that Thackeray originally had the less distant pseudonyms 'Tom Bluster' and 'Examinator', and wrote some more savage things about Forster, whom he had never liked. But he probably realized the unwisdom of publicly attacking a powerful journalist, and converted the assault into a good-natured tap.

## BOOK THREE: I

1. p.356. *a yard of blue ribbon:* the order of the Garter.

2. p.356. *knocked under:* originally to knock the underneath of the table, to signify that one can drink no more. Here obviously to surrender.

3. p.358. *Monsieur Gauthier:* The Abbé Gauthier figures in the accounts of the period as a minor secret agent and diplomat.

4. p.359. *all spent for him in vain:* This diatribe is better suited to the Stuarts generally than to James Edward individually, who seems to have been rather more insipid than this. Although Esmond is a Tory at this point, the view of the Stuarts presented to us, in this last section of the novel, is Whiggish.

5. p.361. *Corporal John:* Marlborough. Swift, in *The Examiner* for example, calls him 'Coachman John'.

6. p.362. *the Imperial generalissimo* and *the Abbé de Savoie* are both, of course, Eugene.

7. p.365. *whether at Rome or at Augsburg:* i.e. whether Roman Catholic or Protestant.

8. p.365. *Dr Sacheverel:* Henry Sacheverel (1674?–1724), a clergyman, impeached before the House of Lords, 1709–10, for having expressed in sermons extreme Tory and High Church views on, among other things, the Revolution. He was attacked by the Whigs, but given only a nominal sentence: suspension from preaching for three years.

9. p.366. *given her name:* Beatrix was named after the wife of James II, Mary Beatrice.

10. p.366. *Teague:* i.e. Irishman, from the anglicized spelling of the Irish

name, Tadhg. Esmond twits the Irishman with the anti-Jacobite song 'Lillibullero', which begins 'Ho, broder Teague'.

11. p.368. *the 11th of September last year:* the date of Malplaquet. The speaker is Anthony Hamilton (1646–1720), who went across to France with the House of Stuart.

12. p.368. *Mr Sterne:* Laurence Sterne's father. Thackeray drew his character, and the subsequent anecdote about his affair with the Suttler's daughter (p. 420), from Sterne's memoir of his father.

13. p.369. *Frank writ:* By a slip of the pen, Thackeray wrote Arthur for Frank, an error which has been much reprinted.

## BOOK THREE: 2

1. p.370. *ryno:* cash.

2. p.378. *never misses a Sunday at court:* Swift, who was regular at 'court and service' on Sundays.

3. p.380. *Guiscard:* the soi-disant Marquis Guiscard, spy, who while being examined before the Privy Council in March 1771 stabbed Harley in the breast with a penknife. Harley survived, and the general sympathy for his injury revived his waning popularity. Guiscard was wounded in the scuffle and died. Thackeray wrote Harvy for Harley here.

4. p.380. *recover:* i.e. her former position.

5. p.381. *tucker:* frill of lace, worn round the neck.

6. p.382. *ten thousand crowns for a tulip:* Tulipomania became proverbial after 1633–7, when it precipitated a national financial crisis in Holland.

7. p.383. *October Club:* extreme Tories. See Swift, *The Journal to Stella*, 18 February 1711, 'A set of above a hundred Parliament men of the country, who drink October beer, at home, and meet every evening at a tavern near the Parliament, to consult affairs and to drive things on to extremes against the Whigs.'

8. p.383. *Diogenes* was the cynic philosopher.

9. p.383. *Alexander*, his great contemporary, conquered *Darius*, the Persian king, and was the only man who could ride the horse *Bucephalus*.

## BOOK THREE: 3

1. p.384. *alibi:* in its literal sense of 'another place'.

2. p.386. *the Exchange:* Thackeray's daughter, in the Biographical Edition of *Henry Esmond*, quotes this extract from his notebooks for *Esmond*:

> '*Exchange.* – There be many exchanges in London, besides markets and the Royal Exchange – as that stately building called the New Exchange and Exeter Change, both in the Strand, where all attire for ladies and gentlemen is sold.'

3. p.386. *I think I could shoot flying:* Thackeray obviously drew on Restoration drama for his picture of Beatrix; here her gay profanity has an echo of Sylvia in Farquhar's *The Recruiting Officer*:

> 'I can gallop all the morning after the hunting horn, and all the evening after a fiddle. In short, I can do everything with my father but drink and shoot flying.'

4. p.387. *Mr Dennis, the great critic:* John Dennis (1657–1734).

5. p.388. *Mr Wilks:* Robert Wilks (1670–1732), the leading actor and manager.

6. p.388. *Eugenio* is Esmond's private joke, drawing on the great topical popularity of Eugene, and also a hint of his own birth (Eugenio means 'well-born'). It also reveals that Thackeray intended to be prepared for the ending of the novel.

7. p.388. *SPECTATOR:* Thackeray's famous parody of the coy, facetious and sentimental style of Steele and *The Spectator*. Apart from the language, Thackeray has imitated the 'problem page' aspect of the journal, and Jocasta/Beatrix is the anti-type of the ideal *Spectator* woman – flirtatious, fashion-crazed and light-headed. The actual *Spectator* paper for this day was by Budgell, but Thackeray has obviously chosen it for the date.

8. p.389. *Tunbridge or the Bath:* She would go to the watering-places at the end of the London season, in early summer.

9. p.390. *Camilla:* Virgil's warrior maid, pseudonym for Mrs Tofts in *The Spectator*.

10. p.390. *Thalestris:* Queen of the Amazons.

11. p.390. *the angel that visited the pool:* See *John* 5. 4.
    For an angel went down at a certain season into the pool, and troubled the water: whosoever then first after the troubling of the water stepped in was made whole of whatsoever disease he had.

12. p.390. *Manilio:* one of the pack used in the card game Ombre.

13. p.391. *Dr Swift's pun:* related in *The Journal to Stella*; Swift saw a sign put out by one who claimed to be able to cure agues spelled 'egoes'. Swift observed that he did not do it 'by a spell'.

14. p.391. *good Mr Shortface:* Mr Spectator often calls himself 'Mr Shortface'.

15. p.392. *I treated her to the fiddles:* as earlier, where Lord Ormonde 'paid the fiddles' for Isabella (p. 226), i.e. paid for the fiddles to play for them.

16. p.394. *rôder:* to prowl.

17. p.397. *his Grace the Duke of Hamilton:* The Duke was pretty much as Thackeray describes him, here and in the thinly disguised peerage entry on pp. 426–8, a Jacobite, Tory and loaded with honours, except that the later estimate of his age ('upward of fifty') is the more correct, and he was not at this period a widower but still married to his second wife. The 'union' referred to was the union of the English and Scottish Parliaments in 1707.

18. p.397. *bit* and *smoke:* used commonly, by Swift, for example, for disguise and detection of journalistic authorship.
19. p.401. *Lubin:* here, as in Prior's epigram 'On his death-bed poor Lubin lies', a conventional name for a countryman.


## BOOK THREE: 4

1. p.409. *Peter Wilkins:* This is perhaps the most commented on anachronism in the novel. It refers to *The Life and Adventures of Peter Wilkins*, 1751, a fantasy by Robert Paltock. The 'Gawries' were flying women, and Peter Wilkins married one.
2. p.411. *where Belinda's cross is:* 'On her White Breast' (*Rape of the Lock*). Thackeray avoids the possibly offensive word.
3. p.412. *My Lord Mohun and I are connected:* They had married cousins, both nieces of Lord Macclesfield. The quarrel over his estate provoked the later duel. Mohun, of course, is of the other party.


## BOOK THREE: 5

1. p.415. *That Great Duke was utterly disgraced:* In 1711 Marlborough was at last brought down by his enemies on the charge that he profiteered from army supplies. His dependants fell with him. He was reinstated after Anne's death, a fact which Esmond does not emphasize.
2. p.416. *his famous Sword of Honour:* In January the Queen presented Eugene, who was immensely popular in England, with 'a diamond sword' valued at £4,500.
3. p.416. *our defeat at Denain:* In July 1712 the French defeated the Dutch under Albemarle. The English commander Ormonde had been secretly ordered not to become involved. Swift's comment to Stella is typical: 'This perhaps may cool their courage and make them think of a peace.'
4. p.417. *never showed the slightest mercy:* In October 1711, for example, Bolingbroke imprisoned fourteen booksellers and printers for putting out libellous matter.
5. p.419. *Doctors Garth:* (1661–1719), author of *The Dispensary*, and *Arbuthnot* (1667–1735), Queen's Physician, friend of Pope and Swift, and himself an author.
6. p.419. *Mr Gay:* John Gay (1685–1732). *Trivia* is a mock-heroic poem about London.
7. p.419. *Mr Prior:* Matthew Prior (1660–1715), poet and diplomatist.
8. p.419. *Button's:* the coffee-house.
9. p.419. *vidi tantum:* I merely saw him. Thackeray was badly disposed to Swift, as the following episode with Esmond reveals, none the less the portrait is a studied one, and Thackeray relies heavily on *The Journal to Stella* in this chapter. Partly it seems to be a failure to understand Swift's irony. He takes the anecdote of the rapist, for example (*The Journal*, 25 July 1711), at face value.

10. p.421. *Omphale:* Queen of the Lydians made Hercules, who loved her, wear woman's clothes and spin flax.

11. p.422. *doubt the Duke of Marlborough's courage:* in *History of the Four Last Years of the Queen*.

12. p.422. *Bouchain:* Marlborough's last victory before his disgrace.

13. p.423. *Mr Leach:* Dryden Leach, a cousin whom Swift set up in business.

14. p.423. *the compter:* i.e. prison.

15. p.426. *mob-caps:* an indoor, deshabille cap.

16. p.426. *in a tie-wig:* The episode is recounted in *The Journal to Stella*. Swift was at this period in fear of the 'Mohawks'.

17. p.426. *my Lord Stair:* John Dalrymple (1673–1747) was the English plenipotentiary at Paris after Bolingbroke had fled to France and taken up office under the Pretender. Accounts of his indiscretions can be found in Walpole's Letters.

18. p.427. *The Hind and the Panther:* as in Dryden's poem, the Catholic and Protestant churches.

19. p.427. *My Cousin Westmoreland:* St John quotes rather unsteadily from Henry V's patriotic Crispin's Day speech.

20. p.427. *Our great King came from Huntingdon, not Hanover:* where Oliver Cromwell was born. St John veers from Jacobitism to Republicanism.

21. p.426. *Duke Hamilton is dead:* This account is again drawn from Swift's *Journal*, November 1712, which also voices a suspicion that Mohun had been set on by the Whigs to prevent any conciliations which the Duke might make as Ambassador in Paris.

BOOK THREE: 7

1. p.436. *the young Duke of Cambridge:* the Hanoverian Prince, later George II.

2. p.437. *Dean Atterbury:* The bishop was sent into exile in 1722 for complicity in Jacobite plots, and died in 1732.

3. p.437. *gossips:* used in an original sense of visitors to a lying-in mother.

4. p.439. *Hexham:* Here, and later, Thackeray refers to it as Hexham. Earlier it was Hexton. Similarly, Lowick, as the name has been spelt previously, in the next sentence is Lodwick. Presumably, when in the flow of writing or dictating Thackeray relied heavily on his memory. He seems also to have been a careless reviser.

5. p.441. *a pair of beautiful old organs:* one instrument with possibly two manuals. The usage is an obsolete one.

6. p.442. *did not set off Prince Eugene:* A number of commentators were surprised by Eugene's plainness when he came to England. Beatrix's reply to this remark is either very deep (she is hinting that Rachel will be his wife) or as far as I can see meaningless.

7. p.443. *To Lorraine:* After the Treaty of Utrecht the Pretender was forced to go to Bar-le-Duc in Lorraine.

## BOOK THREE: 8

1. p.445. *Benedick, the married man:* proverbial for a newly married man, though originally from Benedick in *Much Ado About Nothing.*
2. p.447. *the Atridæ:* the cursed sons of Atreus, Menelaus and Agamemnon.
3. p.447. *Miss Oglethorpe:* Anne Oglethorpe, reputedly the mistress of the Old Pretender.
4. p.454. *five hundred pounds reward:* A reward was offered for the capture of the Pretender by Bolingbroke on 23 June, if he was to be found in England. It was, however, £5,000, not £500. Thackeray gets the figure right on p. 492. The Biographical Edition rationalizes the figure, but the wrong way round, making both these £500.
5. p.454. *Arria* committed suicide as an example to her husband, and *Cornelia* exhibited her sons as her 'jewels'.
6. p.454. *Dr Berkeley's tar-water:* Not a proprietary name. Berkeley was a bishop and philanthropist who wrote tracts on the medical benefits of tar-water.

## BOOK THREE: 9

1. p.456. *Eikon Basilike: The Image of the King,* 'The Portraiture of His Sacred Majesty in his Solitude and Suffering', allegedly written by Charles I, just before his death, but probably by Bishop Gauden.
2. p.458. *Harry's:* Thackeray presumably means 'Frank's'.
3. p.458. *the kingdom of Brentford:* i.e. a worthless realm, and therefore one which can be shared without acrimony, see Cowper, *The Task,* 'So sit two kings of Brentford on one throne.'
4. p.459. *La-Fleur:* This is perplexing, but presumably, still dazed, it is Miss Oglethorpe he calls for.
5. p.460. *yield to the temptation:* His argument was that thereafter no one could consider him trustworthy.
6. p.460. The footnote: This may be deliberately confusing, except for Lady Masham and the Duke of Ormonde, who are later named in the narrative as accomplices.
7. p.462. *Golconda:* in India, fabulous for its diamonds.
8. p.465. *my Lady Viscountess' son:* The plot is complicated here and the details contradictory. The Pretender has arrived in England disguised as M. Baptiste, the Viscount's secretary. On arrival at Kensington he changes with his 'master' and becomes Castlewood, even though he has apparently be seen by the menials of the household. In this paragraph it is implied that Lockwood is both inside the conspiracy and yet unaware of it.
9. p.466. *the soubrette:* the maid.
10. p.466. *Crispin:* the traditional name for the servant in French comedy.

### BOOK THREE: 10

1. p.469. *Lockit and Peachum:* fence and turnkey in Gay's *Beggar's Opera* (1728).

2. p.472. *St Anthony's fire:* erysipelas.

3. p.473. *the Queen's Abigail:* a pun on Abigail Masham.

4. p.475. *Lady ——:* Since the name is given on the next page, there seems little point in this suppression.

### BOOK THREE: 11

1. p.484. *hath broke his staff:* i.e. left office. The staff of office was broken and a new one given to his successor.

2. p.485. *coram latronibus:* a distant allusion to Juvenal's 'Cantabit vacuus coram latrone viator' – the traveller with empty pockets will laugh in the face of the robber.

### BOOK THREE: 12

1. p.494. *scorned Mr Walpole then*: Walpole was disgraced in 1709, yet became under George I and George II the most powerful minister in the realm.

### BOOK THREE: 13

1. p.507. *my dear lord's grandfather:* Esmond uses the term 'grandfather' in the old sense of the word meaning 'ancestor'.

2. p.510. *Boniface:* a landlord.

3. p.513. *'eyes of meek surrender':* Paradise Lost, IV. 494. An example, if any were needed, of the care with which Thackeray chose his quotations; in this passage Milton describes Eve as the 'general mother' with 'matron lip'.

4. p.513. *the kindness of Mr Addison:* as Under Secretary of State, Addison would be in a position to help.

5. p.513. *my son Frank's gallantry in Scotland,* in the 1715 uprising.